THREE GREAT NOVELS
Jemina Shore on the Case

Antonia Fraser

Three Great Novels:
Jemima Shore on the Case

Cool Repentance
Oxford Blood
Your Royal Hostage

First published in Great Britain in 2006 by Orion,
an imprint of the Orion Publishing Group Ltd.

A CIP catalogue record for this book is
available from the British Library.

ISBN-13: 987 0 7528 7302 2
ISBN-10: 0 7528 7302 4

Typeset by Deltatype Ltd,
Birkenhead, Merseyside

Set in Minion

Printed in Great Britain by
Clays Ltd, St Ives plc

The Orion Publishing Group Ltd
Orion House
5 Upper Saint Martin's Lane
London, WC2H 9EA

The Orion Publishing Group's policy is to use papers that
are natural, renewable and recyclable products and made
from wood grown in sustainable forests. The logging and
manufacturing processes are expected to conform to the
environmental regulations of the country of origin.

www.orionbooks.co.uk

Contents

Cool Repentance

For Fred and Simone
and Laverstock
where Jemima Shore was born

'And with the morning cool repentance came.'
Sir Walter Scott

Contents

1

Spring Flowers

'Glad to be back?'

The questioner sounded urgent but the woman putting spring flowers carefully into a low vase merely smiled in reply, said nothing. The deep window to her left was open and from time to time the wind stirred her hair gently as she worked – hair the same colour as the daffodils at her feet. The flowers too stirred in their glass container, when the breeze touched them. The newspaper on the floor held white narcissi with bright red perianths, as well as trumpet-shaped daffodils, whose colour ranged from pale yellow to ochre, and other delicate flowers of the spring; sometimes the newspaper rustled. Everything was bright. Nothing was still.

The curtains of the drawing-room at Lark Manor also appeared to have been chosen with spring in mind. Hanging thickly to the floor, lined and interlined, they were made of yellow and white chintz, while twin gold mirrors, with brackets containing fresh white candles on either side, further reflected the lightness of the sunshine outside. The carpet, patterned and Victorian-looking, was grass green: it matched the colour of the grass exactly, just as the daffodils, blowing and rippling on either side of the drive to the hills beyond, were perfectly co-ordinated with the yellow and white chintz. Where the hills drew back like curtains to reveal a small but distinct patch of sea, that colour was pale azure. But the sea was not forgotten in the Lark Manor drawing-room: small bright-blue cushions, piped in white, reposed on the big yellow sofas by the fireplace, reminding you pleasantly but inexorably of its part in the view.

'Glad to be back?' the person repeated. 'You must be glad to be back.'

Christabel Cartwright gave another smile, not quite as marked as the first, and lifted her eyebrows. She picked up the garden scissors and shortened the stem of a jonquil. There were spring posies and pots of clear blue hyacinths everywhere in the large drawing-room. The flowers which Christabel was arranging stood on a highly polished Sheraton table and would form a centrepiece of the room when they were finished.

'Those are pretty, aren't they? A new variety. Or new to Lark. You were surprised to find them out there by the woods when you went picking, weren't you?'

Christabel Cartwright, a jonquil in her hand, hesitated and then put it down. She continued to inspect the glass vase with concentration.

'Perhaps you wouldn't have planted them? Or if you had planted them, perhaps you wouldn't have planted them just there. By the wood, I mean.'

'I think they're beautiful,' Christabel said at last. Her tone was surprisingly deep for a woman, without being at all husky; it had a charming melodious timbre. 'I noticed them at once.'

'It's just the sort of thing you do notice, isn't it? Flowers, and dogs.' The voice sounded increasingly pressing about it all. 'Didn't you go to the corner of the wood, where they buried Mango, at once? Immediately, I mean. Straightaway? Dreadful smelly old dog.' The person questioning Christabel gave a sudden violent shudder of disgust and the person's tone grew rougher. 'I wasn't a bit sorry at what happened to him.' Perhaps there were tears, one tear, in Christabel's eyes. The person continued in a more satisfied calmer tone: 'Didn't you notice that the trug was waiting for you, and the scissors, your special scissors, all bright and clean?'

Christabel, who had picked up the scissors again, put them down. She did so fastidiously. But then all her movements tended to be precise, as well as graceful. With the modulated beauty of her voice, and her careful management of all gestures, however small, it was easy to believe that she was – or had once been – a famous actress. The tear – if indeed it had been a tear – had vanished.

'What was the first thing you did when you came back?' went on the voice, as though Christabel had given it some sort of answer. 'Do you remember? Can you think back? Oh, do try.' There was a pause.

Christabel looked at the floor. The pile of flowers, with their long thick pale-green stems ranged on the newspaper, had diminished. Out of the glass vase their white and yellow heads were now springing airily like the quills of an ornamental hedgehog. Christabel bent her soft golden head which gave the impression of a kind of halo; in her bright-blue clothes, contrasting with the grass-green carpet, with the white flowers in her hand, she might have been part of an Annunciation scene by Rossetti. Then she picked up the corner of her blue skirt and rubbed the half-moon table on which the vase stood; despite all the care taken, the paper laid down, a drop of water had fallen on the polished wood. Christabel eliminated it.

'Did you take a photograph of Lark with you when you went, by the way? Do cast your mind back. You're getting so forgetful these days. I don't want to sound horrible, but perhaps it's your age, your time of life. You would have taken a special one, your favourite angle perhaps, the corner of the wood, Mango's grave, taken it with your own camera. No, wait.' There was a sharp intake of breath and another laugh. But the roughness had also come back into the voice: the person talking to Christabel looked heated, either in anger or triumph.

'No, wait, it wasn't Mango's grave then, was it? You would hardly have known that corner of the wood was going to be Mango's grave. Seeing as that awful old Mango was still alive when you left him, left him to die. Still, you always did love that corner . . .' The voice trailed away and there was quite a long pause.

'Otherwise,' it resumed briskly, 'there were always the photographs in the press. Newspaper photographs. There were plenty of those.'

Christabel was picking up the last flower from the newspaper. It was a narcissus. She touched her cheek with the fluttery white petal and smelt it. Then she inserted the narcissus deftly into the vase like a bullfighter inserting a banderilla. She stepped back and gazed at her work.

'No one can arrange flowers like you,' said the person thickly: the voice now sounded admiring, almost gloating. 'I've always said that. It's been my firm contention all along.' There was another long pause.

'What a pity it is, a great pity, that you have to die.'

For the first time in the conversation – if such it could be called – Christabel Cartwright gazed directly at her interlocutor. Her eyes were enormous, blue like the distant sea, just a little less vivid than the cushions on the sofas. Round her eyes a network of tiny but distinctly visible lines radiated outwards so regularly that they might have been drawn on to her face; the effect was not unbecoming. Her strongest feature, an indisputably Roman nose, scarcely noticed beneath the radiance of the big eyes.

Otherwise there were no hard lines or planes on her face; everything was soft, some of it a little too soft perhaps – her small chin was almost lost in the folds of the blue and white chiffon scarf which ruffled at her neck. Together the frills and the daffodil hair, waving lightly back from her forehead, gave a slightly eighteenth-century effect: the powdered head of a Gainsborough portrait perhaps. The light powder and delicate patches of pink on her cheeks contributed to this illusion.

Christabel Cartwright, in the sunlight of the Lark Manor drawing-room, no longer looked young: but she did still look oddly girlish. With her pink and white complexion and the pronounced lines on forehead and chin as well as round her eyes, she gave the impression of a much younger woman made up to look old.

Even her figure – although she was quite plump in her soft blue cashmere jersey and skirt – was not exactly middle aged. For her legs remained excellent, really quite astonishingly pretty legs, and in their patterned navy-blue stockings, they commanded attention from the slight heaviness of the hips and bosom which the years had brought.

'No, really,' the voice went on, 'you didn't expect to get away with it, did you? Surely not that. Just to say you were sorry, just to *repent*.' The voice put a very nasty emphasis on the word repent as if describing a most unpleasant activity. 'Was it going to be like the song then, *his* song, cool, oh so coo-ool repentance?' The person picked up a long-stemmed flower and pretended to use it as a microphone: then the voice crooned the last four words slowly, mockingly, gloatingly. 'Was that what you thought – that you would come back, come back here to beautiful Lark, and *get away with it*, did you expect that? I can hardly believe it, even of you . . .

'So you see, one of these days I shall really have to kill you. Just to teach you a lesson. A lesson you'll never forget: that you can't just get away with things. I shall probably kill you before the spring flowers are over. Then we needn't have all those ghastly wreaths at the funeral. Just cut flowers only. Just what you would have wanted.'

Christabel continued to stare with her lovely eyes wide open; they were pools of pure colour: there was no expression in them at all.

'We need some more flowers, don't we – for the study?' Christabel said at length in her low musical voice; she sounded perfectly normal. 'I should have thought of it before. I'll go out and pick some more. There's plenty of time before lunch.'

She picked up the tray and walked in her careful graceful way towards the french windows. At the steps she paused and said with the air of one delivering lines at the end of an act: 'Yes, darling, in answer to your original question, I am glad to be back. Of course I'm glad to be back. I've come back to look after everybody. Everybody – including you.'

Then she walked away into the garden.

The person who had been questioning Christabel Cartwright decided to leave her alone for the time being. Let her vanish alone into the greenness, through the trees, before reappearing on the verge of the drive where the daffodils grew. The person realized that Christabel had forgotten her scissors. It was not too late to do something about that. The person decided to think hard about the scissors and what they might do to Christabel when she came back to fetch them.

2

Back to Normal

The enormous bedroom upstairs was still quite dark, although everywhere in the garden at Lark Manor the sunlight was seeking out the grass beneath the tall trees.

Regina Cartwright, guiding her white horse down the path from the stables to the drive, careful of the surrounding flowers, could see that the bedroom curtains were still drawn. She patted the horse's neck, pulled his head up where he had decided to chomp the grass, and said, rather self-consciously: 'You see, Lancelot, everything's back to normal.'

The remark was caught by her sister Blanche, emerging or rather slouching out of the open french windows of the kitchen. Blanche was dressed in tight white cotton trousers and a sun-top. She wore one sandal, and held the other, which seemed to be broken, in her hand.

'Really, Rina, you are a baby. Still talking to that horse at your age. And does he answer back, then?'

'I may be a year younger than you,' retorted Regina, 'but I used to be in the same form at school, don't forget, so who was the baby then? And by the way Blanche you're far too fat for that sun-top,' she went on more automatically than scornfully. Then her voice changed. 'Those are my trousers, my white trousers, give them back you thieving little bitch, you've swiped them.'

Blanche starting to scream back in her turn at one and the same time turned and fled in the direction of the kitchen windows. Regina on Lancelot thundered after her, now careless of the paths. The shrubs shivered, and shed flowers as the big white horse passed. A host of fallen red camellias lay to mark his tracks.

Even when she reached the kitchen where Blanche had taken refuge, Regina did not dismount from Lancelot but simply urged the horse in through the french windows. Uneasily he stepped onto the cork floor, placing his hooves carefully on the surface as if aware of the heinous nature of the gesture. The animal's enormous shoulders filled the opening making the large airy room, with all its polished wood surfaces, seem quite dark.

It was at this moment that Julian Cartwright, yawning slightly, entered the kitchen by its inner louvred swing doors. He wore a navy-blue silk dressing-gown, piped in white, over blue pyjamas. His dressing-gown was firmly belted in the centre. His dark hair – the same thick dark straight hair which Regina had inherited, but flecked with grey – was neatly combed and his feet shod in dark-red leather slippers. He looked gentlemanly and rather relaxed, despite the early hour, and gave the impression that he would probably always bear himself with similar distinction, whatever the hour of the day.

His words, however, were not relaxed.

'Oh really girls, really Rina, really Blanche, haven't you any consideration at all? You know how Mummy likes to sleep on in the mornings. That noise would wake them in the church at Larminster.'

He did not seem to have noticed the presence of the horse.

'They're awake in the church at Larminster,' pointed out Blanche from her position of advantage behind the polished wood kitchen bar; her tone was extremely reasonable. 'It's Easter Sunday morning. Are you and Mummy going to church?'

'Don't be so silly, Blanche,' Julian Cartwright sounded even more irritated, although whether at the idea of going to church himself or at the idea of anyone going at all, was not quite clear.

'I expect Daddy meant: wake the *dead* at Larminster Church,' suggested Regina from her station on Lancelot at the window. 'Wake Grannie Cartwright and old Mr Nixon and Cynthia Meadows' little sister – that's all the most recently dead we know, and the ancient dead are probably more difficult to rouse. But there could be others from the village—'

'Regina!' Julian Cartwright suddenly shouted in a very loud voice indeed. 'Get that horse out of the kitchen!'

Regina hastily backed Lancelot out of the french windows; he trotted off in the direction of the drive. She shouted something over her shoulder which sounded like '*my* trousers', but could not be heard clearly.

It was a few minutes later that Christabel Cartwright appeared at the entrance to the kitchen, swinging the doors open with both hands so that she stood for a moment as if framed. She wore silver mules edged with swansdown and a thin wool kaftan of a very pale blue, embroidered in white. Her hair, which stood up becomingly round her head, looked as if it might have been blown in the wind, rather than combed. She wore no make-up at all and her face had a slight shine on it. Without concealment of powder, she looked very beautiful, if haggard, and slightly dazed.

Blanche's plump face, with its lack of contours, and mass of fine hair surrounding it, as well as its too-strong nose, showed what Christabel had perhaps looked like long ago – but Christabel must always have had beauty. Blanche at the present time had none.

'What a frightful row!' Christabel began. 'You woke me up.'

'It was all Rina's fault,' said Blanche in a voice which suggested sobs might be on the way if its owner were harshly treated.

'No, not you darling, though by the way Blanche, it's far too cold for those kind of clothes today. It's only April, you know. As for that top – well, we'll talk about that later. No, Daddy woke me up. Yes you did, darling. I was having a beautiful sleep at the time. I know I was. I didn't even need to take a second pill. Seriously, I thought the bull had escaped from the top field.' Christabel, who had sounded rather faint when she first spoke, was now coming back quite strongly. She went on: 'Well, as I am awake, shall we all have breakfast together? Blanche darling? Julian?'

Her eyes fell on a breakfast tray already laid on the bar. The service was of bone china, ornamented by sprigs of lily of the valley, with the exception of the coffee pot, which had a dark-green and white ivy pattern. The voile tray-cloth and single napkin were embroidered with lilies of the valley.

'Whatever happened to the coffee pot belonging to this set?' Christabel demanded quite sharply. There was a silence.

'It got broken,' said Blanche. 'I think Mrs Blagge broke it.'

'Then I think I'll have the ivy-leaf set for the time being,' Christabel broke off and gave a little laugh. 'Sorry, darling – I'm being quite ridiculous. I know I am. But you know how I feel about things that don't match. I just can't help it.'

Julian put his arm round his wife's shoulders and kissed her cheek.

'Goodness, you do look pretty this morning,' he said. 'Doesn't she, Blanche? Eighteen, going on nineteen. Blanche's age exactly. And Blanche is looking pretty good this morning too.'

'She isn't eighteen though', said Blanche in a sulky voice. 'She's forty-seven. At least that's what it says in *Who's Who in the Theatre* and Ketty says actresses always lie about their age. You're only forty-three, Daddy. You're nearer to eighteen than Mummy is.'

'If you're going to be in that kind of mood, I shall feel nearer a hundred,' said Julian. 'Cut it out, Blanche, will you.'

'I really am forty-seven, darling.' In contrast to Julian, Christabel spoke in a pleasant rather amused voice. 'Exactly four years and five days older than Daddy, if you want absolute accuracy.'

'Look darling,' Julian gave Christabel another hug, 'don't worry about the lily-of-the-valley coffee pot. I'll order another one from Goode's or wherever it came from. I should have thought about it before.'

'We did think about it!' exclaimed Blanche, sulkiness suddenly abandoned. 'Ketty and I thought about it. We discussed it for hours. Whether you would want your own tray without the proper coffee pot or another set, all matching, and Ketty thought—'

'A silver coffee pot might have been the answer.' But Christabel's attention had manifestly wandered. 'Where *is* Ketty?' she enquired, that sharper note returning to her voice. 'Isn't she supposed to look after breakfast on Sunday mornings when the Blagges are off? What's wrong with her?'

'Easter Sunday. That's what's wrong with her. Ketty's at her own church in Larminster praying for us all. Especially for *you*, Mummy. She says God never loses sight of any one of us sinners, just like the newspapers. Those were her exact words. She's terribly religious these days; I think it's something to do with the new Pope and the fact he was once an actor. She made something called a novena for you, Mummy. To be forgiven.'

'Are we or are we not going to have breakfast?' Julian Cartwright took the clean folded white handkerchief out of the breast pocket of his dressing-gown and blew his nose loudly. 'And if so, is there the faintest chance of a man having a cup of coffee and perhaps even some decent bacon and eggs before it's time for lunch? Are you, Blanche, going to make it, or am I?'

'I'll make it, darling,' cried Christabel, smoothing her hair back with one long-fingered hand. The nails were long, too, and unpainted, but her hands in general, unlike her face, were the hands of a middle-aged woman. 'Besides, Blanche is going to change into something warmer and more suitable. Yes you are, poppet, this minute and no argument.'

Christabel was already opening the fridge and getting out eggs and limp rashers of raw bacon. She certainly gave the air of knowing where everything was. Even the three attempts she made to find the jar of coffee were done so purposefully that she might have been performing some agreed ritual of opening and shutting cupboard doors.

'This reminds me of Sunday mornings in London,' she said over her shoulder to Julian. 'We just need some Mozart.' Her voice was tender. 'When I was in that long season at the Gray Theatre. We never used to come down to Lark on Sundays then; too exhausting. The girls had to go to school on Monday morning. Ketty went to church: my contribution to church-going was playing the Coronation Mass, and cooking us brunch. Do you remember?'

'I rather think that I used to cook it more often than not.' But Julian's voice too was tender. 'You used to sleep so late, the girls and I would have starved if we had waited for you to put one dainty toe out of bed – and shall I put some Mozart on for you now? Have it wafted in from the drawing-room?'

Christabel set down the frying-pan and faced him: in her high-heeled mules she still looked up at him.

'Happy?' she asked in her low musical voice. 'Happy now?' Her wide blue unblinking eyes met his; he had the illusion that there was moisture in them or perhaps it was in his own. He could smell the strong lily-of-the-valley scent she always used.

'There's no one like you, Christabel.' His voice, unlike hers, was husky. 'You know that.' With one hand Julian grasped the back of his wife's head and pressed his lips hard to hers. His other hand went down towards her breast beneath its thin wool covering.

Christabel stayed quite still for an instant without responding or resisting. Then she gave a minute but quite unmistakable shudder of disgust.

'I'm sorry,' she said very low. This time there were definitely tears. Their eyes met again. They were both breathing quite heavily.

'Back to normal then,' Julian continued to hold her by her head. After a moment Christabel kissed him on the cheek.

'Hello, young lovers!' said a voice from the french windows. 'Happy Easter anyway to the two of you – but you look happy enough already. I've brought some eggs for the girls by the way – we've been having an Easter egg hunt here for the last few years, Christabel, and I thought you wouldn't mind if we continued the tradition.' An extremely tall man, at least six foot five or six, stood there, bending his head much as the horse had done.

'Gregory!' exclaimed Christabel, patting her hair. 'What an unearthly hour to come calling.' The gesture was not coquettish; and she made no attempt to sound pleased. 'And aren't the girls getting a little old for Easter eggs?' she added.

'Unearthly? I've just dropped Mrs Blagge back at the cottage after Mass. Miss Kettering drove herself but refused to drop Mrs B., so I suppose they've had one of their religious rows about the new doctrines again. Now to the Easter egg hunt, and then I'll be away back to the woods – no one is too old for Easter eggs by the way, not me, not Julian, not even you, Christabel.'

Christabel raised her eyebrows and smiled; she resumed her attention to the frying-pan.

'Look, old man, why don't you stay to lunch?' said Julian after a pause. 'After the hunt. You'd be a great help to us, as a matter of fact. You see we've got some people from television coming down; strange as it may seem, they're coming all this way for lunch. And frankly we're dreading it. But if you were here, with all your experience of television—'

'Yes, why don't you, Gregory darling?' added Christabel sweetly from the stove. 'Quite apart from television, you're so good at talking to everyone about everything, and finding out things—'

Gregory Rowan sounded, for the first time since his arrival, uncertain. 'I thought you'd said goodbye to all that kind of thing for good, Christabel. Or is it a retrospective? *Christabel Herrick Remembers*? *My Twenty Years a Star*? *No Regrets Herrick*? Something along those lines perhaps?'

'Don't be ridiculous, Gregory.' This time Julian was definitely cross. 'This is nothing to do with Christabel. It's the Larminster Festival. Surely I don't need to remind you of the existence of the Larminster Festival?'

'Hardly. Yes, thank you, Christabel, I will have an egg. No toast. Yes, I know I should look after myself more and I'm too thin. Both sides please.'

'I know your tastes, darling.'

'Hardly can I forget it,' continued Gregory, easing himself down on to the polished bench, with its bright check cushions, by the kitchen table. 'It's rapidly turning into the Gregory Rowan Festival, I fear. Since that touring company is bringing down one of my plays – their idea, nothing to do with me. I would have so much preferred to write a moving piece specially for the Festival about the night King Charles II spent at Larminster escaping after Worcester. Good rousing local stuff: the village inn, the village maiden, lots of them, a rib-tickling mistress of the tavern, a Mistress Quickly part – would have been good part for you there, Christabel, if you're really making a come-back – exciting new departure style—'

'The Larminster Festival,' said Julian, pointedly interrupting, 'has been chosen by some television company—'

'Megalith,' put in Christabel. 'Cy Fredericks runs it. That's the point. He's a darling. Or rather, he used to be a darling. That sort of thing doesn't change.'

'Larminster has been chosen to feature in a coming series about British arts festivals. From the highest to the lowest.' Julian smiled, more at ease. 'I imagine Larminster comes somewhere near the bottom of the latter category. If not *the* bottom. The presenter, or whatever you call it, is that woman with reddish hair everybody goes on about for being so beautiful and so brilliant, what is she called? She generally concentrates on social causes like housing and unmarried mothers and that sort of thing. She did that huge series last year called *The Poor and their Place*. The arts, we gather, are a new line. What *is* she called, darling?'

But it was Gregory Rowan who supplied the name.

'Jemima Shore,' he said in a thoroughly disconcerted voice. 'Jemima Shore Investigator, as she is laughingly known. General busybody might be a better name. You have to be referring to Jemima Shore. Is *she* coming here? To the Larminster Festival?'

'*She* is coming to Lark Manor,' responded Christabel, placing a perfectly fried egg in a ramekin in front of Gregory; she gave the impression of performing the action in front of a larger audience. 'There you are, just as you like it. Eat up. Never say I don't look after you, darling.'

3

Sea-Shells

On the way to Sunday lunch at Lark Manor, Jemima Shore took a détour which brought her down to the sea. She took along her assistant, the lovely Cherry; Flowering Cherry as she was known at Megalithic House. The famous curves which were the toast of that establishment were on this occasion delineated by a tightly belted mackintosh; it covered Cherry's traditional outfit of white silk pearl-buttoned blouse, buttons hardly adequate to the task imposed upon them, and short tight skirt (Cherry was one of those girls who never noticed the temporary disappearances of the mini-skirt from the ranks of high fashion).

Cherry, who both admired and loved Jemima Shore with all the enthusiasm of her passionate nature, nevertheless felt able to disapprove her inordinate taste for the sea without disloyalty.

'At least she can't plunge in, this time,' thought Cherry, huddling her shoulders as she stood among the pebbles; she looked like a plump little bird, fluffing out its feathers.

Jemima Shore, immaculate as usual in a red suede jacket and dark-blue trousers with long boots – 'That jacket must have cost a *fortune*,' thought Cherry reverently – stood at the edge of the water watching it hiss towards her feet. She looked, Cherry reflected with less reverence, as though she expected a message from Megalith Television to arrive in a bottle.

But when the message came, it was not from Megalith Television and it was not in a bottle. Jemima and Cherry appeared to be alone on the sea-shore. The stretch of shingly beach was not in itself very extensive: the centre of it was a river – the river Lar no doubt, for according to the one signpost Jemima had suddenly spotted on their route to the manor, they had passed through Larmouth. The river was surrounded by groups of trees on either side of its banks where it flowed onto the beach, making a shallow course among the pebbles. The village itself appeared to consist of one pub called The King's Escape (jolly picture of a black-moustached Charles II swinging in the breeze above, empty plastic tables outside), a telephone kiosk and a row of cottages. But the beach was quite hidden from the view of the houses by a turn of the cliff; this made it an unexpectedly secluded and charming place.

Jemima's fast Mercedes sports car, a recent acquisition, was parked on the crunchy pebbles where the grassland gave way to the sea-scape beneath the lee of the cliffs. It was a new crunch which attracted Cherry's attention, although Jemima – 'mooning as though she'd never seen the sea before' in Cherry's words – did not turn her head.

The crunch was caused by a very large, not particularly well-kept, estate car; it was black and with its long body bore a certain resemblance to a hearse. The man who got out of it was however so long in himself that Cherry got the feeling that he might have needed the hearse to house his legs. Like Jemima, he wore very tight trousers, although his – pale cords – were as worn as hers were pristine. Standing together by the sea-shore, with their height and slimness, they resembled two birds, two herons perhaps, visiting the sea.

Cherry was one who, however preoccupied, never failed to assess a male face; she had rather liked the look of this one as he passed. The worn countenance in particular appealed. Cherry was, as she put it, currently into older and worn men (it was fortunate too for her enthusiasm that the two categories so often coincided). Cherry was a great watcher of late-night thirties movies on television, a way of life which had probably started the craze. Of this particular worn face, she had noted as he passed, with satisfaction: 'Like Bogart. On stilts.'

Cherry, watching them at a distance, thought sentimentally that they made a nice couple – 'Both so tall. Though Jem always seems to fancy more the short and powerful type. Is he some dishy country squire, I wonder? Would Jem like that – the lady of the manor? Probably not. Never mind Jemima. Would *I* like it?' Thus Cherry's mind made its accustomed moves towards local romance and its fulfilment, particularly as she had lately decided that a Substantial Older Man (face, but not bank account, well worn) was the kind of interesting new development her life-style needed.

The actual words which were being exchanged while Cherry indulged in these agreeable reveries were rather less romantic.

Jemima Shore had not thought that Gregory Rowan looked in the slightest bit like Humphrey Bogart, although she did have time to notice in a rather more oblique fashion than Cherry that he was quite attractive. And then something happened immediately which made her decide that Gregory Rowan was quite one of the most aggressive over-bearing – and thus unattractive – men she had encountered in recent years.

Gregory Rowan began bluntly enough:

'I hardly think the Larminster Festival is in need of your kind of publicity, Miss Shore,' he said, dragging quite violently on his cigarette as though it was in some danger of extinction.

'And what might my kind of publicity be?' enquired Jemima in her coldest voice, the one she used to freeze unruly – or socially undesirable – interviewees, tycoons wrecking the environment or bland cabinet ministers determined to be jocular rather than truthful.

But Gregory found himself well able to answer the question. To Jemima's considerable surprise she found herself being described as a cultural busybody, a parasite on the body of the arts, and a few other choice terms of abuse – all whilst standing on a cool sea-shore, with the wind whipping her fair hair in her eyes, but hardly disturbing Gregory's own, which was so bushy as to be apparently impregnable to the wind's attacks.

'Why don't you just chuck this programme, Miss Shore? Go away? Go back to London where you belong, and sort out a whole new generation of unmarried mothers who weren't old enough to watch your programme on the Pill – *For and Against*—'

'I'm glad at least you're a fan of my work,' interposed Jemima sweetly.

'Fan! You may take this as you wish, but it's the sort of programme you make, the sort of woman you are – oh, all right, before you speak, *person* if you like – which drove me away from jolly old London to live in the woods of Lark! Gregory Rowan, the Happy Hermit. A good television title? I read your mind. But that is one title you will never see flashing up on your screen. Which is just one reason, having made my choice, why I don't want my retreat polluted by the mating cries of television.'

'Aren't you taking all this rather too personally, Mr Rowan? After all—' This time Jemima was valiantly maintaining her sweetness of manner, as much to annoy as to placate, when suddenly a swoosh of icy water covered her boot and caused her to jump sharply backwards. To her surprise, Gregory Rowan paid no attention whatsoever, either to her jump or to the ingression of the sea. The swirling wave covered his feet in their gym shoes, sought out his ankles, and he did not even move.

Jemima Shore, retreating, continued her sentence, trying to match his own composure. The tide was coming in quite fast, and even Jemima, dedicated bather in a more salubrious climate, did not propose to be involuntarily immersed in the English seas in April.

'After all, Megalith Television is not trying to mate with you, Mr Rowan, merely cover the Larminster Festival as part of a nation-wide series – not at all the same thing – as for your dislike of London—' The waters were softly receding but Jemima kept a watchful eye for the next insurgence – 'it doesn't seem to extend to the West End theatre, I notice?

Or to the production of your plays in London television studios? So that while *you* expect to be sacrosant, West End money—'

Whatever Gregory Rowan would have replied to that was swallowed up by Jemima's hasty and crunchy retreat up the shore at the next wave.

Gregory Rowan watched her. Once again he made no move either to retreat himself or assist her on the pebbles. He merely smiled. His smile gave an unexpectedly pleasant cast to his countenance – that countenance Cherry had aptly characterized as 'worn' – but his words were if anything even more ungracious.

'I suppose you expect me to cry out penitently *touché* and fall at your feet in worship? You've got me quite wrong. It's not London productions of my plays I object to, the more the merrier so far as I'm concerned. Hello, Shaftesbury Avenue, hail to the National! I'll even consider something warm, human and musical at the RSC. Failing that, a permanent rotating series of my plays at the Round House, or if Chalk Farm sounds too pastoral, the Royal Court. And all that goes for television too. How is Megalith's drama by the way?'

'Exquisite,' Jemima put in swiftly. Gregory proceeded as if she had not spoken.

'No, it's Larminster I want to preserve from your ghastly grip. Larminster and its inhabitants.'

'Principally yourself?'

Gregory looked at her as if measuring her. His gaze, if speculative, remained cold. Whatever he was measuring her for, was not she felt, likely to appeal.

'Oddly enough, not,' he said after a while. 'As you've pointed out, I at least have considerable experience of television. And,' he paused, 'I've nothing to hide. But have you thought of the effects a television programme, the sheer making of a television programme, has on ordinary people?'

He lit another cigarette. The water was swirling round his shoes again; Jemima remained out of danger.

'People who do have something to hide? Bruised people? Vulnerable people? There are such people in the world, Miss Shore, even if you, with a toss of your golden head, have no cognizance of them. Let me come to the point. Hasn't Christabel suffered enough from you people? Haven't we all suffered enough on her behalf and through her? Her husband? Her children? Everyone who is or was close to her, some of them very humble people by your standards, Miss Shore, but still people by mine. Vulnerable, bruised people, people who have – forgive my old-fashioned language, so unlike the language no doubt to which you're used – people who have repented what they did. What might television do to them? You might even try thinking sometimes of the meek, Miss Shore – after all it's not Megalith Television that's going to inherit the earth.'

Jemima wondered whether there was any point in reminding this odious man that her name in television as Jemima Shore Investigator had been made by calling attention exactly to the meek – the inarticulate, the oppressed and the helpless. The arrival of Cherry, brightly extending one plump little paw on which lay a small pinkish cockleshell, decided her against it.

'Look, Jem, for you,' she cried. 'For your shell bathroom in London. To join the world-wide collection.' Cherry, goggling huge eyes at Gregory Rowan, was clearly demanding an introduction. Jemima, thinking that Flowering Cherry was welcome to the disagreeable Gregory Rowan, duly made it.

'Jemima brings back sea-shells from all round the world,' Cherry confided. 'And I help her.' Cherry (one of the stauncher characters Jemima knew) was one of those people who managed to look nubile and in need of protection, even in a mackintosh. Possibly for this reason, Gregory Rowan addressed her in quite a different tone, both lighter and warmer.

'You sell sea-shells to Jemima Shore. Hence the name. It's an alias, I suppose. Foolishly, I had always supposed she was born with it. However I'm not sure these particular Larmouth shells are going to qualify. You see, my dear young lady, I've been trying to persuade your boss to cancel her programme. Leave Larminster and its Festival to its own devices.'

Cherry looked quite astonished: she could no more envisage cancelling a scheduled programme without reason than she could envisage anyone not actually pining for that programme to happen, not jumping at the chance to be featured in it.

Gregory Rowan said in his newly pleasant voice: 'Amazed, are you? I see you are. Your eyes remind me of the dog in the fairy story, eyes as big as saucers. Clearly *you* have nothing to hide. Get your boss to explain that remark by the way.'

He swung round. 'Look, there it is. There they both are, as a matter of fact. Have you got good eyesight?'

He was addressing Cherry again but it was Jemima who replied in her cool voice: 'I can see most things pretty clearly, I fancy.'

'Look then. Two gaps in the hills, like bites. Or gaps between huge teeth. The Giant's Teeth we call them round here. You can see the theatre quite clearly: that black turret effect. More like a watchtower than a theatre at this distance. Hence its name. It was supposed to be called the Royal like the old one, but Watchtower just stuck. Lark Manor is more difficult to spot: the light local stone.'

'So close to the sea! The theatre, I mean,' exclaimed Cherry; it was apparent at least to Jemima that Cherry's agile mind had rushed ahead to picnic-time, to time between shooting, to light evenings, to young actors, perhaps, or those not so young, all far from home. Jemima said:

'It's an excellent view. Thank you for showing it to us. An opening shot, perhaps?' she addressed the last remark, at least in principle, to Cherry.

'Locals round here don't like the way the theatre dominates the landscape. So harsh and modern. Unlike Lark Manor which melds into the background. That's why I showed them both to you. It clashes with our quiet rural life, they think with unpleasant results. Like television. Think about it, Miss Jemima Shore, and take your sea-shells home after lunch.'

On this note, Gregory Rowan walked rapidly away. But not, to Cherry's surprise, in the direction of his long black hearse car. He simply walked a little further along the pebbly beach to where a ridge of large stones indicated the highwater mark.

And there, under the stunned gaze of the two ladies from Megalith Television, he proceeded to take off first his thick dark-blue fisherman's jersey and then his battered corduroy trousers. He did not appear to have been wearing anything under these clothes at all; or if he had, he had removed all his garments at the same time. Clad then merely in a pair of old white gym shoes, Gregory Rowan strode back purposefully in the direction of the sea.

Jemima and Cherry could not tear their mesmerized gaze away, and comparing notes afterwards, agreed that they had still expected him to stop on reaching the sea's edge. But Gregory did not check his progress. At first the sea was shallow and merely splashed round his ankles. Then there must have been some shelf and a drop, for he suddenly struck out strongly, swimming along the line of the shore.

The two women watched him silently for a moment, still mesmerized, and then by unspoken agreement turned back in the direction of their own car.

'We-e-ell!' Cherry could hold no silence for very long. To Jemima's irritation her tone was definitely admiring. 'Nothing to hide indeed. What about that? And he didn't even have a towel. Did you notice?'

'I noticed what I was intended to notice,' replied Jemima crossly.

'It must have been freezing,' pursued Cherry. 'And he didn't even pause as he went in. I must say he's quite—'

'I dare say we were supposed to notice that too. Come on, Cherry, stop thinking about old Triton, and find me the route back to Lark Manor. I've got something extremely important to ask you.'

'Triton?'

'Shelley at Lerici, then.'

'But Shelley *drowned* at Lerici!' cried Cherry eagerly; as Jemima was well aware, Cherry had once worked on that notorious series *The Magnificent Shelleys* and could be relied on to get the reference. Unfortunately the literary reference did not have the desired effect of distracting her from the subject of Gregory Rowan. Instead Cherry stopped and began to look back anxiously. He was still swimming strongly and quite fast along the line of the shore; soon he would reach the cliff and the line of jagged black rocks which closed the end of the small bay.

'Jem, you're such a strong swimmer, do you think you should—'

'He won't drown. Of that I can assure you! Come *on*, Cherry, now the thing I want to ask you is this—'

But it was not until they were both back in the Mercedes, sitting, untangling the hair (Jemima), spraying on new forces of *Charlie* (Cherry), that Jemima could thoroughly distract her friend from the black head in the sea.

'Something that man said. Something that puzzled me. He made this very firm reference to Christabel. Christabel and the Festival. Cherry, who is Christabel? Who or what is she? And what connection has Christabel, any Christabel, with the Larminster Festival?'

'Christabel,' repeated Cherry. 'I can't think of any Christabel connected with it at all. Hang on, I've got the actresses' names here. Anna Maria Packe, Filumena Lennox ... And most of the other Larminster Festival names. The Committee.' She scuffled in her large ethnically-inclined tote bag. 'No wait, my God, what am I saying? *Christabel.* Christabel Herrick. *The* Christabel Herrick. The actress. She used to be married to Julian Cartwright, Julian Cartwright, he of Lark Manor, with the lovely deep voice on the telephone, the man we're going to see. Don't you remember? Then she ran off. Oh years ago. There was all that frightful scandal.'

'Scandal? What scandal?'

'Oh, Jem, you're so *ungossip-minded*!' On Cherry's lips this was definitely a reproach. 'But this you *have* to remember. The newspapers wrote screeds about it. It was all so frightfully juicy. And then tragic. But of course that's years ago. I mean, I shouldn't think Christabel Herrick has shown her face down here for years. She wouldn't dare. Certainly not at the Larminster Festival, I mean that would be a *real* scandal.'

'I'm sure you're right, Cherry,' said Jemima slowly.

Behind their backs, the dark head and arms of Gregory Rowan could now be seen heading for the shore, as a shark might be seen cutting through water.

4

Watching Christabel

The person who thought Christabel was getting away with altogether too much these days was really quite disgusted by the scene at Lark Manor that Easter Sunday: with Christabel presiding so airily over the large lunch table.

'Or rather her husband's lunch table,' the person threw in as an afterthought. But the person knew better than to put this kind of sentiment, however justifiable, into words: it was better to hug these feelings to oneself – until absolutely the right moment presented itself. Events this morning had rather proved that, hadn't they? So the person continued to mask both anger and repulsion under an impassive front.

All the same, the person knew that Christabel was really rather frightened by now. Under all that make-up Christabel wished after all she hadn't come back to Lark Manor.

Maybe it would have been better to have stayed in London and been poor and sick and sad and lonely. In spite of having no rewarding work. No marvellous lover. And getting older and uglier and not having beauty creams and hair dyes and perfumes (the smell of her lily-of-the-valley scent filled the house all over again now she was back) and people to wait on her and her lovely dresses such as that soft hyacinth-blue just the colour of her eyes, and *jewels*. How many kinds of blue jewel Christabel was wearing today! A long string of turquoise mixed with *the* pearls with the sapphire clasp, the Cartwright pearls, she'd got them out of the bank pretty quickly, hadn't she? The aquamarine ring, on the other hand, the one she always wore, she'd taken with her when she went. At lunch, of course, she was wearing it on her left hand. Her white hand, creamy and be-creamed, caressing and now once more caressed.

In spite of all this Christabel was going to die and the warm soft round body under the yielding cashmere would grow cold and be put in the dank rich mouldy earth of Larminster Churchyard. So all the creams and lotions and perfumes were not going to save her, and the blue jewels, all of them, all of them save the aquamarine and perhaps that would be buried with her, would go back into the bank.

Christabel had this knowledge now: Christabel was frightened under that sweet sorrowing manner of hers.

'Please don't torture me,' she had said.

Admiring the arrangement of spring flowers in the centre of the dining-room table – scillas and narcissi, blue and white like the china – the person decided not to be in such a hurry to end the game after all. Christabel's torture should not be ended too quickly. The prospect would make up for the fact that there might not after all be spring flowers on her grave, not even tulips, but something full blown like roses; the first big fat creamy roses, the Gloire de Dijon, which grew on the sheltered wall in the courtyard garden of Lark Manor in May. Roses, full-blown roses, were finally much more appropriate to Christabel, the person decided regretfully, than spring flowers. You had to admit that, Christabel's spring was long past.

The person revelled in Christabel's discomfiture and Christabel's secret fear grew.

Jemima Shore, on the other hand, thought that her hostess's aplomb was really quite remarkable. Under the circumstances. The circumstances which Cherry had hastily but vividly outlined to her on the road from Larmouth to the manor. Had the prodigal son been quite so urbane at the feast given in his honour by his father? Certainly this prodigal wife radiated confidence, and even blitheness in her return.

'Of course she is an actress – *was* an actress.' But Jemima, numbering a good many actors and actresses among her friends, knew that emotional control in private life was not necessarily allied to talent on the stage – even with a woman who had once been as celebrated as Christabel Herrick.

Lunch was being handed round by a manservant, an elderly and distinguished-looking man in a very clean white jacket; he was assisted by a woman with tightly set auburn hair, wearing a neat dark dress, who alternately stood at the sideboard and darted out to marshal in fresh supplies of food. From time to time Julian Cartwright issued orders to the manservant in quite a loud voice – he had called him Blagge but the woman Mrs Blagge – as a result of which both Blagges stopped doing whatever they were engaged in and still more wine was poured into the array of bevelled glasses. Christabel Cartwright's precise words could on the other hand hardly be distinguished, but it was noticeable that things moved much faster whenever she did speak; dishes, a delicate egg mousse for example in a blue and white soufflé dish, were whisked round the table again and again; plates were removed, fresh plates were substituted;

it all happened so fast and so deftly whenever Christabel murmured that she might have been whispering some magic password which made the table itself start spinning.

Meat was carved. Spring lamb appeared, presto, on the latest wave of blue and white plates. Mrs Blagge proffered mint sauce and gravy in matching dishes, first to Jemima Shore.

'Madam—'

The hand with which she extended the sauce-boat was quite blotched and claw-like, the hand of an old woman; the striking auburn hair must be dyed.

If only Jemima could be quite sure that Cherry wasn't drinking too much (such efficient service of wine, she felt, plus the presence of such an indubitably glamorous older man as Julian Cartwright presented an irresistible combination of temptations to Flowering Cherry) she, Jemima, could have concentrated totally on Christabel Herrick's, no, Christabel *Cartwright*'s, dazzling performance.

Even the white bandage which Christabel wore on her right hand had an air of elegance: a white kid glove or mitten perhaps. Although at one point Christabel did wince at some inadvertent gesture: had one of her daughters, the sulky little fat one in the unsuitable sun-dress, touched the hand by mistake?

Immediately on hearing the slight cry, Julian Cartwright broke off his conversation with Cherry, perhaps to the ultimate advantage of the latter; since Cherry was leaning forward dangerously in her tight white pearl-buttoned blouse, while her large eyes bore an expression which Jemima for one found it all too easy to interpret.

'All right, darling?' Julian Cartwright called out down the table. The sound of his voice, so redolent of authority that it made a question sound like a command, drew other conversations to a close. 'Christabel, poor sweet, did herself some fearful injury on a pair of garden scissors this morning,' he explained. 'Stabbed herself in one hand in some quite remarkable way, while cutting flowers after breakfast. Darling, do you know, you've never had time to tell me properly how it happened?'

Jemima, professionally trained interviewer, became suddenly and acutely aware that some special tension had been brought into the room by Julian's question. She could not say exactly where this tension was located. After all, everyone in the room gave the polite appearance of listening for Christabel's explanation. Nor could she say further what had stirred her instinct; she only knew that curiosity, Jemima Shore's dominant emotion, had been aroused – curiosity and a strange feeling of apprehension.

Jemima looked down the table and inspected the guests.

The dexterity with which the two servants were handling the meal was made the more remarkable by the fact that it was a large lunch party.

Jemima as presenter and Cherry as production assistant were the only two official guests from Megalith since the director, Jemima's old friend and former assistant Guthrie Carlyle, was still in Greece – shooting the Parthenon for what he assured Jemima was a wholly uncontroversial programme on the Elgin Marbles sub-titled *Ours or Theirs?*

Then there were the two Cartwright girls, who sat together at their mother's end of the table, on either side of a woman whom Jemima assumed to be some kind of governess (although they were surely rather too old for that kind of thing?). This lady was familiarly addressed by the Cartwrights as Ketty, but introduced to Jemima as Miss Katherine Kettering – 'the two names have somehow got combined over the years', She was certainly much at her ease; the girls chattered to her, rather than to their other neighbours, throughout the meal. Fat little Blanche's sulky face lit up talking to Ketty in a way that it never did, Jemima noticed, when Blanche addressed her mother.

'But, Ketty, you remember: the Easter Sunday we all went to the beach and Daddy did press-ups and got sand all over his cricketing trousers—'

The pretty dark-haired daughter Regina, who chose at one point to recite a good deal of Christina Rossetti in the over-loud voice she had inherited from her father, addressed those words also to Ketty. 'When I am dead, my dearest, sing no sad songs for me . . .' and so on and so on. Ketty listened intently and then said: 'Well done, Rina,' as if she had been hearing a lesson.

'Regina,' she informed Jemima across the table, 'has been making a study of Christina Rossetti. She knows most of her work by heart.' 'How delightful,' murmured Jemima, hoping that no one had any plans for recitations of the works of Christina Rossetti by Miss Regina Cartwright aged seventeen in the course of her television programme. As usual, it was Cherry who saved the situation:

'Oh, I adore Christina Rossetti,' she cried happily. 'And Dante – Dante Gabriel, I mean, not the other Dante.' Cherry proceeded to quote at length, by virtue of her past involvement in *Christina and Company – a Rose among the Rossettis*. The series might have been one of Megalith's most noted failures, reflected Jemima, but at least Cherry's education had benefited; and Ketty and Regina were temporarily routed.

Like Mrs Blagge, Miss Kettering had very dark red hair, of a hue which was so bizarre as to be surely dyed; in Ketty's case the hair was strained back into a large thick bun, revealing a pair of dangling green earrings set in big powerfully lobed ears. It was while pondering on the coincidence of two women with the same strange taste in hair dye being in the same room that Jemima realized how much Ketty and Mrs Blagge also resembled each other in other ways. They had the same long thin finely chiselled noses and small firm mouths. Ketty however wore a violent scarlet lipstick; Mrs Blagge none.

Sisters? If so, one sat at the table and drank, Jemima observed, at least her due share of wine. The other served.

On Christabel's right sat Gregory Rowan. He had arrived rather late, with a scant air of apology, into the charming sun-filled conservatory adorned with orange trees in large dark green wooden tubs where the Cartwrights had doled out pre-lunch drinks. His hair was still conspicuously damp, its thickness temporarily restrained, and Jemima had seen Christabel give him a slightly sardonic look on arrival.

'Did you go for a quick one, darling? Quick cooling off?' she enquired. She handed him a silver goblet.

'Had to wash off the taste of chocolate,' replied Gregory. 'Next year *you* can organize the Easter egg hunt. If you're still with us, that is. To the return and the stay of the prodigal.' He lifted the goblet on whose silver surface the chilly contents – champagne and orange juice – had already left white clouds.

It was the only conceivable reference, Jemima noted, throughout the meal and its prelude, to Christabel's past. Christabel merely gave one of her low musical laughs.

Jemima, who was on Julian Cartwright's right, had the Director of the Larminster Festival on her other side. This seemed rather a grand title for the pleasant-faced boy, scarcely older than the Cartwright girls, who introduced himself to her as Nat Fitzwilliam, told her that he was Bridset born, and confided that he had been running the theatre since he left Oxford 'because no one else much wanted to do it.'

The Boy Director was deputed to escort Jemima and Cherry over to the Watchtower after lunch. Jemima observed that whenever he was not coping rather frenziedly with the knives, forks and glasses by his side, as well as the persistent attentions of the Blagges – he hardly touched his wine – Nat Fitzwilliam gazed almost literally open-mouthed at Christabel Cartwright. Jemima could well imagine the effect of the return of such a dazzling creature on a stage-struck youth. How old had he been when she left?

At this point, Jemima discovered with a slight jolt to her interviewer's complacency that Nat Fitzwilliam was not quite the naive amateur of her imagination. It was not so much the list of his credits at Oxford which impressed her – indeed she had a nasty feeling that she might have caught his Chinese (Sung Dynasty) *Hamlet* while at Edinburgh and found it wanting. No, it was the discovery that Nat Fitzwilliam had already directed a play for television, an opera in Holland, and part of a series for the BBC on English poets and their private lives, which Jemima had much admired. All this, while also residing in Bridset and as Nat engagingly put it, 'trying to keep the Watchtower upstanding'. It all went to show that Nat was not only older but also more energetic than he looked.

Next to Cherry sat Julian's uncle, introduced as Major Edgar Cartwright. At first Jemima assumed that the old boy had merely been wheeled into action in order to even up the sexes a little. But Major Cartwright also revealed himself as the Chairman of the Larminster Festival Committee. Jemima expected this information to be followed up by some hard discussion of the subject. Major Cartwright, however, merely leant forward and asked Jemima one question in a very fierce voice:

'This television business: do you pay us or do we pay you?' Having received a roughly reassuring reply – no money need necessarily change hands – he relapsed into a morose silence. This left him free to contemplate Cherry's décolletage with apparent outrage, while every now and then casting a look which Jemima interpreted as acute dislike towards his nephew's wife.

Surprisingly, it was the Major who chose to answer Julian's open question to Christabel about her accident. She had given her little laugh and taken a sip of wine before answering – Jemima noticed that throughout the lunch Christabel's drinking, like that of Miss Kettering (and Cherry), had kept well up with the pace of the Blagges' refilling. Before Christabel could speak, the Major butted in, making his second remark of the luncheon, so far as Jemima was concerned. His voice, like that of his nephew, was commandingly loud.

'The woman's not used to gardening any more, living in some basement in London. That's all there is to be said on the subject.' The Major took a deep swig of his red wine; Christabel drank further of her own glass. At which the Major added something like: 'Damn it', and proceeded to glare round until Mr Blagge refilled his glass. Further draughts of red wine silenced him once more completely. Christabel's fair powdered skin looked rather pink, but perhaps that was the effect of the wine.

It was left to Nat Fitzwilliam, riding with Jemima in her Mercedes after lunch to inspect the Watchtower, to voice the obvious about the very odd social occasion they had just attended. He was able to curl himself confidently into the front seat since Cherry, attempting to hitch a lift from Julian Cartwright, had found herself palmed off with the Major as her chauffeur.

'I always ride with the girls on Sunday,' had been Julian Cartwright's excuse. 'Otherwise the horses wouldn't know it was the Sabbath.' He elected not to hear Cherry's valiant offer of mounting a steed herself – or perhaps a glance at her tight skirt discouraged him from taking her offer seriously.

'Wowee,' breathed Nat Fitzwilliam. Then as if that were not sufficient, he whistled and passed his hand over his brow. 'Wow,' he added. 'What about that? Christabel *Herrick* back at Lark Manor. Why on earth do you suppose she came back? After all these years?'

'Perhaps she repented her wicked ways. Alternatively perhaps she missed the very comfortable gilded cage.' Jemima spoke lightly. As far as she was concerned, the events which had overtaken Christabel Cartwright, or had been provoked by her, lay in the past.

While Jemima admitted to a healthy curiosity on the subject of Christabel's reappearance and the strange combination of graciousness and tensity which the atmosphere at Lark Manor presented, her main concern was with Megalith's seventy-five minute programme on the Larminster Festival. Jemima could see in Christabel's dramatic return a possible obstacle to the successful execution of her endeavour. Already Gregory Rowan, one of the most prominent local residents and one who should certainly feature in the programme, had issued his appeal for cancellation. Now if everyone at Larminster was going to spend the summer discussing the concerns of Christabel Cartwright, it might be very difficult to film the Festival in a relaxed and spontaneous manner.

Nat Fitzwilliam's next remark made her heart sink.

'Do you suppose, since she *is* back, I could persuade her to take part in the Festival? Smashing television for you, of course, and smashing publicity for us. Absolutely transform the programme.' He paused. 'Wowee,' he exclaimed. 'I think *The Sunday Times* might take a piece from me now ... they've turned me down once ... now that I've got Christabel Herrick, the return of Christabel Herrick, to offer ...'

As Nat Fitzwilliam expatiated on these daydreams, Jemima took another look at his cherub's face, its look of candour and sweetness enhanced by the broad brow and wide-set trusting eyes. She realized with some alarm that the cherub's exterior only partially hid the ruthless and empire-building ambitions. Did he cultivate the look of youth to trap the unwary? But Nat had already passed on to the subject of the visit of the touring company, named after its famous theatre of origin, the King Charles at Bridesbury.

'*The Seagull* and that hoary old favourite of Gregory's about Marie Antoinette in prison, showing how she came over all noble at the end,' he was muttering. 'Repertory companies always trot it out if they've got a talented leading actress. Two wonderful parts for *her*, anyway. I believe I could get Anna Maria to step down, she owes me a favour, or if she won't, the bitch, there's always blackmail, isn't there? Then I'll tell Boy Greville that he can't direct the second episode in my series unless he steps down—'

The cherub's eyes were gleaming.

'Look here,' Jemima interrupted strongly, wrenching his attention away from the King Charles Company to his present situation. 'My dear boy, this is all moonshine. What on earth makes you think that Christabel

Herrick *wants* to return to the stage? Isn't it rather the point that she's returned to her family and abandoned the stage? And I should add that Megalith Television is concentrating on Larminster as its typical homespun English festival, not as a major *pièce de scandale.*' Jemima made her words as cold as possible, hoping to punctuate Nat Fitzwilliam's wishful thinking.

'Oh right, right, absolutely. Sorry I got carried away. You're absolutely right. Look, here we are. Park on the left. Then you get a good view of the sea *and* the Watchtower, right in line. As it was meant to be seen.'

Jemima gazed dutifully up at the extremely modern pentagonal building, constructed of blackish stone and darkened glass which loomed above them. Her appreciation was just turning to admiration – at first sight it was one of the most successful modern buildings she had seen – when she received an unpleasant inkling that Nat Fitzwilliam was one of those people who never wasted time in argument, merely proceeded with their plans underground when checked.

'To think, *she's* never even been here!' he was exclaiming fervently as he unlocked the front doors. Jemima could see the empty interior of the foyer through the transparent cinnamon-coloured glass.

'I want you to see it this way,' Nat continued. 'Our little modern masterpiece. Featured in the *Architectural Review* twice. All built with Cartwright money when the dry rot made the old theatre a public hazard. *She* must have had the idea; and then she never saw it finished.'

They crossed the foyer. Jemima did not like empty theatres. She found something creepy about them; even the locked box office, also made of cinammon glass, did not please her. She made a mental note not to allow the architectural properties of the Watchtower to dominate her programme: this was to tell the story of the Festival, not a little modern masterpiece. Even so she had to admit that the stage and surrounding seats – on four of the five sides – were so well constructed as to give the interior of the theatre an appeal in its own right. All the same, all Guthrie Carlyle's shots would show people, lots of people, or would if Jemima had anything to do with it . . .

Nat Fitzwilliam fumbled for another switch and flooded the theatre with more light.

'Can't you just imagine it?' he said gloatingly. For a moment Jemima actually thought he was referring to the television programme she would make, they would make together. But Nat was once more in the grip of his vision.

'Christabel Herrick makes her come-back, directed by Nat Fitzwilliam. Oh, I know she'll do it for me,' he added quickly and joyously, to quell Jemima's objections. 'You see, I was a great friend of Barry's.'

'Barry?' queried Jemima.

'Barry! Barry Blagge! The infamous or famous boyfriend, depending on your point of view. Me for the latter, of course. Barry Blagge! Better known as Iron Boy! Don't you remember: "Coo-ool Repentance"?' He crooned the words as though clutching a mike.

'Iron Boy!' exclaimed Cherry, coming through the doors behind them. 'And that was my favourite of them all, that and "Daring Darling". I told you, Jem. Listen, very quickly, while the old boy parks his car, do you know what he told me on the way here? The solitary remark he made as a matter of fact. That couple, serving that Buckingham Palace of a lunch. Can you believe it? *They're his parents* – Iron Boy's parents.' Cherry's eyes were now as round as mill-stones.

'She runs off à la Lady Chatterley, well, that sort of thing, with the handsome stable lad. That's all he was – Iron Boy was – in those days. And his old parents are still there working at the Manor. They just keep on working. And they're *still* there when she returns . . . Talk about Cool Repentance. Under all that quietness and graciousness, they must absolutely *loathe* her.

'What a weird set-up,' pronounced Cherry, with much satisfaction, adding with that talent for stating the obvious which never deserted her even in moments of greatest crisis: 'I mean, it would never happen in London.'

5

'I'll be Safe'

During May a great many things happened both in London (Megalithic House) and Larminster (the Watchtower Theatre) to advance the planning of Jemima Shore's Festival programme. Most of these things happened more or less on schedule. Even the things which did not happen on schedule, like Guthrie Carlyle and his cameraman Spike Thompson going to the wrong restaurant in Larminster when they were on a reccy – not the one in the *Good Food Guide* – did not in the end impede the development of the programme overmuch. It was an error incidentally for which they most unfairly blamed Cherry: but Cherry was quick to point out that she had booked them into absolutely the right restaurant in the first place; it was pure male chauvinism which had led them to prefer Christopher's Diner (unlisted) to Flora's Kitchen (highly recommended) once on the spot in Larminster.

One of the unscheduled things which was felt to be a hindrance was the constant presence of Nat Fitzwilliam in London. As Director of the Festival being put together in Larminster, rather than the programme being worked out in London, it might have been supposed that Nat Fitzwilliam would have concentrated on the rustic side of things. But this would have been to underestimate the cheerful cherub's capacity to be in both places at once, or at any rate to commute on his motor-bike all too regularly between them.

'That young man will be the death of me,' grumbled Guthrie Carlyle after one of Nat's unsolicited calls at Megalithic House. ('I was supposed to see both Peter *and* Trevor this morning – they're interested in my Sung *Hamlet* at the National – no, no, it's Trevor who's talking musicals and *Middlemarch* at the RSC – but luckily Peter chucked, so that I thought that on my way to see Jonathan at the BBC, I'd just pop in—') 'Correction. This Festival will be the death of me,' continued Guthrie. 'Or if not me, the death of someone probably in the contracts department, in view of Spike Thompson's latest *coup* over his expenses.'

'Wouldn't it be lovely if it was the death of Nat Fitzwilliam?' Jemima spoke wistfully. 'I speak purely professionally, you understand. Just his reputation. I don't want his youthful corpse on my hands, looking all pathetic, appealing to the mother in me. But this morning he gave me most cogently *his* views on *Jonathan Miller*'s views on Shakespeare and I'm not sure that I can take—'

'Have you heard the latest?' Cherry tripped in. 'Our Nat is going to direct *The Seagull* himself. Boy Greville has withdrawn. Personal reasons, *he* says. And that is not all, my friends. *What* about this?' She paused for effect, and who could deny the effect was ravishing – pale-pink T-shirt perilously scoop-necked and pale-pink skirt slit up both sides to reveal plump smooth olive-skinned thighs.

Guthrie whistled appreciatively. 'Wowee, as Nat Fitzwilliam would say. And has Spike Thompson taken time off from his expenses to have the pleasure?' But Cherry for once was not in a mood for tribute.

'Believe or not, she's agreed! Our Nat has fixed it. Christabel Herrick stars! *The Seagull*. And that lovely weepy piece of Gregory Rowan's everyone does at school, *Widow Capet*. You know, Marie Antoinette in prison, thinking about the diamond necklace etc., etc. She'll be Marie Antoinette, yes? Très, très revolutionary France. And *The Seagull*.' Cherry's voice dropped. 'Very, very nineteenth-century Russia.'

'Knowing Nat Fitzwilliam, I wouldn't be a bit surprised if it was exactly the other way round,' observed Jemima tartly. But she was more concerned to digest the surprising and not particularly welcome news of Nat Fitzwilliam's successful recasting. She had no doubt already that the return to the stage of Christabel Herrick – even to the stage of the Watchtower, Bridset, would attract a great deal of interest not all of it purely theatrical in origin. Was this quite what Cy Fredericks had in mind when he had spoken to Jemima of including in her series 'one really superbly insignificant country festival'?

Cy had warmed to his theme: 'Significant in its very insignificance, my dear Jem. A repertory company of the greatest integrity; local worthies, each more respectable than the last, whose wives have never even raised their eyes above another man's feet, sleeping in their seats, the sleep of the just after a long day's work like characters in Hardy, the whole lot preferably in dinner jackets, the worthies of course, not their wives. The wives should be wearing gowns of classical inextravagance in keeping with the plays presented, eternal values kept decently in check. This festival, through the medium of Megalith Television, should symbolize of itself all that makes English cultural country life what it is today.'

Cy had leant back in satisfied contemplation of his own eloquence. 'In short, my dear Jem, the sort of thing that you and I would run a mile rather than attend.' Remembering rather too late that he was in fact recommending Jemima to spend several weeks at such a festival, Cy had added quickly: 'Except in the line of duty, that is.'

Was this new improved version of the Larminster Festival quite what Cy Fredericks had in mind as the significantly insignificant? At the same time Jemima was uneasily aware that Cy Fredericks was hardly going to back out from televising the return of Christabel Herrick to the stage; something to which it would appear that he had inadvertently secured the exclusive rights. Under the circumstances she hardly thought that Cy would stick by his original notion of decent cultural obscurity. Her instinct told her that her own programme was due to undergo roughly the same transformation as the Larminster Festival itself in the immediate future.

And so indeed it proved. Over the next few days Cy Fredericks abandoned the whole concept of the insignificant festival with suspicious alacrity. Larminster and its Festival now became infinitely more central in the whole Fredericks scheme of things and that in turn reflected on the lives of all those concerned with the original programme.

Guthrie Carlyle, swearing outwardly over the damage to schedules, comforted himself inwardly with dreams of prime-time television. Cherry took the opportunity to end – most regretfully – a romance with a craggy forty-year-old producer in another department on the grounds of pressure of work; her secret dreams were of Julian Cartwright's handsomely greying head on her pillow in some Larminster hostelry while Christabel busied herself with her career. Even Spike Thompson, saturnine as ever in his legendary battered black leather jacket, with looks which made his claim to descend from a family of Italian icecream manufacturers named Tommaso at least plausible, spared time from the possible financial implications of such a change to murmur: 'Christabel Herrick, she looks pretty good in her photographs and some of these older women are fantastic.'

'Christabel Herrick, isn't she absolutely into younger men?' enquired a passing secretary innocently. 'I mean, didn't she run off with a randy teenager?'

'Yes, Spike, you'd better keep an eye on your Focus Puller,' concurred Guthrie in a bland voice which was not at all innocent; leaving the secretary to wonder why the great – and greatly fancied – Spike Thompson gave her a wide berth in the Megalith canteen thereafter, despite a series of very straightforward propositions made there on previous occasions.

Jemima Shore for her part found herself with two new tasks. The first was to get to know Christabel Herrick, the distinguished actress who had dominated a generation before abandoning the stage, through the

medium of the Megalith cuttings library. The second was to get to know
Christabel Cartwright, the lady of Lark Manor, in person.

She was half-way through the first task, when she was interrupted by a
telephone call from the object of her researches. Already Jemima had
become torn between morbid curiosity and personal disgust as sensational headline followed headline. Listening to Christabel Cartwright's
delightful low voice on the telephone, she found it very difficult to equate
the two images.

Christabel's call fortuitously set the second task under way, for she had
rung up to propose lunch together. She suggested Larminster – Flora's
Kitchen – rather than her own house on the rather vaguely expressed
grounds that 'there's so much always going on at Lark'.

A few days later at the restaurant Christabel was more explicit: 'We're
redesigning the courtyard garden to make it less *doleful*, there are no
flowers there in the summer, except climbers, which is ridiculous, lots
and lots of peonies I thought, Julian says they take years to establish, but I
said, we've *got* years darling, years and years, at least speaking for
myself . . .'

Yes, thought Jemima, it was certainly very difficult to reconcile the
romantic heroine – or villainess – of the newspaper with this pleasant
pretty well-dressed woman sitting opposite her, rattling on about her
garden planning. Jemima watched Christabel pouring herself a large
vodka from a half-bottle produced somewhat surprisingly from her Gucci
handbag, and thought that was about the only eccentric note she struck.
And even that proved susceptible to explanation.

'No vodka here,' cried Christabel, 'and I can't have lunch without a
voddy, can I? So Poll doesn't mind if I bring my own.'

Poll was a girl with very long very straight hair who served them in
virtual silence, except for occasional low-voiced suggestions. She moved
mysteriously and gracefully, vanishing from time to time into the kitchen
at the back with a swish of her long skirts. Whereupon from the kitchen
much louder noises of furious expostulation usually issued.

'That's Moll,' confided Christabel during one of these bouts. 'She
cooks. And yells at Poll. They're a devoted couple except when Moll gets
one of her jealous fits about Poll and the male customers. They met as art
students. In Florence, you will not be totally surprised to hear.'

The menu featured Botticelli Salad, Boeuf Primavera and Syllabub
Uffizi. Impressionistic figures, roughly based on those of Botticelli, had
been painted all over the walls of the dark little restaurant, giving a
pleasantly cavernous effect. The table-cloths and napkins were made of
Botticelli-printed linen: Jemima found herself staring down at Venus's left
breast, the nipple centrally placed between her knife and fork. All the food
was absolutely delicious, and except for its name, there was nothing
Italianate about it at all.

The house wine was also very good. Poll, unasked, brought a bottle of red and placed it before Christabel. Since Jemima then gently enquired for some white, Christabel was left alone with the red; the level, Jemima noticed, went down quite rapidly, as Poll filled and refilled Christabel's glass silently and deftly.

In the far corner of Flora's Kitchen, appropriately enough in the shadow of the Three Graces, Jemima noticed Spike Thompson having lunch with Nat Fitzwilliam. Poll's long hair drooped and dipped tenderly over Spike Thompson's plate in a way that Jemima thought would not greatly please Moll were she to witness it. Spike, in a scarlet polo-necked jersey under his black leather jacket, was the only truly Italian-looking thing in the restaurant; in contrast to the schoolboy appearance of Nat Fitzwilliam, he looked quite aggressively masculine.

Jemima removed her gaze, banished some unprofessional thoughts on the subject of her cameraman, and concentrated on Christabel. Christabel's fluffy hair was framed rather than covered in the halo of a blue chiffon scarf. A ruffled white blouse under a pale-blue jacket on which a full-blown creamy rose was held by a jewelled pin made her look as ostentatiously feminine as Spike looked masculine. The jewelled pin which held the spray was in the shape of a lily of the valley simulated in pearls and jade. Yet Jemima did not feel that she had dressed with any special care for this occasion; merely that her appearance in general was the result of constant cherishing. The right word for Christabel was glamorous. In that respect she resembled royalty – or an actress.

THE ACTRESS AND THE PLOUGHBOY – that was one glaring headline which came back into Jemima's mind. All that side of Christabel Cartwright seemed quite incomprehensible, looking at her now – unless of course one was inclined to explain the whole history of the world in terms of sex. And that, Jemima, despite being most amiably disposed towards the subject herself, had always supposed to be an error. Perhaps Christabel's history had something to teach her.

According to the newspapers, Christabel Cartwright's torrid romance with Barry Blagge, the handsome red-haired only child of the married couple who worked at Lark Manor, had begun when he was about twenty-one. It was of course nonsense – pure headlinese – to describe him as a ploughboy. Even the columns beneath the headlines themselves contradicted the notion. Barry Blagge, leaving aside his remarkable looks, revealed even at that stage in fuzzy newspaper photographs, had been bright, very bright. He had secured first O-levels and then A-levels at Larminster Royal, hardly a universal occurrence at that quiet school in the early 1970s.

His bent however had not been academic, as various obliging friends had pointed out to various interested newspapers. No, a pop star was what Barry Blagge had decided that he intended to be. There was nothing in his background to explain such an ambition. Mr Blagge was a former soldier who had been Major Cartwright's batman while Mrs Blagge had been lady's maid to Julian Cartwright's mother, Lady May – two sober people. The trouble was that Barry had been born to them late in life. As a result, observers agreed, there had been far too much indulgence there, which they gleefully blamed for what followed: 'Mrs Blagge always spoiled young Barry rotten, gave him everything he wanted, motor-bike when he was sixteen, and then he wore silver bracelets! I ask you, a boy of seventeen in silver bracelets like a duchess. And that ridiculous clown's costume he paraded in about the place. And as for his hair, why didn't his father just make him cut it, cut it himself if needs be, he was in the army Jim Blagge, he knew the score, oh yes, they always gave him everything he wanted . . .' And so forth and so on went the happy prurient chorus.

But the Blagges had not been able to give Barry everything he wanted. They had not been able to make him into a pop star overnight for example. The opportunities in Larminster for singing, even with the most humble group, being naturally somewhat limited, Barry's career had languished. Even so there were those who were sufficiently struck by his remarkable physical appearance – the features of Michelangelo's David set in a halo of profuse auburn curls which gyrated fiercely as he sang – combined with the weird sensuality of his singing, to remember and recount later the odd amateur performances. On the whole however Larminster regarded young Barry Blagge on or off his motor-bike, in silver bracelets, pierrot costumes, singing or silent, with distaste or disapproval.

What the Blagges with their manorial connections could do for Barry was to get him a job, a job of sorts. Hence the ploughboy epithet, although Barry was actually helping to bring in the harvest at Lark.

It was during the long hot summer of 1976, when the Bridset fields were whitening in the sun, that the romance of Christabel Cartwright and Barry Blagge flamed, much as the rest of England flamed in the dry intensity of that legendary weather. Christabel had planned to spend a quiet summer holiday with her daughters, then thirteen and fourteen, after a long season at the Gray Theatre. Instead she fell passionately in love with Barry Blagge. When autumn came she returned to London and the theatre – taking Barry with her.

The whole scandal might still have been contained since Julian Cartwright maintained a front of total reserve. He continued to refer in public to his wife's absence, even their separation, as purely temporary, something to do with the alien world of the theatre, no concern of Julian Cartwright's, the ever-courteous lord of the manor of Lark. In this way he even managed to countenance the undeniable fact that Barry Blagge was living in Christabel's apartment in Eaton Place. 'Being helped with his music,' said Mrs Blagge, caught on the telephone at Lark Manor, and

Julian Cartwright went along with that too. So there the story might well have rested, for lack of further developments. Had it not been for Barry Blagge himself.

Jemima had to admit that Barry Blagge's first exclusive interview with the *Sunday Sink* – headline MY FIRST LADY OF PASSION – made compellingly lurid reading even five years later. There was even a kind of black humour, a bizarre turn of phrase about some of his utterances – if indeed he and not a newspaper ghost-writer was personally responsible for them. With hindsight it was possible to see that it was not out of character for Barry Blagge, an unknown young man in his early twenties, to seek out a Sunday newspaper and insist on delivering his intimate memoirs of a famous actress. At the time the sensation caused both by the revelations and by the flagrancy of the deed itself was enormous.

Would Barry Blagge's career have taken off without this bold stroke of treachery? Probably. The ambition which had caused him to contact the *Sunday Sink* in the first place would surely have enabled him to win through sooner or later – even if you discounted his astonishing looks, reinforcing his voice and lyrics. Within four months of the *Sunday Sink* story, Barry Blagge's first record 'Iron Boy' – a suitable title – got high into the charts. A few months later 'Daring Darling' – another suitable title – reached No. 1. Six months later Iron Boy himself, as Barry Blagge was now mainly known in public, promoting his new record 'Cool Repentance', conquered not only Britain and the United States but most of the rest of the world.

And what of Christabel? At first she continued to work as she had always done, occupying that prominent role on the English stage so ably described by Barry Blagge when he had called her the 'First lady of passion' – if the passion as delineated by Ibsen and Chekhov was of a rather different nature from that envisaged by the *Sunday Sink's* readers. At first, too, there were small gossipy pictures of Barry Blagge attending her opening nights. Later these were replaced by very large pictures of Iron Boy at her opening nights, in a series of his remarkable costumes. As he grew more famous, he made some remarkable statements too on the subject of the theatrical scene. Some of his comments on Christabel's fellow-actors were really rather funny (Jemima guessed by now that the black humour was his own) as well as quite insupportably impudent. Then he discussed Christabel herself – in simpler and more laudatory terms: 'Christabel rules OK.' It all read rather oddly put side by side with the theatrical reviews of the piece in question: her rather subdued Hedda Gabler for example.

As Iron Boy's comments on the person described by some newspapers as his paramour grew more outrageous, the critics, as though not to be outdone, became rather more strident too. Christabel Herrick, their darling for so many years, began to falter in their estimation. Her Hedda

Gabler was merely received coldly – but that could have been the fault of an innately poor production. It was more sinister when the word 'emotional' began to creep into the papers. The reviews became more barbed, with unpleasant undertones. One critic, describing her Portia, spoke of 'liberties with the text on the first night, of the sort we do not associate with Miss Herrick'.

There were no photographs of Christabel Herrick at Iron Boy's concerts, although her face, looking sad and very distinguished, like a French marquise at an eve-of-guillotine feast, occasionally stared out of photographs taken at restaurants afterwards.

Six months after records such as 'Iron Boy' and 'Cool Repentance' had ensured their progenitor world-wide acclaim (that amazing Far Eastern tour, for example, which even Jemima, no connoisseur of the genre, remembered), Christabel left the cast of a new play just before it opened in the West End. Her agent, apparently taken by surprise, spoke gallantly of the need for a complete rest. It did not help therefore when Christabel was subsequently photographed at London Airport on her way to the United States, where Barry was enjoying a further triumphal progress. Her agent's second statement was even more embarrassed than the first. Christabel in this particular photograph looked haggard and much older than what Jemima reckoned roughly to have been her forty-five years. The scarf she wore on her head did not suit her; her eyes looked huge and scared, her nose too prominent. It was as though she knew in advance of the humiliations which awaited her on the other side of the Atlantic.

That was the last picture of Christabel Herrick in the Megalith cuttings library. There were plenty more cuttings of Iron Boy, of course – during the four months he had left to live. Jemima leafed through them with a horrid sensation of nemesis, knowing the grisly end to the story. But there was no picture of the scene when Christabel discovered that Barry had moved into the apartment of a famous black model, six foot tall, nineteen years old and very beautiful – nickname Tiny Georgianne. It seemed that he never even met Christabel when she arrived in New York, but relied on his usual mode of expression, the press statement, to convey to her the news. But of that Jemima could not be sure.

Even the cuttings about Christabel diminished now. Somehow she had obviously struggled back to London, eluding the press at Heathrow, since there was no picture of her arrival. She had been in London, living alone, when the last pictures of Iron Boy were careened all over the newspapers – the day after his beautiful sinuous arrogant body had been cut roughly in half by a lorry, as he rode his motor-bike down the freeway in the Los Angeles dawn, pierrot clothes flying, surrounded by his followers, going from the dawn to oblivion.

Christabel Herrick's statement on Iron Boy's death – no new picture available, just the old distraught one at London Airport – was short and dignified. It spoke with regret of the loss – and that was all. She did not, of course, attend the funeral, which took place in Los Angeles and was marked by hysterical scenes of grief from Iron Boy's fans. Nor, so far as Jemima could make out, did Mr and Mrs Blagge, still of Lark Manor. Nor was any statement from them printed on the subject of Barry's death.

In the cuttings library, Jemima Shore pondered on Christabel's use of the word loss. There was the loss of life, of course – Barry's. Then there was the loss of love – Barry's too – assuming he had ever loved her. And what of the other losses which surrounded this squalid little story? The loss of reputation and dignity to Christabel herself? The loss of security and privacy to her children? The loss of everything to her husband?

Sitting now in Flora's Kitchen, Jemima gazed with something like awe at the smoothly powdered brow before her, the large turquoise eyes eyeing her seductively over a glass of wine, held in a white hand on which a huge aquamarine shone with a shallow blue light. Was it really possible to return, as Christabel Cartwright had evidently done, and bury the past, as securely as Barry Blagge had buried himself in Iron Boy, and Iron Boy was now buried in some Californian cemetery?

She could not help wondering whether Christabel herself felt any regrets for what she had done. Back in the lap of the manor with her rich husband and adoring children, did she ever think back to the events of her lurid past? Jemima sighed. She knew that her Puritan streak, inherited from generations of stubbornly Nonconformist ancestors, shrank away from the spectacle of Christabel's uncomplicated equanimity.

She did not exactly want Christabel to be *punished* for her sins . . . that was a ridiculous notion for Jemima Shore, the famously tolerant liberated lady of the eighties, professionally engaged in comprehending and thus pardoning all around her. Perhaps she just wanted her to feel something, to show something of her past in her manner, in some way to repent.

Jemima pulled herself up sharply. Now that really was a ridiculous word for Jemima Shore to use, straight out of a Puritan past. She would be advocating the stocks for adultery on television next! Jemima was never quite sure whether or not she believed in sin, but she was quite sure she did not believe in public repentance. Jemima set herself firmly to carry out the real task before her. This was not only to get to know Christabel Herrick but also to actually like her – much the best preparation for a successful programme.

Oddly enough it proved remarkably easy to like Christabel: as well as genuine warmth, she had an excellent racy sense of humour which appealed to Jemima. It was not so easy to get to know her. Throughout lunch, Jemima sensed some reserve, some nervousness which made Christabel's original invitation to her seem rather puzzling in retrospect. Had Christabel really asked her to Flora's Kitchen merely to swap amusing stories of theatrical acquaintances and devour Syllabub Uffizi with mutual cries of dietary guilt?

It was at the end of the meal, when Christabel was powdering her nose and looking in the mirror of her gold compact with its jewelled clasp – Cartier no doubt – that she made the first revealing remark of the lunch.

'I'm so frightened about all this, you know,' she said suddenly.

Jemima gave a tactful murmur: 'You mean the stage after so long.'

'That – and other things.' There was a silence while Poll placed the bill between them, her long hair brushing the paper. Jemima, used to entertaining in the way of business, made an instinctive gesture towards it. Christabel swept her hand away: 'On my account.' Without looking at the bill, she thrust a very large tip on top of it and signed to Poll to take it away. Poll, like a witch in *Macbeth*, departed as silently as she had come. The distant shouts of Moll greeted her return to the kitchen.

The restaurant was now empty, Nat Fitzwilliam and Spike Thompson having presumably returned to the theatre.

Jemima's murmur grew still more tactful. 'You mean – also so much public attention – after' – how should she put it? – 'quite a gap. You mean – the loss of privacy. The publicity.'

'No, no,' Christabel leant forward and clutched Jemima's hand across the nymph-strewn tablecloth. Jemima could smell the lily-of-the-valley perfume which wafted from her like a sharp sweet cloud. 'Don't you see, darling, I *want* publicity. That's just why I'm doing it.'

'Well, of course, I do see—' began Jemima. Although nothing surprised her about the general avidity for publicity, Christabel Herrick might under the circumstances have been an exception to that rule.

'I don't think you do. When Nat asked me, I jumped at the chance. He thought he had to persuade me. He didn't. I jumped at it. Even his ludicrous underwater *Seagull* and that maudlin play of Gregory's about Marie Antoinette, never one of my favourites, though it's a good part. I suddenly saw it was the way, the only way.'

'To get back onto the stage?'

'No, to be *safe*.' Christabel's voice was low and very thrilling as she pronounced the words. 'You see, darling, I know I'll feel secure with the eyes of the world upon me. The eyes of television. I'll be safe. Safe at last. Back on the stage. Your programme will be the saving of me.' Her voice grew lower and more tremulous. 'Oh, Jemima, I've been so terribly, terribly frightened, you can't imagine. Locked away at Lark. It's so dangerous . . .'

She broke off. The low door of the restaurant opened. Gregory Rowan, stooping, entered. He was accompanied by the red-haired woman known as Ketty, and the two Cartwright girls, one tall, one short, who stood rather awkwardly at the door.

'Here we are, my dear,' said Gregory with the utmost geniality. 'Your jolly old chauffeur, all present and correct, come to fetch you. I brought Ketty too, partly to do some shopping, partly because she wanted to go to confession.'

'Oh darling, what a shame,' Christabel sounded completely calm. 'I brought my own car. All this way for nothing.'

'Ah, but what you don't know is that Julian has already driven your car back after the County Council meeting. He thought driving might be rather a mistake after your lunch with Miss World Investigator here – you know. Better come quietly, hadn't you?' he added jocularly.

Christabel obediently followed him out of the restaurant. Miss Kettering with Regina and Blanche brought up the rear.

6

'Mummy, Mummy, Mummy'

No one could remember afterwards with any certainty who first suggested having the Festival picnic by the sea. Or rather, when it was discussed in the light of what happened later, everyone seemed to have a different version of how the idea arose.

The Megalith contingent – Jemima, Cherry, Guthrie Carlyle as well as Spike Thompson – received their invitations from Nat Fitzwilliam. This left Jemima with the distinct impression, confirmed by Guthrie, that the initiative had come from Nat in the first place. Unquestionably Nat regarded the occasion as yet another opportunity for exercising his directorial powers. He confided to Jemima that his ideas for *The Seagull* (that production scoffingly described by Christabel as 'underwater') derived their inspiration from boyhood experiences on the Larmouth sea-shore.

'By enclosing the whole production in fishermen's nets, and grounding it in sand, using rocks covered in sea-weed for furniture where necessary instead of that predictably dreary nineteenth-century Russian stuff, I think I'm groping for the symbolism *under* the symbolism of *The Seagull*. But of course I'm not forgetting Chekhov's outward intentions as well, not for a minute. I utterly despise the kind of director who simply forgets about the author altogether. I just want to fuse the two – the inner Chekhov then, the outer Chekhov now. By creating this kind of Russian picnic of us all, the whole Larminster Festival society, I think I shall strike some kind of blow towards that.'

'It all begins to make sense,' said Jemima solemnly.

'It needed doing,' echoed Guthrie with equal gravity. These two phrases had served them well in tight corners before now.

Nat looked pleased. Then a look of slight uncertainty – a rare expression – crossed his face. 'Of course I meant the other way round. The outer Chekhov then, the inner Chekhov now. But you realized that.'

'Of course,' said Jemima and Guthrie together.

At breakfast at Lark Manor on the other hand, Julian Cartwright was busy blaming his daughter Regina for the whole thing.

'For God's sake, Rina.' He spoke in a distinctly testy voice, 'Poor Mummy's already getting absolutely exhausted. You know how tired she gets when she's working. You don't remember? Well you know now. And then this bloody picnic.' He pulled himself up with the air of one who had been sufficiently sorely tried to desert a principle. 'I apologize. This disastrous picnic. We could have had a peaceful Sunday lunch. Whatever induced you, Rina, to suggest it?'

'We always used to have lovely picnics at the sea on Sundays in the summer.' Regina for once sounded as sulky as Blanche. 'Besides, I want to ride Lancelot down to the sea and let the wind flow through my hair.' She shook back her thick black tresses ostentatiously before adding: 'Anyway it was Blanche's idea, not mine.'

'As a matter of fact, Daddy, the picnic was probably Ketty's idea in the first place.' Blanche, in contrast, was in unusually high spirits. 'She wants to meet all the actors in the Festival. She keeps droning on about the old days at the Gray Theatre. And since the Blagges do all the work I don't see it's such a terrible problem for Mummy.'

'Sand in the sandwiches! Tepid coffee, empty lemonade bottles.' Julian Cartwright's handsome face flushed with irritation as he too cried 'Ugh' in his turn. He was so unreasonably bad-tempered that both girls burst out laughing.

'Oh Daddy,' cried Blanche, 'as if Lark Manor picnics were ever like that! No, we shall have our usual sumptuous food, served in our usual sumptuous style, and the actors are going to cook theirs on a huge fire—'

'Which means,' chimed in Regina, 'they will eat up all ours and be rather embarrassed and we will eat up all theirs and not be embarrassed at all. Then footing it featly, we'll all rush into the sea together, all taking hands, chanting "Come unto these yellow sands . . . curtsied when you have and kiss'd – the wild waves whist."'

'Talking of wild waves, you will not be swimming today, Regina. Nor you, Blanche.' Ketty had come into the kitchen, surprisingly quietly, through the louvred doors. There was no expression in her voice. She stood surveying the little breakfast party with her narrow lips slightly pursed. She was wearing a dark-green dress with a full skirt, rather too long for fashion, and two rows of enormous amber beads. Her thick knot of hair was skewered with a tortoise-shell pin. Without her garish lipstick and green eyeshadow, thought Julian, Ketty would really be quite a good-looking woman: but who could imagine Ketty without her warpaint?

'Jim Blagge says there's quite a sharp breeze at the point,' continued

Ketty. 'He went fishing this morning. The tide will be going out at lunch-time. The river makes odd currents at low tide. It's far too dangerous. You could be carried out round the point.'

'It's very hot here, Ketty, no breeze at all,' Julian spoke mildly. 'Very hot night altogether. Mrs Cartwright couldn't sleep at all. In fact I must speak to Blagge about her shutters.' He paused and said in an even more diplomatic voice: 'She was thinking of swimming herself. I think she wants Mrs Blagge to help her find her old bathing-costumes, and there should be some old bathing-caps somewhere too.'

'I'll tell my sister, sir.' Ketty stalked out.

'Of course we're going to swim!' exclaimed Blanche before the doors had swung shut. 'All the actors will swim. I've been talking to some of them. It just makes the day quite perfect if Mummy swims too.'

Julian thought that with her flushed cheeks his elder daughter looked really quite attractive: it remained a pity that she would never be so pretty as Regina (nor for that matter as glamorous as her mother) and additionally unfair that Regina had also turned out to be more intelligent. If only Blanche could discover some real interest in life as Regina had turned to poetry. Not the theatre however. He shuddered.

'Lancelot and I are *definitely* going to swim,' said Regina in a loud obstinate voice.

In the pantry of Lark Manor – a kind of inner kitchen lit by a circular window looking onto the courtyard garden – Mr Blagge counted out rows of bamboo-handled knives and forks, considered suitable for picnics. Mrs Blagge folded a cotton table-cloth printed with a pattern of shells and other artistic forms of marine life; then she began to sort out its matching napkins. Her husband shot her a sideways glance.

'How many does that make, then?'

'Enough,' said Mrs Blagge sharply, setting her lips firmly together much as Ketty had just done. 'The Lark Manor party, including the Major. Mr Rowan of course, as usual. And the television people, as instructed by Mr Julian. I am not catering for the actors. Mr Julian did not mention them. They must make their own arrangements. It makes too much work.'

Mr Blagge fetched down a row of tumblers painted with shells from a shelf – as pretty as plastic tumblers could be. 'I thought I heard you suggesting the picnic to Mr Julian the other day as making less work in the house at lunch-time.'

'What's the difference?' countered Mrs Blagge even more sharply. 'Lunch on the shore, lunch in the dining-room. It's all work, isn't it? But I didn't suggest it. I have no doubt it was Katherine's idea. She's more pleased with herself than ever these days, despite the return of' – Mrs Blagge paused before pronouncing disdainfully, 'Her. You must have heard the high and mighty Miss Katherine Kettering suggesting it.'

'People do say your voices are very similar,' was Mr Blagge's only comment.

Upstairs in her cool bedroom, Christabel Cartwright lay between white linen sheets edged with tiny scallops of lace. The vast bed was left unstirred by her slumbers: she might have been a corpse lying there for all the signs of occupation the bed showed. Her eyes were closed.

Christabel knew exactly who it was who wanted the picnic to take place. She put off as long as possible the moment when she would have to leave the safe and silent bedroom and face the day. She drew the white sheet over her head and thought about what might happen at the picnic on the sea-shore. She thought about swimming in the sea, whether it would be safe to swim in the sea.

A few hours later, on the Larmouth beach, it was a very different Christabel Cartwright who emerged. She was now officially Christabel Herrick – perhaps that was the difference. It was Christabel Herrick who was beguiling the whole King Charles Theatre Company as well as enslaving the more susceptible representatives of Megalith Television – Guthrie Carlyle, for example, and Cherry. (Spike Thompson on the other hand showed no particular signs of joining her court as yet, but remained beside Jemima.)

Christabel even clowned for all their delectation in one of the extraordinary bathing-caps which had been rooted out of some cupboard by Mrs Blagge. She ignored a plainer-looking one beside it. Op Art? Pop Art? With its black and white rubber rosettes springing up all over the scalp, the cap she chose certainly belonged to some vanished era of garish fashion.

'I look like a mad magpie especially with this ghastly vulgar bathing-dress,' exclaimed Christabel. 'All the same, I think I should go the whole hog and wear the turquoise one, don't you? You'll certainly all be able to keep an eye on me in the briny. Make sure I don't sink without trace.'

'Are you really going to swim, Mummy?' enquired Blanche solicitously. Regina, who had ridden down to the shore on Lancelot, kicked her heels into the horse and trotted away down the beach. Jemima noticed Julian Cartwright frowning.

'We'll have to build a monster fire in honour of our leading lady's dip,' said a young actor in striped bathing-shorts and rugger shirt, in whose direction Jemima noticed that Blanche Cartwright had been casting yearning glances. He was called something like Ollie or Obbie Summer-town and Jemima vaguely recognized him from various small parts in television: junior detectives, young policemen, and other budding representatives of law and order. He had already been tearing about the beach gathering driftwood; but Jemima had imagined it was for the benefit of Filly Lennox rather than Blanche Cartwright.

The fame of Filumena Lennox, like that of Jemima Shore, sprang from television. In *Country Kate* Filly's ingenious depiction of a disaster-prone city girl trying to run the farm left to her by an unknown admirer had left a deep impression on the public. She was much less experienced on the stage, a state of affairs she was at present trying to remedy by working with the King Charles Company. It seemed that, unlike some famous television stars, Filly Lennox was able to make the switch effectively. Provincial reviewers – and the odd visiting critic from London – had admired her during the previous season.

Jemima, appraising her with interest (she had to admit to a secret fascination with *Country Kate*), thought that Filly Lennox was a good deal less pretty in real life than on the screen. Her floppy fair hair – presumably she had worn a curly wig in the series – made Filly's nose look rather unexpectedly beaky in a small pointed face. In a way she was not unlike a much younger version of Christabel Herrick, although neither lady would probably have relished the comparison. Only Filly's wonderful eyes, large, hazel, fringed by what were clearly naturally long and black eyelashes, remained to startle.

That – and her figure. Gazing speculatively at what could be seen of it already in white cotton trousers and white T-shirt printed with heart and arrow, Jemima thought that for once Flowering Cherry, the toast of Megalithic House, might have to look to her laurels. She need not have worried. The moment when Cherry threw off her fringed purple poncho, edged with jingling bells, was dramatically superb; and what was revealed beneath more than justified her performance of disrobing.

After that Ollie Summertown decided to stop gathering driftwood quite so energetically and strip off his own rugger shirt 'to get some decent sun before lunch'. As if by chance, he lay at Cherry's feet, and was thus conveniently able to share the sun-oil with which she rubbed her gleaming olive legs and shoulders. Blanche looked wistful. Cherry hoped that Julian Cartwright would feel jealous and oiled Ollie's back.

Filly Lennox, unfazed by Ollie's defection, started to flirt quite blatantly with Gregory Rowan: 'Oh, you should have seen my Baroness Anne in your *Tower*! Well anyway the dress. You see, we had this designer – Knocky Pallett – don't ever work with him – if you'd seen what he did to your lovely play ... somehow he insisted the period was entirely topless ...'

To Jemima's surprise, Gregory Rowan seemed to take to this dialogue with enthusiasm.

'Nonsense, my dear, perfectly historically correct. The part shall never be played any other way in my lifetime. Now can we get down to discussing your costume in *Widow Capet*? No false modesty here, I hope. The girl's a brazen hussy, you realize that. What's Knocky Pallett doing these days, I wonder? We might get hold of him for some last-minute liberating suggestions. Nat, what do you think?'

But Nat Fitzwilliam was sitting literally at Christabel's feet, recapitulating for her benefit the triumph of his Sung Dynasty *Hamlet.* Despite the heat he was wearing an anorak and his habitual long scarf which completed the schoolboy look. An expression of outrage crossed his face at the mention of the name Knocky Pallett, but whether at the mere idea of someone else's liberating influence on his own production or at Knocky Pallett's in particular, was not clear. Nevertheless he did not pause in the flow of his disquisition.

Jemima thought that the whole set of Christabel's face looked rather melancholy now that it was in repose. The lines round her mouth were more obvious and there was a sad downward curve to her lips. Perhaps she did not care for the attention Gregory was paying to the flirtatious Filly Lennox: Jemima thought there might have been a gleam of jealousy there. Christabel was certainly a woman accustomed to being the centre of attention as of right. But it was impossible to tell the true expression in her eyes, behind her dark glasses, as she contemplated Nat. She looked beautiful of course – in her own style. A couple of gold chains strung with real shells set in gold hung to her waist. A leopard-skin printed scarf protected her daffodil hair from the sun. Her long diaphanous robe of the same leopard-skin printed material, worn over a matching sun-top and shorts, made the young things' display of nudity look rather odd – or vice versa, thought Jemima, depending on your taste.

As yet Christabel showed no signs of taking to the sea; although the bathing-costumes and caps discovered by Mrs Blagge – including the despised turquoise ruched number and magpie cap – remained by her side. 'Safe at last' – among a company of actors – she had told Jemima. She did not give the impression of one who felt safe.

A group of the other actors – male – were sitting by the fire discussing the Test Match with great earnestness; such was their absorption that the flames would have died down altogether had it not been for the work of Mr Blagge who ended by coping with both the grand Lark Manor picnic and the actors' barbecue. The actors' voices rose and fell, making soothing patterns, no two phrases absolutely the same, but all phrases remarkably similar, like Bach variations played at a distance.

Victor Marcovich, who would play Trigorin in *The Seagull* and the jailer in *Widow Capet,* looked heavily distinguished on the beach with his fine bald dome and fleshy Roman features. He also looked much older than another actor generally addressed as Tobs, who would play the ageing Dr Dorn in *The Seagull* as well as mopping up a number of revolutionary and aristocratic parts in *Widow Capet.* Tobs told Jemima that in the latter production he had to alternate between wearing a Jacobin cap and a powdered wig; as a result he had a recurrent nightmare of getting the order wrong and going finally to the guillotine wearing a Jacobin cap.

'But at least whatever scene you shoot, you can't miss me. No need to worry,' he told Jemima engagingly. 'I should say my best moment is when I come to hoik *her*' – he indicated Christabel – 'off to the guillotine. You can forget Dr Dorn: there's nothing in it for me, particularly in our Nat's seaside version. In my sou'wester and oilskins I'm probably quite unrecognizable.'

'I'll remember,' Jemima promised.

The most ancient member of the company – and indeed of any company likely to be formed – was Nicola Wain. 'Old Nicola', as she generally termed herself, had survived her legendary amount of years as an actress by dint of an outwardly placid nature which concealed something altogether more ruthless beneath.

'I hear you have a part for Old Nicola in your latest,' she would murmur in the ear of unsuspecting directors – and even, when times were very bad, playwrights. 'Oh you naughty boy, nothing for Old Nicola? That's not what I hear. Trying to pull the wool over my eyes, are you, you naughty boy? Waiting for Sybil Thorndike to rise from the dead, eh? Oh, he *is* a naughty boy.'

Certain roles however Nicola considered to be her own. The jailer's mother in *Widow Capet* – a fearful old revolutionary crone armed with knitting needles – being one of them, she had resolutely imposed herself on the Larminster Festival. Even Nat Fitzwilliam had proved incapable of dislodging her. When it was pointed out that there was nothing remotely suitable for her in *The Seagull* – Tobs as a youthful Dr Dorn hardly needed a geriatric Polena – Nicola had the effrontery to suggest that they should play *The Three Sisters* instead, where audiences always loved to see her in the part of the old nanny. Hastily, Nat had settled for giving her the single role of the jailer's mother, as being the lesser of two evils. He had not reckoned on the fact that being in one production only afforded Nicola an excellent opportunity for 'observing all you naughty boys and girls' as she put it, in the other.

Now Nicola sat on the shore holding forth to Major Cartwright on the subject of Anglo-Indian politics, based on a theatrical tour of the Raj in the early twenties when she had played Juliet. Something about the Major's correct but ancient white summer suit and a straw hat with faded ribbon had obviously excited her. Pointedly, the Major denied ever having been East of Suez: he failed to stop the flow.

Ketty had cornered Emily Jones, the rather sweet-looking girl who would play Masha to Filly Lennox's Nina; Ketty, like Old Nicola, was indulging in theatrical reminiscences, although hers were vicariously based on Christabel's career, not her own. Emily Jones looked younger than Filly Lennox in real life, much as the unknown Tobs looked younger than Vic Marcovich; she was beginning to have a rather desperate air as

Ketty's amber beads dangled closer and closer to her face, when Mrs Blagge acidly recalled Ketty to her duties.

'If you would be so kind, Katherine, there are certain tasks for you as well as Jim and myself.'

If you looked backwards, the tall harsh shape of the Watchtower Theatre could be seen in the distance, looking down from its great height on the sylvan shore, the dark glass of its structure giving the air of enormous eyes keeping an eye on events. But no one did look back – none of the actors, or the other participants in the Festival picnic. Much as Regina Cartwright had predicted, the actors concentrated mainly on the Lark Manor food – asparagus quiches, smoked-salmon cornets filled with prawns, and cold chicken pie cut in slices. They also drank Julian Cartwright's claret which he dispensed personally with a lavish hand. He used the same formula to everyone as he poured.

'A good light Beaujolais Brouilly '76. Sorry about the plastic tumblers but we can't have broken-glass tragedies on the beach. All the same I think you'll enjoy it.'

He was quite right. The actors certainly did enjoy it.

Filly Lennox, who had definitely drunk too much – a great deal too much – became quite pink and giggly. It was in fact Filly who was responsible for one of the few awkward moments of the picnic. After announcing that she was absolutely pie-eyed, she added that she was bound to regret it. Then she started to hum a popular song, filling in a word here and there. It took those present several instants to realise that Filly was happily intoning 'Coo-ool, oh so cool repentance', and several more instants to shut her up, since Filly was quite impervious to winks and frowns. On the contrary, she seemed more than likely to plough right on through Iron Boy's repertory, one song leading to another – until Gregory Rowan saved the day by pulling her back down beside him. Then there was some much safer talk of an expedition to France when the Festival was over – 'I'd love to show you what's left of pre-revolutionary Paris', he was heard to say eagerly.

'I suppose that's France over there, isn't it?' Filly cried, waving a hand towards what was in fact the next Bridset headland. 'Take me to it.'

Emily Jones drank a little too much and, freed of Ketty's attentions, moved closer to Spike Thompson; who nevertheless showed no signs of leaving the side of Jemima Shore. Ollie Summertown drank enough to do some startling gymnastics on the beach, for the particular edification of Cherry and the general edification of anyone else who cared to watch.

'Do you fancy that sort of thing?' Spike spoke quite casually in Jemima's direction. Jemima, who was alone in drinking white wine, took first a sip and then a look. Ollie was currently indulging in a prolonged hand-stand.

'It's rather difficult to tell when he's upside down, isn't it?'

Blanche and Regina Cartwright were both poured half-tumblers of wine by their father. But it was impossible to tell how much he, as host, had drunk. Julian continued to look urbane if slightly flushed. He accepted the frequent compliments of the cast on the quality of the wine with every sign of pleasure. Nat Fitzwilliam alone lifted his glass spasmodically without any sign of noticing what he was imbibing; when Blanche, after colloquy with Tobs, tested this theory by pouring Coca-Cola into his claret, he took a sip quite happily.

Christabel definitely drank a great deal: Jemima watched her. Her hands as she held her shell-painted tumbler trembled. It was possible that her large straw bag also contained a small bottle of solacing vodka.

Vic Marcovich drank the most but without any sign of inebriation at all; until the moment when he threw off his shirt and marched straight off in the direction of the sea, uttering the single superbly articulated word: 'Forward!' The picnic party watched him go. The tide was now very low. His figure, with its fine bull-like shoulders and short muscley legs – it could have been the figure of a wrestler – could be seen for a long while proceeding out across the rippled sands left by the sea.

Suddenly it was as though an emergency warning had been given for the whole party to abandon the site of the picnic as fast as possible. Blanche Cartwright grabbed Ollie's hand as he finished a somersault and before he could object – or cast an eye round for Cherry – pulled him off towards the distant sea. Regina too remounted Lancelot, and galloped off in the direction of the sea: she was reciting Shelley at full tilt as she went. The horse's hooves splashed Blanche and Ollie as Regina passed them. Riding bareback in her scarlet costume, with her black hair flying, Regina looked, thought Jemima, like an advertisement for something – not necessarily something as young and innocent as Regina herself.

Her protests about the tide, wind and water ignored, Ketty proceeded to don a severe but not unbecoming black costume and stalked after her charges in the direction of the sea.

Cherry, distinctly flown with wine and free of Ollie's chaperonage, saw her chance with Julian Cartwright.

'Sware for a swim?' was how the words actually came out. But it did not seem to matter since he evidently looked on the proposition favourably. 'What about you, darling?' he enquired briefly of Christabel. 'Are you going to have a dip?'

Christabel was in the throes of hearing from Nat about his encounter with J.S. Grand, editor of the powerful and prestigious *Literature*, at some elegant First Night supper party in Connaught Square, at which Nat by his own account had reduced the mighty editor to silence with his ideas on Chekhov.

'Jamie Grand is such a darling, isn't he?' broke in Christabel. 'And so amusing. I remember he once said to me that the thing about Chekhov and sex – or was it Turgenev and sex – anyway . . .' Her voice trailed away. She was obviously relieved by Julian's interruption. 'Definitely I shall swim!' she cried with a great deal more energy. 'Definitely. But I make no promise as to exactly where and when. In the meantime why don't you join the lady?'

Nat Fitzwilliam looked a good deal less pleased by Julian's sudden appearance. He announced his intention of going back to the Watchtower to get further inspiration for *The Seagull* from its vantage point 'by seeing the shore as an empty hole' – or perhaps he meant whole, it was not immediately clear.

He was also promising darkly to rethink various Chekhovian characters by viewing them at a great distance. Arkadina, for example.

'Not Arkadina, darling, if you don't mind,' said Christabel sweetly. 'You've thought about her quite enough for one production. Give the others a turn. Why don't you keep an eye on Blanche and our Konstantin instead. Or Gregory and the lovely Miss Lennox? There might be insights into Trigorin and Nina there. Or even Julian and Miss—' she paused and gazed speculatively at Cherry in her gravity-defying costume '—Miss Cherry. So much more rewarding.'

The roar of Nat's motor-bike was heard as he left. Jemima saw Christabel's graceful figure drifting in the direction of the trees at the head of the beach in order to change. She bore a very large straw basket on her arm, containing the despised costumes and caps unearthed by Mrs Blagge. Despite picnic conditions, vodka and Beaujolais consumed in large quantities and her cumbersome burden, Christabel still managed to look immeasurably elegant: she conveyed the impression of a star leaving the stage to the minor characters – purely for the time being.

Filly Lennox now seemed loath to take to the water, even escorted by Gregory Rowan, and murmured or rather giggled a series of rather thin excuses. There was some rather prolonged and playful discussion on the subject of swimming with or without costumes which Jemima found increasingly irritating: why could not Gregory and Filly simply strip off and plunge in and be done with it? But in the end the matter was resolved differently. Filly was not so loath to adjourning with Gregory to the shade of the trees on the far side of the river bank to discuss the matter further: she confessed to the need to lie down. Their figures also vanished. Jemima felt meanly pleased that Christabel had also meandered off in that direction, a fact of which they were evidently unaware.

Jemima found herself alone with Spike Thompson at the now deserted picnic scene – alone except for the Blagges, that is. It was the polite but embarrassing presence of the Blagges which decided her. Taking off her own shirt and trousers, to reveal a new white bikini which she was not at all averse to displaying, she cast an inviting smile in the direction of Spike.

'Our turn,' said Jemima. Spike looked distinctly disappointed when she tugged him off in the direction of the sea, much as Cherry had pulled away Julian Cartwright.

'So many swimmers. Even Her—' Mrs Blagge gestured back to the group of trees to which Christabel had retreated. 'You'd better get the boat, Jim. If you meant what you said this morning about the breeze at the point.' So Mr Blagge departed in the direction of the boat pulled up on a steep bank of pebbles near the river bed. After a bit Mrs Blagge vanished too.

The fire smoked and went out. Only the seagulls still whirled round the deserted picnic site for a while; then they too flew away. The breeze at the point did blow up a little, making a few white crests on the waves outside the bay. The tide started to come in, very fast over the level sands. There was still no one present where the picnic had once been.

Jemima Shore had just changed back into her clothes in the group of trees near the cars, and was busy towelling her thick hair, dripping with sea-water, when the screaming began.

It seemed to come from a little knot of bathers – all men – advancing together through the shallow waters to the edge of the beach. They were moving curiously slowly, staggering slightly. That was because they were carrying something, something heavy. With a sick feeling Jemima recognized the ridiculous black and white bathing-cap Christabel Cartwright had been mocking only a few hours before, and the turquoise bathing-costume.

The person who was screaming was Blanche Cartwright. She was facing the advancing party and their burden.

Blanche Cartwright was screaming: 'Mummy, Mummy, Mummy.'

7

Her Last Hour

In death Christabel Cartwright's face looked quite young and vulnerable. Even her body appeared slighter and more childish than the full middle-aged figure Jemima remembered.

Julian Cartwright and Victor Marcovich were taking it in turns to kneel over her urgently trying to breathe some movement back into that sodden body, or knead some beat from its still heart. For how long? – it seemed like hours. Now Julian was kneeling back on his haunches with a look of despair on his face. Vic Marcovich bent forward again. Ollie Summertown had rushed past Jemima, still in his striped bathing-shorts, to get help; she heard the angry whirr of his motor-bike ascending the track from the beach to the village.

Christabel's eyes were closed. A strand of fair hair escaped the black and white cap and lay along the pale cheek: the sight of that, no longer fluffy, no longer the bright colour of a daffodil, was unbearably touching.

It was at that moment that Jemima realized that she was looking into the dead face of Filumena Lennox, Filly Lennox with her pretty full youthful body, in Christabel Cartwright's vivid turquoise costume. Filly Lennox with her fair hair escaping from Christabel Cartwright's magpie cap. She realized it a split second before she heard the characteristic melodious voice of Christabel herself calling from a distance.

'I'm here. What is it? What's the matter, Blanche? Do stop screaming "Mummy, Mummy" like that, darling.'

But Blanche did not stop screaming. She merely transferred her renewed cries in the direction of her mother, who was now advancing rapidly towards the little group at the edge of the sea, and the body of Filly Lennox where the men had laid her. In contrast to the bathers, Christabel still looked inappropriately smart in her diaphanous leopard-skin printed robe. Her hair stood up from her head like a golden aureole.

'Oh Mummy, Mummy, it's not you, it's not you. I thought it was you.' Blanche's voice rose hysterically and then she burst into tears just as Christabel reached them.

The men who had carried Filly Lennox's body included Gregory Rowan as well as two of the actors. He stood slightly apart from the group round the body. It was to Gregory that Christabel turned, rather distractedly, as though she could not quite take in what had happened, did not quite believe it even now, thought it was all a delusion, a joke perhaps, in spite of the manifest presence of poor Filly's drowned body, lying there on the shore, with Victor Marcovich kneeling beside her, still rather hopelessly massaging her chest.

'Darling, what's she doing in my costume?' she asked. 'And that's my funny magpie hat – I was looking for it. Why did she take it?' Christabel put her hand on Gregory's arm. 'Why is she dressed—'

'Christabel, be quiet, the girl is dead.' It was Julian Cartwright who interrupted his wife as though determined to put an end to these frantic and embarrassing enquiries. He moved and put his arm protectively round her. For a moment Christabel stood thus between Julian and Gregory. Then Gregory moved away.

Like Julian, he spoke heavily, almost wearily: 'She must have changed her mind and swum after me. I teased her about not daring to take a dip. But she wouldn't come. And so I left her. Oh my God, the poor, poor child.'

'That was because she couldn't swim really, or at least not very well.' Tobs sounded pathetically eager as though an explanation of her behaviour might actually bring Filly back to life.

'Yes, she told me this morning she definitely wasn't going to swim. We're sharing digs in Larminster. And then Filly washed her hair specially to look nice at the picnic, so I suppose she took the cap—' Emily Jones began to cry, but quietly, not like Blanche, leaning her head on Tobs's shoulder. 'She was so excited at meeting *you*,' Emily sobbed, nodding her head in the direction of Gregory. 'Properly. Not in the theatre.'

'You see, darling, I fell asleep under the cliffs in my old nook.' Christabel was rattling on, although it was not quite clear whom she was addressing. 'I left my things under the trees in the old place where I always used to change, and then, it was so hot, and I felt so sleepy – all that claret I suppose – we should really serve white wine at picnics in future, darling—'

'Christabel, stop,' said Julian Cartwright in an urgent voice. Jemima realized that Christabel was trembling so hard that her long gold necklaces with their pendent sea-shells shook together.

'When I came back from my nap under the cliff,' she finished more calmly, 'the costume and hat were both gone. I was desperate to swim after my nap. I was livid. I lay down again under the cliff and tried to cool off.'

The arrival of Regina, leading Lancelot through the shallow splashing surf from the opposite direction of the eastern cliff, created a diversion. Still in her red costume, with her wet black hair hanging down her back, Regina looked slightly threatening as though she might carry away Filly's body on her horse's crupper like some modern Valkyrie. When told the news of Filly's death, she turned quite white, and stammered something which was probably a quotation from Webster since it sounded like 'She died young', before lapsing into silence.

Even more bizarre was the appearance of Mr Blagge, rowing his boat towards the shore, up the channel of the river. If Regina had fleetingly resembled a Valkyrie, Mr Blagge had the uncomfortable air of a Charon come to row the dead girl away to some oceanic Hades.

His words, when he heard the news, were spoken in a voice rough and cracked with emotion: 'This is at your door,' he cried turning in the direction of Christabel, adding after a pause with terrible polite incongruity: 'Madam. Our boy, this girl—' he continued wildly, looking round at Jemima and Spike Thompson, then at the still weeping Emily Jones, as though appealing for confirmation. He was wearing a khaki waterproof jacket and trousers which presumably concealed the neat suit in which he had served lunch: the outfit gave him a vaguely military air.

'Jim.' The voice of Mrs Blagge, coming from behind them, sounded very sharp indeed. She had joined them from somewhere in the direction of the cars. At the same time Julian Cartwright with equal authority and a good deal of anger, exclaimed: 'That's enough, Blagge. We must all be careful not to upset poor Miss Lennox's friends further.' He emphasized the word 'all'.

Gregory put a comforting arm round Christabel again. It wasn't clear from her expression whether Christabel had taken in the extent of Mr Blagge's venom: she merely looked rather dazed. Then the arrival of Major Cartwright, still immaculate in his white suit and straw hat, meant that the news of Filly Lennox's death had to be broken all over again. Afterwards he kept repeating angrily: 'But what was the girl doing in *your* bathing-suit, Christabel?', thus making it clear where he thought the responsibility for the tragedy lay.

By the time the ambulance arrived, bringing with it rapid professional – but equally unsuccessful – attempts at resuscitation, the picnic party had been transformed into a very different kind of gathering. The story of the last hour in Filumena Lennox's life had also been pieced together – more or less. Rather less than more, thought Jemima. But that thought she kept to herself for the time being, along with some other thoughts on the subject of the untimely death of a young woman, not totally unlike

Christabel Cartwright in type and colouring, wearing Christabel Cartwright's conspicuous turquoise bathing-costume and magpie hat.

Gregory Rowan was the last person who had actually spoken to Filly Lennox – on the shore among the trees – but he was by no means the last person to have seen her. Several people had caught sight of her in the sea or at any rate of the striking black and white hat bobbing about in the water; but of course everyone had assumed they were looking at Christabel.

After Gregory Rowan had left Filly, he had waded into the sea in his favourite place, under the western cliff, on the other side of the river which divided the shore in half; he had deliberately swum away from the merry gathering on the other side of the little bay. 'For peace,' he said. Jemima guessed that he had also privately decided to dispense with a bathing-costume, in his preferred fashion, and had not wished to advertise the fact. So that when Filly decided, literally, to take the plunge, she had gone to look for him in quite the wrong direction.

Ketty volunteered that a figure in a black and white cap had passed her, striking out rather slowly, in view of the waves, in the general direction of the point: 'I *did* think it was rather unwise.'

Ketty, in her tight-lipped way, was obviously very shaken by the incident, and evidently blamed herself for not warning the girl about the tide and the currents. 'Believing it however to be Mrs Cartwright and believing she would remember – she couldn't have forgotten that – she used to swim there all the time – once – believing it was my duty to look after the girls ... Besides, Jim Blagge was out there somewhere with the boat. He should have helped her.'

But Jim Blagge was one of the few people who had apparently not seen Filly in her magpie cap, Julian Cartwright being another.

Blanche confirmed that she had seen Filly swimming – 'But it was Mummy, I knew it was Mummy, that was the whole point.' Blanche was on the verge of howling again before Julian Cartwright curtly indicated to Ketty that she should put an end to these hysterics.

Regina's contribution was briefer: 'I swam alone and saw no one and nothing.' Then she added illogically: 'I thought it was Mummy anyway,' and burst into tears. But unlike her sister, she cried quietly.

All the actors had swum in the end, or at least paddled, with the exception of Old Nicola and Major Cartwright. After lunch, at which she had drunk at least her fair share of claret, Nicola had adjourned to the upper shore. Here she had plonked herself down on a comfortable chair unwillingly abstracted by Mrs Blagge from the Cartwright Land-Rover. Robbed of the company of the Major – who rapidly backed away from the prospect of a further tête-à-tête on the subject of the British Raj – Nicola settled down to a little post-prandial sport with the triumphant words: 'Time to watch you naughty boys and girls.' Out of a dark-grey plastic bag which had itself seen better days, she had produced a shapeless mass of knitting of roughly the same colour. (It was part of their power struggle that Nat Fitzwilliam was quite determined Old Nicola should not produce her own knitting on stage during *Widow Capet*: but she had by no means conceded the point.) And then Old Nicola had noticed Filly Lennox staggering towards the sea.

'Staggering, my dears. I'm afraid there's no other word for it. The poor girl was quite – well, you know. She was laughing too, and singing. That Iron Boy song you wouldn't let her sing before, "Cool Repentance". Not that she had anything much to repent about, the poor little duck. And some of the other Iron Boy songs. She looked very happy. I dare say it was a very happy death. We should all try to look at it like that.'

This picture of Filly Lennox, weaving and laughing her way towards the sea, Ophelia-like, singing snatches of songs – worst of all the banned songs of Iron Boy – upset everyone anew. Jemima saw that Tobs's eyes were wet.

'Of course *I* knew it wasn't Christabel!' continued Nicola. 'I wasn't fooled for a moment. Much smaller bottom. We all spread out as the years pass, don't we my dear?' The old woman turned to Christabel with a well-delivered conspiratorial look. 'And you really have lived well over the past few years, haven't you? Which is funny, because my friend Susan Merlin told me you were absolutely starving in a garret—'

Some of the members of the company remembered amid the general embarrassment that Christabel for one had been strongly opposed to the introduction of Old Nicola into the Larminster Festival. 'She's a positive croaking raven; give me Susan Merlin any time even if she can't remember more than one line in three . . . at least that line comes from the right play . . .' Old Nicola had evidently nosed out Christabel's hostility.

Now feeling that she had created enough trouble for one day, Nicola finished her account of Filly's passage to the sea by timing it precisely, 'Four o'clock. On the dot. I looked at my watch. No, I never make that kind of mistake.' In a lower voice, she added: 'And wasn't one of you naughty boys giving her a bit of a cuddle in the sea? Or was it just a girl giving her a helping hand? I've got eyes in my head, you know. At least it wasn't you, Major, do you remember, you went for a walk onto the cliffs, spying on all the pretty girls where they were changing, I saw you, you old rascal.'

Major Cartwright, curtly denying the motive, did admit the walk. And since Old Nicola did not name the cuddler – or the helper – and nobody had mentioned encountering her in the sea, that parting shot was not thought to be particularly important by the company in general: merely part of Old Nicola's general propensity towards malice. Jemima Shore, who did note it vaguely, pushed the remark to the back of her mind for the time being.

After Nicola lost sight of Filly Lennox, the girl had been alone.

Alone with no one to warn or help her, she had taken the treacherous route to exactly where the currents made by the river debouching its subterranean waters were most dangerous. Somewhere out there a sudden freak wave breaking – not an uncommon occurrence – must have taken her by surprise, filled her mouth with water, then her lungs . . . No one of course had seen her getting into difficulty or waving for help or heard her shouting – if she had been able to shout. No one said it aloud but everyone remembered how much Filly had drunk in the course of the picnic. Perhaps she never knew quite what was happening to her. Or perhaps Filly Lennox had waved, waved and struggled desperately for survival, and everyone near her had merely interpreted it as a cheerful salutation from Christabel Cartwright.

That had been Victor Marcovich's experience: and he, like Ketty, blamed himself passionately for the mistake, convinced that he might have done something to save Filly had he known.

'The trouble was I was pissed,' he groaned.

'We were all pissed,' Ollie corrected him. 'I lost the little girl altogether, she vanished. Which one was it? Blanche, the fat one—' He seemed unaware of Blanche's continued presence, standing beside Ketty. 'I dived off in search of you—' He looked towards Cherry, standing in her once-gay purple poncho, which now had the air of a funeral garment.

'It's all rocks out there, and little bays and inlets at low tide. You do lose sight of people.'

'Yes, I lost sight of you altogether', put in Cherry rather plaintively. 'Where were you? Where did you go?'

Julian ignored her. Then his calm air of authority suddenly broke and he too groaned: 'Oh my God, the poor girl, why did we swim at all? Why didn't I stop you?'

It was Tobs who was in the worst state of all: for it was Tobs who had found Filly's body floating on the surface of the sea, the face half-covered with water; the waves were propelling it inexorably towards the shore.

One of the ambulance men said, before Filly's body was rushed away to hospital, still in the vain hope of resuscitating it: 'It *is* very dangerous swimming out at the point at low tide. Someone was drowned here I believe a couple of years ago. Also from London.' There was a very faint note of reproach in his voice.

After that no one had much to say. Breaking the news to the world in general and Filly's family in particular was obviously the next painful task to be faced. And breaking the news to the world at any rate – wasn't that at least in part the concern of Nat Fitzwilliam as Festival Director? It was also the concern of the Festival Chairman. Major Cartwright departed in his Bentley to inform such bodies as his Festival Board, with a view to preparing a statement on the whole distressing episode.

'As Chairman, it was my duty to come to this festivity,' he commented gruffly to no one in particular. His gruffness appeared to hide some strong emotion, presumably disapproval of the whole Bacchanalian nature of the picnic. In the meantime, what of the Festival Director?

Nat Fitzwilliam – oddly enough, no one had thought of him in the course of the crisis. He had last been seen, still in his scarf and anorak, heading for the Watchtower Theatre where he had intended to view the shore from on high and seek further inspiration . . . first of all, someone had to tell *him.*

Guthrie Carlyle, as representative of Megalith, volunteered for this disagreeable duty. Jemima Shore, in exchange, agreed to shoulder the burden of breaking to Cy Fredericks, head of Megalith Television, the news of the tragedy which had just struck at his Larminster Festival programme. Cy Fredericks was certainly the right person to handle the whole public mourning which would follow the lamentable decease not only of Filumena Lennox, but of 'Country Kate'.

But it rapidly transpired that Guthrie Carlyle had the best of the bargain. There was the noise of another motor-bike arriving, and Nat Fitzwilliam appeared in person at the head of the beach.

'I passed an ambulance,' he began. 'And then you were all standing there on the beach for so long after the swimming stopped. I saw you. I was watching you all the time. From the top of the theatre.' Jemima suddenly noticed the large pair of binoculars slung round his neck, half-hidden by his scarf.

The person who hated Christabel also noticed the binoculars. The person thought it would be a pity if it turned out that Nat Fitzwilliam had witnessed certain things through those binoculars. The person was really very sorry indeed about the death of Filumena Lennox, which had been a stupid mistake, and just showed the foolishness of giving way to impulse after so long. The person thought: you could certainly lay that death at the door of Christabel; if she had not come back to Larminster in the first place, none of this would have happened.

8

Late at Night

'What are *you* doing, flapping round here?' The question was directed at Nicola Wain – with no pretence of grace – by Christabel Cartwright. Indeed, the old woman did have something of the air of a bird, if not a vulture or a raven, still something vaguely ominous, a rook perhaps; with her bright little black eyes, and her long nose which gave the effect of a beak.

It was very hot in the conservatory at Lark Manor, although the glass windows were all flung open. Nicola was wearing no stockings. Her legs, beneath her dark print dress, looked aggressively white and at the same time gnarled, patched with veins and other bumps. Christabel's beautiful shapely legs were also bare but beneath her pristine pleated white cotton skirt, worn with a pale-blue silk shirt, they looked smooth, tanned, expensive – legs which were caressed daily by lotions and creams, things which, even in her hey-day, would never have come within reach of the old actress's purse.

The emphasis on Old Nicola's legs was due to the fact that she had stretched them out on one of the comfortable chaise-longues in the conservatory. The rich foxy scent of the regale lilies, standing everywhere in pots, filled the air. The summer cushions had lilies printed on them: just as in winter the cushions had a pattern of ferns.

'It was your sweet little girl invited me up,' confided Nicola. Christabel's eyes fell on a silver tray, placed on a low stool beside the chaise-longue; plates still bore the remnants of a delicate yet tasty meal. 'She knows I'm not very comfortable in my room at the Spring Guest House. Old Nicola does like to be comfortable at her age, well *you*'d understand that, and the little duck suggested Mr Blagge should collect me in Larminster along with the shopping and just give Old Nicola a little, just a little taste of honey. Then she's talked to Mrs Tennant the manageress at the Royal Stag. Tonight that nice Mrs Tennant is going to squeeze me into a room, just a *wee* room, at a price an old lady can afford—'

'Then where *is* Blanche, since she has so kindly made herself your hostess?' Christabel had recovered her composure, but it was noticeable she still made no pretence of welcoming Nicola. For that matter the old woman remained stretched out on the liliaceous cushions without any attempt at moving.

'Little Blanche? Oh, I imagine *she's* still at the audition.' At which point Old Nicola helped herself to the remaining sandwich, popping it neatly into her mouth like a seal swallowing a fish. 'Nat is reading for the new Nina this morning. Poor little Filumena. But still, the show must go on, mustn't it? And so say all of us.' Old Nicola polished off the last macaroon with equal delicacy and even greater relish. 'As you know, my dear, I'm not in *The Seagull*, but I should have thought you at least might have wanted to be there. To see how the little duck makes out. And she *is* a little duck, too, I think it's a lovely idea to have your own real-life daughter playing Nina, even if she has absolutely no experience.

'I said so to Vic Marcovich only this morning, who didn't quite see it that way, I must admit, but then he wouldn't, would he?' Old Nicola somehow managed to munch and speak at the same time. 'Bloody unprofessional were the words he used – if you'll pardon the expression. Shall we say he's been just a *wee* bit disappointed all along that our dear Anna Maria never got to play Madame Arkadina after all? You came along at such *very* short notice, and you were *such* a big star. So we needn't pay any attention to that naughty old Vic, need we, after all he and Anna Maria are just like two kittens in a basket—'

Then Nicola went on to demolish the last two tiny creamy éclairs.

'*What* are you saying?' *Blanche* as Nina? It was at that moment exactly, almost as though Christabel's anguished cry had given him his cue, that Julian Cartwright strode into the conservatory. He was accompanied by Ketty and Mr Blagge.

'Blanche as *Nina*?' He hurled the words at his wife. Ketty looked extremely nervous, Mr Blagge wore a slightly sardonic expression, and Julian Cartwright looked plainly furious. 'Is this *your* doing?' he added.

'Over my dead body!' Christabel answered, in a voice approaching a scream. 'She can't *act*. At school Blanche couldn't even play the Gentlewoman in the Lady Macbeth sleep-walking scene, and God knows that's no test of ability. Never ever have I been so embarrassed in the whole of my life sitting there. She even got her lines wrong: "It is an accustomed action with her to seem thus washing her hair . . . " and then the whole school burst into roars of laughter. And *then* she went and gave her name on the programme as Blanche Herrick Cartwright, when her middle name is actually May after your ghastly mother.' In her hysteria

Christabel did not seem to have grasped that she and her husband were actually on the same side.

Only Old Nicola, finding a sponge finger she had previously overlooked, continued to bear an expression of placid happiness.

About the same time, telephoning from a rather less elegantly furnished room in a Larminster hotel, Jemima Shore was trying to explain to Cy Fredericks just why the casting of Blanche Cartwright as Nina in *The Seagull* would be a total disaster. From the point of view of Megalith Television, that is. It would also, in Jemima's opinion, be a disaster from the point of view of the Larminster Festival, the King Charles Theatre Company, the present production of *The Seagull,* and last and possibly least, the future of Miss Blanche Herrick Cartwright on the stage. But since Cy Fredericks notoriously did not recognize any point of view other than that of Megalith, it was hardly worth mentioning these further considerations.

'As it happens, Blanche Cartwright is not a dish and she's not a doll either,' Jemima was explaining as patiently as possible. She kept her voice down. Cy Fredericks, like Julian Cartwright, had a tendency to shout when aroused and she did not wish to encourage him: the conversation had already lasted twenty minutes. 'But that's nothing to do with the case. You see, Cy, while you *don't* have to be a dish or a doll or a fruit or a chick to play Nina, you *do* have to be able to—'

But the word 'act' was quite drowned by Cy Frederick's amiable roar down the line:

'It helps, my dear Jem, it helps,' he boomed. 'Think of us old men leaning forward glassy-eyed in front of our sets, all passion spent, and then suddenly – what do we see? We see a lovely young woman, daughter of our greatest British actress – yes, yes, I know, she's been retired for ages, but *we* are old, don't forget, we remember her – and this lovely young woman is making her début. And where is she making her début, I am asking you? Why, on Megalith Television! Jem, already, I tell you *already*, I am reaching for my handkerchief.'

Jemima prayed for patience. Her voice grew lower still. 'To begin with, as I told you from the beginning Blanche Cartwright is *not* a lovely young woman. She's a stocky, rather plump, teenager, who, when she's fined down in a year or two, will be lucky if she's half as good-looking as her mother is now—' Jemima ignored an interruption which sounded like 'the first fresh dawn breaking' and ploughed on relentlessly: 'She's stagestruck and she's sulky and she's jealous of her mother, and Cy, listen to me for a minute, just listen, none of these things matter in the least compared to the fact that SHE CAN'T ACT FOR TOFFEE! I was there at the audition. It was PAINFUL.' Jemima allowed herself at last a higher register on the final words.

Satisfied she had secured if only for a moment Cy's attention, Jemima moved in for the kill: 'Listen to me, Cy. Something is going on here. Something I don't understand. Something unpleasant. Someone has set this girl up, or rather set up the production and Christabel Herrick along with it. You see, *someone* suggested Blanche should read for Nina in the first place, and now everyone denies it.

'It certainly wasn't her mother, let alone her father, who hates all things theatrical for obvious reasons, and the girl herself says she simply got a telephone message from the Director telling her to turn up for the audition. The Director – Our Nat – utterly denies having sent the message, and I must say I very much doubt whether he would take any step quite so liable to ruin his precious production. The death of Filly Lennox was trouble enough, with all the publicity it caused: the post-mortem showing death by drowning, and the coroner's inquest – accidental death, but still most unpleasant, with all those revelations about wine drunk at the picnic. Then the funeral and then back to the rehearsals and no Nina. But *he* thought it was Christabel's own personal request to include Blanche; he got a tip-off that she was on the point of withdrawing from the production altogether, because of Filly's death and all the newspaper coverage, unless Blanche got the part.'

Jemima paused. It was time to use her trump card: 'There's some kind of plot here, Cy, a conspiracy and I don't want Megalith to get mixed up in it.'

'A plot!' There were two words Cy Fredericks recognized in any language; one was 'plot' and the other was 'conspiracy'. Associated with the name of Megalith, these were a lethal combination. After that double invocation, it was not really too difficult for Jemima to get her way. Was that not indeed one of the reasons why Cy Fredericks employed her? Trumpet, cajole, bluster – and on occasion break down and weep as he might, he could rely on Jemima Shore not to give in to him, if she believed that by so doing a programme would be ruined.

On this occasion Cy Fredericks ended by giving Jemima *carte blanche* to deal with Nat Fitzwilliam. Megalith would finally withdraw from the filming of the Larminster Festival – having honourably weathered the death of Filly Lennox – if Blanche Cartwright was allowed to play Nina.

Under these circumstances the footage of film already taken would be consigned to that special limbo reserved for fragments of Megalith programmes which had been scrapped. This included rehearsals of *The Seagull* which was well advanced and early rehearsals of *Widow Capet*. The same would go for the long interview already filmed with Nat Fitzwilliam and the short interview with Major Cartwright as Chairman of the Festival (so short it scarcely amounted to more than two questions and three hostile looks). Even some of Spike Thompson's fine work on Larminster sunsets illuminating the Watchtower Theatre in Blakean fashion would similarly be scrapped.

Jemima apprised Spike Thompson of Cy Fredericks' decision. They were sitting in the bar of the Royal Escape at the time. Spike was drinking Scotch. He offered Jemima a drink.

'Come on, my lovely love, what shall it be? You can't be serious with all that white wine you keep knocking back, no better than cat's piss in a pub like this. Come on then, what's your heart's desire?'

'Truthfully, champagne. But at the moment, nothing. I have to go back to the Watchtower to have a little talk with Our Nat which *may* be awkward, then on to Lark Manor for a talk with Little Blanche which *will* be. Champagne wouldn't help.'

'You don't mean she got the part? Guth and I had an idea of covering the audition, but Jesus when she came on – the poor kid – it was pathetic. Look, darling, if you're worried, I could drop a word in Equity's ear—'

But in the event Jemima found her interview with Nat Fitzwilliam unexpectedly easy. While her interview with Blanche she decided to postpone to another day, to let at least one night pass before crushing the poor kid's ambitions.

Nat Fitzwilliam was sitting in the third row of the stalls, gazing raptly at the stage, on which for once nothing whatsoever was to be seen. He did not hear Jemima approach: the theatre was thickly carpeted in cinnamon-colour which extended all over the seats and walls, making it in some ways more like a cinema than a theatre.

Jemima had found the dark-glass front doors unlocked. A girl with long straight hair was sitting in the little glass booth which served as a box office. For a moment Jemima had the impression that all girls in Larminster had the same drifting hairstyle and were attired in the same pre-Raphaelite patterned muslin. Then she realized she was gazing not at Poll's double, but at Poll, she of Flora's Kitchen, herself.

Poll, away from Moll, was surprisingly chatty, to the point of being effusive. She confided to Jemima that bookings for the Festival were brisk and that the death of Filly Lennox had not affected them, despite her popularity as a television star; newspaper reports of the drowning had simply called further public attention to the event itself. Above all, declared Poll, the general public wanted to be on telly.

'It's perfectly super!' she exclaimed. 'They all want to be there the nights you're filming. No problem with a full house at all. I've explained everything just as they said. Reduced visibility, cameras in front of their noses, bright lights. It doesn't seem to put them off one bit. They're all interested in just one thing – will they see us? The audience, that is. Nat's a bit depressed about it all, to tell you the truth. For a moment he thought they were more interested in television than in Chekhov, his Chekhov that is. Which would be absurd.'

'Absurd,' echoed Jemima.

'Anyway he's in the theatre,' Poll added, 'seeking inspiration.' Was she serious? It was impossible to tell. Jemima headed for the auditorium.

'Oh, by the way,' Poll called after Jemima, 'see you later?' For a moment Jemima was disconcerted. Then she remembered a tentative rendezvous with Spike Thompson – and Guthrie Carlyle of course – at Flora's Kitchen to discuss the latest developments in *l'affaire Nina*. She supposed that either Guthrie or Spike must have booked a table – probably the latter who, since the original mistake which had taken him to the interior cuisine of Christopher's Diner, had proved a regular customer at Flora's Kitchen. Since food at Flora's Kitchen, although delicious, was not served at rustic prices, Jemima had a momentary loyal pang for Megalith's bank balance. Then she reminded herself that the regular eating place of Cy Fredericks, representing management, was the Connaught, arguably the most expensive restaurant in London. Why should Spike Thompson representing the workers – and after all Spike was nothing if not a worker – fare any worse?

'See you later,' she echoed to Poll.

'Not a word to Moll then.' A grin which was quite roguish lit up Poll's pale elfin features. 'I'm moonlighting here. Helping Nat out of a hole. We're mates. We lived together for a couple of years, one way and another. Moll can't take that. She's—' As Poll indicated the cutting of the throat, Jemima hastily promised silence.

So into the soft dark cinnamon-coloured world she passed.

Nat started up when she touched him on the shoulder.

'Oh, Jemima.' He looked for a moment slightly surprised, then he looked delighted.

'Poll told me you were communing—' she began.

'I wanted to see you anyway,' he exclaimed, jumping up from his seat which folded silently upwards. 'There's something I'd rather like to talk to you about.'

'Nina, I suppose? Blanche Cartwright – look, I'm afraid, Nat, that Cy Fredericks won't wear that at all. And I agree.' Even as she spoke Jemima realized that for once Nat was not thinking about Megalith Television. The tone – almost cajoling – with which he addressed her showed that it was she, Jemima, not Megalith, who was the object of his attentions. Now Nat twisted the fringes of his white scarf, in what he seemed to imagine was a beguilingly youthful manner, as he addressed her.

'No, no, not about Blanche as Nina. Whose idea was that anyway? Someone who wanted to ruin the whole production, I'll bet. Blanche was absolutely hopeless of course. Emily Jones is our Nina, that's for sure, which leaves Masha – I see a kind of severe sailor-suit here, by the way, in contrast to Nina's mermaid costume – the sea-creatures and the creatures of the land. And wonder of wonders Anna Maria Packe will do it, despite being chucked as Arkadina: says she adores the part, always has, which means she really adores Vic Marcovich. Boy Greville's coming too. That's the only flaw. He should have directed it, but under the circumstances I felt I must—'

'What will Boy Greville *do* here?' demanded Jemima desperately, wondering where all this was leading.

'Oh nothing. Fuss. Take pills.' Nat sounded quite unconcerned about it all. 'He's married to Anna Maria you see and a frightful hypochondriac. He won't do anything. Just look on. He'll like that, I can assure you. He likes being an onlooker, it doesn't tax his health.' Nat sighed. Then he began to plait the fringe of his white scarf as he resumed: 'It was about something quite different I wanted to talk to you, Jemima. Something much more personal. You're such a calm person. Yes you are. *Calme, volupté et luxe*...' Nat let his voice trail away as though *calme* was the operative word here, *volupté* and *luxe* merely bonuses which Jemima could take or leave as she wished.

'You have this wonderful outside-inside calm,' he went on. 'And so I'd love to cast you as Volumnia in my green-green *Coriolanus*, the one I'm going to do at Edinburgh.'

'Green-green?' she questioned, momentarily taken aback. But she should have realized that Nat's personal approaches always related in some manner to his career.

'Yes, I'm terribly excited about my discovery: green is absolutely the key to *Coriolanus*. All the different greens; from hope to envy – you do see how exciting it will be? Faces, costumes, sets, all green. And you could be my Volumnia.'

'My greenish silence?'

'Oh you're wonderful, you're teasing me,' Nat cried. 'And don't worry about your age by the way: it's your *inner* age I'm after and that's perfect. No, seriously, I'd love to talk to you properly. Alone. Just you and me. I feel we should get on terribly well away from all this, the narrow artificial world of the theatre.' Nat waved his hand grandly, as though to sweep away all his productions; past, present and to come. 'Could we have, do you think, dinner together?'

But Jemima had other plans for her evening. Dinner plus a full exposition of the green-green *Coriolanus* – possibly even worse than the traditional dissertation on the Sung Dynasty *Hamlet* – was not at all what she had in mind. She said so: that is to say, she said that she had other plans for the evening while indicating placatingly that she might well be free the next night.

This merely meant that Nat returned to his cajolery. 'I could even help you with your investigations, you know.' Jemima began to curse the persistence which was undoubtedly Nat's dominant characteristic. 'I'm quite a good investigator myself,' was his next remark – the tone only barely modest. 'A natural talent for observation, an eye for detail. I'm an onlooker too, although in quite a different way from Boy Greville.'

'Oh, I'm sure of that,' Jemima replied sweetly. 'But you see, I'm not making any investigations at the moment – except into the workings of your production for Megalith. I mean, what else is there to investigate round here?'

A rather curious expression crossed Nat's face: for once he did not rush into the breach. It was as though smugness was struggling with caution – or perhaps some uglier emotion was at work. Smugness, of a limited nature, won.

'I could tell you something about being an onlooker – my sort of an onlooker,' he said after a pause. 'I was an unlooker for example on the afternoon that Filly died. An onlooker through my binoculars. What do you make of that?'

Jemima, from having been exasperated and even bored by Nat's advances, became suddenly alert; she did not necessarily want to betray her interest to Nat.

'I should really ask you what you make of it,' she spoke quite lightly. 'Whatever it is you're referring to.'

'Supposing I saw something through my binoculars, something rather odd, something which didn't seem odd at the time, but in retrospect, thinking it through, right down to the sub-text, which is what I like to do with everything and is I think one of my strengths as a director—' Jemima's heart sank as Nat appeared to be returning to his well-worn theme but she was prepared to hear him out. However just then Nat broke off:

'Oh, come on, Jemima, let's have dinner. And then I'll talk to you in depth about Volumnia. I know I can persuade you that being in my production will give a further integrity to your career. Think about it. Volumnia *is* Jemima is Volumnia.'

It was the last sentence which was fatal. One thing was quite clear: Jemima was definitely not Volumnia, but Jemima. Nat was obviously trying to lure her with his references to investigations: conversation at dinner would be angled heavily towards the green-green *Coriolanus*.

'Tomorrow,' she said firmly. 'Not tonight. Any other night.'

'Tomorrow then, eight o'clock. It has to be Flora's Kitchen of course. I used to work as a waiter in Christopher's Diner and a close acquaintance with their kitchen . . .' Nat, to her relief, agreed without further protest to a postponement.

'So what did you see?' Jemima could not resist asking jokingly at the last minute.

'Ah, interested in spite of yourself!' The teasing note had returned to Nat's voice. 'We might discuss it tomorrow – and then we might not. Tell me one thing, do you promise to think very very hard about Volumnia tonight? Think about it all tonight? And then, if you're favourably disposed tomorrow, and I know you will be—'

'I won't have a wink of sleep,' Jemima swore solemnly.

'In that case—' The same odd expression – half-complacent, half-greedy – crossed Nat's open boyish face. 'I will tell you something. You're not the only person interested in this particular piece of information. And yet the funny thing, the hilarious thing, is that I actually saw nothing. My mind was very much on my production, you realize. Using my binoculars, I was busy conjuring up new images, juxtaposing the reality of the beach and the trees and the sea with Chekhov's inner reality. It was only afterwards, when I tried to make sense of the macabre patterns of that dreadful afternoon, that I noticed it. I saw nothing where I should have seen something, or to put it another way, just a little discrepancy between text and sub-text. Once again part of my director's instinct, I suppose. Now if we worked together on *Coriolanus*—'

'Quite so,' interrupted Jemima hastily. 'We'll talk about all that tomorrow. One last thing though – I don't suppose you've discussed all this with anyone else as yet? Or have you?'

Nat smiled back at her. Now the greedy look was quite apparent on his face. It occurred to Jemima suddenly that what she saw was the look of a predator, the expression of one who had been, or was about to be, preying on someone else.

All Nat said was: 'Haven't I? Let's see about that too tomorrow. Sleep well, Jemima Shore, or rather dine well and then think, think deep about Volumnia. Green. Green-green. It really is the key to everything you know.'

On which mutually unsatisfactory note – Nat having failed to persuade Jemima to have dinner and Jemima having failed to pump Nat – they parted.

After all, Jemima had dinner with Guthrie alone. Spike Thompson, whom she had expected to be present, was busy despatching spools of *Widow Capet* rehearsal and Bridset countryside by rail to London. Cherry, much to her surprise, had been invited to sample the delights of The French Lieutenant in neighbouring Dorset by Major Cartwright.

'Totally new place, can't be too careful,' was the rather strange form the invitation took. Cherry wondered if she was supposed to taste the food for the Major and see if it was poisoned. However, under the circumstances – after all the Major was unarguably an older man and a substantial one to boot – she had felt it right to accept.

Poll, serving in Flora's Kitchen, was as deft and silent as before: her conversation with Jemima in the Watchtower might never have taken place. When Nat Fitzwilliam himself came in with Anna Maria Packe and Victor Marcovich (no sign of Boy Greville), Poll scarcely acknowledged his presence beyond depositing the Botticelli menus on the table. Moll in the kitchen remained raucous but unseen.

There was nevertheless some feeling of tension, expectancy in the air.

When the Cartwright party swept in and occupied a large table on the opposite side of the restaurant, Jemima felt she had known all along that they were coming. It turned out to be Blanche's birthday. To celebrate the occasion, she was trying out a new sartorial style: she wore a man's hat, a baggy checked jacket over a shirt and a flowing tie, and what looked like baggy trousers beneath. Hat and all, she was, Jemima feared, imitating Diane Keaton in the film *Annie Hall*. Christabel elegant in contrast, in a mauve linen dress and matching bandeau covering her fair hair, looked relaxed. She kissed Nat Fitzwilliam, then Vic, then Anna Maria warmly and passed on. Julian Cartwright, in spite of the heat in the restaurant, kept on his jacket over the dark silk polo-necked jersey: he did all the ordering. Gregory Rowan made the jokes. Blanche looked happy if hot. Evidently unaware of her dismissal as Nina, she waved ecstatically at Nat. Then she took him over a large chunk of birthday cake and hugged him. Ketty and Regina were on the whole silent.

Jemima Shore, suddenly feeling the whole Larminster scene to be claustrophic, left as soon as she could. She had a quick drink – more white wine – with Guthrie at the bar of the Royal Stag and decided to retire to her bedroom. The Cartwright party was arriving at the hotel for some final celebration as she mounted the stairs. She heard Julian Cartwright's loud authoritative voice. She wanted to be alone.

But when she opened the door of her suite, she was not alone. There was someone waiting for her. Spike Thompson was sitting there, quite at his ease, in the most comfortable chair in the room, wearing jeans and a blue top which might or might not have been a kind of vest. Through the door, she could see his black leather jacket was laid carefully on the bed – which was very large, a four-poster and advertised as having been occupied by King Charles II on his escape from Worcester. He had not bothered to draw the curtains of the rooms more than half-way.

'I think you said champagne was your heart's desire.' There was a bottle cooling in a silver container beside him. 'I paid for it in cash, by the way.'

'Ah. Cash. Now that *is* serious.'

'Exactly. Now why don't you take off your clothes, and then take off mine, unless you'd prefer it to be the other way round? I want this to be your treat, starting with the champagne.'

'If this is to be my treat,' said Jemima thoughtfully, 'I think one or other of us should wear your black leather jacket.'

In the end it was Spike Thompson who took off the clothes and Jemima Shore who wore the black leather jacket. Spike Thompson also opened the champagne. Neither of them remembered to close the gap in the curtains.

It was a long time later that Jemima raised her head from Spike's chest, her fingers clutched into the nests of black curly hair.

'Spike?'

'Mmmmm.' He tightened the grasp of his arm, equally hirsute, about her.

'There's a light on in the theatre.'

'Fuck the theatre. This is television.'

Nat Fitzwilliam, when he went back into the Watchtower Theatre, also found someone waiting for him, someone sitting silently in the front row of the stalls.

'Who is it?' he called from the back of the auditorium. But the figure, apparently gazing fixedly at the empty darkened stage, did not answer. It was very dark and still in the theatre: the lights which Nat had switched on did not illuminate the silent figure where it sat and to Nat, suddenly nervous, it had something of the horrid immobile air of a guy, a guy waiting patiently for the drama to begin.

'Who are you?' Nat called again, walking quickly forward. 'And how the hell did you get into the theatre?' His voice sounded sharp, even commanding, but he was twisting the ends of his white scarf as he spoke.

'Oh, I know where the key was left,' said the person suddenly, rising up from the seat, and pulling Nat's white scarf from between his hands. Taking advantage of Nat's surprise, the person most efficiently then placed the scarf round Nat's neck and pulled it tight, tight, till his round eyes began to pop out of his head, and his poor bragging tongue started forth.

The theatre was quite quiet and no one saw the person who had just murdered Nat Fitzwilliam leave the the Stage Door and go away.

Nat Fitzwilliam remained sitting, sightless, on the edge of the seat of the stalls where he had fallen, the white scarf twisted round his neck. After a while his body keeled forward and pitched down on to the floor. His body made no sound, resting on the thick theatre carpet. And when the seat, relieved of its burden, clapped back again upright it made no sound either.

9

Forbidden Thoughts

It was Julian Cartwright who broke the news of Nat Fitzwilliam's death to Christabel. He intended to do so with that gentle deference which characterized his treatment of his wife. At the time Christabel was immured alone upstairs in her white bedroom whose windows looked to the sea. She was in that trance-like state half-way between sleep and the anguish of the day in which she might linger for hours if not called by Mrs Blagge.

When rehearsals began, Christabel's orders had been precise: 'My breakfast tray exactly two and a half hours before rehearsal, darling – not a minute earlier, not a minute later. I like to have a bath, find my face again, recover from those wretched but essential pills. And I want the female Blagge to bring it, no, not you, Blanche darling, no Rina, of course not, and above all not Ketty – the female Blagge is the only one of you who won't talk at that time of day. Silent disapproval is ideal at that time in the morning, because it really is *silent.*'

Julian Cartwright had not offered to bring the tray himself and thus ran no risk of being repulsed.

Now he stood beside his wife's large bed, gazing down at her in the semi-darkness. The day was overcast: the sultry night had ended in a small storm and a shower of rain, freshening the heavy green summer garden: so there was no sunlight to eat its way through the chinks in the curtains. All the same Julian could discern the soft contours of his wife's body under the bedclothes; she slept, as she always had, he remembered, well over on the right side of the bed, although there was now no rival occupant to disturb her repose. Had she slept like this too during those years away, those years when – surely her bed then had been all unruly –

These were forbidden thoughts. Putting them from him, Julian touched Christabel's shoulder lightly.

She stirred and muttered something like 'Curtains'. Seeing that her eyes were still tightly shut, Julian suddenly bent down and kissed her naked shoulder where he had touched it, as though to soothe the mark away.

Christabel gave a little cry, opened her eyes, cried out again more strongly, and then stopped. She looked quite frightened as she clutched the white sheet across her breasts, only partly concealed by the white silk nightdress. Julian sat down on the edge of the bed.

'Darling Christabel, listen to me.' He did not attempt to touch her again.

'What time is it?' Christabel sat up more fully, and tried to squint at the little lapis lazuli and gold clock on her bedside table. 'What time is it? Have I overslept? Where's Mrs Blagge?'

'Listen to me, my dearest. The police have telephoned from Larminster. There's been an accident. I want to prepare you.' For once Julian's voice was really low; his tone, as ever, was reasonable.

He was violently interrupted by screams coming from the landing. The voice was that of Blanche. The cry – 'Mummy, Mummy' – was the same primitive wail which had announced the discovery of Filly Lennox's body on the seashore.

Blanche came running into the bedroom. She was wearing very tight jeans and a T-shirt, with her fair hair pulled tightly into a ponytail. Julian had an automatic reaction: Blanche shouldn't wear jeans or pull her hair back, even last night's baggy outfit had been better. Then Blanche's story came tumbling out at high speed:

'He's dead! Murdered! Vandals came in the night! They killed him – and now—' She began to weep copiously, hurling herself across the silk coverlet embroidered with spring of lily of the valley. 'I'll never be an actress now, I know I never will.' As Blanche's weeping turned to howls, Regina's much taller and slimmer figure, also clad in jeans, was seen rather wistfully standing in the bedroom door.

'Come in, Rina, come in, don't hang about there,' he called out impatiently. 'Mummy's awake. You can see that. Ordinary rules don't apply. Besides—'

Regina stepped tentatively into the bedroom. Her eyes were full of tears.

'Oh Daddy,' she began. 'The pity of it—' She stopped as she saw that Julian's arms were struggling with Blanche's prostrate form, half-comforting her, half-trying to lug her off Christabel's bed. Regina too began to cry.

About the time that Julian Cartwright with the help of Blanche was breaking the news of Nat Fitzwilliam's murder to Christabel, Miss Kettering was performing the same office for the Blagges.

Mr and Mrs Blagge were together in the main kitchen; Mrs Blagge was setting Christabel's breakfast tray. Ketty watched her sister for a moment in silence.

'Give over, Katherine,' muttered Mrs Blagge rather irritably. 'Give over watching me, why don't you? Haven't you got any of your own work to do?' Mrs Blagge folded a tiny voile napkin and made it look like a butterfly. 'If I don't call her in good time before rehearsal—'

'No need to hurry yourself, Rose, no need whatsoever. There won't be any rehearsals from this time forward. Not for Her at any rate. For others more worthy, there will be. After all sin will not triumph.' Ketty's tone was solemn but beneath it, something approaching glee could be discerned. Mrs Blagge was bent over the fridge, searching out a minute pat of butter.

'What's that you say, Katherine?'

'Thought better of it, has she then? No rehearsals? Repented her wicked ways?' If Ketty sounded a note of subdued glee, Mr Blagge was positively jovial.

'Nat Fitzwilliam, he's dead. Mrs Nixon and Joan found him this morning when they went to clean the theatre. A terrible sight! Strangled with his own scarf. It's all over Larminster. They got the police of course, but he was quite dead. Must have been dead for hours. Somebody must have broken in. May God Have Mercy on His Soul.' Ketty crossed herself.

Mrs Blagge did likewise. Mr Blagge did not move. Then the jug he was holding crashed to the floor and splintered into fragments as though some unseen force had prised open his fingers. He made no attempt to pick up the pieces.

'Barry! He was just the same age as our Barry – and now they're both dead – well, at least it's fair – when you think—'

'We agreed that we'd never talk about that, Jim,' interrupted Mrs Blagge. 'That's forbidden, Jim, to think about that, about those days.' Mr Blagge subsided.

'Broke in, you said?'

'Well, they must have broken in, mustn't they?' observed Ketty in a pious voice. 'We are not dealing with the supernatural here, Jim, and he was not likely to have let in his own murderer was he? He was a foolish boy, but he was not that foolish.'

'So the key wasn't used?' Mr Blagge's voice was hoarse.

The two women looked at each other; their expressions were unwontedly sympathetic.

'What's that, then, Jim?'

Mr Blagge sat down heavily at the kitchen table, the debris of the jug crunching under his feet.

'Last night. While you, Katherine, were having dinner with them in that arty-crafty place they love so much with the mucked-up food and those two hens who run it, Rose went to call on Father O'Brien and Mrs

Lang – I stayed in the car. Then *She* asked me to fetch her shawl from her dressing-room. Found a teeny weeny draught in the restaurant' – Mr Blagge cruelly imitated Christabel's beguiling tones – 'and of course Mr Julian had first rushed off to look for it. Came back without it. No key to the theatre – forgot about asking for it, in all his hurry to look after *Her*.

'So then I was called from the car to make the second visit. The key was produced by Master Nat – he was having dinner there too you know – and into the theatre I go. Very cheeky he was too, when I asked him for the key. Gave him a piece of my mind right back, I did. I wasn't standing for that from young Nat. I don't care who heard me.'

'Into the theatre, Jim! Why you might have been killed,' gasped Mrs Blagge ignoring the references to Nat's cheekiness. There was something quite self-righteous about her exaggerated anxiety.

'That is, not into the actual theatre,' Mr Blagge corrected himself carefully, 'through the Stage Door, where I picked up the key of her dressing-room, and ended up with the aforesaid shawl . . . The only thing is . . .' he hesitated. 'When I returned the shawl, Mr Julian told me not to bother to give young Nat back the key. I was very glad not to have to hand it back to that cheeky bastard, I can tell you. He'd left the restaurant by that time with the bald actor, the one who plays Sergeant Bartock on telly, and some woman. I saw them crossing the square to the Royal Stag on my way back.

'"Leave it under the big stone by the dogs' drinking-trough," he said – Mr Julian, that is. "Mr Fitzwilliam will pick it up later. It'll be quite safe." So forth went I out and deposited it, just as he, Mr Julian, had requested.'

Already there was something about Mr Blagge's words which smacked of the prepared statement.

'And so you did, Jim?' Mrs Blagge prompted him.

He nodded.

'Then you've done nothing to reproach yourself with. Even if it wasn't a break-in. You were just obeying orders. Mr Julian's orders.'

'Ah, but Rose, anyone could have seen him,' Ketty resumed her most pious voice. 'You must bear that in mind. Anyone could have heard you, Jim, come to think of it.'

'Heard me! Heard Mr Julian, more like. It was he what was making the arrangements, don't you forget it. A voice like a bull, as She has so often put it—' Mr Blagge now sounded quite agitated.

'Be that as it may, I prefer to look upon the bright side of things, myself,' Ketty in contrast was all sweetness.

'And what might that be?'

'The end of Her return to the stage. No more attention for Her.' Ketty smacked her lips. The gesture appeared to remind her of the need for bodily sustenance in this difficult time. She helped herself most adroitly to a piece of toast from Christabel's tray and buttered it. Mrs Blagge frowned.

'Let Her sleep,' declared Ketty with confidence as she munched. 'Poor Nat. I remember his mother, Maisie Johnson; I was at school with her. We should have a Mass said for him, Rose, you talk to Father O'Brien about it. Father O'Brien's very interested in everything to do with the theatre – I'm sorry, Jim, I know your opinions, but it's true. They're not all bad people – you should have met some of the ones I met in London – perfect ladies and gentlemen.' Jim Blagge made no comment but looked unconvinced. 'Still, I'd like to see Her face when she hears the news that the production has been cancelled.' Ketty went on cheerfully.

Miss Kettering was however to be denied that satisfaction.

The verdict of the Larminster Festival Committee, as represented by Major Cartwright, on the subject of cancellation was clear enough. Major Cartwright's statement, for him, verged on the eloquent.

'Can't be done. Glad to be shot of the whole business, myself, police crawling all over the place, not as bad as those television johnnies of course, no, nothing could be as bad as that. At least you know where you are with the police, at least the police are doing a job of *work*.'

Major Cartwright glared at Gregory Rowan, to whom these remarks were being addressed, as if he might disagree.

'Oh quite,' responded Gregory earnestly. 'Give me murder and the police over a straightforward television programme any day.'

'Absolutely, my dear boy, absolutely.' The Major was delighted by this unexpected support. 'You know where the police are, and they know where you are. Whereas television! Tripped over a damn camera myself, the other day, and went for a burton. Good as murder any day, show you the bruises if you like. At least the police never trip you up – it's not their job to do that. All the same' – the Major's expression became more melancholy – 'can't be done. Lots of bookings, local interest, *county* interest. Insurance wouldn't play for one thing. Have to get another director I suppose and face the music. Godawful play anyway, even with *this* director, and he was born in Larminster.'

'There are of course *two* plays to be considered,' Gregory suggested.

'That's right. *Two* godawful plays and we need a new director for both of them,' pondered the Major in a voice of exceptional bad temper. Some sense of Gregory's role in the Festival then appeared to penetrate his consciousness. 'Not yours, old boy,' he added graciously. 'No question of that. Always love your plays. Always have. No! It's all this French Revolutionary nonsense. Historical twaddle. Not my phrase, by the way, but Fitzwilliam's own. The last time I saw him he used that very expression to me – historical twaddle, he said, play only saved by his own first-class production.'

Gregory, with an air of unruffled good-humour, suggested that far too much twaddle was seen in Britain, both on the stage and above all on television. He pointed out that Boy Greville, a highly experienced director with a particular knowledge of his, Gregory's, work, and a real ability to hunt and destroy twaddle wherever he found it – notably and most urgently in Nat Fitzwilliam's productions – was actually present in Larminster. Might it not be a good idea to employ him? The Major agreed. They parted on terms of the utmost amiability.

Cy Fredericks, on the telephone to Jemima Shore, began like Major Cartwright by expressing a strong desire to be shot of the whole business – the business in this case being Megalith's involvement in the Larminster Festival.

'My dear Jem,' he roared indignantly down the telephone, 'they can't keep on dying like this.' Anything that seriously impeded a Megalith programme in the making – that is, one with large sums of money already invested in it – was apt to be regarded by Cy as a deliberate campaign against his own personal survival. Clearly the unscheduled demises of Filumena Lennox and Nat Fitzwilliam fell squarely into this unfortunate category. 'They can't keep on like this and not expect Megalith to pull out. We had a special meeting this afternoon to discuss it all – where were you, by the way Jem, canoodling in Bridset, helping the handsome Spike to despatch his film, if what I hear is correct?'

'On the contrary, I was helping the Bridset police with their enquiries,' replied Jemima in her coldest voice. 'And so was Spike. We're expecting to be arrested at any moment. Then you'll have to stand bail for us both for the sake of your programme – and as we shall then naturally elope, it could be a very expensive business.' Why was Cy's information service always so tiresomely up to date? She made a mental note to find out who had betrayed her and if it was Cherry, to condemn her to a lifetime of dating eighteen-year-olds.

'For you, Jem, nothing is too much!' Cy was heavily gallant. 'As for our friend Spike, nothing *has* been too much for him in the past – the sight of his expenses in Capri on that dreadful deep-sea-diving Axel Munthe film still floats before my eyes on sleepless nights – so I suppose his bail would be merely one more colossal down-payment.' His tone changed. 'Anyway, you will be pleased to know, my dear Jem, that we've decided to go ahead with the programme for the time being. Less emphasis on the production itself. More emphasis on Christabel Herrick's return to the stage on the one hand, colourful local pageantry on the other. In short, we've decided that it would look bad if we pulled out now. We are artistic patrons, Jem, never forget, as well as businessmen. We have hearts as well as pockets, and we are prepared to dip our hands into both.'

'I never do forget, Cy,' murmured Jemima. The image of Cy dipping his hand into his heart was an irresistible one; she hoped Cy might use it in his next application for a television franchise. 'I think you've made the right decision,' she added more strongly. 'Boy Greville's a perfectly competent director and he happens to be already on the spot.'

'Exactly. I made the same point to Guthrie: at least there's no need to fly him here from some expensive Greek island, which is what we had to do with Guthrie himself. But no more deaths, Jem please, no more deaths. The next time you ring me with the bad news that Christabel Herrick has fallen off a cliff or taken an overdose or been shot point-blank in her dressing-room, you and Spike must expect to interrupt your Bridset idyll. Permanently.'

'The next time!' exclaimed Jemima. 'What makes you think there will be a next time?' Her tone suggested she might be referring more to her relationship with Spike Thompson than to future tragedies involving the Larminster Festival. As soon as she rang off, however, Jemima's thoughts turned away from Cy's teasing to the sadder and more sinister topic of Nat's death.

The Bridset police had treated his death as murder from the start. An incident room had been set up at Beauport under the general command of the county's senior detectives at Bridchester: however the driving force behind this particular investigation was destined to be the Beauport-based Detective Inspector Matthew Harwood. The pathologist's post-mortem report was one of the few concrete pieces of evidence available to him. It gave the cause of death as strangulation and when pressed for an opinion – in the nearest pub to the mortuary – the pathologist had placed the time of death between eleven p.m. and one a.m.

There were no signs of breaking into the theatre: the key to the Stage Door had therefore presumably been used, since the front doors were locked and the locks had not been forced. Since one key to the Stage Door was also missing from beneath the Lady May Cartwright Memorial stone drinking trough, where Mr Blagge had placed it, the inference was generally made by the public that this was the key which had been used.

Not, however, by the police. In the formidably bulky shape of Detective Inspector Harwood, the police were a great deal more cautious. In questioning his witnesses, Detective Inspector Harwood was very careful to give no opinion whatsoever as to which key might have been used to enter the Watchtower Theatre. There were, he pointed out, several other keys to the Stage Door. Nevertheless local gossip in Larminster continued to concentrate on that particular key placed by Mr Blagge under the stone on the night of the murder.

'Anyone could have seen him' – it was an echo of Miss Kettering's pious cry. 'The types you get about here in the summer . . . Vandals . . . Hippies . . . Layabouts.' It was comforting to be able to blame some casual criminal, drawn from the outside world: the very existence of a theatrical Festival was felt to have some sinister bearing on the crime. Theatre audiences, if not to be totally identified with hippies and layabouts in the local imagination, were not exactly held to exclude this category either. Robbery was widely suggested as the motive, the box office proceeds as the target. Larminster gossip thus ignored the inconvenient detail that no attempt to enter the box office, let alone rob it, had in fact been made. After all, if the murder had not been committed in this random manner for mercenary motives, it must have been deliberately planned. In Larminster. Possibly by a Larminster resident. This was a forbidden thought.

For precisely the same reasons, the distraught members of the King Charles Theatre Company preferred to believe in the notion of a Larminster murder – a local person of known bad character perhaps – whose identity would be uncovered as quickly as possible. Robbery remained an element in the story which the actors told themselves, although they were rather more cynical about the likely proceeds of the theatre box office.

'I mean, it's not exactly Shaftesbury Avenue, darling, is it?' Thus Anna Maria Packe to her husband Boy Greville.

'I hope no one thinks *I* killed him to get the job,' Boy Greville spoke in a voice of acute anxiety. 'Nat was utterly ruthless. Everyone knows that. The way he got rid of us both when the lovely lady Christabel made her unexpected entrance – blackmail – nothing else. Yet in the end one forgave him.'

'Someone didn't,' Anna Maria said lightly: but she sounded reassuring. This was her habitual tone when addressing her husband just as his habitual tone when addressing anyone at all was one of acute anxiety. A mutual interest in the anxieties of Boy Greville was indeed the basis of their long and on the whole not unhappy marriage. From time to time a peculiarly tempestuous love affair – or a peculiarly demanding lover – would withdraw Anna Maria altogether from Boy's side; there had been several separations and even on one occasion (for who could resist Marty Bland?) a projected divorce. Physical separation from Boy did not however free Anna Maria from her responsibility as general consultant on his anxieties, a role he considered she could still carry out to his satisfaction so long as she remained at the end of the telephone.

Boy was not insensitive: all his consultations pertained entirely to his own problems and he was most scrupulous in not referring to Anna Maria's own situation. Nevertheless it was the persistent nature of these calls which had always persuaded Anna Maria so far that it was easier to live with Boy Greville than at the end of his telephone line.

'Someone had it in for him.' Detective Inspector Harwood, had he but known it, agreed with Anna Maria Packe. He made the remark quite casually to Jemima Shore in her sitting-room in the Royal Stag. 'We don't buy the idea of burglary, of course. No evidence for it whatsoever. Not a thing touched. Nor vandalism for that matter. I mean, think what a self-respecting vandal could have done to those seats! The mind boggles. And the glass. Frankly I'm always surprised that a glass theatre in Larminster doesn't suffer more. You sometimes get these young lads streaking up from Beauport on their motor-bikes. Still, it doesn't. One or two incidents, I believe, nothing very much. Quiet little place, Larminster. Even the Festival brings you a quiet sort of visitor. Quiet Americans. Quiet Germans. Quiet Japanese – well, that's only to be expected. Even the occasional quiet Italians. The noisy sort go to Stratford, I suppose.'

Detective Inspector Harwood had already interviewed Jemima offi-cially, as indeed he had interviewed all those present in Flora's Kitchen on the evening of Nat Fitzwilliam's death. The time of Nat's departure from the restaurant was easily established as ten o'clock. He had then had a drink in the bar of the Royal Stag with Anna Maria and Vic Marcovich, before announcing his intention of returning to the theatre. He also mentioned to Vic Marcovich that he would use his own front-of-house key instead of picking up the key deposited by Mr Blagge, since he had forgotten where Julian Cartwright had suggested it should be hidden. He had said this in the full earshot of all those in the bar of the Royal Stag at the time.

Also in the full earshot of those same people in the bar, Vic Marcovich had criticized Christabel Herrick for demanding her shawl so capriciously in the first place: 'Lady of the Manor, First Lady of the Larminster Festival – which is it to be?' But that ungallant remark belonged to the whole area of background material relating to the case.

No one suggested Vic Marcovich had murdered Nat Fitzwilliam. For one thing he had an unimpeachable if slightly disreputable alibi: he had spent most of the night with Anna Maria Packe in his room 'discussing the production'; as if that was not alibi enough, they had received constant calls from Boy Greville on the house telephone throughout the night hours on the subject of Boy Greville's latest allergy, probably aroused by one of the house plants in the lounge of the Stag. For another thing, Vic Marcovich had no motive.

'And the question of motive brings me to you, Miss Shore.'

'Me?'

'Well, you've a reputation for these things, investigations I mean. I know all about you from my little brother Gary in London – not so little these days, two inches taller than me, Gary Harwood, if three stones lighter, the one who looks like Elvis, or so the girls tell me, and works for Pompey of the Yard. Jemima Shore Investigator . . . and not only on the telly. Am I right or am I wrong?'

'Ah.' Over the years it was true that Jemima had enjoyed a pleasant working relationship with Pompey of the Yard, Detective Superintendent Portsmouth as he had become, formerly Detective Chief Inspector John Portsmouth of the Bloomsbury Division; her relationship with his dashing sidekick while in Bloomsbury, Detective Constable Gary Harwood, had had its pleasant moments too. Her connection with Pompey had begun when she had interviewed him on television in connection with an appeal for a missing child. Subsequently there had been investigations – she was not too modest to admit it – where the confidence of the public in the familiar appearance of a telly star, combined with Jemima's own intelligence and curiosity, had enabled her to solve certain cases which had baffled the more conventional workings of the police.

'I spoke to Gary this evening, as a matter of fact. Nothing official. What's happening in the Third Test, you know the sort of thing.' She did. 'And he said "That Jemima Shore, give her enough rope and—"'

'Go on,' Jemima prompted him sweetly.

'"Give her enough rope, Matt," he said, "and you can watch the Test to your heart's content – because she'll solve your case for you."'

'Ah,' said Jemima Shore again.

'What I need to know, Jemima, is this.' After these combined mentions of Pompey, Gary Harwood and cricket, their friendship was clearly progressing. 'Who *wanted* him out of the way? What's going on here? It doesn't make sense. No debts. We've checked that. No obvious clues. No vicious ex-girlfriends for example. We've checked that too. No romances in the cast – not gay either so far as we know. A girl in his flat in London who seemed devoted to him, very upset at his death, anyway she had an alibi although we didn't quite put it like that, at the theatre with her sister. Professional rivalry? That director, the nervous one, who's taken over – he doesn't look a murderer for my money and anyway if his wife's story – *and* her lover's by the way – is to be believed, he was busy telephoning about his asthma all through the night! Theatrical people. I ask you.' Detective Inspector Harwood shook his massive head.

Jemima thought back to a certain conversation with Christabel Cartwright in Flora's Kitchen.

'On the stage, I'll be safe.' And so she was safe – up to the present time. But Filly was dead, and so was Nat Fitzwilliam. These could no longer be forbidden thoughts. She had to talk to someone about Christabel. And that led her to Gregory Rowan, Gregory who had made no secret of his hostility to Megalith Television on her arrival at Larmouth, but was now suspiciously amiable.

'I'd like to help you, Matt—' said Jemima with her angelic smile, the one she kept for ravishing television viewers when she was discussing importantly boring topics like the Common Market. 'Unofficially, of course.'

'My money's on the playwright,' added Matt Harwood suddenly and rather unexpectedly. 'Had a row with Fitzwilliam over his production of his play. Left for home about eleven o'clock to go for a *swim*! Then went straight back to his cottage. *Swimming!* What kind of an alibi is that? Still, I dare say you will tell me that playwrights never do want to kill directors over productions of their plays.'

Jemima saw no reason to tell him any such thing. But since she had no wish to lower his opinion of theatrical people still further, she merely agreed aloud that it would be a wise move for him to talk further with Gregory Rowan. Privately she decided to go and call on Gregory herself in the cottage in the woods. She thought she would go alone. She did not mention this plan to Detective Inspector Harwood.

10

A Real Killer

'Let me help.'

Gregory Rowan put out his arm, an arm so darkly tanned and knotted with muscles that it might have belonged to a sailor, and gripped Jemima by the elbow. She trod water desperately. For a moment he supported her altogether.

'It's the current,' she gulped, 'I'd no idea. I'm quite a strong swimmer. And it's very cold.'

He could just as easily have pulled her under: they were alone, far out from the shore; the beach was deserted. But that was a mad thought, produced by panic. He had saved her, not pulled her down.

Afterwards he said: 'You see. Nobody takes this current seriously. That poor girl – you probably see now how easily it can happen. Anyway you're a beautiful swimmer. You just needed a little help. Even you.' Gregory smiled. 'Even Jemima Shore Investigator.'

Jemima smiled too. 'I was out of my depth.' They were back at his cottage and she was smoking a cigarette, which had Gregory but known it, was another sign that she had felt, even for one moment, out of her depth. So far as she could recall, she had not smoked one cigarette that year.

She had first begun to feel out of her depth when Gregory had greeted her unexpected arrival at Old Keeper's Lodge – in fact a cottage – with extraordinary cordiality. Unlike Detective Inspector Harwood, she was not herself inclined to 'put her money on the playwright'. It was to talk about Christabel that Jemima had decided to pay her surprise visit to the cottage – Christabel and her friends, Christabel and her enemies. In order to find out who might have had reason to kill Nat Fitzwilliam – possibly because of what he saw from the Watchtower concerning the death of Filly – it was necessary to go back to the beginning and find out what was or had been frightening Christabel. Gregory was her best potential source of information about the past at Lark Manor: but she did not expect the interview (she used the word automatically) to go very easily.

On the other hand she did not herself rate Gregory as a suspect. Or if by any chance Gregory had killed Nat, Jemima could hardly believe that it was for the reason that Matt Harwood proposed. Fitzwilliam's contempt for *Widow Capet* had been much discussed; phrases like 'this middle-class, middle-brow and middle-aged hit' had been quoted, the latter being a remark Nat had chosen to make to Old Nicola of all people, with the predictable result that it had received a wide circulation. Nevertheless if Jemima judged Gregory's character right, this kind of behaviour in a young director was more likely to inspire Gregory to verbal attack in public than murder in private; even if the death of Nat had resulted in the restoration of the original director and sympathetic interpreter of Gregory's works, Boy Greville.

As for the death of Filly, Jemima could not of course imagine any reason at all why Gregory should wish to remove her from the Larminster dramatic scene. Filly's death had considerably weakened the cast of *Widow Capet*: Anna Maria Packe was too old to play Paulinot, the jailer's daughter. Emily Jones, who was the right age, was as yet far too weak a stage presence to compete with Christabel as Marie Antoinette in the famous scene between the two women, which even Nat Fitzwilliam had admitted stood most effectively for the Old France versus the New. What might have been memorable theatre with Filly Lennox involved, would now be sadly tame.

And Gregory killing Filly by mistake for Christabel? Ah, there was the rub. There was a great deal about the strange tangled emotional situation at Lark Manor yet to be unravelled. This was one reason why Jemima had not yet shared her suspicions concerning Filly's death with the police, despite the growing warmth of her friendship with Detective Inspector Harwood.

'He wouldn't want to hear it. It's only supposition. After all there's no *proof*,' she told herself, to explain her reluctance, knowing full well that this was not the true explanation. The truth was that Jemima Shore Investigator, tantalized by the strange situation at Lark Manor – above all by the 'cool repentance' of Christabel Cartwright – wanted first crack at solving the mystery herself.

Gregory's cottage was predictably book-furnished, shelves everywhere, and books also in heaps on the floor and resting on sofas like sleeping cats. Jemima noticed a number of books about Restoration Drama and what looked like an eighteenth-century edition of Rochester's erotic poetry (an admirer had once presented her with something similar). A good many of the books looked as if they came into the valuable category of the very old; others fell into the expensive category of the very new.

The books, whether leather-bound or modern, did not however look dusty. And there was nothing dirty or even shabby about the cottage. The thick woods rising behind Lark Manor had parted to reveal this little patch of green order within the luxuriant chaos of the trees, with a cottage – a Hansel and Gretel type of cottage – in the middle of it. Inside the cottage there was the same feeling of order at work within chaos.

As she looked round, Jemima's eye fell on a large framed photograph of the lady of Lark Manor herself. It must have been taken many years ago: the two solemn-eyed girls at Christabel's side, holding up the ends of her wide sash, were mere children. The photograph was not actually on Gregory's desk but facing it. On the desk, however, was another smaller photograph of Christabel in a gold frame. Her hair rippled out of the picture: she smiled into the camera, at Gregory, at Jemima Shore. That photograph too came from some past era. A further quick glance round the room revealed at least one other picture of Christabel, more of a family snapshot than a posed actress's photograph. It included the father of the family, Julian Cartwright.

Jemima thought that the presence of so many large and obvious photographs of Christabel Cartwright ought to make her task of questioning Gregory on the subject rather easy. The fact that none of these photographs was at all recent – all of them must certainly antedate the Iron Boy affair – could also be considered helpful.

At this point Gregory suggested going swimming.

'And then we can talk all you like, Jemima Shore Investigator,' he ended with a slightly ironic smile; but he still showed absolutely no sign of his earlier hostility. 'And you can ask me all the questions you like. Isn't that what you've come for?'

Somehow Gregory's professed willingness to be interrogated, like his friendliness, gave him an advantage. It crossed her mind to wonder which of them was really going to pose the questions and gain the needful information: who, whom? Once they were back in the cottage, after rattling up from the beach in Gregory's large black hearse-like car, she continued to feel out of her depth, and not only because of her recent chilling experience in the water.

The truth was that Gregory exerted some kind of odd influence over her, she had to face that, and had done so since that first abrasive meeting on the beach. Then he had displayed the rare power to rile her – she, Jemima Shore, whose great asset as an interviewer was the fact that she was never riled, no matter what the provocation, using on the contrary her cool composure to rile others where necessary in the cause of her investigations. Now he was persuading her to smoke and drink whisky before lunch, something which was even rarer; many of Jemima's best friends felt that her whole legendary composure could be summed up by the glass of chilled dry white wine she was so fond of drinking.

Spike Thompson, for example, had been able to convert Jemima neither to whisky nor to cigarettes, under far more intimate circumstances: on him she had imposed her own demand of champagne, and, where cigarettes were concerned, had merely watched while Spike had rolled his own choice of smoke; naked and happy she had gazed at the ceiling and smelt the slightly sweet smell of pot drifting by without any inclination to share it.

The thought of Spike suggested to her, irritatingly, that she was possibly rather attracted to Gregory in a tiresome Beatrice and Benedick kind of way, which scarcely fitted her plans for Bridset relaxation. Jemima, being a free woman, made it her practice to do exactly what she pleased in that direction; especially when she was, by her own reckoning, fancy-free – as she was at the present time. Doing what she pleased, she decided, might include an uninhibited Bridset Idyll with an energetic cameraman, but it definitely did not include any kind of involvement with the provoking and doubtless complicated Gregory Rowan.

Nevertheless the ability of Gregory to intrigue and tease and annoy her suggested to Jemima, from experience, that she was not absolutely indifferent to him in the mysterious sphere of sexual attraction. She therefore made a resolution not to allow these tentative thoughts on the subject of his physical attraction to go any further; she backed it up with a further resolution to keep this resolution. She was here to talk about Christabel.

It was therefore rather a pity from the point of view of both these resolutions that conversation about Christabel led at once to the topics of love, infatuation and even, though it was not explicitly stated as such, sex and Gregory Rowan. None of this exactly helped to quell Jemima's personal interest in the subject.

A further surprise awaited her. Gregory spoke quite simply when she questioned him about Christabel and the past. His irony as well as his hostility were temporarily dropped. There was an air of relief about his confidences as though he positively enjoyed making them. Was it the magic of the trained interviewer at work, even with a man as sophisticated as Gregory? Or was it, as Jemima soon concluded, that Gregory welcomed any opportunity to talk about Christabel Cartwright?

'I loved her madly. I loved her to distraction. Shall I put it like that? When she ran off with that ghastly ginger-haired lout, my heart stopped.'

'Was that really all he was? Iron Boy? Just a ginger-headed lout. No one here will talk about him – for obvious reasons.'

Gregory considered. 'Am I prepared to talk about Iron Boy? Probably not. Am I even prepared to be fair about him? The answer is, once again, probably not. He was ginger-headed and he was a lout; but he did have a kind of mad vitality, at any rate when he was a boy; people, all sorts of people, had a good time in his company. Beyond that, there's really nothing to be said for him at all. Back to my heart, if you don't mind. It really never started again. Not until she came back to Lark. And even then the old ticker is not what it was . . . How about that? Is all that sufficiently dramatic for you? I am a playwright you know, and as such, unlike some of my contemporaries, frequently accused of too much plot and melodrama in my works.' Gregory smiled calmly before continuing: 'Oh, by the way, perhaps I should add that I also love Blanche and Rina Cartwright. Quite as deeply. And Julian. In many ways I love him the most of all. He's much the nicest character in the Cartwright family: the only unselfish member of it, for example.'

'So that's why you stayed here all those years? Why you never married?' It was irresistible; the curiosity of Jemima Shore Investigator would not be stifled.

Gregory looked rather surprised. 'It's why I stayed here, of course. But I was married. To Anna Maria, yes, *the* Anna Maria, Anna Maria Packe of the King Charles Theatre Company. You might say that I've always had a thing about actresses—'

'Natural perhaps in a playwright,' Jemima put in encouragingly.

'Except that's not the real point. Anna Maria was still at Central School when we got married. It's probably the other way round: the kind of woman who attracts me tends to become an actress.'

'And that is?' Jemima supposed she must number quite a few actresses among her friends, although she did not generally think about them in this category; this was because in her experience actresses, like actors, and most other categories of professional person, were infinitely varied in their personalities. But she was interested to hear Gregory's answer.

'Emotional. Insecure. Vulnerable. Above all the latter. Beneath all the emotion, in need of care and protection.'

Jemima had not been notably struck by the emotional vulnerability of Anna Maria Packe while in Larminster, as the actress to-ed and fro-ed contentedly between her director husband and her actor lover, satisfying both no doubt, and herself most of all. She said so, as delicately as possible.

Gregory hastened to agree with her.

'That's really why it broke up. She was far too tough and so was I. Anna Maria's much happier looking after Boy, with all his interesting hypochondria. And I—'

He stopped. 'But this isn't why you've come, surely. To talk about the past, my past with Anna Maria. The facts about Christabel and me can be quickly told. They're public knowledge, after all these years. We had a wonderful flaming romance during the run of *Lombardy Summer* – my first really successful play – and it was the summer, the long hot summer of 'fifty-nine. It continued on Broadway in the autumn, that extraordinary season for me, *Lombardy* such a hit, and of course Anna Maria safely tucked away at Stratford, no chance of joining me.

'But,' he stopped again, then plunged on, 'I also wanted to be free. I didn't put it like that to myself of course: I told myself that I was an artist, needed to live alone, all that kind of rot. So – one fine day, when we were all back in London, and my new play had opened, and flopped – the only one that ever did – *Tower*, it became an instant classic by the way, never stops being revived to loud critical, where-did-we-go-wrong? applause. Nothing like the failures they themselves have caused to turn on the critics, but that didn't help me at the time. Nor poor Christabel, who played Baroness Anne, one of her few failures. And she wasn't going to be able to revive it again and again over the next twenty years, was she? So one fine day, she upped and married Julian Cartwright.'

'But he wasn't part of the theatre?'

'No, no, he was just her devoted admirer, her rich young man, she used to call him. He was always around. Christabel wanted security, she said. I took it to be financial security she was after. I was bitterly hurt. She'd always sworn to me that she couldn't go to bed with Julian, not my type she used to say, not my type, darling. *I* was her type. I thought.'

'But you came here? You came and lived here? So that in the end – she had both.' Jemima felt she must tread with extreme care. But she no longer felt out of her depth. Many things about the household – and its attachments – at Lark Manor were becoming clear to her.

'Yes, she had both. Financial security from Julian, and a good deal of emotional security as well down the years. Emotional security also from me, encouragement, understanding with her career. More parts. Knowing all about the theatre, which Julian couldn't, or didn't care to do. I found, you see,' he said simply, 'that I couldn't live without her. And Julian too, I liked him. He liked me. I made her happy. We both of us possessed her. Julian is an extraordinary man. I don't know if you realize that. Besides, I too was having my cake and eating it. I had my own kind of family life at Lark, especially after the little girls were born. And I had my freedom. It suited me. It suited everyone.'

Until Barry Blagge came along – or rather grew to his precocious manhood, thought Jemima. But this thought she did not put into words. Gregory too left it unspoken.

'I *have* come to talk about Christabel,' she said aloud. 'Now there is a vulnerable person. For many reasons—' She meant to concentrate the conversation on Christabel's elopement with Iron Boy and her surprising cool return. But it was as though Gregory, having once decided to put the character of the younger Christabel in perspective, the Christabel with whom he had fallen in love, was reluctant to let it go.

'You're right! Women never seem to understand that,' he exclaimed.

'Christabel always has been extraordinarily insecure, full of self-doubt, self-dislike even, even at the height of her fame, even before all – well, all of that, when she was one of the best-known actresses on the British stage. Oh the doubts, the agonies! About her looks, the loss of youth – that was the attraction of Iron Boy, the confidence it gave her, much more than the mad physical infatuation of the gutter press's lurid imagination. I suppose too she had an irresponsible good time in his company, and she could forget she was an ageing actress, forget everything. After she ran off, I used to think about her new life in the watches of the night. I used to imagine Barry was like Comus, surrounded by his crew of unruly midnight revellers. You know – "What hath night to do with sleep?"'

'Wasn't Christabel rather oddly cast as The Lady? With her "virtuous mind, that ever walks attended By a strong siding champion Conscience——"' Jemima, who had got a First in English at Cambridge, was not averse to quoting Milton herself.

Gregory smiled. 'I should have known better than to bandy quotes with you. It was Barry I was referring to, not Christabel. "Virtuous mind" – I fear not. In any case my Miltonic visions owed a great deal to my stupid insomnia and that's a thing of the past I'm glad to say. Isn't it odd? I've slept like a top ever since Christabel returned. No comment, please. To return to Christabel herself and her insecurity, when he, Iron Boy, ditched her – took Comus's rout somewhere else, if you like – in one way it was the dream of guilt, or self-hatred come true. In another way it totally destroyed her. I believe she was scarcely sane when Julian went and found her and fetched her down here, so he told me.'

Jemima saw her opportunity. (It was time to put aside those tentative thoughts on her own behalf about Gregory: no one who on his own confession specialized in vulnerable women was going to be drawn to Jemima Shore, that golden goddess of television. It was lucky that the Spike Thompsons of this world had a different method of assessing vulnerability.) Murmuring sympathetically, she encouraged Gregory to explain to her the circumstances of Christabel's return: how Christabel had simply telephoned one day, a short desperate call to Julian and asked him to take her back – 'to make a fresh start'. And he had just driven up and fetched her, just like that – 'I told you he was a saint.'

'How did everyone here take it? In this secluded place – the return of the prodigal – if one may put it like that. How did you take it for example?' It was her gentle persistent television interviewer's manner.

Gregory paused and then laughed. 'It sounds ridiculous but at first I felt quite violent. When I first saw her, that day, at Lark, the most perfect early spring day, cold wind from the sea but sunshine, the wind blowing the first daffodils in the drive, and her hair – the wind blowing the beautiful hair, still beautiful – and she so charming, little jokes, just the same, I was amazed by her lightheartedness. She only showed one pang of emotion and that's when we had to tell her that her dreadful mangy old spaniel Mango had died. For some reason Julian had kept that news from her. It was Christabel who adored that dog; Julian couldn't bear him; that was another thing Julian and I had in common: we loved Christabel and loathed her spaniel. I was surprised he even kept Mango after Christabel left, but perhaps he had hopes that Mango would lure her back to Lark. Instead Mango ran out on the main road in her absence, nobody looking after him properly I fear, and got killed. She asked to see the grave, the place where we buried him in the woods. Apart from that, nothing, just little jokes.

'So you see,' he paused, 'for one terrible moment, I wanted to do her some frightful physical injury. I almost wanted to kill her for all the suffering she had caused. So stupid. As I told you, I love her. I'll always love her. You can't kill people like Christabel for what they do. You see, somewhere deep down, she does it to herself worst of all.'

Jemima thought of the elegant pampered woman: the woman who had come back to Lark Manor with impunity to find everything just the same – except for the death of an old dog – and wondered privately if that was actually true. To Gregory, she continued: 'And the children? Regina and Blanche, how did they take it?'

'Resentful at first. Extremely. But they got over it. They'd both seen their mother in London, of course, over the years, although Julian wouldn't let them visit her alone, always sent Ketty along to ward off evil. Evil in the shape of Barry Blagge. Once they grew older, they chose not to meet Barry of their own accord. It was embarrassing for them: the Blagges, you see, they were still there at Lark as servants; I think Rina felt it even worse than Blanche, although it's difficult to tell with a reserved girl like that. Nowadays, I hasten to say, everything's fine with the girls. But you can imagine why I didn't at first want television, in the shape of you, Miss Jemima Shore Investigator, coming down here and upsetting the applecart.' He smiled again.

'And the Blagges?' pursued Jemima. 'To me, that's almost the most amazing part of all. She ran off with their only child and they stayed here. In the same place.'

'Ah, how little you understand of our delightful country ways! This was their home, wasn't it? They looked after it long before Julian married Christabel. There have always been Blagges at Lark, there were Blagges long before there were Cartwrights, for example. Major Cartwright's father, Julian's grandfather, only bought the property some time in the eighties, but there are Blagge graves in the churchyard stretching back into the seventeenth century. Jim Blagge had been through the war with Major Cartwright: excellent brave soldier, by the way. Resourceful and courageous. "A real killer, Blagge was," the Major is fond of saying:

strange to think of that distinguished elderly man handing round the meat and two veg behind his chair as he says it. No, it was she who was the interloper, Christabel, the actress, the woman from the outer world.'

He added: 'The Kettering sisters are local too. Two bright farmer's daughters. Only Rose married Jim Blagge and went into service, and Ketty, the younger sister, became first the girls' nannie, then housekeeper and general factotum when she went with them to London and Christabel was working all the time. She was quite stagestruck in those days. Finally, with Christabel's departure, Ketty was queen of the roost at Lark – with only Rose Blagge to keep her in her place.

'Julian never kept her in her place.' Gregory lit yet another cigarette: 'Too grateful to her for sticking around and preserving order. Ketty was a good-looking woman in her day, handsome rather; the frightful Barry Blagge looked rather like her, I always fancied, only those strong straight features and red hair came out better in a man. Ketty's not so old, either. And she always worshipped Julian. Christabel used to tease him about it – in the old days.'

'And then Julian Cartwright took Christabel back,' said Jemima thoughtfully. 'In spite of everything. Didn't he – well, think of the effect on the Blagges and Ketty?'

'They were appalled, of course. It might have been different if Christabel had shown some true signs of repentance – by Ketty's and Rose Blagge's rather narrow Catholic standards, that is. They love sinners – in theory – so long as they acknowledge their sins. A sort of Mary Magdalen act would have been acceptable, perhaps. Hair turned grey, some modern form of sackcloth and ashes. Instead – well, Christabel carried it off with her usual style, her hair looked better than ever and her clothes ran their usual gamut from Zandra Rhodes to Bellville Sassoon with not a touch of sackcloth anywhere.

'I said Julian was a kind of saint,' he went on. 'But haven't you ever noticed how saints can be curiously insensitive to the sufferings of lesser mortals caused by their own sanctity? I wrote rather a good play on the subject once, although I say so myself. *Holy Margaret*. They're reviving it at the National in the autumn: you should try to catch it. No, Christabel was Julian's obsession, just as she was mine. He'd never lost it. He jumped at the chance to succour her. As for the Blagges and Ketty, he just assumed they'd share his feelings, in so far as he thought about it at all. And he'd been brought up in a certain way, hadn't he? Kind as he is, to him, after all, and this is going to sound ghastly and old fashioned, but for him finally Blagges and Ketty were just servants. His servants.'

As you were both her servants: but Jemima left that thought unspoken too. As she drove back through the Lark woods and down the end of the Manor drive, she pondered on a number of things. She pondered on Christabel's enemies: there certainly were plenty of those to be found in and around Lark Manor. In particular she pondered on the whole matter of servants and the extraordinary intimacy which Cartwrights, Ketterings and Blagges had all shared in this beautiful Bridset valley, after Christabel's departure. Until Julian Cartwright, the master, one day shattered the whole thing by casually restoring Christabel to favour.

Mr Blagge, the father of Barry. Jim Blagge: 'a real killer'. *The* real killer? Jemima was still turning over the two phrases in her mind and picturing to herself Jim Blagge rowing his boat like Charon over the Styx – was it Jim Blagge Nat had seen through his binoculars, paying the penalty for it with his life? – when the telephone rang in her hotel suite.

It was Detective Inspector Harwood. He was proposing a cup of tea on his way home.

'Something to report to Jemima Shore Investigator,' he said jovially. 'Blagge, you know, the butler fellow from Lark Manor, the father of the late unlamented pop star, I believe, the one the good lady ran off with. We have a witness who saw him leaving the Watchtower Theatre.'

'To get Christabel Cartwright's shawl—' began Jemima, still rather confused by the way the telephone call had broken right into her own thoughts on the subject.

'No, no a second visit about an hour later,' Detective Inspector Harwood sounded increasingly jolly. 'More like eleven o'clock. While the Cartwright party were still carousing at the hotel. Now why, I wonder, did Mr James Blagge not mention that little fact in his statement to the police?'

Jim Blagge: a real killer? Jemima put the telephone quietly down and awaited the visit of Detective Inspector Harwood with something much closer to melancholy than the policeman's own cheerful mood.

11

Arrested Rehearsal

Everyone was in a very tense mood at the rehearsal of *The Seagull* which took place two days later. It was doubly unfortunate that Megalith's tight camera schedule demanded that this particular rehearsal be filmed. Jemima agreed to reason with Cy Fredericks on behalf of Boy Greville but without much hope of success: she was well aware that further postponement would be financially disastrous for Megalith on top of the delays already incurred by what Cy Fredericks termed rather crossly down the telephone 'these wretched deaths'.

It could never be said that the services of Spike Thompson and the rest of the crew all installed – more or less contentedly – at the Royal Stag were to be secured at light cost. Moreover the profits of Flora's Kitchen would, Jemima felt, bear some close relation to the losses incurred by Megalith Television, since none of the crew condescended to eat any-where else once it was discovered that Flora's Kitchen was listed in the *Good Food Guide* as 'expensive but worth it – if you have the money and decide to lavish it on lavish Bridset food given pseudo-Florentine names and served in pseudo-Florentine surroundings'. Spike Thompson and the rest of the crew found it, on behalf of Megalith, a decision easy to make: so after a bit Moll and Poll, with fine appreciation of the workings of the market, thoughtfully put up their prices.

At least Spike Thompson proved a tower of strength during the filming of the rehearsal. Guthrie and Jemima felt deeply grateful to him for the usual mixture of unflappability and ferocious energy which he displayed – and he cut a reassuringly urban and flamboyant figure as he darted behind the camera and then away, in his scarlet polo-necked jersey beneath the black leather jacket. The sound engineer on the other hand was in a highly neurotic mood – possibly induced by a prolonged diet of over-rich food – causing him to groan over tragic noises of interference from the Larminster traffic, inaudible to anyone else; he also grumbled perversely about the isolation of the theatre and its proximity to the shore. At one point he even complained that he was picking up the cry of a seagull.

'Isn't he rather overdoing it in his appreciation of Emily Jones's performance as Nina?' murmured Guthrie to Jemima. 'Every time she declaims, "I'm a seagull", I suppose he mistakes it for the real thing.'

Everyone – except possibly Spike – was in a tense mood, and everyone had their problems. The Megalith lighting crew, for example, had not formed a notably high opinion of the lighting system at the Watchtower, nor had they exactly sworn brotherhood with the theatre's stagehands. Guthrie Carlyle reminded himself that his problems lighting the Parthenon for his non-controversial programme, *The Elgin Marbles – Ours or Theirs?* had been worse, the Greek crew getting thoroughly excited over something; possibly the non-controversial subject matter, possibly the length of the lunch-hour, he never dared enquire.

'On the other hand at least the Parthenon itself stayed put,' he reflected gloomily. It was fair to say that within the Watchtower theatre no one very much stayed put, even someone like Old Nicola, who had no part to play in the rehearsal itself. Lacking a role in *The Seagull*, she had nevertheless infiltrated rehearsals early on, accompanied by her ancient grey plastic bag full of knitting. Even Nat Fitzwilliam had lacked the requisite energy to stop her; and under the new regime of Boy Greville, any threat of removal was met by: 'Oh that poor sweet Nat! What a little genius, wasn't he just? He didn't mind Old Nicola being here, but if you feel differently dear, if you don't quite feel the confidence yet dear, never you mind, you just tell Old Nicola first thing and she'll go quietly.'

So Old Nicola knitted on, regaling listeners with anecdotes of bygone *Seagulls*, mainly featuring her own performances. She claimed to have played Nina and Masha on alternate nights in one season at Stratford.

'And I bet she got the two parts mixed up half the time,' Christabel had been heard to comment. 'Fiendish to play with. She always was, even when she just had one part to remember.' She spoke just within earshot of the older woman, whose hearing, where her own interests were concerned, remained quite acute.

Now the presence of the television crew galvanized Old Nicola into fresh activity. Somehow she always managed to be sitting knitting in exactly the path of the camera and had to be moved at the last minute. In moving, she showed an infallible instinct for selecting a seat which would prove to be in the direct path of the next shot.

'Off you go, my old darling. On your way again,' Spike would shout blithely. Guthrie felt less tolerance.

'Can't we lose her?' he muttered desperately. 'Like forever?'

'By putting her head in her own grey plastic bag?' suggested some other member of the crew enthusiastically. Jemima heartily agreed with the sentiments: she was being personally badgered by Old Nicola to interview her for television on *My Wonderful Long Years in the British Theatre*: 'You could just let the cameras roll and Old Nicola would give it to you; no need for any of your cutting and editing, I can assure you; Old Nicola knows by this time just what interests an audience.' But she declined to join in the jolly discussions about Old Nicola's possible fate; superstitiously, she remembered wishing some dreadful doom to overtake Nat Fitzwilliam. Old Nicola, for all her cunning and trouble making, looked quite physically frail: another 'wretched death', even the natural death of an old lady, was the last thing that Megalith needed.

Boy Greville clearly felt that he had problems enough as director today, without tackling Old Nicola. The extreme agitation which he displayed in private life on matters such as his health, gave way to such a violent nervosity in public when he was working, that Jemima wondered at first how any of his productions ever succeeded in opening. Yet Boy Greville had an excellent reputation as a director over a number of years, and actors were said to like working with him. Jemima could only suppose that they exerted themselves extra frantically on his behalf, in order to try and alleviate at least some of the worst of his sufferings.

'I can't go on with this sort of thing much longer,' he had been heard to groan to Tobs, who at his tender age was having undeniable problems with the character of Dr Dorn: 'The strain on me, personally: you can't imagine—' Tobs straightened up the painful hunched back with which he was attempting to convey Dr Dorn's burden of years, and tried to comfort his director.

Today however the strain was universal. Emily Jones wept a little, and her voice, always a little too high when she was nervous, did take on a kind of bird-like screech in Nina's speech with its reiterated phrase 'I'm a seagull' which gave all too much point to Guthrie's aside.

No doubt the television cameras were adding to the production's troubles by making everyone additionally nervous but it was difficult to believe that anything by Boy Greville, adapted at the last minute from a production by Nat Fitzwilliam, could ever have gone very smoothly. Nat's 'underwater' conception still haunted the production in the shape of certain costumes, as well of course as the set itself, with its unlikely-looking plaster rocks and realistic-looking – because it was real – fisherman's netting. At least Boy had got rid of the sand from the set, which was driving everybody mad, including Mrs Nixon and Joan who were in charge of cleaning the theatre.

There were a number of good reasons why the set could not be replaced. There was the time element: the Larminster Festival was due to open with the production of *The Seagull* at the Watchtower in under a week's time. There was the expense element: the finances of the

Watchtower were shaky enough already, despite contributions from friendly local magnates such as the Cartwrights and the work of the Festival Committee, without the expense of scrapping one whole set and building a new one.

'Committee wouldn't stand for it. Nor would the Chairman,' Major Cartwright, who was the Chairman, told Cherry. He had taken a marked fancy to her, choosing to use her as his conduit of information to Megalith as a whole. His passion was expressed in a series of invitations to meals at expensive restaurants rather further afield than Flora's Kitchen. To the Royal Harbour Hotel at Lar Bay, the Queen Mary at Bridchester, Giovanni e Giovanna, improbably to be found just outside the tiny rustic village of Deep Larkin, Major Cartwright drove Cherry at high speed in his Bentley without speaking. The food was always delicious. All this atoned to Cherry, in some measure at least, for the failure of Julian Cartwright to cast any glances at all in her direction.

'Just have to grin and bear it. That's what I always say anyway about a night at the theatre.' So the Major closed the subject of any possible further expense on the Larminster production of *The Seagull*.

Leaving aside the humorous properties of the play itself – and Nat Fitzwilliam had given the company several interesting lectures on 'Chekhov and the Harmonious Laughter of the Future' – Cherry thought the Major would probably find a good deal to grin about in *The Seagull* production, if that was what he wanted. There might have been even more, if Boy Greville had not insisted on altering at least some of the more ludicrous 'underwater' costumes, where it could be done cheaply.

Thus Emily as Nina was no longer dressed as a mermaid and Vic Marcovich as Trigorin had thankfully got rid of his Neptune's trident, as well as adding extra garments of a rather more conventional nature to the brief golden loincloth required by Nat. No one had ever discovered why Trigorin was to be played as a sea-god: and now it was too late to find out. Ollie Summertown, however, still wore Konstantin's original white sailor-suit, although with the short trousers lengthened (he rather fancied himself in it, he told Cherry, what with his new Bridset tan, and was sorry that his knees were not after all to make their début on television). And Tobs clung to his sou'wester and oilskins which he had decided lent to Dr Dorn what he described as 'an old tar's dignity – I'm a kind of ship's doctor I think'.

Christabel too still wore her original costume. Since this was made of becoming white muslin, over a large hoop skirt, it did give her a suitably nineteenth-century air, especially once the festoons of dark-green sea-weed were ripped off the skirt and bodice. Christabel therefore looked appropriately Chekhovian and even elegant, at a distance: the special grace which she brought to every stage movement was underlined by the sway of her huge skirt.

In herself, however, Christabel was not nearly so poised. Her face, seen close-up through the camera lens, looked drawn. She was more nervous than usual on stage and inclined to dry. In such an experienced actress – at any rate in terms of the past – it was difficult to believe that this was the effect of the television cameras. Besides it was odd that Christabel should falter now: Megalith had already filmed two other rehearsals, and Jemima had noticed that Christabel had been one of the few to be virtually word-perfect from the start – 'off the book already', Nat had said proudly, as though he had learnt Christabel's part for her.

It was more plausible to seek the cause of Christabel's strain in the renewed police questioning of Mr Blagge, underway at the present time. It was true that if Mr Blagge had indeed been the hidden element of fear in Christabel's household, she should by rights have been relieved at his disappearance, at any rate as far as Beauport Police Station. Perhaps it was the uncertainty which was responsible for her anxiety: when they broke for lunch, Jemima was among those who wandered over to the Royal Stag with Christabel, and among those – not a few – who noticed the alarming amount of vodka she consumed. It was left to Old Nicola, who had managed to wander along too, to make some loaded remarks about actresses who drank during rehearsal in her young days and what had become of them – 'Not still acting in their eightieth year like Old Nicola, dear, that I can tell you; they lost their looks first of course . . .'

The Blagge developments had been outlined to Jemima the day before by Detective Inspector Harwood, over the tea-cups in her tiny chintzy hotel sitting-room. There he told her that Jim Blagge was well known locally to have conceived a violent hatred of the theatre, and of all things theatrical, as a result of the career of his son Barry. That this career had actually ended with Barry's death in a road accident was hardly the fault of the theatre; and Iron Boy had been a pop star not an actor. However this was not a distinction that had bothered Mr Blagge among his Bridset cronies. Neither of the Blagge parents had had any real contact with Iron Boy after his elopement with (or abduction by) Christabel; she belonged unarguably to the theatre – so it was the theatre which had led to Barry's death. If not logic, there was a certain natural justice in his resentment.

Mr Blagge's paranoid dislike of the theatre had found a new focus in the person of Nat Fitzwilliam. Had not Nat been a school friend of Barry's? Nat had gone to university and with his superior education should have somehow saved Barry from his fate instead of corrupting him (this was Mr Blagge's version of events). Worse still was the emergence of Nat as Director of the Larminster Festival – the local boy made good when their own Barry was lying in his California grave. Worst of all was the return of Christabel to the stage, directed by Nat himself. Mr Blagge had ascribed the actual responsibility for that return to Nat. He had told his friends, with a knowledge born of his intimate position in the Cartwright family, that without Nat, 'she'd never have had the cheek to do it – not even Her'.

All of this, as Detective Inspector Harwood judiciously acknowledged, added up to no more than current Larminster gossip. He had not come to tea, he assured Jemima, merely to regale her with a lot of old tabbies' talk. The threats of violence made by Blagge against Fitzwilliam were more serious, the evidence of Blagge's second visit to the Watchtower Theatre more serious still. The visit had been witnessed by two strangers to Larminster with no personal knowledge of Blagge or his situation. Their timing was also unshakeable, based on a particular news bulletins on the car radio: so there was no question of their confusing Blagge's innocent first visit with this alleged second sortie.

'Threats of violence?' Jemima queried. She cast her mind back to the only two occasions when she had been aware of Mr Blagge and Nat being in close proximity. One was the original Easter Sunday lunch at Lark when the Blagges had handed round the food: the other was the occasion of the fatal picnic at Larmouth beach. In both cases Mr Blagge had, as far as she was concerned, concentrated entirely on serving food and drink. She had certainly noticed nothing untoward or threatening in his attitude to Nat Fitzwilliam.

But then, thought Jemima wrily, did one ever notice very much about the reactions of the various serving figures at a party, if one was a guest oneself? It was as though one expected their function somehow to dehumanize them, rob them of natural feelings of disgust and envy. Whereas the exact reverse was much more psychologically probable. Her mind went back to Gregory's recent revelations of Julian Cartwright's insensitivity. Mr Blagge no doubt felt even more violently towards Nat Fitzwilliam for having to hand him dishes, and pour him wine at Sunday lunch at Lark Manor. While Nat had sat there, his eager cherub's face pressed forward, utterly unconcerned about the emotions of his erstwhile friend's father dispensing claret over his left shoulder.

Detective Inspector Harwood was able to confirm these vague suppositions in a surprisingly accurate way. By instructing Jim Blagge to get the key of the theatre to fetch Christabel's shawl, Julian Cartwright had obliged Blagge to seek out Nat at the table where he was dining in Flora's Kitchen. This mission had turned into a highly unpleasant encounter when Nat had refused, apparently wilfully, to interrupt his conversation with Anna Maria and find out what Mr Blagge wanted. The older man's pale face had flushed visibly.

'Mr Marcovich who was the third party present was very particular about this detail,' Detective Inspector Harwood told Jemima. 'No mere figure of speech, he assured me. The colour of fine old port was how Mr Marcovich expressed it. And he gobbled like a turkey. After that it became a case of What The Butler Shouted. Mr Blagge actually threatened to thrash Nat, adding for good measure, "if not something worse".'

'We have several witnesses to the fact that he lost all control,' pursued the Detective Inspector. 'But then he does have these fits of sudden explosive rage, they tell me; has done, ever since the war. Terrible thing, uncontrollable rage. Rage and strength. Jim Blagge had both.'

At this moment, as the Megalith cameras focused on the Watchtower stage, Mr Blagge was being questioned at Beauport Police Station. Jemima knew that in the first place he would merely be asked for a further explanation of his movements. Matt Harwood and his team of detectives would be bearing in mind that famous police catchphrase: 'Method: Opportunity: Motive'. So far Mr Blagge had proved to have both Opportunity and Motive. The Method by which Nat had been killed was also obvious – strangulation by his own scarf. It remained to connect Mr Blagge, with his Opportunity and Motive, to the Method. Matt Harwood had assured her that the Bridset police would be quite as rigorous as those in London in applying the Locard exchange principle:

'I daresay that our friend Pompey has made you familiar with it,' he conceded kindly. 'And I hope young Gary bears it in mind as well. A criminal always leaves something at the scene that was not there before—'

'And carries away something that was not there when he arrived,' finished Jemima. Pompey had indeed made her familiar with the phrase. He was particularly fond of it. So, according to the aforesaid exchange principle, Mr Blagge's clothing on the night of the murder would be tested by a kind of giant hoover – for particles from Nat's clothing, and particularly Nat's long white silk scarf. While fibres of Nat's scarf and other clothes would be similarly 'hoovered' for tiny but tell-tale traces of Mr Blagge's garments.

The quiet remorseless police process going on at Beauport was certainly in marked contrast to the furore which had by now developed inside the Watchtower. Jim Blagge too was doubtless meeting with the traditional guarded politeness of the police, whereas there was precious little politeness left inside the cinnamon-coloured auditorium of the theatre.

The costume parade which had begun the morning gave way to a short rehearsal of the last act and then a run-through of the play. In the third act of *The Seagull* Christabel dried twice. Boy Greville ran his hands through his long greying hair in despair, like some ageing wizard whose spell was failing to work. Emily Jones's voice, when it was not trembling, rose higher and higher. Tobs's impersonation of a hunchback Dr Dorn failed to please despite his protests: 'But I spent the day at an old folks' home *studying* them,' he exclaimed indignantly. Finally Vic Marcovich decided off his own bat to deliver all his lines in a completely new manner reminiscent of George Sanders in *All About Eve*. It gave a very odd twist to Trigorin's famous speech about the creative process of a writer and made it sound as if he was talking about a gossip column.

The last phenomenon reduced Boy to the verge of collapse, and he had to be helped from his seat to take some special herbal remedy for when things went really wrong.

Megalith, in the shape of Guthrie as director and Jemima as presenter, had agreed in advance that at least one day would be spent in filming 'work in progress' – in order to contrast the unfinished rehearsal with the final achievement of the First Night. The trouble was, as Guthrie groaned to Jemima, there was altogether too much work and too little progress about this particular rehearsal. Boy's official attitude to the run-through of the last act was that since the first three had gone so abysmally, by the law of averages, the fourth act must go better.

It went much worse. The famous scene between Emily Jones as the fallen Nina and Ollie Summertown as the despairing Konstantin shortly preceding his suicide had about as much tension in it – as Vic Marcovich whispered to Anna Maria – as the reunion of a rice pudding and a treacle tart. Vic was still smarting at the rejection of his George Sanders turn and in no mood for generosity; all the same the comment elicited an embarrassed snigger from those members of the company who overheard it.

'All this should make a wonderful contrast with the First Night,' Cherry observed brightly to Jemima, who wondered not for the first time whether Cherry's gift for stating the obvious was all good.

Just as Vic Marcovich was getting into his stride, his George Sanders manner forgotten or at any rate held over, Boy Greville got a sudden frightful new kind of headache – possibly the onset of his first migraine, but who could be sure? Anyway, he said it was quite different from the nagging low-grade headache he generally endured. His anguished cry and the startling way in which he clapped his hands to his head was, Guthrie and Jemima decided, the most effective bit of acting they had seen all day. They had it on camera, of course. They might even decide to leave it in. Anna Maria cut an interesting figure too, tripping over Old Nicola's knitting as she rushed wildly into the auditorium with a sachet and a glass of water.

The television crew, who had elected to behave angelically all day – even the sound engineer ceased to hear both buses and seagulls through his head-set – suddenly chose the last act to turn into the proverbial work-to-rule demons. Guthrie had been contrasting their behaviour most favourably with that of his disaffected Greek crew: now this fit of patriotic fervour gave way to something more like nostalgia for the vanished glories of the Parthenon programme. The crew would not agree, for example, to run over their supper break by even one minute. Thus it was by no means sure that Megalith would be able to complete the filming of the final scene, the vital moment at which Christabel would react to the noise of Konstantin shooting himself off-stage. For this a dramatic close-up was planned.

It was a case of the whole crew agreeing to this extension or none. Spike raised Mephistophelean black eyebrows to Jemima across the auditorium, smiled ruefully, and put his thumbs down. Jemima suspected the lighting-men of obduracy, as part of their enjoyable guerrilla warfare with the Watchtower stagehands. However there was never any point in suffering additional frustration over these matters; it was all part of the interesting tapestry of English television and had to be accepted as such, along with weather which washed out summer harvest filming in Constable country or played gentle sunshine on the Brontës' moors just when you wanted a Heathcliffian thunderstorm. The actors, most of whom had worked in television and were used to the phenomenon, were equally philosophic.

'We'll just have to take a chance.' Whatever his private thoughts, Guthrie sounded equally resigned.

Emily successfully – well, more or less – declaimed Nina's last speech: 'When you see Trigorin don't tell him anything . . . I love him. I love him even more than before . . .' Her voice did evince its unfortunate little wailing note from time to time, but at least she looked suitably wan and very pretty, still wearing the navy-blue dress with a sailor collar which Boy Greville had substituted for her mermaid's outfit.

Now Christabel was seated on her plastic rock; she had changed from her white muslin into her own clothes – a pale-blue shirt and navy-blue pleated skirt which showed her excellent legs in their narrow-thonged white sandals. Jemima thought that she had the legs at least of a young girl (although Emily Jones, who was a young girl, had rather thick legs, not entirely hidden by her long skirt).

Trigorin gazed at the stuffed seagull before him. Just as planned, a loud noise was heard off-stage. Jemima just had time to think that it did not sound very like a shot, when two things happened.

The supper break was officially reached, so the plugs were pulled and the crew stopped filming. And Blanche Cartwright rushed on to the stage. It was, in its way, a splendidly timed entrance, except for the fact that the camera was no longer turning.

Otherwise Blanche had everyone's fullest attention, from her mother, who gave the most perfectly startled look of any Madame Arkadina reacting to her son's shot off-stage, right down to Old Nicola, who awoke very startled from a little snooze in her seat and started to scrabble frenziedly for her knitting.

Blanche was crying: 'They've got him, they've arrested him. The police have arrested Mr Blagge. Mummy, they're saying it was Mr Blagge killed Nat. Mummy, you've got to do something, it's all your fault, Mummy, you should never have come back.'

12
Weak Flesh

The arrest of James Roy Blagge, 63, chauffeur, of Stable Cottage, Lark Manor, Bridset, for murder created a major sensation in Larminster. In a way it was an even more shattering – and thus exciting – event for the local inhabitants than the crime itself. Something about Nat's shady theatrical career, it had been vaguely felt as the weeks passed, must have contributed to his fate: his departure from Larminster to university had already marked him out as different and, on his return as Festival Director, he had made no effort to ingratiate himself with Larminster society other than that section of it represented by the Festival Committee.

Jim Blagge was different. They all knew Jim, and they all knew Rose Blagge too, as they had known Rose Kettering, and still claimed to know Katherine Kettering, for all her grand airs up at the Manor. Father O'Brien, the Larminster parish priest, went up to Stable Cottage to comfort Rose Blagge. He reported that she had collapsed totally when the police arrived with a warrant for Jim's arrest. It had been in one way fortunate that Rose's sister had been visiting her at the time, and could succour her, although less fortunate that Ketty was accompanied by Blanche Cartwright, so highly strung at the best of times; before anyone could stop her, Blanche had run screaming from Stable Cottage, grabbed her father's Land-Rover and driven to Larminster and the theatre, where she had broken the news of the arrest in dramatic terms now known to the whole of Larminster.

Ketty was praying with her sister when Father O'Brien arrived; he had subsequently asked to see Mrs Cartwright but had been told by Mr Julian Cartwright that she was unavailable. Father O'Brien added that Mr Julian Cartwright himself had been extremely kind and promised to do everything in his power to help the unfortunate Jim Blagge: give support in the magistrate's court, stand bail if there was any chance of that, and all the rest of it.

'Of course I know Blagge's innocent, Father,' Julian exclaimed testily in his loud voice which penetrated, had he but known it, the darkened bedroom upstairs where Christabel lay resting and thus rather removed the point of his next remark: 'All the same, my wife mustn't be disturbed: we don't want to bring her into this, any more than is absolutely necessary. She's got her performance to think of, two of them. It's not as if she was involved personally in any way in this ghastly business.' Julian Cartwright glared at Father O'Brien as if defying him to contradict this assumption, and for one moment looked remarkably like his uncle the Major.

Father O'Brien tried to conceal his disappointment. He had much looked forward to a good talk with Christabel Cartwright, consoling or at least condoling. But for Jim Blagge's sake, and because he was a tactful man, at any rate where Protestants were concerned, he murmured something non-committally soft and Irish.

Secretly, Father O'Brien cherished a very different attitude to Christabel from that of the Blagges and Ketty. In theory, of course, he deplored the flagrant adultery which had led to her disappearance with the Blagges' son – although he had never actually met young Barry, having arrived in the parish a few months after their departure. But Father O'Brien was also a dedicated admirer of television, a medium which he was convinced was directly guided by the Holy Ghost in view of the vast benevolent influence it exercised in the world. Old people comforted, the lonely solaced – but these were minor benefits. Above all, in Father O'Brien's opinion, high moral values were upheld on television: look how the evil were punished nightly for their sins on the television news, while at the same time you could learn to recognize the devil and all his works, with a choice of channels, in the safety of your own home. Even Cy Fredericks, in his wildest fit of euphoria, would not have advanced for Megalith Television alone some of the claims which Father O'Brien, in his study at St Bede's presbytery, took for granted about the whole medium.

Christabel Cartwright was the nearest that Father O'Brien had ever come to the baleful world of the enchanter. He had greeted the news of her return to Lark Manor, broken to him in accents of horror by Rose Blagge, with public gravity but private excitement. Father O'Brien was one of those who dropped by the Watchtower Theatre box office at an early stage and enquired after a seat on the night that the television cameras would be present. Poll, encased in the darkened glass booth, had been quite shocked by a priest wanting to come to the theatre in the first place, let alone on the First Night: she assuaged her feelings by making him pay for his own seat, and the top price too. This in turn rather shocked Father O'Brien who thought that the performance of his parish duties – in this case witnessing the public penitence of Christabel Cartwright – should come free.

The advent of Megalith Television to Larminster, followed by Christabel's resumption of the stage, he regarded in general as a striking example of the power of prayer; Father O'Brien having offered up Mass for Christabel and her family and in the course of it mentioned something of the sort to the Almighty: 'For her own good, and the good of her darling girls, and the good of the whole community. Let the sinner be seen to repent in public, preferably not on BBC2, which Thou knowest O Lord is not too clearly received in the presbytery . . . Acknowledge her sin like the publican in the Bible,' added Father O'Brien hastily, lest God, at the sound of his familiar complaint about the presbytery television set, should lose interest in Christabel Cartwright's artistic future.

Julian Cartwright, unaware of the maelstrom of yearnings in the priest's breast, simply repeated to Father O'Brien that he would do his best for Blagge. As for Mrs Blagge, she was of course excused any further duties in the house until she saw fit to return. Ketty too might stay with her as long as she liked.

'Though God knows the girls need her too,' he concluded wearily. Father O'Brien, in a rush of sympathy quite at odds with his usual romantic appreciation of the situation at Lark Manor, realized that Julian Cartwright had come to look quite a lot older and sadder since his wife's return to the stage.

'All the same, Mrs Blagge comes first, I insist on that,' Julian finished. Father O'Brien then wondered whether perhaps Blanche . . . perhaps a word or two from him . . . he was not of course her parish priest, no wish to poach on the Vicar's preserves, but if he could be of any help, since he was right here at Lark . . .

'There's nothing for a priest to do. Of any persuasion.' Julian Cartwright sounded crisp. Soon Father O'Brien found himself being escorted out of the beautiful light drawing-room where Julian had received him, with its blues and greens, and its view of the sea, in the direction of the front door. But as they passed the open door of Julian's study – a glimpse of manly dark reds and browns was to be seen through it – Julian appeared to think better of his decision.

'A quick whisky, Father, before you go?' His tone, if forced, was suddenly much more friendly.

The priest and Julian had actually just had tea, which had been brought them by Regina Cartwright, in the absence of Mrs Blagge, Ketty, and of course Christabel. Father O'Brien said that the pretty curly-handled Rockingham cups reminded him of the china his mother had had when he was a boy in Ireland; diplomatically, he ignored the stained cloth where Regina, carrying the tray and looking rather magnificent as she did so, like some kind of dark-haired caryatid, had nevertheless managed to slop tea everywhere.

'The cups that cheer but not inebriate, wait on each . . .' Regina had murmured as she deposited the tray. Father O'Brien, unaware that she was quoting Cowper, was nonetheless quite willing to follow the cheering cup with an inebriating glass. Julian ushered him into the study and splashed a good deal of whisky into the heavy-bottomed Waterford glasses.

At Julian's request Father O'Brien then dutifully admired an enormous portrait of Julian's mother, Lady May, as a young girl, in riding-costume, whip at the ready, dog at her feet, some enormous louring white stately home in the background, painted by Sir John Lavery. But as an Irishman, Father O'Brien had never been able to see the British aristocracy as part of the divine plan: he was busy looking round for portraits of Julian's wife, not his mother. He was rewarded immediately by one glamorous photograph and one family group including the girls as well as Christabel (if Father O'Brien had been on calling terms with Gregory Rowan, he might have been surprised to discover exactly the same photographs abutting Gregory's own desk, in the rather less grandly decorated surroundings of Old Keeper's Lodge).

Julian Cartwright leant back easily in his large tobacco-brown leather chair: the heavy velvet curtains of the study, their colour matching the whisky in his hand, partly shrouded the view and ensured that very little of the summer light filtered through into the handsomely sombre room. What Julian Cartwright wanted to explain to Father O'Brien was this: when Blanche had burst out in her dramatic denunciation of her mother at the end of the Watchtower rehearsal, she was above all not to be taken seriously. Julian supposed that Blanche's words might have caused some shock and alarm in Larminster – Father O'Brien, he was sure, never gossiped, nor did he, Julian, but it had to be faced that there were many 'less heavily employed people than us, shall we say, Father', who did little else.

The fact was, Blanche was absolutely devoted to her mother, Julian continued in the kind of voice he used for reading the lesson in church (not Father O'Brien's church). But it happened that she was just at the age when she took things very much to heart, and Blanche had this silly childish habit of speaking her mind, or what appeared to be her mind. The arrest of Mr Blagge, whom she had known and loved since babyhood, more or less in front of her eyes, had quite upset her balance. Whereas her sister had many more resources with which to deal with the situation.

'Rina is more the dreamy type, you know, reads a book and rides her horse, has even been known to do both at the same time, read a book *on* a horse—' Julian laughed rather more loudly perhaps than the joke warranted, but Father O'Brien hastened to add his own polite soft chuckle. 'The trouble with Blanche is that she has not yet found her own niche. With Rina being so much more bookish, intelligent one might even say, Blanche needs to develop her own interests—'

'The theatre maybe, I believe she has talent, like her mother? Television—' The moment he had spoken, Father O'Brien realized that he had made an error. It was too late. Julian Cartwright had already drained his whisky and ignoring the fact that Father O'Brien had barely begun his, was jumping to his feet.

'Hardly the theatre, I think, Father.' He sounded both cold and furious at the same time. 'It was somebody's mischievous suggestion that poor little Blanche should read for a part at the Watchtower which upset her balance in the first place. Sheer trouble making. My wife was very upset about it too. We were united on the subject. Neither of us feels that Blanche is suited in any way to a life in the theatre.'

Julian was now walking so fast on his long legs, out of the front door in the direction of the priest's old black Rover, that Father O'Brien, much shorter and quite a bit stouter, could hardly keep up with him.

'Oh, I hardly think Miss Kettering meant to make trouble,' Father O'Brien managed to pant out, just as they were reaching the car. 'She only wanted her dear little girl to have her own chance – just as her mother had done. So she sent a little message. That nice old Miss Nicola Wain helped her. All *quite* harmless.'

Once again Julian stopped. His resemblance to Major Cartwright this time as he fixed Father O'Brien with a ferocious look was so marked as to cause the priest to take a nervous step back. He had never cared for Major Cartwright, ever since it had come to his ears – via the intelligence service of Mrs Blagge handing round the food – that the Major had described him over lunch as 'that confounded Holy Roman busybody.' The Major's daunting expression persisted in Julian as he repeated several times:

'I see. So that was it, was it? I see. So that was it. Ketty set that one up. Ketty thought of that little plan.'

Father O'Brien was at last free to bustle into his car and drive away – rather too fast, under the circumstances, rattling over the cattle grid on the drive. Julian watched for a moment and then turned on his heel and walked back through the front door.

'Ketty,' he roared. 'Ketty. Come here, will you! I want to have a word with you. Ketty!'

But Ketty did not answer. Perhaps she was still over at Stable Cottage with her sister Rose, or perhaps she was at the top of the next flight of stairs where years ago she had set up a little sewing-room to make or alter the girls' clothes, with the sound of the sewing-machine drowning that of Julian's voice. Or perhaps she was in her bedroom, along the landing, between those of Regina and Blanche, and managing to sleep through his calls. At any rate she did not answer.

Everything was very still inside Lark Manor. The early evening air hung heavy and silent in the beautiful tidy rooms. Where was everyone? There was no sign of Regina, for example – but she had probably ridden Lancelot down to the sea. Blanche had spent the morning sobbing loudly in her room after the previous day's outburst; either she was asleep, or she had gone out – at any rate no sound came from her room. Gregory sometimes came over from his cottage in the woods at this time of day to collect his milk and have an early drink with Julian. Today there was no sign of him.

Finally Julian Cartwright's voice too fell silent. His last words had been a raucous cry of 'Ketty'. Any chance Christabel had of enjoying a peaceful nap in the tranquillity of the manor would surely have vanished altogether at the sound of that stentorian voice. But in fact Christabel Cartwright was lying awake.

She was awake and frightened. She wished that Boy Greville had not decided to rehearse the other scenes which did not include Madam Arkadina, in order to give Christabel a rest from her ordeal. She wished she was at the Watchtower Theatre, in her little modern dressing-room, gazing at her face in the harsh light of the electric bulbs round the mirror, dragging at the grease-paint on her face with cold cream.

She wished she were anywhere except alone in her bedroom at Lark Manor.

The person who had thought all along that Christabel could not just come back like that and expect to get away with it knew that she was alone. The person knew too that Christabel was frightened. The person decided that the right moment had at last come to put an end to Christabel. Extinguish her. Above all put an end to her soft pampered body, that body which had betrayed her and everybody else close to her, because it was the desires of Christabel's warm greedy body which had taken her away from Lark Manor, caused her to fly away with Barry Blagge about whom nothing good could be said except that he had thick red hair and an enormous—

The person stopped short at the next word, because even to use it in the person's thought, such a coarse, such a rough crude physical word, aroused bad feelings in the person, feelings from the past which the person did not wish to experience again. It was better to concentrate on purely helpful thoughts of how to obliterate Christabel's body, the body which had entertained Barry – the person felt calmer now: there was no temptation to dwell on exactly how Christabel's body had entertained Barry Blagge.

The person began to croon the old familiar litany of hate: if only Christabel's soft skin had not betrayed her like that when she could have spent all her life so happily in the luxury of Lark Manor, with her nice husband and the nicest most convenient lover in the world in the shape of Gregory Rowan – for that's what he had been, had he not? Then there were her loving daughters, oh such loving little girls, worshipping the ground – and the stage – their mother trod on. All thrown away, thought the person, for who could pretend that Blanche and Regina would ever worship their mother again? Who could expect them to?

Christabel's career too – all thrown away. Younger actresses had come to take her place, or actresses who were never half so good like Anna Maria Packe – that failure, the failure of her career too could be blamed on Christabel's weakness. Certainly it was quite ridiculous, the way that Christabel thought that by repenting, she could simply resume her stage career just like that . . .

If only Christabel's body had not grown greedier with the years. If only that spoilt soft flesh could have tolerated, just once in a while, the embraces of her own husband – instead of which Christabel's treacherous body, Christabel's *weak flesh*, had caused her to shrink and turn and turn away, and lie passive and reluctant in her husband's arms. While all the time in the arms of Barry Blagge—

But here the person checked the dangerous thoughts again.

Moving very quietly in the empty house – for the person knew every board, exactly where every stair creaked, and how to listen for every door that might open, the person began to lay plans for the death of Christabel. Once Christabel had had a perfect life. She had thrown it all away. Now she should have a perfect death.

No one would ever know that it had not been an accident, the way the person planned it. After all, the person had drowned Filly Lennox – a mistake, admittedly, and everyone had believed that to be an accident. As for Nat Fitzwilliam, who had got altogether too close to the truth about the girl's death with his prying binoculars, that rather unpleasant death was being blamed on Mr Blagge.

The person, now in a room upstairs, quietly rummaging for something essential to the person's plan, paused for a moment to consider the whole question of Mr Blagge. He was now in police custody. If Christabel's death was made to seem like a proper accident, he might still be blamed for the murder of Nat. The police were such idiots: Jemima Shore Investigator was not quite such an idiot, but, even so, the real truth was unlikely to strike her. For one particular reason. The person smiled. The idea of fooling Jemima Shore was by no means displeasing to the person.

So how did the person feel about Mr Blagge being blamed? It was important to decide before these preparations went much further. The house was empty now but you could not expect a house the size of Lark Manor to remain empty forever, on a late summer's afternoon. Oh, it would be terrible, the most dreadful pity, for the person's plan to kill Christabel to be ruined at the very last moment!

On the whole therefore it was best to proceed and let Mr Blagge take his chance . . . after all this time, the person had no particular feelings about Mr Blagge either way. The person merely hungered for the end of it all: the resolution of the tragedy. So the person proceeded with quiet and deadly preparations for the death of Christabel.

Julian Cartwright, rushing from the back of the house, collided with Gregory, coming from the front. Gregory was breathing hard and looked alarmed. There was no sign of his large car in the drive.

'It's Christabel, it sounds like Christabel,' he said. Julian said nothing, but pushed past him and started to run again, through the wide open french windows of the kitchen, towards the hall. After a moment, Gregory, his tall figure towering over Julian's, ran after him. Both men stopped at once when they got to the hall. The first person they saw was not Christabel but Ketty.

Finely dressed as ever in a dark patterned crêpe dress, and wearing her usual jangling earrings, Ketty was standing in the middle of the hall, looking up the well of the stairs. It was remarkable, in view of the formality of her frock, that she was wearing no shoes; her feet were large and well formed: the toe-nails, painted dark red, showed incongruously through the stockings. Christabel, above them, was wearing a pale-blue silk peignoir, the material so light you could see the shape of her soft ample body, her breasts, quite clearly. Her pale hair was in disarray; it looked as if she had just got out of bed. She was leaning on the balustrade. She looked both startled and frightened.

'My darling! You screamed! Are you all right? I heard you scream,' Julian ignored Ketty and rushed on up the stairs.

'I did scream,' said Christabel slowly; her low voice was not quite steady. She too like Gregory was breathing very fast. Julian put his arms round her. The slight involuntary check with which she met his embrace was painfully noticeable to the two watching below. 'I heard a noise in the house. I thought I was alone. It was only Ketty. She gave me a fright, that's all.'

'I'm sure it wasn't me that made any noise,' Ketty spoke in her usual grimly self-righteous voice; alone of those present she seemed quite unperturbed by Christabel's distress. 'I took my shoes off when I came back into the house from my sister's, so as not to cause a disturbance when certain people were resting.' Ketty stared defiantly, first at Gregory, then back up at Julian. Then she added in an even more emphatic voice: 'I'm sure there is nothing about *me* that should frighten Mrs Cartwright.'

13

Simply Guilty

At the remand hearing in Beauport Magistrates' Court the police – in the shape of Detective Inspector Matthew Harwood – opposed bail for James Roy Blagge. This, coupled with the very serious nature of the offence with which he was charged, was sufficient to convince the magistrate that the accused should be kept in custody.

'And a good thing too!' Matt Harwood commented to Jemima Shore, when Jim Blagge, neatly dressed and impassive, had been taken back to the prison at Bridchester on a seven-day remand. 'Bail-for-murderers indeed, which my little brother Gary tells me is becoming quite the fashion in London's fair city these days. Here in Bridset we think there is just one place for a man suspected of a violent crime, and that is a nice cosy prison cell. Just in case.'

'Just in case he does it again? Or just in case he decides to do a bunk on a boat from Lar Bay?'

'Just in case,' repeated Matt Harwood, sounding rather pompous. Then he softened. 'There are a good many things a man on a grave charge can do if he's left at liberty, you know, apart from the above. Not only tampering with witnesses. He can do away with himself, for one thing. It's been known to happen.'

Jemima, remembering the erect silver-haired figure of Mr Bragge in the court, appreciated the policeman's point. Self-destruction must be a real possibility – if he had indeed murdered Nat Fitzwilliam as the police contended; murdered him in a fit of spontaneous and uncontrollable rage, brought on by the younger man's casual contempt on the night of the murder, his long-term insolence – or worse still insolent indifference – in the months preceding it. And all rooted in Mr Blagge's paranoid hatred of the theatre itself, of which he had made no secret since his son's departure. Such a man might well wish to put an end to an existence irredeemably wrecked by his own violent impulse.

Mr Blagge was certainly not likely to vanish abroad – for where would he go? What would become of Mrs Blagge? His whole life was here in Larminster and up at Lark Manor, as Gregory had explained. Nor was there any possibility of Mr Blagge tampering with witnesses: the strangers who had witnessed his second visit to the theatre had already given their written statements. Anyway the case against him rested strongly on the forensic evidence.

It was a classic case of the Locard exchange principle at work, Matt Harwood told Jemima happily: he suggested that she should let Pompey of the Yard know all about it when she was next in touch with him. 'We're not so dim in Bridset, you know, not dim at all.'

Minute fibres of Nat's white scarf had been discovered on Mr Blagge's jacket, and Nat's own clothing had revealed similar tiny traces of Mr Blagge's dark jacket. Faced with this unassailable evidence, Mr Blagge had broken down at his second questioning and admitted to paying a second visit to the Watchtower, while the Cartwright family was still celebrating in a private room at the Royal Stag.

When he had presented himself in the foyer of the hotel, Julian had told him to cut along, the car would not be needed for at least an hour or so. So he had been unable to resist returning to the theatre – knowing where he had deposited the key – and 'giving that young man a piece of my mind'.

Mr Blagge even went so far as to admit that in the course of this process, he might have come close to plucking at Nat's scarf, might actually have given it a tug, especially when the young man in question waved him away, refused to speak to him, talked about Mr Blagge interrupting his precious meditations . . .

'His precious meditations!' snorted Mr Blagge, indignation once again overcoming him at the memory; with his face flushed, he looked altogether a more dangerous animal than the impeccable butler-figure he generally presented to the world; the detective questioning him noted how quickly his anger could erupt. 'As if he was in church, as if he was some kind of holy being. When he was only sitting in the theatre, wasn't he? I told him, I told young Master Nat—'

But Mr Blagge still maintained firmly and steadfastly that he was not responsible for Nat's death. Had not in fact strangled him with the white scarf, despite the evidence of his handling it.

'They often do that, murderers,' said Matt Harwood comfortably to Jemima Shore afterwards. 'Admit everything but the deed itself.'

Mr Blagge had then added that he had been vaguely conscious of someone else outside the theatre, a man, waiting, lurking in the shadows.

A man who would have noticed him put back the key under the stone trough, and would then have been able to enter the theatre unobserved.

'That's the man you should go for,' Mr Blagge told the police, still truculent. 'The person who was watching me. That's the person who did for Nat Fitzwilliam, that's who. I put the key back, second time as well, and now it's missing. The murderer took it. That's who.'

In desperation he went even further: swore that Nat himself had left the theatre again shortly after Blagge for a breath of fresh air – 'Told me I'd interrupted his thoughts! *His* thoughts! And what about *my* thoughts? What was I supposed to think when young Nat Fitzwilliam cheeked me in front of the whole of Larminster inside that restaurant? Fresh air indeed! Yes, he needed fresh air all right, I'll grant him that. And I heard him come out of the front door of the theatre too. Heard those great doors opening as I was crossing the square back to the hotel. Anybody could have used the Stage Door then. Anyone who knew where the key was. What about that man then, the other fellow?' Mr Blagge concluded truculently.

But: 'They often say that too', Matt Harwood told Jemima. 'Someone else was around at the same time, someone unknown with exactly the same opportunity, who actually committed the crime.' And he pointed out how easy it would have been for Blagge to dispose of the key somewhere where it would never be found. There were also no witnesses to confirm the presence of a third party lurking in the shrubberies, nor had anyone else seen Nat Fitzwilliam leave the theatre for a breath of air, if indeed he had.

Jemima Shore, for her part, wished she could feel so totally convinced about the guilt of James Roy Blagge. It would have made life so much simpler. Instead, her instinct was troubling her; that famous instinct, merrily castigated by both Cy Fredericks ('Your lady's instinct, my dear Jem, always so expensive, what is it asking for this time?') and Pompey of the Yard ('My wife suffers from the feminine instinct too; you could say we both suffer from it'). But Jemima knew by experience that this instinct was not to be derided.

The single word 'instinct', drawing the fire of such quizzical males as Cy Fredericks and Pompey, was in fact not quite accurate. It was more that Jemima possessed a very strong instinct for order. This would not let her rest so long as the smallest detail was out of place in the well-regulated pattern of her mind. On this occasion the small detail which was troubling her, and would continue to do so naggingly until she resolved it, was Christabel's distress at the televised rehearsal and her continued nervous state since Mr Blagge's arrest. Jemima had suggested rather flippantly to Matt Harwood that Mr Blagge might be being held in custody 'just in case he does it again'. But there could be no question of

Mr Blagge attacking anyone while he was in the cells at Beauport. What then was frightening Christabel Cartwright?

The best way to find that out was to ask the lady in question. Jemima would use as an excuse for a meeting the need to discuss the new shape of the programme. She found that television provided an excellent cover for investigations of a very different nature, because the victims themselves were so eager to submit themselves to interrogation; the demands of the medium apparently vindicated in their eyes inquisitive approaches which Jemima herself would never have tolerated from a comparative stranger.

So Jemima invited Christabel to lunch at Flora's Kitchen. Inflamed by Cherry's descriptions of her gastronomic adventures with the Major, Jemima did for a moment flirt with the idea of roaming further afield, tasting the delights of Giovanni e Giovanna at Deep Larkin, for example, or even voyaging as far as The French Lieutenant just across the county border. In the end she rejected both plans: Giovanni's Special Bridset Spaghetti (Lar Bay mussels) and The French Lieutenant's *Coupe Sarah*, about both of which Cherry had waxed lyrical, would have to wait for another occasion for Jemima's seal of approval.

There was the complication of rehearsals as the First Night of *The Seagull* approached (and *Widow Capet* was billed to open the following week). More than that, Jemima wanted Christabel to be exceptionally relaxed and confidential at this particular meal. Such an insecure woman – Jemima was increasingly inclined to take Gregory's estimate seriously – would be at her least guarded on familiar Larminster ground. Elsewhere, she might be tempted to give a performance, as it were, to Giovanni if not to Jemima Shore.

But as she faced Christabel across the Botticelli-printed tablecloth at Flora's Kitchen, Jemima did not find her noticeably relaxed. She could not help contrasting this jumpy nervous woman with the confident charming Christabel who had first introduced her to the restaurant. Her clothes were still perfectly chosen in their feminine way; full skirt of a very pale pink, echoed by the deeper pink rose on her jacket lapel, cream-coloured silk blouse tied in a floppy bow at the neck, and pearls. The great aquamarine ring still flashed on her finger, as though to remind anyone in danger of forgetting that Christabel's unblinking eyes were the same translucent tropical-sea colour. So was her eyeshadow, for that matter, and one noticed that fact too.

Critically, Jemima wondered whether Christabel wasn't wearing too much make-up for that time of day – and that particular restaurant. Her cheekbones were prominently high-lighted with rather harsh blush-on powder; frequent dabs from her gold basket-weave compact, with its diamond and lapis lazuli catch, did not serve to soften the picture. Her over-heavy mascara made her lashes look rather spiky. Next to Christabel,

Poll's scrubbed powderless face, as she swept on her silent way producing the Florentine – or pseudo-Florentine – food, had a welcome freshness.

It would not be long before Blanche Cartwright would represent a prettier, as well as a younger version of her mother. This reflection was inspired in Jemima by Blanche's sudden eruption into the restaurant in the middle of lunch. She demanded some cash from her mother. She sounded jolly rather than hysterical and it suited her; her cheeks were pink, and a new short layered haircut drew attention to the heart shape of her face. Evidently Blanche was reconciled with her mother, at least to the extent of taking her money; her outburst at the Watchtower Theatre appeared to have had some kind of purgative effect. Even in her man's – or rather boy's – clothes of shirt and white knee-length shorts she looked rather pretty, now she had lost weight.

It was Regina Cartwright in her father's Land-Rover who dropped her mother at the restaurant – she had recently passed her driving test and Jemima had a feeling that the days of Rina's teenage passion for the horse Lancelot might be numbered. Striding away from her mother, black hair swinging on her shoulders, Rina looked both beautiful and confident. In the three or four months Jemima had known her, she too had changed out of all recognition. The girls had both emerged from the summer's ordeal strengthened and rather improved; it was the mother who languished.

One memorable aspect of Jemima's first meeting with Christabel was however still present. She continued to dip into the vodka bottle concealed in her expensive handbag. Guiltily, Jemima was rather glad, she presumed that drink had loosened Christabel's tongue on that previous occasion and hoped it would produce the same effect on her today.

Jemima insisted that this was her lunch – 'Megalith's lunch', she said with her sweet wide television smile, the one that made people who watched her on the box, men and women, fall deeply in love with her and decide she was really a very sweet person. She ordered a carafe of red wine for Christabel and a glass of white wine for herself.

But as it turned out, Christabel was not to be drawn. All the wiles of Jemima Shore Investigator, the practised tricks of the professional interviewer, failed to secure any form of personal revelation from her. In particular she declined to respond to references to their original conversation. Had Christabel felt 'safe' back on stage, as she had hoped to do?

'Oh darling, it's no good asking me that. Safe! I'm always so terribly terribly nervous before a First Night. A bundle of nerves. Not safe at all. Ask anyone. I'm on the verge of quitting the profession – again!' Christabel added with a ghost of her old humour. It was really the only light moment in what was otherwise purely a defensive operation.

'But something was frightening you—' pursued Jemima. 'You told me.'

Christabel looked at her quite steadily for a moment, her huge eyes appeared to glisten with tears.

'Oh it's too late to talk about all that now, darling,' was all she said. She hesitated. 'Maybe I should have talked to you about it more then. It all seems so long ago. If I had, darling, well, all sorts of things might have been different. But now – well, it's too late, isn't it?'

'Too late for what, Christabel?' In her desperation, feeling the brief moment of confidentiality passing away, Jemima became bolder. But at this Christabel merely opened her blue eyes even wider in a parody of surprise.

'Too late to go back, darling. That's all. That's all I meant. One can never go back in life, can one?'

You did! Jemima longed to cry in frustration, seeing Christabel's face settling itself into a mask of polite non-cooperation. She still looked infinitely sad, but at the same time remote. In a moment she would be waving the dreaded powder compact again, powdering her nose for the third time, as one who shakes dust in her pursuer's face. You came back! But the words died on her lips. She could not risk antagonizing her at this stage. The question of Filly Lennox's death was crucial.

Afterwards Jemima was to regret bitterly not pressing Christabel Cartwright further on those few melancholy words, so much at variance with her public air of cool – and maddeningly successful – repentance. If Jemima had done so, might not Christabel have broken out from behind the pathetic painted mask? And if so, would Christabel have been 'safe'? – what she declared she so much wanted to be at their first meeting. Or was it already, as Christabel now so sadly said, 'Too late'?

At the time Jemima was too concerned to satisfy herself on the subject of Jim Blagge's guilt or innocence to turn aside.

'Christabel,' she said urgently. 'There's one question I must ask you. Do *you* think Mr Blagge murdered Nat? Is he quite simply guilty? Should I accept that fact? Supposing he did, and I must admit that the police evidence against him is very strong, is it possible – wait for it – that poor Filly Lennox was murdered too? Deliberately drowned: murdered in mistake for you? Mr Blagge went out in the boat on the day of the picnic. Does Mr Blagge hate *you* too? For the sake of –' now she had to come out with it 'for the sake of his son?'

At this point Jemima fully intended to shock. She did not intend to let Christabel drift back into her gracious reticence. And there was something deeply shocking about voicing her theory – to the woman whom Mr Blagge had perhaps intended to drown in Filly's place. Even so Jemima was quite unprepared for Christabel's reaction.

She fainted.

When Jemima told Spike Thompson about it late that night, as they lay together in the four-poster bed conveniently provided by the Royal Stag, it suddenly struck her that the faint – a dead faint, off the chair to the floor, carrying glasses and cutlery with it – might have been a protective measure. After all Christabel never had answered Jemima's question about Filly's death. Nor for that matter about Jim Blagge's guilt. Yet if it was a protective measure, who was Christabel so concerned to protect?

At the time Christabel's startling physical collapse made it easy for her to escape from Jemima's inquisition: 'I'll go back to the theatre and rest,' she murmured. 'Terribly silly of me, darling. I've been overdoing it. Two productions. Poor little Filly's death. Then Nat. And the strain of the arrest.'

Christabel would not let Jemima summon Regina to drive her home and reacted even more strongly to the idea of Jemima's telephoning Julian at Lark. Blanche, who could be seen inside a bow-windowed Larminster boutique opposite, trying on a pair of velvet knickerbockers, was the only person Christabel agreed to have contacted and sent after her to her dressing-room. So Jemima had to let her go.

Spike, prepared to take a lazy interest in the subject of Christabel's faint during a temporary lull in the night's proceedings, encouraged Jemima in her suspicions. 'These actresses are up to any old trick. I could tell you a thing or two about actresses. But then you, my lovely, are also up to any old trick, aren't you?' But the thought of Jemima and her tricks turned Spike's thoughts away from Christabel Cartwright and once more to that activity with which the gallant Spike always liked to fill as many as possible of his off-duty hours when on location.

He did spare one Parthian chauvinist shot for Julian Cartwright: 'I can't get over her old man taking her back like that. Screwed all over the press by a pop star – and then it's welcome-home time when he ditches her, and-did-you-have-a-good-time, darling? I wouldn't stand for it in my missis, I can tell you,' said Spike virtuously. 'I'd give her a proper going over.'

'Not all men are the same. And not all women either. If I was Christabel Cartwright, it would drive me quite mad to have to come back to Lark as penitent Magdalen.' The conversation might have gone further – for Spike's Parthian shot had started an interesting train of thought in her mind. But by now Spike had succeeded in turning Jemima's attention too from Christabel Cartwright; for the rest of the night, Jemima was entirely possessed by Spike, the touch and taste and feel of him.

What with one thing and another, it was not until the next day that Jemima fully analysed her conversation with Christabel. She was now in renewed conclave with Matt Harwood. It was time, she decided – the time was really overdue – to confide to him her suspicions about the death of Filly Lennox and her instinct that Christabel, while still fearful, was nonetheless protecting some person close to her.

But Detective Inspector Harwood, in his most reasonable voice, merely asked for proof of all these female fancies. He freely admitted that a good many people had had the opportunity to kill Nat Fitzwilliam, including, if she wished to consider them, the entire large Cartwright family party installed at the Royal Stag on the night of Blanche's birthday. Gregory, Ketty, the Cartwrights in force, they had all been there milling about in the hotel: Mrs Tennant, the manageress, had given them an empty suite on the first floor – Jemima's suite was the only other one in the hotel – out of local loyalty.

Up there however the party had rather fizzled out. The suite was stuffy because it was not in use. At Christabel's request Gregory had then gone downstairs to rout out the champagne which Flora's Kitchen had not been able to produce before leaving for his late-night swim. Christabel had been overcome with exhaustion – 'or maybe something stronger' said the Detective Inspector – and during Gregory's absence, which had been quite prolonged, had at Julian's suggestion retired to the bedroom to lie down. Blanche, removing a few of her hotter garments and unbuttoning her shirt as she went, had then taken the opportunity to flit off to find Ollie Summertown. She had ignored Ketty's protests – 'It's my *birthday*, Ketty, and anyway it's *not* indecent – some people think it looks pretty' – and after a bit Ketty had gone to look for her. Julian agreeing that it *was* very hot had gone out for a breath of air. Regina went down to the lounge to look for a book . . . the Detective Inspector was happy to give Jemima as detailed an account as she liked of their various movements.

It all amounted to this, said Matt Harwood: many people had had Opportunity and Method to kill Nat Fitzwilliam. Only Jim Blagge had had Motive. Only Jim Blagge had had close physical contact with Nat Fitzwilliam on the night concerned. Only Jim Blagge admitted paying Nat Fitzwilliam a late-night threatening call. Jemima was really the only person in Larminster who had any doubts about Jim Blagge's guilt.

Curiously enough, this was not actually true. There was another keen-eyed observer in Larminster who was not quite satisfied that Jim Blagge had murdered Nat Fitzwilliam. This was seventy-nine-year-old Nicola Wain. The old actress, with only her role in *Widow Capet* to consider, was left with a good deal of liberty on her hands as rehearsals of *The Seagull* grew more intense. Knitting, as Old Nicola often remarked, gave her plenty of time for thinking 'and also watching all you naughty boys and girls'. It also gave her plenty of time to figure things out, movements, noises, statements which did not add up.

The room to which she had moved at the Royal Stag, a room about which she constantly complained to anyone who would listen ('No bathroom *en suite*, well, dear, at my age . . .') lay at the top of the service staircase on the first floor. Admittedly the room's single window overlooked the back of the hotel instead of the pretty square which was Larminster's chief beauty and contained the Watchtower Theatre, set among mature trees, in one corner of it. Even Mrs Tennant, the manageress of the Royal Stag, who was an optimist, had had to agree that the view from Old Nicola's room – over the back entrance of the hotel and the courtyard which served as a car-park – was not inspiring. On the other hand she had firmly rebutted the notion that the service stairs, adjoining Old Nicola's room, would prove to be an unpleasant source of nocturnal disturbance.

'No one uses them at night,' Mrs Tennant had assured her querulous guest, at the time of her arrival. 'But we just can't lock them, dear, because of the Fire Regulations. You never know when someone might not need access. In an emergency, that is.'

'Exactly,' Old Nicola had grumbled at the time, as though an emergency was just the kind of needless disturbance she gloomily predicted. Yet in its own way, Old Nicola's sojourn in her little first-floor room had not been unrewarding. Either Mrs Tennant's reassuring remarks about the service stairs not being used except in an emergency had turned out to be inaccurate or perhaps the occasion when they had been used recently had been considered an emergency by the person concerned. Either way, Old Nicola was really quite pleased with the new piece of information which had come her way as a result of her room's geographical location.

As the dress rehearsal of *The Seagull* approached and everyone else grew more and more frantic, Old Nicola began to reach a certain rather interesting conclusion. For, as she told herself, there was really nothing wrong with 'these poor old wits' – wits which had certainly kept her afloat in her own profession, by fair means or foul, for over sixty years.

It remained for Old Nicola to decide exactly what use she should make of this discovery. After a period of thought, spent by the old woman knitting ostentatiously in the lounge at the Royal Stag – the sight of the battered plastic bag from which the knitting emanated began to madden even the good-natured Mrs Tennant – Old Nicola went upstairs to her room. Once there, she locked the door, and placed her knitting, bag and all, in the solitary armchair as carefully as if it had been a child. Then Old Nicola sat down at the tiny writing-desk and began to write a letter.

Although Old Nicola had frequently complained to Mrs Tennant about the size of the desk and the inadequate light above it, on this occasion she looked positively happy as she penned the words in handwriting which, as she often told herself, was really quite remarkable for her age. She did not however think that the person to whom she was addressing the letter would feel quite so happy at receiving it – despite the care with which it was written, and the clarity of the handwriting.

14

Happy Ending

The dress rehearsal of *The Seagull* was not going to be filmed for television. Too like the real thing the next night to be dramatically interesting, Guthrie decided.

'Unless there's a disaster,' contributed Cherry brightly. 'We don't want to miss that, do we?'

'Don't we?' Jemima sounded cold. It was now impossible to enter Cherry's bedroom at the Royal Stag for the reek of fruit – nectarines and peaches – and flowers – mainly fat richly-scented crimson roses sent down from Major Cartwright's greenhouse and garden at Larksgrange. The Major had also started to quote poetry to Cherry over the dinner-table although otherwise his conversation remained strictly gastronomic. In the cosy depths of Giovanni e Giovanna the previous evening, he had recited Tennyson's Song from *The Princess*: 'Now sleeps the crimson petal, now the white . . .'

At the end: 'I wrote that,' said the Major sternly. Cherry, despite months spent working on *Tennyson: The Tortured Years* had not contradicted him, which Jemima told her was very disloyal. Jemima feared the worst: was Flowering Cherry's long quest for the Substantial Older Man in danger of coming to a happy ending?

'We haven't missed many disasters yet,' was Guthrie's gloomy comment. He had just learned from London that the first of his non-controversial programmes about the Elgin Marbles – *Ours or Theirs?* – was held to be such political dynamite by the Greek government that they had locked up an entire Megalith crew (coincidentally out in Greece at the time the programme was shown, harmlessly filming *Sappho: A Woman for Our Time*). Most unfairly, he felt, Cy Fredericks blamed the entire expense of bailing this crew out of prison on Guthrie. As a punishment he was threatening to pare down Guthrie's editing time for *In a Festival Mood: Part IV: A* Seagull-*by-the-Sea*.

Only Spike was blithe. This was because in the absence of any filming, he had a free evening which meant he could get over at last to The French Lieutenant for dinner. Its prices sounded promising – if not from Megalith's point of view. He took Jemima's refusal to accompany him (conscientiously she felt she must attend the dress rehearsal) in good part. Spike took food almost as seriously as Major Cartwright: in a way it was a pity they could not eat together as their tastes in this matter at least were very similar.

Guthrie, Cherry and Jemima sat together centrally, but towards the back of the wide amphitheatre, which fanned out from four sides of the pentagonal stage. Gregory came and sat beside Jemima. A good many rows nearer the front sat Julian Cartwright, Blanche and Regina. Ketty was with them.

Gregory whispered to Jemima that he was most surprised to see Julian. 'He never used to come anywhere near a dress rehearsal in the old days. Not invited for one thing. Didn't want to come either, I dare say. Made a polite supporting appearance at the first preview, if there was one, and then a gracious supporting appearance at the First Night. Otherwise he left it at that – apart from picking up a good many bills for large dinners at expensive restaurants when required. As a matter of fact I never thought even in those days Julian was really all that much in love with the theatre as a whole. It was Christabel he loved. When he secured her by marriage, that patient courtship paid off, the *raison d'être* for all that theatre-going had vanished.'

Gregory smiled. He added, still in a low voice: 'Ironically enough, I always thought that made Julian rather a good sort of husband for a leading actress. Certainly better than an actor would have been – no competition, no rival First-Night nerves in the home. Until events proved me wrong.'

But Julian *was* a good husband, thought Jemima; it was Christabel who had not been a good wife. What was more, she guessed that Julian's presence tonight was due to a laudable desire to support Christabel yet again on the eve of her come-back to the stage.

The lights dimmed, to a sharp cry from Boy Greville – he had warned Jemima earlier that dress rehearsals had an extraordinary effect on the nerves in his spinal cord and he often found himself going into spasms just as they started. His production of *The Seagull* was clearly to be no exception to this painful rule.

Apart from the physical agonies suffered by the director, the first act of the dress rehearsal really went remarkably well. Boy Greville had to lie flat on the thick soft pile carpet of the auditorium. Gallantly, he observed that it was one of the great consolations of his affliction that theatre floors, especially modern ones like the Watchtower, provided an ideal arena for recuperation. He spoke warmly of the Olivier at the National in this context as though recommending an expensive private nursing-home.

'Like dock leaves growing near nettles,' Cherry piped up: her new passion for imparting pieces of country lore, where previously she had concentrated on literature was, Jemima thought, another bad sign.

The company advised Boy to think of himself, and not worry about the production. 'Lie back and enjoy it, like rape,' added Vic Marcovich. In view of what was known about Boy's general passivity, and in view of Vic's special relationship to Boy's wife Anna Maria, this jocular remark if well meant, was felt to be in rather poor taste.

Still, the play went on. In their efforts to atone to Boy for this latest blow of fate, the actors did as well, even better perhaps, than if their director had attended the rehearsal in the more conventional upright position. As a result, the performance was singularly free from those petty theatrical disasters of the sort to be expected and even welcomed at a dress rehearsal because they seemed to promise a trouble-free First Night. 'Dangerously smooth,' Vic Marcovich described it. 'Hope it's not a bad omen for tomorrow.'

In particular Christabel shone. In view of what happened later, the few people who had been present would remember this last shimmering of her talent with agonized regret for what might have been. Guthrie announced in the first break that Christabel was using her voice as if it were a musical instrument whose range was being explored for the first time at the hands of a master. 'A clarinet perhaps,' he suggested enthusiastically, the image clearly taking hold. Jemima, trusting that he would not expect her to incorporate any such sentiment in her commentary, did not speak. She was still deeply moved by what had happened on stage, and wanted to collect her wits before joining the unofficial Critics' Forum.

'Violin!' cried Cherry.

'Bassoon maybe? Christabel's voice is quite deep.' This was Gregory. Cherry shot him a reproachful look. Jemima felt grateful.

All the same, Christabel's voice was peculiarly sonorous and varied that evening. Her performance radiated exactly the kind of automatic careless charm, followed by sudden vulnerability and frightened hungry reclaiming of the wandering Trigorin, which the part of Arkadina, the actress playing the actress, had always seemed to Jemima to require. Gone were all the hesitations and nerves of previous rehearsals. Christabel Herrick was back. Christabel Cartwright was forgotten.

Even Old Nicola, never one to shower a fellow-actor with compliments, acknowledged that. But then Old Nicola was in an unwontedly seraphic humour that evening. Her knitting too was less maliciously orientated, less audacious in its attacks on the ankles and elbows of passersby. It remained incarcerated in the old grey plastic bag at her feet most of the time. Old Nicola did not even attempt to knit during the first three acts of *The Seagull.*

'Just as well. I would have murdered her if she had,' muttered Guthrie.

'You keep threatening that kind of thing,' complained Jemima. 'You know Cy's strong views about a director's individual responsibility. If anyone does in Old Nicola we shall have our programme cancelled and it will be all your fault.'

Guthrie snorted. But really, it had to be admitted that Old Nicola was not in a tiresome mood at all, and as a result no one had any proper excuse for wanting to murder her. If she was not, all the same, an absolutely ideal member of a small audience, this was because Old Nicola had a habit of chuckling audibly whenever she herself perceived one of the jokes. These perceptions of Old Nicola's concerning the humorous side of Chekhov had not by any means been shared by the late Nat Fitzwilliam nor by Boy Greville subsequently.

Old Nicola had nevertheless proved quite remorseless in her note-giving after rehearsals: 'You naughty boy, you should really listen to Old Nicola, you know. I've known them all in my day, Stanislavsky, Komisarjevsky, all the Russians. I even went to Moscow. Have I ever told you about the time I was in the audience when Stalin came to the theatre. Now when Stalin laughed, you see, everyone had to laugh . . .'

But neither Nat Fitzwilliam nor Boy Greville, disappointingly, was prepared to show undue interest in Stalin's contribution to Russian humour. Besides, Old Nicola's reminiscences were growing more daringly fantastic every day. Since she even claimed to have been bandaged by Chekhov's own hands ('He was a perfect duck, Chekhov, he was a doctor you know, and when I accidentally tripped over at a rehearsal and fell . . .'), perhaps too much credence was not to be given to her memories.

Now her chuckles punctuated the performance like a persistent low cough, irritating when the performance flagged, unnoticeable when it was at its height. During the second break, on the eve of the last act, Old Nicola first went and exchanged some remarks with Blanche, then sidled up to Jemima. Gregory had moved and was chatting to Julian and the girls.

'Isn't she quite perfect tonight?' Old Nicola put her face with its bright bird's eyes and bird's sharp beak very close to Jemima's. 'Christabel, I mean. I've just been telling that sweet little Blanche; never mind about Nina, her chance will come, I'm so pleased for Mummy. I do hope everything will go right for tomorrow. After so long, you can't help being worried for her, can you? Wouldn't it be just tragic if anything went wrong? Just when everything's coming to a happy ending for her?'

'What could go wrong?' Jemima was afraid she sounded irritable but she found Old Nicola oozing sympathy even more intolerable than she was grumbling. 'Other than a bad performance. And I don't think Christabel is likely to turn in one of those, do you? Or are you suggesting she can't do it twice?'

'Oh no, dear, no, no, no. Please don't misunderstand Old Nicola. My, some of you clever ladies from television can be sharp sometimes, can't you? Not all of you, though. My friend Susan Merlin was interviewed by a young lady, a *very* pretty young lady, the other day on her memories of the theatre – though Susan is really quite a newcomer to the stage compared to me, and you didn't want *my* memories, but we'll let that pass. Be that as it may – we'll talk about it later, dear – Susan said that this young lady was really terribly sweet and gentle and helpful to her, in spite of being so pretty. Still I suppose it takes all sorts in television, doesn't it, as well as in life?'

Jemima had not survived the repeated fruitless attempts of the press to stir up rivalry between her and her female contemporaries on television in order to succumb to the poisoned darts of Old Nicola.

'I think that's so very true,' she said in her warmest television voice. 'It certainly does take all sorts. And not only in television. The theatre too. Now tell me all about *Widow Capet* and your part in that. I'm sorry that in the end we went for filming just the one production—'

Normally, any mention of this appalling dereliction of duty by Megalith was enough to set Old Nicola off on a tirade. An interview with Gregory was being included, but no clips of the play itself (which might have shown the old woman in her famous role as the jailer's mother). It had turned out to be too expensive to film both productions and do them justice. But on this occasion, Old Nicola's own version of a high good-humour was not to be shaken.

'Well, dear, there's not much to tell, is there? Otherwise I suppose we'd find ourselves telling it to all you clever girls and boys on the box, wouldn't we? To tell you the truth, I'm not quite as thrilled with the part as I was. I've done it many many times, you know, really created the role for that nice Gregory, at his own personal request. But that was a long time ago. The stage is not like television, dear: here today, gone tomorrow. It's a very hard life. So you may be interested in hearing, dear, *on or off the box,* that Old Nicola is going to retire.'

In its way, it was a startling declaration. And Old Nicola made it not with regret or complaint, but with an air of triumph. What, no more Old Nicola besieging young directors with her irresistible demands for parts? No more Old Nicola giving those same unwary directors endless notes after rehearsal on the proper way to get the production right – which meant listening to her tales of bygone triumphs? And what about her flat in Fulham, hers for so many years, whose ever-increasing rent was one of Old Nicola's most persistent laments? What about the cost of living, another personal affront to Old Nicola's survival, especially since she was blessed with an equally ancient companion, in the shape of an enormously fat grey cat called Thomas. Jemima had seen his photograph: from his girth and insolent expression, it came as no surprise to her to learn that Thomas could only exist on a diet of minced best steak and fresh fish, salmon being a particular favourite. Jemina, who had always thought she liked all cats, wondered if she might find herself making an exception in the case of Thomas.

'Oh no, dear, it won't be a disaster financially, not at all,' Old Nicola hastened to reassure her, her complacency even more marked. 'You see, someone is going to look after Old Nicola in future. Someone who can *well* afford to do so, plenty of money, when you think how Old Nicola herself has to live. But how good of you all the same to think of my Thomas, my dear, and his special diet; I shall tell Susan Merlin that you have a heart of gold under your' – Old Nicola paused – 'up-to-date exterior. Yes, Thomas and I will be able to afford lobster in future – something he has never yet tried, but I have a hunch he may take to it.'

'A gift?' enquired Jemima delicately. From the bustle on stage, the next and last act was going to proceed at any moment.

Old Nicola looked immensely sly and at the same time very pleased with herself. 'A gift? Not quite, dear. A reward, you could say. A reward to Old Nicola for having sharp eyes, and a clear mind in her eightieth year, and being able to put two and two together and still make more of it than most of you young people. Yes, you may not believe it, but I shall be eighty on December the sixteenth. Jane Austen's birthday and people have often pointed out that I have exactly the same talent for observation.' Old Nicola clearly awaited some comment from Jemima on this coincidence.

But Jemima's instinct as an investigator was at war with her respect for Jane Austen. The latter won. She said nothing.

'Of course I also know all about the theatre and its little ways,' went on Old Nicola, sounding disappointed. 'After all these years. It was really most fortunate I moved my room to the Royal Stag when I did, in spite of the manageress making such difficulties about giving me a proper light. It even turned out lucky in a way that my room overlooked the back entrance to the hotel although I trust you will not mention the fact to Mrs Tennant.' The old woman, in her newly bonhomous mood, gave a conspiratorial chuckle. 'Fortunate too that I kept my eyes open at that picnic, no naps for Old Nicola in the afternoon, even though she is in her eightieth year. Eyes open and mouth shut, that's the way to get rich, dear.'

For a moment Jemima had the strongest possible feeling that Old Nicola was going to confide in her exactly what it was that she had seen. She held her breath. The Stage Manager appeared at the edge of the stage.

'Right, Boy?' he called. From his prone position, Boy Greville raised his arm on high in assent, in a gesture of the dying Siegfried, and the house lights were dimmed.

'Miss Wain,' whispered Jemima urgently, 'what was it you saw? Who is it who is making you this handsome gift?'

But Old Nicola merely put up her thin gnarled finger to her lips, and went 'SSSh' in a self-righteous way. Then she scuttled away to one of the side rows of the theatre, away from the central block, taking her plastic bag with her. She was still smiling. She looked both greedy and cheerful, like a gourmet cat who expected to be fed on lobster for the rest of his life.

After the theatre, Old Nicola was not to be seen. She must have gone straight back to her room at the Royal Stag, across the square. Jemima looked for her for as long as decency allowed, but that was not for very long. There were the actors to be congratulated and encouraged, and even more to the point Boy Greville to be brought back from the verge of despair. Although everyone else agreed that the dress rehearsal had gone wonderfully well, even worryingly so, Boy Greville declined on the one hand to believe this, and on the other hand prophesied woe on the morrow.

It was not until he reached Flora's Kitchen where a special late dinner had been arranged for the Cartwright family that Boy became remotely content. Jemima walked across the square to the restaurant, with Christabel's expression at the very end of the last act haunting her.

'What's that?' she had exclaimed, at the sound of the shot off-stage. Tobs, as Dr Dorn, had made a very passable stab at comforting her: 'That's nothing. It must be something in my medicine chest that's gone off. Don't worry.' Christabel had then sat down and pretended to be comforted. But all the while Christabel's expression, her over-wide eyes, had remained stamped with some terrible premonitory fear. When Dr Dorn confided to Trigorin at the end of the play: 'Take Irena Nikolayevna away from here somehow. The fact is, Konstantin Gavrilovich has shot himself', you knew that she already experienced the tragedy within her.

It was as well that dinner at Flora's Kitchen was rather demanding with Boy needing not only spiritual reassurance but medical remedies. (Moll coped with the latter, sending Poll out from the kitchen with some strange vegetable concoction of her own, her raucous voice shouting, 'See if that will shut the bugger up.') Otherwise Jemima might have had to live with that image of Christabel's expression throughout the evening. As it was, everyone was relieved when dinner, begun late, broke up early, with the prospect of a First Night ahead. Julian Cartwright it was who masterfully tore Christabel away, and announced in his loud voice that he and Christabel had booked rooms at the Royal Stag for themselves and the girls: 'Christabel certainly needs a proper sleep, as she says, and Lark is not very comfortable at the moment, in view of poor Mrs Blagge's condition.'

'Can't I drive back by myself, Daddy?' began Regina. Ketty silenced her.

'This is much nicer, Rina,' she said firmly. 'Please say thank you nicely. Daddy has been his usual thoughtful self.'

'I'm thinking of Mummy as well,' Blanche contributed in a virtuous voice. 'I'd like to stay, if it makes things easier for Mummy.'

It transpired that the suite in which the Cartwrights had been allowed to continue their party on the night of Blanche's birthday – and Nat's death – was still empty. Christabel was to sleep in the inner bedroom, Julian on a bed in the sitting-room, 'to give her maximum rest' as he put it. The girls and Ketty had been found rooms on an upper floor.

All these domestic arrangements appeared to have a warming effect on Gregory. He offered to buy Jemima a drink at the bar – champagne, why not? – and when the bar was closed, suggested jovially that they should adjourn to her suite and order it there. This suggestion, in view of the possibility that Gregory might find Spike Thompson already installed in her sitting-room, black leather jacket and all, or worse still in her bed, black leather jacket and everything else discarded, Jemima was obliged to turn down. She found herself feeling distinctly regretful about this, which both annoyed and unsettled her. And when she did get upstairs, there was no sign of Spike, which annoyed and unsettled her still further.

Old Nicola, when she had first reached her bedroom some hours earlier, had been in an altogether more contented frame of mine. So she was fast asleep when the person who was supposed to reward Old Nicola for her sharp eyes and ears entered her room by means of Mrs Tennant's pass-key. Certainly the last night of Old Nicola's life had been a very happy one. As the person placed the dark-grey plastic bag over Old Nicola's head and fastened it tight with the flex of her despised table-lamp, perhaps she was dreaming of lobster, of proud Thomas tasting the first consignment with his fastidious pink tongue.

At any rate Old Nicola made no noise as she died, in the small room at the top of the service stairs in the Royal Stag Hotel.

15

Your Lady's Instinct

In all the terrible furore which followed the discovery of Old Nicola's body – by Marie, the hotel chambermaid, bringing her morning tea – nothing was more painfully vivid to Jemima Shore in retrospect than her conversation with the Chairman of Megalith Television. Somehow breaking the news to Cy Fredericks was an even more traumatic experience for Jemima than Marie's prolonged if natural hysterics (she was only sixteen) and Mrs Tennant's equally natural hotelier's agitation.

At first Mrs Tennant showed herself a model of calm; but her nerves grew progressively more ragged with the inevitable influx of a large work force of policemen and their associates. The doctor on call to the police, who arrived at the same time as a Detective Constable from Beauport, was actually well known to her, because he happened to be the hotel doctor too. Mrs Tennant thought this only made his behaviour in using the front staircase more outrageous.

'Doctor Lamb ought to know how dreadful all this is for us!' she exclaimed to the nearest sympathetic audience, which happened to be Jemima Shore. 'What will the guests think? What will the Cartwrights think? Mr Cartwright was so upset to hear the news: he said he'd break it to his wife personally when she awoke. I'm afraid Miss Kettering had already got it from Marie before I made her lie down upstairs, the noise when she dropped the tea tray woke her, and then it was too late to stop the young Cartwright girls finding out. Regina went terribly quiet, but Blanche was quite hysterical, I always say she's the feeling one—' Then, in her nervous state, Mrs Tennant concentrated on the essential difference between the front staircase and the service stairs, as though by upholding this distinction, she could avoid further dire troubles for the Royal Stag Hotel.

The cause of death – asphyxiation – was not too difficult for Dr Lamb to suggest, especially as neither Marie nor Mrs Tennant had removed the plastic bag. Marie, after one horrified look, had fled screaming for Mrs Tennant. The manageress, rushing up the stairs – 'Hush, Marie, for goodness' sake, you'll wake Mrs Cartwright; and Marie, what *have* you done with that tray?' – had fallen back at the grim quiet sight on the pillow. No wonder poor Marie had backed away. It looked as if some lumpish grey cuckoo had entered Miss Wain's bed.

Mrs Tennant had the presence of mind to touch her hand, and on finding it cold, she felt for her pulse. Finding none, she felt next, for a heart beat – equally in vain. She did not however attempt to remove the plastic bag – something Mrs Tennant could not explain to herself afterwards, but for which, since nothing could have been done for the old woman anyway, the police were duly grateful.

At least it was some consolation to Mrs Tennant that Old Nicola's body was taken away down these back stairs when Detective Inspector Harwood finally authorized its removal. Her corpse was now encased in a protective black plastic covering – so much cleaner and newer-looking than her own grey knitting-bag had been, but equally a shroud; it looked shrunken by death into a very small size indeed. The room itself, after being subject to the most thorough scrutiny that the wit of Matt Harwood could devise for fingerprints and other clues, was then locked up. Now all the patient investigations, takings of statements, siftings, collations of evidence which had taken place after the death of Nat Fitzwilliam would begin all over again.

All of this was still not more testing to Jemima – perhaps because the routine of police work had become familiar to her – than the ravings of Cy Fredericks.

'You were quite right. He actually blames me for the old bird's unfortunate demise.' Thus Guthrie Carlyle, reeling away from his own call. 'The man is out of his mind. He seems to hold me personally responsible for what he calls "an extraordinarily high death-rate – even by your standards" of the population of Larminster. Naturally, he's cancelling the programme. I expected that. But what the hell does he mean – an extraordinarily high death-rate by *my* standards?' Guthrie ended angrily.

'I'm sorry about the programme. After all your work. Our work.' Jemima herself was more weary than angry after her own forty-five minutes of telephonic hysteria. 'I think he's referring to the fact that one of your Greek crew, you know, the one you nicknamed Two-and-Twenty Misfortunes after the character in *The Cherry Orchard*, had died in a car crash. His widow has just worked out a way of suing Megalith—'

Guthrie groaned. 'Stop, stop. Just do me a favour and never mention any aspect of Hellenic civilization whatsoever, alive or dead, to me again. I want to lead the rest of my life as far removed from the Glory that was

Greece as possible.' Jemima wondered whether this was a tactful moment to break it to Guthrie that Cy Fredericks proposed to substitute for Larminster, as Part IV of *In a Festival Mood*, an eight-day Gaelic song contest on a remote island off the west coast of Scotland. In spite of his last bold words, she decided against it.

In the course of the conversation Jemima herself had had with Cy, almost the only serious charge which he did not hurl down the telephone was that of high treason. She could only suppose this was because Cy had yet to discover political overtones to Old Nicola's death – no doubt he soon would. Words like 'betrayal' and 'conspiracy', always high on his list of expletives, tripped off his tongue. After 'conspiracy', 'lack of all consideration for Megalith Television' sounded rather tame, but was clearly intended to be an equally lethal insult on Cy's lips.

Jemima, who had seen out these storms before, waited till there was a pause, because Cy was recovering his breath and then struck back: 'Cy,' she began in an ominously quiet voice, 'an old woman, a very old woman, as it happens, has died – been murdered, I gather from my friends the police. She was also a singularly unpleasant old woman and was probably blackmailing her killer. This old woman also happened to be an actress and she happened to have a part in one of the two productions in a Festival programme being televised by Megalith. All of this is most unfortunate. I agree with you. It's most unfortunate for Megalith because we've wasted a lot of money – and time and trouble, incidentally – on this programme and now I agree with you – *I do agree with you*, Cy, it has to be scrapped.'

Jemima gathered momentum: 'It's also unfortunate for the Larminster Festival because they've now suffered two fairly macabre murders on the eve of opening, and yet they can hardly just cancel the whole affair, just like that, with all the tickets sold out, mainly to see Christabel Herrick, and suffer financial ruin. It's even more unfortunate for the King Charles Theatre Company – think of what they've been through. Their director dying on them and now a member of the company stricken down, even if she was only in one production and replaceable: at this moment the wretched Boy Greville is trying to get hold of Susan Merlin who's played the part before, and who he wanted to cast originally anyway. Most of all, you could reasonably say it's unfortunate for Nicola Wain who died on the eve of what she fancied would be an affluent retirement and will probably be mourned by nobody but her cat.

'But none of this, Cy,' Jemima slowed down as she delivered her peroration and raised her voice a couple of decibels (she also did not think Cy's silence would last much longer for she could hear strange snortings and pantings down the line as of a great beast seeking to free itself from control), 'none of this, not one single element of this, amounts to a conspiracy against Megalith Television. I did not kill Nicola Wain. I did not kill Nat Fitzwilliam. Nor, I would dare swear, did Guthrie Carlyle. Nor did Cherry Bronson. I would even hazard a view that Spike Thompson, whatever his expense sheets, is not a murderer and,' she threw in inspirationally, 'I am quite prepared to be his alibi if necessary. In view of all these manifest facts, Cy, and in view of your attitude to me and my colleagues this morning on this distressing occasion, I must ask you to accept my immediate resignation.'

There was a long horrified silence, with no snortings or pantings at all. Then Cy said, in what for him was a whisper: 'Jem, Jem, you haven't – you haven't got another job? Breakfast Television? The BBC? No, Jem, you couldn't have done that to me, not you, Jem. The BBC? My God, what are they paying you? It's an outrage. Public money . . . I shall raise questions . . .' His voice rose, 'Listen, do nothing, Jem, do nothing at all until I have seen you. I am coming down this afternoon in the Rolls, straightaway. Miss Lewis,' he was by now shouting, 'tell Leonard I shall be going down to – to – well, wherever it is, find out where the festival film unit is, Miss Lewis, well, where is it? Find out, woman! Don't ask me *which* festival film unit, all right, *all right*, yes, of course, I know there are several, I commissioned this series, didn't I? The one lucky enough to have the company of Miss Jemima Shore. Tell Leonard I shall be leaving at two o'clock for it, wherever it is, and yes, yes, I will be back for dinner. Dinner at Mark's Club, but please telephone Lady Manfred and ask her to make it nine o'clock instead of eight-thirty—

'My poor child,' he then crooned loudly but tenderly down the telephone, 'my poor Jem, of course you've had a terrible time—'

It was with the greatest difficulty that Jemima convinced Cy that not only had she no other job in view, but also that his presence in Larminster, even with the incomparable Leonard at the wheel of the Rolls, would only make matters worse than they were already. The conversation thus ended amiably but sharply with the news of Guthrie's exile to the Western Isles ('You will know how to break it to him, Jem, your lady's instinct') which showed that Cy was once more quite himself.

As Jemima predicted, the Festival Committee were in no position to cancel their programme, even if they were so inclined. The tickets were mainly sold, and the Festival had thus to pursue its course, unassisted by the presence of Megalith Television – and of course Miss Nicola Wain. The latter was easier to replace as an attraction than the former. Susan Merlin did indeed respond most sweetly to Boy Greville's appeal, and promised to arrive 'word-perfect' within a few days: Which is an advantage I think I can say I have over poor Nicola. She was always a slow study, but then of course she was really quite a few years older than me, even if she didn't like to admit it . . .'

The news of the departure of Megalith Television spread rapidly through a Larminster already appalled by Old Nicola's decease – but more by its locale than anything else. Like the arrest of Jim Blagge, anything concerning the Royal Stag and its manageress struck straight at local sympathies.

'Poor Ivy Tennant, when she's worked so hard to build the place up . . .' These words were heard far more frequently than: 'Poor Miss Wain'. Old Nicola was chiefly known as an actress for her appearances in Dickens serials in which she generally played some appropriately witch-like character: the impression of malice she conveyed had not been contradicted in real life by her behaviour at the Spring Guest House and the Royal Stag itself. Even the kind-hearted Mrs Tennant found it difficult to say many nice things about her guest, while Marie was a good deal more explicit: '"Late again, dear," she would say, sitting up in bed like an old bat. I often wanted to throw the tea things at her head. And in the end that's just what I did, except that her head—' At this point Marie collapsed in loud howls.

The retreat of Megalith from filming the First Night was quite another matter. Father O'Brien for example found it very difficult to reconcile himself to this working of the divine will. His Christian resignation was further tested when Poll, doing a heroic stint at the theatre box office, absolutely refused to refund him for his ticket, an exchange which he requested on the grounds that the television cameras would not now be present.

'The rules say that I have to tell ticket-holders in advance that the programme will be filmed. But they don't say I have to compensate them if it won't be filmed,' she maintained firmly, her long hair swishing the seat plan in front of her like a soft broom. 'You'll just have to grin and bear it, Father, won't you,' said Poll, all unaware that she was advocating Major Cartwright's own recipe for getting through a night at the theatre.

Compared to Cy Fredericks, Major Cartwright was really a model of reason and good sense.

'Much of this sort of thing go on in the West End theatre?' the Major enquired of Gregory. Taking his silence for assent, he went on: 'Humph. Thought so. Wonder how you ever get a show on at all.'

'It is fair to say our disasters generally occur on the First Night itself,' Gregory replied diplomatically.' Rather than shortly before it.'

'Bit quicker off the mark here, eh? Not quite the backward provinces, are we?' And the Major gave a ferocious chuckle.

So far as the Festival was concerned, that was that. The Major's mixture of of taciturnity and authoritarianism enabled him to deal with such potentially recalcitrant bodies as the press and his own committee with admirable despatch. His address to the actors of the King Charles Company was certainly a model of its kind:

'Bad show' pronounced the Major from the stage of the Watchtower to the assembled company: 'See that you give a good one tonight. Damn sure you will. Like the war. Ensa. The Windmill. We never closed.' The mention of the Windmill seemed to recall to the Major some more urgent appointment, and shortly afterwards he was seen whirling away in his Bentley, with Cherry's dark head in the passenger seat. It was left to Boy Greville to calm the understandable nerves of his actors along more orthodox lines, a task made easier by the fact that a real slap-up disaster, as Anna Maria observed, always brought out the best in him. It was noticeable that throughout the day and the night which followed it, Boy never once referred to his own physical condition nor sought any remedy for it.

Jemima Shore was still in her suite at the Royal Stag by the late afternoon, although most of the clearing-up of the abortive television proceedings had already been done. Spike Thompson generously offered to stop over – 'We could have a real evening, dinner together, sea-food spaghetti at Don Giovanni's, or whatever it's called. Steak maison – £2 supplement, the best claret, champagne to round it all off, my place or yours. I'll pay, no, honest, my love. It would be my pleasure, I can't say fairer than that, can I?'

He could not. Jemima still rejected the offer. She bid an affectionate farewell to Spike and watched his jaunty departure, black head held high, thumbs stuck into the pockets of his black leather jacket, with genuine regret; she would miss them both – the man and the jacket. But Jemima needed solitude, a pause for vital recollection. She needed desperately to think back over all that had taken place in Larminster and around it, if she was not to betray her famous 'lady's instinct' as Cy termed it. In short, the abandoned pagan nymph of Spike Thompson's nightly revels had to take second place to that sterner character Jemima Shore Investigator.

Jemima sighed. And put her mind firmly to work on the whole vast problem of the Larminster murders: she knew she would not think about Spike again until her 'lady's instinct' had come up with at least some kind of interim solution.

No solution was for the time being offered by Detective Inspector Harwood. Jemima managed to snatch a few minutes of his beleaguered time over a cup of tea at the Royal Stag. He looked tired, lifting his tea-cup automatically, as though it was the twentieth cup he had drunk that day – which was possibly true. The murder of the old woman following so closely that of Nat Fitzwilliam, and the arrest of Jim Blagge had obviously come as a shock to the police. It was likely that Mr Blagge's solicitor would now make representations for him to get bail, which under the circumstances the police would probably not oppose.

'A maniac loose? That's what they're saying in Larminster, Jemima. Yes, only a maniac would kill a young man and an old woman, and for what? That's what we don't know, Jemima, assuming the two killings are linked. But what is a maniac? You tell me that. Mad or sane, these murderers never much want to be caught by the police, do they? Take X who killed Fitzwilliam, for we'll rule out the chauffeur for the moment. He took good care to cover up, didn't he? Maniac or no maniac. Take X who killed the old lady – the same X as we now think, this X wore gloves and was very careful indeed to leave no traces behind. No clues. Not altogether mad, you see. Not mad enough to be caught. Not so far. Whatever the do-gooders will say when he or she comes to trial.'

Jemima who had no intention of arguing about the definitions of criminal insanity with Detective Inspector Harwood, if she could help it, asked instead: 'So what now? The police never give up. That I do know.'

'They do not.' Matt Harwood sounded quite shocked. 'Hard work, that's what happens next. Hard work. Routine questions. Taking all the statements of the residents in the hotel on the night in question – a good number of them members of the Cartwright family, I understand. Funny – or not so funny – the way they keep recurring, isn't it? They were all here the night Fitzwilliam was killed too. Oh we shall plod on all right. We may be slow, but we are very very sure. We'll get him – or her – in the end.'

'And suppose there is another murder in the meanwhile?' suggested Jemima. 'My instinct tells me . . .' She realized she had gone too far.

Detective Inspector Harwood shot her a look which somehow reminded her of Cy Fredericks – Cy in one of his more chauvinist moods. Matt Harwood's next words also reminded her of Cy Fredericks.

'If your feminine instinct tells you there's going to be another murder, maybe the same useful instinct will tell you who's going to do it and to whom. Then you can go ahead and prevent it.' On which note of jocularity the Detective Inspector departed.

Jemima decided not to attend the First Night of *The Seagull* now that there was no television work to be done. She had seen a superlative performance from Christabel the night before: she doubted it could be matched tonight, especially under the traumatic circumstances of another death striking at the company. She was not sufficiently thrilled by any of the other actors to see them twice outside the line of duty – not even Vic Marcovich whose Trigorin had been very impressive or Anna Maria Packe who had turned in an appealing Masha. It was a pleasure not to have to gaze on the rocks and fisherman's netting further. Besides the First Night at the Watchtower would be a morbid occasion, she suspected. She was not surprised to learn that Julian had taken his daughters back to Lark Manor. He himself planned to return later, 'But if not, well, Christabel has Gregory to support her, doesn't she?' he observed to Jemima on his way out of the hotel. Christabel herself had returned to Lark for a short rest, fleeing the confusion of the Royal Stag. Then Gregory had driven her back to the theatre.

But Jemima's famous instinct was letting her down in allowing her to stay in her suite at the Royal Stag, instead of attending the First Night at the Watchtower. For the person who had long sought to destroy Christabel, killing three people in the process, had just chosen that particular occasion to put an end to her once and for all. After some heart searching, the person decided that Christabel should die as she had lived – in the full public eye. So that everyone should see and understand that there was no real forgiveness possible: that no one could ever come back if they had done the things that Christabel had done.

Jemima Shore, as yet unknowing of this decision, sat in her suite and pondered on all the murky circumstances surrounding the cool repentance of Christabel Cartwright. She had just, dazedly, reached a solution – a horrifying solution – when there was an imperative rap on her door.

Jemima came with a jolt out of the dream, nightmare really, into which her own reasonings had plunged her. Automatically she looked at her watch and was further startled to find it was very late. *The Seagull* must be well on its way by now. The door was locked – Mrs Tennant had insisted on that after the murder.

'Who is it?' she called, looking round for the key.

'Miss Shore, I must speak to you. It's desperately urgent. Please let me come in.'

Jemima recognized the voice of Miss Kettering.

16
Death of a Seagull

Ketty's sharp tapping interrupted a very long train of thought in Jemima. It had been punctuated – unpleasantly – by bursts of music from a radio played much too loudly in the room above. Pop music. Somewhat against her will Jemima recognized the tunes because they had once been so colossally popular that it had been impossible to avoid contact with their demanding monotonous beat. One of these tunes which she recognized was 'Cool Repentance'.

Was it the Iron Boy record being played? She could pick up – could not really fail to pick up whether she liked it or not – the repeated long-drawn-out first syllable 'coo-oo-ool, oh so cool repentance', but she could not recognize the voice of the singer. Some of the other Iron Boy hits were played, including 'Daring Darling' and 'Iron Boy' itself, but then she could also hear some of the Rolling Stones' numbers. During the brief pauses, however, when she could hear the disc jockey talking, Jemima found it was 'Cool Repentance' which stayed beating in her head and would not go away.

It was not a soothing experience. Lying back on the chintz-covered chaise-longue in the sitting-room, Jemima contemplated asking Mrs Tennant to have the offending radio turned down: on reflection she decided that the unfortunate manageress had endured enough for one day. Then it occurred to her that the chambermaid Marie had been installed in the empty room above her to recuperate. Marie too had had an unpleasant experience. If pop music on the hotel-room radio contributed to her recovery, then perhaps she should be allowed to play it. Even loud.

Feeling virtuously fair-minded – and also rather cross – Jemima set her mind back to work, to the tune of the loud beats coming from above.

It was a question of the past, and of things in their proper order.

Where had it all begun? It had begun, properly, with the moment when Christabel had confided her fears to Jemima: how she would only be safe again back on stage, 'with the eyes of the world upon me . . . Oh, Jemima, I've been so terribly, terribly frightened . . . Locked away at Lark. It's so dangerous . . .' Then Gregory had arrived with Ketty and the girls. So Jemima had never really discovered where the mysterious danger lay, beyond the fact that it was clearly somewhere close at hand – connected with Lark Manor itself.

After that there had been the picnic. She passed certain images back through her mind, as though replaying the key moments of a television programme. Christabel, with Nat Fitzwilliam at her feet, the young man talking away, the older woman's attention wandering. Jemima had spotted an oddly upset glance in the direction of Gregory, himself chatting cheerfully away to Filumena Lennox.

Gregory, who had tried to warn Jemima off originally at their first bizarre encounter on the sea-shore: 'Why don't you just chuck this programme? . . . Have you thought of its effect on people with something to hide?' He had pretended that he had been trying to protect Christabel's privacy. Had it after all been Gregory himself who had something to hide? Was it possible that it was Gregory whom Christabel had feared all along?

Gregory had been in Larminster on the night of Nat's death – had no subsequent alibi beyond swimming as Matt Harwood had scornfully told her – and it was certainly feasible for Gregory to have entered the Royal Stag last night, since security, under Mrs Tennant's easy-going eye, was lax to non-existent. In many ways Gregory fitted the bill very well – all too well for Jemima, since she discovered in herself considerable reluctance to postulate Gregory's guilt (she hoped that this reluctance could be attributed to instinct – the right kind of instinct).

Gregory had disliked Nat Fitzwilliam: he had made no secret of the fact. Gregory was a successful playwright, with no visible dependants, who had plenty of money to spare to support Old Nicola in her chosen retirement. So far, so good. Or rather, so bad.

But all of this had to be based on a foundation-stone of hatred – hatred not of Nat, nor yet of Nicola, but of Christabel. Was it really possible for Gregory Rowan to hate Christabel Cartwright? Hate her so much that he had planned to drown her? And in so doing had tragically and mistakenly put an end to the life of a young girl – a girl with whom he had been openly flirting only an hour before?

'Come with me and see pre-revolutionary Paris.' Jemima had overheard his offer. Most of the rest of the picnic must have heard it too. Gregory of all people had not expected Filly – rather than Christabel – to be wearing the magpie hat. For it was Gregory who had tried to persuade Filly to swim and, as he thought, failed. He had strode away towards the west cliff to swim by himself – wearing nothing but a pair of tennis shoes, no doubt. Or had he? Was this what Nat had seen through his binoculars? At one point it had seemed that Nat must have focused on something connected with Mr Blagge and his boat; now Mr Blagge's boating expedition had turned out to be quite innocent – just what it purported to be, a rescue expedition in choppy waters, at his wife's suggestion. So what had Nat seen – not seen – through his binoculars? 'I saw nothing where I should have seen something.' Gregory not under the west cliff at all . . . for Gregory was by now cutting through the waters to the east like a black shark . . . Was this – 'just a little discrepancy between text and sub-text' – what Nat had tried to discuss 'several times with the person concerned' receiving an answer, which 'wasn't satisfactory either'. Old Nicola too, she had glimpsed something as she sat on the beach – an unknown 'helper' or 'cuddler' there in the water close to Filly; she had never referred to the incident again – was it Gregory Old Nicola had observed?

Another image flashed on to her personal screen: Gregory in his cottage, telling her with perfect good-humour: 'It sounds ridiculous but at first I felt quite violent . . . She only showed one pang of emotion and that was when we had to tell her her dog Mango had died . . . For one terrible moment, I wanted to do her some frightful physical injury. I almost wanted to kill her for all the suffering she had caused . . .'

'Coo-oo-ool, oh so cool repentance' beat and wailed and rocked above her for the second time: that really must be Iron Boy singing it. She thought: was it really possible for anyone to come back as Christabel had done, abandoned first by Iron Boy, then by the world, and not arouse devastating murderous passions in the injured?

Jemima began to list them to herself. First of all, her children, but was Regina really for all her literary allusions to be classed as a potential matricide? A modern version of Electra, perhaps, with Christabel as Clytemnestra? She decided to hold on that one and passed on to Regina's sister. Blanche had evidently been most resentful of her mother when Jemima first visited Lark and theoretically the Nina incident should not have helped their relationship; yet she had the impression that mother and daughter had seemed much closer lately. Jemima thought of Blanche, over-heated in her Annie Hall outfit on the night of her birthday, and in any case physically most ill-suited to such a parody of masculine clothing: she had certainly improved since then.

Jemima decided to hold on Regina and Blanche and pass on to the rest of the Lark Manor circle. Jemima was patiently reviewing the various characters involved: the Blagges . . . after all, no. Ketty – in love with Julian Cartwright, said Gregory, hating Christabel's return which had demoted her in the household . . . yes, perhaps . . . All of a sudden the music above her head came to an abrupt halt.

Footsteps were heard instead. Then voices. Then a door banged.

Evidently Mrs Tennant had come to claim Marie, or at any rate restore peace to her hotel.

The shock of the sudden silence, for one instant quite as shocking as the endlessly reverberating noise had been, had a most surprising effect on Jemima. It was as though she had suddenly seen everything exactly reversed: silence was shocking, noise the norm ... She began, with rising excitement, to look at all her own images from exactly the opposite point of view, to ask herself a whole new set of questions, questions which she knew at last were getting close to the heart of the mystery.

Cool repentance ... but was it really possible in any couple for a wife to be quite so bad, a husband quite so good, as Christabel and Julian Cartwright seemed respectively to the outside world? Was Christabel really so complacently composed, Julian really so doggedly adoring as they appeared in public? Had she really felt no shame at what she had done to him, her loving husband of so many years, the younger man who had married her when Gregory would not? More to the point, was a man, any man, really going to accept such flagrant behaviour and for so many years. She thought – nostalgically, as she lay on the chintz chaise-longue – of Spike. Chauvinist Spike who had not been able to understand Julian's husbandly meekness: 'I'd give her a proper going-over.' In vain Jemima had responded: 'It would drive me quite mad to have to come back to Lark as penitent Magdalen.' Suppose that secretly ...

Following this train of thought proved very interesting indeed to Jemima Shore.

She conjured up a whole new set of images. She remembered the Sunday lunch table. Julian giving the orders. Julian, the lord of the manor, very much in command of his household. She reviewed again, still patiently, the picnic on the shore. She concentrated on Julian's assiduous control of absolutely every detail of the picnic, the melancholy which seemed to underlie Christabel's attitude to him, more than melancholy, almost a feeling of shrinking from him.

She remembered Gregory's words: 'I was very surprised. She always said he was not her type: she called him her rich young man. Security, I suppose.' 'Not my type,' Christabel Herrick had said of Julian Cartwright ...

She ran through still more of her conversation with Gregory in her mind. His surprise when Julian had agreed to fetch Christabel, the guilty woman, down to Lark immediately. Why had he rushed up to London so promptly? Why had he brought her down to secluded luxurious Lark, the house she had willingly abandoned? Gregory had given his own explanation: Christabel had been 'totally destroyed', 'scarcely sane', when Julian had fetched her – for Gregory was Julian's friend as well as Christabel's. 'Julian Cartwright,' he had loyally told Jemima, 'is much the nicest character of the Cartwright family.'

Jemima wondered about other things. The death of Nat Fitzwilliam. Nat who had intended to focus his binoculars on the sea-shore from the Watchtower to view the production 'as a whole' and to concentrate on the character of Arkadina in particular: until Christabel had jokingly suggested that there had been enough concentration on Arkadina for one production, and that focusing on Blanche and Ollie, Filly and Gregory, or even Cherry and Julian, might provide more useful insights – into the characters of Konstantin, Nina and Trigorin . . .

The death of Nat Fitzwilliam, and that figure in the shadows. That figure – a man – alluded to by Mr Blagge, who knew well where to find the key, because the topic had been discussed in Flora's Kitchen: and knew also just as well as Mr Blagge how to throw it away afterwards so it would never be found. A man who noticed when the Cartwright family and their attachments were ostensibly upstairs in the Royal Stag finishing off Blanche's birthday elebrations, but in fact proved on examination to have been widely dispersed as the evening wore on. All this at a time when beady-eyed Old Nicola, also installed on the first floor near the service stairs, could easily have witnessed an unscheduled flitting from the hotel. Aroused by the noise on the service stairs, she could have looked out of her little back window and seen *someone* – who? – leaving the hotel by the back entrance and the car-park . . . basis for blackmail later. Old Nicola: who was expecting someone 'who can well afford to do so' to provide for her for the rest of her life. 'Someone who can well afford to do so, plenty of money, when you think how Old Nicola herself has to live.'

And then at last Jemima saw it all: instinct helped her to take the last step, where first instinct, then reason, had guided her originally along her path of discovery. She saw it all in one appalled and appalling glimpse in which past and present combined.

Plenty of money. Lark Manor. The lap of luxury. Julian Cartwright. Regina Cartwright. Blanche Cartwright. It all came down to this: could Christabel be forgiven for what she had done to her husband and family? Hadn't Christabel said it herself on their second meeting in Flora's Kitchen: 'It's too late. One can never go back.'

It was at this point that Jemima heard Ketty's imperative knocks. Still startled, slightly shaking in view of the new path along which her thoughts were rapidly carrying her, Jemima undid the door. She took a step back.

Ketty was an astonishing sight: her dark-red hair, normally strained back into its thick bun, was falling round her shoulders. Her eyes were hardly touched with their usual garish eyeshadow; her quivering mouth was quite devoid of its harsh red lipstick. She was wearing a cardigan over her dark dress which was misbuttoned: everything about Ketty's outfit, in contrast to her usual style, had the air of being very hastily assumed.

'Miss Shore, let me in. It's urgent. Really urgent. Otherwise I wouldn't have come. I've driven from Lark. I took the Jaguar – he's got the Land-Rover. I've never driven it before. It's outside. Not very well parked. Oh, my God—' Ketty sat down suddenly on the chaise-longue. A glass of white wine was on the table beside her. She drained it. She did not seem to notice it was not water.

This new defenceless Ketty, looking at least ten years younger than the formidable governess of Lark Manor, was such a surprising apparition, that it took a moment for Jemima to rally her thoughts. Then she realized the full import of what Ketty had just said:

'*Who*'s got the Land-Rover?'

'*He's* got the Land-Rover. Julian. Mr Julian. He's going to the theatre. I know he is, and oh, Miss Shore, you've got to help us.' Ketty was by now trembling violently as though in delayed reaction to her drive.

'How do you know he's going to the theatre?'

'Where else *would* he go? But to her.' Ketty looked up desperately to Jemima, her large face incongruously framed by her mass of rippling auburn hair like the hair of a forties film star: her eyes were imploring. Yes, there was no doubt about Ketty's feelings for Julian Cartwright. 'And that's not the worst of it,' she went on. 'His pistol's gone. *That's* the worst of it. That's why I came to you. I know where he keeps it and it's gone. The drawer in the study was open after he left, when he rushed out of the house—' Ketty gave a sob.

'Oh, Miss Shore, he's been so patient, so terribly terribly patient through it all. I'm frightened—'

'I'm frightened too,' said Jemima grimly. 'Come on. We're going to the theatre.'

Taking Ketty's hand, she guided her down the staircase and out of the hotel, ignoring Mrs Tennant's bewildered face behind the reception desk. With Ketty's hand in hers, Jemima felt for one absurd moment like the Red Queen tugging at Alice: but she was well aware that the situation in which they were all involved was tragic not absurd.

Together they walked, half-ran and then ran across the pretty little square which separated the hotel from the theatre.

The glass of the pentagonal theatre was thoroughly illuminated. Across its central facade hung an enormous white banner. It concentrated on essentials: TONIGHT, it read, CHRISTABEL HERRICK IN 'THE SEAGULL'. There was no mention of such details as the author's name, the director, let alone the names of any of the other actors in the King Charles Theatre Company.

But when Jemima entered the theatre itself – rushing past the surprised attendant who exclaimed: 'I thought you telly people were all gone' – Christabel Herrick, the star of the occasion, was not visible on the stage. Jemima shoved Ketty down into a vacant seat on the left-hand aisle (she thought it must have been one of Megalith's unused seats, but it had in fact been vacated at the first interval by Father O'Brien, who had returned home to watch one of his favourite programmes on television). Jamie Grand, the powerful editor of *Literature*, was sitting in the same row: as usual when he was at the theatre – as opposed to reviewing a book – there was a pleased expression on his face; an unknown blonde girl was next to him. Neither of them took their eyes off the stage for a moment but Jemima saw another face look up at her with a frog-like air of injured astonishment at the disturbance. She recognized a London critic, come down to Larminster to witness the return of Christabel Herrick to the stage. There was no sign of Julian Cartwright in the crowded and darkened auditorium – but that was not where she expected to find him.

Trying to catch her breath, Jemima surveyed the stage. Emily Jones was at the beginning of Nina's last speech: 'I'm a seagull . . . No, that's not it. I'm an actress . . . I'm a seagull. No, that's not it again . . . Do you remember you shot a seagull? A man came along by chance, saw it and destroyed it . . .' She was ploughing on gamely and not unsuccessfully, if much faster than had been planned at rehearsals. Ollie Summertown as Konstantin was sitting listening to her.

There was still time, time to get round to the back of the stage.

'Slow up, Emily, slow up anyway for your sake as well as mine,' Jemima prayed desperately. 'Nina does not gabble.' And she turned and ran back out of the theatre, round to the Stage Door, in past an equally stunned door-keeper – 'Well, hello there Miss Shore, I thought—' But Jemima did not stop. She knew now exactly what had happened, what might happen. She got to the wings of the stage. Still she did not see the man she was looking for, Julian Cartwright, nor the woman, Christabel.

Emily had reached the end of her speech and ran down the steps which, for lack of a proscenium arch, stood for french windows on the set. Konstantin was still tearing up his manuscripts: ending his work preparatory to ending his life. In the absence of a desk, he had to take them out of a seaman's canvas bag. It was a long-drawn-out process. Jemima noticed that Ollie's hands were trembling.

At that moment there came a loud report from the direction of the dressing-rooms. A look of amazement followed by slight embarrassment crossed Ollie's face: as though he feared that he had somehow shot himself prematurely and would get into trouble for still being on stage tearing up manuscripts when he should be officially dead off-stage. There was a faint disconcerted rustle in the audience as though some of those who prided themselves on being Chekhovian *cognoscenti* were having the same reaction.

But Jemima had no further time to consider what was happening on stage. She looked round frantically. She still could not see any sign of

Christabel, although any minute Madame Arkadina was due to make her last entrance and Trigorin and Masha were already in place.

It was Julian Cartwright who provided the solution to the mystery of Christabel's whereabouts. He came slowly towards Jemima from the direction of Christabel's dressing-room. Vic Marcovich and Anna Maria, who were waiting to enter, stared at him. The voice of Dr Dorn could be heard on-stage: 'That's strange. The door seems to be locked . . .' Without the benefit of his aged-up appearance, Tobs still sounded oddly young.

Julian Cartwright moved like a sleep-walker. But his voice when he spoke was as clear and strong as normal. So that a good many members of the audience must have heard him when he said:

'Get everyone out of here. No, don't go into the dressing-room. Christabel has shot herself.'

Inside the star's dressing-room, with all its as-yet-unopened good-luck telegrams and all its sweet-scented flowers from Lark Manor, all the flowers she loved, lay Christabel Herrick. She was still just conscious enough to be aware that she was dying at last, killed by her own hand as she had always intended, shot, immolated, ended.

Then the person who knew that Christabel could never be forgiven for what she had done, closed her eyes. The person who hated Christabel died together with her, and at the same instant and in the same body. United in death, all her voices, good and evil, ruthless and repentant, found peace at last.

17

Obsession and After

They pieced it together afterwards, all of them. Christabel, the person who had killed three times, once in a sudden fit of murderous jealousy – Filly Lennox, a younger rival; twice to protect herself from the consequences of her crime – Nat Fitzwilliam who had seen something through his binoculars, and Old Nicola who had seen something else from her vantage point at the Royal Stag hotel. Christabel, the schizophrenic murderess. Christabel, the person who hated herself for what she had done, and so in the end thankfully destroyed herself.

The people who pieced it all together included Jemima Shore, who had reached the truth in a flash of illumination at the end – but too late to save Christabel from her final desperate act; Julian Cartwright, who knew only too well about his wife's unbalance but feared to face its consequences; Gregory Rowan, who had talked so convincingly to Jemima about Christabel's self-hatred – Christabel as her own worst enemy – and yet likewise feared to face the agonizing truth.

'I think we were both blinded, Julian and I, by the fact of her leaving us,' Gregory told Jemima. 'We were obsessed by her absence, by what she had done by abandoning us. So when she did return, we were determined that everything should be just the same: it had to be. Back to normal. That was our motto. You see, it was our conspiracy to pretend that everything was back to normal, not hers. She was merely acting out what we wanted her to be. And giving a superb performance, too. That extraordinary radiant composure, which the world took for brazenness – acting, all of it. Beneath it all, she was terribly frightened, must have been frightened of going mad, frightened of what she might do if she did.'

They were once more by the sea, on the beach where Jemima had first met Gregory Rowan and he had told her harshly to go back to London – where television belonged. Behind them rose up the pale Bridset stone of

Lark Manor and parallel to it the darker shape of the Watchtower Theatre, but neither Jemima nor Gregory looked back. It was one of those late summer days when you knew that autumn would not be long in coming; a cold wind raked the sea and sent iron-grey shadows scudding across its rippled surface. Jemima dug her hands into the pockets of her elegant red suede jacket and shivered. She was thankful Gregory did not suggest swimming.

Jemima had come to say goodbye to Gregory Rowan at the Old Keeper's Lodge, and found him surrounded by books and packing-cases. Some kind of move was evidently contemplated. She did not comment on the fact nor did he. He simply said: 'Come, on, let's get out of here and go down to the sea for a breath of good Bridset air. I find the woods rather claustrophobic these days.'

They were out of the cottage before Jemima remembered about the many photographs of Christabel which had surrounded Gregory's desk on her previous visit; she wondered what he had done with them. That was another thing she would not ask.

Now she spoke into the wind, in the direction of the sea, without looking at Gregory: 'She told me she was frightened, frightened of being left alone at Lark, the first time we had lunch together. Of course, at that time I thought – I imagined – so many people had good reason to wish her ill, to resent her return—'

'I can imagine what you thought, Jemima Shore Investigator. Betrayed husband, abandoned daughters, sinister servants, even perhaps menacing playwright.' But Gregory's smile, that odd smile whose sweetness had surprised her on their first meeting, robbed the words of offence.

'*I* never suspected you,' replied Jemima, loyally and more or less truthfully, for after all it had been Matt Harwood not her who had put his money on the playwright, and if she had suspected Gregory just for one moment towards the end, then it was only during that strange long-drawn-out process of thought, to the tune of the hotel radio, by which she had reached her ultimately correct solution . . .

'I suppose she really had her first breakdown when I left her, or anyway didn't want to marry her. I wanted my own selfish solitary life,' Gregory continued slowly; he too preferred to look out to sea. 'Julian rescued her then. He married her and looked after her. She recovered; back to normal, you could say. He thought he could do the same thing after the departure of Iron Boy. That really did drive her mad – Julian told me so himself when he went up to London to fetch her. But he was so sure that she'd be all right when he got her back to Lark – he couldn't see, he didn't want to see that Lark, with all its memories, the daily reminder of what she'd done, cooped up with the resentful girls, condemned to be waited on daily by Barry's own parents, was the worst place for her. Even the dog she adored had been killed in her absence, without her to look after it –

that must have made her feel so guilty. Her thoughts alone must have driven her mad, the voice of her own conscience.'

The virtuous mind that ever walks attended
By a strong siding champion Conscience –

Jemima quoted. 'Do you remember? Those lines from *Comus*. I questioned whether Christabel was altogether well cast in the part of The Lady. I was wrong. She *did* have a conscience, if not a virtuous mind.'

'Yes, why do we always assume that it's only the virtuous who have consciences? In my injured pride, I was wrong about that too.'

'That's why she was so keen to get back on the stage I suppose,' said Jemima. 'To blot it out. "I'll be safe," she said to me: she meant safe from herself, and her own terrible instinct towards self-destruction.'

'But she didn't only destroy herself!' Gregory exclaimed. 'That's the horror of it.' He swung round and looked at Jemima. His eyes were full of tears. 'She drowned that poor little girl, just because I laughed and flirted with her at a beach party and offered to take her to Paris, and because Filly was young and pretty and a good actress and the centre of attention – all the things Christabel herself had once been. Filly was going to play Paulinot in *Widow Capet*. She would have been sensational in the part too, Christabel knew that. She knew all about the theatre, never forget that, she knew that in the famous confrontation scene between Marie Antoinette and Paulinot, what the late Nat called the 'Old-France-versus-the-New Number' it was not necessarily going to be Christabel who wiped the floor with Filly.'

'Old Nicola was on to that like a flash,' commented Jemima. 'I think she must have had her suspicions about Christabel from the first and decided to keep them to herself in case they proved profitable. Sitting on the beach and "watching all you naughty boys and girls" as she used to put it, she may even have spotted Christabel taking her surreptitious swim. I suppose Christabel wore one of the other less conspicuous suits and hats unearthed by Mrs Blagge: in the general confusion after the death of Filly no one would have noticed one wet bathing-dress more or less, and of course when Christabel reappeared on the beach, she was still wearing that flowing leopard-skin printed robe: it was easy to change back into that. But she had taken off her scarf and combed her hair. I remember it stood out from her head like a golden halo—'

'Halo!' exclaimed Gregory.

'Let's get back to Old Nicola,' Jemima hastily steered the conversation away from Christabel's personal appearance. 'She made some rather odd remark, I seem to recall, about a person unknown either "having a cuddle, or else being helpful" in the sea, and then never repeated it, which was unlike her usual style. She was certainly well aware of Christabel's jealousy for Filly – "knowing about the theatre and all its little ways after all these years" – almost the last thing she ever said to me. The professional jealousy of an older woman for a younger was all too easy for her to divine, because she was eaten up with envy of Christabel herself. Christabel pretended to be resting in the inner bedroom on the night of Nat's death: Old Nicola must have spotted her slipping down the service stairs, when she was padding along to that distant bedroom she used to moan about.'

Jemima stopped. There had been enough grief and guilt. She had no wish to add to Gregory's.

'It must have been far more difficult for Nat to guess the truth,' she went on, knowing that the subject of Nat was a safer one to raise. 'At first he could have had no idea of the implications of what he'd seen through his binoculars that fatal afternoon on the beach.'

'Or not seen,' put in Gregory. 'Wasn't that the phrase he actually used?'

'Exactly. I imagine he found Christabel was missing from her resting-place, the one she said she went back to when the turquoise bathing-dress was missing. You remember the poor fellow had had one of his typical ideas for inspiration – he would gaze at her from the Watchtower and by being at a great distance derive some further insight into Arkadina's character.'

'Typical indeed,' commented Gregory.

'The thing about Nat, as we all know, is that he had this incredible persistence. Not for him to desert a plan, and watch Blanche and Ollie, you and Filly, or even Julian and Cherry as Christabel suggested. I dare say he focused on her – or where she should have been resting under the cliffs – quite relentlessly, in his dotty way expecting to understand something more about Chekhov at the end of his binoculars. And once he appreciated that Christabel's statement didn't agree with what he had seen, he would have worked on the problem. He was also – dare I say it now he's dead? – the most frightful little opportunist. He too – like Old Nicola – might even have been contemplating some superior kind of blackmail. Some kind of deal along the lines of: "You help me with my career and I'll keep quiet about what I suspect." He was awfully smug, even gloating to me about his own "investigation" as he had the impudence to call it. I had the distinct impression even then that something nasty was afoot. But Christabel had no intention of leading her professional life for the foreseeable future in the power of Nat Fitzwilliam. Besides, how could she trust him? So she deliberately worked out a way of getting rid of him.'

'It figures,' was all Gregory said.

'At least Filly's death was an impulse,' Jemima finished. 'You must never blame yourself for it. It was a murderous impulse from an unbalanced person who lost control. A maniac.'

'A maniac!' cried Gregory. 'But a maniac who knew exactly how to cover her tracks, how to put on a superb act. Between us, we had written the act for her, hadn't we, cool repentance, and she played it to perfection. I never knew her act better in a part of mine, not even at the beginning, the time of *Lombardy Summer*, Christabel in her twenties, so fair and little, nothing to her but a pair of eyes and a pair of legs, I used to tell her, both of them beautiful. Oh God, what's the point . . . ?' It was his turn to stop. 'Those early memories are the worst of all. It's better all round to concentrate on the other side of the picture. All the damage she did, the wanton deaths she caused. She may have been mad at the end, but she was also a murderess three times over.'

Detective Inspector Matt Harwood of the Bridset Constabulary took very much the same line in his farewell interview with Jemima.

'We should have got her in the end,' he pronounced firmly. 'We always do, you know. Well, nearly always. We never give up. She wanted to be safe, you say, but she would never have been safe from us. The case would never have been closed.'

From her experience of the police, Jemima thought that was true. Nobody in the end, not even Julian Cartwright, could have saved Christabel from that thorough remorseless process of police investigation. But by then Christabel herself would surely have been dead – dead by her own hand. She would not have waited for the net of the law to close and tangle her, as the fisherman's netting on *The Seagull* set had tangled the unfortunate stagehands trying to dismantle it.

'But I could have saved her!' Jemima exclaimed. 'If only I'd trusted my instinct earlier. I knew she was a terrified woman – she nearly confided in me once, and that was long before she'd killed anyone; I realize now she was simply contemplating suicide, trying to fight down the urge. Then, as she said herself at our second lunch: "It's too late now." She'd already killed once, knew she might have to kill again. It's an awful thing to confess, Matt – but I too was put off by the apparently brazen manner of her return. The gracious hostess presiding at Lark Manor, the unhappily silent daughters, the wronged husband – it all stuck in my gullet rather. And by the time I'd worked it out correctly, trusting my instinct at last, seen that matters were exactly the other way round, well, it *was* too late, wasn't it? That ghastly night at the theatre. It was too late to save her from herself. If only—'

'Suicides,' interrupted Matt Harwood in his comforting voice. 'They'll always do it in the end, you know. If they really intend to. And we must believe that the lady in question did so intend.'

'Yes, but in that frightful way, Matt! Shooting herself with a pistol in her dressing-room, in front of her own husband's eyes.'

'Ah, but Jemima, she was an actress, wasn't she?' It was not clear whether the Detective Inspector meant by this to explain Christabel's presence in a theatrical dressing-room, or the dramatic manner of her self-inflicted death. In either case, thought Jemima, it was not an inappropriate epitaph for Christabel Herrick.

She could leave it to Detective Inspector Harwood and the Bridset police to clear up the intricacies of procedure in the wake of Christabel's death: the dropping of charges against Jim Blagge was one priority. It was probably not much satisfaction to Jim Blagge to have his story about the mysterious man in the shadows beside the Watchtower Theatre at last believed, since the police had treated it so cavalierly in the first place. But at least he could point out certain details which explained Christabel's 'Method' as well as confirming her 'Opportunity'.

The 'man' for example had been wearing a hat and some kind of jacket – hence Mr Blagge's subconscious assumption of the male gender in his reference to the glimpsed figure. The 'man' – Christabel in disguise. It was Jemima who pointed out to the police that Christabel would not have had to look very far for a rudimentary form of masculine disguise that hot night in the suite at the Royal Stag hotel. The memory of Blanche, faintly ridiculous in her man's clothes, was one of those illuminating images which had come to her when she was recapitulating the whole tragic story to herself, on the night of Christabel's suicide. Jemima recalled to the police that Blanche had been wearing her Annie Hall outfit when she left Flora's Kitchen: Ketty confirmed that Blanche had left behind the hat and jacket when she went out to search for Ollie Summertown, ostensibly because she felt too hot, actually because she considered an unbuttoned shirt more seductive. Afterwards, Christabel did not even need to dispose of the garments – she could leave them in the suite and rely on Blanche to pick them up again.

Then there was the re-examination of the forensic evidence by the Home Office laboratories which would prove – to the police's official satisfaction – what Jemima had seized upon by instinct. According to Locard's exchange principle, traces of Blanche's checked jacket found on Nat Fitzwilliam's clothes, hitherto explained by the fact that Blanche had hugged him in the restaurant when she had presented the birthday cake, would now take on a more sinister light. The examination of the evidence relating to the death of Old Nicola had only just started by the time of Christabel's suicide: that too would be thoroughly analysed. Jemima Shore Investigator could set off for London while the Bridset police were still patiently at work.

'In any case,' added Matt Harwood, at the door of Jemima's Royal Stag sitting-room, 'would you really have wanted to save her? Save her to stand trial? She was a maniac, yes, I'll grant you that, quite a lot about that is coming out too, now – now when it's too late to do anything about the deceased persons – specialists' opinions in the past, when she was in London, before her return to Bridset. But she was a triple killer too, wasn't she? Guilty but insane if you like. But Broadmoor – how would she have stood for that? Christabel Herrick. A woman like that.'

It was an unexpected view for a policeman and Matt Harwood seemed to appreciate her surprise.

'I'm speaking quite unofficially, you realize,' he said with a wry twinkle. 'Now don't you go and tell my little brother Gary what I've just said, let alone Pompey of the Yard. Whatever would he think of us in Bridset if he thought we conducted our affairs along those kind of lines? Officially in Bridset, same as anywhere else, the law is the law and murderers must be apprehended and brought to trial and the police are there to do it.'

Jemima heard his heavy footsteps going down the corridor in the direction of the stairs – the service stairs. Either Detective Inspector Harwood was a discreet man and did not wish to add to Mrs Tennant's distress further by manifestations of police presence, or else he was a busy man, who simply wanted to go about his business as fast as possible in the most convenient way. She thought how Christabel must have twice slipped along that corridor, leaving the bedroom of her suite by its unused outer door, unused, but easily and quickly unbolted. She too had wanted to go about her business as fast as possible in the most convenient way – the business of murder.

One of the people who helped to piece together what had happened was Christabel Herrick's widower, Julian Cartwright. Jemima learnt the details of his statement and some of the other macabre circumstances of the last few months from Gregory Rowan: Julian Cartwright had not wished to say goodbye to Jemima Shore. Secluded at Lark Manor with his daughters, supported by Ketty and the Blagges, Julian Cartwright presented the same face of dignified silence to the world as he had done when Christabel eloped with Barry Blagge.

Gregory Rowan told Jemima of Christabel's last note to Julian – three words only: *Darling, forgive me.* 'He showed it to me afterwards: it was on her special writing-paper, that very pale azure paper she loved, in her huge sprawling handwriting, blue ink too. Even when the police had finished with it, it still smelt of her special scent, lily of the valley . . .'

It was the discovery of this note lying in his study, with the pistol gone from its drawer, which had sent Julian on his last frantic expedition to rescue Christabel. She must have left it some time during the afternoon, when the family returned to Lark from the Royal Stag, Christabel ostensibly needing to take refuge from the loud confusion of the police *mêlée* at the hotel; she must have descended from her darkened bedroom with its thick white curtains blotting out the view of the sea, the sea where Christabel had drowned Filly Lennox not so long ago. Christabel was cunning: Christabel remembered where Julian kept the key to his private drawer. Christabel was also mad and left behind one last plea for her husband's forgiveness.

If Julian had not taken the girls over to see Gregory, so that there should be no sudden noise in the house while Christabel rested, he might have found the note earlier. And then he might have been in time to stop Christabel ... stop Christabel putting the pistol to her head just as he entered the dressing-room ... one last translucent unblinking sea-blue regard and then one lethal shot which instantly destroyed both Christabel and all the beauty she had once had in her husband's eyes.

Jemima asked Gregory: 'Will he ever recover, *can* he ever recover?'

'Wasn't what he'd already gone through almost worse? Because it was perpetual secret fearful anticipation. The unacknowledged dread of her suicide, or at least that she would do herself some injury. There was some odd incident with her garden scissors at Easter, just after she first came back. We don't quite know what happened. Maybe she tried to stab herself and drew back. She was in two minds – literally, I suppose – up till the very end. One afternoon, I'd come over to Lark and suddenly heard her scream. Julian heard it too and came rushing in from the courtyard garden. He thinks she may have planned to take an overdose then, she'd been rummaging in the various bathroom drawers upstairs, thinking she was alone, and at the last minute somebody disturbed her. Ketty. Pussy-footing about with no shoes on – and seething with jealous resentment – because Julian had said there was to be no noise in the house while Christabel was resting.'

'But the murders?' cried Jemima. 'Did he have no inkling that Christabel was responsible – because if so ...' She left the sentence ominously trailing.

Gregory considered. 'Filly – no, definitely not. True, it was Christabel who originally suggested the picnic, the picnic where she fully intended to shine with all her old sparkle, captivate everyone left right and centre, only to find herself upstaged by Filly – but then Filly's death was not premeditated, and afterwards, in the light of the tragedy, everyone forgot who had proposed going to the beach *en masse*. It was Christabel too who suggested going back to the Royal Stag to continue Blanche's birthday celebrations upstairs – "Mrs Tennant will do anything for me, darling" – I remember it so clearly, Julian's objections, Christabel overruling them. Now *that* was premeditated.

'So was her "rest",' he went on. 'To give herself the opportunity she needed to get to the theatre and do in the wretched Nat; just as she originally asked for her shawl to get the key out of him, make sure it would be available for her. She was lucky there, of course – she could hardly have known that Mr Blagge would return to the theatre and divert all suspicion to himself; as it was, she narrowly missed running into him.'

'The man in the shadows,' quoted Jemima. 'The one in whose existence the police declined to believe.' In her mind's eye she saw Christabel that night, Christabel deftly picking up Blanche's discarded jacket and hat, maybe even suggesting herself with a casual word that Blanche would look prettier without them for Christabel was always commenting on Blanche's clothes. Christabel the professional disguising herself swiftly and effectively – if not from the prying eyes of that other professional Old Nicola. Christabel watching Nat leave the theatre by the front door for his breath of air. Christabel deftly picking up the key of the Stage Door deposited for the second time by Mr Blagge, and after the murder throwing it far away or perhaps burying it in the woods, as she buried the responsibility for what she had done. Christabel still dressed in Blanche's checked jacket and Annie Hall hat pulled down over the mauve scarf which masked her fair hair; Christabel melting back into the shrubberies and trees round the Watchtower; Christabel who had just ... but this time Jemima did not share her thoughts with Gregory.

'And the second night in the Royal Stag,' pursued Gregory, 'the night she needed to spend there to shut up Old Nicola once and for all – that was premeditated too. Even so, the plan might have gone wrong if she'd had to share a bedroom with Julian. But then – she knew her Julian. He was a gentleman. He would sleep in the sitting-room on a sofa, wouldn't he, rather than disturb Christabel's precious rest on the eve of a First Night. She knew where Mrs Tennant kept the pass-keys; in fact she knew a great deal about the Royal Stag. In the old days, she and I—' Gregory coughed. 'Well, we needn't go into that now. Suffice it to say that she knew where Old Nicola was sleeping. And that everything was always easy for Christabel where Julian was concerned. She had only to ask and he granted it for her.' For the first time Gregory sounded more angry than distraught.

'So in answer to your question,' he continued, 'no, Julian had no real inkling of what Christabel had done. Julian was a man with an obsession, and his obsession was Christabel. He could see that she might destroy herself but he could not see anything or anyone beyond that.'

'So he won't recover. He can't.'

'My dear Jemima Shore Investigator!' Gregory had picked up a series of flat stones and was skidding them enthusiastically across the surface of the sea. But now the tide was going out quite rapidly across the flat sands. There was no danger today of a sudden wave engulfing Gregory's tennis shoes or Jemima's red sandals whose high heels were already slightly scuffed by the Larmouth pebbles. 'My dear Jemima, how little you know about the nature of obsession. Maybe there should be an investigative programme on the subject. You might find it interesting – 'Obsession and After' – how's that for a title?'

'Compulsive viewing.'

'No, Julian will recover,' Gregory went on as if she had not spoken. 'First Christabel had to come back, then she had to be gone for good, both things being essential to his recovery. Perhaps he'll even marry Ketty one day. Stranger things have happened. Life will be easier for him that way. He's had his great love, hasn't he? He'll settle for a comfortable life and Ketty and the Blagges between them will make him very comfortable indeed.'

'And his daughters too?'

'Ah, not so. Julian will be even more comfortable because his daughters won't be anywhere near Lark. Rina's going to try for Oxbridge in the autumn, which she should have done in the first place, and – wait for it – Blanche is going to Central School!'

'Blanche – an actress!' Jemima was amazed. 'I don't believe it. Think of her disastrous audition as Nina—'

'Ah, but Christabel was alive then.' Gregory could now speak her name quite calmly. 'Christabel who was determined her daughters should not rival her by following her onto the stage. Blanche always messed up anything to do with her mother hence *The Seagull* fiasco but when Ketty and I visited her at school, she did jolly well – so long as her mother wasn't in the audience. That's why Ketty tried to get her the part of Nina secretly, without her mother knowing. No, the Cartwright girls are going to be perfectly all right.

Major Cartwright was also going to be perfectly all right. For it turned out that he had had the brilliant foresight to insure the Larminster Festival specifically against the collapse, illness, breakdown or any other form of non-appearance of its star, Christabel Herrick, leading to cancellation of the Festival. No one could deny that Christabel's death constituted one form of non-appearance and it was equally undeniable that the entire Larminster Festival had had to be cancelled following the tragic events of the First Night. At least the Festival would not be showing a financial loss.

'May actually make more money. May be better off than if we'd sold all the seats,' the Major told Jemima with gruff satisfaction. 'Confounded Festival generally runs at a loss. Been spared altogether this time.' It was clear that the Major felt that he had been spared more than just financial loss – several long evenings at the theatre had also been averted, when it would have been necessary, in the Major's own heroic phrase, to grin and bear it.

Jemima dared to ask him why he had taken this prescient course. 'Unstable woman, my nephew's wife,' replied the Major. 'Drank too much. Eyes far too wide apart as well. Saw a good deal of that kind of thing in the war.'

On the other hand, the Major had not exactly turned out to be the Substantial Older Man of Cherry's dreams. That is to say, on their parting, the Major had asked for Cherry's London telephone number: but he seemed to have in mind the sort of gastronomic forays which had so much enlivened Cherry's Bridset life (as well as threatening her nubile figure with dangerous new proportions) rather than installing her as the châtelaine of Larksgrange.

'Used to know a little woman just like you in the Blitz,' he told Cherry in what for him passed for a sentimental speech. 'Like to tell you about her one day. What do you think of this place near the old Berkeley Hotel – Langan's Brasserie?'

'It's very trendy,' answered Cherry cautiously.

'Oh I know that, damn it,' the Major sounded impatient. 'Have to take the rough with the smooth. But is the food any good?'

As Gregory stood beside Jemima on the beach, where the tide had now slithered out so far that he could no longer throw stones across the sea, he too, like the Major, brought up the subject of the future.

'Maybe I'll come up to London more often. Lark is over for me. I have to find another hermitage – perhaps I'll find a hermitage convenient for the capital if such a thing exists. A commuter's hermitage. I might ask you out to dinner, Jemima Shore Investigator. Would you accept?'

Jemima thought of their conversation in Gregory's cottage and gave her famous smile, the lovely wide deliberate one which made people of both sexes think she was a sweet person and fall in love with her on television. 'I warn you,' she said. 'Vulnerable I may be, but emotionally insecure I am not. Not in the slightest. And I've no intention of starting now.'

'Oh don't apologize,' Gregory gave a grand wave of the hand. 'I was thinking of changing my type anyway. Keeping up with the times. Isn't it supposed to be good for one's art? You would know about that sort of thing.'

He took her hand and found she was clutching a sea-shell. She had found it in the pocket of her red jacket. It was the souvenir cockleshell which Cherry had presented to her that first Sunday morning by the sea.

Gregory bent and kissed the hand which held the shell.

'Would you accept?' he repeated. 'I might ask you to more than that. Do you like France?'

'Pre-revolutionary Paris?' enquired Jemima. She was still smiling but by now it was the unforced smile familiar to her friends.

'Yes, if you like. Other things might follow. We could discuss that.'

'Paris anyway,' said Jemima Shore.

Oxford Blood

For Diana of the Barn ways
with love

'Noon strikes on England, noon on Oxford town.
Beauty she was statue cold – there's blood upon her gown...'

James Elroy Flecker

Contents

1

A Dying Woman

'It was kind of you to come at such short notice,' said Sister Imelda to Jemima Shore. 'We thank you for it.' She fixed her large pale blue eyes on Jemima in a long look in which no expression could be detected; nevertheless it was evident that some kind of judgement had been made. 'It won't be long now,' she added.

'Of course miracles can happen.' Sister Imelda gave a brief rather wintery smile as though acknowledging that the words, serious in her case, might be construed in others as some kind of jest. 'She might just live out the week. But in fact we don't expect her to last more than another forty-eight hours.'

'I'm not that busy—' Jemima Shore spoke deprecatingly. Afterwards she wondered if she had subconsciously expected Sister Imelda to waive aside her disclaimer. After all Jemima Shore was in most normal senses of the word extremely busy. For one thing she was in the midst of planning her next series of programmes and as usual Cy Fredericks, the ebullient Chairman of Megalith Television, was engaged in a campaign to infiltrate some of his own ideas at an early stage.

'So that they will grow up along with the series, my dear Jem. All of us in the melting-pot stage together. You know that I wouldn't dream of disturbing matters later on.'

Keeping Cy's ideas, and Cy himself for that matter, out of what he chose to call the melting-pot stage (not a phrase she would have applied to it herself) of her new series, was clearly absolutely imperative. To defeat Cy demanded a good deal of time and energy. But the alternative, Cy's victory, was undoubtedly worse. Particularly in view of the fact that Cy wanted Jemima to follow up her highly successful series about the elderly and poor with a probe into the lives of the youthful and rich, while

Jemima wanted to investigate the meaning of middle age. There was quite a difference.

To make matters worse, Jemima's nubile PA – Flowering Cherry, as she was known, the toast of Megalithic House – was in the throes of an unhappy love affair with an older man whose wife approved but whose analyst frowned upon the alliance. While this imbroglio could not be said to impair Cherry's professional efficiency (nor for that matter, Jemima noted, her appetite) it did mean that tears tended to drip over the typewriter, the engagement book and even the matutinal box of Danish pastries with which Cherry was wont to prop up her strength. Weeping Cherry would now be a more appropriate nickname, thought Jemima, torn between affection and irritation. What Cherry needed was distraction; she made a mental note to check the marital (and psychological) status of the men involved in her new series with special reference to Cherry's needs.

On the other hand Jemima Shore Investigator, as she was known through the wide success of her eponymous television series, was in no need of further distraction herself. The last programme of her recently concluded series had been titled *How Does the Day End?* It had culminated in a furious discussion about euthanasia. Jemima Shore (and Weeping Cherry) were still dealing with the correspondence arising out of that one – to say nothing of the prolonged stir in the media. So what with programmes from the past and programmes for the future, it was fair to say that Jemima Shore Investigator was in every sense of the word extremely busy.

While Jemima Shore certainly did not expect Sister Imelda to appreciate the whole of this, she had perhaps anticipated some anodyne remark from the nun in answer to her own self-deprecation; something along the lines that it was always the busiest people who managed to make time.

'I'm not all that busy—'

'No, perhaps not,' was what Sister Imelda actually said, quite briskly. 'Perhaps you are not really busy at all compared to Nurse Elsie, because she is busy dying. And we are trying to help her die in peace.'

'You're quite right,' responded Jemima, feeling ashamed of her original impulse and speaking suddenly in a much warmer tone. 'It is much more important what is happening to her. And anything I can do to give her peace of mind—'

'Peace of mind. Ah Miss Shore, that can only be given by God.' Another gleam of frost from Sister Imelda. The long starched veil she wore was set back upon hair which was visibly white. Her complexion however was quite rosy, set off by the watchful blue eyes which were the dominant feature of her face.

Sister Imelda was the Matron of Pieta House, a Catholic Hospice for the Dying. She was, Jemima knew, a professed Catholic nun as well as a nurse. It was difficult to know whether her clothes corresponded to a nun's habit as modified by the decrees of Vatican Council II, or an actual nurse's uniform. Sister Imelda wore an unfashionably long grey skirt, which left several inches of severe grey stocking visible, ending in heavy grey shoes with straps across the instep. The long stiff white veil gave the air of a nun, that and the black rosary at Sister Imelda's belt, jostling almost carelessly with her keys. But her starched white apron, decorated with the traditional nurse's safety pins and little watch pinned on the broad smooth unindented breast, belonged entirely to a hospital matron. A large flat silver brooch with some engraving on it was pinned centrally on her veil; Jemima expected it to be a badge of office. Actually the engraving, rather badly done, was of Michelangelo's statue of the Pieta.

In spite of all this Jemima, who had attended a convent school in youth and was in principle fond of nuns, decided to regard Sister Imelda as a nurse. She was not particularly fond of hospitals and unlike nuns counted no nurses among her friends.

'You appreciate that Nurse Elsie asked for you after she saw one of your programmes on television. You referred to the question of peace of mind for the dying then of course.'

'I hope that didn't matter. It is rather a loose phrase.' Jemima gave her famous sweet smile, the one that made people watching her on television think what a charming person she must be in private.

'Oh, on television, Miss Shore, I've definitely heard worse.' Sister Imelda smiled in her turn. She had very large unnaturally clean-looking white teeth. Perhaps they were false – Jemima remembered from her own convent days that nuns' teeth were always ill-fitting either out of economy or, as was believed among the girls at the time, as a form of penance; but Sister Imelda did not give the impression of one who would easily tolerate inefficiency either in false teeth or anything else.

Sister Imelda stopped smiling suddenly. The teeth vanished from view. There was a very slight pause or even perhaps a hesitation. But when Sister Imelda spoke again she was even brisker than before.

'And then of course there is the question of absolution. You might help her with that too—'

'*Absolution?*' In her capacity as a leading television investigative reporter Jemima had fielded some strange requests from the public in her time. But to provide absolution for a dying woman in a Catholic hospice was certainly the oddest she had yet encountered. 'Surely a priest would be more suitable?'

'Oh please, Miss Shore.' Sister Imelda raised one hand. Like her teeth, her hands were almost unnaturally clean and white: where were the traditional red signs of washing and scrubbing, common to both nun and nurse? Sister Imelda's hands resembled those of a top-class surgeon, not least because they were notably big hands for a woman. 'Nurse Elsie has of course made a full confession. We live next to the Priory here, you know. At any hour of the day or night the Fathers come if they are needed; it's part of what the Hospice is able to offer.' Sister Imelda gave another of her tiny significant pauses. 'But – absolution is another matter. It's not automatic. I should explain—'

Jemima wondered whether she herself should explain something to Sister Imelda. Having been educated at a Catholic convent (although not herself a Catholic) she was perfectly well aware of the rules governing Catholic confession. Absolution – forgiveness for past sins given by the priest, standing in for God as it were – did not necessarily follow confession; but in all the years when Jemima, half envious, half scornful, wholly in love, had listened to her friends' confidences on the subject, she had never heard of anyone being refused it. Penances could and did vary, of course, in proportion to sins declared. 'The five Sorrowful Mysteries of the Rosary! Rosabelle, whatever have you been up to?' That had been a typical half-envious, half-gleeful comment.

But to refuse absolution to a dying woman?

'It can't be long now.' By all the rules of the Church, Jemima failed to see how Nurse Elsie Connolly, dying slowly and inexorably here in Pieta House, could possibly have been denied the ultimate forgiveness by a Catholic priest. It made no sense. What crime could poor old Nurse Elsie have committed? No, wait – *anyone* could commit a crime, as experience had certainly taught Jemima Shore. But if Nurse Elsie had committed some sort of fairly serious crime, why on earth had she not confessed it before? Undoubtedly the good Fathers from the Priory came round regularly to hear confessions, quite apart from the sudden flurry when one of the many failing inhabitants of Pieta House was judged to be on the very brink of death. As Sister Imelda had pointed out, that was one of the important services provided by the Hospice.

Jemima decided that if she was to be of any help in the situation – which was after all why she had postponed an important planning meeting where she intended to worst Cy Fredericks once and for all – she had better come clean with Sister Imelda. Swiftly she explained the facts about her background.

The effect was remarkable. Sister Imelda did not exactly warm to Jemima – it was doubtful from her stance whether she knew how to do so, except perhaps towards the very sick. But she did drop altogether that air of cool superiority which had hitherto distinguished most of her remarks.

Sister Imelda's tiny bare office was furnished solely by a Crucifix, a vast but out-of-date calendar featuring the Pope, and, rather surprisingly, a crudely coloured picture of the Princess of Wales holding her first baby which at first glance Jemima had taken for the Madonna with her child.

Leaning across the ugly wooden desk Sister Imelda spoke urgently to Jemima:

'Oh, thanks be to God' – manifestly she meant it – 'a Catholic.'

'I'm not.' cried Jemima.

'No, no, I realize that. A Catholic education, I was going to say. You understand the problem. You'll help us. I know you will. It's all Father Thomas. A saint you know. A dear good man as well. But ever since he came back from Biafra – such terrible things endured and even worse witnessed. No sense, you know. No sense about this world at any rate.'

Jemima Shore had an inkling that where Sister Imelda was concerned this was the ultimate criticism; there was a clear implication too that Father Thomas might well turn out to have no sense about the next world as well. But Jemima made no comment. As a practised interviewer, she recognized the need for silence, an irresistibly interrogative silence.

'Restitution, yes.' Sister Imelda's confidences marched on. 'Of course that is one of the conditions of confession. To make restitution if one can. Without that, there can in theory be no absolution. The thief for example must give back his ill-gotten gains before he can be absolved. If he is still able to do so. That is the teaching of the Church. But in this case – even supposing it's all true, which I very much doubt – that Father Thomas should land us in this! So many things at stake. The Hospice itself. Our foundation – when you think who's involved.' Sister Imelda shot a quick nervous look at the picture of the Princess of Wales, giving Jemima the impression once again, if only fleetingly, that this was some kind of contemporary ikon. Then she visibly reasserted control.

'You'll help us, Miss Shore, I know you will. Help us – and of course,' she added in a less hurried voice which was nevertheless not quite calm, 'help Nurse Elsie.'

Sister Imelda rose. The smiling image of the Princess fluttered as she did so, in a breeze caused by her starched white veil, her starched long white apron and even perhaps the flap of her long grey skirts. The image of the Pope was made of heavier material and remained static.

'Sister Imelda, could you amplify—' Jemima rose too. But Sister Imelda was by now thoroughly restored to tranquillity, which also meant authority.

'No, Miss Shore, I think it is only fair to let Nurse Elsie tell her own story. I apologize if I have seemed over-emotional.' Another glance towards the Princess of Wales, but this time the expression was austere, even condemnatory. 'This has been a trying time for the Hospice. But I expect you are used to dealing with that kind of thing on television. Please follow me, Miss Shore.'

The first thing which struck Jemima Shore about Nurse Elsie Connolly was the charm, even prettiness, of her appearance. She had expected a skeleton of a woman. Nurse Elsie, with a smooth skin and two long plaits

161

of hair lying down on either side of her pink nightdress, certainly looked an invalid – she was extraordinarily pale for one thing – but she resembled the kind of invalid described in a Victorian novel who may linger for years of interesting if bed-ridden life.

Nurse Elsie was in fact sixty. Jemima learnt this from her very first remark, as though in answer to her unspoken question.

'My sixtieth birthday! Jemima Shore comes to visit me. Now that's a real present.' The words, like Nurse Elsie's appearance, were quite girlish. But the voice itself was faint and Jemima perceived that immediately after speaking Nurse Elsie gave a kind of gasp as though the effort itself had nearly extinguished her. Jemima wondered what kind of pain-killers she was being given. If faint, she sounded quite lucid.

Jemima produced the small arrangement of strongly perfumed freesias which she had carefully commissioned beforehand at her favourite flower-shop in Notting Hill Gate. A perfectionist where flowers were concerned, Jemima knew that nothing annoyed busy nurses more than having to cope with a vast bouquet of ill-assorted blooms immured within crackling cellophane, demanding the instant production of a vase.

Nurse Elsie smiled with obvious delight. It was almost as though she had recognized the perfection of the choice as well as appreciating the nosegay – and perhaps as an ex-nurse herself she had.

'Like you.' Her voice was even fainter. 'So pretty.' Nurse Elsie put out her hand and laid it on Jemima's wrist. It was a claw.

Memento mori, thought Jemima. The skeleton was not after all so far below this poor woman's skin; and above the perfume of freesias, mingling with the obvious hygienic smells of the sick-room, she detected for the first time some other smell, more lingering, more distressing.

Yet the rest of the scene was pretty, charming, like Nurse Elsie herself in her pink nightdress, almost cloyingly so. There were pink blankets, pale pink flowered curtains – a pattern of hollyhocks and lupins – pale green walls. The screens which stood around a bed at the far corner of the room were made of the same ruched material.

There were about six other people present in the ward, all lying down. One woman – Jemima imagined she was a woman – with a broad swollen face and very short black hair, raised her hand. Perhaps she was waving. On the off chance, Jemima waved back. The hand sank and a look of puzzlement crossed the broad face.

A large crucifix hung above the door and on the opposite wall there was a reproduction of Fra Angelico's St Francis feeding the birds. A coloured picture showed Pope John Paul II walking with the Queen in the corridor of Buckingham Palace; both parties faced the camera with smiles of almost aggressively healthy confidence in contrast to the sick women below. Some tasteful flowers – a few carnations and a great deal of greenery chosen almost too obviously to harmonize with the colour scheme of the room – stood in a large dull white case on a plinth beneath the crucifixion. Little bouquets and vases flanked most of the beds, and most of the women boasted at least two photographs on their bedside tables.

In spite of this, Jemima was quite unprepared for Nurse Elsie's own array. It might have been a shrine, the resting-place of a saint, there were so many flowers. Some of them were certainly dead, others like Nurse Elsie herself decomposing. But some were like Jemima's own little nosegay, evidently fresh.

The photographs in frames which ranged from plain perspex to silver – quite a few of those – were all of children, very young children, often babies.

The claw scratched at her palm.

Nurse Elsie was smiling at her again.

'My babies,' she said.

'*Your* babies—'

'My babies. All of them. I was a midwife, you know. Didn't they tell you?'

'No, I didn't realize. A nurse was all they said.'

'A midwife. A state registered midwife. *Later* a nurse. The first month. I used to look after my ladies for the first month. Longer sometimes. Eleven weeks. Those were twins.'

Nurse Elsie moved her eyes in the direction of one particular photograph. It was one of those with a silver frame.

'The Fergus twins. You've read about them I expect.' Nurse Elsie gave another gasp and closed her eyes. She panted heavily, frighteningly. Jemima wondered if she should ring for help as Sister Imelda had told her she might do in case of need.

Nurse Elsie's lips moved. She was saying something else. 'Nor – Nor – Nor—' What was it she was trying to get out?

'Naughty,' she managed at last. Her voice strengthened a little. 'Naughty. Always in the papers. Little devils. Very *naughty*.' Nurse Elsie's eyes closed and there was silence. The dark woman with the broad face waved again and Jemima waved back.

The hold of the claw strengthened.

'Naughty. That's what I wanted to tell you. I've been very naughty, no, *wicked*. I want to put it all right. You've got to help me, Jemima Shore. Just as he says.'

'He?' But Jemima knew the answer.

'Father Thomas. He says I've got to put it all right before I die.'

'Never mind about Father Thomas,' said Jemima gently. 'You can tell me anything you like, you know. I won't tell anyone else,' she added.

Something like a spasm crossed Nurse Elsie's face.

'No, tell, tell,' she whispered urgently. 'You've got to tell everyone. Tell a lawyer, anyway. That's what Father Thomas said. You must get me a lawyer. The wrong has got to be put right. Otherwise I shan't get absolution. I shan't die in peace.'

'Tell me then,' said Jemima, still as gently and quietly as she could.

'And you'll bring me a lawyer?'

'If that's what you really want.'

'A lawyer tomorrow—'

'Well, I'll do my best. The day after, maybe.' Jemima spoke with the guilty knowledge that it would certainly not be tomorrow, a day already cluttered with a host of highly important meetings and leaving no time for amassing stray lawyers, let alone paying another visit to the Hospice herself.

'It's got to be tomorrow. I'm not going to last very long. I know that. I wouldn't let them give me my medicine this afternoon so I could be clear. It won't be long now.'

Nurse Elsie closed her eyes once more. But this time there was no silence. On the contrary she began to speak aloud in a rapid, low but perfectly lucid voice. It was as though she had long rehearsed in her own mind what she had to say.

'When the little baby was born dead,' began Nurse Elsie, 'the boy, the boy they'd always wanted, I thought my heart would break, my heart as well as theirs. She went into labour early, they couldn't find the doctor. But they got hold of me; I was on another case in London not far away. I did everything but the baby died. I couldn't tell her. I left it to him. And it was he who said to me, "Nurse Elsie, we have to get her a baby, another baby. I feel so guilty. A proper live healthy baby. Nurse Elsie, would you help us?"'

'And that's when it all began. The wickedness.'

2

Bedside Conference

Jemima's next discussion on the subject of Nurse Elsie also centred round a bedside. Only in this case the bed was Jemima's own and it was Jemima herself who was in the bed, or rather lying across it. Unlike Nurse Elsie however, Jemima was not wearing a primly pretty Victorian nightdress but an exotic towelling-robe, honey-coloured like her hair, and beneath that nothing at all. And unlike the ward at Pieta House with its long row of bed-ridden figures, Jemima's bedroom contained only one other occupant.

This was a lawyer called Cass Brinsley. While Jemima lay on the bed in her robe slowly stroking Midnight, her sleek black cat (who responded with a complacent raucous purr), Cass Brinsley sat fully dressed in an armchair beside the bed. One could also say that he was formally as well as fully dressed, since he wore a black jacket, striped dark trousers, a stiff white collar with a spotless white shirt, and a black silk tie with delicate white spots on it. Neither party however, the honey-coloured woman on the bed or the formally dressed man in the armchair, seemed to find anything strange about the contrast.

'What you are saying, darling, is that there was a switch in fact. A deliberate fraud was perpetrated.' Jemima noticed with amusement that where professional matters were concerned, Cass Brinsley quickly reverted to the language of the law courts. The contrast between Caspar Brinsley, the precise almost over-deliberate barrister, and Cass, the astonishingly uninhibited lover, never ceased to intrigue her. She eyed his formal clothing so clearly destined for a day in Chambers speculatively and wondered just for a moment what it would be like . . . just once . . . a seduction . . .

Quickly and rather guiltily Jemima Shore reminded herself that Cass Brinsley, seducible under these circumstances or not (probably not), was also not the only one with a busy schedule. Jemima returned with determination to the topic under discussion. At the same time, Midnight, who seemed jealously to have sensed a distraction in her thoughts, gave a mew and Jemima stroked his back too with renewed concentration.

'I'm not saying there was a switch, Cass. She's saying it. Nurse Elsie. By chance the other mother she was looking after was going to give the baby for adoption anyway. I got the impression she was unmarried – a tragic case, Nurse Elsie called it. Anyway it was a cloak-and-dagger delivery. Something that wouldn't happen in these days of easy abortion to say nothing of the Pill. The other baby was also a boy. So she switched babies. She wants me to bring along a lawyer – that's the word she uses by the way, I think it's probably the word used by the batty priest Father Thomas. I suppose in fact it would have to be a solicitor?'

Cass nodded.

'A commissioner of oaths is what you would need. She'd have to make a deposition and it would have to be sworn. A solicitor can act as a commissioner of oaths – so a solicitor would do.'

'And then? Where would I go from there?'

'And then, my darling, assuming what you tell me about her health is correct, you would be left with a sworn deposition concerning events which took place over twenty years ago, made by a retired midwife, who was dying of cancer at the time. A woman in great pain and certainly under the influence of a great many drugs, if not literally sedated at the time she spoke to you. Added to which she'll almost certainly die on you the moment the deposition is made, if she lasts that long.

'Jemima,' continued Cass in a tender voice, reaching forward and taking her hand, 'stop stroking the insufferably demanding Midnight and listen to me: this is really not one for you. What exactly do you hope to achieve? Especially when you think of the people involved.'

'That's exactly what Sister Imelda said – the Matron of the Hospice – the starchy one. "Think of the people involved."' Jemima scratched Midnight's furry throat as the cat stretched luxuriously. Cass grabbed her hand again and the cat leapt suddenly and angrily off the bed.

'Darling Jemima, answer the question. What do you hope to achieve? I know you love your cat more than you love me. That has been established.' Cass's tone was the sweetly reasonable one that Jemima assumed he used in court for a difficult witness.

'Peace of mind for Nurse Elsie, I suppose,' Jemima spoke rather doubtfully.

'"Only God can give peace of mind,"' quoted Cass. 'Sister Imelda's line. I rather like it. I shall try it on my clients. Certainly justice being done doesn't always give it.'

'You're right to question my motives, Cass,' went on Jemima with still more uncertainty. 'I certainly don't want to cause great misery to a whole lot of people on account of something private they once did years ago. Jemima the Avenger – absolutely not. If I'm to be honest – it's curiosity as much as anything else. Can her story be true?'

'Jemima Shore Investigator!' pronounced Cass. 'I knew it. Your dreadful inquisitiveness.' He looked at her and thought how beautiful she always looked after making love; how beautiful in her loosely tied robe, with her famous hair, so much admired on television, now in total disarray and no make-up on her face. What Jemima Shore did not know about the cool and reserved Cass Brinsley was that he sometimes surreptitiously turned on television at night, in the middle of working on a brief, in order to watch Jemima. The sight of the dazzling poised intelligent image on the screen combined with the memories of the evenings – nights – they had spent together filled him with a mixture of possessive jealousy and frustrated lust.

Cass judged it wise to keep these feelings a secret from Jemima. Possessiveness in any form he knew to be her bane – as indeed in theory and in practice up to the present time it had been his too.

Two uncommitted people.

Besides, he had a foolish feeling that a great deal of the British nation also felt this way about Jemima Shore's image on television – without the excuse of knowing her, as it were, in the flesh.

That was another point. Cass hated to be one of a crowd. After one of these bouts of secret jealousy he generally solved the problem of the lust if not the jealousy by taking out any one of a number of attractive available girls (Cass disliked pursuing women) and vanishing temporarily from the list of Jemima's admirers. He never knew if she minded – his absences, that is.

Cass, like Jemima, withdrew his attention rather guiltily from these secret thoughts to the matter in hand.

'Tell me, darling, do you believe her story?' It was the witness box again.

'At first sight it's incredible, isn't it? People don't do such things, as Judge Brack said of poor old Hedda G. Listen to what Nurse Elsie suggests happened. That you-know-who, a highly responsible man – he's held every conceivable post in the government from Defence Secretary to the Environment – got this midwife to procure a live baby, a son, in place of his own child that died. And then calmly went ahead and made the substitution, and has lived quite blithely with the situation ever since. As has his wife. And no one has ever suspected. It's incredible.'

'So you don't believe her,' said Cass, still in his judicial voice, putting the tips of his fingers together.

'Ah, I didn't say that. I haven't been absolutely idle, you know. For one thing I have looked the family up in the peerage – no, you're quite right, Megalith didn't run to such a thing but it does now, since Cherry was quite thrilled to go and purchase one at Hatchard's. It's quite cheered her up – given her all sorts of ideas about her love life.'

'Cherry flowers again?' Cass had heard about the untoward intervention of the analyst.

'Exactly. She's heavily into peers now by the way. Her daydreams have gone up several notches in the social register. It's convenient for her that so many of the peers are quite ancient: you know Cherry's perennial yearning for the Substantial Older Man. Even handier, Debrett gives their dates of birth. Also their residences. She's found one Duke of fifty-seven, that's Cherry's ideal age, who's been married four times and is currently divorced, with two residences in the South of France. Her dreams know no bounds. No children too. Where was I?'

'Another noble family. One child.'

'One child indeed. Where our noble family is concerned, there was an enormous amount at stake – purely in terms of title, if you like that sort of thing. The title has to go through the male line and the present Marquess has no brothers or sisters. His father and his uncle were both killed in the First World War, uncle very young and thus unmarried. After that you have to go way off to a remote cousin, third cousin, something like that. Brilliant Cherry, by now thoroughly over-excited, went to the British Library and checked on a Debrett of 1959, before this boy was born. Fortunately Debrett makes it easy for you by printing the name of the heir presumptive in capital letters. Otherwise even title-oriented Cherry might have had difficulty in tracking it down. So guess who the heir was in 1959?'

'The traditional New Zealand sheep farmer or Los Angeles taxi driver, who would suddenly have become the Marquess of St Ives?'

Jemima frowned. 'No, not a sheep farmer and not a taxi driver. Very much not. Lord St Ives' heir was – no, I won't even ask you to guess, because it's so incongruous. Andrew Iverstone!'

'Iverstone!'

'Yes, Iverstone. The family name is Iverstone. Lord St Ives' full name according to the industrious Cherry, is Ivo Charles Iverstone, Marquess of, etc.'

An unjudicial look of pure surprise crossed Cass' face.

'Andrew Iverstone: that fearful Fascist! I can see you might want to do him out of a title. To say nothing of his yet more dreadful wife. No, wait, that was a remark of pure prejudice, Jemima, forget it. The sheer dreadfulness of Andrew Iverstone is still absolutely no proof that Lord St Ives carried out a crime to rob him of his inheritance.'

All the same Cass thought of the austerely handsome face of the former Foreign Secretary, type-casting for the kind of elegant detached aristocrat beloved of old-style Hollywood movies, and contrasted it with the florid rabble-rousing image of Andrew Iverstone. On behalf of Lord St Ives, Cass Brinsley shuddered.

'Shall I go on?'

'Proceed, Jemima Shore Investigator. So – no children for the Marquess and Marchioness of St Ives – or rather none till this boy. St Ives must be going on seventy now. So he was fifty-odd when the child was born.'

'Correct. But there had been a child, three children in fact, two boys and a girl, all born much earlier, two listed as born and died on the same day, the first lived a little longer. Then this child. Lord St Ives was fifty at the time and more to the point Lady St Ives – she's in Debrett too, being the daughter of a lord, very convenient so I could look her up too – she was forty-six. It was definitely the last chance.'

'All this for a title? As it happens, I've always admired Lord St Ives – his stand over Africa for example. If you must have aristocrats, he's always seemed to me a good advertisement for them.'

'Nurse Elsie said it was all for her – for his wife. What she called the wickedness. I should tell you that. Very emphatic about it in so far as she had the strength to be emphatic about anything. He loved her, couldn't bear another tragedy. She's very much around, by the way, Lady St Ives. A good woman. Known to have visited the Hospice, and of course Nurse Elsie herself, quite recently.'

Cass whistled.

'So your old bird, inspired by her priest and aided by some friendly neighbourhood solicitor or whatever, provided by her favourite television star Jemima Shore, who just happens to have a tame lawyer handy—' he cocked a quizzical eyebrow at Jemima who with an innocent smile continued to stroke Midnight, returned and now sunk into some distant purrless paradise '—aided by all this, your old bird intends to bring fear and unhappiness into the lives of what is laughingly known as one of our great families. But is in fact a retired highly honourable and distinguished politician, and a lady in her sixties who according to your nurse never knew anything about it in the first place. All this to push the vast wealth and estates of the St Ives family, including historic Saffron Ivy, in the direction of that rabid racist Andrew Iverstone.'

'You're the lawyer, Cass. What *about* justice? Justice *and* peace of mind?' asked Jemima with a smile.

'I'm not a lawyer in this bedroom. Who is to say that in a sense justice hasn't been done ? After all if Lord and Lady St Ives had adopted a child – no, I'm wrong, titles can't go to adopted children. Nor entailed estates for that matter. I imagine Saffron Ivy is entailed, or in some kind of trust on the heir male. That Holbein! Andrew Iverstone to own that Holbein! I digress. What I'm trying to say is this: If Lord and Lady St Ives had been less grand, less wealthy, they could simply have adopted a baby like any other childless couple. And that is what they have, in effect, done. Twenty years ago. Leave it, Jemima darling, leave it and forget it.'

'I can't leave it. Forget it, yes. Leave it, no. You see, I promised. And it was my programme which started it.'

'*Your* programme? I thought the priest started it.'

'My programme. The one about peace of mind for the elderly and how they should be allowed to die in peace.'

Cass groaned. 'Oh my God, the ghastly power of television. You mean those few casual words of yours inspired an old nurse who had sat on a secret for twenty years, suddenly to up with it and spout it out to a priest in the confessional.'

'I mean just that,' said Jemima unhappily. 'The penultimate programme in the series was called *Peace of Mind.*'

'Peace of mind! What about the mother? What about the boy, for heaven's sake? We haven't even mentioned him. What's his name, for a start? We keep calling him the boy – but he's virtually grown up.'

'Saffron is his name, like the house. Lord Saffron, I think, or Viscount Saffron, that's the courtesy title of the heir. Nurse Elsie just refers to him as Saffron.'

'A very grand adoption. From bastard to viscount. And imagine a boy brought up to all of that – yes, I know I'm a member of the Labour Party but I've got humanitarian feelings – imagine such a one being suddenly told he's nobody. He must be quite grown-up.'

Cass Brinsley stood up and checked his watch.

'My God, look at the time. Jemima darling, you are irresistible. All the same, I absolutely must go.' Jemima smiled and rolled gracefully off the bed, abandoning Midnight so that she could throw her towelling arms around Cass.

'Ouch, no fluff. No honey-coloured fluff, if you don't mind. And not too many red-gold hairs either. As I was saying—' Cass picked carefully at his dark sleeve '—you are irresistible. And you are also in a hole, which happens to you but seldom. So what I will do for you is this. I will come down to the Hospice with you on Saturday. Can't possibly manage it till then. I won't take a statement or anything like that – I'm not a solicitor. But I will sort of spread my authority around, persuade that Matron of the foolishness of all this talk, about the law of slander – good point that. See the priest if necessary. It's your peace of mind I'm worried about, by the way, not Nurse Elsie's.'

'Angel – and to hell with the honey-coloured fluff.'

Jemima launched herself and Cass Brinsley ducked, retreating rapidly.

'Let them know we're coming,' he called, 'with any luck Nurse Elsie will be dead by Saturday and the whole problem will be solved.'

As it happened, Cass Brinsley was right as, in his legal way, he was right about so many things.

Nurse Elsie survived through Wednesday and Thursday; according to Sister Imelda – who spoke in a typically unemotional voice on the telephone – the prospect of Jemima's return with 'a legal adviser' had indeed brought about some kind of miracle. Nurse Elsie had rallied.

She was so much recovered that according to Sister Imelda she proposed to receive some visitors on Friday – old friends.

'But she's living for *your* visit,' Sister Imelda gave a dry cough. 'That's what she says, Miss Shore. You do of course realize that Nurse Elsie remains a dying woman, could in fact die at any time. These little rallies, in our experience, seldom last very long. However, we expect you and – Mr Brinsley, is it? – on Saturday as arranged. Goodbye, Miss Shore.'

Mr Brinsley and Miss Shore spent Friday night together at Jemima Shore's flat. It seemed convenient that they should set out for the Hospice together. On Saturday morning however, just as Jemima was pulling on the honey-coloured robe, the telephone rang. It was Sister Imelda.

The news she wanted to impart was that Nurse Elsie Connolly had died peacefully if unexpectedly on the previous afternoon. Peacefully, and only unexpectedly in the sense that Nurse Elsie had had a visitor sitting with her at the time.

'Distressing but hardly surprising: she was dead before Father Thomas could be fetched to give her the last rites.'

'A visitor?' Jemima knotted the robe around her and listened rather confusedly to the sound of her bath running in the next room, the bath in which she had intended to lie planning their whole course of action at the Hospice.

'The Marchioness of St Ives was sitting with Nurse Elsie at the time of her death,' replied Sister Imelda; Jemima wondered if it was pure imagination on her part that she heard an undercurrent of triumph in the Matron's voice.

'It was so very sweet of her to come all the way from Saffron Ivy when she heard that Nurse Elsie was asking for her. But then Lady St Ives is such a remarkable selfless person, as we have found here at the Hospice. And she was the very last one to be with her. Nurse Elsie must have been so pleased by that. Lady St Ives and Nurse Elsie were after all such *very* old friends. Another old friend also came, one of Nurse Elsie's ladies – as she used to call them. But Lady St Ives was the last.'

This time there was no mistaking her tone. Jemima stood by the telephone, still holding the receiver, and wondered if the Matron's normally impassive face was wearing the same expression of cool satisfaction.

'So you see, Miss Shore,' concluded Sister Imelda, 'Nurse Elsie did after all die in peace, just as you wished. You must be glad to know that.'

The Matron rang off. But for some time after the noise of the telephone had been reduced merely to a steady sound not unlike Midnight's raucous purr, Jemima remained standing with the white receiver in her hand.

3
Nothing Wrong with Money

By the end of an agreeable weekend, telephone mostly off the hook, Jemima Shore had come to agree with Cass Brinsley that Nurse Elsie Connolly's death was providential – and natural. Jemima's feeling of unease when Sister Imelda broke the news on the telephone that Saturday morning, she was now prepared to ascribe to her own over-heated imagination, inspired by the atmosphere of the Hospice. The death was providential because it freed Jemima of further responsibility towards the matter.

'Yes, I know you have this famous instinct, darling,' Cass said patiently. 'But unless you're suggesting that that grim Sister actually went and murdered the poor old nurse—'

'Hastened her death,' Jemima put in; but she already sounded doubtful. 'Nurse Elsie was dying anyway. No, no, I'm not exactly suggesting that.'

'Then was it the boy's mother, the gracious Marchioness of St Ives no less?'

'No, no, of course not.'

'Because according to the nurse's story, and that's all you have to go on, my love, Lady St Ives didn't know anything about the substitution in the first place. So she didn't even have a motive.'

'She could have realized something was wrong later,' Jemima countered. 'We've agreed that the boy himself must be about twenty now. Twenty years is a long time in which to bring up somebody else's child and suspect nothing. It depends a good deal on what the boy looks like, of course. I never got a chance to ask Nurse Elsie about any of the details. We all know what Lord St Ives looks like even if we do tend to see him in terms of Marc's cartoons, a series of long thin terribly aristocratic lines, that long straight nose and single narrow line for a mouth. But what about her? I have an image of a typical English lady of a certain type forever meeting her husband at airports with a brave smile.'

At which point Cass Brinsley said very firmly, 'Enough of this. I'm going to distract you forever with an enormous therapeutic draught of Buck's Fizz. I have in mind filling one of your numerous television awards to the brim: there must be a silver goblet amongst them.'

'Unfillable statuettes in the main, I fear.' All the same Jemima allowed herself to be distracted.

Under the circumstances it was hardly surprising that by Monday morning Jemima was in a very different frame of mind. She certainly did not expect to hear of the late Nurse Elsie Connolly again, nor of Sister Imelda of Pieta House, still less of the youthful heir Lord Saffron. Besides, Monday morning was to be the occasion of a full-dress confrontation with Cy Fredericks on the subject of their rival concerns – crabbed age, in the case of Jemima Shore, or at any rate the approach of same, and youth 'full of pleasance' in the case of Cy Fredericks. The nature of the new series had to be decided shortly, or at least the nature of the first programme.

It never did to have your mind in anyway distracted when confronting Cy, as Jemima knew to her cost; while the information, derived from Cy's secretary via Cherry, that Cy Fredericks was currently pursuing a gilded moppet called Tiggie, filled her with additional dread. Cy Fredericks' romantic attachments were closely monitored by those in the know at Megalithic House, since all too often they provided the vital clue to what otherwise seemed a totally irrational enthusiasm for a particular programme.

If only Cy would stick to Lady Manfred! thought Jemima as she wheeled her little white Mercedes sports car into the Megalithic car park. Cultured, music-loving, above all gracefully *middle-aged*, Lady Manfred demanded no more of Megalith than a generalized support of the opera, of which Jemima for one thoroughly approved. But an attachment for the notorious Tiggie Jones (Tiggie forsooth! could anyone with a name like Tiggie bode well for Megalith?), twenty-three-year-old Tiggie, the darling of the gossip columns according to Cherry, Tiggie of the long legs and roving eyes, according to the photographers, that was definitely bad news. It also helped to explain why Cy was being at once devious and obstinate in his determination to make a programme tentatively entitled – by him – 'Golden Lads and Girls'. (Had he, Jemima wondered, ever read the actual poem from which the quotation came? The conclusion might come as a surprise to him.)

Cy Fredericks' opening ploy at the meeting was also his valediction.

'You deserve a holiday, Jem, and this, *in effect*, is going to be it.' Jemima pondered inwardly on the potential menace contained in those two little words 'in effect' on the lips of the Chairman of Megalith.

Outwardly she merely smiled sweetly, that charming smile which made people watching television think what a nice warm human being she was.

'I'm afraid I don't find the idea of investigating a lot of poor-little-rich kids at university quite my notion of a holiday. It's now the eighteenth of January. How about that programme on the growth of feminism in the West Indies? An interesting subject and an interesting location. I could be ready to leave for preliminary discussions in a week or two. First stop Barbados.'

There was a short silence. Cy Fredericks was clearly remembering that he himself had just rented a luxurious villa on that very island and wondered whether Jemima was aware of that fact. (She was: his secretary had told Cherry, who had told Jemima.) Cy solved the problem in his usual galvanic fashion.

'Jem, my dear Jem,' he murmured, leaning across the vast desk and grasping, with some difficulty, her hand. 'We've been too much out of touch lately. We need to talk, really talk. Miss Lewis!' he suddenly shouted in a voice of great agitation, dropping the hand and gazing rather wildly round him. 'Miss Lewis! Are you there?'

There was an acquiescent noise from the outer office. Although Cy had in fact a perfectly efficient intercom, he never seemed to have the necessary leisure to master it.

'Miss Lewis! When am I next free for lunch?'

Miss Lewis, a neat young woman in a silk shirt, check skirt and well polished brown boots, entered hastily, bearing a leather diary which she deposited in front of her employer. Cy gazed at it for a moment with an expression of outraged disbelief and then, in silence, proceeded to score out a number of entries with great violence. Finally he looked up and beamed at Jemima.

'So! For you, Jemima, I drop everything. We shall have our heart to heart. Exchange of souls. Lunch on February the twenty-eighth.'

'I can't wait,' said Jemima.

Negotiating the white Mercedes once more out of the Megalith car park that afternoon, Jemima was wearily aware that the chances of her *not* spending a few cold winter weeks in and around Oxford University to say nothing of the other equally unpleasing (to Jemima Shore) haunts of the young and rich, were rapidly diminishing. To console herself, and while away the time in the heavy traffic she put on a tape of *Arabella* and waited for her favourite song beginning: 'Aber der Richtige . . .' 'The man who's right for me, if there is one for me in all this world'. But the thought of the right man coming along put her uncomfortably in mind of Cass Brinsley: did *he* think *she* was the right woman . . . Could anyone, even a lawyer, be quite so detached? It was to distract herself from these – essentially unprofitable – thoughts that Jemima jumped out of the car in a traffic block and bought an evening paper.

At the next lights she glanced down at the headlines, particularly glaring this evening, accompanied by a large photograph. The next moment she found herself staring, the car still in gear, her neck still craning down. It took some frantic hootings all round her to tell Jemima Shore that the lights had turned green and that the heavy crocodile of lorries, trucks and cars was supposed to be rattling forward once more up Holland Park Avenue.

The newspaper photograph showed a handsome young man, very young and very handsome: the flash bulb had perhaps exaggerated the dramatic effect of the wide eyes and high cheekbones, the thick hair, apparently black, a lock falling across the forehead. Even so the looks were sufficiently startling to make Jemima suppose for a moment she was gazing at the face of a pop star. And the rather wide mouth and well-formed lips confirmed the impression of a pop star to a generation brought up on the ultimate pop-star looks of Mick Jagger, although this young man was more distinguished, less roguish-looking than Jumping Jack Flash. His clothes too were more deliberately Byronic: he was wearing something which looked like a white stock above a ruffled shirt. It was not, to Jemima at any rate, a very sympathetic face. Or perhaps the expression of arrogance was, like the contrast in the looks, purely the creation of the flash bulb.

A pop star in trouble. For the young man in question had been photographed leaving some court or other. It was the caption which corrected Jemima's error, and the text beneath it which caused her to stare and stare again at the newspaper.

OXFORD BLOOD SAYS 'NO REGRETS'
'Gilded Rubbish' – Magistrate

Twenty-year-old Viscount Saffron, undergraduate heir of former Foreign Secretary, the Marquess of St Ives, pictured leaving Oxford magistrates' court yesterday, where he was fined £750 with costs. He was among other students found guilty of causing damage to the Martyrs Hotel, Cornmarket, Oxford, after a student party following an exclusive (£50 a head) Chimneysweepers' Dinner of the 'Oxford Bloods'. High-living Lord Saffron, heir to what is estimated to be one of the largest landed fortunes in Britain, told reporters that he had 'no regrets' about the damage caused to the hotel, 'since he had plenty of money to pay for it'. Lord Saffron added with a laugh: 'There's nothing wrong with money, so long as you don't earn it.'

Jemima, as she sped forward once more amid the hooting cars, felt sick then angry. Oxford Blood indeed! You scarcely needed a knowledge of the latest unemployment figures – which some sardonic newspaperman had in any case thoughtfully placed alongside the lead item concerning Lord Saffron – to be disgusted by such a gratuitous display of upper-class insolence. Jemima felt herself in total sympathy with the remarks of the magistrate who referred feelingly to behaviour 'unacceptable in supporters of a football club' and all the more disgraceful in someone who had been raised 'in such a privileged manner' as Lord Saffron.

The magistrate was also particularly incensed by the fact that Oxford Bloods called their function the Chimneysweepers' Dinner, thus mocking what had once been a decent profession for a working man; many people, he opined, would regard these young people themselves as mere 'gilded rubbish', at the bottom rather than the top of society. And this was the type of delightful young person Cy Fredericks expected her to study in his precious *Golden Lads and Girls* programme. By the time she reached her flat, Jemima had worked herself into a royal rage which even Midnight's soft purring welcome round her ankles hardly assuaged.

She studied the story in the newspaper in detail – nearly a thousand pounds' worth of damage had been caused by the so-called Oxford Bloods at their Chimneysweepers' Dinner (presumably its members, unlike Cy, did know how the 'Golden Lads' rhyme ended). Lord Saffron had the pleasure of paying that sum as well as the fine. Glasses and plates had been smashed: well, that, if not edifying, was not so surprising, and various other pieces of minor vandalism carried out; but the principal item consisted of repairs to a marble mantelpiece which had been deliberately attacked by Lord Saffron with a hammer. Hence the fact that the case had been brought against him personally rather than the various other members of the club.

About that damage, young Lord Saffron had been theoretically penitent, or at any rate his lawyer had been so on his behalf. Outside the court however he had positively revelled in the destruction of something he castigated as 'artistically beyond redemption and fortunately now beyond repair'.

Jemima took a cold bottle of white wine out of the fridge and looked out of her wide uncurtained windows towards her winter balcony. Delicate exterior lighting made it into another room. A large pot of yellow witch hazel was flowering. Daring the cold Jemima pulled back the glass, cut a sprig, and put it in a little vase at her elbow. Soon the delicate sad perfume was stealing into her nostrils.

She would run a bath, allow the Floris Wild Hyacinth oil to challenge the *hamamelis mollis*, sip the wine, listen to Mozart (Clarinet Quintet, guaranteed to soothe and transport) and in complete contrast to that, yes, she would glory in the new Ruth Rendell, hoping it was one of her macabre ones ... She would forget *Golden Lads and Girls*. She would forget the odious and arrogant Lord Saffron. Above all she would forget Cy Fredericks ...

So that when the telephone rang as though deliberately intending to thwart these plans, Jemima knew, absolutely knew, that it was Cy. White wine to her lips, she allowed the answering machine, a serene robot insensitive to both slight and triumph, to take the call.

'This is Jemima Shore,' cooed the recorded voice back into the face of the real Jemima. 'I'm afraid I'm not here . . .' The perfect twentieth-century double talk.

She then expected Cy to do one of two things: fling down the receiver with a strangled groan (he quite often did that; after all it was the dreaded technology, something he did not trust as far as he could see it) or simply leave one deeply reproachful word on the machine: 'Jem.' The implication of this one word was quite clear. 'Where are you? I need you.'

But it did not happen like that. When the message began, with Jemima's serene recording finished, there was a burst of music, which sounded like reggae, then some giggles. Light not very pleasant giggles. Then the impression of a hand somehow stifling the giggles. After that, silence – the steady silence of the track. Jemima waited, curiously disquieted, for the click-off indicating the end of this non-existent message.

She analysed her disquiet. Her home number was supposed to be a closely guarded secret, at any rate from members of the public who might be expected to express various unwelcome degrees of rage, admiration or even lust, following her programmes. So that such a call was on the face of it slightly surprising. On the other hand the unknown gigglers might have hit upon her number by complete coincidence.

Then Jemima felt her skin prickle. The track was no longer silent. A light androgynous voice had begun to sing softly into the machine: 'Golden lads and girls all must,' it lilted, 'Like chimneysweepers come to dust.' There was a pause. A giggle. 'You too Jemima Shore,' added the voice. 'You too.' The message was over.

In the interval Jemima's Mozart tape had, unnoticed, come to a stop. So she found herself at last sitting in silence. And the wine in her glass had become warmed by her fingers. Nothing was quite so pleasant as it had been before the telephone rang. It was possible of course to play the tape again and listen to that sinister, silly little message once more, concentrate on the voice, see if she recognized it. But that would be to give the matter too much importance.

Instead, Jemima wrenched her thoughts away from the tape and back to her work. 'Golden lads and girls' indeed. As a more relevant piece of masochism, she did re-read the evening paper including that chilling declaration from Lord Saffron: 'Nothing wrong with money so long as you don't earn it.'

It was then that Jemima took a sudden resolve, spurred on as it were by her mingled indignation towards Lord Saffron and her dislike of the unknown telephonic intruders.

Two could play at that game.

She dialled Cy's private number. He answered with alacrity, which in Jemima's experience meant not so much that he was free but that he was engaged talking on at least two of his other lines, and was picking up the private one purely in order to still its clangour. She had analysed the situation correctly.

'Jem – one moment – Venetia—' (into some other demanding mouthpiece). 'Is that you? One moment, Jem, one moment – darling, one moment – No, New York, I hear you, *ne coupez pas, ne coupez pas.* Miss Lewis, where are you?' he suddenly bellowed. 'Please take this call from New York.'

Miss Lewis' calm voice speaking to Jemima Shore was quite a relief, and once Jemima had made it clear she was neither the switchboard of the Carlyle Hotel in New York, nor that of the Hotel Meurice in Paris, both of which Cy was apparently trying to engage in word play, they were able to have a pleasantly sardonic exchange on the subject of Cy's telephone habits until interrupted by his next bellow:

'Miss Lewis, Miss Lewis, what is the Meurice doing in New York?'

'Mr Fredericks—'

'Speaking perfect French too,' Cy proceeded. 'Not a trace of an accent.'

All in all, it was sometime before this international cat's cradle was unravelled. Finally Jemima was allowed her own exchange with Cy.

Threatened as she was by New York, Paris, Lady Manfred and some other plaintive little female voice which could be heard bleating occasionally: 'Cy, Cykie, Cy', Jemima made her call brief.

'You're right, Cy, right as ever. I think there is a good programme in the "Golden Lads" story – or at any rate something worth investigating further.'

'Jem!' explained Cy with ebullience, dropping the receiver, or at least one of the receivers he was holding, with a crash. When normal service was resumed: 'I knew you would see it my way.'

'The evening paper made me see it your way.'

'Oh yes, most exciting.' Which told Jemima that Cy had not yet read the evening paper.

'When you do read it, you'll see why I thought I'd start with the Oxford Bloods, as I believe they're called.'

'Most exciting, most exciting!' Cy continued to exclaim. This was surely carrying blankness a little too far even for Cy. His next words provided the clue.

'You don't have my memo?'

'Memo? What memo?'

'Miss Lewis, Miss Lewis!' Clearly the bellowing was about to begin.

Either to obviate it, or because Miss Lewis had an unspoken alliance with Jemima on the subject of Cy and his lightning projects, Miss Lewis now broke firmly into the conversation.

'I think Mr Fredericks is referring to the memo concerning Miss Tiggie Jones,' she observed in a neutral voice. 'Although he has not yet finished dictating it. In fact he has not gone beyond the first paragraph. However I understand Miss Tiggie Jones is to act as a' – delicate pause from Miss Lewis – 'a student observer on your new programme.'

Complete silence from Jemima Shore.

Into this silence the plaintive female voice of one of Cy's telephoners, which had happily fallen still in the last few minutes, was heard again.

'Golden lads and girls all must,' sang the little voice, 'Like television come to dust.' Something like a giggle followed. 'Ooh Cykie, I've been listening to every word.'

With an unpleasant feeling Jemima recognized not only the giggle but also the androgynous singer of her anonymous telephone call.

The feeling of unpleasantness was intensified when Cy Fredericks cried out with pleasure:

'Tiggie! Darling, where have you been? I've been trying to reach you on the telephone. We have so much to discuss—'

Then to Jemima, still on her end of the line, as though introducing two people at a party:

'Jemima, I really must introduce you to Miss Tiggie Jones.'

4

Staircase Thirteen

'That staircase will be the death of someone,' said Jemima Shore. She added fiercely as she nursed her ankle: 'After our recent encounter I only hope it's young Lord Saffron. Staircase Thirteen, I see. Most appropriate.'

'How about Tiggie Jones?' suggested Cherry. 'Supposing she ever gets as far as Oxford.' Cherry had accompanied Jemima down to Oxford in the latter's white Mercedes. That was because Tiggie Jones, billed to introduce Jemima to *'le tout Oxford'* as Cy Fredericks put it, had failed to show up at Holland Park Mansions on time. Or anything like on time. After waiting an hour, Jemima with difficulty resisted the temptation to make a vengeful call to Cy. Instead she had summoned Cherry from her office.

'Come and hold my hand among the golden ones.' Nothing loath, Cherry had arrived with great swiftness, pausing only to exchange a high-necked clinging jersey to something more in keeping with the spirit of youth as she understood it – which meant a T-shirt both clinging *and* revealing. As a result Cherry was now shivering at the bottom of a staircase in Rochester College, Oxford. And Jemima, who had just fallen down the same staircase, was trying to comfort her – 'No, go on, Cherry, take my coat, I've got my left-wing fury to keep me warm' – as well as rub her own ankle.

The first steps were made of stone. Dark, vanishing upwards above their heads, the rest of the staircase was made of wood, which creaked from time to time despite the fact that no one was using it. It was difficult to negotiate not only because it was steep and badly lit, but because the distance between the treads was so high. Jemima had stumbled at the top of the last flight and had only broken her fall by clutching the thin wooden rail.

The staircase ended in an arch. It was very cold in the stone interior and slightly dank. The presence of a bathroom to their left and a lavatory to their right was also unaesthetic. A further staircase leading downwards had a cardboard notice reading: TO THE WASHING MACHINE. DO NOT USE AFTER 11 P.M. C.L. MOSSBANKER. Someone had scrawled: 'To hell with that' beneath it. Someone else had added: 'And high water.' A further hand still had added: 'I'm pissed off with late night Lady Macbeths trying to wash it off after getting it off.' Jemima had a feeling the dialogue was only just beginning.

It was difficult to believe, in view of all this, that the arch in front of her eyes formed part of a façade rated by some as the finest thing Hawksmoor ever did, outstripping the glory of neighbouring St John's.

The next excitement was the appearance of a man they assumed to be Professor Mossbanker, from the fact that he emerged from the ground-floor rooms beneath the arch, which bore his name in gold letters.

The professor was blinking and rubbing his eyes. Then he replaced the large thick spectacles, which with their heavy black rims made him appear almost the caricature of the absent-minded academic. Looking at Jemima with some surprise and at Cherry in her T-shirt with disbelief, he asked abruptly what time it was.

Jemima told him.

'How odd!' he exclaimed. 'People generally fall down this staircase at night. That and the infernal washing machine leave one no peace. What is the compulsion, I wonder, which makes modern youth want to wash so noisily? And at night.' On which note he turned on his heel and retired back into his rooms. The heavy door shut.

'I think he's done that sporting thing.' Cherry sounded rather uncertain.

'Sporting thing! I don't call that very sporting. He could at least have given us a glass of dry sherry—'

'No, Saffron just told us. When you slam your door it's called sporting your oak or something. Look, it's got no handle. You can't open it from outside. There's an inner door as well. Saffron had the same set-up.'

'Like *The Light of the World*,' commented Jemima, who was an admirer of the Pre-Raphaelites and intended to visit Holman Hunt's celebrated picture in Keble College chapel after lunch, if she could hobble there. At the same time, agreeable memories of other sported oaks in her Cambridge days, doors in men's colleges shut not so much in her face as behind her back on entrance, rather agreeable memories, came back to her.

The sudden arrival of a tiny girl dressed as some kind of clown in a white ruffled pierrot top and very baggy white trousers worn over high-heeled black shoes, distracted them both. The clown figure rolled her huge dark eyes, delineated in black, panda fashion, in Jemima's direction and sucked her finger. Her very short very black hair was topped by a conical hat with a pompom. It was not clear whether this childishness was genuine and thus mildly unfortunate, or assumed and thus extremely irritating.

'Jemima, forgive, forgive,' whispered the clown. 'You've no idea of the *perils* I encountered on my journey. Oh, if only I had been with you! I know I would have felt so *safe*.'

As Tiggie Jones carried on in this vein, rolling her huge eyes the while, Jemima wondered how it was that this diminutive creature, apparently lacking in all intelligence, always managed to put her so neatly at a disadvantage. I mean, how did you cope with the annoyance of being called *safe* by someone you believed to be a mere ten years younger than yourself if that?

'And didn't you just adore him? Isn't he foxy? Tiggie was murmuring. 'Saffer. What a naughty boy. Still we can't *all* be good all the time like you.'

'This is unbearable.' Jemima Shore pronounced the word quite distinctly. There was a short silence into which Cherry contributed the diplomatic sentence: 'Poor Jem's twisted her ankle coming down this lethal staircase. She's in agony.'

'Oh poor *darling*!' The next moment – Jemima never quite knew how it happened – Tiggie had somehow produced a long cashmere scarf from about her person, possibly from around her tiny waist, and easing off Jemima's pale leather boot, had most deftly bound up the swelling ankle.

'Now you've got to have a rest.' A faint flush of effort touched Tiggie Jones' pearly white cheeks, allowing Jemima to perceive that much of the whiteness was due to liquid white make-up. 'And a glass of champagne. For shock. Proffy will simply have to provide.'

Before Jemima could stop her, Tiggie had banged boldly upon Professor Mossbanker's heavily shut door – his sported oak. After a few moments, and a few more bangs, the figure of Professor Mossbanker reappeared. Jemima waited for his wrath to fall. To her surprise, the professor's face actually cleared.

'Antigone, it's you,' he said with some warmth. 'Did Eugenia get back from Washington last night? I've just read the paper she read in Rome in December at the Conference of Classical and Psychological Studies: Neurosis and Anxiety as depicted in fourth-century Greek vases. Excellent, quite excellent.'

But the professor, despite an evident affection for his colleague Professor Eugenia Jones, mother of Antigone, still did not have any champagne. 'Alas poor Academe, alas poor Academe,' he cried. 'And especially poor Proffy! Why don't you try our rich young man upstairs? I could do with a glass myself. Make sure it's cold, won't you?'

But the professor, if he had no champagne, did have a very comfortable sofa, from which he hastened to dump a weight of learned periodicals and papers. Then he sat down on it. Jemima, who had imagined the sofa had been cleared for her, then sat on a much less comfortable chair with a certain wry amusement. It was left to Tiggie to fetch the champagne. It did come from upstairs and was borne down by its owner, the occupant of the top room – none other than Viscount Saffron.

So for the second time that day, and after all too short an interval, Jemima found herself gazing into the handsome, sulky, strangely un-English face of that notorious Oxford Blood, putative subject of a Megalith Television programme.

'Is there going to be a party?' enquired Professor Mossbanker, breaking the slightly embarrassed silence. Even Tiggie now seemed to suspect that Jemima's previous encounter with Saffron had been something of a failure and that had she been present – as hired by Megalith – to perform the introduction it might have gone better. The professor alone amongst them displayed a mixture of elation and curiosity, as though he were an anthropologist about to witness strange tribal rites. Jemima thought it surprising that a don, however remote from reality as the professor appeared to be, should not have had his fill of parties, living as he did on the same staircase as Saffron. Or perhaps scientists – it appeared that Proffy was some kind of scientist rather than an anthropologist – were not invited to parties.

But Tiggie Jones cleared that one up. 'Proffy loves parties, don't you? He says he got to like parties in the war when he was a spy. Weren't you, Proffy? Apparently parties are awfully important for spying. But *I* think it's because he's got so many children. He finds parties outside the home rather peaceful compared to life inside Chillington Road. He hates the young, of course, having so many children, but he does love champagne!'

'How many children do you have, Professor Mossbanker?' Jemima was relieved to find some conventional subject on which she could make polite conversation with the man obliged by Tiggie to be her host. At which a look of deep suspicion crossed the professor's face.

'Oh, the usual number, the usual large number,' he said quite crossly. 'I don't know why people always expect me to have that kind of information at my fingertips. You should ask Eugenia if you're really interested.'

'Eleanor,' put in Tiggie, blinking her panda eyes. Jemima realized she was trying hard not to giggle. 'Eugenia is my mother. Eleanor is your wife.'

'Eleanor, I thought I said Eleanor. You confused me, Antigone.'

'And Proffy, you have eight children.'

'Exactly, the usual large number.'

'Amid the wonders of Professor Mossbanker's philoprogeniture, one question remains,' remarked Saffron in his habitually languid manner. 'Am I going to open this champagne here or am I going to carry Jemima

Shore heroically back up the staircase to my rooms? A terrifyingly macho thought, but I might impress you, Jemima, and then we could re-create it for television. It would do wonders for my image, a little tarnished at the moment: you know, the monkey lord, *Greystoke* and all that, so sweet.'

Jemima smiled coldly. She had the feeling she looked much as the professor had done a few moments ago when asked the exact number of his children.

The next thing she knew, Saffron had whisked her up in his arms and was carrying her quite fast back up the steep staircase. He was surprisingly muscular: Jemima, slim as she was, was tall. Saffron's languid manner and pale complexion were something of a delusion. Besides, there had been some sporting equipment about in his rooms, otherwise more noted for the smell of expensive Rigaud candles and the sight of empty champagne bottles. Jemima had noticed a cricket bat in a corner (was it quite the season, this icy spring?), a tennis racket and a couple of squash rackets.

'I boxed for my school,' murmured Saffron in her ear. 'I always thought it would come in useful.'

Back in his rooms, Jemima sat down on another sofa – a more elegant one this time, covered in dark green velvet with a lot of patchwork cushions – and gazed up at him. Yes he could have been a boxer, once you got over the illusion of effeminacy, or perhaps decadence was a better word. Saffron's shoulders were not particularly broad but he was tall and wasn't that nose slightly flattened out? It was certainly not the perfect aristocratic shape of her imagination.

Then from her new position on the sofa, she saw something she had missed on her previous visit. Standing on the table beside her was a framed photograph, a family group. The background was a large country house, late Elizabethan – Saffron Ivy itself. The figure of Lord St Ives, so familiar from the newspapers, was easy to recognize, and the woman next to him with her hand on the head of a large dog was presumably his wife. But what attracted Jemima's attention was the figure at the end of the row, a figure dressed in nurse's uniform; allowing for the time lapse and the harrowing conditions under which she had visited her at the Hospice, she was almost sure that she was gazing once more at the features of Nurse Elsie Connolly.

'Oh, that,' said Saffron carelessly, 'that's my parents' Silver Wedding. I was four at the time – the happy afterthought. *Very* happy, at least for them. Look, there's my cousin Andrew Iverstone – you know, the famous Fascist beast, looking sick as mud at my mere existence. Sixteen years later he still hasn't forgiven me for being a boy. And Cousin Daphne.'

'Who's the other boy holding your hand? He looks a little older.'

Saffron sounded even more cheerful. 'Oh that's my cousin, Jack Iverstone, Cousin Andrew's son. He would be looking forward to getting the lot if it wasn't for me. He's at Oxford too, as a matter of fact. In his last year.'

'And does he hate your guts as well?'

'Christ, no. Jack doesn't hate anyone's guts. He's a member of the SDP and it doesn't go with gut-hating. Pure reaction against Cousin Andrew of course. With parents like that, *you* would be a member of the SDP.'

Jemima forbore to say that she had indeed flirted with the possibility not so many years ago, before returning to her traditional Labour stance – and without Jack Iverstone's excuse. Instead she asked: 'And the woman at the end of the row, the nurse?'

There was a tiny pause, so brief that Jemima even wondered afterwards whether she had imagined it.

'Oh, that was someone, an old retainer if you like, she used to be around a lot in my childhood; my mother was quite ill after I was born, quite depressed I believe, despite the Super-Happy event; something to do with her age I daresay.'

'And is she still around? The nurse. I mean, we could interview her,' Jemima improvised. 'Part of your privileged background. A live-in nurse at the age of twenty.'

'Privileged! Nurse Elsie ... You have to be joking.'

Saffron had abandoned his usual languid tone for a kind of bitter briskness, 'No, as a matter of fact, she's dead. Died the other day. Of cancer. I went to see her. It was horrible. Very upsetting. My mother forced me to go and see her. The trouble with my mother, she's a saint, and she expects everyone to do likewise. Only it's no trouble to her, and a great deal of trouble to the rest of us. In short I wish I hadn't gone, for any number of reasons, and if Ma hadn't bullied me I would have got out of it altogether because Nurse Elsie died suddenly the day after I visited her.

'As if there weren't enough members of my family crowding about her anyway,' he went on. 'Nurse Elsie produced my cousins as well as gorgeous me; in fact her invaluable attentions were about the only thing Cousin Daphne Iverstone and my mother had in common, and they both competed in being sentimental about her. So if Cousin Daphne went, Ma had to go, and if Jack and Fanny went to say the final goodbye, I had to go. What rubbish. Nothing to do with death.'

In spite of all her good resolutions, Jemima found herself feeling both excited and apprehensive. For the first time that day, young Lord Saffron had genuinely engaged her attention. She was determined not to let the opportunity drop, determined not to return to the tedious (to her) subject of his luxurious Oxford life-style. She was wondering how to frame her next question when she heard hurried footsteps on the stairs. Expecting either Tiggie or perhaps Cherry mounting a rescue operation, Jemima saw instead a tall thin young man whose appearance was so essentially English that you could have mounted his photograph as a travel poster. With curly brown hair, rather small blue eyes, a longish nose and high healthy colour, the stranger had the air of an eighteenth century gentleman, except for his clothes which were distinctly modern – jeans and a baggy brown jersey over a check shirt. He also had a pile of books under his arm.

'At the champagne already, I see, Saffer—' Then the stranger noticed Jemima and paused.

'Miss Jemima Shore,' said Saffron in a silky voice. 'May I introduce my cousin Jack Iverstone? He probably wants me to subscribe to something thoroughly decent. In which case I shall refuse. He also comes fresh from a lecture by the look of him which always has a deplorable effect on the temper.'

'Oh don't be so affected, Saffer,' said a girl's clear voice from the doorway. 'As if you'd ever been *near* a lecture. Good afternoon, Miss Shore, I'm a great admirer of your work, particularly that programme *The Pill – For or Against?* It certainly needed saying. Why should we all drop dead for the sake of some international chemists? Now listen Saffer, you've got to come and have lunch with us. Oh, I'm Saffer's cousin, Fanny Iverstone, by the way, Miss Shore. You see, Saffer, Mummy's come down to talk to Jack about his wicked political views – or wicked according to her and Daddy. We thought you would distract her—'

'Certainly *not!*' exclaimed Saffron. 'This is going too far, even for you, Fanny. You out-boss Mrs Thatcher sometimes, besides not being nearly so pretty. *I* am having lunch with Jemima Shore. She's going to do wonders for my image on television.'

Fanny Iverstone turned her eyes – clear blue like her brother's – on Jemima Shore. In other ways too, she was like a girlish version of Jack Iverstone, Jemima thought, with her fresh complexion plus a few freckles, paler pink cheeks, and shoulder-length curly brown hair tied at the back with a bow. Her expression, however, was not particularly girlish.

'Miss Shore!' cried Fanny. 'Now why don't *you* have lunch with all of us? We're having lunch at *La Lycée*, in any case wonderful material for your programme – anybody who can afford the Lycée mid-week has to be a golden lad or laddess.'

Jemima noted that Fanny Iverstone knew all about her programme. She was coming to the conclusion that everybody in Oxford knew everything they cared to know about anything they cared to know about. Which left a good deal unknown.

'Which college are you at, Fanny?' she asked politely. Although not suitable for the *Golden Lads* programme – there was something far too sensible about Fanny, even her clothes were quite sensible – her remark about Jemima's previous series had struck an agreeable chord. Maybe when Jemima had researched the *Golden Lads* sufficiently, and assured

Cy it would not make an interesting programme, she could return to Oxford and make something of this new intelligent generation of women undergraduates, the post-*Brideshead* types, living in colleges in equal numbers and on equal terms with the men. Fanny Iverstone would be most suitable material for that.

'Good heavens, I'm not *at* Oxford,' exclaimed Fanny cheerfully, shattering this dream. 'At the school Mummy sent me to, they raised a cheer if you got a couple of O-levels, let alone A-levels. No, I'm doing shorthand typing at Mrs Bone's.'

'All the same Fanny *is* at Oxford,' commented Jack. 'Wherever Fanny *is*, she's *at.*'

'I'm looking after my little brother!' Jemima thought Fanny was probably not being ironic. 'And my little cousin too,' she went on in the same fond voice, 'except that's impossible.'

Then Fanny returned to a more bracing tone.

'Come on, Jemima – may I call you that? I've seen you so often on the telly. Do come to lunch. Mummy's not nearly as terrible as the Press make out. And then she simply adores Saffer here; it's her dreadful snobbishness I fear, the future head of the family and all that. *She* doesn't object to his wicked ways one bit. Unlike us.'

And yet Saffron was convinced that Daphne Iverstone's husband Andrew hated him, thought Jemima, if not on the surface at least deep down. Had hated him since birth. Did Daphne Iverstone really not resent Saffron's late appearance in the family tree? Out of curiosity about the Iverstone family rather than some finer professional instinct towards the programme, Jemima accepted the invitation to lunch. At all events it would be a relief to leave Staircase Thirteen, with its slightly sinister atmosphere, for the peace of a comfortable restaurant.

5

Fight Before the Death

In the course of lunch Jemima decided that Fanny Iverstone was wrong. Mrs Andrew Iverstone was worse, really much worse than the Press made out. What made her worse was not the nature of her neo-racialist politics, which seemed to have been fairly accurately reported, but the odious whimsicality with which she presented them. There were references to 'horrid freezing old England' and the 'sweet negroes, why do they want to come here and get pneumonia, the poor darlings? I wish someone would give *me* a lot of lovely money to go to Jamaica.'

'Blacks, Mummy.' Jack Iverstone looked at his plate as he spoke. 'Blacks, Mummy, not negroes.'

'I know, darling, I know. And I know you have lots of lovely friends like that. That marvellous cricketer. But that's different. You can't compare someone who looks divine in white flannels, someone at *Oxford*, with some illiterate monkey straight off—'

She's going to say it, thought Jemima, she's going to say, straight off the trees. I don't believe it. In 1985, in so-called civilized society. Then Fanny Iverstone saved the day as Jemima suspected she had done on more than one occasion.

'Oh come on, Mummy,' she said brightly. 'You know how you loved going to India and staying with that Maharajah. Didn't you and Daddy go tiger-hunting on your honeymoon?' This certainly had the effect of stopping Mrs Iverstone in her tracks and changing her tone from one of persistent whimsicality to that of nostalgia, even tenderness.

'Ah but Sonny Mekwar was different, quite different. A thousand years of breeding went into that man. You knew it immediately you saw him play polo for example. Such an aristocrat. Some of those Maharajahs go back almost as far as the Iverstones, you know.'

'Crooks and robbers. Successful crooks.' Jack spoke as before, looking at his plate.

'What was that, my love?' Jemima thought she detected a sharper note beneath Mrs Iverstone's honeyed sweetness.

'I was referring to the early history of the Iverstone family. I thought you were too. The first Iverstones were robber barons who managed to terrorize their neighbours in East Anglia sufficiently to acquire large amounts of land . . .'

Throughout this conversation, Saffron had remained quite silent, occasionally eyeing Tiggie Jones. The latter had insisted on joining the lunch party in her usual imperious fashion on the grounds that she had been sent down to Oxford by Megalith in order to accompany Jemima Shore, and could not desert her.

'I'm your *chaperone*, Jemima,' Tiggie had said with a roll of her eyes. 'I can't let Saffer just abduct you and not protest.' That however was not the full extent of her interference with the lunch arrangements. When Tiggie discovered that the party would be at least two men short, she promptly roped in Professor Mossbanker. He was now having an earnest conversation with Cherry about classical ethics in the television world, a subject on which Cherry was enchanted to give her views, having unaccountably never been asked before. To Jemima's expert eye, the professor was very promising Cherry-material, being sufficiently advanced in years, and certainly substantial, if you counted an Oxford professorship; which Jemima guessed Cherry, distracted from the Dukes, now would. The father of eight children was certainly substantial, in some sense of the word.

Then Tiggie had routed out Saffron's neighbour at the top of the staircase, a dark-haired young man, not unlike Saffron himself in build and type, if less handsome, whose name no one (except presumably Saffron) seemed to know. At least the unknown had a large appetite. Jemima asked his name and, between mouthfuls, the unknown said something that sounded like 'Bim'. After that she let him get on with his food.

But the unknown's appetite prompted Jemima to wonder: who was paying the bill for this large lunch party at Oxford's most expensive restaurant? If the answer was Megalith Television, then the idea of paying for Daphne Iverstone's lunch stuck in her gullet. On the other hand it seemed unfair – at least by normal standards – to make Daphne Iverstone pay a huge bill for what had originally been a family lunch party, whatever her political views.

The question was suddenly solved.

In the middle of the conversation, Saffron stood up. He did so before the unknown 'Bim' had finished his double ice-cream (Professor Mossbanker, the other sweet-eater, had eaten very fast, so fast in fact that his spoon had on occasion been seen to skim an extra scoop of ice-cream off his neighbour's plate).

'All this talk of ancestors is so terribly exhausting, it reminds me that I simply must go and have a sleep before my tutorial at five. No better preparation, don't you think? A fresh mind and all that.'

'No essay again, Saffer?' But Jack Iverstone sounded indulgent as well as reproachful.

'My dear Jack! You know I've been in London for days ... My magic moment in court left me with an urgent need to recover. Then I had to go home to pacify Pa and Ma. Adieu, one and all. Oh and by the way, Cousin Daphne, don't worry about the bill. I've signed it. Nobility obliges.'

Lord Saffron sauntered off. Jemima watched his retreating back. Reluctantly, she had to admit that he had a certain style. To her annoyance, however, she still had not the faintest inkling whether Daphne Iverstone loathed or adored the boy who had dispossessed the claims of her own husband – and son – to inherit Saffron Ivy. To that extent, the lunch had been a failure, since Daphne Iverstone had been too busy discoursing on race to address Saffron, and he had been too busy gazing at Tiggie Jones. So much for her famous detective instinct. This meditation was interrupted by a very loud clear voice somewhere at the front of the restaurant.

'There goes Saffer, the biggest shit in Oxford,' said the voice.

Lord Saffron's steps did not falter.

'There goes Saffer the Shit,' repeated the voice. 'Come on, aren't you going to break up this restaurant too? And then pay up with Daddy's money?'

Jemima now focussed on a table at the front of the restaurant, to be compared with their own in size, except that all those sitting at it were apparently young. There was no Daphne Iverstone figure, let alone a Professor Mossbanker. The most noticeable figure – because of his remarkable colouring – was a young man with a shock of violently red hair, and an accompanying pallor which was almost morbid. He reminded Jemima, still in her pre-Raphaelite mood, of the dying poet Thomas Chatterton in Wallis's portrait. Oddly enough, the girl next to him was also red-haired, but the colour more russet, the pallor less pronounced. The man next to her was also striking, not so much through his colouring but because he was exceptionally big; the huge shoulders and thick short neck of a rugger player, or at least that was the impression he gave.

'Rufus Pember,' Fanny Iverstone spoke with something like a groan, 'and that frightful heavy of his, Big Nigel Copley. Worst of all, Little Miss Muffet Pember is along as well. *Now* what's going to happen?'

Afterwards Jemima found it difficult to remember exactly what did happen, or rather the order in which it happened. Did Saffron turn and hit Rufus Pember first? Or was the whole fight set off by Tiggie Jones, who scurried to the distant table, surprisingly fast on her tottering high heels, and slapped Rufus Pember in the face? At all events, both blows were certainly struck, followed by other blows, as Big Nigel Copley lurched and blundered to his feet, revealing his breadth to be fully matched by his height. And at some point the innocent Bim got involved, cheered on by Tiggie but receiving quite a lot of punishment at the hands of Big Nigel as a result.

Jemima found herself watching the faces of the group at her table. Daphne Iverstone's prim little face – she had incongruously rosebud looks, a rosebud faded and dried up with the years but still recognizable for what it was – looked ardent, excited. As Saffron felled Rufus Pember, who fell with a crash on a nearby table, sending glass and forks flying, Daphne Iverstone gave a kind of sigh. She certainly did not hate Saffron even if her husband did. This looked more like the adoration to which her daughter Fanny referred.

Fanny herself had an air of weary tolerance as though she had witnessed plenty of such incidents among undergraduates in expensive Oxford restaurants (as no doubt she had). Cherry screamed and clutched Professor Mossbanker's hand, a situation he accepted with equanimity, patting the little hand briefly before pouring on with his conversation. His own participation in the proceedings was limited to the expression 'tribal rites' which he repeated several times with evident satisfaction, before returning to his dissertation on wartime parties at the Dorchester, on their importance in bringing to an end all proper Anglo-American understanding.

Only Jack Iverstone looked absolutely horrified at what was happening. After a minute he jumped up, crying something like: 'Why *will* he do it?' and then 'For Christ's sake, Saffer.' So saying he rushed over to the fray, which was being watched helplessly by two young French waiters, definitely too slight to deal with the burly figures of the contestants. Tiggie herself had by this time retired to the sidelines, or rather the lap of one of the other lunchers not involved in the fracas – one could only assume he was a previous acquaintance as Tiggie seemed much at home in her situation, sucking her finger and cheering on Saffron. Saffron himself, in spite of the blows landed on Rufus Pember, was beginning to get very much the worst of it at the hands of the huge Copley, while Bim remained prone on the floor.

'It's disgusting!' said a woman in a brown velvet hat very loudly at the table next to Jemima's. 'Why doesn't someone do something? We haven't come here to watch a fight.'

'They should all be sent into the Army,' remarked her companion, a middle-aged man, grimly. 'These young fellows need a good sergeant-major to take the stuffing out of them. When National Service ended – criminal, I said so at the time—' Jemima stopped listening, but not before the woman in the brown velvet hat had contributed something about the waste of taxpayers' money.

It was Jack Iverstone in fact who ended the fight, ended it just as the proprietor – a very small and very angry Frenchman – announced his intention of sending for the police. With admirable courage, Jack pushed his way between the contestants and put his hand on his cousin's chest.

'You bloody fool, Saffer. Do you want to be sent down?'

Saffron stared back, dishevelled, panting, and said nothing.

'Do you want to make the headlines in the *Post* every day?' went on Jack.

'Come on then, man,' said Saffron after a minute, in an approximation of his usual languid manner, inhibited by breathlessness, 'let's leave this unholy mess. Oh yes, yes, I'll pay—' thrown in the direction of the proprietor '—Viscount Saffron, Rochester College.'

Staggering slightly, but with his shoulders squared, Saffron headed for the stairs as though the mess of wine and glass and food he left behind him simply did not exist. Jack Iverstone hesitated, looked round where his party still sat, stunned, at their table, and then went after Saffron.

'See you later, Saffer!' called out the man named Bim suddenly from the floor.

'See you in Hell!' shouted a voice from the rival table. Was it Rufus Pember or the enormous Nigel Copley? Or one of the others at the table who, to do them credit, had not joined in the affray. 'We'll get you, you—' a stream of obscenities followed. 'And when we get you, Saffer, there won't be anything to help you, not Daddy's money, not *The Tatler*, nor the Queen.'

'Aren't they terrible?' Daphne Iverstone's voice cut sweetly across the invective, like some light soprano joining a bass ensemble. 'I don't think people like that should be allowed to eat in good restaurants, do you, Miss Shore? Poor darling Saffer. He's led a very sheltered life, you know, with such elderly parents, wonderful people of course, but so old when he was born. He was terribly protected. I did try to warn Gwendolen. I wonder if he was quite *ready* for Oxford.'

There was a sublimity about Mrs Iverstone's blindness to her young cousin's failings – well, almost a sublimity. No question but that she adored him. No question also but that there were a great many other people presently within Oxford who did not.

The lunch party – what there was left of it – dispersed. Jemima came upon Jack Iverstone unlocking his bicycle from a nearby railing as she left the restaurant. Saffron had vanished.

'Are you going back to Rochester?' she asked.

'No, to the Bodleian,' he answered rather shortly. Then as if to apologize for a temporary lapse in courtesy, he added with a smile: 'The Bodleian is a wonderful cure for bad temper.' Then: 'So what did you think of Rochester, Miss Shore?'

'It's a beautiful college. Architecturally.'

'Oh quite. I'm at St Lucy's myself.' And Jack Iverstone rode away on his bicycle.

That night anyone within Rochester gazing at Hawksmoor's exquisite façade would have seen one patch of darkness among the lighted archways: Staircase Thirteen alone was not illuminated by an overhead light inside the arch. The impression given by this dark gap might have been mysterious and even slightly sinister. Unless a watcher reflected that a missing light bulb, far from being an abnormal phenomenon in the archway of an Oxford college, was in fact nothing out of the ordinary, given the relative durability of light bulbs and the lack of housekeeperly attention to detail in such surroundings.

It was silent on Staircase Thirteen. Visitors were not admitted to Rochester after 11.30 p.m. (although no check was made as to whether all the many visitors freely admitted throughout the day had actually left). Rochester's own undergraduates and dons were of course at liberty to move freely about the college, its two main quadrangles and the newly built library all night if they so pleased. The library, a recent gift of a rich Turk, reposed beyond the Hawksmoor quadrangle, all glass and steel, looking like some vast beached ship or ark which had sailed into classical Oxford on some vast flood tide, and been deposited there unable to float away again. There were still lights burning in the library.

After a while the wooden steps of Staircase Thirteen creaked a little as though someone was ascending. But then the steps creaked sometimes of their own accord when there was no one there at all. When a door opened on the top landing, the noise was considerable. Saffron's voice, indistinct, and his characteristic arrogant laugh could be heard. Tiggie Jones' voice was higher and clearer. She was laughing too, though giggling might be a better word. Tiggie was saying something like: 'Oh Saffer, don't, don't be a naughty boy.' There was scuffling and more laughing. The door shut.

Then there were footsteps, heavy footsteps, descending.

After that, there was a gasp, a stifled cry or shout, then a heavy protracted crash, as of a body rolling over and over down a staircase. Then there was complete silence.

Nothing happened at all. No door opened on the various landings. Professor Mossbanker's door remained shut, which was just as well for something which looked horribly inert and lifeless lay right across it, and it was doubtful that the professor could have managed to open it in any case.

After about five minutes the creakings resumed. Someone was coming very carefully and softly indeed down the stairs. There was a noise as of a body being dragged down the stairs to the basement.

A few minutes later the deep cyclical hum of a washing machine was heard from the depths of the building, the noise loud and sepulchral in the night silence.

The washing machine continued to revolve ardently, but its noise could not of course wake the dead man lying beside it. It was not until sometime later that Professor Mossbanker, in the absence of lights, stumbled down to the basement. In the darkness of the launderette the light of the machine glowed at him. He stood staring at it for quite a long time, as if not quite comprehending what he saw. Then he bent over the dark shape at his feet, much as the prowler had done earlier.

Professor Mossbanker gave a deep sigh, or something more like a sob than a sigh.

6

No Long Shadows

The police came to the conclusion that Bevis Ian Marcus (known to his friends as Bim) had died as a result of a late night fall down a steep staircase in Rochester College.

The nickname 'Bim' was not actually used by anyone at the inquest. It would have doubtless seemed too cosy, too intimate for such a grim occasion as an inquest on a twenty-year-old undergraduate who had broken his neck following some kind of party. Those who gave evidence included Miss Antigone Rose Jones, twenty-three, of Launceston Place, SW, Saffron Ivo Charles Iverstone, commonly known as Viscount Saffron, twenty, of Rochester College, and Professor Claud Lionel Mossbanker, of Chillington Road, North Oxford. Sundry other undergraduates, female as well as male, who had seen Bevis Ian Marcus on the last evening of his life gave evidence. These undergraduates rather self-consciously also referred to him as Bevis, since that was what the coroner called him. One of the girls, who was at Rochester, sobbed a bit, thinking how Bim had hated the name, virtually denying its existence, pretending his real name was something like Brian, and how he would have hated the coroner announcing it like that, so persistently, for all the world to hear.

But then the girl, Magdalen Mary Irina Poliakoff, twenty, (known to her friends as Magda), was already tremulous with guilt over the death of Bim. It was her belief that if she had not rejected Bim's invitation to the cinema on the grounds that she had an essay to write, he, Bim, would not have fallen down the fatal Staircase Thirteen.

Magda Poliakoff needed little prompting to share this feeling of guilt with the coroner.

'But in any case you thought he was drunk?' asked the coroner, a doctor with a cynical view of the drinking habits of undergraduates. 'Quite apart from the question of your work, Miss Poliakoff, the real reason he turned you off, as you have just put it, the deceased that is, was because he had been drinking. Drinking, in your opinion, all day.'

'Since lunch,' and Magda Poliakoff shot a defiant look at Saffer and Tiggie Jones sitting on the opposite side of the small court room. 'She – whoever she is – forced him to go to lunch, actually put her arm round his neck, pulled him away. I mean I was just sitting there when it happened. And then of course – well, you know what *he's* like—' She transferred her trembling but still venomous gaze to Saffron! 'Er – *Bevis* wasn't like that. Like them. He was jolly poor. And he worked jolly hard. Most of the time, anyway. If only he hadn't been on the same staircase as *Lord* Saffron. People like him shouldn't be allowed places at university when there are plenty of other people—'

'Now Miss Poliakoff,' said the doctor firmly but kindly. 'We are here to establish the truth about Bevis Marcus' death, if we can, not to discuss the merits or otherwise of the admissions policy of the University.' He paused and then went on: 'Can I take it then, Miss Poliakoff, that by seven p.m., Mr Marcus was in your opinion too drunk to know what he was doing?'

It was the question of the bruises as Jemima reported to Cass Brinsley later that day, sitting in their favourite local restaurant, Monsieur Thompson's, in the dell at the end of Kensington Park Road.

'Certainly he died of a broken neck caused by a fall. The medical evidence is quite clear on that point. But what caused the fall? Was there a fight? At the top of the staircase causing the fall. But of course Bim had had some kind of punch-up, totally drunk, earlier in the day. The police are satisfied it was an accident. A tragic – but not atypical – undergraduate accident, they called it. No second fight.'

'Saffron denied it strongly,' Cass pointed out. 'And Miss Tiggie Jones – my God, what a sexy-looking girl! Are those eyelashes real? – Miss Tiggie backed him up. They finished drinking, because they finished the last bottle of champagne, no less, and Bim stumbled away – Saffer's words – to his own room – as they supposed. Shall I ever meet her, do you suppose?'

'I very much doubt it.' Jemima sounded cold. 'Since I hope not to meet her again myself. And I doubt whether Tiggie Jones features a great deal in Lincoln's Inn Fields, wandering about on her own, singing a happy song.'

'Ah well. The point is, does that mean she's a liar as well?'

'To be fair, not necessarily,' said Jemima who saw herself as someone who always did try to be fair. 'It was all very mysterious as well as tragic. But the coroner was sufficiently satisfied to go for accidental death.'

'As you know, Professor Mossbanker, or Proffy, as your beguiling friend Miss Tiggie calls him, found the body in the middle of the night, having been aroused by the noise of what he called the infernal washing machine. Apparently he's always carrying on about the noise it made if used late at night. A few minutes later – he was very clear about it – Saffer accompanied by Tiggie came *down* the staircase. Of course she shouldn't have been in the college so late, but under the circumstances the professor wasn't going to complain. In any case, everybody at Oxford seems to turn a blind eye to that kind of thing these days, officially that is. Their story was that Tiggie wanted to go to the loo on the ground floor and Saffer was escorting her.'

'A likely story?' queried Cass.

'Not altogether unlikely, given the lack of bathrooms and loos in the former all-male colleges at Oxford. I've never seen such squalor. That's one advantage we had in all-women's colleges, bathrooms; but I digress. Not an altogether unlikely story. Look at it like this. If Saffron had really had a fight with the unfortunate Bim, thrown him or caused him to fall down the staircase, I can't believe he would have waited till he heard Proffy emerge, and then come down the stairs plus Miss T. He would either have tried to help straightaway, the decent reaction, or kept well clear of the proceedings altogether.'

'Then there's the whole question of Miss Tiggie and the fight, isn't there?' pursued Cass, pouring Sancerre purposefully into his own glass, and after a gentle reminder into Jemima's too. (As Cass normally had excellent manners, Jemima privately put this aberration down to distracting thoughts of Tiggie Jones.) 'I may be prejudiced in her favour by her eyelashes,' went on Cass, unaware of these cross reflections, 'but supposing Bim did fall or was pushed down the staircase in Saffer's presence, would Tiggie really have let him calmly return to his own room, leaving Bim in a crumpled heap at the bottom, right at the bottom, in the launderette?'

'I'm not so prejudiced that I can't agree to that,' Jemima was sipping away happily at her refilled glass. 'She'd have swooped down on him like some dreadful little bat and given him some terrifyingly predatory form of First Aid. However that's not the real mystery. The real mystery to me is why Bim Marcus set the washing machine in motion. The police think he was badly concussed. Crawled there, set it in motion and then died. It's still odd. But concussion – and alcohol – does odd things to you.'

'Interested in this investigation, darling?' Cass was only half teasing. When Jemima's unofficial criminal investigations took over from her official sociological ones for Megalith, she was apt to have even less time for Cass for a month or two: Cass Brinsley, finding himself for some reason put in mind of the big black eyes and long black eyelashes of Tiggie Jones, thought he would like to have notice of an extended period of absence on Jemima's part. To give such notice was not exactly in their (unspoken) contract of a liberated relationship; any more than Cass had given Jemima notice of finding Flora Hereford, the new pupil in his Chambers, astonishingly attractive.

Jemima however had somehow suspected it and reacted by having a devil-may-care affair with a handsome cameraman at Megalith. Well, she was not called Jemima Shore Investigator for nothing. Sometimes Cass even wondered whether some more permanent arrangement might give him yet more joy, much less heartache. In what should such an arrangement consist? There was one obvious kind of arrangement . . . Cass, wryly certain that such a thought had never crossed Jemima's own mind, put it resolutely from his own.

'I'm interested in the investigation, yes,' Jemima, blithely unaware, cut across his thoughts. 'The nurse's story grabbed me from the start, as you know. I'm not talking about exposure here, of course: Saffron's secret is safe with me, if it is his secret. But I can't rid myself of a feeling – my famous instinct rears its head here – that it's not altogether a coincidence that Bim Marcus died on Saffron's staircase, as a result of a quite unforeseen association with Saffron. They weren't even friends. Tiggie pushed Bim into the party. The police won't buy it – evidence not instinct is what we are after, my dear, as Detective Chief Inspector Gary Harwood of the Oxford CID informed me – but I'm privately wondering whether the right man actually fell down that winding staircase. Let's just suppose someone thought *Saffron* was lurching down to his room, and instead got the wretched Bim in the darkness – the two men were quite alike in an odd way, the same height and build – then we have to think of anyone who would wish Saffron ill. Quite a few in Oxford no doubt, though murder is perhaps going a bit far. What is more, if Saffron is or rather was the target, *that* brings us back to Nurse Elsie's death bed revelation,' concluded Jemima triumphantly.

'I follow your argument about Bim and Saffron on the stairs. You mean, no one could have expected Bim to be up at that time? But I still don't get the Nurse Elsie connection.'

'Don't you *see*, darling? I know you think I'm obsessed with Nurse Elsie – instinct again, and you feel about my instinct roughly as does Detective Chief Inspector Harwood—'

'Not all your instincts,' interposed Cass mildly.

Jemima paid no attention but swept enthusiastically on. 'Don't you see that Nurse Elsie revealed Saffron to be a kind of changeling, the happy accident, whose appearance, late in his parents' life, did horrible Andrew Iverstone and horrible Daphne Iverstone out of their inheritance? And by implication, that nice fellow Jack, I have to admit. That's a lot of enemies. Saffron is not married, has no children; if he died on that staircase, Andrew, and in the course of time Jack, would still inherit Saffron Ivy.'

'That's true whether Saffron is a changeling or not,' pointed out Cass.

Jemima sighed.

'I know. I have to say that I still don't get the connection. I just think there *is* a connection between Nurse Elsie and the Rochester College death. For one thing, there were so many of the Iverstone family at the Hospice those last days – quite out of the blue. Saffron himself revealed that he'd been there, and Daphne Iverstone, she was there too. From what Sister Imelda said, I think she came on the last day of all. She referred to another old friend, "One of Nurse Elsie's ladies", and that could have been Daphne. Then there were the Iverstone brother and sister.'

'So what is the next step, Jemima Shore Investigator?'

'Oh, to forget it all,' responded Jemima. 'What else?'

Jemima Shore, while she was as good as her word for the rest of the evening and night, found herself rapidly reminded of Rochester College at Megalith Television the next morning. This was because she received a letter. The envelope was fairly undistinguished other than that it bore the crest of Rochester College, Oxford; this revealed the foundation to be something vaguely episcopal and not, as Jemima had romantically supposed, connected to the poet Rochester. The quality of the envelope was thin and white. The writing paper within was, on the other hand, nothing if not distinguished.

To begin with, the paper was so thick as to give the momentary illusion of parchment, and its very thickness brought a glow in the tint of the ivory. Then there were great curly black swirls in the address, which was so heavily engraved that the letters positively stood out from the paper. Luckily the address itself could afford to be inscribed in this lavish fashion since it scarcely constituted a space problem. The address read simply: SAFFRON IVY. There was no mention of a neighbouring town, not even a county, let alone anything as common as a postal code (or telephone number).

Jemima read on with interest. That very morning a conference had taken place at Megalith in which she had utterly failed to shift Cy Fredericks from his profound conviction that, as he put it, 'these Golden Kids are Big Bucks, and I don't mean our expenses, I mean our sales. Have you seen the *Brideshead* figures? We can make *Brideshead* look like peanuts. They were just a bunch of actors. We've got the real thing.' So discussions about the *Golden Lads and Girls* programme meandered on; no scheduling as yet, apart from a general feeling that summer was the time to get to grips with that kind of thing. 'Girls in long dresses, nothing punk. And those long boats,' murmured Cy, lowering his voice for once, as if in deference to the scene he was summoning before their eyes. 'Punts,' suggested someone helpfully. 'Nothing punk,' repeated Cy with a wild glare in the direction of the speaker before continuing: 'Long shadows across the July grass. No long shadows across their future, these are Golden Kids – remember, Miss Lewis, make a note of that line – *no long shadows*—'

'Long dresses, long boats, long shadows, I mean, *no* long shadows,' murmured Guthrie Carlyle, Jemima's old friend and potential director of this epic. 'Will it be a long programme to match?'

'What's that, Guthrie?' asked Cy Fredericks sharply. One could never count on Cy's total absorption in his own flow of words, reflected Jemima, especially if there was any hint of disloyalty in the room. Cy had uncanny hearing for disloyal echoes. 'The programme, like all Megalith programmes, will be exactly the right length,' he swept on, 'not a minute more or less. And I mean *artistic length.*' He looked round as if to ask Miss Lewis to inscribe that thought too on her tablets, but by now more exciting matters called, and Miss Lewis had vanished to sort out a flurry of messages from New York.

The main result of the conference was to rechristen the programme *Golden Kids.* This was to avoid the possible charge of sexism implicit in Shakespeare's line, which by placing the word 'Lads' before 'Girls' might be held to suggest that the 'Girls' were mere appendages to the 'Lads'. Guthrie had in fact floated this suggestion as a joke, but finding it enthusiastically endorsed by Cy (who was always desperate to avoid sexism, if only he could put his finger on what it was) Guthrie quickly took the opportunity to atone for his previous levity by proposing it in earnest.

'How about *Oxford Bloods?*' suggested Jemima at one point, 'or even *Bloody Oxford.*'

'Jem,' said Cy reproachfully, 'I had expected better from you. This is not a bloody programme.'

So *Golden Kids* it was. Everyone felt a good deal of progress had been made, and as Cy had to leave for Rome – or as he absent-mindedly described it, New York, until Miss Lewis coughed and corrected him – the meeting broke up.

Jemima was left wondering whether she should have pointed out that the Oxford academic term ended in June. In July, the long shadows in Oxford would be falling on innumerable tourists, while the Golden Kids played elsewhere, departing in long aeroplanes for the long shores of the Mediterranean, the Far East and the United States.

She now gazed at the short note beneath the ornate Saffron Ivy address and thought that under the circumstances a polite invitation from Lord Saffron to lunch in Oxford was not unwelcome.

'Ooh, watch it Jemima,' was Cherry's reaction. 'Supposing he sports that oak thing once you're up there.'

'I shall of course ask him to keep his oak thing to himself,' replied Jemima sweetly. 'In any case I intend to direct operations from a suite at the Martyrs Hotel. Could you be an angel and book it for me? A nice large suite, so that Lord Saffron and others can keep their distance. Megalith owes me a nice large suite for working on *Golden Kids.* And get onto that man, what's his name, that don who went on television the other night calling for more compulsory admissions from comprehensive schools in arts subjects – what *was* his name? Barber or something similar. He's got this campaign called COMPCAMP. I'm not going to let *Golden Kids* get by without a suitable class struggle.'

Jemima was reminded of these bold words a few days later when she found herself sitting with Saffron at lunch in what was in fact a very small and unfashionable restaurant off the Broad.

'For some reason my name is mud in most Oxford restaurants,' explained Saffron plaintively; he also fluttered his eyelashes in a flirtatious way which, whether joking or not, for a moment reminded Jemima of Tiggie Jones. 'And as you know the Martyrs have banned me for my lifetime, or their lifetime, whichever shall be longer. I feel the Lycée won't give me the big hand in future. Luckily when I came here before, I had the wit to book myself in as Colonel Gadaffi and they haven't twigged yet, beyond thinking I'm rather young for a military man. Alas, I can't even set foot in your lovely suite, I fear. I could shin up those pillars, I suppose, and lope in through your balcony. You have *got* a balcony? Looking on the Broad – looking *at* the Martyrs Memorial, oh that's the best one. What a relief. Anyway so far as I am concerned, life at Oxford is just one class struggle.'

Jemima, in spite of herself, had to laugh. But Saffron merely pressed her hand.

'No, I do so understand what Marx meant. The class struggle! When will it ever end? I ask myself. Only the other day Tiggie and I and a few others took ourselves off to the Highgate cemetery to visit the dear fellow's grave. Vodka and Blinis were judged appropriate, though as Poppy Delaware pointed out, who is a Marxist, albeit a Catholic one, something German like beer and bratwurst would really have been more appropriate. Ah, Marx! What a prophet. It's seldom a day I don't think about him, as one tries bravely to keep one's head *above* beer and bratwurst, with due respect to Poppy.'

Saffron, presumably with this admirable objective in view, had ordered champagne on arrival, what he described to an unsurprised waitress in smock and jeans as the Colonel's special. Now he poured it yet again (he was, Jemima noticed, an attentive host; perhaps all the Oxford Bloods were, since they were used to playing the role to each other; or perhaps Saffron had been trained to it since childhood by his parents).

'As if I didn't have enough to contend with, what with the class struggle and beer,' Saffron continued in the same genial voice, 'on top of it all, somebody round here is trying to kill me.'

7

Blood Isn't Everything

'Look, Jemima, I'm going to hire you. That's the point. What are your rates? You're going to find out who's trying to kill me. It would also be quite nice in an off-beat kind of way to know why. Who would want to kill poor little me?' Again Saffron's look of mock innocence reminded Jemima of Tiggie Jones. She did not mention that fact to Cass Brinsley, to whom she related the conversation later that day by telephone. I don't want to inflame him further, thought Jemima sternly. In any case, what Jemima did relate was quite enough for Cass to be getting on with.

'And you let him?' gasped Cass incredulously. 'You let him hire you? As his own personal private investigator. May one enquire the price?'

'You may,' answered Jemima. 'We've struck a bargain. If I discover what's going on, he's going to give a huge donation to the Radical Women's Settlement for Single Drop-Outs. If I fail, he gets to take me to Ascot.'

'Why the Radical Women's Settlement? That's the one you filmed in January, I take it.'

'To be honest, I thought it was the cause he would most dislike,' replied Jemima. 'Originally I considered CND, but unfortunately he actually supports it, although for all the wrong reasons. He told me the noise of the American bombers from the aerodrome near Saffron Ivy disturbs the sweetness of his slumbers. Of course, it's a good thing he supports it,' Jemima added hastily. 'But you see what I mean about it being annoying.'

'Quite,' said Cass who was a multilateralist.

'The real point, darling, is that I am now properly enthusiastic about *Golden Kids* – even if *my* reasons are all the wrong ones,' went on Jemima. 'All the reccying I'm doing, interviews with absolutely everyone in Oxford including dons from Professor Mossbanker whom I adore to Kerry Barber whom I'm hoping to adore because he's so worthy, it's all now a cover. So naturally I feel much better about it all.'

Although Jemima had worked out for herself that the killer – accidental or otherwise – of Bim Marcus had probably been aiming at Saffron, she was taken aback to find that Saffron himself had made the same calculations and come to the same conclusion. An intelligent and quick-witted Saffron was not quite what she had expected to find. Still less had she anticipated finding him sympathetic. Yet away from his friends, the newspapers, away from his *public*, one might almost have said that sympathetic was what Saffron was. The poses were dropped. And the story he unfolded was in itself sufficiently startling and upsetting to deserve some sympathy in its own right.

'Someone's trying to kill me,' he repeated. 'At first I couldn't take it in. The brakes failed on my car. Yes, I know I'm not the world's safest driver, but I do look after the car, and if I don't Wyndham does – he's the old chauffeur at Saffron Ivy. It was Wyndham who finally convinced me that something very odd had been done to the car; he put it down to Oxford undergraduates of course. All the same: "You could have been deceased, my lord" he pronounced with great solemnity, Wyndham having the bearing of a bishop rather than a chauffeur. There were one or two other odd incidents too, but of course I was getting pretty jumpy about everything. Then Bim was killed.'

'When did all this start?' asked Jemima. 'I take it you don't count the fight in the restaurant. The man with the red hair and the appropriate name of Rufus, plus his enormous friend. *That* wasn't an attempt on your life?'

'Rufus Pember and Big Nigel Copley.' Saffron laughed in a brief return to his airy manner. 'Oh yes, they would like to kill me all right. I must write to the Vice-Chancellor about it. Where did it start? A girl, I believe. Muffet Pember, to wit, but this is not sex and violence. This is *serious*.'

It all began, Saffron told her, on the terrible day he went to see Nurse Elsie at the Hospice.

'If only Ma hadn't made me go – but as I told you, she made such a point of it. Said Nurse Elsie was asking for me specially – you bet she was – wouldn't die happy unless I went. Then that ghastly place. No, I know it's a wonderful place and all that. But Nurse Elsie, her hand like a claw clutching mine – that was what was ghastly. Like a skeleton from the past. Isn't it odd? I'd always hated it even more when she came to look after me sometimes when Nan was on holiday. And she used to bring Jack and Fanny to stay sometimes. She *looked* at me so oddly, I swear she did. Hugging me when we were alone. Telling me I was her own special little boy. Touching me all the time when we were alone. Nan hugged me of course, but there was something creepy about the way Elsie did it. I knew it was wrong. Children always know things like that, don't they, even if they don't know *why*.

'And now here she was, this terrifying skeleton – hanging on to me – and telling me – she was a lunatic – she was telling me – of all things—' Saffron was sounding increasingly incoherent, even hysterical. All the same, Jemima was astonished when he leant forward and without bothering to push aside the glasses or the champagne bottle, now three quarters empty, simply buried his face in his hands. The large green bottle rocked to and fro twice and then fell heavily over. The remains of the drink began to bubble out and flow goldenly across the table.

Jemima saw that Saffron was crying.

When he finally looked up, however, his expression was quite steady. 'Such a relief to tell someone,' said Saffron after a while. He took Jemima's hand and pressed it.

'You haven't told me anything yet.' Jemima spoke gently; after all she knew – who better? – exactly what he was going to say. What she had not known till this minute was the fearful strength of Nurse Elsie's dying obsession – if that was what it was. It had never occurred to Jemima, famous instinct for once at fault, that Nurse Elsie, as the days passed and death came nearer, with no lawyer arriving, might have passed on her story to anyone else. Yet she *should* have known it of course: when Sister Imelda referred to Nurse Elsie's 'peace of mind' at the end, Jemima *should* have realized that Father Thomas had granted absolution – which supposed some form of revelation to someone. To how many others did Nurse Elsie tell her story, was the unspoken question in Jemima's mind, even before Saffron told of his own interview with the dying woman.

'Why me?' was what Jemima said when Saffron had finished relating Nurse Elsie's story. Then she received her second surprise. Saffron spoke flatly, as though all his emotion had for the time being been drained away.

'Because you knew already. That's true, isn't it? You were going to bring a lawyer. Expose the whole thing. Aristocratic fake. Phoney lord. Those were going to be the headlines on television.'

'For heaven's sake,' exclaimed Jemima, 'who on earth told you that? It is true I was going to bring a lawyer—' She stopped. What had she intended exactly? Oh wise Cass! she thought, why didn't I listen to you before I got involved in all of this? Too late now to step back. 'That was to bring comfort to a dying woman,' she went on carefully. 'The priest wouldn't give her absolution unless she made restitution, as it's called. Making a statement to a lawyer – he wasn't a solicitor by the way, so he wasn't a commissioner of oaths, just a barrister friend of mine – that was a kind of well-meant sop.'

Something else struck Jemima. 'Phoney lord, aristocratic fake. Those were never Nurse Elsie's words. Who else have you discussed this with –

your parents—' she paused delicately. After all, one of the main points of Nurse Elsie's story was that Lord St Ives had proposed the deception; he might have been motivated by a desire to spare his wife pain, but the consequence would be to deprive Andrew Iverstone – or more likely his only son Jack – of his inheritance.

'It's not true. Don't you understand?' Saffron said this very fiercely. 'It's not true! Of course I haven't told Pa. As for Ma, it would kill her. She's in a pretty dickey state anyway.' Now it was Saffron's turn to pause. 'As a matter of fact I did tell Tiggie. Not the truth, of course. Just that you were trying to rake up some scandal about me. Spill dirt all over me. And *she* put the point about television. She's into that kind of thing. After all, she screws Cy Fredericks, doesn't she? Or maybe she doesn't. With Tiggie, who knows? She said she'd fix it.'

'Fix me?'

Saffron gave her his disarming smile. 'Fix the programme if you like. Get Megalith so involved with me, your original Oxford Blood, that they wouldn't even want to expose me – not that there's anything to expose,' he added quickly.

'Ah.' One thing which Jemima had tucked away in the corner of her mind as not-to-be-forgotten and one-day-to-be-investigated was the reason for Tiggie Jones' hostile 'anonymous' telephone call. As for Cy Fredericks – to adapt the words of Saffron, who cared if he was screwing Tiggie or not – but in either case she understood the passionate advocacy of the *Golden Kids* programme which had infuriated her; clearly Tiggie was putting pressure upon him.

'So how does it all fit in? The murder attempts – if that's what they were – and Nurse Elsie's story. In view of what she said, why should anyone want to *kill* you—' Jemima stopped rather awkwardly, then decided that she might as well be frank. 'Wouldn't it be better for an interested party' – that was a delicate phrase – 'to *expose* you?' That was somehow less delicate, but Jemima ploughed on: 'Expose you as not being your father's real son?'

'Don't you see, that's for you to find out. All I know is that there have been these attempts. The car; that night when poor Bim died. And they all began when that horrible old woman died.'

'In short,' Jemima ended up telling Cass Brinsley, in a voice which she hoped was as disarming as that of Tiggie Jones, or Saffron himself, 'In short, I've agreed to go to the Chimneysweepers' Dinner at the beginning of next term as his guest. I'll pretend to be researching the programme. But actually I'll be there as a kind of protection. In case someone has another go.'

'Will you be wearing a gun?' enquired Cass. It was his turn to sound cold. He began to appreciate the irritation Jemima had felt at his interest in Tiggie Jones (although that was of course totally platonic, mere sociological interest in one so young, so bizarre – and admittedly so pretty). Was it possible that Jemima fancied the odious Saffron? 'Phoney lord' – yes indeed.

Reflecting later on this conversation with Jemima, Cass angrily hoped that Saffron would turn out to be the son of a butcher and then quickly corrected himself, realizing that this was a concept highly insulting to butchers. The trouble with Jemima was that she was so convinced that her head ruled her heart, that she never seemed to notice her extreme vulnerability to any rash suggestion on the part of the aforesaid heart, added to which, what was all this heart nonsense anyway? Saffron was an extremely handsome as well as extremely arrogant young man, and when had Jemima ever been averse to a handsome man, young or old?

Absolutely resolved to put all these thoughts away from him, Cass Brinsley reached for his telephone book and looked for the number of Flora, that pupil in his Chambers about whom Jemima had been so surprisingly suspicious. He then wondered idly what Tiggie Jones' telephone number might be and whether Cherry could be persuaded to disgorge it ... When Jemima returned to London, he would try to dissuade her from further involvement with Saffron, involvement beyond the call of professional duty to the programme. Nothing personal. Merely his concern for Jemima's own best interests.

But it turned out that Jemima's own concern for her best interests did not exactly tally with that of Cass. During the academic holidays, Cy Fredericks' appetite for the *Golden Kids* programme was further sharpened by various exciting encounters with Tiggie Jones (faithfully reported to Cherry by Miss Lewis, who ran a nice line in quiet bitchery behind her agreeable Sloane Ranger exterior). And the beginning of May found Jemima once more installed in her suite at the Martyrs Hotel. What was more, she was preening himself in the mirror, preparatory to attending the Chimneysweepers' Dinner on the arm of Lord Saffron.

'Preening' was the word because she was not going to wear a gun to dinner, she was going to wear a new Jean Muir outfit consisting of wide flowing crepe culottes, a silk blouse, and a crepe jacket cut like a very grand cardigan. Jemima was now trying the effects of a scarf against the soft grape-coloured folds of the blouse. She was sufficiently distracted not to notice a large packet on her desk until it was almost time to sally forth.

Inside the packet was a book and a note. Jemima frowned. The title was not immediately seductive to one about to cut a swathe (in a new Jean Muir dress) among the notorious Oxford Bloods. She read the note first.

Study it, Jemima Shore Investigator. I actually went as a blood donor over Easter at Saffron Ivy because Ma is the local President or whatever, so my good blue blood was in demand, to prove giving blood is harmless in spite of AIDS. The Prince of Wales had just given *his* even bluer blood, and I was out to please poor old Ma. After recent events. I do have my nice side, you know. Except my blood wasn't blue exactly, it was AB like a reader of *The Times*. Which, according to the uniformed vampire who took it, is a fairly rare group. At least she made me feel my blood was socially useful even if I wasn't. Something else the vampire said made me ask Ma what her group was, and she said: 'O, I think, darling, same as Pa's.' 'Oh no, Lady St Ives' says the vampire importantly, that's not possible . . .' which set me thinking. Of course blood isn't everything, I hear you say. Or isn't it?

The paper was the familiar crackling parchment headed by the curly words 'Saffron Ivy'. There was a similarly curling S as a signature. A scribbled PS read, 'Why don't you come to the above noble pile? If you and I both survive the Chimneysweepers. You could say it would be for the sake of the programme.'

The title of the book (which had the book-plate of the Rochester College library) was *Medical Jurisprudence and Toxicology*. A marker had been put in a chapter entitled 'Blood Grouping'. Page 349 contained a simple table, so simple in fact that even Jemima Shore, who had been woefully or perhaps wilfully stupid at science at school, could not fail to understand it. The table, entitled 'Derivation of Offspring After Landsteiner', illustrated a sub-section called 'Blood grouping in cases of disputed paternity'. There were three headings in the table: 'Groups of Parents', 'Groups of Children' and 'Exclusion Cases'. Under 'Groups of Parents' Jemima traced down to O. The only possible blood group of children whose parents' own blood groups were both O, was given as O. The blood groups A, B and AB were specifically excluded from possibility.

That seemed clear enough, rather horribly clear in fact. In case it wasn't, there was a further Note appended: 'A and B agglutinogens cannot appear in the offspring unless present in the blood of one or both parents. This is common to the theories of von Dungern and Hirszfeld, and of Bernstein.' So if the table was correct – Jemima glanced at the date of the book – and if she had understood the table aright and if matters concerning blood groupings were really quite so simple, and above all if Lady St Ives had got it right about her own and her husband's blood group, then Saffron could not be his parents' natural child, because the A and B agglutinogen, whatever that was, could not be present in the offspring of two O group parents. According to Landsteiner, von Dungern, Hirszfeld, old uncle Bernstein and all. The date of *Medical Jurisprudence and Toxicology* was 1950 and its author was one Glaister.

How odd, how truly ironic, if Saffron's blood, to which he paid such store, proved in the end to be a fatal liability!

Was it that simple? Could it be that simple? A good deal seemed to rest on the evidence of Lady St Ives, speaking off the cuff at some function which was only vaguely official; after all she could have easily been mistaken about her husband's blood group if not her own. Jemima remembered a recent case of a baby's disputed paternity which had been settled by blood tests taken from the two possible fathers; but details of the process had not been given. What was an agglutinogen anyway and could a blood test lie? Questions like this made a bizarre contrast to the evening ahead of her when the only blood likely to be under consideration was the aristocratic blood of the participants. At least she hoped it was.

And that blood was not actually going to flow. At least she hoped it wasn't.

8

Dress: Gilded Rubbish

Jemima's first reaction to the sight of the assembled rout of the Oxford Bloods at the Chimneysweepers' Dinner was that for once the newspapers had not exaggerated. The theme of the evening, Saffron had informed her, was to be taken from the magistrate's remarks at the end of the Martyrs case in which he himself had featured so prominently. 'Gilded rubbish' were the words used by the magistrate, and 'Dress: Gilded rubbish' was printed at the bottom of the Chimneysweepers' ornate invitation. Jemima herself could not have thought of a more exact description of the medley of peacocks which confronted her. It was as though a Beckett play was being enacted by a set of Firbank characters.

The club, for obvious reasons no longer welcome at the Martyrs, had taken refuge in a slightly down-at-heel restaurant on the edge of the river called The Punting Heaven, which was presumably prepared to overlook the Oxford Bloods' fearsome reputation for the sake of pecuniary reward. Now these sparkling tramps — was that Tiggie Jones emerging from a scanty parcel of newspaper sprayed with glitter dust? — congregated on the small lawn in front of the restaurant. Some of the Bloods were sprawled on the grass and champagne bottles already rolled among the gilded dustbins with which the path to the river was artistically lined.

Had the Bloods actually arrived in the enormous dustcart, suitably gilded and hung with other golden dustbins, which jostled with Jemima's white car at the edge of the lawn? Or was it perhaps for display purposes only? Was it indeed a genuine municipal object, decorated for the evening, or somebody's bizarre creation? Jemima touched it. Papier mâché and paint: characteristically superficial glamour. The structure began to sway perilously even to her light touch, and she backed away lest this *oeuvre* come to dust even before the Chimneysweepers' Dinner had begun. Along its flank was painted the insouciant motto: 'Gold is all that glitters' – another characteristic touch.

At the side of the river a series of punts were chained together. Although it was only the beginning of May, it had been a sunny afternoon, the temperature quite hot once one got out of the wind, and Jemima had noticed a number of boats being poled enthusiastically up the Cherwell, amid the pollarded trees whose outlines were being rapidly blurred with green. She imagined that these chains were strong enough to withstand any attempts of similarly enthusiastic Bloods to take to the river after dinner. Jemima trailed her fingers in the river. The water was icy.

Afterwards, in view of what happened, Jemima came to look back on the comparative serenity of the early evening with a kind of awed nostalgia and her own part in it later with something like amazement. Did she really sit with Proffy on the bank of the river under a full moon riding high across the water meadows discussing whether the rich were happy, with a goblet of pink champagne in her hand? (To hell with the new Jean Muir dress.) While all around them, stretched out in the deep shadows left by the moon's pathway, the bodies tumbled and caressed like nymphs and shepherds in a Poussin landscape. Most of their fragile sparkling clothing had in any case been crumpled or torn away, so that classical garlands or brief wisps of trailing material were all that some of them were wearing. Occasional laughter from that direction, the creaking of the chained punts and a splash – a bottle? a glass? – indicated that the boats, if captive, were still being put to some use.

At this point Jemima decided that champagne was responsible for a good many of the excesses in her life, but this was one of the oddest. It was true that she had decided politely not to tumble or be tumbled with the rest of the nymphs: although one particular undergraduate rather reminded her of Cass and there was always of course Saffron . . . Cass's ridiculous jealousy on that subject had, to be honest, been rather counter-productive. She also received several invitations, rather, she thought, as one might be invited to dance. But since she had reached her thirties without participating in an orgy (unless you counted certain scenes in a jacuzzi on the West Coast of America which she didn't) it seemed a bad plan to start a new way of life in the purlieus of Oxford University. Deep as the riverside shadows might be, Jemima had a feeling that the harsh light of the *Evening Post*'s gossip column, to say nothing of *Jolly Joke*'s vicious searchlight, would somehow manage to penetrate them. On the other hand she had to admit that the decision was a cerebral one.

It was extremely tempting to go with the exotic hedonism of the evening – fortunately the presence of Proffy and the particular subject which they were discussing kept her attention more or less concentrated on the conversation to the exclusion of thoughts about the shadows, beyond brief amused reflections that Cy's cameras should really be present for such an occasion. Oh well, she had no doubt that the Oxford Bloods would recreate the scene, if asked, with enthusiasm when summer came. If this was their style in early May, what on earth would June bring forth? The aggressive heat of The Punting Heaven had driven her out of doors; no doubt similar scenes were being enacted inside amid the wreckage of the flower-decked tables. The gold music of *Rheingold* being played very loudly indoors ('*Rheingold*! *Rheingold*! Tumty ta-ta') covered other sounds.

'We always play Wagner at Chimneysweepers' bashes,' explained Saffron, 'because it's so cheerful. Besides, it covers up the noise of breaking glass a treat. Do you suppose that was why old Wags wrote it?'

The presence of Proffy, and indeed of various other more senior guests, was a surprise to Jemima, until she realized wryly that their participation – and indeed her own – was intended to rehabilitate the Oxford Bloods' somewhat tarnished image. (That impulse had however evidently exhausted their plans for reform.) There was, for example, an older woman present, rather handsome, with greying dark hair worn in a bun, and a beaky, almost Roman, nose. Her gold lamé dress, judging from its cut, might have been newly acquired for the occasion, since it was in the height of the current fashion; on the other hand it was the sort of dress that a woman like this might have had in her wardrobe, regardless of fashion, for the last twenty years. The same could be said for her prominent necklace of large amber and jet beads. Although she appeared to be rather silent compared to the rest of the company, Jemima had the impression of a strong personality; one of those people whose presence at any particular gathering marks it, without one being able to define exactly why.

The multiparous Mrs Mossbanker? It turned out that the handsome woman was in fact that mysterious Professor Eugenia Jones, mother of Antigone, alias Tiggie – she who had been last heard of returning from the States. Curiously enough, Proffy had addressed her consistently as Eleanor, which if Jemima remembered rightly was actually his wife's name.

Studying Eugenia Jones, one could see where Tiggie's looks came from, if not her particular sense of style. She was also quite short, like her daughter, although her flowing golden robe gave her an air of dignity. Who was Jones, Jemima wondered, and what was his profession? She would have to ask her friend Jamie Grand, currently visiting professor at a new college founded by a shy millionaire apparently entirely for Jamie's delectation since it provided vast funds for lavish dons' dining, but none for the sordid everyday needs of undergraduates. Jamie combined a fierce insistence on the highest standards of academic criticism and study with an endearing propensity to gossip, an activity which he pursued with exactly the same informed seriousness, expecting others to do so too.

Thinking of Jamie and the tabs he kept on society – with both big and small S – Jemima was at least not surprised by his presence among the older guests. A little blonde girl, of the sort of which Jamie appeared to have an endless supply, hung on his arm. A large gold fez crowned the countenance whose veriest frown could cause a shudder in the literary world (to quote *Time* Magazine – and Jamie often did).

'Who's Jones?' blurted out Jemima without preamble. At exactly the same moment Jamie said: 'Do you know Serena of Christ Church?' He swept on: 'Isn't it enjoyable hearing that? I'm old-fashioned enough to adore it. These days I only go out with girls from the best men's colleges, or rather the former men's colleges that were formerly the best. Rachel of Magdalen, Allegra of Trinity, I don't know anyone at Balliol yet unfortunately.' He turned to Serena of Christ Church.

'Do you know anyone at Balliol, my dear? Blonde of course. About your height and weight.'

'I don't want to distract you but I was wondering about Jones, Eugenia's husband. Tiggie's father,' broke in Jemima before Serena of Christ Church could answer.

'Ah, that Jones. The ideal husband. In the sense that he was never there when she was wanted. Or so Eugenia once told me, in not quite so many witty words. He vanished before my day. No, I can't tell you anything about Jones. I've sometimes suspected Eugenia of inventing him. She's certainly been totally happy ever since in a so-called unhappy personal situation, as you are doubtless aware. Eugenia is one of those women who thrives on personal unhappiness. It leaves her plenty of time for work – after all, think how successful she is. And then Eleanor has all the domestic responsibilities. Which are considerable where Proffy is concerned, to say nothing of the butter mountain of children.'

So, when Jemima was swept away from the heat of The Punting Heaven to the moonlight of the river bank, she was for the first time aware that she was on the arm of the lover – the long-term lover according to Jamie – of Professor Eugenia Jones; as well as the abstracted husband of Eleanor, and still more abstracted father of innumerable Mossbanker children. By now she was curious enough about Eugenia Jones to make a mental resolve to interview her for the programme – difficult to see how she could be fitted into *Golden Kids*, other than as the mother of Tiggie Jones, which might not be the most tactful approach, but Jemima would think of something. Eugenia Jones herself had vanished discreetly after dinner before Jemima could have more than the briefest exchange with her. Nevertheless, her impression of a strong personality had been confirmed. Although their conversation in recollection was not particularly scintillating, at the time Eugenia Jones managed to invest slightly commonplace remarks with something of her own dignity.

One of Jemima's personal preoccupations, based on her own past, was with long-term extra-marital relationships, particularly from the woman's point of view – the other woman's point of view, that is, when the man was married and she was not. A serious programme on the subject would have been impossible so long as her painful long-drawn-out relationship with Tom Amyas MP prospered – if that was the right word, which on the whole it was not. And now? She still did not imagine that Professor Eugenia Jones would welcome an overture based on such a premise. All the same, the connection between her own success and that time early in her career at Megalith, when she fought down jealous thoughts of Tom's domestic routine with hard work, was not to be denied. Had she ever quite forgotten the pain of the moment when Tom was obliged to break it to her that Carrie, his wife, was pregnant? And yet Professor Jones had presumably had to endure that kind of scene with extraordinarily regularity in view of the amazing fertility of Mrs Mossbanker. Maybe Jamie was right, and it had allowed Eugenia Jones to get on with her own work uncluttered with domesticity.

Compared to Professor Eugenia Jones, Fanny Iverstone was not such a surprising guest. (And maybe Eugenia Jones was only here to have a glimpse of Proffy? However improbable the thought, Jemima knew from personal experience that nothing of that nature was ever totally improbable where the so-called 'other woman' was concerned.) Fanny was after all a young girl living in Oxford, and a not unattractive one, even if she was not quite in the same dazzling class as two ravishing girls introduced to Jemima merely as Tessa and Nessa. In the old days such girls would have been marked down as arriving from London; nowadays all the prettiest were probably at the University.

Saffron was rather uncharacteristically vague about who had invited Fanny, to the extent that Jemima was led to expect he had actually done so himself at some earlier date, before seizing the opportunity to bring Jemima as well. It had to be said that the style of 'Gilded Rubbish' did not suit Fanny's looks and perhaps it was for that reason, or perhaps she was generally discomforted by the company, but in any case Jemima found Fanny much less ebullient than on the famous occasion of the Lycée lunch. Tiggie Jones was exactly the sort of girl who shone at a party like this, and there was Tiggie – shining. Shining also was Poppy Delaware, a girl so like Tiggie (except for the colour of her hair, which was partially blue and partially orange) that Jemima wondered if they might not be sisters until she realized that the effect of the glittering tattiness of the costumes as well as the short-cropped hair-cuts of both sexes was to make everyone young look rather alike.

All this made it very easy to recognize another surprising guest,

Daphne Iverstone, and wait – *could it be*? yes it was: Andrew Iverstone MP, Mr Rabblerouse himself. With his broad build and heavy shoulders, his pink face and fast-receding light curly hair, Jemima disgustedly thought that Andrew Iverstone resembled nothing so much as a big white porker; certainly his looks, arguably representing some kind of Anglo-Saxon stereotype, constituted no kind of advertisement for the sort of racial purity he was fond of advocating. And yet it was always said that he possessed the kind of charm which made the unwary overlook the precise import of his views until it was too late, and some kind of implicit approval had been given. Jemima however had never met him and did not wish to do so now.

Only Jack of the Iverstone family was missing. But then the Chimneysweepers' Dinner was scarcely his form. He was after all in no sense an Oxford Blood.

'Not one's bright idea, I assure you.' Saffron spoke in her ear. 'I can't bear him, the old Rabblerouse. Some other bright spirit invited him and Cousin Daphne. Almost as tactless as Bernardo Valliera inviting Muffet Pember.' Saffron pointed to where a man, looking vaguely South American, was clothed in bonds of tinsel wound round the rather small base of a leopard-skin jock strap; he had his arm round a girl in a gold mask and high-heeled gold boots, with a skimpy leopard-skin bikini in between. From her russet-coloured hair which was left free, Jemima recognized Muffet Pember, sister of the aggressive Rufus.

There was, Jemima had realized from the first, a certain amount of fairly discreet drug-taking going on. Discreet in the sense that no one had actually offered her some of the various little substances being shared around: cocaine presumably – another expensive taste like champagne. There appeared to be an unwritten law by which the 'adults' such as the Iverstones, Eugenia Jones and Proffy were ignored in this connection, and they themselves in turn ignored it. Bernardo Valliera, on the other hand, whether he thought his South American blood granted him some immunity, was not being particularly discreet in whatever it was he was pressing upon Muffet Pember.

Saffron however seemed quite indifferent to that aspect of the situation and Jemima had to admit that she never actually saw him involved in it; as far as she could make out, champagne – and a great deal of it – was enough for him.

'At least Muffet is pretty enough outside as you can observe for yourself,' he went on, 'if all venom inside. But Cousin Andrew is so terribly unaesthetic, isn't he? I wish he would wear Muffet's mask, which incidentally I take to be disguise from brother Rufus' righteous fury if he finds out she's come to the dinner. So likely Bernardo won't tell everyone in Oxford. As for Cousin Andrew's celebrated views, give me the West Indians any day. There's a fantastic black girl at New College –

unfortunately her radical prejudices make her reject all my advances. Looking at Cousin Andrew makes one realize all over again that blood isn't everything.'

It was the only allusion he made to the note and the book on her dressing-table.

The presence of Andrew Iverstone had the effect of making Jemima concentrate more than she would perhaps have done otherwise on Professor Mossbanker's ramblings on the subject of wealth and happiness. She still hoped to avoid the social burden of an introduction to the MP but it was not quite so easy. Andrew Iverstone had not maintained a prominent position in public life over a number of years by undue sensitivity on social occasion where liberals were concerned. Particularly when they had access to the media. His invitations to 'a civilized lunch' issued the day after a journalist had criticized him savagely in public were notorious: somehow the journalist was never quite so savage about Andrew Iverstone again.

'Of course I can't bear the fellow's views, perfectly ghastly but you have to admit he's not afraid to meet his critics. Never mind, the lunch was delicious – gulls' eggs! and a fantastic claret later – all the same I gave him a frightful bashing' – Jemima had heard this speech on more than one occasion. The lunch guest never seemed to notice that Andrew Iverstone's public utterances, unlike their own, remained quite unaltered by the frightful bashing he had received.

Now Jemima found herself receiving the treatment.

'Miss Shore, I would never have expected to find *you* at an evening entitled "Gilded Rubbish".' Even in his dinner jacket – no fancy dress risked – Andrew Iverstone gave the impression of lifting an imaginary hat to Jemima.

'But darling, I told you, Jemima is really absolutely one of us.'

Daphne Iverstone, prettily dressed in spotted powder blue and white chiffon, twittered from somewhere near her husband's elbow. Andrew Iverstone ignored her.

'It's providential. I was so interested in that programme of yours about Asian women and the dramatic conflict between our culture and theirs. You might be surprised to learn how many Asians regard me as a kind of father confessor. They really do want to return to their own culture.' Andrew Iverstone twinkled his little eyes and his fair eyelashes, short but very thick, fluttered. 'I thought we might discuss the matter over a civilized lunch.'

'How truly kind. Actually my programme was about the assimilation of Asian women, bearing in mind their traditional values. I think you must have another programme in mind. I should hate to have lunch, especially a civilized lunch, under false pretences.'

It was helpful that throughout this exchange Proffy had not ceased philosophizing on the subject of Dives and Lazarus. Jemima turned back to him with relief. Proffy was capable of drinking from an empty glass without noticing; he could also cheerfully eat off an empty plate while talking, as well as dipping his spoon into his neighbour's pudding as he had done at La Lyceé. None of this diminished the rapidity of his conversation. Jemima did not notice what happened to the elder Iverstones as the more orgiastic aspects of the evening began to develop. But as she sat herself gracefully down on the river bank alone, Proffy suddenly appeared from nowhere. He picked up the conversation concerning wealth again as though it had never been interrupted.

'Dives – a very happy and contented man!' he exclaimed several times, pumping the night air with his hand. 'Whereas Lazarus undoubtedly needed the services of a psychiatrist, supposing he could have afforded one. People don't understand that it's most agreeable wearing purple and fine linen, particularly if you have a beggar at your gate to eat up your crumbs. Purple for the rich man: oh yes, indeed. When Saffron succeeds to that Elizabethan gem, perhaps I shall try to persuade him to allow me to come and live at his gate as the token beggar to ensure him happiness, yes, yes – but what about the children?' he paused, then rattled on. 'Not perhaps with all the children. I don't think Eleanor would like it either. Lazarus has no family in the Bible. But I shall be there, with my official sores for his dogs to lick. I wonder what *kind* of dogs they have at Saffron Ivy? Rather large dogs I daresay. No, on second thoughts, I think I will persuade Eugenia to bring the children, at any rate during the holidays, they're fond of dogs I expect, children are so sentimental about animals, and they can take some of the burden of being licked off me. Take them for walks and that sort of thing!'

'Didn't the story of Dives and Lazarus end rather badly?' enquired Jemima, 'for Dives, that is. Didn't Dives find himself in Hell, looking up at Lazarus in Abraham's bosom?'

'My dear girl,' cried Proffy. 'Surely you don't believe everything you read in the Bible. A highly corrupt text. I assure you Dives was immensely happy until the day of his death, when he was promptly received into Abraham's bosom as a reward for his kindness to Lazarus.'

'Money, like blood, isn't everything—' began Jemima. She was stopped by the sound of a loud splash or perhaps two splashes, coming from the river. There was the sound of wood crashing on wood and some kind of splintering, as it might be two boats colliding. From the noise of it, a fight was taking place.

There were shouts. Jemima distinctly heard the word 'Pember' and then: 'Look out – Christ, what *have* you done?'

Then a girl's hysterical voice cried out: 'It's Saffer. He's covered in blood. I think he's dead.'

9

An Envious Society

The screaming girl was Fanny Iverstone. As she ran out of the shadows, Jemima saw dark patches on her gaudy dress: patches of blood, black in the moonlight. At that point, as if on some ghostly cue, the moon went behind a thick black cloud and for a moment the only light came from the coloured dancing globes of The Punting Heaven, still streaming across the lawn as the noise of the *Liebestod*, which had succeeded *Rheingold* (ancient Flagstadt? modern Linda Esther Gray?), bellowed out.

'They've got him, they've got him,' she was crying. 'Proffy, *do* something.'

The continuing sense of chaos was made worse by the fact that the grandeur of the music, the glorious voice of Flagstadt (yes), went on soaring above it all. When someone at last saw fit to switch off the home-made Wagnerian tape, special to the occasion, the babble of cries and voices left behind sounded quite puny in the silence.

Fanny went on sobbing hysterically as Bernardo Valliera – recognizable by his leopard-skin – and another man called something like Luggsby ran towards the river. Proffy, who had stood quite still and for once silent through all this as though in a state of shock, eventually put his arm round her. The emergence of the revellers from the grass and a couple from the most distant punt, both male it appeared, together with a powerful searchlight turned onto the scene from the boats, meant that the evening had lost all its classical Poussinesque magic. A comparison to Stanley Spencer was more appropriate. Several of the girls were shivering. Everyone was suddenly aware that it had become very cold.

It seemed an extraordinarily long time before the ambulance arrived. Before that, Saffron's motionless blood-stained body was borne out of the bushes at the edge of the bank where he had been found lying by four of his friends, using the door of the boathouse as a kind of bier. As the searchlight fell on his face travelled across his body, still partly clad in its gold finery, the Wagnerian comparison to Siegfried was irresistible; would his arm suddenly rise and would he sing of the past before dying?

Who was his Brunnhilde? Fanny Iverstone? But she hardly looked the part; not romantic enough. Tiggie Jones in a way-out modern version? Or perhaps Muffet Pember who, mask abandoned, was sitting distraught on the grass, quite alone, dishevelled red hair round her shoulders. She looked infinitely pathetic in her leopard-skin bikini; nobody had thought to put a coat round her shoulders. Jemima, who wanted to do something to help and was frustrated by her inability to think of anything practical, went and covered her with her cardigan.

Muffet looked up. Her first words reminded Jemima that Muffet's correct role in *Götterdämmerung*, if she was to pursue the comparison, was that of Gutrune, bride of Siegfried and sister of Siegfried's slayer Gunter.

'Everyone thinks it's my fault,' she sobbed. 'But I didn't tell Rufus I was coming here. I'm not such a bloody idiot, am I?' Muffet gazed rather angrily at her. It occurred to Jemima that Muffet, apart from her unusual Pre-Raphaelite colouring, was not really all that pretty: her brown eyes were quite small; her neat little nose was quite sharp and snipey. When one looked at her closely Muffet Pember looked more shrewd than naive. Perhaps she was not so pathetic after all. Jemima remembered Saffron's words: 'all venom inside'.

'Do you mean that it was your *brother* who attacked Saffron?' asked Jemima sharply. Beyond the fact that Saffron had been assaulted with a boat hook and had a large gash on the back of his head, Jemima had not managed to gather many details of the attack. Despite the great loss of blood – the AB group blood – from the scalp wound he was however very much alive and his pulse was strong.

'No, of course it wasn't,' said Muffet, sounding even more indignant and less woebegone. 'It was just an awful coincidence. Rufus and Nigel and their friends came up the river in a couple of canoes to – well, I don't know exactly what they came to do' – slightly coy tone – 'and before they could do anything, before they even landed, Fanny found Saffer all covered with blood. I know it sounds rather odd,' Muffet finished lamely. 'But it was just an awful coincidence. I mean, why should Rufus use a boat hook?'

'Why indeed?' asked Jemima rather grimly. Muffet seemed to imply that other methods of assault – the fight in the restaurant for example – were lawful. At this point they were joined by Fanny Iverstone, hysterics now remarkably vanished and a coat – Proffy's ? No, too smart – flung over her stained dress. Under the circumstances Jemima admired her control, as she had admired her breezily bossy character on the occasion of their first meeting. It took some strength of character to be smoking a cigarette by the river, when you had discovered the blood-stained body of your cousin a very short time before. Even if Fanny's hand was shaking, her conversation made sense. Nor did she seek to blame Rufus Pember.

'*Somebody* must have had it in for him,' said Fanny. 'But not necessarily Rufus. He was just lying there. And then I heard the splashes. The trouble is, you know what Saffer's like. People absolutely loathe him. All that money. And then he never tries to hide it, when most people here are so poor. Lots of people hate Saffer who've never even met him. I'd hate him myself, I expect, if I'd never *met* him.'

'Well you don't hate him, do you? Not exactly.' Muffet still sounded sulky. Nor was she apparently grateful for Fanny's defence of her brother. Altogether, not a very appealing little character, thought Jemima.

The next day Jemima related this conversation on the telephone, along with all the other lurid details of the evening, to Cass in London. Considering Cass' doleful prophecies about Jemima's presence at the Chimneysweepers' Dinner, he was remarkably tolerant towards her revelations, showing more interest in the possible identity of Saffron's attacker than in Jemima's own experiences during the evening. The jealous cracks about Saffron were also missing.

It was not until later, when she was walking with her usual aesthetic satisfaction down the long curve of the High Street on her way to visit that well-known moralist Kerry Barber at St Lucy's, that this absence of jealousy struck Jemima as significant. A sense of fairness in Cass – one of his marked characteristics as curiosity was hers – meant that he generally abandoned any questions concerning her private life when his own would not bear examination. So Jemima, ineluctably, began to wonder who . . . All at once the elegance of the curved street, paraded graciously down towards Magdalen Bridge like an Edwardian beauty at the races, failed to move her. Ignoring for once the classical façade of the Queen's College, she felt like Emma during the Box Hill expedition: 'less happy than she had expected'.

Jemima put her mind resolutely forward to the prospect of her encounter with Kerry Barber at St Lucy's. The bells of evensong were sounding as she passed St Mary's, the University church, and soon other bells began to chime in. Jemima did not imagine that the groups of the young – all undergraduates? at any rate all young – lounging and scurrying along the pavement were on their way to evensong. Nevertheless, for all the evening sunshine now casting its romantic stagey shadows on pillar and alley, there was something uncomfortable at the heart of the idyll. At any rate to Jemima's fancy; another kind of disquiet replaced the vague dissatisfaction about Cass's absent affections.

An open car, small and red and noisy, passed her: the driver and the male passengers were wearing white. A girl in the front seat, wearing pale blue, waved: it was Fanny Iverstone. Jemima waved back. Fanny at least had perfectly recovered from the events of the previous night, even if Saffron was lying in the Radcliffe Infirmary, eight stitches in his scalp, but otherwise not as badly injured as that glimpse of him white-faced on his bier had seemed to indicate.

It was this sight of Fanny which jolted Jemima towards the source of her own disquiet: at least about Oxford. It was all very well for Cy Fredericks, as chairman of a commercial television company, to talk enthusiastically about 'a post-*Brideshead* situation', followed by his famous pronouncement: 'these Golden Kids mean Big Bucks'. But the various attempts on Saffron's life (for so she certainly regarded them) cast rather a different light on the social situation at Oxford University, 'post-*Brideshead*' or otherwise.

Some person or some people hated Saffron enough to wish him dead, or at best very severely injured. Leaving aside the mysterious business of Bim Marcus' fall, an attack with a boat hook was not to be put in the same category as some form of undergraduate jape on the river. The kind of jape for example that Rufus Pember and Nigel Copley had stoutly sworn they intended to carry out that night, only to be thwarted by some previous more murderous intrusion.

'Saffer is a shit' had pronounced a huge and dripping Nigel Copley: Saffron's claim to this noun was evidently received wisdom in the Copley/ Pember set. Big Nigel had been hauled with some difficulty out of the river where he had attempted to hide beneath his own overturned canoe, following the discovery of Saffron's body. 'But we wanted to abduct him, you know, not to kill him.'

'*Abduct* him ?' Jemima heard one of the dinner guests exclaim, possibly Bernardo Valliera, because he added: 'This is not South America, my friend.'

'Duck him, he said. *Duck* him,' Rufus Pember, equally wet but somehow more composed, interrupted. 'Duck him. A good old-fashioned British custom.' He glared at Valliera. In Jemima's view, not every red-haired person justified the reputation of their kind for aggression; Rufus Pember however, for all his physical resemblance to the dying Chatterton, certainly did.

For the time being Jemima suspended judgement on the involvement of Messrs Pember and Copley in the attack on Saffron. (Although she certainly did not believe a mere ducking had been intended: who would take canoes late at night, travel a mile upstream, merely to administer a ducking ? It made no sense. So to Rufus Pember's aggressive quality, she added a capacity for quick thinking: Copley's admission had been neatly turned.)

But now as she reached Holywell, and the long secure wall of Magdalen, she considered Fanny's words anew: 'Lots of people loathe Saffer who've never even *met* him.' Was that uncomfortable thing at the heart of the idyll simple human envy? In an age of grants, declining, and unemployment, rising, it was easy to see how some undergraduates might actively envy Saffron for his advantages. Not only the media found themselves in 'a post-*Brideshead* situation'. Many students came up to Oxford, envisaging themselves enjoying their own mini-*Brideshead* existence for a year or two, before setting down to a more serious way of life. Oxford was a place of great expectations. What happened when those expectations were disappointed? Great envy? Even, perhaps, great hatred? For that matter what price the classless society based on merit which many might hope to find at a university if nowhere else in Britain? The cars, parties, dinners of the young and rich ensured them not only a sour spotlight within the university, but the rather more appreciative attention of the media in the world outside. Jemima reflected that Cy Fredericks' enthusiasm for Golden Kids was really quite typical: you could not imagine him mounting a whole programme on the lifestyle of comprehensive-school students once at Oxford, with due respect to the views of Dr Kerry Barber whom she was about to visit.

Jemima's conversation with Proffy came back to her. Who was to say what Lazarus actually *felt* about Dives, as he ate up the crumbs from the rich man's table? And maybe being forbidden to give Dives a glass of water afterwards, an instruction from Abraham, was one of the pleasurable experiences of his (after) life.

As Jemima reached the porter's lodge of St Lucy's College, she was thinking that money – and blood – had a lot to answer for. Blood! That unlucky word again. Better to concentrate on money.

'Money and where it comes from, money and where it goes to,' Kerry Barber was saying a few minutes later as he lay back in an ugly modern chair which was ill-suited to the large panelled room in St Lucy's famous Pond Quad; he was airing long rather good legs clad in a pair of crumpled white shorts. Dr Barber had evidently just taken part in some active game although it was difficult to make out exactly what, since the single thing his room had in common with Saffer's was the amount of sporting equipment littered about. 'Did you see my piece on the redistribution of Britain's wealth as reflected or rather *not* reflected in the average income of an undergraduate's parents? "Grants should Get up and Go". Shocking, quite shocking.'

Kerry Barber jumped up and poured Jemima another large sherry. It was of excellent quality; very dry and if you liked sherry, delicious. Jemima felt it would be ungracious to say that she actually hated sherry, when Barber was such a generous host. Furthermore, he clearly did not drink himself, but took occasional swigs at a china mug bearing a symbol of international goodwill; goodness knew what it contained.

All in all, he was really a very decent man. It was only under gentle pressure from Jemima – the trained interviewer – that he revealed he had spent the afternoon playing squash with paraplegics; further discreet questioning, centred on the mysterious china mug, elicited the fact that he gave the money he would otherwise have spent on drink to the Third World.

'It's a decision Mickey – my wife – and I took years ago and you'd be surprised how it mounts up.' He smiled rather sweetly. 'You see we both enjoyed a drink before – and we try not to cheat by pretending to drink less as the years go by. If anything, as Mickey pointed out, we might be drinking *more*. So many of our friends are drinking more these days. We notice it at our own parties, where of course we try to keep the drink flowing as much as possible. Mickey seriously questions whether the price of three glasses of wine each is enough to put in the box at the end of an evening. Judging from our married friends, at least one of us would be an alcoholic by now – if we drank that is. But which is it to be?' He smiled. 'Statistics suggest Mickey but as she has the lower income that doesn't seem quite fair.'

Jemima, self-consciously clutching her own second sherry, looked nervously round the room. Was there a box – the box – visible? She thought she saw something which looked like a collecting box near the door and made a mental resolve to donate handsomely to it (the price of a half bottle of champagne at least) on departure. In the meantime, as Kerry Barber was much the most decent person she had met in Oxford, with the possible exception of Jack Iverstone (Proffy with his views on Dives deserved the epithet of engaging rather than decent) Jemima looked forward to his confrontation with the so-called Golden Kids on the programme. What would the Oxford Bloods make of his policy concerning drink and the Third World? Why, their donations if made along the same lines would keep several African states going for months . . .

She wondered if any of them had crossed Kerry Barber's path. The answer, under the circumstances, was slightly surprising.

'Lord Saffron, as I suppose we must call him, although the sooner that sort of thing goes the better. Yes. He came to me for economics his first year.' Jemima realized rather guiltily that it had never even occurred to her to enquire what subject Saffron was reading; or was it an indictment of his own deliberately frivolous approach to the University?

'He's rather bright, you know,' went on Kerry Barber, still more surprisingly. 'Good mind. Much brighter for example than his cousin Jack of our college. A good man, but almost frighteningly conventional in his thinking. To make up for that dreadful father, I suppose. Hours in libraries and very few minutes of original thought.'

'What's he reading – Jack?' enquired Jemima.

'Oh history of course,' replied Kerry Barber in what for him passed for a malicious remark.

Jemima grappled with the unexpected phenomenon of Saffron being naturally intelligent.

'You don't mean he actually did any work?' she asked incredulously.

'Good heavens, no! And it's perfectly disgraceful that he hasn't been sent down. A prime example of the sort of thing COMPCAMP would put an end to. Coming from a comprehensive school, he would of course—' And Dr Barber launched into his favourite subject. To Jemima's general satisfaction, however – for was he not now saying exactly what she wanted him to say on the *Golden Kids* programme? Provided she could somehow get it past the eagle eye of Cy Fredericks. Cy had a tiresome habit of returning to Megalithic House after weeks of absence in some luxurious haunt, as though by instinct, just as a programme-maker was trying to slip a fast one past him at the editing stage.

All the same, she judged it right to leave after about twenty minutes of elucidation on the aims of COMPCAMP. She did so as gracefully as possible, pausing at the door of the room to deposit a five-pound note in the collecting box.

'For my two delicious sherries.'

'Good heavens, you could have had many more for that!' exclaimed Barber generously. 'Are you sure you don't want to come back? I feel I've only just scratched the surface of our discussion. COMPCAMP is such an important issue.' He sighed as though Jemima was perhaps not the only television interviewer to back away through his door, leaving the depths of his campaign unprobed. 'Ah well, another time. But I must say I envy you having the forum of television for your views.'

'We'll share it,' promised Jemima, generous in her turn, vowing inwardly to defeat Cy even if it meant bribing Miss Lewis to muck up his return flight arrangements for the first time in her life.

Jemima wandered back into Pond Quad still thinking about envy. She gazed rather distractedly into the large round stone-built 'pond' itself, with its statue of St Lucy, Virgin and Martyr, in the centre. As a result of undergraduate binges St Lucy sometimes had to endure further forms of martyrdom. She was currently wearing a large painted notice on her bosom: 'St Lucy votes SDP.' Below someone had written: 'I know. That's why they killed her.' How old were the golden carp in the pond supposed to be? Old enough not to want to go on television programmes, whatever the motive. Old enough not to envy any of the hurrying undergraduates who thronged the quad.

One of the undergraduates stopped and smiled at Jemima.

'Are you going to feature the fish in your programme? They *are* golden.'

It was Jack Iverstone. He was carrying a pile of books, as on their first acquaintance in Saffron's rooms, and Jemima was reminded of Kerry Barber's judgement: 'hours in libraries and very few minutes of original thought'. She decided to put it down to the natural disdain of the economist for the historian.

'I've just been to see Saffer,' he went on. 'I must say he has the strength of ten. Enormous gash in his head and he's asking me to smuggle in some champagne for a celebration.'

'A celebration?' queried Jemima incredulously. 'What on earth can he have to celebrate beyond being holed up in the Radcliffe?'

Jack Iverstone continued to look at her with his easy charming smile. But there was now something quizzical about the smile which she did not quite understand.

'You know Saffer,' he said after a pause. 'He celebrates the oddest things. Why don't you ask him yourself?'

10

Intellectual Advantages

It was Jemima's intention to visit Saffron as soon as she got her interview with Proffy out of the way: she thought it would be good to be able to contrast the Mossbanker way of life with that of the heroically abstinent Barbers, for she somehow doubted whether Proffy and his clever wife Eleanor had a collection box in their North Oxford house – that is, if Proffy's appetite for food and drink at the Lycée restaurant and The Punting Heaven were anything to go by.

She still wondered at the nature of Saffron's celebration and the meaning of Jack Iverstone's quizzical glance as she collected her car from the Martyrs car park and drove up St Giles, leaving Rochester College, Saffron's theoretical residence, on her right (and the Radcliffe Infirmary, his actual dwelling on her left). Arrival at the Mossbankers' house, however, drove these thoughts out of her mind. Chillington Road was a pretty tree-lined backwater, part of a network of similar roads off the Banbury Road. Thus the exterior of the Mossbankers' house, despite the ugliness of its late-Victorian architecture, was agreeably tranquil, softened as its façade was by blossom, the door masked by a weeping tree. The interior on the other hand was the reverse of tranquil. In fact Jemima's first reaction was to decide that marriage between consenting Oxford intellectuals should probably be banned for the future (unless sworn to be childless).

To begin with, the combined force of Mossbanker children was in itself daunting. Were there only eight of them? Alternatively were these tow-headed infants and occasional tow-headed adolescents really all Moss-bankers? So many of them seemed to be the same age. Jemima had not thought to enquire from the Professor whether the Mossbanker Eight included twins or even triplets: but then what made her think he would have known the answer to such an essentially domestic question? As

Tiggie had expressed it on their first meeting, he liked *having* a lot of children (the children themselves he rather disliked).

However, it was not so much the sheer mass of Mossbankers which persuaded her that intellectuals should not be allowed to marry each other. Nor did she necessarily ascribe the untidiness-beyond-parody of the North Oxford house, books and potties competing for attention, frequently doing an exciting balancing act in the same pile, to the presence of an intellectual mother. After all, take the case of Jemima's fiercely clever friend, Dr Marigold Milton, whose students were notoriously terrified into an appreciation of English literature which lasted them for the rest of their lives no matter how they tried to get rid of it. Marigold Milton had as a matter of fact given birth to four children, making a point of reading Proust between pangs of labour (she was a quick reader), yet her house was so exactly polished that even the students wiped their feet reverently on entering it, before having their essays merrily pulled to pieces.

No, it was apparently the fatal combination of both Mossbankers which made life in Chillington Road such an ordeal: Jemima knew that Eleanor Mossbanker had as Proffy's pupil gained her own First in something or other before leaving scholarship for parturition in a dedicated way. For the effect of this union of intellects was, as Jemima quickly discovered, to make the Chillington Road house a kind of debating chamber concerning the education, past, present and to come, of the numerous Mossbanker offspring, into which any unwary newcomer was immediately plunged.

Proffy let her into the house, trampling on a small bicycle as he did so (admittedly the alternative would have been to hurdle it). He guided Jemima towards the sitting room, negotiating various physical hazards – a carry-cot, another bicycle and two satchels – in the same ruthless manner.

'Eleanor is just giving him—' he look closer '—I mean *her*, an intelligence test to see whether the last report from the local comprehensive has anything to be said for it at all. Can any child of ours, can any child, really not be able to read at the age of eight?'

'Ten, Proffy, actually,' said a sulky voice emanating from one of the tow-heads. Jemima got the impression that Proffy's boasted dislike of the young might actually be reciprocated.

'Exactly!' cried the Professor with the triumphant air of one who had just proved a point. But the dark Egyptian head bent over the blonde child was surely that of Eugenia Jones. While Eleanor Mossbanker had to be the fair Saxonesque beauty, heavy but not unbecomingly so, some years younger than Eugenia, with a baby in a sling round her neck (which also contained a couple of books). Not for the first time the professor had mixed up their names.

It was Eleanor Mossbanker who proceeded to give Jemima a warm but hasty welcome. The welcome was hasty because she wasted no time in scrabbling in the sling for one of the books, the baby giving a single regal shriek at this interruption to its dignity.

'There, what did I tell you?' she demanded, as though continuing some previous conversation, although as far as Jemima was aware, they had never met before. 'Isn't that a ridiculously unimaginative poetry book for a child of seven? At that age I was reading Yeats, or at any rate—'

'For God's sake, Eleanor!' shouted Proffy quite angrily – and for once there was no doubt who he was addressing. 'You *chose* that school.'

'You did, Mum, honestly,' said one of the tow-heads, looking up with a mild expression from a rather noisy television set for a moment or two. 'Proffy chose St Albert's and then it was your turn and you chose Mandells.'

'But I've never even been there,' countered Eleanor Mossbanker heatedly, poking the offending poetry book back alongside the regal baby and adjusting the sling.

'Of course you've never been there,' contributed another tow-head, also flat out on the floor in front of the television. 'That's because you've always been to St Albert's by mistake, thinking that was the school you chose.' Then he turned the sound up on the television. No wonder Proffy went to parties to get away and drink champagne, thought Jemima.

'Could you all be a bit quieter while we're watching telly?' the first tow-head threw over his shoulder.

'Sigi and Lucas are taking part in a controlled television experiment to see if watching television six hours a day interferes with their enjoyment of reading the classics,' explained the Professor. This left Jemima wondering wearily how on earth she was going to detach him sufficiently from the fascinating topic of his offspring's mental development in order to discuss her own television programme. Champagne might once again be the answer.

One of the further ironies of the Mossbanker household was that compared to the ancient splendour of, for example, Rochester College, it gave the impression of great penury as well as discomfort. No wonder Proffy had fantasized at the Chimneysweepers' Dinner about a house at Dives' gate. Jemima did not imagine eight children left a great deal to live on out of a don's salary, particularly one who enjoyed champagne.

In the event the question of the programme did not arise. For at that moment the figure of Tiggie Jones, clad in very small pink shorts covered in butterflies, darted into the room through the French windows. Some iridescent butterflies gleamed in her dark hair. She posed for a moment, head on one side, pinky-purple lips pursed, as though considering the order of kisses, before laying her long lashes against Jemima's cheek, then Proffy's, then Eleanor's, finally her mother's. The Mossbanker children she ignored, much as they ignored her.

'I've just come from seeing Saffer,' she pronounced. 'Such foxy news.' There was a pause. 'We're going to get married,' she said. 'Don't you envy me?' continued Tiggie, with her pretty little cat's smile, addressing no one in particular. 'I'm going to be Lady Saffron. And I'm going to be terribly, terribly rich.'

There was a sharp intake of breath somewhere in the room.

'No—'

'Stop it, Eleanor,' said the professor.

But it was Eugenia Jones, still half crouched beside an infant Mossbanker, who now gazed in evident horror at her daughter.

'Antigone, you can't be serious! This is one of your jokes. Proffy, *do* something!'

It was odd, thought Jemima, how women were constantly asking Proffy to *do* something – as Fanny Iverstone had urged him to *do* something after the discovery of Saffron's body at The Punting Heaven – and yet here was a man whose detachment from awkward reality was sufficiently marked for him to regularly and unabashedly mix up the Christian names of his wife and his mistress. Engaging as Proffy was in conversation, Jemima suspected that there was something quite sweetly selfish at the heart of his lifestyle, for all the physical impression he gave of heavy patriarchal reliability.

Perhaps it was the perpetual hope of discovering this phantasmagoric reliability which had kept Eugenia Jones in thrall to him for so long. Weakness or selfishness in a man was often a most successful grappling-hook ... why else had Eugenia Jones remained devoted to Proffy throughout so many years, including the years when he married his brilliant pupil Eleanor and procreated all those tow-headed children; the children to whom Eugenia was now administering intelligence tests?

'I think your mother means something like: you're throwing yourself away.' Proffy spoke in that slightly irritable tone which Jemima noticed he tended to adopt when obliged to form part of a conversation as opposed to holding forth in more light-hearted monologue. 'Considering all your intellectual advantages,' he added, 'that kind of line of attack.'

Was he being serious? Intellectual advantages! Tiggie Jones, the toast of the gossip columns (which would be lost without her if she married, or again perhaps not), Tiggie, the happily idiotic Golden Kid, Miss Tiggie who was or was not screwing Cy Fredericks, in the words of Saffron himself – Jemima was interrupted in these reflections by Eugenia Jones.

'Antigone, have you no shame?' The fierce voice was worthy of Dr Marigold Milton herself, ringing the editor of *Literature* to complain about a misprint in her review. 'You got a very good Second, but touches of Alpha there in certain papers, admittedly in English—'

'Your mother means that you would have got a First if you had done any work at all. And now you're throwing yourself away on a very rich man, two years or so your junior, so that you will eventually endure the unspeakable fate of being Marchioness of St Ives, mistress of Saffron Ivy. I think that's what your mother means.'

'Oh Mum!' cried Tiggie in a tone of sheer exasperation. It was the first time Jemima had heard her speak without any affectation. She even sounded quite fond of her mother. But then Jemima was seeing Tiggie through new eyes in more ways than one. A good Second in English. For a moment, thinking of the constructed personality Tiggie now displayed, hedonism not to say sheer silliness and irresponsibility strictly to the fore, Jemima found herself agreeing with Eugenia that Tiggie was doing something called wasting her opportunities. Then she pulled herself up. Wasn't Tiggie actually using her so-called intellectual advantages to get exactly what she wanted? A rich husband. Purple and fine linen for the rest of her life. Or at least until they divorced – and then a good lawyer would probably see to it that the supply of purple did not diminish for Saffron's ex-wife.

The exasperation, and the naturalness, passed quickly from Tiggie. 'Saffer and I are going to settle down. We're going to be old folks. Isn't that sweet?' And she did a little pirouette, setting all the gauzy butterflies in her short dark hair a-quiver. 'We're going to have lots and lots of children just like you, Proffy. Mum, don't be cross. You'll *love* the library at Saffron Ivy. You can live in it if you like. You can have a wendy house in the library. A sort of hut. Think how adorable.'

'I know the library at Saffron Ivy,' was all Eugenia Jones vouchsafed by way of reply.

'Oh really,' said Tiggie incuriously, 'I didn't know you'd ever been there. *I've* been there.'

'There was a life on earth before you were born, Antigone,' said Proffy.

Eugenia Jones herself did not speak again but turned back to the Mossbanker child on the floor, who had by now joined the ranks of the television viewers and was highly indignant at being recalled to an intelligence test (the upbringing of the young Mossbankers, thought Jemima, unlike that of Tiggie Jones, was full of intellectual disadvantages). But Jemima saw that Eugenia Jones' eyes were full of tears.

Even more astonishing, Jemima surprised on Proffy's own face a look of absolute despair. The look was purely momentary, transforming Proffy's normally benign if eccentric countenance into something really rather tragic as if a mask had been applied. Then he relaxed, blinked and patted Eugenia on the shoulder. The whole incident had not lasted more than a few seconds.

It was not time to press Proffy on the subject of Golden Kids. Jemima departed as rapidly as possible, unnoticed by the majority of the Mossbanker family, feeling that a visit to the putative bridegroom was now indicated. As to the motive behind his unlikely engagement, as Jack

Iverstone had suggested with that quizzical gleam in his eye, 'Why don't you ask him yourself?'

Her first sight of Saffron however had the immediate effect of driving his engagement from her mind. She thought instead of his blood. That was because Saffron, although propped up on high pillows, and smiling at her quite strongly, was demonstrably still wired or tubed or taped up to some form of blood transfusion.

'AB blood like readers of *The Times*.' Jemima remembered all over again the note sent to her at the Martyrs on the eve of the dinner, which circumstances had not yet allowed her time to discuss with Saffron, let alone investigate its contents for herself. Was now the time to discuss it when blood – presumably AB, the fairly rare group – was so obviously being replenished in his veins? On the other hand, perhaps Saffron still felt too weak to discuss a subject which was potentially so painful. While Jemima hesitated, she heard the sharp sound of a crackling uniform behind her, and she was accosted by a woman's voice speaking with great command and indignation in a strong Scottish accent. Jemima swung round. This was clearly a very senior type of nurse. She was also black.

'Ye may be his relative or ye may not – I'm thinking this laddie has an unco' lot of relatives all of them gairrls—' she pronounced the word with relish '—only one visitor at a time, relative or no relative; and that in visiting hours.' The nurse stopped. She stared at Jemima Shore. Then she beamed. There was no other word for it.

'Jemima! We met in Glasgow when I was doing my training. Do you ken that? Young black nurses, a whole lot of us. Suella May Mackintosh, that's me. What was the series called now? *New Scottish World*? Something like that.'

Jemima beamed back. *New Scottish World* had been a very early series, and an embarrassing memory as it had pleased neither new nor old Scottish worlds, due to her handling the subject of colour with insufficient directness from which she had learned a valuable lesson. At least it lived on in the memory of Suella May Mackintosh, now a formidable hospital Sister. In a matter of minutes she had secured the privilege of a short uninterrupted interview with Saffron.

The patient himself regarded these negotiations with a sardonic air. 'And you think I'm privileged, Jemima Shore,' was what he said eventually. 'Would you like some champagne? Faithful Cousin Jack brought it. I bought it and he brought it.'

Why not, thought Jemima, if only to expunge the taste of Kerry Barber's exquisite sherry. She had never got as far as a drink at the Mossbankers', and in any case Ribena had been the only visible liquid refreshment.

'I hear I have to congratulate you,' she said as she sipped a glass of vintage Bollinger (just as well the rich Saffron had paid for it and not the poor-but-honest Jack) out of a plastic hospital toothglass. 'Tiggie told me, in the process of telling her mother.'

'I'm going to settle down.' Was it her imagination or did Saffron sound slightly defiant, compared to Tiggie who had sounded plainly ecstatic at the thought of her purple future? Jemima also noticed that Saffron did not even bother to enquire how his prospective mother-in-law had taken the news. Furthermore: 'We're going to settle down' – that was Tiggie's version. 'I'm going to settle down' – that was Saffron's.

'This last attack decided it,' said Saffron.

Jemima leant forward impulsively and squeezed the hand free of the tubes, lying docilely on the light hospital blanket. 'I'm sorry, Saffer, I wasn't much of a protector, was I?'

'Not much you could do against a bloody boat hook, was there?'

'So you remember? In which case—'

'Oh Christ no—' wearily '—the police asked me all that till our darling Scots Sister drove them away. They're after Pember and Copley of course, except they can't prove it. She's great, isn't she, our Sister? Took particular pleasure in turfing out dreadful Cousin Andrew by the way, who insisted on dropping by out of hours in the hopes of finding me moribund, and thus transforming him at one sweep into being The Heir. I'm sure Sister Mackintosh recognized him. Spoke in her broadest Scots accent, and when Cousin Daphne had the cheek to ask her what island she came from, replied: "Glasgow, madam, and what island might you be coming from yourself?"'

His vitality flagged: 'No, I remember nothing. Nothing at all. Dinner, the end of dinner. Cousin Andrew's ghastly speech: ghastly but I have to admit quite witty. Conversation with Cousin Daphne, who definitely was not witty: unless you think the suggestion that Jack is sowing his wild oats in the SDP is in itself a form of wit. She sometimes hints after a drink or two that I might do worse than marry Fanny thus keeping everything in the family; I've put paid to that one at least. Fanny is a good girl, but I would rather marry Mrs Thatcher. Dancing to the *Liebestod* in a carefree way, possibly with Tiggie, possibly with Fanny, or was it Poppy? I can't even remember that. Then nothing more. Not even going down to the river. Or with whom. Apparently it's quite usual with a blow on the head. I may remember later.'

Jemima thought again of *Götterdämmerung*. Would some woodbird's song suddenly awake this Siegfried to a full memory of what had gone before? In which case would he recall the actual identity of the person who had made the murderous attack on him with a boat hook?

'And Tiggie? Your marriage – are you very much in love?' As she spoke, Jemima realized the question sounded perfectly pathetic.

'Rather an adorable idea, don't you think?' Saffron had become frivolous again although his eyelids with their long black lashes had begun to quiver as though with exhaustion. 'We get on, you know. We think alike. We want the same kind of life. As to love, I'm not sure I'm into love. But then nor is Tiggie. So that's all right. We'll probably live at Saffron Ivy when I've finished here. If they let me finish. And have children. That's the whole point. I don't want to be an aged parent like Ma and Pa.'

'Saffron—' Jemima paused. If he was putting the whole strange matter of the blood groups behind him, who was she to raise it? And yet it was Saffron who had sent her the book on medical jurisprudence. Was this decision to marry and settle down a bold declaration that he was the one true heir to the St Ives title, no matter what a crazy midwife might mutter?

'But there is one other thing, Jemima.' Saffron smiled engagingly. 'I thought you might find out who I am. If I'm not who I think I am, if you get my meaning. Very secretly. Just between you and me. Check out that odd blood group thing. You're still my sleuth, remember.'

'I can't handle it,' he went on. 'No, not the violence exactly. Not knowing who I am is worse. It was after the – the dread revelation of Nurse E., that I bashed up that foul mantelpiece in the Martyrs. I had to take it out of someone, or something.'

'An innocent victim?' queried Jemima.

'You should have seen it,' said Saffron sternly. 'That mantelpiece was definitely not innocent. Look, you're coming to Saffron Ivy. We'll have a big engagement weekend, ask everyone, including Tiggie's mother and Proffy as her escort. He's insisting on coming: he loves high life. Then you might do some sleuthing there. All the same I'm quite sure I am *me*. That's why I'm going to marry Tiggie and have as many children as the Mossbankers.'

At least Tiggie and Saffron were united in their aim, thought Jemima: a Mossbanker-size family. But she ought to refuse to have anything more to do with Saffron and his identity. Why not let the matter rest? Get on with the programme and treat Saffron purely as a Golden Kid ... Yes, she definitely ought to do that. It was absolutely against her better judgement that five minutes after leaving Saffron, she found herself seeking out Sister Suella May Mackintosh.

'Sister,' began Jemima Shore Investigator. 'Now that I've happily bumped into you again after all these years, I wonder if you can help me over something to do with a new programme. It's a little matter of blood groups: how would I get certain information? Just quite privately, you understand.'

11

Who He is Not

For one whose life had been spent in a world of blood, or at any rate test tubes thereof, Professor Mavis Ho looked remarkably fresh and trim. In the tiny over-heated office off the main buildings of the Kensington Hospital into which she escorted Jemima there were flowering plants. Professor Ho herself wore a flowered dress and white court shoes with a slight platform sole: with her white handbag, square, clean and authoritative on her desk, she bore a certain resemblance to a member of the Royal family, a resemblance encouraged by her pleasantly gracious smile; except since she was Chinese, perhaps Professor Ho should be compared to an Empress Dowager rather than a Queen Mother.

'It may sound a strange mission,' concluded Jemima, as she drew to the end of her story: a carefully edited version of events. She supplied no proper names, nicknaming Saffron Moses for good Biblical reasons; she merely related the theory of the baby swap and the facts of the blood groups. Then she explained how 'Moses', now twenty, had stumbled on the old story by chance, with obviously distressing consequences. 'It may sound strange, but as Moses-in-the-twentieth-century-bulrushes' put it to me, he does want to find out who he is.'

Professor Ho considered for a moment, neatly coiffed head on one side. How calm she was, what a sense she projected of internal serenity, sitting in her little hot beehive with its uncomfortably glaring plate-glass window; beneath them the various denizens of the Kensington – a teaching hospital – scurried about, much as the undergraduates had scurried in Oxford. Except that the hospital surroundings, built in an amalgam of styles at an amalgam of dates, ranged from the dreary-but-functional to the plainly-temporary-but-long-standing. Here were no colonnades, no Hawksmoor façades, no green quadrangles, no ancient somnolent carp, above all no dreaming spires or at least only one, above the Victorian arch of the most antique part of the building. All the same Jemima thought that Professor Ho was far closer to the image of the sage dispensing wisdom from some inner fount, than either of the two university professors – Mossbanker and Eugenia Jones respectively – Jemima had recently encountered.

Proffy manifestly lived in chaos: his rooms at Rochester had demonstrated that before ever she set foot in Chillington Road. Eugenia Jones' personal life seemed to bear the marks of a kind of personal chaos: what with a disappearing husband, in Jamie Grand's smart phrase 'the ideal husband, one who was never there when she was wanted'; then there was the wanton daughter who had singularly failed to live up to the heroic name of Antigone, but had emerged from her academic background with her sights determinedly set on a rich husband.

Jemima did not think she was merely carried away by Professor Ho's mandarin appearance. That was as incidental to her personality as Sister Suella May Mackintosh's colour was to hers. Thus Professor Ho incarnated the intelligent balanced English lady of a certain age, while Sister Mackintosh stood for the fiercely bossy – but golden-hearted – Scottish nurse. (It was perhaps no coincidence that contact with one lady had led Jemima, through a trail of experts, to the other.)

'I wonder, Miss Shore, if you quite appreciate the situation with regard to your Moses – I take it he's not in fact Jewish by the way? So far as you know that is.' Jemima shook her head. Professor Ho continued in her measured manner: 'You see, you will not be able to tell him who he is. You may be able to tell him who he is not.'

Jemima sighed. 'He's torn, our Moses. He's not a fool, in spite of behaving in a very foolish manner. Most of the time. On the one hand he was curious enough to latch on to the question of the blood groupings – to get some book out of the college library, Glaister I think it's called as I told you, and to ask me to take the matter a little further. On the other hand . . .'

'It would be a great shock to a young person,' finished Professor Ho kindly, 'to find out that he was in effect an adopted child – which is what Moses may turn out to be – having believed himself to be the biological child of his parents for twenty years.'

'I think Moses wants some kind of certainty about his identity. I don't think, oddly enough, that he plans to make any kind of use of this certainty, given he can achieve it.'

'Not so odd, perhaps. If by doing so he robs himself of a great deal of family money.' Professor Ho's tone remained amiable.

'Especially when he has been brought up to enjoy an extravagant lifestyle. At least that is the impression you gave me.'

Jemima had a vision of Saffron, last seen lying in hospital offering vintage champagne; or Saffron the Oxford Blood, gyrating to the music of the *Liebestod*, at the Chimneysweepers' Dinner, tickets £50 a head.

'An extravagant lifestyle covers the situation.'

'The interesting thing about your Moses is that he does not let the matter lie.'

Jemima hesitated. 'I have the impression that it's to do with his inheritance, his true inheritance,' she said after a while. 'He's been brought up in this way, with such an emphasis on what he has inherited, or is about to inherit. Now the whole thing is cast in doubt. *Is* there anything hereditary about blood? Your kind of blood.'

Professor Ho smiled, looking more like a Chinese Queen Mother than ever.

'In one sense blood is the most hereditary thing there is – my kind of blood, as you put it. Blood groupings. I take it you don't mean my ethnic Chinese blood. It's all to do with blood corpuscles and agglutinogens as you discovered from Glaister. You can have no agglutinogens present in the blood: that's called O. Or you can have A agglutinogens present, or B, or both A and B. As I've explained to you, everyone takes a bit from both parents. That is why your young man – and you assure me his grouping is definitely AB – falls into a comparatively rare category.'

'It's AB. That at least is certain.' Jemima had established this in conversation with Sister Mackintosh, in connection with a so far totally imaginary programme on the subject of blood donors and the National Health Service. The question of Saffron's blood group had been raised ostensibly in order to demonstrate a point she was trying to make.

'You see, to form AB, he must have one parent who is A and another parent who is B,' pursued Professor Ho. 'Now A is the most common category among white British people – O being the second most common. Forty-six per cent of the white British population are A, whereas forty-four per cent are O group. But B is relatively uncommon – eight per cent I think. I'd have to check it in Mourant.' She tapped one of the pile of text-books which jostled with the flowers on her desk, then could not resist opening it. 'Yes, eight point six per cent.'

'If AB demands not only one B parent, but also B in combination with an A, you can see that the chances of an AB child diminish rapidly,' she went on. 'Three per cent of the British population according to Mourant's work on blood frequencies. Among the Mongoloid races, and thus among Chinese immigrants, B is much more frequent. As a matter of fact my own blood grouping is B.' Jemima wondered whether this, for an expert on blood groupings, was a matter for congratulations, and whether she should proffer them.

Professor Ho continued: 'I repeat, among white British people, B is comparatively rare. The reason I asked you whether the name Moses had any significance other than purely Biblical was because you also get a much higher incidence of the B blood group among Jewish people; it varies, but it can be as much as twenty-five per cent.'

'As far as I know, Moses so-called is not Jewish. Not Chinese either,' Jemima added with a polite smile. Saffron with Jewish blood? In so far as it was possible to define the physical characteristics of Jewish blood, it could not be ruled out. With that black hair and faintly olive complexion, Jemima had felt all along that there was something of the Mediterranean about his appearance – as opposed to the copybook Englishness of his cousins Jack and Fanny for example. The conventional idea of a Jewish appearance in English terms was often no more than that – something of the Mediterranean or the Middle East, something which had come home to Jemima when visiting Israel and being frequently unable to tell Jew from Arab among the indigenous population.

'Higher too among Greeks – fourteen per cent as opposed to eight per cent in the UK. The increasing presence of Greek Cypriots in this country after the Turkish invasion means that the Health Service needs more B group blood donors than before. There's a particular disease called thalassaemia – Colley's anaemia – to which they're subject.'

Greek? Greek Cypriot? Yes, Saffron could well have Greek blood, Greek Cypriot (or for that matter Turkish) if one was simply into some ethnic guessing game based on his appearance. All of this was however to do with who he was or might be rather than who he was not.

'At any rate what you're saying is clear,' replied Jemima. 'If Moses' parents are both group O, as his mother has stated, then they cannot be his *biological* parents. So I suppose it's back to me to try and establish that one way or another.'

'It's really quite simple – or a case like that is simple provided you're quite sure about the parents. Since 1969 blood tests have been allowed in court cases of disputed paternity – to exclude a given father of course, from paternity. As Moses' father would be excluded in court from being the biological parent, given the circumstances: not to prove parenthood, only to exclude.'

'How strange that these agglutinogens in our blood should be more strictly hereditary than anything else. After all, physical characteristics or talents like music are not necessarily passed on to children. You can have a red-haired parent without having a red-haired child, but you can't have a B group parent, without having something of B in the child, be it AB or I suppose OB. How strange that blood should be so important.'

But Jemima saw from Professor Ho's expression that she did not think it particularly strange that blood should be so important.

'It's back to me,' she said hastily, 'and I've got to establish the truth of the parents' blood groups. Any suggestions how I should go about it?'

Professor Ho relaxed. 'The mother is likely to be right about her own group, especially if she lost a number of children before this one. Three, you said. She might even be O Rhesus Negative to her husband's Rhesus Positive: the antibodies which clash produce a built-up and would account for the series of deaths. The first child should have been all right, did you tell me there was one live birth?'

Jemima shook her head. 'Not as far as I know. No, wait, one born live who died about three weeks later. And it was the first child.' She remembered the details of Nurse Elsie's story and from the peerage.

'That first child could have died for quite different reasons not associated with blood. After that the problem of Rhesus Negative and Rhesus Positive would build and build.'

'And the father?'

'Is he old enough to have been in the forces in the war? People had to carry their blood group with them on a disc.'

Lord St Ives had been in the army: an MC came to mind after his name, and memories of the gallant war record which had made this otherwise somewhat austere figure acceptable to the Tory party in years gone by: 'Ivo got all his men back from St Nazaire, one of the few who did—' the words floated back to her from some television documentary compiled when he became Foreign Secretary. But she could hardly ring up the War Office to establish his blood grouping on the strength of this. The most inventive (and invented) programme for Megalith would hardly cover such an eventuality. No, wait . . .

One possible answer came to her.

'Professor Ho, could you just repeat to me what you told me about the Greek Cypriot community and that disease, the need for more B group blood in the UK as a result? I see a possible programme here. At least, one I could look into. That could be useful.'

'Useful to your Moses? Or useful to society?' asked Professor Ho.

'Both,' said Jemima firmly.

Not so much later Jemima, back in her flat, was pouring a placatory coup of champagne for a slightly sulky Cherry.

'Yes I know, I know darling, whatever will I think of next!'

'Are we *really* going to make this six-part series called "The National Blood"?' enquired Cherry. 'In which case I'm applying for a transfer.' But she drank all the same.

'Why not?' asked Jemima with spirit, repeating to Cherry as to Professor Ho: 'At least it's useful.'

'You promised me a good time among the Golden Kids,' Cherry grumbled, 'and now you're talking about a lot of blood. Which reminds me that Cy is back, and according to Miss Lewis, after yours. Blood that is. Wants to know why shooting hasn't started on the aforesaid *Golden Kids*. That's because he's sold the programme in the States *and* another couple similar about the Golden Kids of France and Germany – I guess that has to be West Germany, but as Miss Lewis said, you never know with Cy, he could pre-sell a programme about the Golden Kids of East Germany when he's in the mood.'

'Does he know about Tiggie Jones' engagement to Saffron? Now there's a piece of news for you. 'Jemima waited smugly to see the effect of her little surprise on Cherry. 'You could even call it a Megalith romance since Tiggie was allegedly the researcher on the *Golden Kids* programme. As to shooting, even Cy Fredericks can hardly expect us to shoot our hero in hospital having been beaten up with a boat hook. Not very golden.'

'Saffron and Miss Tiggie! Engaged!' Cherry sounded even more startled than Jemima had expected. She really looked quite astonished, her eyes round as saucers. 'Now that really does take my breath away.'

'You mean – because of Cy?'

'That and other things.'

Cherry looked at Jemima, began to say something more, stopped herself and then said with perhaps rather more vigour than the occasion warranted: 'I never liked that girl.' She went on: 'Now tell me the questions you want me to ask about individual blood groups for this so-called programme.' Cherry sounded quite kind.

A couple of evenings later Jemima found she also surprised Cass Brinsley with the news of Saffron's engagement. But then Cass was in the middle of a case and in that slightly captious mood she had come to associate with such situations. No doubt she herself was similarly abstracted – not to say irritable – when in the midst of shooting. All the same Jemima had to confess that his captiousness came as a slight disappointment when she herself had been looking forward quite eagerly, no really very eagerly, to seeing him following her return from Oxford.

'I always knew that girl would come to a bad end. Her lashes were far too long for perfect honesty,' said Cass crossly.

'*Is* it a bad end to marry a very rich young man?' Jemima thought of Proffy and Eugenia Jones' rather similar objections to her daughter's match.

'It depends what you want.'

'And what do you want, Cass?' It was quite a light-hearted remark but since it was already late, and they were sitting on the deep sofa in Jemima's flat, listening to *Don Giovanni* (Losey film version) Jemima half expected some romantic rejoinder. It was almost the end of the opera: with one ear cocked, Jemima heard the Commendatore dragging Don Giovanni down to hell, as the pious sextet rejoiced over his damnation. She rather thought her Don Giovanni might drag her down to bed . . . Instead of which Cass answered quite seriously:

'What do I want, darling? Oh God, I wish I knew. Look it's late. Don G. has gone to hell and this case is getting to me. I'll call you tomorrow. OK?'

He gave her a quick firm kiss on the mouth, touched her lightly on the breast and got up.

A few minutes later Cass was gone. A few minutes after that Midnight came complacently through the cat flap and flumped himself down on Jemima's lap, purring loudly and stretching his black paws to her face. Midnight did not care to share Jemima's favours with other admirers.

Jemima once again felt oddly disconcerted, that Emma-at-Box-Hill feeling which had overcome her in the High Street at Oxford. Whatever the nature of their relationship – so carefully undefined – she had been looking forward to going to bed with Cass that night.

The presence of Midnight, large, furry and sensual nibbling at her cheek with his delicate tongue, only emphasized the absence of Cass.

Better to think about blood. Saffron's blood. Jemima found Mourant, the book presented to her by Professor Ho, the title: *Blood Relations* and the sub-title *Blood Groups and Anthropology*. Perhaps Mourant would send her to sleep. She began, rather firmly, to read the preliminary remarks about visible characteristics such as the shape of eye or colour of skin fixed solely or partly by heredity and came to the passage:

'In contrast to these visible characteristics, research during the present century shows that there is a class of invisible ones, fixed by heredity in a known way at the moment of conception, immutable during the life of the individual, and observable by relatively simple scientific tests. These are the blood groups . . .'

Curiously enough, someone else was at that very moment also thinking dark thoughts about Saffron's blood. In a way these thoughts might have benefited from the absolute clarity brought by Mourant; as it was, they consisted of a great swilling wash of anger brought about by the knowledge that Saffron was not what he seemed, seething like a tide in the basin of an uneasy brain without any possibility of escape. Relief would only come through the spilling of that same blood, the interloper's blood.

Bim Marcus had already paid the penalty for a mistake. The boat-hook incident had been a sudden impulse and as such had not really deserved to succeed. Planning was the essence of success. As Jemima restlessly put aside Mourant, and took up a P.D. James she had already read twice (its title ironically enough was *Innocent Blood*), the other person thinking about Saffron that night decided on what might turn out in the end to be the best plan of all.

12
Love and Hate

Jemima Shore woke up about five o'clock. Neither Mourant nor P.D. James had ensured heavy slumbers. At first she was surprised to find herself alone and murmured rather sleepily: 'Cass.' Midnight too was absent: some dawn prowl had claimed him.

An hour later, sleep being impossible, Jemima feeling remarkably discontented decided on a dawn prowl herself. The thought of Richmond Park in the early morning, green, quiet and empty, was suddenly extremely tempting. She pulled on a white track suit and filled a thermos full of coffee. She thought of a private breakfast picnic among the bracken; perhaps there would be deer; she could not remember which season it was which brought the deer to join the solitary picnickers.

Jemima driving fast – too fast – in her Mercedes, had forgotten the early morning string of horses and riders which usually filed into the park at that hour. She came to a rapid halt. Then at the traffic lights she found herself drawn up beside one especially magnificent glossy horse, a chestnut, which took its rider way above the height of the low sports car.

Jemima looked up. The rider was male, and like the horse, quite young and very glossy with thick hair not unlike the colour of his horse's coat.

She smiled.

'I like your horse.'

'I like your car.'

'Swap?'

'Horses are worth more than cars, even Mercedes. What will you give me to make up the balance?'

Jemima considered. The lights were changing.

'I could give you a cup of coffee, but then what would you do with your horse?'

'You know,' began the rider, 'you look rather like—'

241

The light was green and Jemima shot forward. What with Cass and Mourant and Midnight, none of whom had proved themselves to be particularly rewarding companions during the night hours, she began to wish that she had rather a different nature. Why not, for example, take off into the bracken with a handsome and unknown young cavalier and forget the cares of the world, or at least the cares represented by the foregoing three names for the length of one morning's idyll? Why not?

'Because I wouldn't have enjoyed it at all,' said Jemima sternly to herself as she laid out her solitary picnic in the bracken, car abandoned, some time later. 'That's why. What a perfectly ridiculous idea anyway. As it is, I'm already covered in bracken, so think what it would have been like . . .' Jemima drank her coffee and did think, just for a moment, what it would have been like.

Whether she was right or wrong about the anonymous cavalier would never be known, but she was still brushing fronds off her track suit when she entered Megalithic House. What was more, she was by now rather late, having encountered heavy traffic on her way from Richmond Park. The various traffic blocks gave Jemima plenty of time to ponder on a number of things, including whether there was a special God who deliberately sent down heavy traffic when you were late already and not for a reason that everyone in the world would consider a good one.

Cherry, looking remarkably appealing in a pink cotton boiler-suit, many top buttons left untouched and a tight belt to clinch her figure at the waist, gazed speculatively at Jemima as she entered.

'Messages first or a cup of coffee? You've just been having coffee? In Richmond Park? I knew it had to be something perfectly ordinary like that. Ah well, here goes. Cy of course. Three times, and I dare say Miss Lewis fended off some other of his reckless enquiries after your whereabouts before they reached me. Cass telephoned. Twice. Sounded agitated, if not as agitated as our Chairman. Says he missed you at home. And Saffron. Last but not least. First, he's out of hospital, back in his college. Second, the engagement weekend at Saffron Ivy has been fixed: bank holiday weekend at the end of May.'

'Anything else?'

'Oh yes. A man telephoned. Nice voice. Wondered if you drove a white Mercedes sports car. He thought he might have seen you in Richmond Park this morning.'

'What a weird enquiry!' said Jemima in her most innocent tone.

'That's what I thought. So I told him you drove an old black Ford and were anyway away filming in Manchester.'

Cy Fredericks accepted with surprising equanimity Jemima's proffered explanation of a game of squash, and then a traffic delay driving from the squash club. It was the word club which seemed to soothe him.

'The Squash Club!' he cried. 'Most exciting! Jemima, you must take me there sometime. Can one eat there late as well as early?' Luckily Miss Lewis entered before Jemima had time to sort out a suitable reply.

As to Cy's keen enquiries about the progress of the *Golden Kids* programme, Jemima was able to stop them at source by her double revelation of Tiggie Jones' engagement and her own invitation to Saffron Ivy.

'We'll be *shooting* there?' asked Cy in a specially reverent tone which he reserved for any conjunction of Megalith cameras and the more gracious aspects of English life.

'No, no, all shooting in Oxford.' Jemima knew it was the moment to stand firm. 'I've got the whole thing lined up.' She took a chance. 'You didn't read my memo. We centre round the Commem Balls at the end of June. St Lucy's is having a big Commem this year – it's their turn – and Rochester is having an ordinary Ball, which I'm assured won't really be ordinary at all. We feature Saffron with Tiggie Jones, the future Lady Saffron, on his arm or anyway somewhere respectable like an arm, then the whole lot of them: the Golden Kids at play. Just what you wanted. Then we move to St Lucy's which is on the river: plenty of punting. Remember how keen you were on punting.'

Cy Fredericks looked uneasy but Jemima thought it was more in reference to the unread (and as a matter of fact as yet unwritten) memo than at the prospect of Megalith cameras going punting. Which should actually have worried him more.

'Tiggie Jones to wed,' he said at last. 'I shall never understand you English girls. Never.' Jemima thought it diplomatic not to probe further into that statement. Nor did Cy Fredericks seem in any mood to amplify it. It was his kind of obituary on the future Lady Saffron.

The ten days or so before the Saffron Ivy weekend were spent by Jemima both at Megalith and Oxford in a frenzy of official activity as the *Golden Kids* programme suddenly became a reality – a hideous reality said Guthrie Carlyle in one of his daring *sotto voce* remarks at a planning meeting, and 'that bloody programme' was heard on more lips than just Jemima's. All sorts of questions had to be answered rather quickly, ranging from the practical to the theoretical.

For example, was Spike Thompson (Jemima's favourite cameraman and many other people's favourite man) available? It was generally agreed that Spike would display an unrivalled mastery over the shadows on the long grass and Laura Ashley dresses and doomed youth and fingers trailing out of punts and ancient stone walls and all that sort of thing. He would also deal expertly with pop music, heavy metal, rock music, and sundry other concomitants of the modern world which Jemima, if not Cy, was well aware went with a successful Commem Ball. Spike could also be relied upon not to raise his camera – nor for that matter his eyebrows – at some of the more lethal habits of doomed youth, the exotic cigarettes to be puffed, the exotic white substances to be sniffed. In short Spike Thompson was, so far as Megalith was concerned, Thoroughly Modern Cameraman.

'Champagne yes, if it's around, the rest of it no,' observed Guthrie Carlyle wisely. 'You can't drink and drug. At any rate not on a Megalith programme.'

As for Spike's expenses: 'Even Spike can't do much with a lot of students' snack bars,' suggested some optimist. For Spike Thompson's expenses while on location were legendary; so that people sometimes swapped anecdotes about such trips at eventide in the Blue Flag, as Henry V predicted that the men who outlived Agincourt would recall St Crispin's Day.

'I'm not sure we'll be moving exclusively in the snack bar set. The programme *is* called *Golden Kids.*'

'But not *Golden Cameramen,*' retorted the optimist wittily. Jemima exchanged glances with Cherry. It was in both their minds that introducing Spike to La Lycée – and how could it be avoided? – was rather like showing an Alsatian into a butcher's shop.

As to the theoretical side, it became increasingly obvious that there were two programmes here. One was the programme beloved of Cy Fredericks – the *Golden Kids mean Big Bucks* programme which was undeniably the type of programme he had successfully pre-sold in those parts of the world – the more luxurious parts – which he had recently visited. The other was the kind of socially investigative programme beloved of Jemima Shore and Guthrie Carlyle in which the lifestyle of the Golden Kids would be contrasted with that of the vast majority of the undergraduates eating in Hall, living off grants or, rather, struggling with inadequate grants, finding even coffee an expensive luxury and never touching a drop of champagne from one end of term to the other.

'This is where Kerry Barber is important,' explained Jemima. 'He's our link. For one thing, he's not only boycotting St Lucy's Commem Ball but leading a protest outside it, a protest against the price of the tickets, that is. He thinks the money should go to the Third World and is prepared to say so to camera. He's also going to provide us with some undergraduates of the same way of thinking. We've got permission to film at St Lucy's as well as Rochester, so the Barber protest should be quite an effective contrast.'

'Jem, my gem,' began Cy Fredericks warmly, 'you're doing wonders here as you always do. Rounded, human *and* humanitarian: I can see already how this programme is shaping. All the same, our motto here at Megalith has always been hard-*nosed* not hard-*grained* reporting.' He paused, giving everyone at the meeting including himself just time to wonder exactly what the difference if any between these two terms might be, before he rushed on: 'What I'm saying, and I think – Miss Lewis, is this right? – I *think* I'm quoting from my address to NIFTA last fall – the essence of interesting controversy on the screen is equality of protest.'

Miss Lewis' silence being taken as assent, Cy beamed even more warmly, particularly at this last statement gained a great deal of muttered encouragement from all those present, delighted to have such an unexceptional sentiment with which to agree.

'So, my gem, please no uncouth types in blue jeans given our air time for their causes . . .'

'I'm afraid I can't guarantee the elimination of jeans from the programme altogether,' interrupted Jemima sweetly, allowing her gaze to roam the room before resting briefly on her own designer-jean-clad thigh. 'But I should tell you that the principal protestor at St Lucy's on the night of the Commem will be Jack Iverstone, who is of course Saffron's cousin. Is that what you meant by equality of protest?'

Everyone agreed afterwards that it was a noted victory for the cause of the good in the perpetual – and not unenjoyable – war waged between Cy and Jemima on the content of her programmes. But as a matter of fact the victory, if it was such, had been engineered by Fanny Iverstone. In the course of her various expeditions to Oxford, Jemima had found no difficulty at all in securing the agreement of assorted undergraduates to appear on the programme promoting assorted views. But although the views were varied, the declared motive for agreeing to appear was generally the same:

'I thought I might go into television after I've gone down,' confided the innocent. The more sophisticated eyed Jemima keenly and asked details of graduate training schemes at Megalith. It all came to the same thing: most people at Oxford, like Kerry Barber, were perfectly prepared to share what they imagined to be Jemima's forum of the air.

Nevertheless Fanny's approach took Jemima by surprise.

Perhaps it should not have done. After all Fanny was an indefatigable organizer. Saffron was really quite right to compare his cousin to Mrs Thatcher – except that the latter had actually been at Oxford as an undergraduate whereas Fanny, as she had cheerfully admitted on their first meeting, had had no education at all. The thought occurred to Jemima as they sat in the dark plate-glass window of Bunns, Oxford's most fashionable café. Fanny was drinking an extraordinarily expensive cappuccino while Jemima toyed with an orange juice (equally expensive). In view of Fanny's forceful character, it was tragic that foolish Daphne Iverstone had taken no interest in her education. With education, Fanny might have gone far. Correction: Fanny would – somehow – go far; of that Jemima felt sure. The question was, in what direction?

Jemima certainly could not imagine her married to her cousin Saffron, although she would have made an excellent Marchioness of the old-fashioned school; but the pair of them would have driven each other to desperation. Jemima only hoped that the dominating streak Fanny had inherited from her father – at present concealed under the softness of girlhood – would not lead her in the same political direction as Andrew Iverstone.

It was Andrew Iverstone who constituted the problem for Jack, confided Fanny. That and his political ambitions.

'Can you imagine what it's like for him, being the son of Old Rabblerouse? For Jack who won't allow any violent emotion whatsoever to surface? Quite apart from being ambitious to save the world and all that sort of thing. So it's twice as important for Jack to make his name as for anyone else. You must feature him on your programme. Doing his thing. This protest with that rather dishy tutor who eats nuts, in his shorts and sandals. Just so everyone can see he doesn't agree with Daddy. Please, Jemima.'

'What about you, Fanny?' asked Jemima curiously. 'Do you mind being the daughter of Old Rabblerouse, as you kindly term him?'

'It's different for girls, isn't it?' Fanny gave her confident upper-class laugh which was possibly more charming now while she was still young than it would be when she got older. 'I'll change my name when I get married. For me, frankly, it's much worse being Mummy's daughter. All that ghastly debutante stuff and the match-making! I ask you. In this day and age. Quite a relief when the Prince of Wales finally got married, I can tell you. If only the other two would follow suit. Prince Andrew, as you may suppose, is Daddy's ultimate idea of what a hereditary leader figure should be.'

'I gather she even had cousin Saffron in mind.' Jemima spoke carelessly.

'Who told you that?' Fanny sounded – and looked – quite put out.

'Oh just gossip! said Jemima hastily. 'Poppy Delaware, someone like that.'

'She should talk. She's been after him for ages. Oh well, now Tiggie Jones has got him. For the time being. We've been bidden, you know, to the great engagement weekend. And Mummy and Daddy. All very feudal: political differences to be strictly put aside: blood is thicker than politics.'

'For the time being?' questioned Jemima, catching at one of Fanny's seemingly careless remarks. 'You don't think the marriage will last?'

Fanny gave another of her confident smiles. 'Did I say that? I didn't exactly mean it wouldn't last if they did get married. I just meant that they're not married yet.' But Jemima had the impression that this time Fanny's jauntiness was slightly forced.

'Many a slip between engagement and lip,' Fanny went on, 'or at least where that couple is concerned. Tiggie Jones is going to have to give up one or two of her bad habits, for one thing.'

'Her universal displays of affection? Or as she put it herself once to me, I just love love. Is that what you had in mind?'

'Oh absolutely,' replied Fanny in a tone of voice which made it quite clear that it was not.

It was noticeable that Jack Iverstone, whom Jemima interviewed about the programme in his rooms at St Lucy's, took rather the same line about the engagement. Fanny was perhaps animated by a certain feminine jealousy. Jack had to be acquitted on that score. Nevertheless he frowned over the prospect, that deep rather weary frown which from time to time marred his cheerful face and made one see the anxious politician he would one day become.

'Trust Saffer to pick on the one girl who can be guaranteed not to pull him together.'

'You don't like Tiggie?'

'Tiggie isn't someone you like or dislike. She's a perfectly idiotic force of nature, if such a thing is possible. I just think they're far too alike. That dreadful capriciousness of hers and those mad ideas of his – did he ever talk to you about his Marxism? Marxist! *Saffer*! Who even has his shoes cleaned by Wyndham, at least fifty years his senior. It's all part of his plan to provoke, and Tiggie, in so far as she has any plan, has roughly the same idea. You have to have one sane one in a marriage. It's terrible when people think alike and they're both wrong.'

He stopped at Jemima's expression.

'Yes, I am thinking of my own parents, if you're interested. My mother's lifelong adoration of my father – they married when they were both twenty – it's one of his chief problems. No one at home has ever argued with him.'

'Except you.'

'Except me. And I don't argue, I reason. But you won't find me reasoning with him at the coming weekend. I shall rein it all in – keep it perhaps for your television programme,' Jack said with a slight smile. 'It's going to be grisly enough without a father-and-son confrontation. Cousin Ivo will be giving us his celebrated impersonation of a very parfait gentleman, as a result of which he was able to appear as our most popular Foreign Secretary for years, in spite of being quite a tough customer underneath it all. Cousin Gwendolen needs no impersonation to be the very parfait English lady.' He shuddered.

'Such politeness all round! When we stayed there as children and my father was making all those terrible speeches about immigration in the seventies. Just *The Times* handed over to you at breakfast: "Jack, your father's making the headlines again." Perfect politeness, no reproach. I wanted to *die*. I was so embarrassed I couldn't read it and had to sneak into the library later. I used to be sick before coming down to breakfast in anticipation.'

'And Fanny? The same?'

'Good God, no! Fanny's much more straightforward. "Has Daddy been spouting tosh as usual?" she'd say brightly. And help herself to the rest of the sausages. Fanny's one of the strongest characters I know. And I don't mean physically.'

'I take it there'll be a great deal of politeness around this weekend. Including your father.'

'Oh yes, you know Daddy's manners when he wants things to go well. At Saffron Ivy there'll be so much politeness about on the surface that we'll all be swimming in a great dish of rich cream. But what about the hatred underneath? You should worry about that, Jemima Shore Investigator.'

Jack leant back in his large worn green armchair, the bottom of which was visibly sagging. He had installed Jemima in the only vaguely new chair in the room, something which had evidently arrived, but none too recently, from Habitat. His mantelpiece was crowded with cards of various societies, mainly of a political nature, amongst which Jemima noticed the official programme of the Union. The contrast with his cousin Saffron's mantelpiece at Rochester was marked: there she had glimpsed practically no traces of Oxford life at all (unless you counted Chimneysweepers' menus) but a number of rather grand engraved invitations to London parties. Her eye lit upon a rather pretty water-colour of a house hanging to the left of the fireplace, much the most attractive object in the room. Jemima recognized Saffron Ivy.

'Nothing that happens in a house like that can be all bad,' she said. But afterwards she would always swear that even at the time some frisson, some faint expression of her famous instinct, had warned her that these words were, like those of the Megalith spokesman on the subject of Spike's expenses at Oxford, absurdly optimistic.

13
Saffron Ivy

There were a number of cars drawn up in the sweep of the drive which
ended with a flourish in front of Saffron Ivy like the dramatis personae of
a play. Jemima saw a Rolls, not a new Rolls, at least fifteen years old
Jemima guessed, but so beautifully kept and shining that it gave the
impression of being a treasured yet still useful antique, like an
immaculately polished dining-room table. Drawn up alongside was a
sharp little mini, navy blue with tinted glass windows. Jemima thought
the mini might belong to Fanny Iverstone. There was also a rather fine
motor-bike, probably a Harley Davidson, since it was remarkably similar
to that owned by the legendary cameraman Spike Thompson and thus
occasionally ridden pillion by Jemima Shore (amongst others). Next to
that was a Porsche.

Then there was a dusty grey Cortina, looking like a poor relation: Jack
Iverstone? Beside it Jemima recognized Saffron's car, a Maserati, dashing
and rather too ostentatious like its owner; in case she hadn't, the final
note of ostention was presented by the initial S on the driver's door and a
coronet over it. The back seat of the Maserati had a jumble of cassettes on
it and some white and frilly garments spilling about. Tiggie's presumably,
not Saffron's. Would his car be unpacked as well as his suitcase? Jemima
remembered Saffron's description of the chauffeur Wyndham 'looking
after everything in my car'. That led her to Saffron's account of the
original attack, the fixing of the car. Jemima shivered.

Above her head, above the surrounding flat but gracefully wooded
landscape, a vista of greens beneath an enormous bowl of grey sky, rose
up the imposing shape of Saffron Ivy. To Jemima there was something
menacing as well as palatial about its magnificent façade. She felt that the
rich and newly respectable Iverstones, who dragged Robert Smythson

from the employment of Bess of Hardwicke to build the house, did not intend their robber baron origins to be entirely forgotten.

The front door opened and at the head of the steps stood a welcoming figure in T-shirt and jeans. Saffron. She assumed it was Saffron. The informality of his clothes was, she thought, in pleasing contrast to the formality of the late Elizabethan façade. The welcoming figure then trotted down the steps and revealed itself to be a good deal older as well as stouter than Saffron.

Slightly startled, Jemima put out her hand. Instead of taking it, the T-shirted figure deftly possessed himself of her car keys and before she could protest, was burrowing in the back of her car for her luggage. Her suitcase emerged with its conspicuous labelling (ordered by Cherry – but that was really no excuse) JEMIMA SHORE. Jemima found that she was gazing at the T-shirt, strained over an impressive chest, which also bore a piece of conspicuous labelling.

I'M BINYON she read.

The jean-clad figure looked down at her suitcase, tapped his chest and smiled even more broadly.

'Good afternoon, Miss Shore. We've both of us nailed our colours to the mast, as it were, haven't we? But then in a manner of speaking, we're both in the same line of business. If you don't think me presumptuous.'

Jemima, even more baffled, smiled back, her beautiful smile of all-purpose sweetness which was particularly useful when total strangers accosted her, apparently confident of recognition.

'I'm Binyon' – the chest was tapped again – 'Binyon the swinging butler.'

Some vague memory stirred.

'And of course I don't need to be told who you are. Label or no label. You're just like you are on television. Very friendly.' Binyon shepherded Jemima up the steps. 'The staff are so excited. What with his lordship's engagement and your arrival.'

To be accurate, thought Jemima, out of the two of them it was Binyon who was the friendly one. And what was a swinging butler anyway? Unless it was simply a butler who wore jeans and a T-shirt in the afternoon. Jemima found she was oddly disappointed; atavistic snobbery no doubt, but she had been expecting the sort of butler you saw on television – except that Binyon seemed to indicate that he *had* been on television. Oh well . . .

'His lordship is in the library,' said Binyon. At least that was a conventional butler's observation. And the library, the famous Saffron Ivy library founded by some intellectual Iverstone in the early eighteenth century, was everything of which a romantic might dream: tooled leather, dark bindings, deep embrasures by the windows, heavy chairs, a large globe, a beautiful deep desk, it was all here. So for that matter was his lordship: not Saffron, however, but Lord St Ives, jumping up with extraordinary briskness from his chair and lolloping to greet her, as though a second's delay might indicate a fatal degree of impoliteness.

At the same moment, a large labrador, so pale it was almost white, started towards her. The dog, unlike Lord St Ives, was remarkably fat which perhaps accounted for the discrepancy in their respective gaits. The words 'well-preserved' might almost have been coined for Lord St Ives: he was so spare as to suggest that the familiar cartoons which showed him as a series of narrow straight lines were in fact portraits not caricatures.

While the dog sniffed slowly and cynically at Jemima's high-heeled shoes, as though little that was good could be expected from them, Lord St Ives shook Jemima's hand with a particular kind of energetic delight. Jemima found it oddly familiar until she realized that she had watched him displaying it on the television news, on numerous occasions, as he greeted world leaders when he was Foreign Secretary. The more the ensuing talks were expected to be 'controversial' in the words of the newscaster, the more pleasure Lord St Ives evinced; he had the air of running into a friend from his London club. How different, how very different was the Cy Fredericks style of greeting! The Chairman of Megalith was apt to welcome even those he knew well with a very slight air of unease beneath his rapture, as though they might have gone and changed their name or in some other way subtly betrayed him since their last meeting.

Then Jemima saw that Lord St Ives had not been alone in the library. At the far end, an elderly woman was struggling out of a deep leather chair, similar to that from which Lord St Ives had sprung with such trapezoid agility. Finally she was able to stand up with the aid of a stick, two sticks. Jemima, recognizing Lady St Ives from Saffron's photograph at Rochester, thought that she actually seemed years older than her husband. This was partly because Lady St Ives, like the dog, moved slowly and had pure white hair. She wore spectacles, secured with a cord round her neck; Lord St Ives' hair on the other hand, in line with his general air of preservation, retained a kind of sandy colour which made Jemima suppose he must have looked much the same even as a young man. How old *was* he? How old was *she*?

The most surprising thing about Lord St Ives was that even now he was actually an attractive as well as a charming man: something to do with centuries of having things your own way, thought Jemima suspiciously. But then Lady St Ives must have had her own way too: perhaps illness had prevented her from developing this particular kind of allure; Jemima remembered Saffron's references to his mother's health.

In the meantime Jemima was being briskly guided to the far end of the library by her host; managing however to take in the famous Lawrence of

The Strawberry Children, which showed a little girl and boy holding a basket of fruit between them, on the way.

Jemima shook Lady St Ives' extended hand which bore a number of splendid but slightly dulled diamond rings. (Was it *nouveau riche*, she wondered, to have one's jewellery cleaned? Jemima neither possessed a lot of precious jewellery nor coveted it – except perhaps the odd emerald; so far the offer of an odd emerald had not come her way.) Lady St Ives wore a handsome diamond brooch pinned to her flowered dress, as well as three rows of pearls; the brooch was similarly dulled. The pearls looked superb.

'We're all so excited, Miss Shore,' Lady St Ives echoed her husband's words. 'And Binyon has been polishing the silver as he only does when the Queen comes.'

'Rather more so!' exclaimed Lord St Ives gaily. 'He's been practically polishing us.'

Jemima saw an opportunity to get at least one mystery solved: 'Yes, do explain to me about Binyon.'

'Oh we thought you might know him' – surprise from Lady St Ives. 'From the telly—'

'Nonsense, my dear, she's much too grand.'

'Yes, but he's Binyon.' Lady Ives turned to Jemima, quite eagerly: 'Binyon, the singing butler.'

'Oh *singing*, you said singing. Singing, not swinging.' Puzzlement from Lady St Ives.

'I don't think Binyon swings. What would he swing from? But he has a very nice voice. Rather like John McCormack, we always think.'

Jemima was distinctly relieved to find that Binyon, jeans or no jeans, was no new breed of butler, but had simply entered an amateur talent competition on television. He had won a series of rounds culminating in an exciting final in which Binyon the Singing Butler had defeated Mirabel O'Shea the Crooning Cook.

'At least, that's how the papers described it,' confessed Lady St Ives. 'But Mirabel O'Shea, while being an absolute darling, all twenty stone of her, we loved her, Binyon invited her down here afterwards with her children, there wasn't a father, all the same she wasn't exactly what you'd call a cook. She'd been frying bacon and eggs in a motorway café, you see.'

'Nonsense, my dear, move with the times! That's exactly what you'd call a cook these days.' Lady St Ives did not answer her husband but instead displayed to Jemima an enormous and very ugly television set, facing her chair, to which they had all been glued during Binyon's weeks of fame. Above it hung an exquisite double portrait of a mother and child, the mother with a mass of powdered curling hair, the baby with its fat white arms thrown upwards; once again Jemima had seen so many reproductions of the picture that she found the sight of the original, sited so cosily above the television set, slightly disconcerting. The label read: 'Frances Sophia, Marchioness of St Ives and the Honble Ivo Charles Iverstone'.

Lord St Ives followed the direction of her gaze. 'Sir Joshua. We think ours is better than the one in the National Gallery. So did K. Clark, I'm glad to say.'

'It's ravishing. *She's* ravishing.'

'Oh, Frances Sophia. I'm afraid she was no better than she should be – you remember Greville's phrase.'

'Of course. And the baby is delicious,' replied Jemima firmly, who had never read Greville, but did not intend to be wrong-footed, at least not on that score, by her host.

'The baby – Ivo Charles – he grew up to be the corrupt MP, I fear. And a terrible gambler. Fox's friend.'

'We used to think Saffron looked rather like him as a baby,' volunteered Lady St Ives. There was a small quite unmistakable pause: Jemima was quite sure about it. Then Lord St Ives gave a light laugh.

'I do hope the resemblance is not carried through. As far as I am aware, gambling at least is not among my son's vices.'

'But he used to love playing *Vingt et Un* as a child, when we all went to Bembridge.' What further reminiscences Lady St Ives might have produced of Saffron's childhood – the topic was after all not absolutely without interest – was not to be known, since the subject himself now arrived in the library.

Saffron was dressed in white cotton trousers, rather tattered, and ending as though more by chance than design at the knee, and a scarlet vest. He was browner than Jemima remembered and, she had to admit looked remarkably handsome. He also had an air of health. It was difficult to believe that he had so recently been in hospital; in fact with his tanned skin, thick black hair, considerably longer, flopping over his face, and his slanting black eyes, he looked more like a gipsy than ever; a stage gipsy from a musical comedy perhaps.

Tiggie on the other hand, in baggy khaki shorts and a mud-coloured shirt, looked for the first time drab, not a word which Jemima would ever have thought to apply to her in London. Compared to Saffron, she had the air of a hen bird: she had had her hair cut very short and her skin remained pale. The only sparkling thing about Tiggie on this occasion was the conspicuous ring on her finger. Diamonds, yes, and emeralds, or rather one great big emerald. This ring really did gleam and was either brand new or had been recently cleaned. But the nails on the small pale hand which bore the weighty ring were dirty. Jemima was surprised; she had the impression that the fairy creature she had first encountered at Megalith had been immaculately clean beneath her bizarre get-up.

Saffron gave his mother a light peck on her papery cheek; then he gave Jemima a kiss on both cheeks, followed by a hug. He was hot and sweaty like a young horse which had just run a successful race.

'Tennis, darling?' enquired Lady St Ives, with a doting look, as though to explain this condition and at the same time boast of it.

'Fanny and I have just beaten Jack and Cousin Andrew.'

'Andrew must have hated that!' pronounced Lord St Ives with much satisfaction. 'He used to be frightfully good. Didn't he play in doubles at Wimbledon, my dear?' Lady St Ives looked rather vague as if the subject of anyone else's tennis other than that of her son's did not interest her.

'I don't think Jack liked it very much either,' said Saffron. 'He always used to beat me. But Fanny's terrific. Serving like Martina Navrati-whatnot. Tremendous at net too.'

'Oh darling, do you think you should – your head—'

'Oh Ma!'

'What about you, Antigone?' Lord St Ives asked kindly. Jemima noticed he exhibited the same courtesy to the young as to the old, and was especially gallant to his future daughter-in-law.

Saffron answered for her. 'Tiggie doesn't play.' Tiggie cast down her eyes, so that the long lashes which Cass had admired fluttered on her pale cheeks. 'I hate games,' she said in a voice which was scarcely above a whisper.

Saffron took her hand and held it. The pair of them were standing directly beneath *The Strawberry Children* – subtitled: *The Honble Miss Iverstone and her brother with a basket of fruit*. Then he dropped the hand and turned to Jemima.

'Well, I love games. There's going to be a return match. Come and watch. Cheer me on. You're on my side, you know you are.' Saffron's bold black eyes challenged Jemima: there was something febrile about him today, as new and marked as Tiggie's passivity. It was a sexual statement.

'My dear boy, I'm certainly on your side.' Lord St Ives put his arm around his son's shoulders. Jemima wondered if he had perhaps known what Saffron was up to, and decided that he probably had: not much passed by Lord St Ives. Seeing them side by side for the first time, 'father' and 'son', she was struck by the similarity of their stance; Saffron had evidently copied his father's bearing, even some of his mannerisms, from childhood. Although physically they could hardly have been less alike, the one so dark, the other so typically English, Jemima ruminated on the interesting resemblances which 'nurture' not 'nature' was able to bring about. She had known other adopted children, come to think of it, who had grown to resemble their 'parents' so strongly, that people sometimes refused to believe in the truth of their adoption.

'You're avenging all the times Andrew used to beat me,' said Lord St Ives.

'Quite apart from Jack beating *me*,' replied Saffron. 'All the cousins are terrifically athletic; or anyway they try very hard. To make up.' Saffron sounded quite complacent.

'To make up for what?' Jemima asked innocently, although she knew the answer; but she felt an urge to prick the complacency, a radical urge which she instantly regretted when Lord St Ives, who had not held Russians in play for nothing, picked up cudgels. Or rather, he appeared to gaze at the cudgels beneath his nose and find them instantly delightful.

'Why, to make up for being dreadfully poor of course, whereas we are dreadfully rich!' he exclaimed, with his usual zest. 'It *is* unfair. Don't you think so, Miss Shore? Of course you do. That we should have all this—' he gave a wide gesture embracing not only the Reynolds, the Lawrence, and several thousand books in their majestic bindings, but also Binyon who had at that moment entered and was standing, still clad in his eponymous T-shirt, at the door. 'I expect you want me to feel guilty. Oh Miss Shore, I do, I do.'

'Ivo, why are you being so silly?' Lady St Ives suddenly enquired. 'You know you don't feel guilty at all. The hereditary system is absolutely indefensible, except that it happens to work brilliantly. I've heard you say it countless times.'

'Oh my dear, don't give me away,' said Lord St Ives tenderly. 'I only say that in the House of Lords; you've been listening to my speeches which I really don't advise. Nobody listens to my speeches in the House of Lords.'

Lady St Ives continued to look gently reproachful.

'Besides, I think Miss Shore is referring to primogeniture, aren't you, Miss Shore? Why should I sit in glory here at Saffron Ivy while for example poor Cousin Andrew pigs it in Henley?'

'I did ask a question,' said Jemima sweetly. 'But I don't think it was exactly that one.'

'But Ivo, Daphne and Andrew don't live *in* Henley, no one lives *in* Henley—' began Lady St Ives.

'*Façon de parler*, my dear, *façon de parler*. I have to admit that one good defence of the hereditary system does seem to me the fact that I live here and Cousin Andrew doesn't. But then I'm prejudiced. Now what about that tennis?'

'The players are on the court, my lord.' It was the solemn voice of Binyon, once again sounding, if not looking, like the butler of Jemima's dreams. 'Mr Valliera is playing with Miss Fanny in place of Lord Saffron.'

'No he bloody isn't!' exclaimed Saffron. And so they all went and watched the tennis, leaving Jemima with various images in her mind, some of them concerning Saffron, some Tiggie, some both; and some thoughts about Lord St Ives and the hereditary system. She did not think that Lord St Ives had been altogether joking when he defended his inheritance on the grounds that he was worthy of it, whereas his cousin was not. That substitution all those years ago . . . she had expected to find it quite implausible in the face of Lord St Ives' famous courtesy and 'parfait' manners, in the words of Jack. But Jack was right: there was something quite steely there underneath it all.

The last thing she had learned concerned the passionate affection which was borne towards Saffron by his parents – not only Lady St Ives, but Lord St Ives as well. There was something quite naked about the devotion he had momentarily exhibited when he put his arm around Saffron's shoulders. Jemima dreaded to think what would happen to this elderly couple if anything happened to him. And this time she was not pondering on the fate of the Iverstone inheritance.

14

Tennis is About Winning

It came as relief after these subterranean fears, to watch the open rivalries of the tennis court. When the St Ives party arrived, Proffy and Eugenia Jones were sitting in two ancient deck chairs beside it. Their heads were close together.

Jemima had the impression that some rather earnest colloquy had been interrupted, certainly not of an amorous nature and probably not connected with the tennis match either. Both stood up as Lady St Ives, walking with difficulty, arrived. Eugenia Jones looked extraordinarily melancholy and, unlike Lady St Ives, in no way conveyed that kind of indulgent affection towards Tiggie which might have been expected on such a celebratory occasion. More than ever she seemed dependent on the ebullience of Proffy who gave the air of cosseting her, as a bear might protect some smaller breed of animal. This kind of possessiveness in public away from home was no doubt intended to make up for his defection to the side of Eleanor in marriage.

On this occasion Eugenia simply ignored Tiggie and walked in the direction of St Ives as though to speak to him. In a neat manoeuvre, Proffy somehow managed to outflank her:

'A word—' he began.

'Later, later. After tennis. I know words. They lengthen into sentences. To say nothing of speeches. Then we shan't get any tennis.'

'Oh Ivo, are you going to play?' cried Lady St Ives.

'If anyone will play with an old man like me,' replied Lord St Ives genially. 'A geriatric doubles, perhaps, after this dashing match is over.' He settled himself down, as though the matter was decided. Jemima was nonetheless left with the impression that the tension within Eugenia which Proffy had in some way tried to relieve, had not subsided.

The tennis court itself, Jemima was amused to note, was more in the tradition of Lady St Ives' jewellery, antique splendour now much dimmed, than of anything more professional. Andrew Iverstone did indeed allow himself some fairly barbed references to the superiority of the court in – or rather near – Henley. Lord St Ives bore it all with great humour as he sat in a deck chair, itself not in its first youth, his face shaded by an aged straw hat, whose faded ribbon doubtless proclaimed membership of some exclusive club to which Andrew Iverstone had never belonged.

'Can't you get your people to look at this court, Ivo?' shouted Andrew Iverstone eventually, when he failed to return a modest lob from Saffron which landed in one of the more obvious craters.

'What people, my dear chap? I don't have any tennis people, I fear. This court was made before the war. *En-Tout-Cas*.' He gave the name exquisite French pronunciation. 'I must say it's lived up to the name. Until today that is.'

'I'll give you the name of ours,' grunted Iverstone, smashing a good low forehand drive from his daughter unexpectedly to Saffron's backhand and thus winning the point.

'Such charming people' fluted Daphne Iverstone in the vague direction of Gwendolen St Ives. 'Old-fashioned manners which I think make such a difference—'

'Be quiet, will you, Daphne, when we're playing.' Andrew Iverstone's politeness, in its own way as much a part of his public character as that of Lord St Ives, evidently did not stretch as far as the tennis court. Some of the other young sprawled temporarily by the court. They included Bernardo Valliera who proved to own both the Harley Davidson and the Porsche (how had he transported *both* to Saffron Ivy?). The dusty Cortina however did not belong to Jack who said cheerfully he could not afford a car, but to Proffy. The smart little Mini was a recent present from Saffron to Tiggie. Then the young departed for the croquet lawn which lay at some distance, sufficiently far for the gales of laughter which punctuated play to have a charming rather than irritating effect upon the ear.

Iverstone was at net where he made an imposing bull-like figure, his great red forehead gleaming with sweat; there was no doubt that he was still a formidable tennis player, and Jemima could well imagine that he had once been in the top class. In spite of his weight – in any case much of it still gave the impression of being muscle – he looked fit enough. Jack looked quite puny beside him and was, as he wryly admitted, still regularly beaten by his father on that immaculate Henley court.

'Since Daddy is a master of the chop shot, the slice, the top spin and all other similar ploys.'

'Tennis is about winning, my dear boy' was Andrew Iverstone's comment on this. All the same, Jack was a good player, with style and ease.

Jemima glanced at the spectators. It was odd how Eugenia Jones kept her glance quite rigidly fixed on Andrew Iverstone and to a lesser extent Jack, her tension if anything increased. She remained silent throughout. Proffy on the other hand took an active interest in the game, shouted encouraging comments, applauded, and generally revealed himself in the rather unlikely role of a tennis buff. Although his ceaseless chatter might have put off some players, it was in a way preferable to Eugenia Jones' unhappy silence. Jemima turned back to the court itself.

The wonder was that Saffron and Fanny had taken the first set; perhaps knowledge of local conditions, in the form of the court's bad patches, had helped them, Jemima reflected wryly. If Saffron in his tight white breeches and red vest looked like a stage gipsy, he played tennis more like a stage bullfighter in the sense that his tennis had the air of being conducted largely for the benefit of the spectators. There were frequent smashes, many of which landed against the rusty old netting at the end of the court, rather than anywhere more conventional within the white lines.

At any rate Andrew Iverstone and Jack took the second set quite easily, six-one. Although Jemima could not help noticing that Iverstone took advantage of every doubtful ball to call the score in his own favour, without any interference from Jack: it was so characteristic of the man. Even when the Iverstones were leading four-love against Saffron and Fanny, Andrew Iverstone insisted that a particular ball of his daughter's had been out although Jemima could have sworn that there was a tiny puff of chalk from the bedraggled court. Jack did nothing. After all, what was there for him to do? Only Saffron, with a deliberate swagger, carefully dropped the next few balls which came his way just over the net.

'Just to make sure, Cousin Andrew.' It was in fact this method which secured Saffron and Fanny their solitary game, since it defeated both Iverstone at the back of the court and Jack who waited for his father to take them.

None of this seemed to make much impact upon Tiggie, sitting on the grass at the side of the court and wearing a large flowered cotton sun bonnet – where had she found it? – which accorded oddly with the rest of her khaki outfit. She was totally docile, to the extent that Jemima wondered if she was actually aware of the play in progress.

The third and decisive set began. It did not seem likely that Saffron and Fanny would find their original form again. Tiggie's head in its large bonnet drooped. But it so happened that Saffron and Fanny, having gone a long way down at the start of the set, with Andrew Iverstone (and to a lesser extent Jack) grimly determined to pulverize every ball, now began to pull back.

This was partly due to Fanny's steady strong play: Saffron's comparison to Martina Navratilova was perhaps going a little far, but there was certainly something of the same determined masculine style about

Fanny's tennis. Jemima discerned for the first time a distinct resemblance to her father in the stance of the well-muscled but shapely legs, for example, which were not particularly long but twinkled across the court at an astonishing pace to bat balls down the tramlines beyond her father's reach.

Saffron's smashes were also beginning to find their mark just inside the court instead of a yard outside it; and similarly his first service actually produced some aces, as well as the usual ration of ineffectively hard shots which left the aged net shaking as they slammed into it.

The score in games was now five-four to Saffron and Fanny, Saffron having just held his service with a triumphant last ace. Now Andrew Iverstone himself was serving, with Jack a slightly deferential figure at net. Jack's air of deference was in part due to the fact that his father's service had become just slightly erratic with age: although Iverstone was still capable of delivering balls with an amount of top-spin which made them highly challenging to return, he was equally capable of an apparently inexplicable double fault. In such a case, Iverstone's temper, like his service, could be erratic.

Now a series of these double faults from Iverstone had brought the score to deuce. Then Fanny in the right-hand court passed Jack at net with one of her well-placed drives. Andrew Iverstone glanced briefly and very angrily at the ball: for one moment Jemima thought he might actually call it out – although the ball was in by inches. Instead he said nothing. It was left to Saffron to sing out the score:

'Advantage Lord Saffron and Miss Iverstone, that popular young couple. Set point. Don't feel nervous.' Jemima thought it singularly tactless of him. After all, everybody realized it was set point. Nobody else commented. Saffron, still very much at his ease, crouched slightly to receive Andrew Iverstone's service.

It was at this very moment that Tiggie, for no particular reason that anyone could see, suddenly jerked into life. Her head came up and she stared at the court. Then she started to laugh and clap with uninhibited frenzy:

'Saffer, Saffer, ooh Saffer,' she clapped again, 'I've got something for you, Saffer.'

Jemima realized rather belatedly that Tiggie had to be stoned; not necessarily stoned out of her mind, but certainly stoned beyond the permissible level of a spectator at a tennis match. The symptoms which Jemima would soon have identified in metropolitan London had been so alien to the mellow environment of Saffron Ivy that she had failed to recognize them. Pot? Cocaine? Probably the latter, since Tiggie now seemed to be miming some form of sniff for the benefit of her fiancé. Jemima wondered what Andrew Iverstone's reaction would be. It was not likely that this kind of interruption would be tolerated for very long by a man who had told his own wife to be quiet when he was playing a point. And at a crucial moment in the match.

Afterwards it was difficult to decide whether Tiggie's frenzied clapping, her cries of 'Saffer, oooh Saffer', had actually caught Andrew Iverstone in mid serve. As a matter of fact, he had probably already delivered the serve when she broke out into her little birdsong. All the same, fairly or not, the fact that the ball went into the net on the first service seemed not unconnected with Tiggie's cries.

Immediately Iverstone served again, too quickly perhaps. That service too foundered. In this low-key fashion the third and decisive set had been won by Saffron and Fanny.

In the prevailing silence – no one dared clap – Tiggie gave a loud titter: 'Oooh, there it goes again. Into the net. End of the set.'

At this point three things happened more or less simultaneously. Saffron flung up his racket in a whoop of triumph (the racket, unlike the net, was gleaming new): 'Six-four to the good guys. Well done, Cousin Fan.'

Lord St Ives went with great speed behind Tiggie's chair and started to help her up with the words: 'Come along, Antigone my dear.'

And Andrew Iverstone, with astonishing viciousness, aimed a ball hard at precisely that bit of wire netting which protected Tiggie's frail figure from the game's onslaught. 'Little bitch!' he shouted.

That in itself might not have mattered so much had the Saffron Ivy netting been of the high quality of, say, the Iverstone court at Henley. Only too clearly, it was not. The impact caused a large section of the blackened netting to fall to the ground, amid an unpleasant hail of rust. The ball itself struck Tiggie just as she was obediently rising to Lord St Ives' command. Shock, more than pain, must have caused her to give a short scream. Tiggie opened her large eyes and sucked her finger.

Jemima involuntarily looked towards the court. Andrew Iverstone stood panting and flushed as though struggling to master himself and resume the mantle of his manners. And on Jack Iverstone's face she saw a surprised look of absolute disgust, presumably at his father's behaviour, so strong as to amount to something close to hatred.

Jemima sighed. She pitied him.

'Daddy, don't be such a bad loser.' Fanny's bracing voice came as a positive relief. Jemima watched, fascinated, as the mask of impasssivity came down again on Jack's face; there was now no trace of the strong emotion he had exhibited only a moment before.

'I'm terribly sorry.' Andrew Iverstone's voice was musical in its apology; he made a theatrical gesture with his hands. 'How could I be such an oaf? Fanny's quite right. I'm the most awful loser.' He made it sound as if this was a charming eccentricity on his part. 'Antigone, are you all right?'

But Tiggie was being helped towards the house by Lord St Ives – 'I'll be back later for my game' – and Saffron, whose high spirits were quite unimpaired by recent happenings, was busy trying to do a breakdance on the court.

'Jemima, can you do this?' he called. Saffron made no attempt to follow Tiggie, nor for that matter did her mother. When Lord St Ives finally returned, dressed in ancient white flannels which in no way diminished his air of battered elegance, it was to find the little party at the court, spectators and exhausted players, waiting in a silence which still had a great deal of awkwardness about it.

'Now for the Golden Oldies!' cried Saffron, whose gyrations were by now quite unnerving.

'Personally, I need a fast runner for a partner, one who's going to take every shot in the front of the court. My dear boy, if *you're* to fill that role—' Lord St Ives looked pointedly towards Saffron, who was still standing on the top of his head '– do take care.'

'We'll take you on, Ivo. Fathers and sons. Jack and I against you and Saffron.' Andrew Iverstone stood up. He still looked heavily flushed. Jemima could understand why Daphne Iverstone began a tremulous protest.

'Oh darling, you know what the doctor said—'

She expected Andrew Iverstone, in spite of his state, to administer a sharp snap to his wife. Instead of which Iverstone hesitated, then smiled affably and sat down again.

'Damn it, she's right. Doctor's orders. Three sets and no more. As I intend to play tennis vigorously for the rest of my life, I have to pay attention.' He added pleasantly: 'I'll umpire. Take my revenge that way.'

That left Lord St Ives looking for a fourth player in the direction of Fanny, or perhaps Jemima. But Jemima, although she secretly rather fancied her tennis, thought that the opportunity for observation on this occasion was not to be missed. Tennis as a guide to character was a favourite preoccupation of hers. (Cass and Jemima for example had an on-going singles match in which Cass beat Jemima by strength and Jemima beat Cass by stealth.) She thought that she might get to know a little more about the character of Lord St Ives in the game which followed. The ruthlessness which must lie beneath the charm might perhaps be more clearly exhibited under the pressure of the game.

Who then was to be the fourth? Fanny and Jack together, it was felt, would make rather an uneven game: there were more polite references from Lord St Ives to his geriatric tennis. At which point Proffy suddenly stood up and said: 'I'll play.'

For the first time Jemima realized that he was wearing white tennis shoes (one black lace, one brown) with his loose grey flannel trousers for a purpose: she had imagined this detail to be further engaging proof of his absent-mindedness. Eugenia looked startled, gave the air of being about to say something: a third feminine protest to be joined to that of Lady St Ives which had failed and that of Daphne Iverstone which had succeeded. Then she sat back again in silence without speaking.

Proffy gambolled on to the court, looking more than ever like a bear that had lost its way: but he was obviously prepared for the game quite apart from the shoes, for he produced a pair of gold-rimmed plastic-lensed glasses from a pocket which he substituted for his habitual black-rimmed ones. Jemima remembered her original estimate of Proffy as a man whose absent-mindedness merely applied to those details of life which did not interest him (such as his wife's Christian name) and decided it had been correct.

She focussed her attention on the game. Yes, Lord St Ives could be said to be a ruthless, or at least competitive, player: although to be fair he was not nearly as competitive as Proffy, some of whose line calls were strangely reminiscent of those of Andrew Iverstone in the previous match – or perhaps the gold-rimmed spectacles were not as efficient as they looked. Otherwise she noted that Lord St Ives had a quick rather old-fashioned way of serving, with no great throwing up of the ball; true to his promise, he left all the running to Saffron; lastly his net play was lethal.

Jemima watched Proffy's surprisingly hard forehand drives being killed time and time again by Lord St Ives at net in a way that left even Jack – a fast runner and a fit one – no opportunity to reach them. Proffy's way of dealing with this was simply to hit harder – but he still aimed straight at Lord St Ives, as though mesmerized by the tall spare figure at the net. And Proffy's despair was comical.

'Insane, insane,' he kept muttering. 'Can't help aiming at him, can't help it.'

Since Lord St Ives continued to despatch these balls within his reach, Saffron twice won his service, erratic as its style remained. Jemima thought that Lord St Ives looked more like a gun at a shoot, polishing off driven grouse, than a tennis player. Then she remembered that he had been a noted shot in his day: no doubt an excellent eye explained his lethal performance, even at the age of seventy.

At this point a hard ball sent by Proffy actually hit Lord St Ives on the shoulder. As Proffy began to lumber forward, apologizing profusely, and Saffron galloped towards his father, Andrew Iverstone suddenly called out from the sidelines: 'That's your point, Proffy.'

'For heaven's sake, Daddy,' began Jack.

'Of course it's their point, Andrew. I'm aware of the rules. And I'm perfectly all right. No, Gwendolen, please do not call Binyon.' But for once Jemima had actually seen Lord St Ives' genial surface ruffled.

After this incident, there was a distinct rise in the level of the game's tension, which Jemima attributed directly to the presence of Andrew Iverstone sitting implacably, still rather flushed, behind the court's rusty netting.

Jack and Proffy were now leading five games to two, these two games representing Saffron's service. The games however had been closer than the score indicated: Lord St Ives in particular had played with still greater keenness following Proffy's blow and Andrew Iverstone's intervention. Proffy's own shots were getting wilder and rather less hard, as if the blow had upset him far more than his host, and something of the edge had gone off Jack Iverstone's play, possibly for the same reason. Lord St Ives and Saffron were definitely the improving couple, and only lost the seventh game after a series of deuces and a call from Proffy which was to say the least of it dubious.

It was Lord St Ives' turn to serve.

'He wants to win,' thought Jemima, 'or rather he does not want to lose.'

Then Andrew Iverstone called Lord St Ives' second serve out, just as Proffy, playing in the right-hand court, took a swipe at it. The swipe went into the net.

'Out,' he repeated.

'Balls,' said Saffron in a tone which was clearly audible.

'I must say I thought it was in,' said Jack in a mild tone to no one in particular.

Proffy panted and said nothing.

Lord St Ives said nothing either but simply crossed to the other court and prepared to serve again. The score was now love-fifteen. Lord St Ives served a double fault – very quickly, both balls delivered and into the net almost before Jack was ready to receive them.

Love-thirty. He recrossed, and served once again, too low, too quick, and straight into the net. But the second serve, surprisingly fast and also surprisingly deep, actually hit the white line close to Proffy's feet and Jemima herself saw the puff of chalk. The ball, both its pace and depth, obviously took Proffy completely by surprise; for one thing he was standing far too forward. He made no move to hit it.

It was this lack of movement which encouraged Andrew Iverstone to call out again from his deck chair: 'Out.'

'Was it out?' asked Lord St Ives in quite a sharp voice. He spoke to Proffy.

'Oh yes, absolutely out, absolutely. Wonderful serve all the same.' Proffy, apparently unaware of what was going on, spoke with great enthusiasm. 'Wonderful serve, but out.'

Love-forty. And set point.

Then Lord St Ives picked up a tennis ball and with much more grace than his cousin Andrew Iverstone at the end of the previous match, but with very much the same intent, hit it in a high parabola above the net. The ball bounced somewhere way outside the court. In no sense could the shot be interpreted as a serve.

'Set and match to you,' said Lord St Ives. 'Or rather we'll give it to you. I shan't bother with my second service.' He handed his racket to Saffron. 'Carry that for me, will you, old fellow? My shoulder is a bit painful.'

He walked off the court.

'You're quite right, Andrew,' were his next words, said with extreme good nature to the MP, still sitting in his deck chair. 'We really must get our court seen to. Will you give Gwendolen that address?'

Tennis, thought Jemima, was not the only game being played at Saffron Ivy. Some grimmer, more secret contest was also being played out.

15

Drawing Blood

Tiggie reappeared at dinner. She sat beside Saffron. She looked terrible and spoke not at all. It must have represented a considerable effort, Jemima thought, to have come down to dinner at all under these circumstances. Above the heads of the affianced couple hung another Lawrence, a sketch for the big double portrait of *The Strawberry Children* in the library, two youthful heads: compared to Tiggie, the Honble Miss Iverstone looked healthy and enchantingly pretty.

There were eighteen people at dinner, stretching down the long table, with its weight of glass and silver; the latter included a rococo silver centrepiece which on close inspection proved to represent a tortuous grove of trees, liberally entwined with the ivy which formed the family's crest. Ivy was also to be found on each separate dinner plate, together with the Iverstone family motto, whose Latin caused Jemima a moment's earnest but ultimately useless concentration.

'It means something like "Like the ivy, I protect my own walls",' said Lord St Ives genially, noting the direction of her gaze. 'Which is of course absolute nonsense, since ivy, if anything, pulls walls down.'

'A good motto, nonetheless. Haven't you rather lived by it?' Seeing Lord St Ives look slightly taken aback Jemima added with a politeness to match her host's own: 'As Foreign Secretary, I meant.'

Binyon, serving dinner, was assisted by a young man called Stephen, wearing a dark suit which did not fit, and an elderly man wearing a similar suit which did. Retainers. Assisting Lord St Ives – and Binyon – to protect the walls. To Jemima there was something faintly distasteful about an elaborately served banquet at which most of the guests were in their late teens and early twenties: the sight of the elderly retainer bending low to proffer a soufflé dish to Saffron with the words – 'Haddock Soufflé, my lord' – struck her as against the natural order of things in which youth should minister to age.

'Come on, Saffer, don't take it all,' said a rather jolly young man simply called the Gobbler sitting opposite him; the Gobbler's interest in food was one of the running jokes of the Saffer set, Jemima observed, so that even the simplest remark of this nature issuing from his lips was greeted with gales of laughter. Everyone felt very disappointed if the Gobbler did not fill his plate to overflowing; just as the Gobbler showed equal disappointment if those around him did not try to seize the food back off his plate. Jemima had inadvertently contributed to the fun before dinner by mentioning a new series about gourmet food to be mounted by Megalith in the autumn.

It was pure courtesy which had led her to mention that there was an opening for a researcher on this particular series when the Gobbler made the more or less obligatory enquiry about openings in television, since she could hardly imagine the Gobbler or indeed any of those present at Saffron Ivy (except possibly Fanny) being able to hold such a job down.

'Is that the sort of thing that interests you?' The question was quite innocent. But as a result, when the hilarious laughter died down – Jemima thought Poppy Delaware would literally choke, she laughed so much – an extra running joke was added on the subject of the Gobbler and his television career.

'The Gobbler must do some research' became a rallying cry at the sight of any dish, to the untiring amusement of all the Oxford Bloods. From Jemima's point of view it was a relief to contemplate the only two outside guests, both male, both Cambridge dons, one quite young called Shipley and one very old called Leek. (Jemima dreaded to think what the Oxford Bloods would have made of such names, had they been the slightest bit interested in anybody's concerns at the dinner table other than their own . . .)

The dons were sitting at the other end of the table, on either side of Lady St Ives. The function of Shipley was to make conversation to Eugenia Jones about classical tragedy. The function of Leek, less exhausting, was to listen to Proffy who addressed him about the problems of the Albanian Resistance in World War II over the head of a passive pretty girl called Nessa, last seen at the Chimneysweepers' Dinner, who seemed to be loosely attached to Bernardo.

Jemima surveyed the table and took a deep breath. She thought that the presence of the two dons, loquacious and silent respectively, would make the next stage of her investigation easier than the reverse. All the same, there was a certain risk in what she proposed to do. It was not a question of Cherry's briefing: she trusted Cherry to the hilt, even though Cherry's enthusiasm for the subject had not matched that of, say, the Gobbler, for gourmet food. No, the problem was Saffron. In order to carry out her plan, she had had to enlist his help. Even if she had not, he would soon have guessed her intention, so that to take him into her confidence was in another sense essential. All the same, she hoped that Saffron would keep a cool head.

Jemima had come to agree with Kerry Barber about the quality of Saffron's intelligence, even when it was cloaked with some deliberate affectation of idiocy. Yet there was nothing very cool about him this evening. On the contrary, he was in dangerously high spirits: she thought that already he had drunk more than most people would drink in a whole evening. Saffron drunk and indiscreet was capable of wrecking the whole plan.

At that moment, Saffron leant forward and in a voice which was almost perfectly casual asked: 'I say, Jemima, what's next?'

'Next?' Jemima excused herself politely from a conversation with Jack Iverstone about the possible unification of the SDP and the right wing of the Labour Party.

'When you've finished with us Golden Kids –' an audible groan from Jack '– all right, holy cousin, *we* didn't call ourselves that. We're Marxists, as you know, or we were last term.'

'Oxford Bloody Marxist!' said Jack which for him sounded quite rude.

'We're anarchists now, Saffer,' Poppy Delaware interrupted sternly. 'Don't you remember that night after the Talking Heads concert? 'We got out our manifesto.' Poppy looked ravishing in a loose but extremely well-cut white linen dinner jacket, wing collar and narrow black tie; the only thing which was visibly anarchistic about her was her wildly streaky hair, in which silver and orange were only a few of the colours visible. Jemima knew that it was despicably sexist on her part but she could not summon up enormous interest in Poppy's political views; on the other hand, she would like to know where she got the dinner jacket.

'Anarchists, OK, yah. Well, what are you going to do next, Jemima?' Saffron was not to be deterred.

'Now for something totally different. I'm working on a programme about blood as a matter of fact. No, not noble blood this time. Everybody's blood.'

She was conscious of the presence upstairs of that invaluable text-book, *Blood Group Serology*, 5th edition, procured by Cherry, together with Mourant's *Blood Relations*. What had the maid thought when she unpacked them? (They were placed conspicuously on her dressing table next to her make-up instead of beside her bed with the other books, as though of a vaguely pharmaceutical nature.) Jemima launched into her theme. Blood transfusions . . . The need for more and different kinds of blood in the National Health Service . . . blood groupings . . . ethnic frequencies . . . types of formerly rare blood becoming more frequently needed in a society in which immigrants play an increasing part . . . to say nothing of the whole new problem of AIDS.

Once again Saffron played up admirably. He referred to his own recent blood transfusions at Oxford and even managed to make the announcement of his own comparatively rare AB group sound like a characteristic boast.

'It's surprising how few people do know their own blood group.' Daphne Iverstone was a helpful if unexpected ally. 'I remember working for St John's – we all thought it should be compulsory to carry it on you.'

'Had to be in the war, of course,' grunted Andrew Iverstone. 'But I'm not sure we want any more bureaucratic rules here, do we?' It was noticeable how his wife brought out the worst in him, his normal courtesy perceptibly flagging. But he was also badly placed at the table: the preponderance of males brought about by the presence of the two unattached dons meant that he had ended sitting next to the Gobbler – scarcely a marriage of true minds; he had Eugenia Jones, still being lectured by Shipley, on his right.

Daphne Iverstone hesitated; Jemima saw her struggling with natural reluctance to contradict her husband on anything. It was Fanny on the Gobbler's other side, who came to the rescue. She leant forward.

'Don't be silly, Daddy. When it saves lives. Think of accidents and things like that. I learnt all about it with the Guides. You can't give someone any old blood transfusion, you know. You have to be sure of the group first.'

Daphne Iverstone took heart.

'And precious time is wasted while you take a test. But if you know the group—'

'So what is your group, my dear Fanny?' Andrew Iverstone was once more sounding gallant.

There was general laughter as Fanny hesitated. Finally she burst out laughing in her turn.

'How awful! I've forgotten. I promise I knew once.'

Jemima pursued the opening.

'This is one of the things I'll be considering, of course. Should we carry cards? As servicemen did in the war. For example, let's see how many people, if any, round this table do know their blood group, A, O, B or AB. And as a matter of interest if we get enough figures, whether the pattern conforms to the national average.' She started with her new ally, Daphne Iverstone.

'A – A positive actually. That means I'm Rhesus positive.' The nice young man next to her called Ned who was said to be a wonderful cricketer shook his head, bemused by the turn the conversation was taking. Fanny, opposite, came back gamely with A.

'I'm sure it was A. Is A rare too?' she enquired hopefully.

'A and O are the two most common English groups.' Daphne Iverstone sounded delighted to be able for once to put her daughter down. In so doing she did Jemima's work for her.

'That's really one of the points of my programme. Groups like B, which used to be comparatively uncommon, under ten per cent, are becoming more common with immigration; hence the need for more blood of these rarer groups within the National Health Service.'

Andrew Iverstone, whose ears had evidently pricked up at the sound of the word immigration, leant forward in his turn.

'How very interesting, Miss Shore. I don't think I'd appreciated that, in spite of my special study of this kind of subject. Isn't this an example of the way British society is simply not able to *cope* with large influxes of alien races, whose very blood cannot mix successfully?'

But Fanny, for one, was having none of that.

'Oh, come on Daddy, let's go round the table,' she interrupted brightly. 'I think it's a fascinating new kind of game. Maybe we should all go off and have blood tests or something.'

Jemima's eyes met those of Saffron across the table. This was not quite going the way they had intended. Or was it? As she hesitated, Bernardo Valliera, sitting next to Fanny, suddenly and surprisingly volunteered that his own group was O. There had been some accident playing polo as a result of which he had derived this information. Jemima, remembering from one of the maps in Mourant that virtually the whole of the South American population were group O, felt a glow of pleasure that Mourant was working out so exactly: she beamed at Bernardo.

'Now we go round the table,' said Fanny. 'Tiggie, you next.'

But Tiggie, unsurprisingly, did not know her blood group. All she did when asked was sink her head on Saffron's shoulder with the words: 'Ooh, horrible. I hate it when they take your blood, don't you? I hate needles. They should be like vampires. They should *suck* it. Sucking is lovely—'

This time it was Saffron who effected the interruption, passing the question on to Poppy who said she had absolutely no idea, but offered the fact that she was a Pisces as being an alternative and perhaps preferable line of enquiry . . . At which point Saffron interrupted even more firmly, as a dangerous babble of zodiacal chit-chat could be heard coming from Tiggie, which Poppy showed every sign of picking up.

Luckily the elderly don called Leek did know his blood group – O. Nessa next to him smiled, fluttered her eyelashes and said nothing; she seemed not to believe that any serious question could possibly be addressed to her. Proffy, who was rattling away, paused just long enough to pronounce: 'A, A, pure Alpha' before rattling on again. Lady St Ives, suddenly grasping the subject at discussion, plunged into it with some enthusiasm, much as Daphne Iverstone had done, based in her case on her presidency of the local Red Cross.

She confirmed that her own blood group was O and pointed out that when in doubt in an emergency, O group blood was administered since it contained no clashing agglutinogens. Then she went on to talk about the difficulties experienced with new ethnic groups who had immigrated to the local towns, especially the east coast ports: 'We need more B blood.'

This time Jemima did not look at Saffron. She was desperately anxious that the question should continue to run on round the table to where the object of the whole exercise sat at the head, listening to proceedings with his usual air of impartial benevolence. So that she was not much disappointed when first the don called Shipley and then Eugenia Jones passed, neither betraying any particular enthusiasm for the subject, before returning to Shipley's disquisition on classical tragedy.

Andrew Iverstone, however, threatened to wreck the whole show. He had been frowning, first at Daphne, then as he listened to Lady St Ives' own little lecture.

Finally, when asked the question, he said lightly: 'Oh something thoroughly British. A, I think.'

'No, it isn't, darling!' cried Daphne Iverstone. 'B. Definitely B. B negative. I remember because when the children were born, and there was some question, there might have been difficulties.'

'Oh Andrew,' Lady St Ives sounded quite enthusiastic. 'Maybe you will give us some of your nice B blood.'

There was some laughter from those who realized the significance of what had just been said. Andrew Iverstone joined in.

'Serve me right. Patriotism is not enough. You have to have the right blood too. Daphne, my dear, thank you. Your frankness may save my life in a car crash.'

The question was passed to the Gobbler whose mouth was full and who did not attempt to answer it.

Fanny had already answered. It was Jack's turn.

'I don't know. But I can easily work it out having done biology at A-level. If Daddy is B and Mummy is A then I must be AB. And so must you, Fanny.'

Again Professor Mossbanker paused just long enough in his peroration to Leek to say: 'He's quite right, quite right', before rattling on again.

Oddly enough, nobody commented on Jack's statement, although Jemima nervously thought that someone at least might have worked out its implications as regards Saffron with his O group mother. But perhaps she overestimated the guests' interest in the subject.

'My own group is A, A positive like Mrs Iverstone,' said Jemima quickly. 'And now Lord St Ives—'

Her host sat back in his chair, eyes half shut, and sipped his claret in a leisurely manner as though trying to decide on the vintage, information he must however already have had at his fingertips.

'My blood group? Oh, I'm afraid I've no idea, no idea at all,' said Lord St Ives.

Jemima's heart sank at his answer – had all this charade been for nothing, other than to establish that Andrew Iverstone was full of 'non-British' blood which might be good for his soul but not helpful to her investigation? Then there was a discreet cough from her left shoulder.

'Excuse me, my lord, Wyndham says your blood group is A. He remembers from the war.' It was Binyon. Jemima saw the elderly retainer at his elbow nodding with satisfaction at having preserved this precious information for so many years.

'So it was. If Wyndham says so. He was my batman in the war,' Lord St Ives confided to Jemima.

'And Miss Shore,' continued Binyon loftily. 'My own group is A, like your own. Wyndham's is O. Stephen from the farm doesn't know his,' he added apologetically. 'Now I've made that five Os and five As, counting the servants, which I hope you don't think irregular, in your little experiment. Mr Andrew Iverstone is of course B as we have learnt from Mrs Iverstone and there are the ABs—'

Someone had to say it. 'Like readers of *The Times*,' broke in Jack, 'I'm delighted to be an AB.'

'Since we're brother and sister, I suppose I'm one too,' said Fanny. 'I suppose it's a family thing.'

Brother and sister.

Jemima looked across at Saffron, sitting on the opposite side of the table under the Lawrence portrait of the Iverstones. A family thing. She suddenly realized something, in that heightened atmosphere of relationships based on blood, an overwhelming and obvious truth, which had been hovering just outside her consciousness for so long.

It was strange. Once this truth was apparent, not latent, it seemed so obvious to her that she was amazed that she had not seen it, or at least suspected it from the first. Unfortunately for Jemima Shore Investigator it was a truth which, far from helping to unravel the mystery of Iverstone family life, only served to entangle it further.

As Jemima put it to Cass, when the events of the weekend had passed into history, unhappy history: 'It was the picture which gave it away. That on top of Fanny's words. And the definitive discovery that Saffron was not his parents' child. An O and an A can't produce an AB – It's in *Blood Serology*. I looked it up later. Their children must be either A or O: AB and B are what is called "impossible phenotypes".'

'You certainly drew blood there, Jemima Shore Investigator. To coin a phrase,' commented Cass. 'Congratulations.'

'But it was the picture really,' pressed on Jemima. '*The Strawberry*

Children: you know the one, you know the picture if not the name. All red fruit and pink ribbons. You've seen it reproduced all round the world. Miss Iverstone and her brother. He's not named for some reason: I asked Lord St Ives and they think it was because he died shortly after Lawrence painted the picture. But his name was of course Saffron.'

'They're brother and sister,' said Cass, who was talking about the picture.

'They're brother and sister,' repeated Jemima, who was not. 'I looked across at them at dinner and it was quite clear. They were sitting next to each other because they're engaged; there was some joke about it: apparently it's the old-fashioned thing.'

'Saffron and Tiggie Jones!' exclaimed Cass incredulously. 'Brother and sister!'

'Half-brother and sister, to be accurate. It has to be so. And then of all extraordinary things – almost as if she read my mind, Eugenia Jones leant forward and said to me down the table in that rather gruff voice of hers, disconcerting coming from such a little woman: "If you're really interested in statistics, I believe my blood group is B as well, I believe that of many Greeks is so." And of course that figured too. One of Saffron's parents had to be B.

'So you sat there—'

'I sat there in that incredible dining room – that's where the Holbein is by the way, much smaller than you'd expect but even more powerful – being handed endless food by Binyon. I sat there and I looked along at Eugenia Jones in her red velvet dress, same as she wore at the Chimneysweepers', and I *knew* they were both her children. It changed everything.'

'You mean, it should have changed everything,' replied Cass sombrely. But then he was speaking after the weekend was over.

16

A Tragedy Must Take Place

Up till the night of the dinner party, Jemima had never thought of Saffron as being somebody's child; only as being nobody's child, unless of course he was the lawful child of his parents, something which had now been ruled out. Suddenly he had a mother: that gipsy look, how marked it was in Eugenia! And it was Greek of course, not gipsy. Jemima had been right: Saffron did have something of the Mediterranean about him. Eugenia's classical scholarship had distracted her from the fact that she had actual modern Greek blood.

Not only did he have a mother, he had a half-sister. Did Eugenia Jones know she was gazing in her sad abstracted way at her own son? Jemima, remembering her horror and dismay at Tiggie's impetuous announcement of her engagement, believed that she did know.

Under the circumstances, this reaction and the look of despair which Jemima had surprised on the face of Proffy, to say nothing of the melancholy which possessed Eugenia here at Saffron Ivy, were easy to understand. All that fell into place. Eugenia's evident apathy made Jemima wonder what steps she now proposed to take. Was it possible that she was actually going to allow Tiggie to marry her own half-brother, something which was considered genetically dangerous in the modern world, and even worse in the world of classical tragedy which Eugenia Jones might otherwise be deemed to inhabit. Was classical tragedy the clue? Did she feel there was a dreadful inevitability about these events, that a tragedy must take place ... ?

But then how was Eugenia Jones to stop the match? Only by telling her daughter the truth, and that meant, in effect, telling Saffron the truth.

That also meant telling Lord and Lady St Ives the truth, or rather Lady St Ives, if one accepted Nurse Elsie's story of her ignorance. And there was a further consideration: how was such a secret to be kept? How, for example, was Cousin Andrew Iverstone to be kept in ignorance of news which left him, and Jack after him, heir to the Marquessate of St Ives with all that implied? It might be that Eugenia Jones, seeing her son in a position of vast wealth and privilege, had hesitated to deprive him of it. In that case she had indeed found herself between Scylla and Charybdis, the mythological rock and the whirlpool dreaded by ancient mariners.

On the one hand she sacrificed her daughter, like a Greek maiden to the Minotaur; on the other hand she dispossessed her son ... there was doubtless still some further mythological comparison amid the plethora evoked in her mind. It was at this point that Jemima became aware that Binyon, impeccably coated in a tailcoat and striped trousers, was offering her asparagus, with the air of one who had been doing so for some time.

'Our own asparagus,' he said confidentially; for Binyon, as Jemima had observed, seldom missed even the slightest opportunity for conversation with those he served. 'In case you're wondering, Miss Shore.'

'Wondering? Yes, I was.' Jemima helped herself with an automatic smile in the direction of the butler, now in full butlerian fig. But that hardly seemed the right thing to say to Binyon, who accepted her remark with a discreet, a very discreet but still perceptible, air of surprise.

She corrected herself. 'I meant, I was *hoping*.'

Binyon passed on to Daphne Iverstone; he now looked, with equal discretion, satisfied.

It struck Jemima that throughout her stay so far Binyon had treated her not only as an honoured guest, but also as an ally – an ally from their shared television world. So that in a subtle way he was both anxious for her behaviour to be correct and gratified when it was.

Then this was forgotten as the full implications of her discovery – or rather her intuitive flash concerning Tiggie and Saffron, flooded over her.

Poor little Tiggie, how wan she was, how woebegone, how unlike the odiously affected but high-spirited creature who had seduced Cy Fredericks, engaged the admiring attention of Cass Brinsley and driven Jemima mad at Oxford. Did she have some inkling that her glorious destiny was about to be snatched from her? Jemima recalled her words at the Mossbankers' house: 'I'm going to be Lady Saffron. And I'm going to be really really rich ...' She remembered also those other revealing snatches from Saffron about Tiggie: 'We think alike. We want the same kind of life.'

It was as though Saffron, in all the atmosphere of hereditary claims in which he had been brought up, had felt himself claimed by his own family, and mistaking one thing for the other had been impelled to bond Tiggie to him.

Who knew? The question reverberated in her mind as she gazed across at the Strawberry children opposite with their dark eyes and high cheek-bones, so similar to those of Eugenia Jones. Then there came another more startling thought, distracting her sufficiently to take another enormous helping of the home-grown asparagus, so that Daphne Iverstone, did she wish for more, was left lamenting. Jemima was assuming all along that her own intuitive discovery meant the end of the projected marriage. What on earth had led her to that conclusion? For one thing, she had no proof, only surmise; for another, even if proof were advanced – an admission of the truth by Eugenia Jones for example – was she, Jemima Shore, about to play God, an avenging god at that, as Cass had pointed out right at the beginning *a propos* Nurse Elsie's revelations? 'Justice is for Almighty God' – Sister Imelda's words. Jemima had entered the fray out of curiosity, not to right a wrong. She had stayed to investigate – and protect Saffron.

In any case was it really so terrible for half-brother and sister to marry? Stranger things must have happened in the history of the aristocracy, to say nothing of the history of the average country villages. Memories of delving into the history of birth control before her programme *The Pill: For or Against* came back to her: there had been long ages, almost to the present day, when the absence of effective birth control of any sort must have led to such embarrassing problems on more than one occasion.

Jones. Who *was* Jones? Tiggie was older than Saffron, a fact on which the gossip columns had not failed to comment, when printing rumours of the impending engagement. If the mysterious Jones was the father of Tiggie, who then was Saffron's father? She gazed down the table at that great progenitor, Professor Mossbanker. Was *that* possible? Ironically, enough, Proffy's blood group – A, which fitted – now became as interesting to her as the blood group of Lord St Ives had formerly been.

At this moment, the rest of the meal having passed in a kind of daze for Jemima while she accepted food in continuing large quantities as a method of covering the desperate sorting of her thoughts, she was aware of a soft voice at the end of the table trying to engage her attention.

'Miss Shore,' Lady St Ives was saying, leaning down the table. 'Isn't it lovely? Binyon will sing for us after dinner.' Jemima realized that Lady St Ives was actually doing that old-fashioned thing of catching her eye; as a result of which the ladies of Saffron Ivy were expected to abandon the dining room to the gentlemen.

The sight of Lady St Ives' pale drawn cheeks, her thin throat hardly concealed by the rows of pearls, and a green silk evening dress, rather grand, the colour too bright for her complexion, reminded Jemima that the truth, if disclosed, would cause pain to far more people than merely Tiggie and Saffron. It would be a vicious stone to throw into any pool, and pain and astonishment and shock and scandal and fear would spread in rings.

Fear. The word recalled her sharply to the original reason for her visit to Saffron Ivy. Someone was trying to kill Saffron. How and where did the surmise of his true parentage fit into this scheme of things?

With a purpose which she hoped was not too apparent, Jemima sought out Eugenia Jones in the White Drawing Room as the ladies settled themselves down for their period of ritual planned waiting. It was noticeable how the style of the White Drawing Room rendered some costumes so much more appropriate than others. Lady St Ives settling her wide emerald green taffeta skirts and picking up a large bundle of embroidery, possessed an unconscious grace which she had not displayed throughout the day. Fanny Iverstone, in a pale pink dress with a wide white collar which owed a great deal to the current fashions of the Princess of Wales (although their figures were markedly different), suddenly looked elegant; her healthy plainness vanished. But Tiggie, in a white chiffon dress, no petticoat but a trail of sequins laid across it, and a bedraggled feather in her hair, looked like a little ghost. There was no place for her at Saffron Ivy.

'Gommer's dress,' exclaimed Fanny, as though she read Jemima's thoughts. 'I've got it. You're wearing Gommer's court dress, Tiggie.' She sounded quite angry. 'And you've torn it.'

At once Tiggie, in her chiffon, stood and sketched an impertinent little dance in front of Fanny; she did it all without speaking, like some chiffon-draped Squirrel Nutkin in front of a conspicuously irritated Brown Owl. But she was much hampered by her shoes: battered white satin court shoes, several sizes too big. The long white kid gloves, with their pearl buttons, were also too big.

'Doesn't the dress look charming on Antigone?' enquired Lady St Ives to the world at large. 'It belonged to Ivo's mother,' she added into the general silence. 'Darling Gommer. How we all loved her.' Her voice trailed away.

'We used to be allowed to dress up in her clothes as children. On special occasions. If we were very careful.' Fanny still sounded sulky. 'Such a pity if it were ruined now.'

Daphne shot Fanny a look in which the warning was unmistakable. It was the look of the poor relation down the ages. The look meant: don't overstep the mark. It's Tiggie's dress now – or it will be. And one day, who knows, we will depend on her favour to come here. If we come here at all.

The full dislike which both ladies harboured for Tiggie was equally unmistakable.

Jemima was just thinking how ironic it was that Tiggie's dress, deemed by her so inappropriate, had actually turned out to be, as it were, the dress of the house, when Tiggie made her first pronouncement since they had entered the White Drawing Room.

'I think I'll just go and have some sleepy-byes,' said Tiggie. She half danced, half stumbled towards the door, catching her foot in its battered white satin shoe with the pointed toe in the train as she did so. (Gommer St Ives' shoes? Presumably.) There was a tearing sound.

Fanny cast her eyes up to heaven. Daphne Iverstone hummed. Lady St Ives kept her eyes on her embroidery. Jemima, seeing her opportunity, sat down hastily beside Eugenia Jones, who, as ever where she was concerned, had not sought to intervene or even speak to her daughter.

'She's very like you—' Eugenia Jones creased her lips slightly. 'To look at, I mean,' continued Jemima. 'But then I suppose one always thinks that, if one knows only one parent.'

Eugenia Jones inclined her head.

'Perhaps Tiggie is after all very like her father?'

Eugenia Jones looked at Jemima with her enormous dark hooded eyes, eyes which despite being surrounded with a network of wrinkles, were still beautiful. She wore no make-up whatsoever: the effect was in one sense to make her look haggard beyond her years; but in another way the untouched olive skin, if one ignored the lines, the full mouth and fine firm chin, were ageless and might have belonged to a much younger woman.

'Tiggie's father died before she was born. I was never able to compare the two.'

The words were sufficiently abrupt to encourage Jemima, rather than the reverse. She felt some kind of advantage coming her way.

'How sad.'

'Sad?'

'For you of course. But I actually meant: how sad for Tiggie never to have known her father.'

'At the time – I was very young – it seemed more important that I did have her, than that she did not have a father.'

'And now?'

'Don't you find, Miss Shore, that being stuck with the decisions we make when we are too young to understand their possible consequences, is one of the most disagreeable aspects of middle age?'

Then Eugenia Jones unexpectedly gave Jemima a most ravishing smile which eradicated the heaviness of her face and transformed it.

'What am I saying? You are so much younger than I. What do you know of these things?'

At that point, before Jemima could answer, the gentlemen appeared at the door of the White Drawing Room, preceded by Binyon bearing a tray which bore three categories of glasses: heavy tumblers of whisky, delicate champagne glasses and smaller tumblers which appeared to contain barley water. The choice of drink proved something of a test of character, even if it was not so intended. Both Lord St Ives and Andrew Iverstone took whisky, both Lady St Ives and Daphne Iverstone refused altogether.

Saffron took three glasses of champagne, deposited one dexterously in front of Jemima and then preceded to sit at her feet nursing the other two. Fanny Iverstone and Poppy Delaware, and most of the other girls, took champagne; Jack Iverstone, alone of the young men, chose barley water.

A little later all were once more concentrated on the figure of Binyon as the butler, standing in a position of advantage in the middle of the drawing room, began to sing with that mixture of melody and confidence which had once held fourteen million television viewers enthralled. Binyon, like the great John McCormack on whom, according to Lady St Ives, he modelled himself, had a tenor voice. And Jemima (who had once been presented with a McCormack record by Jamie Grand, a self-acknowledged expert on the subject) could see that the resemblance had been cultivated. It amused her to find this McCormack of the eighties dominating the after-dinner scene at the noble house of Saffron Ivy with his performance, so that there was no possibility of conversation, and all on the strength of his telly triumph. It was a splendid butlerian triumph of the times in which Downstairs finally succeeded in subjugating Upstairs (Jemima, for example, was longing to continue her conversation with Eugenia Jones) through the medium of television, just because they both shared it equally.

'Fear no more . . .' sang Binyon, his fine chest rising and falling.

Jemima looked round. Fear. Saffron had settled his back comfortably against Jemima's knees which she found slightly embarrassing but not disagreeable. Tiggie had not reappeared. On a particularly sentimental song, Daphne Iverstone took her husband's hand: he did not disengage it. Jack and Fanny sat slightly apart from the rest of Saffron's friend, although Fanny at least had been very much part of the Oxford group in all the earlier festivities.

Fear. She felt it. Someone in this room was frightened. Was it Eugenia Jones, frightened by the whirlwind which she was now reaping? Lord St Ives? His part in all this remained an enigma, if one that Jemima was determined to solve in the future. But she could not imagine pure fear as such ever holding this man in its grip. Proffy? He had placed himself beside Eugenia Jones on arrival in the drawing room; now he was leaning back and was either fast asleep or shamming sleep. Jemima remembered that Proffy like Eugenia Jones was a passionate lover of opera: it was possible that he did not regard the singing butler with, for example, the same indulgent approval as Lady St Ives. As for the lady in question she was definitely asleep: quietly dozing over her embroidery.

> Golden lads and girls all must
> Like chimneysweepers come to dust.

Jemima shivered. How odd, how morbid, that Binyon should have chosen that particular song on which to end his recital, in view of Saffron's unpleasantly publicized involvement with the club making use of that name. Perhaps it was innocent. Or perhaps it was deliberate: perhaps Binyon, no more than the rest of the world, did not love his employer's wild young son for the extravagances of his privileged youth, having witnessed them first hand.

Binyon gave a ceremonial bow. There was a flutter of applause. Lady St Ives gave a slight start and clapped in her turn. Proffy had clapped loudly from the beginning. His eyes however remained shut. Shortly after that the evening broke up. That is to say, the bright young things, including Fanny, proposed to vanish to some distant ground-floor billiard room now fitted up as a music room where it was understood they would play their 'horrible tunes' – Lord St Ives' cheerful phrase – out of earshot, as late and as long as they liked. Only Jack said he would prefer to go to bed.

'Oh *Jack*!' exclaimed Fanny. 'Just for once, why don't you unwind?'

Jack gave a comic shudder.

'Unwind to the sound of Saffron's thousand-pound amplified torture chamber? I shall be fresh for tennis – and revenge – in the morning.'

'I shan't be long,' remarked Fanny rather vaguely as though some explanation was due to her brother.

'I'll be along later,' said Saffron. 'Bernardo – the key—' He tossed across a large key. There was something almost too carefully casual about his voice. 'Something I have to do.'

All in all, Jemima was not totally surprised when, about fifteen minutes after she had entered her vast dark bedroom, with its canopied bed, the door opened silently.

Saffron entered. He was still dressed in the white ruffled shirt he had worn beneath his dinner jacket, but had taken off the tie. The shirt was open to the waist. His black eyes glittered. Jemima thought he was rather drunk.

'To what do I owe this honour?'

'The West Bedroom? I thought you were in Lady Anne's Bedroom. You might have told me. I've just been invited rather sharply to leave by Cousin Daphne. As if I should want to seduce *her*.'

He was definitely drunk.

'Your luck is out. You're about to be invited equally sharply to leave the West Bedroom.'

'It's pretty, isn't it?' said Saffron inconsequentially, touching the faded chintz in a pattern of wisteria which was hung everywhere in the room. 'I think this is the room where I had my first fuck—'

'Saffron—'

'Or was it the Elizabethan Bedroom? Do you know, I think I've had someone in every room in this house. Except the servants' bedrooms, of course. And even one or two of those—'

'Saffron, will you spare me? Your reminiscences. And your boasting. Both.'

'Sorry. Gone too far. Really very sorry.'

Jemima said nothing.

'Don't you fancy me, Jemima Shore? I rather thought you did. Don't fancy the bastard?' Saffron put his arms around Jemima from behind and held her for a moment, pressing himself against her. 'A bastard. That's what I am, aren't I? You know it's true. We discovered it. You and I. The blood thing doesn't work. I am a bastard. Rather romantic in literature. I'm not so sure in real life. *Don't* you fancy me?'

Jemima still said nothing.

'Wouldn't you like to be in that bed with me? Cheer me up? I'm drunk of course. But not that drunk, not *too* drunk. Just say the word and I'll come back. I'll creep in. Lights out. No one will ever know. Go on. Say I can come back. Don't worry. I'm not going to force myself on you. Rape isn't my thing, you know.'

Jemima, Saffron's arms still around her, feeling the dreadful possibility that the treacherous flesh might somehow betray her, remained silent. It was the best she could do.

'Don't say anything then. I'll come anyway.'

'*Dont,*' she said at last.

'You don't mean that.'

There was another pause.

'Yes, I do.' Then she added: 'But Saffron, I'm *sorry.*'

'I know you are. Bless you for that anyway.' He sounded more sober all of a sudden. 'You go to sleep in your great big bed,' said Saffron gently. He kissed her and this time she did not resist, but kissed him back, a consoling, passionless kiss. He went.

All the same, long after Saffron had gone, Jemima found herself lying awake. Worse still, she discovered that oddly her ear was still slightly cocked for the discreet click of an opening door.

Her door did not open. But sometime in the night hours, she did hear the distinct noise of a door opening and shutting somewhere else along the corridor of the big silent house. Jemima surmised, sardonically, that Saffron might be trying his luck elsewhere. Or might just conceivably be joining his lawful if thoroughly stoned fiancée, Tiggie Jones, in her drugged slumbers.

Jemima finally fell asleep.

In her dream she was aware of a body, a warm body, sliding into bed beside her. Somebody was pulling up the thin silk of her nightdress. Someone was touching her. She felt a hard, hot body against hers . . . she had no idea what the time was when out of the mists of sleep, Jemima was aware that somewhere along the way, her dream had turned into reality. Someone was touching her, but touching her on the shoulder, on the cheek. Someone was pulling at her, whispering to her.

The light snapped on.

Jemima found herself gazing at Saffron. He was wearing a red towelling robe and nothing else. He looked ghastly.

'Jemima, please come, please help me. It's Tiggie. Something's happened to her,' he was saying. 'You must help me. I think – think she's dead.'

17

Two Unlucky Lives

Jemima followed Saffron in his red towelling robe down the broad darkened corridor, oil paintings of bygone Iverstones dimly glimpsed, nearly to the end where a big uncurtained window looked onto the park. Tiggie's bedroom – inconsequentially Jemima noticed the name 'The Butterfly Room' on the open door – had one light burning by the bed. The bed was smaller than Jemima's, canopied in soft white material on which butterflies were lightly printed.

On the walls there hung various pictures made up of brilliant butterflies, pinned down in deep frames. On the bed lay the little butterfly, Tiggie Jones, with her hand stretched out as though in appeal. She was naked except for a pair of tiny white briefs; her body was so thin that she had the air of a naked child asleep in a picture. Her eyes were shut. There was no sign that she was breathing.

Jemima ran forward and felt her pulse. There was no pulse that she could find. She felt her flat infantine chest; it was still. Then Jemima stumbled on something at her feet. It was a syringe. She pushed it aside, then, more carefully, picked it up between finger and thumb and put it on the table. The syringe lay next to a glass paper-weight containing a butterfly whose spread wings were the colour of viridian.

Tiggie's body was not cold, but it was not completely warm either. There was a cool damp feel to it.

Jemima pulled one of the sheets over Tiggie's body, leaving her head still exposed as it lay half on, half off the white pillow.

'A doctor. Saffron, you must get a doctor at once.'

Saffron turned, hesitated.

'Tigs. Is she dead?'

'I don't know.'

'She is dead.'

'Get a doctor for God's sake! He'll tell you.'

'Yes, yes, I'm sorry. Look—'

'I'll stay here. In case—'

'OK. And – thanks.'

It seemed to Jemima an age before Saffron returned although probably not much more than fifteen minutes had passed while she sat in a low embroidered chair beside Tiggie's bed in the Butterfly Room.

Twice Jemima touched Tiggie again and felt if there was a pulse. She could find nothing. She believed the body was growing cooler. She began to try and order her thoughts a little.

Tiggie was dead. Jemima had not much doubt of that. But Tiggie had not been dead long. How had she died? Her eyes were closed. Had she administered some fatal dose by mistake and in the mists of a narcotic dream passed from life into sleep and from sleep into death. Or . . .

When Saffron came back he was dressed: jeans, an old green jersey and trainer shoes. That reminded Jemima that she was only wearing her silk nightdress and a thin kimono over it; she was barefoot. Grey light was beginning to steal through the thick curtains, chintz patterned in butterflies. Jemima like Tiggie was growing cold. It seemed another age in which Saffron had put his warm arms around her and tried to take her into bed.

'He's coming. The doctor. I've told Pa. He'll be along. He's dressing and waking Binyon to let in the doctor. We're letting Ma sleep.'

'What happened? To Tiggie.'

'She's still . . . ?'

'I'm afraid so. What happened? After you left me.'

'I was drunk. You know that. Christ—' Saffron put his hand to his brow. He had dressed but he had not combed his hair; the effect was to make him, like Tiggie, look very young. 'It's odd, I don't feel at all drunk now. Anyway, what happened? First, I went back downstairs to the old Billiard Room and drank a good deal more. A lot of champagne. A lot of whisky. We watched this horror video which Ned brought. Called *The Girl-eating Ghouls* or something like that. Did somebody have some coke? Probably. I was too drunk to care. At some point they all went to bed. I roamed about a bit. I like this house at night. Even as a child – look, the point is I don't really remember. I think I attempted to pay a social call on Nessa, rather forgetting that old Bernardo was here, but he *was* here, or rather he was there, and they didn't seem to welcome the idea of a party. Then I went back to the old Billiard Room. It was empty. Played some music, The Clash, *Thriller*, that kind of thing. I may have ended on Wagner. Then back up here. A call on Tigs. When I found her.'

'You saw no one else? When it was late, I mean.' Why was she asking him these questions?

'No one. No, wait. How odd. I did see someone else. I saw Fanny.'

'*Fanny*? What on earth was she doing? Or was she just paying what you call a social call, like everyone else?'

'Fanny? I doubt it. She's quite prim, Cousin Fan. No, she was carrying a pile of sandwiches of all ridiculous things. She said it was to put outside the Gobbler's room. As a joke.'

Then Lord St Ives arrived, and almost immediately after that the doctor accompanied by Binyon. Jemima, after a discreet explanation of her presence, judged it the moment to withdraw.

Soon the telling would have to begin, first of all the telling of Tiggie's mother – would she be found in the arms of Proffy? Did it matter? Did anything make it any worse or better now that her child was dead? Then the telling of the house-party, followed by its disbanding. Then the telling of the world.

The worst moment, the very worst moment of all, so Jemima told Cass afterwards, was the next morning when Eugenia Jones broke down and started screaming.

'She chose Lord St Ives as her target – words like "your bloody, bloody family" – but I felt it could well have been anyone there, anyone in the house, the house itself. She became like one of her own Greek characters, Medea perhaps.'

'Except that Medea killed her own children. And Eugenia Jones' child killed herself!' Cass pointed out.

'Or did she? I don't know. *Did* she? Oh Cass!' Jemima felt herself starting to cry again. 'That poor little girl. I should have done something. I knew something was wrong. Something was wrong about the whole weekend. But then, what with the proof, if you call it that, that Saffron was illegitimate, and the discovery and I do call it that, about Eugenia Jones being his mother—'

Cass hugged her again.

'You'll find out what happened. And at least there'll be some justice.'

'Justice! Where was the justice in a twenty-four-year-old girl killing herself by – or possibly being killed by – an enormous overdose of heroin acting on a great deal of alcohol.' Jemima, in spite of herself, found the tears coming again.

'I keep thinking of her, her little interventions at the tennis match. That evening in her white dress. Like Ophelia.'

'Come on. Who could have done it? Think of that. Are you sure she didn't kill herself?'

'Not sure. The police, by the way, are quite sure that she did. Accidentally. Not suicide. They say they have much experience of these things, alas, and you can't expect drug addicts to behave rationally or self-preservingly in any way. They gave me the impression of having a pretty poor opinion of the said addicts, including, I may say, poor Tiggie.'

'But you don't agree?'

'It's Saffron,' said Jemima slowly. 'He's positive that Tiggie didn't use heroin all that much, plenty of cocaine however, and when she did, she sniffed it. She hated needles. I remember her saying it about blood tests. Why couldn't blood be sucked out instead? You see, there were no other syringe marks. Even the police admitted that.'

'How did they account for that?'

'There had to be a first time. And this was it. It was unhelpful that Tiggie had been in such a daze all day. All her friends agreed about that: the police talked to them. And she had been taking a lot of coke: they all had to agree about that too. So the combination was lethal, with the drink as well.'

'Where did she get the syringe?'

'That was rather unhelpful too. Only her prints on it. Wait. No, that's odd, isn't it? Why no prints of the person who sold it to her?' Jemima felt her spirits revive. 'But if the syringe was wiped clean after she was killed – injected with this enormous dose, that is on top of a lot of cocaine – the murderer had only then to plant her prints on the syringe with her hand.'

'The Press has been ghastly, hasn't it?' interjected Cass. 'Poor Lord St Ives. Poor Lady St Ives. I even feel sorry for Saffron, something I never expected to be. The engagement weekend: the stately home. The dashing, now tragic, young lord with his handsome face and his evil reputation. It's all been jam for them.'

'The Press! No worse than Eugenia Jones' denunciations, and in a way better, because more impersonal. There and then in the great hall the next morning, the young gathered forlornly with their suitcases. Binyon trying to organize them into their cars like a portly sheep dog. Both the girls, Poppy and Nessa, were crying. Fanny looked frightful and I thought Jack was going to be sick.

'Then Eugenia Jones comes flying down that great wooden Elizabethan staircase, feet clacketing as she came. I thought she was going to slip at first, black hair all over the place – yes, you're right, she was like Medea. Then she starts on Lord St Ives.'

'Didn't anyone try to stop her?'

'Lord St Ives stood for once like one frozen. Nobody else had the wit or courage. Perhaps Binyon might have had a go – but he was lugging suitcases outside. So she went on and on. Saying things like: "You should have done something" over and over again, "You should have stopped her." Finally Proffy appeared and put his arm around her. He said something to her. I think it was in Greek. He sounded very tender. And he took her away. I didn't see her again.'

'I'd like to say something tender to you, in Greek if you like, and take you away. Jemima, why don't we have a holiday? I'll talk to my clerk. I'll take you to Greece—'

'I've got to solve it,' said Jemima doggedly. 'Besides, believe it or not,

I've still got to make this programme: *Golden Kids.* Yes, Cy Fredericks thinks it has become something called sociologically reverberating. That's the next stage up after being socially relevant, it seems. To compensate, I'm going to solve the mystery of Saffron's birth if it kills me.'

'Because it has killed Tiggie?'

'In a way. And probably that boy at Rochester, Bim Marcus. And nearly killed Saffron. Can I bear that holiday in mind to see me through?'

'You can. And now let me give you something else to bear in mind to see you through.'

They went into Jemima's bedroom. It was a reunion, but unlike most reunions it was all sweet not bitter; both Jemima and Cass wondered afterwards as they lay in the huge white bed with its airy views of the tops of the Holland Park trees why they ever found it necessary to try other views of other trees in other bedrooms and elsewhere. But neither of them gave voice to the thought. It was not in the contract.

Immediately after Cass left, Jemima, who had been half-feigning half-feeling sleep, leapt up and pulled on her honey-coloured robe. Action would blot out all such reflections which unlike the reunion were half sweet, half bitter. Cherry. Cherry and Jamie Grand, in that order. Cherry, superbly efficient (unless her love life was in chaos) could be entrusted with this new mission over the telephone, but Jamie Grand needed more dulcet treatment.

To Cherry, Jemima outlined her latest task, only to be greeted by a most un-Cherry-like gasp.

'But it's only a birth certificate, Cherry,' pleaded Jemima. 'You've done this before. Don't you remember that case we had? The little girl. You were so brilliant, darling darling Cherry—'

'What do you mean, Jem, done this before? Who has ever looked for a birth certificate for a baby born probably under the name of Jones somewhere in London?' Cherry spluttered. 'When I've got this new wonderful fellow in his late forties, just getting over his third marriage, and his third wife's cooking, all he wants is to eat out, hold my hand, and forget.'

'All that food should strengthen you,' replied Jemima soothingly. 'Which reminds me that I've got a new contact for you at Oxford, to do with the *Golden Kids* programme. He's called the Gobbler, but don't let that put you off. I think you're going to have a lot in common.'

'Jemima—'

'After all, you do know the baby was a boy. And the date of birth, twenty-eighth October 1964.'

'Isn't that fantastic? We know he's a Scorpio. The sexy sign. But I daresay you knew that already, didn't you?'

Jemima maintained a short dignified silence; Cherry had a feline ability to discern the possible direction of Jemima's fancies which simply could not be encouraged.

Then she said in her most winning voice, which she knew would not fool Cherry for an instant: 'I have found out one or two other things which will be helpful. London is certainly the place, Nurse Elsie definitely mentioned London – she did talk of the other mother being "not far away". You see Saffron was officially born in the St Ives' London house, which was then in Bryanston Square – they've sold it long ago of course. Hence Nurse Elsie as the private midwife, hence the opportunity to practise the deception which couldn't have been carried out in a nursing home, let alone a hospital. Nurse Elsie had also delivered the other mother very recently, Eugenia Jones we now think, when Lady St Ives' labour started prematurely. Start with the local Registry office for Bryanston Square.'

'And work out. Start with Jones and work – where do I go from Jones, Jemima? Smith, Brown, Robinson—'

'Concentrate on the date. Children have to be registered by law within six weeks of their birth. So the time span isn't too large. Also the new baby, the illegitimate baby who is now, we think, Saffron, can't have been much older otherwise somebody would surely have smelt a rat. As for the name, I think she almost certainly did use her own name: its very anonymity must have been attractive. And it is after all an offence to register under a false name. You can get into all sorts of trouble.'

'Let's hope the Joneses of the world weren't in an especially productive mood in October 1964' were Cherry's last gloomy words.

Jamie Grand was invited by Jemima to lunch at Monsieur Thompson's on one of those frequent forays to London from Oxford which his interpretation of a sabbatical year as a visiting professor did not preclude. Unlike Cherry, Jamie was highly responsive to Jemima's request for information, especially when she prefaced her invitation with the words 'This is about gossip not literature, Jamie.'

'What a relief,' he sighed down the telephone. 'There was a time when Oxford itself was more like that. I'm trying to use my short stay to re-educate them. Serena of Christ Church is a nice girl but she will keep asking me about W.H. Auden . . .'

'Eugenia Jones. The life and loves of Eugenia Jones.'

'Beyond Proffy?'

'Before Proffy. Jones, the mysterious Jones. What happened after his death, which actually occurred, Eugenia told me, before Tiggie was born.'

'It won't be difficult just at the moment. Everyone's terribly sorry for her. She's totally shattered, one hears. Added to which Eleanor Mossbanker is pregnant. Again.'

'An unlucky life.'

'Eugenia or Tiggie?'

'Both, I suppose. Two unlucky lives . . . I actually meant Eugenia.'

A few days later Jemima's impression of Eugenia Jones' unlucky life was thoroughly confirmed by the tale spun out – not without a certain rueful relish, it had to be admitted – by Jamie Grand at Thompson's.

'Your friend Marigold Milton was a great help. That woman has a talent for gossip which is very much underdeveloped. She remembered a number of absolutely vital rumours about Eugenia twenty years ago which even I had quite forgotten.'

Over exquisite portions of fish in various delicate vegetable sauces, Jamie Grand talked of passion, passion and Eugenia Jones.

'A very passionate undergraduette. Was one still permitted to use that word in the fifties? Perhaps not. At all events, a brilliant mind, a brilliant career ahead and an astonishing capacity for indulging in the most hopeless love affairs on the side. She might have been a man, her capacity for divorcing her judgement at work from her judgement in bed was so absolute. Names? I could name a few—'

Jemima allowed him to amble on. One loved or loathed gossip, but in Jamie's company one simply had no choice but to share his preoccupation.

'But then something more serious started,' pursued Jamie. 'We're now at about nineteen sixty. An affair with a married man. Something she didn't talk about, something which obsessed her. She was in London by then, working on her first book, travelling a good deal to Greece. A slightly different circle of friends. Her movements were much less circumscribed. You know what Oxford's like, or *should* be like. Not much individual freedom there, freedom from gossip. There was even one rumour – here Marigold Milton was useful – that Eugenia, with that fine classical mind of hers which always seems to excite amateurs of secrecy, was mixed up in some kind of intelligence work.'

'A spy? Eugenia Jones?' At one level all this was difficult to reconcile with the Eugenia Jones she knew, or had at least encountered quite frequently over the last traumatic months. And yet she had to recall that mysterious sense of power which Jemima had sensed in her from the first, that feeling of impenetrability – only a rare public flash of anguish after her daughter's death.

'Nothing so crude as a spy,' went on Jamie. 'At least according to Marigold Milton. Perhaps a report here, a mission. Greece in the late fifties – an interesting place. It was odd the way Tiggie came along, and the mysterious Jones was married and killed off all in a short space of time.'

'You think he never existed?'

'That's what everyone thought at the time. It was fiction, a graceful fiction, to have this child by her lover and bring her up, but not unduly challenging the Oxford authorities by unmarried motherhood. To which place she now returned. And settled down. Little Antigone at her knee.'

'Is this when she meets Proffy? Proffy we know was in intelligence in the war – he's never made any secret of it. As a scientist he was much in demand. There may have been a connection there.' Jemima was aware of a strange unaccountable feeling of disappointment. This meant that Proffy, father of so many, was also Saffron's father. Why was she disappointed? Why was she surprised? It was surely the logical explanation, had always been the most logical explanation of Saffron's parentage, given that Eugenia was his mother. She already knew that the blood groups fitted.

'I guess so. She certainly met him. Sooner or later he must have replaced the original married lover and become the new obsession. The only thing about that is that Proffy didn't marry her, Eugenia. Why did he wait, except out of sheer absent-mindedness and then marry Eleanor some time later?'

'No time off?' Jemima had to cross-question Jamie if she was to establish the truth of Eugenia's movements throughout 1964. But she had no intention of confiding to him the reason for her interest; that would be altogether too much jam, too irresistible for Jamie, too unfair to Saffron himself. 'No intervening love affair?'

'No new love affair that I could discover. A change of pattern. After all she was married, well, widowed by now. A small child. But there was time off. One more year taken off, or six months perhaps to write a book. But the book never appeared.'

Jemima tried not to show her relief, or her excitement.

'And that year was?'

'Nineteen sixty-four or nineteen sixty-five. Around then.'

'Jamie, you're an angel,' cried Jemima with a warmth which surprised both of them. 'If only I was ten years younger and at Oxford.'

'Oh Jemima, you're absolutely no use to me,' said Jamie Grand in mock horror. 'W.H. Auden is the least of your demands. So what's it all about? I'll have some more of this excellent Puligny Montrachet while you answer,' he added.

'Oh gossip, Jamie, gossip. Just gossip ancient and new.' And Jemima called the waiter.

Jemima was still in a good humour, and in a state of excitement when she walked back to her flat from Monsieur Thompson's. Midnight greeted her with a reproachful rub round the legs and shot savage looks at his cat bowl – which happened to be full, having been filled to bursting by Mrs B. Midnight however never failed to imply that there could be yet further supplies or fresher supplies of food, if Jemima really cared.

As Jemima went to scratch him, the telephone began to ring.

It was from a call-box.

'Jemima,' began Cherry in an urgent voice. 'I think I've found something very odd. You see, slogging my way through the Joneses, and a fertile lot they were, I fear, it suddenly occurred to me we were looking in the wrong place.'

'Not London?'

'London all right. But not births. Deaths not births. One child died, right? The real St Ives baby died. And the false baby was put in his place. So there had to be a death certificate for the real baby. Only it would be under the false name. Are you with me?'

'My God, Cherry, I *am* with you!'

'So listen to this, Jemima. I then went through the death certificates at the same time. Male babies called Jones. Not at all difficult. No luck at Marylebone, but when I got to Kensington, guess what I found?'

'One dead male baby called Jones. Who died on or about twenty-eighth October and was born shortly before.'

'No. Not one dead male baby called Jones. One dead male baby called Saffron. Saffron Jones, to be accurate. Born on twenty-sixth October and died on twenty-eighth October 1964. Mother's name Eugenia Jones. Now guess the father's name.'

'You're the investigator. You tell me.' Jemima held her breath.

'Ivo Charles,' said Cherry in a voice of triumph, 'Ivo Charles, as in Ivo Charles Iverstone, Marquess of St Ives in the big red peerage. Ivo Charles. Get it?'

Into the silence came the pip, pip sounds of the call-box phone and Jemima was left gazing at the instrument in her hand as the harsh burr of disconnection eventually replaced them.

18

Your Father

'My father!' said Saffron uncertainly as though trying out the words for the first time. Then he repeated with more strength: 'My father. My father.'

Finally Saffron laughed. 'This is ridiculous, isn't it? What you're saying, quite simply, is that my father – the father I've known all these years, Ivo Charles, Marquess of St Ives, is actually—'

'Your father,' completed Jemima in her turn. 'Your naturally biological father. As well as in a weird kind of way, also your adopted father. I've worked it out now. The birth certificate, or rather the birth certificate and the death certificate, thanks to that genius Cherry Bronson Investigator, began the unravelling.

'It goes like this,' she continued. 'There were two babies. One was your mother's, I mean Lady St Ives' baby, this is getting confusing but you know who I mean—'

'It's definitely too late to think of Eugenia Jones as my mother,' said Saffron firmly. 'Go on.'

'This baby dies at birth on the twenty-eighth of October, but is smuggled a way by Nurse Elsie, and buried under the name of Jones – Saffron Jones, as it happens. They used *your* real date of birth and its own date of death for the certificate. Then there's the true Saffron Jones – that's *you* – who was born to Eugenia on the twenty-sixth of October and substituted for the dead baby. So it – he – you grew up as Lord Saffron.'

'Both of them my father's sons.' Now Saffron sounded almost angry. 'The most shocking thing about all this, more shocking than anything else you've told me is that my father, the most upright man in Britain as he is famously regarded, my father had an affair, a long long affair with Eugenia Jones. Including when my mother was having a last desperate stab at having a baby.'

He stopped.

'Oh Tiggie. Oh Christ, poor Tigs – is what you're saying that Tiggie was my sister?'

Jemima nodded. 'Your full sister. I thought at first she was your half-sister. But now I think that there was never any Jones, ever. Just a hidden love affair. And a child. And then – perhaps when the affair was nearly over, another child.'

'*Christ*. It's unbearable. The hypocrisy of it.'

They were in Saffron's rooms at Rochester. A huge poster-size picture of Tiggie, panda eyes and all, taken by some fashion photographer Jemima guessed, gazed down at them. Someone – Saffron? – had written RIP underneath it.

The room had a desolate feel to it. There was a pile of unopened letters and notes on the table and some books. None of the invitations on the mantelpiece looked particularly recent, nor were there any empty champagne bottles to be seen; the cricket bat still reposed in the corner of the room with the tennis rackets and the squash rackets. They were neatly stacked, and did not look as if they had been in recent use. The sight of an enormous golfing umbrella, open and sodden, spread across the hearth rug reminded Jemima that outside the Hawksmoor quad was equally desolate, with driving squalls of cold rain, of the sort that Cy Fredericks for one would never believe could belt down in Oxford in June as the summer term reached its climax.

What were they to do if it rained throughout Commem week? Could even the legendary skill of Spike Thompson create idyllic punting on the river, the balm of a summer night, the rising luminosity of an Oxford dawn when rain was beating down on all parties concerned? 'No long shadows', had been Cy Fredericks' firm instructions. Like King Canute, Cy Fredericks might have to bow to the inexorable force of the English climate.

Saffron, hunched in a T-shirt bearing some message of vaguely revolutionary – or perhaps satirical – import, and torn white track-suit trousers, bare feet (his soaking sneakers put to dry by a small smoking fire) now looked merely depressed as well as angry. The resemblance to Eugenia Jones that fatal weekend at Saffron Ivy, was marked. And his height came from his father. The B blood and the A blood. Ah well, thought Jemima, at least he gets his brains from his mother. A for aristocratic blood and B for brains. She still found it irresistible to think in terms of blood grouping.

On the other hand one could hardly suggest that Lord St Ives had no brains, no intelligence, no cunning, no shrewdness . . . She wanted to tell Saffron about her recent lunch with Lord St Ives then decided against it. Saffron had enough to bear, enough to sort out.

Lord St Ives had responded to her invitation to lunch with his usual enchanted – and enchanting – courtesy. In spite of Jemima's determination not to be put in thrall by the old fox's charm, as she put it to herself, she found herself believing that her invitation had totally transformed a rather dim day at Saffron Ivy.

'How delightful . . . we never did get to know you . . . tragic weekend . . . how *is* my son? I assume you've seen him at Oxford since the funeral that is.'

'I will be seeing him.'

'Good, good . . . Such an admirable influence.' The flattering phrases flowed on, then: 'Gwendolen would so much like to meet you again' – but I didn't ask her, thought Jemima in a panic – 'however, as you know, she never comes to London these days . . . Her health, alas . . . Another time at Saffron Ivy . . . When you feel ready . . .'

Curiously, Lord St Ives showed no signs of asking Jemima what the lunch was about. It was only when Jemima suggested Le Caprice that Lord St Ives exhibited some degree of interest. Le Caprice was convenient for what she conceived to be his Mayfair/St James's/Whitehall orientation and she wanted to be on her ground not his.

'Le Caprice? The smartest restaurant in London! That does sound exciting. I expect my son goes there. Ah no, alas. Please excuse the selfishness of an elderly man, Miss Shore, but I'm afraid I must insist on being the host at this luncheon. For one thing it's much too late for me to learn to be paid for by a lady; I should be in the most dreadful state throughout, wondering what I dared eat and drink without ruining you. No, I'm sure your salary is enormous. But secondly you must indulge me and allow me to be seen with a pretty woman somewhere where it will add enormously to my prestige. What a fillip it will give to my reputation to be seen with you!'

Lord St Ives suggested Wilton's. Jemima, feeling out-manoeuvred, agreed.

As smoked salmon followed by lamb cutlets (Lord St Ives) and dressed crab (Jemima) were brought with a stately courtesy equal to Lord St Ives' own, by waitresses like ageing family nannies in white overalls – here at last were the traditional retainers of her dreams – Jemima wondered desperately whether the whole lunch would pass without her being able to step out of this warm bath of politeness.

In the end it was Lord St Ives who turned the topic of conversation from a mixture of gardening and Tory politics ('what kind of roses do you suppose Mrs T. admires? Huge strong-growing hybrid teas, I fear') to something more personal. First he waved on the raspberries:

'Yes, yes, you must – raspberries for Miss Shore, a nice large helping and lots of cream. Some Stilton for me.'

Then he looked at her directly. She thought for the first time that Lord St Ives had a very sad face in repose. She still could not see Saffron's features in his, Saffron having the full mouth of his mother, Lord St Ives the narrow mouth beneath the straight nose of the crusader. But those mannerisms which she had once thought 'nurture not nature' and the figure, the long legs and narrow shoulders, all these Saffron had inherited from his father.

'My son, Miss Shore,' said Lord St Ives in a gentle voice, 'I think you want to talk about my son. He *is* my son, you know.'

'I do know that – now.'

'But you doubted it.' There was a long pause. Then Lord St Ives went on, still in the same quiet tone: 'Nurse Elsie, Miss Shore. A very indiscreet woman, at least when she was dying. She told my wife she had seen you. Without saying why: just that you were interested in her story. Gwendolen passed it on to me. I – shall we say I held myself in readiness, Miss Shore? Then things began to fall into place. Your interest in Saffron, for example. Other things: that conversation about blood groups at dinner; altogether too pat, too convenient. Am I correct?'

Jemima nodded.

'That wretched woman.' Lord St Ives heaved a sigh. 'But then who am I to judge someone dying of cancer?'

'Who wanted to make her peace with God,' concluded Jemima. 'I'm not a Catholic, but who are we to judge her harshly for that?'

'"Never trust a Catholic servant," Gwendolen's mother, old Hattie Wiltshire, a frightful dragon, used to say. "Sooner or later the Pope starts giving them orders instead of you." That's going a bit far perhaps, but in this case perhaps justified. Nurse Elsie's peace did cause a great deal of strife for the rest of us, didn't it?'

'At least the truth is known. That's a good thing.' Jemima sounded more convinced than she felt.

'Is it? I envy your certainty, Miss Shore. A lifetime in politics has taught me that truth can be just as damaging as lies. A depressing conclusion, perhaps. Ah well – you are not here to listen to my political reminiscences. Who knows this particular truth? You know it. Does my son know it? Andrew and Daphne Iverstone?' He gave a slight grimace.

'Nurse Elsie told Saffron the first part of it. It was terribly upsetting for him, naturally. He half believed it, half rejected it. I think it was partly responsible for him going off the rails. All that business with the restaurant.' She tried not to let an element of reproach creep into her voice. 'Now I can tell him the second half of it. The other Iverstones – no, they don't know.' Jemima devoutly hoped this was also the truth. 'I'm going down to Oxford to see Saffron.'

'Do you judge me very harshly? I see you do. Before you go down to Oxford, Miss Shore, let me tell you a story. A love story if you like, a love story of long ago. Or perhaps a story of guilt.'

Then Lord St Ives, in quite simple language, his affectations of enchantment and enthusiasm dropped, told Jemima the story of the married man, the rising Conservative minister, who encountered the unmarried young woman, the beautiful and intelligent young woman, quite unexpectedly, by one of those improbable coincidences which should never have happened, might never have happened, in the course of their shared work.

'The Ministry of Defence. I was Minister for Defence in the late fifties, not for long, but long enough. And Eugenia, you've probably heard this, worked for them for a period. Someone from another world. I'd never really known anyone, any woman that is, like Eugenia before. Such wildness, such passion. There'd been occasional – well, flings – Gwendolen always in the country, no, I don't want to apologize for them – but never love. I'd always wanted to love someone: and then I loved her.'

'You loved her. Did you also want to marry her?'

'There was never any question of that. I could never leave Gwendolen. How could I? An innocent woman. What had she ever done wrong?'

'Did Eugenia want—'

'She said not. I don't know. At any rate she accepted it was impossible. I took her once to Saffron Ivy: a risk, that. My mother-in-law was dying. Gwendolen went to be with her. The excuse was to look at the library, that's what the servants were told. I've no idea if they believed it. Oddly enough, I think it was then that Antigone was conceived. And then Eugenia insisted on having the baby. I helped her. Jones was invented of course: a convenient fiction, his birth and equally convenient death.'

'I worked that out.'

'It was after that, after Antigone's birth, we parted. Did you work that out too? Gwendolen was so terribly unhappy. She knew.'

'She knew about Eugenia?' Jemima was startled.

'Not in so many words. She knew something was up. Don't people always know that sort of thing? But someone told her something: I've always suspected Daphne Iverstone, as a matter of fact. So we parted, Eugenia and I.'

'But then – Saffron – and the other baby which died. Very much the same age. Born within forty-eight hours of each other.'

'Wasn't it odd? Almost as if it was fated. By chance once more, I met Eugenia again. I was Foreign Secretary by then. There was some visiting Greek dignitary, some banquet. Gwendolen was in the country. We took the chance, the risk. One night, not even a night. I went back to Saffron Ivy full of guilt. And a few days later – need I go into this further? – the other baby was conceived. Gwendolen had lost so many children. But she was determined to have one last chance. Even the doctors didn't want her to try.'

'That baby died.'

'I nearly went mad. Gwendolen was hoping for so much in spite of the doctors. And it was then that the idea came to me. Nurse Elsie was looking after Eugenia too: in a way it was strangely easy. You see, Eugenia once again refused to have an abortion. I couldn't make her, I thought it was a mistake. The affair was over, she was making a new life. She was just beginning to see Proffy; he had, I think, just fallen in love with her. The baby was going for adoption. I was half crazy, I admit it. All Nurse Elsie had to do was tell Eugenia her child had died.'

'So Eugenia didn't know what had really happened to her child.' Jemima was astonished.

'Not then, not for years. Our paths didn't cross. We took care in fact to avoid each other. Myself in London or Saffron Ivy; Eugenia in Oxford; we never had any friends in common, that was part of the fascination, I suppose. It never occurred to me that Antigone's path would cross with Saffron's: the one thing I never thought about. And yet somehow, by another kind of strange fate, they seemed drawn to each other.'

'When did Eugenia know? I got the impression that she did know. That she regarded the engagement with horror as a result.'

'Nurse Elsie. Told her too on her deathbed in her grand confessional mood. She sent for Eugenia after sending for you.'

So that was the other woman, thought Jemima, who came on the last day of all to the Hospice. I suspected Daphne Iverstone.

'As for the engagement,' pursued Lord St Ives, 'we were both appalled. But separately. I tried to speak to Eugenia about it, but Proffy wouldn't let me meet her. He's quite jealous of her in his Pasha-like way. So I wrote to her: a carefully guarded letter, because for one thing I did not think the truth should be committed to paper, suggesting that the matter would be sorted out at Saffron Ivy. My plan was to put them off without revealing the truth: they were both so young, so capricious, it could happen naturally. This engagement came from nowhere, one of Saffron's schemes. We could sort it out. I could sort it out.'

Jemima thought: and in its own tragic way, it was sorted out at Saffron Ivy. But she did not say so.

None of this did she think it right to pass on to Saffron.

There was one last question for Lord St Ives.

'Forgive me, your wife? You said people always know. Did she know this too?'

'There was a time: he was such a dark little baby, she used to comment how odd it was. Then a time came when she never mentioned the subject of his looks. After that she began pointing resemblances to Saffron in the Iverstone family portraits, almost as if she wanted to reassure herself. They say a mother always knows. But then, Miss Shore, to me she *was* his mother.'

'As you were his father.'

'In exactly the same way,' concluded Lord St Ives firmly. 'In exactly the same way.'

'And in addition to saving your wife, you saved your estates. So you protected your own walls.'

'Like the ivy, in the family motto? That's also true. But now, Miss Shore, would you have wanted Saffron Ivy to pass to Andrew Iverstone?'

'A nice liberal dilemma. But now there's Jack of course. He's a decent fellow.'

'Very decent. Almost too decent I sometimes think; as though he was repressing quite different feelings. But I could hardly have expected Andrew and Daphne to have a son like Jack, could I? Heredity is certainly a very odd thing.'

It was Lord St Ives' last word on the subject of the Iverstone family.

To Saffron in Oxford, Jemima said:

'Don't judge him too harshly – your father.'

'I don't want to judge anybody!' exclaimed Saffron fiercely. 'And I don't want to be judged either. Let him try to come the heavy father on me now, lectures about my way of life, no way, that's over.' He laughed angrily and leapt up with a kind of furious grace, which reminded Jemima of his antics on the tennis court.

'Let's have some champagne.'

Jemima shook her head. 'I don't want any. I'm meeting the cameraman and the director, down by the river at St Lucy's. Much need for Megalith mackintoshes.'

'Oddly enough, I don't want any either. You may not believe this, Jemima, but I'm absolutely fed up with all that shit. Golden Kids and all that. I'm thinking of going straight. Cousin Jack will be amazed. He's always given me moral lectures about waste and the family honour. I'm actually thinking of *working*.' He made it sound as unlikely an activity as going to Xanadu.

'And one last thing, Jemima, I'm not taking part in that fucking programme. You can tell Megalith Television to go and stuff themselves. Let the others get on with it: there are plenty of Golden Kids in Oxford. The Gobbler, Poppy and the rest of them. No lack, whatsoever. But you can include me out, in the immortal words of Sam Goldwyn.'

Saffron stopped. 'So what do you think of that, beautiful but icy Jemima?'

'I'm not icy. Just cold. I find I prefer Cy Fredericks' idea of Oxford with golden sunshine playing on the arcades rather than puddles: dreaming spires, not spires teeming with rain.'

'You look icy. Icy towards me.'

'As a matter of fact I feel quite warmly towards you.'

'Not disappointed about your programme?'

'It's only television,' said Jemima lightly, hoping that the lightning, dispatched by Cy Fredericks, would not come to strike her dead. 'As a matter of fact, I think it's probably the first sensible decision you've made in your life.'

'I'll come to the Commem. I mean, I'm not aiming to become a monk, for God's sake. It's my own College, I've got the tickets.' He paused. 'But I haven't got a partner, have I?' There was a silence. 'Jemima—'

'I'm working, Saffron,' said Jemima hastily. 'You may have opted out of *Golden Kids* but some of us are not so lucky. Do you realize that if I don't make this programme successfully, this darling of my boss's heart, he could send me to the Siberian equivalent of the saltmines, which in Cy's case could be making a six-part series of programmes about Common Market attitudes to the EEC?'

'I thought the Common Market was the EEC.'

'That's my point.'

'Not as much fun as a programme about the Radical Women's Settlement. To which I was once going to give some money if you acted as my private investigator.' Saffron hesitated. 'Jemima – have you thought about all that?'

Jemima wondered what she should say. She had indeed thought about 'all that'. She had gone through over and over again both in her head and with Cass the various murderous attacks, one successful but hitting the wrong target and one failed. Bim Marcus who died on Staircase Thirteen, Saffron attacked with the boat hook at the Chimneysweepers' Dinner. And then there was Tiggie, fatally injected with a massive dose of drugs, Tiggie who feared the needle and yet had died by it. She was beginning to see a connection, in terms of the various people who had been present on all three occasions; the names of those who had the opportunity led her inexorably to the motive, the obvious motive. Envy.

But these thoughts too she did not wish to repeat to Saffron. A taste for murder was said to grow, like other tastes. Tiggie was gone but Saffron still lived. She wished that she could pen her suspects together, pin one of them down, abandon the others; at the moment it was still risky to see them as more than a group, those who had had the opportunity on all three occasions.

Bim Marcus' death could have been encompassed by anyone in Oxford at that time; they only had to walk into Rochester – which was not difficult – and then lie low until the dead of night. The murderer or murderess could then lurk somewhere else in the college, and leave easily, at leisure, when the college gates were open.

If envy was the key, as she had felt all along, then the Iverstone family certainly had the strongest motive. Had Nurse Elsie possibly confided the truth about Saffron's parentage to one of them as well as to Jemima and Eugenia Jones? Daphne, Fanny, or even Jack. Andrew Iverstone was a ruthless man, no one denied that, and she had glimpsed his naked hatred for Tiggie as he slammed the tennis ball at her. Andrew Iverstone had been in Oxford at the time of Bim's death, and at the Chimneysweepers' Dinner and at Saffron Ivy. So for that matter had Daphne Iverstone, although it seemed even more far-fetched to suspect her, twittering innocent as she appeared. No, of the two Andrew Iverstone was the far more likely. Technically, Fanny Iverstone had had the opportunity, having been present on all three occasions. But while Fanny was slightly more plausible as a killer than her mother, she was also demonstrably very fond of Saffron, and she surely had to be ruled out on those grounds alone.

As for Jack Iverstone, he had to be ruled out for two reasons: first he had not been present at the Chimneysweepers' Dinner, and secondly sheer niceness must make him the least plausible member of that Iverstone branch to emerge as a murderer.

Nothing more could happen. Or so Jemima had confidently told Cass in London. Inwardly she was by no means so sure.

Jemima took a decision.

'I'll come with you. Or rather, you'll come with me. Stay with me. You'll be good cover for my sizzling exposure of the *jeunesse doré*, particularly now you've elected to leave their ranks. You'll protect me.'

Her unspoken thought was: And I'll protect you.

19

Supper à Deux

Megalith's luck was out. Or at least as far as the weather was concerned. Tantalizing sunshine succeeded the rainstorms early in the week, and then the day of the St Lucy's Commem and the Rochester Ball – and the first filming for the *Golden Kids* programme for that matter – was marked by a downpour in the morning.

Jemima thought there was after all a kind of beauty about the rain-washed spires, and the heavy blue thunderclouds looming over the dome of Christ Church and Magdalen tower had some kind of Constable effect; but the huge marquees in the quads of those colleges which were about to have, or had just had a ball, conveyed all the cheerfulness of a rained-out fête, as rain fell persistently on the canvas. The boats, both punts and canoes, drawn up and chained by St Lucy's, had an especially depressing air; a young boatman was bailing them out with a misanthropic expression.

Traditionally a Commem Ball ended with punting on the river at breakfast time as the sun rose on the tired revellers – an idyllic scene which Spike Thompson had absolutely promised to get in the can for the benefit of Cy Fredericks' romantic sensibilities concerning Oxford. With a gloom worthy of the boatman's, Jemima wondered whether rain would stop play.

She met Fanny Iverstone in the hairdresser's.

'Oh, it'll be all right on the night,' said Fanny confidently, reaching for a copy of *Taffeta* and adding it to the pile of glossy magazines on her lap. 'It always is, isn't it? I've been to dozens of Commems. God just does this to frighten us. I've got the most groovy dress, Brown's, it cost a fortune, Mummy paid, she approves of Commems, I think they remind her of her youth. She definitely brightens up at the thought of them, as though they were the last bastions of civilization.'

Fanny laughed: 'Which is quite funny, really, when they cost a packet, the dinner's disgusting, you generally quarrel with your partner or lose him more likely or fancy someone else's partner, they last for ever, and end up at six in the morning with everyone totally pissed and, worse still, most people sick as dogs. Some civilization.'

Jemima shuddered. Could Spike Thompson be trusted to make this unpromising material into something more like an advertisement for, say, an upmarket shampoo?

She could not resist asking Fanny: 'Then why go?'

Fanny looked at her in surprise, her blue eyes opening wide. 'Oh, one has to *go*,' she said. 'It's just that one doesn't expect to enjoy oneself very much. That's all.' And she turned her berollered head happily back to the cosy vitriol purveyed by *Taffeta* magazine.

Jemima thought it was time for an urgent conference with her director and her cameraman. Guthrie Carlyle had vanished but she found Spike Thompson at St Lucy's in the rooms of Rufus Pember, who turned out to be Chairman of the Ball Committee, with Nigel Copley, as a committee member, also present. She had not seen Rufus, except fleetingly in the High, since the night of the Chimneysweepers' Dinner when he had appeared with Nigel Copley from the river. The memory of that secret expedition upstream – even if Rufus and Nigel had to be acquitted of the attack on Saffron, on the evidence of Fanny Iverstone – stirred in her momentarily other thoughts about that night and the possible move-ments of other participants in the drama. The police, after some initially strenuous inquiries, had for want of any real evidence against anyone, abandoned the investigation. Privately Detective Chief Inspector Har-wood gave it as his opinion that it was a typical piece of undergraduate folly which had gone wrong. He did not exactly say: 'Let them lay about each other with boat hooks, if they like, so long as the honest citizens of Oxford are left in peace.' But Jemima got the impression that the thought lay somewhere at the back of his mind ... Then her attention was distracted by the merry sight of Spike Thompson and Jimbo, the sound man, recording as they put it, 'some useful wild track of champagne corks popping'.

'Who pays?' enquired Jemima sternly.

'Jemima! You ask me that! These lovely boys are paying, aren't you boys?' Spike seemed to have had a hypnotic effect on Rufus and Nigel, or else they were already glazed with champagne-tasting on behalf of the Ball Committee, for they nodded agreement.

'This is going to be the greatest Commem Ball ever. And that's official. Right, boys?' Rufus and Nigel nodded again. 'You name it, they've got it. Bands. They've got bands. All the big names: Glenn Miller—'

'Style of Glenn Miller,' interrupted Rufus Pember, showing a moment's anxiety at the enthusiasm of his new friend. 'Glenn Miller's dead.' He paused. 'Isn't he?'

'Of course he's dead! But he lives again in the person of this fabulous guy with this fabulous band. Then there's Boy George and the Culture Club – no, sorry mate, the *new* Boy George and the *new* Culture Club. This lot's going to be big, right Rufe? And the latest reggae band. What's the name of the latest reggae band? It doesn't matter. They met a man who met Bob Marley; they have to be good.'

Rufus nodded more happily, as Spike Thompson reeled off the names of a further five or six famous bands or groups or singers ending with one singer whose sex Jemima never did quite work out since he or she was described as looking rather like Mick Jagger's younger brother, but sounding more like Marlene Dietrich.

'Something for everyone,' said Jemima diplomatically. But Spike Thompson was not finished yet.

'And the fireworks! And the sideshows! There are exotic sideshows: strip-tease; both sexes. No, correction, all three sexes. Correction again, this is the eighties, all four sexes. A disco, a dancing bear—'

'No, the bear can't come. It's got a previous engagement,' put in Nigel.

'Pity. I was planning the shot. Anyway, all-night videos in the Junior Common Room, videos of an advanced nature, I take it. As for the Senior Common Room, God knows what will be going on in the Senior Common Room, some of these professors are ravers.'

'*We* organize this Ball, you know,' said Rufus, slightly stuffily. 'The undergraduates. It's nothing to do with the dons. We do it all – our committee. We organize everything from the champagne' – he looked pointedly at the bottles, now empty – 'to the security, to keep out the gatecrashers.'

'Of course you do, mate, no offence meant. And it's all going to be recorded by Megalith Television. Immortalized.'

Jemima wondered when the moment would come to break it to Spike that whatever turn his nocturnal activities might take, he was not expected to bring back shots of 'advanced' videos to Megalith Television . . .

'And all this for one hundred guineas a double ticket,' ended Spike brightly. 'I mean, it's given away, isn't it? I'm surprised you have so much trouble with gatecrashers. You'd think they'd be glad to pay.' Ah, that's my boy, thought Jemima. For a moment Spike had had her slightly worried. The price of the ticket reminded her that she needed to discover the final details of Kerry Barber's demonstration outside St Lucy's against the price of the aforesaid tickets and in favour of aid to the Third World. She looked into Jack Iverstone's rooms. Instead of Jack, she found Kerry himself, scribbling a message on Jack's desk.

'His father's ill,' Barber told Jemima cheerfully over his shoulder. 'They've telephoned through. Some kind of attack brought on by high blood pressure. It almost makes a rationalist like me believe in God when the bad guys start getting it.'

Under the circumstances, Jemima saw no need for any conventional expression of sorrow. Nor was she particularly surprised, remembering that sweating flushed bull-like figure on the tennis court. Playing competitive tennis, even limited to three sets, was certainly no way to combat high blood pressure.

Jemima was more surprised when Jack Iverstone arrived that evening at her suite at the Martyrs Hotel, just as she was changing for the ball – or the programme – and announced that he was carrying on with his protest.

'No, I'm going through with it. It's important to me. My chance.'

'But Jack,' protested Jemima, 'your father—'

'It's a put-on. Fanny agrees with me. She's carrying on with her plans. We had a frightful row on the subject of Kerry Barber's demo. He said I was making a fool of myself. I said I could live with that. Then he changed tack and said I was making a fool of him. The idea of me appearing on television riled him, you see: he thinks he has the media all sewn up. Now he produces this convenient attack and I'm supposed to come running.'

Shortly after Jack Iverstone departed, Saffron himself arrived. In his dark green tail coat with its white facings – the mark of an Oxford Blood – he looked extraordinarily handsome; the slightly gaunt appearance he had presented since his accident, and still more since Tiggie's death, suited him. With the thick black hair flopping across his forehead, slightly too long for the conventional idea of one who wore a tail coat in the evening, Saffron looked for a moment more like a musician, a young violinist perhaps, than a rich young undergraduate come to escort a lady to a Commem Ball.

Because Jemima was wearing a ball dress of roughly the same colour – bottle-green watered taffeta, off the shoulder, with flounces and a very full skirt – she had to admit to the mirror that they looked curiously well matched. Even her white shoulders matched the white facings of his coat.

It's a great pity I'm not into younger men, thought Jemima, as Saffron kissed her quite hard on the lips. This is all very well, but I've got more serious things to do like make a programme. And more serious people to kiss, for that matter. All the same, she responded to the kiss with an enthusiasm which took her – and perhaps Saffron too – by surprise.

After a bit, they broke apart; green eyes met black ones. Jemima patted her hair, in a gesture she only used on television when she was extremely nervous.

'Eyes like a cat,' said Saffron. 'Do you scratch like a cat as well? I have a feeling you might.'

'Dinner, Saffron. You're taking me to dinner. We queue for our dinner tickets, right? And then take our places in the tent. It's all in with the ticket, I gather, which it jolly well should be. We're not going to film that, so there's plenty of time.' She was speaking too quickly. 'The demo doesn't get going till about eleven. That's where I catch up with Spike. And you're not coming to that with me.'

'I thought we'd have some pink champagne in my room at Rochester first, supper *à deux*,' said Saffron carefully. 'And some lobster. I've studied your tastes. We're having our own ball, as you know, but I've bribed a member of the committee with an extra bottle to let me keep the key to my own room. All the rooms are supposed to be doled out to the eight hundred jolly people as sitting-out rooms but I didn't fancy that very much. As for the official Commem dinner, why don't we give that a miss? Not exactly an inspired menu, with Rufus Pember at the helm, and another eight hundred people at St Lucy's milling about in a tent like the vegetable show at the Spring Fair at Saffron Ivy.'

Saffron took Jemima over to Rochester under the shade of an enormous black umbrella. Even so, her long green taffeta skirts swished in the puddles of St Giles and she feared for her very high-heeled green satin sandals. Then Jemima went swishing up the winding staircase of Staircase Thirteen and climbed to the top, past Proffy's door (the oak, she noted, was firmly sported) all the way to Saffron's room at the top. It was in half darkness: then Jemima realized that the top of the vast tent which filled the Hawksmoor quad, on which the rain was gently rattling, obscured the window, through which she had once been able to look down on the green sward, the fountain and the Fellows' Garden beyond.

Saffron slammed the heavy door.

'We don't want any interruptions from eager beavers of this college, male and female, having their first and only night out of the year.'

He opened the pink champagne and poured it into a silver mug which looked like a christening mug – Jemima turned it round and saw the engraving: Saffron Ivo Charles 28 October 1964. She also saw that the room was filled with white roses, Virgo, the kind of greenish-white rose she loved.

'More study of my tastes.' She drank. She wondered whether he would get the date on the mug changed to the twenty-sixth, and thought he probably would not. She drank again.

Afterwards Jemima blamed the champagne (a thin excuse however from a champagne drinker, so perhaps it was the scent of the white roses) for the fact that after a while Saffron persuaded her that her taffeta dress was really too wet to be worn, that the dress needed hanging up to dry if it was to feature properly on Megalith Television in a couple of hours' time, and really all Jemima needed to do was to step out of it, and then the problems of the world would be solved, or at least for the time being, and even if they weren't, the evening would be off to a very good start . . . So Jemima did step out of the green taffeta dress, which left her, roughly speaking, in her stockings and high-heeled green shoes, all of which Saffron much appreciated, and shortly after that Saffron and Jemima adjourned to his bedroom, a small untidy cell off the sitting room, with a scarcely made bed, none of which made any difference to the pleasure and variety of what followed, the endless pleasure, the remarkable variety.

'Christ!' exclaimed Saffron, a good while later, sitting up in bed with his black hair in chaos. 'There's somebody trying to unlock the bloody door.' There was a good deal of other black hair all over his body, and as he jumped up and snatched at the red towelling robe, Jemima was reminded of how at Saffron Ivy she had thought he looked like a gipsy; no longer like a musician, he was much more like a gipsy, a healthy muscular young gipsy. Saffron ran into the other room, leaving her in the little cell. Jemima sank, sensuously, beneath the duvet. Then she thought in her turn: 'Christ, my *dress* is hanging up in there.'

She heard Saffron say: 'My dear Proffy, I've got special permission.'

'From the Dean, Saffer?'

'Have some lobster, Proffy,' was Saffron's reply. 'And some pink champagne!'

It seemed a very long time indeed before Saffron returned to the bedroom, in the course of which Jemima had begun to wish she had not also left her little gold bracelet watch in the sitting room, as well as her green crystal drop earrings (all of which must be extremely conspicuous, unless Saffron had had the wit to conceal them). The watch became increasingly vital. If the worst comes to the worst, thought Jemima, the programme comes first, and if I ever doubted it, witness the fact that I'm going to have to stalk into the sitting room starkers except for a pair of green sandals, and assume my clothing as graciously as possible, under the watchful eye of Professor Mossbanker as he guzzles the lobster, in order to get to St Lucy's on time to film Kerry Barber's demo.

But it did not come to that. Saffron returned.

'Proffy! He sure has a nose for a party. And for lobster. And for champagne for that matter.' Saffron heaved a sigh. 'Most dons give the Commems a wide berth. But I believe the old boy was simply moseying about the Staircase looking for refreshment.'

Jemima did not enquire about the dress. She only hoped that Proffy's legendary absent-mindedness extended to overlooking a ruffled green taffeta ball dress swaying gracefully in the window of Saffron's room. She was busy trying to replace Jemima, happily reckless lover of Saffron, with that other Jemima, presenter of Megalith's *Golden Kids* programme.

As Jemima and Saffron sped, under the great black umbrella, from Rochester, down the Broad and Long Wall to her rendezvous with Spike outside St Lucy's, they passed a series of other revellers, the men in dinner jackets – wing collars were clearly in fashion, and the occasional tail coat – the girls all in long dresses which would have satisfied Cy Fredericks.

'Gatecrashers!' pronounced Saffron with pleasure. 'The serious fun starts once dinner is over. In fact that is the only real fun of a Commem, gatecrashing it. Rochester's security is hopeless – anyone can get in if they want to – but St Lucy's is a good challenge: you can swim across the river, carrying your clothes in a plastic bag, I did that to Magdalen one year. On the other hand they're wise to the river. St Lucy's roof might be better: where it touches the botanical gardens; the chapel is too steep. There's a rumour that they're going to use hoses on the roof, which makes it even more fun. Added to which there's another rumour that Nigel Copley's brother was in the SAS, so that they're going to use SAS methods, or borrow the SAS on an amateur basis to keep out gatecrashers – which makes it even more fun, and more of a challenge. In fact I rather think I'll have a go—'

Jemima stopped.

'Saffron, whatever your plans are, you can gatecrash Buckingham Palace for all I care, but don't tell me. I've got a programme to make. In short, this is where we part. Do I make myself plain? If I see you, I don't acknowledge you. It's Falstaff and Prince Hal, only you're Falstaff and I'm Prince Hal.'

'I know thee not, young man?'

'Precisely.'

'You knew me.'

'I did. And you knew *me*. Very lovely it was. Goodbye, Saffron.' She kissed him on the cheek, then turned and crossed the road to St Lucy's.

Saffron called something after her: 'I'll be there. It's a promise. Meet you at Pond Quad at dawn. A definite rendezvous.'

Jemima looked back. He was waving and blowing a kiss.

'See you,' then she called back: 'Take care!' It was her last sight of Saffron, vanishing back up Long Wall in the direction of Rochester.

20

Dancing in the Quad

As soon as Saffron was gone, Jemima was caught up totally in the concerns of Megalith Television, beginning with the filming of Kerry Barber's extremely visible demonstration, which straddled in front of the great mediaeval archway gate of St Lucy's. The effect, in view of the fact that Kerry Barber and his fellows were wearing T-shirts, jeans, baggy trousers and suchlike whereas the revellers visible inside were in formal evening dress, was to give the impression of peasants demonstrating against their feudal lord. The demonstrating peasants included not only Jack but an older woman, chic in khaki dungarees, whom Jemima guessed to be Kerry Barber's admirably teetotal wife Mickey. Then there was a girl Jemima dimly recognized and only pinned down later as Magda Poliakoff, she who had given evidence at the Bim Marcus inquest.

'All this,' said Jemima to Guthrie Carlyle happily, 'is going to look very good on our programme.' There was a brief interval while two would-be gatecrashers, both male and rather small, were unceremoniously evicted from St Lucy's.

'I told you it was no good saying you were from the *Observer*,' Jemima heard one say to the other indignantly. 'Who cares about the *Observer* at a Commem?'

'You said you were from the *Daily Mail* and you got slung out too,' hissed back his companion. 'On account of the fact that there are eighty or ninety people from the *Daily Mail* there already.'

Then Megalith, in the guise of Guthrie and Spike Thompson, were able to set to in earnest and film some splendid shots of Kerry Barber's banners – most of which mentioned the price of a Commem ticket – ONE HUNDRED PIECES OF SILVER was the most effective – in contrast to the plight of the Third World. The rain made it even more effective.

Jack Iverstone was unaccustomedly tense during his brief interview on camera with Jemima – with a background of St Lucy's, plus a banner reading ONE NIGHT'S FUN FOR YOU, ONE YEAR'S FOOD FOR THEM. Either he was suffering from anxiety about his father or else the medium of television had robbed him of his habitual ease of manner. Jemima was relieved when the interview was over. Jack vanished, possibly depressed by his performance, and did not rejoin the demonstration. Then Megalith was able to move inside the defended portals of St Lucy's and mingle with the lawful – or mainly lawful – crowds as they danced sedately to the new Glenn Miller, jived to the new Boy George, swayed to the people who once met a man who met Bob Marley, twisted (and shouted) in Luke's Disco, admired (and cat-called) at the strippers of all four sexes or repaired to the Junior Common Room for the sake of the advanced videos. Or simply vanished into the sitting-out rooms for the sake of wine or women, song being freely available outside in all varieties.

In all of this Jemima never spared a thought for Saffron. She was busy, doing a job, if not the job for which she had been sent into the world, at least a job which she enjoyed doing. She talked to Fanny Iverstone (who looked very pretty in her Brown's dress) and to Poppy Delaware (whose dress, at least by the time Jemima met her, was failing down, but she also looked very pretty in it or out of it). She did not talk to Muffet Pember (whose partner had cut his hand on some glass, thus convincing Jemima that Muffet, or at any rate her partner, was in some peculiar way accident prone).

She found the Gobbler, preparatory to interviewing him, only he was in the pond under the statue of St Lucy's at the time, consuming gulls' eggs on a plate as the fountain played on his fair and foolish face. So the programme had to be made without the spoken views of the Gobbler on being a Golden Kid. There was only this striking illustrative shot of the Gobbler at play which many people afterwards thought was the finest shot in the whole film, and a still version of which was used on the cover of the *TV Times* and a whole host of other magazines but for which the Gobbler's parents, who turned out to be Very Important, were still trying to sue Megalith Television long after *Golden Kids* had picked up the last of its many inevitable awards.

All of this was to come. Jemima and camera picked their dainty way past rather a lot of people who had just been or were just going to be sick, particularly as the evening progressed, but the cameras avoided all of that, unlike the sight of the Gobbler at play. For one thing it was not really very socially relevant or as Spike Thompson sagely observed: 'Who needs Golden Kids losing their Golden Dinners out of their Golden Gobs? What's happened to the smashing bird in a red dress who promised to dive into the pool starkers once we get that fat boy out of it?'

Copulating couples were however not utterly ignored. As Spike observed to Jemima: 'This might be a witty voice-over situation for you, my love.'

'Sex in, sick's out,' was the way Guthrie Carlyle summed it up.

In the early hours of the morning the rain stopped and the fireworks went up into the night sky.

For the first time Jemima, gazing at them restlessly – she hated fireworks in principle as dangerous and wasteful yet found them irresistible – thought of Saffron. She wondered if he had indeed tried to gatecrash St Lucy's and if he had succeeded. There had been no sign of him. Of those she knew, Jack Iverstone had never reappeared, and Fanny Iverstone, glimpsed early on looking rather flushed in her Brown's dress dancing in Luke's Disco, had long since vanished.

At about two o'clock a great cry went up in Pond Quad: 'Ahoy there!' Then: 'They're on the roof!' Then to the delight and excitement of all those lucky enough to be inside St Lucy's, two figures in black hoods and darkened clothing were glimpsed on the sloping roof of St Lucy's chapel. The invaders' situation looked perilous enough already, but then the firehoses began to play upon them. Although some of those at the Ball also got drenched – 'Oh fuck off!' shouted an indignant girl of elfin appearance wearing a sprigged muslin crinoline, when the water sprayed her – it was thought by the rest to be a small price to pay for the fun.

The invaders slid ignominiously down the roof.

Saffron? Jemima rather hoped not.

It was only later that she learnt that the so-called invaders had actually been security men, the recriminations about the hosing down afterwards being so violent as to lend some credence to the theory that they were out-of-hours SAS men.

It was not until the dawn, a luminous dawn, with mist rising off the river, and the first intrepid revellers climbing into the punts, reckless of the rainwater, and the pretty skirts – or perhaps they were sufficiently dishevelled anyway – that she began to wonder seriously where Saffron was.

Jemima leant her head on Guthrie's shoulder.

'Breakfast, my love? You look as if you could do with kidneys, bacon, sausages, kedgeree, scrambled eggs, and whatever is the rest of the menu which I have in my pocket. Spike's going to take some shots of the river now the boats are out. He doesn't need you any more. Then an overall picture of the aftermath.'

St Lucy's was beginning to look like a battlefield, as recumbent bodies, the survivors, lay about, sleeping, unconscious, twined round each other. Bottles were everywhere. Somewhere one of the bands – or was it Luke's Disco? – was still loyally playing.

'No thanks, I have a previous engagement. I think I'll wander off.' Jemima looked again at the scene of mayhem before her, more like Dutch peasants at the kermis, than anything more classically graceful – no shades of Poussin here.

'I wonder who won this battle? And who lost?'

'We won it. Megalith Television won it,' said Guthrie smugly.

'There seem to be a great number of losers.' Jemima pointed to the inert bodies, corpses as they seemed, strewn around them. 'One wonders whether some of these will ever wake again.'

I must look for him, she thought. Then: Saffron – he broke his promise. Why? Did he fail to gatecrash after all? Then with more urgency: Saffron: why didn't he come?

For the first time since she had parted from Saffron, she thought of the possible dangers to him in this great Oxford night of rout. Where were all those who might wish ill to Saffron? Where for that matter was Saffron himself?

At Rochester College, there was the same feeling of the battle lost and won, the same slightly morbid impression of corpses, as Jemima, now wrapped in a vast Chinese shawl against the cool of the morning, stepped her way through the quad to Staircase Thirteen. She had received, with Saffron, a pass to leave Rochester and return: finding she had lost it, Jemima expected the man at the gate to raise an eyebrow; instead she was waved on with a resignation singularly at variance with the paranoia recently exhibited at St Lucy's. If security was the standard by which a successful Oxford ball was rated, no wonder Rochester's was considered to be inferior.

As she clambered up the high winding stone staircase, Jemima wondered if she would find Saffron too in some kind of passive state of post-revelling (and post-coital) contemplation. Perhaps he had merely gone quietly back to bed after leaving her at St Lucy's. Or perhaps he had found other possibilities for enjoyment at Rochester . . . Nevertheless the sense of unease which had oppressed her since dawn at St Lucy's became stronger as she reached the top of the stairs and saw that Saffron's door was open. She noticed that several of the other doors on the staircase were shut (although Proffy's on the ground floor was for once open; perhaps he had finally gone home to Chillington Road, having sufficiently slaked his appetite for lobster and champagne).

Jemima went into the room. It was empty. She went through into the tiny bedroom and stared. Saffron was lying on the bed, dressed in his white evening shirt and black trousers, only the white tie had been undone and lay loosely round his neck. His eyes were shut. One sleeve had been rolled up. Otherwise the resemblance to the body of Tiggie was uncanny.

Jemima ran forward and supported his head, realizing as she did so, that Saffron, unlike Tiggie, was breathing; his body was warm. But the pulse, when she felt it, was very faint.

'It's not true!' she cried aloud and started to pull at Saffron's body, slapping his cheek, tugging at his shoulders. Once Saffron's lips opened a little but otherwise there was no movement. He was in a coma, a drug-induced coma, Jemima recognized that only too well. The question was, how did she reverse it? What should she do, now, immediately? Did she dare leave him and fetch help? After that, she would work out how on earth he had got himself into that coma.

'Saffron,' she said aloud again. 'Saffron! Wake up, Saffron, you've got to hear me.'

There was a very faint noise behind her. Jemima realized for the first time that she was not alone with Saffron.

She whirled round. There standing in the doorway of the tiny room, watching her and blinking slightly in his usual mild manner behind the black-rimmed spectacles, stood Professor Mossbanker.

'Proffy,' she began, 'thank God. We've got to get help. Will you telephone – you've got a telephone downstairs? We've got to save him—'

Then she stopped. She saw that in his hand Proffy was holding a syringe.

'You found that?' she questioned, still feeling confused. 'What are you doing here, Proffy?' she said in a stronger voice. 'What are you doing with that syringe?'

'I didn't expect you to be here,' Proffy spoke with an odd kind of detachment. 'Why did you come?'

'I came *back*,' Jemima spoke urgently, 'and thank God I did. And now we've got to get help, we've got to save him.'

'Oh you'll be able to save him all right.' Proffy continued to speak in the same casual tone. 'If you think he's worth saving, that is.'

Then Jemima for the first time fully understood.

'You!' She hesitated and then said in an uncertain voice: 'You – the murderer?' Jemima took a step backwards. She was not sure at the time whether it was a protective move towards Saffron or a defensive one on her own account.

'Precisely. Rather an unexpected discovery on your part, I fancy.' Proffy spoke in his familiar rapid unemphatic tone; he continued to stand there blinking behind his spectacles. He might have been congratulating – or reproving her – on some slight matter of scholarship. Then he put down the syringe and removed his spectacles. For a moment his eyes, his whole visage, looked naked and rather innocent. Then she realized how cold his real manner was, had perhaps always been behind the friendly bumbling veneer.

Jemima felt an instant of pure panic. Proffy had tried to kill Saffron or was preparing to do so. He had – she grappled with the thought – killed poor little Tiggie. Her thoughts went further back as she struggled with the implications of it all: he had probably also killed Bim Marcus. Proffy:

a double murderer. A would-be triple murderer. Was it likely that he would now spare her?

Yet Proffy still made no move towards her. In a way his stillness, his air of ease, was more sinister than if he had displayed openly the violence which must lie within him. She supposed that she ought, nonetheless, to prepare herself for self-defence, some kind of defence. She was tall and quite strong: Proffy was on the other hand, if a lot older, a lot taller and a lot heavier. On his own testimony he was a killer, even if the weapons he had chosen hitherto had been secret ones.

Jemima took a deep breath.

'Why?' she asked crudely. She had some vague memory that hostages were supposed to engage terrorists in conversation in order to defuse a violent situation. Even stronger was her obstinate desire to know the truth – if it proved to be the last thing she ever found out.

'Why?' replied Proffy, twisting his heavy spectacles in his hands. 'I suppose I thought the world would be well rid of him.'

'Wasn't it a case of being well rid of – *them*?' To her own ears, Jemima's voice sounded distinctly tremulous. Above all, she wanted to give an impression of calm authority.

'Ah yes, them. So you worked that out. Very good, very good.' There was the same surreal atmosphere of academic congratulation.

'The deaths of Tiggie and Bim Marcus. Aren't I right? Wasn't it all part of the same—' she hesitated again. 'The same plan,' she finished.

Proffy ignored the question.

'Why?' he repeated, instead. 'Why indeed? A long story, a long story from the past. But not, I think, the story you anticipated, Jemima Shore Investigator. My impression was that you were altogether too carried away by other aspects of it all . . . Ah well, it doesn't matter now.'

Proffy put his spectacles on again and gazed at her. 'You look frightened, I see. Not surprising I suppose under the circumstances. All the same, no need to be frightened, no need at all. It's over, all over.'

'Why?' demanded Jemima desperately.

Proffy continued to consider her. 'Yes, I daresay the enquiring mind ought to be encouraged. In theory if not in practice. Since it no longer matters to me, I will indulge myself – and you – by explaining. We might go downstairs.'

Much later, Proffy said to Jemima: 'While you're waiting for the police I think you'd better let me have the syringe.' He blinked at her one last time. 'I shall go outside. I've always been fond of parties, you know. Give my love to my wife and—' he stopped. Then: 'Eugenia' he pronounced. It was not quite clear whether he was aware of his surprising triumph in getting the names the right way round.

Outside in the College, once the sun was fully up – too late for the ball, it was going to be a beautiful day – strong and competent men in the shape of the porter's workforce, started moving purposefully about. Plates and glasses, innumerable bottles, were collected and packed away, from innumerable suppers, breakfasts, in tent and quad, arcade, staircase and endless sitting-out rooms. It was now time to persuade the few last revellers of Rochester that the Ball was now well and truly over. As Jemima had suspected, one or two of the bodies, whether single or entwined with each other, were extremely reluctant to awake, and even more reluctant to move. One in particular was hard to rouse, the dark head sunk on the chest, a body lying in the corner of the big tent in the main Rochester quad.

'Come along, sir, come along. Time to go now, sir. Come along.'

The porter shook the recumbent reveller by the shoulder without effect and passed on to the next body.

Twenty minutes later there was a call from one of his associates. 'Fred – can't seem to get any reaction out of this one. Out for the count.'

The head porter called back: 'We'll put him to bed, then. If he's one of ours.'

'Fred, come over here will you. I don't like this. He's – well he's cold. Quite cold.' There was a new urgency in the voice.

'Who's cold?'

'It's the professor! Professor Mossbanker. Fred – I think we'd better get an ambulance. Quick. There's this syringe!'

'OK, right then. You go and telephone for an ambulance. That's the second time this morning. Well, we once had three after a Commem. I ask you. And they call it fun.'

'This is serious, Fred. I think he's dead!'

To some of the revellers walking unsteadily in the streets of Oxford, on their way to the river, on their way back from it, the wail of the ambulance passing down the Broad, bearing Proffy's lifeless body on its ride to the hospital, was like the last music of the long night.

21

Purple for the Rich Man

Afterwards, back in London safely reunited with Cass, Jemima still shivered at the thought of what followed. But it was the thought of Proffy's strange mild calm which caused the revulsion.

'He seemed quite fatalistic about everything. Oddly dispassionate. All he really wanted to do was get it over – my questions – and then as we now know, go outside and kill himself. I got the impression that he was hardly interested in me; I certainly don't think I was ever in any danger.'

'I'm glad of that.' Cass put his arm around her shoulders.

'You see, for him the game was over: the *party* was over. He answered my questions, almost with a shrug. Said that he'd drugged Saffron when he came to drink the champagne.' Jemima forbore to mention to Cass the question of the green dress. How ironic, she reflected privately, that Proffy the cool murderer, the former secret agent, the chemist who knew how to kill, should have failed to deduce from the presence of a ball dress hanging up in the sitting room that Saffron was entertaining its former occupant in the bedroom ... she thought of his formidable mixture of jealousy, ruthlessness and absentmindedness which had defeated her investigation for so long and turned her in the direction of the Iverstones, more especially the ever-decent Jack. Or perhaps Proffy was so used to female clothing draped round Saffron's rooms and even his car (she remembered the Maserati at Saffron Ivy bestrewn with white frilly underclothing) that he paid no special attention to one dress. It was after all part of his picture of Saffron, the careless sexuality of arrogant youth, the picture which he had determined to destroy.

'And now he was coming back to finish off the job. Just as he killed Tiggie,' Jemima said aloud.

'Envy!' exclaimed Cass. 'All that in the name of envy!'

'Envy after all can kill,' said Jemima. 'Can be destructive as well as self-destructive. He warned me, and that was his own piece of arrogance, on the night of the Chimneysweepers' Dinner. He was talking about the parable of Dives and Lazarus. What makes you think Dives wasn't happy? he said. Purple and fine linen: who wouldn't want to be dressed in purple and fine linen? What makes you think Lazarus didn't envy Dives his lot? That gave me the clue to the attacks on Saffron – a killing hatred based on envy was at the bottom of them. But I was obsessed by the hereditary element in it all, the fact that the Iverstone family were bound to envy Saffron and, if anyone, would want him removed. That tension I felt at the tennis match – the tension which was really between Proffy and Lord St Ives: I was determined to put it down to Andrew Iverstone's jealousy of his cousin. Andrew Iverstone, Daphne, Fanny, even the ever-decent Jack – they were all present at the various attacks and had an opportunity—'

'But Jack wasn't present at the Chimneysweepers' Dinner,' objected Cass.

'Yes, but he too could have canoed up river, as did Rufus Pember and Nigel Copley. That wouldn't have been impossible. What I knew all along, but failed to connect, was that Proffy had the best opportunity of all. Saffron's car, for example, the original attack, parked outside Rochester and in various car parks near the college; who had better opportunity than Proffy to fix it? And then the death of Bim Marcus: Proffy was even able to report finding the body with perfect impunity. No one needed to enter Rochester and lurk till the small hours, when the murderer actually lived there – right on the same staircase, Staircase Thirteen.'

Cass frowned: 'Why the washing machine? That always struck me as being so odd. If it was Proffy, why didn't he just do the deed and retreat back into his rooms? Why set the machine on and alert everybody to his presence?'

'Of course I should have realized all along the importance of that clue,' agreed Jemima. 'I felt instinctively at the time as you know; thought the police were a little too easy about it all – the machine was on, with Bim's prints on it; ergo he set it off. No, that was Proffy's cunning way of distracting our attention from his presence. The machine was put on deliberately to give him the perfect excuse to discover the body. Any prints or awkward traces he might have left – all taken care of.'

'In view of his feelings about youth – by the way, who said he liked the idea of children and hated the young?'

'Tiggie,' said Jemima.

'Perceptive. In view of these feelings it must have given him sardonic pleasure to use the legend of his own intolerance concerning the machine. Everyone knew he hated being woken up by it. But let's go on. Saffron Ivy, yes, I see he had every opportunity there. You said that he never shared Eugenia Jones' bedroom.' Cass frowned again. 'But the Chimney-sweepers' Dinner! Didn't he take a risk there? You mean he just went from your side, attacked Saffron, and returned. A cool customer, indeed. Not only at the end.'

'Till the very end. He encouraged me to telephone for a doctor from his room. Outside we still heard the music playing, and the sun must have been coming up, except the shadow of that huge tent blocked the light. I saw the photographs: Eleanor Mossbanker and all those tow-headed children and a huge photograph of Eugenia Jones. Those dramatic looks she handed on to her children – to Tiggie, and to Saffron.'

'Why did the attacks start *then*? Surely he had always known about Saffron and Tiggie—'

'No, no that's the whole point. He never knew. It was the Nurse's story which gave it away.'

'Nurse Elsie strikes again.'

'She did indeed. She told Eugenia about Saffron's – her baby's – actual whereabouts, Eugenia having believed for twenty years that the baby died shortly after birth. That was such a shock that Eugenia confided in Proffy simply for the sake of sharing the shock with somebody. But of course at the same time she had to tell him about Lord St Ives being the father of Saffron. Otherwise none of it made any sense – the switch of the babies I mean. Proffy's a very jealous man you know, *was* a very jealous man. Up till Nurse Elsie's revelation he'd always imagined that the baby which died was his child, because it was conceived just at the start of their relationship. Eugenia, knowing his feelings on the subject, let him believe it.'

'What about Tiggie?'

'Oh that was before he knew Eugenia. Proffy went along with the original story concerning the mysterious Jones. And now, with one fell swoop he learnt that his mistress had betrayed him sexually at the very beginning of their affair. What was more, she had in effect lied to him for twenty years. Worse still, it was clear that she must have always preferred Lord St Ives. You see, it was Eugenia who had refused to marry Proffy, not – as I'd always imagined – the other way round. Lord St Ives was the great love of Eugenia Jones' life; or the perfect masochistic emotional situation if you prefer it, the one man she could never hope to marry, the man who would never leave his wife . . .'

'So now Proffy found that this boy, this arrogant rich privileged boy, where his own children were poor and numerous, was not only the son of his mistress, but also the son of his mistress *and* her lover.'

'Exactly. Instead of hating Eugenia, as might have been logical, he transferred his hatred to the boy. So that it was easy for him. And he decided to kill him. Eliminate him from Eugenia's life.'

'Purple and fine linen – and death – for the rich man,' commented Cass. 'With the compliments of Dives.'

'Except that poor little Tiggie was the one who got killed, Tiggie and the wretched innocent Bim Marcus, killed for the coincidence of one wasted day of high life. Tiggie did for herself when she got engaged to Saffron. I suppose the spectacle of Tiggie, Eugenia's daughter, about to become rich and famous, as she herself boasted, to enjoy all that wealth, that house, those possessions, everything that belonged to the man Eugenia had preferred, was too much for him. Proffy reckoned he could make that death look like suicide, knowing the amount of drugs that Tiggie took. As with Saffron. Who would seriously question it? A death from drink and an overdose of drugs on the night of a Commem Ball – all too probable, especially with Saffron's reputation.'

'The hatred of the old for the young. Must be all too easily encouraged by life at Oxford. If it's there in the first place.' Cass shivered.

'Don't forget that the Kerry Barbers of this world, who are also to be found at Oxford, are a much larger part of it in fact,' Jemima pointed out. But Cass, for the time being, was not thinking of the Kerry Barbers of this world.

'Finally he killed himself. And you let him do that. You got a doctor for Saffron, but you didn't get the police for Proffy. Was it to save the scandal? Was it for Saffron? Or did you think you wouldn't be able to convince the police?'

Jemima took Cass's hand. 'No, not for Saffron. Nor even for the St Ives family. As for the police, I would have tried my best, although it might have been difficult. No, it was for her, Eugenia Jones. She'd made a mistake, if you call love a mistake, twenty years earlier. And that mistake came to cost two lives, three if you count Proffy himself, and it nearly cost the life of another, Saffron. She had to live with the knowledge that her lover had killed her daughter and tried to kill the man she now knew to be her son.'

'Did she suspect *anything*, anything at all before it happened?'

'There were a good deal of strong emotions floating about at Saffron Ivy that weekend, which fooled me at the time,' admitted Jemima ruefully. 'That is, I picked up the emotions and attributed them to the wrong people. Not only at the tennis match. Eugenia Jones is another example: that night when the butler was singing, I felt fear in the room, fear very strongly present. I thought it was Lady St Ives but that must have been Eugenia's fear for her daughter.'

'So she knew?' asked Cass.

'Maybe she didn't know. But she feared. It was the thought of what she must have feared, as well as what she endured later, which made me think that she had the right now to come to terms with it all in secret. To recover her peace of mind, if she ever can, outside the baleful light of public scandal.'

'The peace of mind Nurse Elsie sacrificed at her death.'

'Peace of mind is for God to give: that's what Sister Imelda told me originally. I'm beginning to think she was right. I'm not sure who else but

God, about whose existence I remain anxiously doubtful, will give it to poor Eugenia Jones. Whatever she may have suspected before, she now knows the full truth about Proffy. It's been hushed up for the rest of the world, a simple suicide while the balance of his mind was disturbed etc. There's no proof of what happened, after all, and of the various parties concerned, including Saffron, none of them want the truth to be exhibited to the world. Then there's poor Eleanor Mossbanker and those wretched children to be considered: suicide is better for them to live with than murder.'

'You saw Eugenia Jones?' asked Cass.

'In Oxford. Briefly. She asked to see me. Said it wouldn't take long and that she wanted to ask me a question. She came to the Martyrs.'

Jemima thought of that last interview. Eugenia Jones looked quite haggard. She also seemed to have shrunk in height. In her black clothes – official mourning for Proffy? – she resembled a middle-aged Greek peasant woman more than a distinguished academic.

'Did I do wrong?' asked Eugenia Jones abruptly. She refused to accept a drink or even coffee, and sat quite stiffly on the edge of her chair in the hotel suite. 'It began with love. Was that wrong?'

'Why do you ask me? Of all people.'

Eugenia Jones smiled faintly. She had a charming smile; Jemima had noticed before how it lit up her slightly heavy features.

'You know all the facts. There's no one else I can talk to. Besides, you seem remote from love. I thought you might have a detached view.'

'I can't and won't judge anyone in all this,' said Jemima Shore honestly. 'Except Proffy, and he's beyond all our judgements. Certainly not you.'

Eugenia Jones stood up. 'No absolution then.'

'No need for it, as I can see it.'

'Wise girl,' commented Cass, when Jemima related this (although she chose to omit for some reason that comment on her remoteness from love). 'So now Saffron goes forward to be the next Lord St Ives.'

'And that's right too,' said Jemima staunchly. 'That's justice. He *is* his father's son after all. And his mother's son too – at least that's the line he's taking. I mean Lady St Ives. He doesn't want to see Eugenia Jones and she doesn't want to see him. I daresay he'll be reconciled to his father in time, if only for Lady St Ives' sake. It's over: the past will be left in peace, or at any rate that bit of it.'

'How are they all? Your suspects. Your former suspects, I should say.'

'I haven't seen Jack Iverstone since his father's death; I still feel guilty at having wondered at the end whether a jealous murderer's nature lay beneath that decent exterior.'

'Jack – I wonder if he's glad or sorry that he finally revolted on that last night and chose to demo with Kerry Barber when it must have been fairly clear that his father was dying,' mused Cass.

'Being Jack, he'd be sorry, very sorry. No, correction, the new Jack is probably deep down rather glad. Otherwise his father would have died and Jack would never have proved to himself that he *could* revolt. Except publicly, of course. But being a member of the SDP was nothing compared to his inability to speak up when his father was actually present. Think of that tennis match, for example. Now that Andrew Iverstone's off the scene, he can happily pursue that moderate political career for which he is so eminently suited. But Fanny, believe it or not – I'm taking Fanny into Megalith Television. As a secretary in the first instance; I'm sure she'll rise rapidly. I'm determined to save her from the twin curses of a right-wing background and an inadequate education.'

'And Saffron?'

Jemima smiled. 'Recovered. He has nine lives, like Midnight here, even if Proffy has used up a good few of them. He swears he's going to work next term. No more Oxford Bloodiness.' She bent to stroke the cat, feeling for some reason that it was necessary to add: 'I haven't seen him recently you know.' She was aware that she was very slightly embarrassed.

At the same moment, Cass was producing a sentence, which exhibited a similar awkwardness; nonetheless Jemima got the impression he had been rehearsing it for some time. 'Jemima, I've got something to say to you. First I think you should know, I don't know quite why I think this, but I do – that Tiggie and I, once or twice, you know, while you were in Oxford – she was so wild, sweet but crazy, it meant nothing. Not to either of us.

'Cherry must have guessed,' he added, 'or at least suspected. Because I had to ask her for Tiggie's telephone number. I take it she didn't tell you?'

Jemima thought of Cherry's slightly odd, even strained reaction to Tiggie's engagement, one of those things she had filed away at the back of her mind to be explained one day. Now she must either reward Cherry with flowers for her discretion or – that too was something which could be filed away for a later decision; on the whole Jemima thought she would probably send Cherry flowers.

Cass seemed to have nothing more to say.

There was a long silence while Jemima, her head bent, continued to stroke Midnight as though his life depended on it; after a bit his heavy raucous purr filled the silence. As a matter of fact, during the silence Jemima was not thinking of Midnight at all but was reminding herself of fairness, justice, equality of opportunity, personal freedom, individual liberty, possessiveness-is-theft, and many other fine concepts, all in an effort to prevent an enormous wave of furious indignation and jealousy sweeping over her and knocking her right off her elegant perch on a rock, as she saw it, way above such horrible human passions.

To break the tension, Jemima jumped up and pressed the button of her cassette player. The melody from *Arabella* filled the room: 'Aber der

Richtige . . . The one who's right for me . . .' Jemima switched it off again.

Finally she said as lightly as she could manage: 'Investigating the past is not always a good thing. As witness all the fearful troubles caused by Nurse Elsie's efforts to bring it to rights.'

'Jemima, leave that damn cat alone,' said Cass, putting his arm round her. 'That's only the first thing I have to say to you. The second thing is: if the past is best left alone, and I agree, how about, as you might put it, investigating the future? Our future, to be precise. I am proposing a new arrangement.'

'Had you in mind some *legal* arrangement?' enquired Jemima cautiously. She still gazed steadily in the direction of Midnight, but allowed herself to rest against Cass.

'Why not? I am a lawyer,' replied Cass.

'Then I shall investigate it.'

'Is that a promise?'

'No promises at the beginning of an investigation,' said Jemima Shore.

Your Royal Hostage

For Tasha – princess over the water
with love

Contents

1

Innocent?

'We don't want to hurt her. We must remember that. All of us. She is, after all, innocent.' There was a brief pause. Then the man who called himself Monkey repeated firmly: 'She is innocent.'

He raised one eyebrow – the right, a familiar habit – and then smiled at them, lifting the left side of his upper lip as he did so to exhibit a flash of long slightly yellow tooth. It was as though he was willing them to agree.

The girl who called herself Lamb found that she was becoming increasingly fascinated by these physical tricks on the part of Monkey. No one was at first sight less like his chosen code name than Monkey (any more than she herself resembled a lamb); yet the more Lamb studied him, the more she found something significant about the choice. Monkey, for all his bulk, had something simian about him, with his long upper lip and flat splayed nostrils: a friendly monkey of authority who gazed at you calmly from his cage until you wondered which of the two of you dwelt in the outside world.

Similarly Fox was at first sight a somewhat languid young man, with a pale complexion and of slight build, most unfox-like; closer inspection revealed an oddly sharp nose and bright, small deeply set eyes. Even his slight build was belied by his surprisingly long and muscular arms. Also Fox could be cunning, as Lamb had learned, cunning as – well, cunning as a fox. As for Beagle: but it did not do to think about Beagle. So Lamb stopped herself thinking about Beagle, stopped thinking anything at all about him as she promised herself to do, and concentrated once more on Monkey.

'Well, isn't she? Of course she's innocent.' Monkey happily answered his own question as one delighted at solving a difficulty. That was another familiar trick; Lamb imagined Monkey had used it to effect in innumerable committee meetings in the past. And after all, what was this except a committee meeting? If a committee meeting in rather an odd place of rather an odd sort.

Nobody else had spoken or showed any signs of doing so. So Monkey went on: 'Quite a pretty story in the *Standard* this evening, by the way. Anyone read it?'

Lamb looked down automatically at the evening paper which lay on Monkey's lap although she had in fact seen the lunchtime edition. The original headline had been moved to the second half of the page. All the same, she could still read the words: PRINCESS: WEDDING SCARE.

The story itself, as Lamb knew, having studied it earlier, was fairly insubstantial. Something to do with the route the wedding cortège would take. But since no one yet knew officially what that route would be, it could hardly amount to a serious scare. There had been numbers of similar stories – or non-stories, if you like – recently: PRINCESS: WEDDING SNUB (Some extreme Labour councillors who had refused to subscribe to a local wedding present).

PRINCESS: WEDDING HOPES (Some extremely loyal tenants on a grand country estate who believed the young couple would spend their honeymoon nearby).

PRINCESS: WEDDING EXCITEMENT – what on earth had that been about? Certainly nothing which was actually very exciting. The arrival of an unusually large number of American tourists in the capital perhaps. Just as PRINCESS: WEDDING FEARS might refer to the fact that exactly the same unusually large number of American tourists were staying at home . . .

All that these numerous headlines went to prove was that any combination of the two words 'princess' and 'wedding' was deemed, probably rightly, to sell larger numbers of newspapers than for example a similarly recurring combination of, say, 'government' and 'spending'; the public appetite for weddings having grown rather than diminished with the most recent example, that of the Duke and Duchess of York. In short, Princess Amy was News. Or rather, when in the process of getting married, Princess Amy of Cumberland was News.

Up to this point, to be frank, the media had been strangely unaware of the potential news value of this particular twenty-two-year-old girl. The Cumberlands were after all not a particularly important branch of the Royal Family. Although the Duke of Cumberland himself, as a king's son, had retained his place in the succession, his marriage to a Catholic princess meant that his three daughters were actually outside it. None of this had seemed to matter very much at the time. The Duke, a bachelor soldier as it seemed, had surprised everyone by marrying at the age of fifty, and surprised himself even more by producing three daughters; the youngest, Amy, being born when he was already scurrying towards the end of his uneventful life. The children of the Duke's royal siblings being already grown up when the Cumberland Princesses were born, the latter had in effect skipped a generation.

As a soldier the Duke had once referred to a previous holder of the title – 'Butcher' Cumberland of Culloden – as 'a damn fine general who understood how to deal with the natives' – remarks which caused a sensation in Scotland where he happened to be at the time. Otherwise he had led a life of almost total obscurity so far as the Press was concerned. As for the Duchess, the fact that she had been a French princess, related to half the royal families in Europe, had somehow never cut much ice with the xenophobic English Press.

Ah, but a wedding! And the wedding of a princess who was in effect an orphan (never mind the continued existence of her mother)! And the wedding of a princess who was not only an orphan, but also the youngest of three sisters . . . What was more a Catholic wedding – in Westminster Cathedral – made a nice change, it was generally agreed, from the Abbey and St Paul's; as well as providing excellent opportunities for interdenominational tolerance to be paraded in these ecumenical days. Already the possibilities so far as the Press was concerned were infinitely exciting, with words like 'Cinderella' produced in all sorts of hopefully tactful combinations: if you could not after all exactly term the Princesses Sophie and Harriet of Cumberland 'Ugly Sisters', you could somehow hint that poor little Princess Amy had been neglected since her father's death; surely she must have been neglected, since she had been so signally neglected by the Press . . .

It was fortunate from the point of view of contrast that Princess Sophie, pop eyed, lively and rather bossy, had married an unnewsworthy Scottish landowner. Then Princess Harriet, melancholy, wraith-like, bonily beautiful like her mother but not particularly photogenic, had married a French businessman without a title (where did she *find* a Frenchman without a title? In any case, title or no title, a French businessman was if possible less newsworthy than a Scottish landowner). All this made Princess Amy's match with a real live prince, admittedly European, but a genuine prince for all that, shine yet more brightly.

What was more, Princess Amy, little (she was 5' 3"), unpretentious (well, why not?), stay-at-home (she had no job that anyone could remember) Princess Cinderella-Amy, had captured a prince who could by a little stretching of the imagination be described as the richest young man in Europe. The fact that Prince Ferdinand, being thirty-three, was also a Prince with a Past, was almost too much joy.

No wonder that AMY MEANS I LOVE YOU, according to one enterprising if inaccurate newspaper headline, and a lot of enterprising if inaccurate T-shirts and buttons subsequently. (Curiously enough, it was the combination of Amy's blameless past and her poverty, together with Ferdinand's blameworthy one and his wealth, which had suggested the match to certain ageing royal relations in the first place; thereafter at various Royal Family gatherings and other weddings, a certain amount of discreet promotion had taken place.)

Lamb sighed and fingered the AMY button on her own brightly coloured handknit jersey. Beagle had described wearing the button as a cynical gesture when he pulled the jersey quite roughly over her head that famous night, the night she had temporarily decided not to remember.

'But I do love Amy,' Lamb had protested, 'I love her in my own way for what she's going to do for us—'

'Us?' queried Beagle, touching her; he was delighted and she thought surprised to find that she was naked under the thick garishly patterned wool.

'Us. Innocent Rights.'

'I love her in my own way for what I'm going to do to her – no, that's a joke, Lambkin. Believe it or not I've loved little Amy from a respectful distance for years.'

Monkey had finished speaking. He picked up the *Evening Standard* and turned to the City pages.

'As a matter of principle, I don't think she's innocent and nor does Pussy here.' It was quite unexpected for Tom to speak like this. He did not generally say much at meetings, having been introduced comparatively recently by Beagle.

Pussy was a distinctly large middle-aged woman. Her code name was actually Cat, but they had all given in lately and called her Pussy since she insisted that she preferred it. Certainly 'Pussy', with its comfortable overtones of fireside and hearth, suited her appearance. That meant that Beagle's friend, introduced to them as Tom, had been able to adopt the code name of Cat. Except that he had, slightly humorously, announced that if the previous Cat was a Pussy, he was undeniably a Tomcat. So that Tom was how he was generally known.

'No real names, if you please,' Monkey had put in on this occasion. 'Sorry to be tiresome but if Tom's your real name—'

'Oh but it's not,' replied Tom blandly, 'just a *nom de guerre*.'

'All the same, I believe Beagle did call you Tom.' In his charming way Monkey could be very persistent.

'Cut it out, Monkey.' Beagle used the slightly crude tone he tended to adopt towards Monkey as if determined, however pointlessly, to shake him from his chairman-of-the-board composure. 'Supposing we say that Tom's real name is double-barrelled? Will that satisfy you? And let's say his Christian name is hyphenated. Will that do?'

'Hyphenated as in Tom-Cat. But not actually Tom-Cat, of course.' Tom smiled with a charm equal to Monkey's own.

Now Lamb turned her attention back to the argument concerning the innocence or otherwise of Princess Amy. This particular argument had occurred once previously (before Tom joined them). Lamb wondered what Monkey felt about the subject being thrashed out all over again, especially since time was on this occasion short. And they had to decide on the next meeting before they parted.

Of course they had all discussed the subject of Amy herself, discussed it very thoroughly at the first of their regular meetings. It was the other middle-aged woman in their group, the one known as Chicken, who raised it. (And Chicken did have something suitably scrawny about her appearance: even if, in view of her age, Hen might have been even more appropriate.)

Lamb knew more about Chicken than she knew for example about Tom. Something in Chicken's manner, a mixture of diffidence in the details of everyday life and confidence when on her own subject, reminded Lamb of one of her teachers at school. And sure enough, Chicken had revealed herself to be a retired teacher, if from a very different kind of school from the one Lamb had attended. What a thoroughly nice woman, what a reliable person, that would be the first reaction of most people to Chicken. As it had been to Lamb's teacher, known as Miss Ursula. Yet Miss Ursula had contained something oddly desperate inside her outward shell of responsibility; witness the fact that she had got into the papers for assaulting the woman with whom she lived not many years after Lamb left school. Was there then something desperate struggling inside pleasant, slightly didactic Chicken?

'Of course some people would reckon us *all* to be desperate, especially since—' But once again Lamb stopped herself thinking along those dangerous lines. Instead she cast her mind back to the previous argument about Princess Amy. Monkey had been cheerfully patient with them all, although Lamb suspected that he had intended to bring in an 'innocent' verdict all along. Chicken had delivered herself of a well-turned little historical lecture on the attitude of the British Royal Family to animals. In the course of it, she mentioned King Charles II: 'a lover, as we know, of spaniels.'

Beagle interrupted: 'And a few other things too, ho ho.' That had mercifully leavened the serious atmosphere – and equally mercifully, cut Chicken short.

Without Tom, Pussy had merely clicked her tongue over a Press story, unproved, that Princess Amy had commissioned a coat of rare white Arctic fox. Other than muttering: 'She may be innocent but she's a spoiled brat,' she had not played much part in the discussion.

It was Fox, who for all his bonhomie, had proved quite persistent in his personal condemnation of she whom he termed 'our little Royal Madam'; until Monkey cozened him out of it.

Lamb had said little or nothing on that occasion. So that now she thought she would come to the aid of Monkey.

'After all she's never hunted; Princess Amy.'

'And she loves dogs. How sweet. She loves all animals. Even sweeter. We *know* all that, Lamb.' Tom was becoming uncharacteristically vehement. 'But surely you realize that a princess is more than just a nice little girl. She's a *symbol*, Lamb, ever heard of a symbol? And a symbol, Lamb, is *never* innocent. Lamb felt quite alarmed by Tom's expression: why was he looking at her in that particular way? Lamb was increasingly frightened by Tom, even if he was Beagle's friend.

'This is all quite unnecessary, Tom.' It was remarkable how Monkey could pull a meeting to order, even by a gesture like putting a *Standard* beneath his arm, even a meeting as weirdly placed as this one. 'I merely mentioned Princess Amy's innocence in the context of the fact that we have to be careful, extra careful, not actually to harm her. Or harm anyone for that matter. It would hardly do for us, my dear Tom, who oppose all violence and mean to say so publicly in our own way, to be accused of any form of real violence ourselves. It's especially important in view of the radical nature of The Plan, critical in fact . . . But we've been through all that, haven't we? After all we're not *petrol*-bombers!' exclaimed Monkey in a voice of disgust although the subject of petrol-bombing had not actually been raised. 'So that the general question of Princess Amy's innocence is surely irrelevant.'

Monkey stood up. 'This is my stop.'

The Tube train shuddered slightly as it came into the station.

'Next week same time but on the Northern Line between Golders Green and Leicester Square. It's a good long line; we can use it right down to Kennington if necessary. Usual procedure for joining each other. I'll get on the train at Golders Green station. One stop each in reverse alphabetical order this time which starts with you, Tom, at Hampstead and ends with Beagle at Euston. Watch for me in the last carriage as the train enters the station. We'll work down if we have to, once we're all gathered. Follow my lead. When I judge we're safe, I'll open my *Standard* at the City pages.'

'What about Mornington Crescent?' questioned Fox plaintively; he was studying his Tube map. 'I see I'm to get on at Mornington Crescent—'

Monkey smiled at him. 'Follow the map, my dear Fox, that's all.'

'Actually, I get on at Mornington Crescent,' remarked Chicken to no one in particular. As so often with Chicken, she sounded politely superior.

The Tube doors slid open.

In stately fashion Monkey descended from the train. The others watched him go, a heavily built man in a dark-grey pin-stripe; the sort of man you would not be surprised to see wearing a bowler or at least carrying a furled umbrella. But Monkey had never so far carried an umbrella since the presence of an umbrella was the emergency signal to abandon the meeting. As for the bowler, that was the final signal for the disbanding of the group.

The others watched him go and remained silent. It was against the rules for anyone to speak to anyone else once the meeting was over, except for Chicken and Pussy, who used their agreed cover as a couple of middle-aged ladies to continue to chat.

In this way it was not breaking the rules, only breaking the spirit of them, for Pussy to remark aloud to Chicken in a small defiant voice: 'I still think I'm right. Of course she's guilty. Youth is simply no excuse.'

2

No One to Blame
but Herself

PRINCESS: WEDDING SCARE: Jemima Shore was relieved to find that headline in the *Standard* which she bought at Tottenham Court Road Tube station. She did not bother to read any further. Another made-up tale about these tiresome nuptials. All the headline meant to Jemima was that the story, her story, was not yet out.

For Jemima Shore Investigator had just been sacked by Megalith Television. That was the plain truth of the matter, however much lawyers, spokespersons and purveyors of official statements might attempt later to wrap it up, for one reason or another. Undoubtedly Jemima Shore, the star reporter of Megalith, was News (much as Princess Amy getting married was News). Television companies like Megalith were also on the whole News, especially when enjoyable things were taking place, like management coups, or the arrival of so-called hard-faced businessmen and the abrupt disappearance of household names from the company's employment – household faces might be a better phrase under the circumstances. The combination was liable to prove irresistible to the Press: thus Jemima was under no illusions but that her peremptory dismissal would make the headlines when it emerged.

By the time the train reached Holland Park station, however, Jemima was wondering just why she had been relieved not to find the story in the *Standard* lunchtime edition. It was after all merely postponing the evil hour. The story had to come out sooner or later. So she bought the late edition from the wooden booth outside the station just to show that she could face it, whatever it contained; it also occurred to her that her flat in Holland Park Mansions might by now be ringed by Press and though that too had to be faced, it was just as well to be warned.

PRINCESS: WEDDING SCARE had now been moved to second place in the *Standard* but there was still no sign of the headline she expected. What form would it take? Could she expect something as mild as JEMIMA QUITS? Unlikely. Fleet Street had its sources inside Megalith as well as everywhere else. TV STAR 'SACKED' was the best she could hope for, the inverted commas round the word 'sacked' being a delicate protection against the possibility of Jemima suing them just in case the story was not true.

But the story *was* true. Jemima Shore spared a wry thought for Cy Fredericks, the recently departed Chairman of Megalith Television. O Cy, O Tempora, O Mores . . . O Cy, O Cy's mores which were not always absolutely open to ruthless inspection. Yet in spite of this, Jemima could not rid herself of a certain fondness for her former Chairman, despite the manner of his abrupt departure from the board which had led indirectly to her own dismissal. It was a dismissal brought about directly by Jemima's public declarations of loyalty for Cy. In short, as the hard-faced businessman had pointed out, more in sorrow than in anger (for he had studied Jemima's ratings on the eve of the interview) Jemima had no one to blame but herself.

One way and another, Jemima was inclined to agree with that verdict. Why on earth had she agreed to speak up for Cy – at his own urgent request – without paying more attention to the dark, and not-so-dark hints dropped by his knowledgeable secretary Miss Lewis on the subject of Cy's future plans? She had even told the board that she would not continue to work for Megalith if Cy was ousted, believing Cy when he assured her that this was purely a formality, and would enable him to defeat the powers of hard-faced darkness threatening him, without delay.

And now where were Cy Fredericks and Jemima Shore respectively? Cy Fredericks was somewhere in America with an enormous golden handshake to arm him in a future life which turned out to be remarkably well organized in advance, considering the apparent suddenness of his fall at Megalith. Jemima Shore was trudging back from the Tube to her flat in Holland Park Mansions (dashing white Mercedes sports car, like Megalith, a thing of the past, because, in some mysterious way, like everything else it turned out to belong *to* Megalith). Redundancy payment if any was certain to be the subject of long, long argument between Megalith's lawyers and her own, just supposing she could afford such a thing. In short, Jemima Shore, like a good many of the rest of England, was out of a job.

She turned to the inside page of the *Standard*. Yes, it had to be the day when she read about something else she had been dreading, dreading proudly in silence for several weeks. She found herself gazing at a wedding photograph. But this was no royal wedding, no bride in white tulle and diamonds on the arm of a chocolate soldier in Ruritanian uniform. Where the groom was concerned, Jemima Shore was gazing into the face of a man she knew, no newspaper creation, in fact until recently had known very well indeed.

'I wonder what happened to his spectacles? He must be wearing contact lenses,' she thought irrelevantly.

The bridegroom was one Cass Brinsley, a barrister who had been Jemima's steady lover for a period not long enough in her opinion, too long in his. The bride, who was called Flora Hereford, was also a barrister and had once been a pupil in Cass Brinsley's chambers. Jemima angrily reflected that Flora Hereford, wearing a dark high-necked dress with a small white collar, looked *extremely* pleased with herself. As well she might. After all, she'd been after Cass for years. And now she'd got him.

LAWFUL MATRIMONY ran the witty caption under the happy couple. Really, the Press these days and their headlines; what with PRINCESS: WEDDING SCARE almost daily, and now this . . . Furthermore: 'What a dull dress to wear at your wedding! I wouldn't dream of wearing anything quite so lacking in style as that,' was Jemima's next uncharitable thought. And then something most unpalatable occurred to her: 'How on earth would I know? I've never been married.'

Immediately after thinking this, in spite of herself, Jemima found a wave of horrible emotion sweeping over her as she walked down the broad silent street, still clutching the paper folded back at the fatal photograph.

Unhappiness? Yes, perhaps. Jealousy? Yes, definitely.

Oh Cass, thought Jemima, Cass, you should have waited. At which point the honest unpalatable voice spoke again in her ear: but he did wait, didn't he? He waited for months, almost a whole year after his declaration in the direction of marriage, and what did you do? You wouldn't say yes, you wouldn't say no. Cass's very own words.

It was only after that that Flora Hereford got him. That one-off programme about child-brides in Sri Lanka, the trip he begged you not to make – 'not *another* eight-week stint without a telephone call' – she could hear Cass's voice now, and her own defensive reply: 'Is it my fault if you're always out when I'm in?' 'But I'm always in while you're away,' retorted Cass grimly. Added to which the programme had never even been shown, concluded Jemima ruefully, and now it never will be. Ah well, no one to blame but myself.

Jemima Shore decided that these were definitely the most depressing words in the English language. As they resounded in her ears, she took another peek at the photograph, as a result of which honesty once more made her admit that Flora Hereford was really a very pretty girl wearing rather an elegant dress; she was also several years younger than Jemima.

No one to blame but herself. She had a ghastly feeling that this was turning out to be what Cherry, Jemima's former aide at Megalith, a nubile but tearful lady, would term a crying situation. Was she going to manage to get up the stairs and into the flat before the gathering tears flowed? Jemima reached the flat. As she put her key in the lock, she could hear the telephone ringing.

For one wild moment – it was something to do with the sheer unreality of *that* photograph – she thought: 'Cass!'

Midnight, Jemima's sleek muscular black cat, a smaller version of a leopard, purred raucously at her ankle. In attempting to reach the telephone, Jemima stumbled over Midnight who squawked pathetically and then knocked over a vase of flowers left by Mrs Bancroft, her cleaning lady, to cheer her up.

The telephone stopped just as she reached it. At which point Jemima Shore finally burst into tears. Midnight had just forgiven her, in token of which he leapt heavily on to her lap, claws out, when the telephone rang again. It was Cherry, speaking from Megalith. Jemima gulped as she answered.

'Jemima, you're *crying!*' Momentarily Cherry spoke in a voice of astonishment that anyone bar herself could dissolve into hopeless tears; above all, that legend of invulnerability, Jemima Shore. Then, being a person of much good sense when not in floods of tears, Cherry reverted to her usual brisk tone: 'Good news and bad news. Which do you want first?'

Jemima gave another gulp.

'All right, here comes the bad news, and it's not all that bad, because it's what you expected. The story is out about you being given the push, this place is like a madhouse, telephones never stop ringing, etc., etc. You can imagine it all for yourself, general flap on about what you will say, and as to that, you can expect the hounds of Fleet Street baying at your door any moment, I fear.'

'Thanks for the warning, Cherry. You're a brick, as usual. I'll call you when—'

'Don't you want to hear the good news? Here it comes anyway. You know the Royal Wedding? How could you not know the Royal Wedding? How could any of us not know the Royal Wedding? Well, whatever you may feel about the Royal Wedding, it's an ill wind, because Television United States, no less, TUS, that is, are doing a special on it, imagine that, a whole special on our very own British royal nuptials, and they want you to be the anchor person. One of the anchor people. Rick Vancy will be the other.'

'And you call this good news?' enquired Jemima in a cool voice from which tears had however noticeably departed.

'Jemima, think of it! Dollars, delights, coverage, work, and *Rick Vancy*. Don't you *adore* Rick Vancy? If not, pass him on—'

'What interests me far more than Rick Vancy, and he interests me only mildly, is *why* TUS is making a special on the Royal Wedding. Any clues?'

'Oh, I think they imagine there's going to be an incident, you know what Americans are like. An assassination or something like that,' said Cherry airily, 'nothing serious, nothing to bother you.'

'Cherry, what on earth gave you that idea?'

'Only that the man I spoke to, some London-based chap with a boyishly enthusiastic voice, kept asking if you had a cool head and could guarantee to keep that same head in a crisis.'

Jemima burst out laughing. 'Really, Americans! They are absurd. The idea of anyone, anyone at all, wanting to assassinate poor little Princess Amy, or even the chocolate soldier, unless some aggrieved husband takes a pot-shot. I mean, it's a wedding, don't they realize that? Just a wedding, a perfectly ordinary wedding, dolled up in fancy clothes, dolled up in its details mainly by the Press. After all, we've had two of them, royal style, recently, without any trouble at all. Weddings! Really!'

'Mmm, weddings. On the subject of weddings—'

'It's all right, Cherry, I saw. Nice photograph. Nice girl.'

'She has bad legs,' said Cherry loyally. 'Now getting back to the other much more important wedding, Jemima, I really think—'

'No, Cherry, definitely no. I'm going to have a rest period, a long, long, rest period. Then I'll probably become a probation officer, if they'll have me, and end up Dame Jemima, deeply worthy, with her wicked past in television long ago forgotten. Look, forgive me, we'll talk, there's someone at the door. Pressing the bell *and* banging, by the sound of it.'

Actually, there were three people at the door. One was pressing the bell, one was banging and one was leaning so eagerly forward that he fell into the room as Jemima opened it. All three were male. All three were smiling. Jemima took a deep breath.

Then the telephone began to ring again. More to avoid talking to her three new knights than for any more positive reason, Jemima picked it up. The voice was, in Cherry's phrase, boyishly enthusiastic. The accent was American. The voice had been talking for a few minutes with Jemima making automatic responses, as she wondered exactly how much whisky she (a non-whisky drinker) had in the flat for this particular Press emergency, when she heard the words: 'exclusive interview'.

'Why me?' Jemima, once again acting automatically, did not repeat the words 'Cumberland Palace' to the waiting ears of the knights of the Press. What she did say was: 'Fifty-five minutes. That's a hell of a long time for anyone, let alone . . .'

More enthusiastic boyish confidences. Then: 'Both of them?' Jemima paused. 'Just her might be better. Or one at a time. It *is* exclusive? Perhaps you'll tell me just how you worked this magic when we meet.'

Some time later as Jemima poured the last drops of the whisky into the glasses of her knights, now installed quite cosily in her flat, with no sign of leaving, she was able to remark quite innocently: 'As for myself, I think

I'll open a bottle of champagne. If there's one in the fridge. No, I'll keep the one you kindly brought for another day, when it's cold, thank you very much . . . After all, I really do have something to celebrate, don't I? . . . No, not *freedom* exactly, more like a new life. I'm working on the Royal Wedding. For TUS. With Rick Vancy. Didn't you know? Well, of course I had to keep it absolutely quiet from Megalith. This is all strictly off the record, I need hardly say, please keep it to yourselves, at any rate till the public announcement. It would be so embarrassing if it leaked out. You will promise I won't read all about it in the papers tomorrow morning?'

There *was* some cold champagne in the fridge. After the first knight had opened it with a flourish, Jemima sat sipping it with a most innocent expression on her face. It crossed the mind of the second knight that her expression was in fact not unlike that of the elegant black cat purring loudly on her lap. The third knight was busy wondering how soon he could get away and telephone his paper from the call box he had noticed at the corner of the street.

He tried to imagine the headline.

ROYAL WEDDING SENSATION? Yes, why not?

3

Amy Means Trouble

Princess Amy, breakfasting in bed at Cumberland Palace, read the headline ROYAL WEDDING SENSATION with an agreeable quickening of interest and was correspondingly annoyed to discover that the story actually concerned rival television companies.

She pouted. When she was alone Princess Amy's pouts made her look sulky if sensual; her full lower lip extended and drooped, and her nostrils – perhaps already a little too wide – flared. In public, however, Princess Amy had quickly learnt how to transform 'the pout' into something not so much sulky as sweetly disappointed, and thus rather delightful.

The Princess was wearing a short cotton nightdress in the form of a man's shirt, trimmed with white lace. The nightdress itself was her favourite colour, known to the Press as Amy Blue ('Amy Loves Blue – and so will you' promised one feature in a woman's magazine). In fact the colour was nearer to turquoise or even green. The open front of the nightshirt revealed Amy's surprisingly large and full breasts – surprising, that is, only because they did not accord with the girlish image the Press were busy imposing upon her, and thus even when discreetly covered up by day or safely moulded in evening dress, generally took observers by surprise.

The rest of the bedroom, including the narrow wooden four-poster in which Amy herself lay, was decorated in shades of the same colour, something with which even Princess Amy's healthy twenty-two-year-old complexion found it difficult to contend. On the walls, a set of watercolours in oval frames showed a series of eighteenth-century princesses – Amy's relations – in white muslin and blue sashes. Their costumes acted as an unintentional reminder of how much more flattering this kind of garb was to a young girl than a turquoise nightshirt.

There was a quick low knock at the door and a dark-haired girl who looked to be some years older than Amy, poked her head round the door. The Princess dropped the paper and gave a shriek.

'Ione, don't tell me you're here already – what on earth's the time?'

'Good morning, Ma'am. No, it's early, honestly it is, I thought I'd get on with all those letters, and then something came up—'

Amy interrupted her with a groan. She had just looked at the pink enamel and gold clock by her bed. 'Oh God, Ione, I *know* I promised to be down. We were going to plough through them together, I *know* we were. For God's sake, don't tell Mama when she wakes up, please, please, please—'

'The Duchess has gone to Plymouth, Ma'am, to the naval base.'

'Goodness gracious: she actually went! No headache?' The Duchess of Cumberland's inability – through sudden 'illness' – to carry out public engagements was celebrated in her family.

'Well, what would *you* do if you were a royal widow with nothing to do?' charitable Princess Harriet had once asked of her more critical younger sister.

'I'd take a lot of lovers,' replied Princess Amy bracingly. 'It's so *wet* of Mama to be boringly faithful to Papa's memory. With the aid of the bottle.'

'Her Royal Highness went by helicopter at six o'clock this morning,' confirmed Ione, to whom all these facts were well known; she spoke without expression. 'From the lawn. I'm surprised you didn't hear it.'

'Of course I didn't hear it, Ione, you coot. A helicopter would have to land on my *bed* at six a.m. to wake me, as you perfectly well know.' Amy stretched so that her breasts half fell out of the open nightshirt; she did not bother to button it up.

'Ione, my angel, my good angel, listen, I've *got* to telephone Ferdel. Then I promise I'll be right with you. All morning.'

'No problem,' said Ione Quentin easily, 'I'll be downstairs.' She turned and stopped. 'There is just one thing, Ma'am –'

But Princess Amy had already turned to the telephone.

'It can wait,' said Ione after a moment, seeing that the Princess was already chattering away.

'ROYAL WEDDING SENSATION', she was reading from the headline of the *Daily Exclusive*. 'And then nothing about *one* at all. Quel drag, Ferdel, yes?'

Her fiancé, corralled for the pre-wedding season in the Eaton Square flat of an absent aunt – an aged foreign Royal who had played some discreet part in the promotion of the marriage – laughed in what he hoped was a sympathetic manner and did not pursue the subject. He was wondering whether Amy had noticed the latest instalment about his previous relationship with Mirabella Prey in the gossip column of the same newspaper.

'Don't forget – AMY MEANS I LOVE YOU,' Amy was saying now as a light farewell, quoting the familiar text of the buttons (although she had quite failed to make Ferdel himself wear one).

'Nothing about one at all.' Prince Ferdinand sighed. That Amy should be so fortunate . . . It was all very well for Amy, cast as the public's favourite virgin (although that certainly wasn't true in private as Ferdel had every reason to know, Amy having admitted to one lover, with Ferdel suspecting at least one other). But Ferdel, aged thirty-three, was somehow expected to exhibit the man-of-the-world allure derived from an exciting past, without actually having lived this past with any specific individuals. These kinds of ridiculously unreal expectations could only be harboured by the British public, he reflected mournfully.

Ferdel sighed again and thought of Mirabella Prey. *Hélas.* He would miss her. That is to say, he would miss the nights, all of them. He certainly would not miss the days, hardly any of them. No one could possibly want to spend their days with Mirabella Prey, except as a prelude to the nights: Mirabella, with her well-publicized passion for wild animals, Mirabella who was inclined to stock her house with pets some of whose mating habits were even more savagely exotic than those of Mirabella herself.

That confounded cheetah, for example. It was the cheetah which was the peg for this morning's story in the *Daily Exclusive* (generally, but not always accurately, known as the *Clueless*). TROUBLE ROYAL it read. WILL FERDY CHEET-HER? ran the second headline. The writer then went on to enquire with pseudo-innocence whether foreign Prince Ferdinand intended to bestow a second cheetah on his young English bride Princess Amy, following that first cheetah so generously bestowed upon the foreign film star Mirabella Prey, she of the noble passion for the animal kingdom. For most people, however, the headline with its nasty implication of post-marital betrayal on the part of sophisticated Europeans, would be the point of the story. Ferdel hoped that his young English bride had failed to notice the item.

Naturally Princess Amy had noticed it: this was because she read the gossip column of the *Clueless* (as well as those of the *Mail* and *Express*) sedulously each morning. She had done so since her early teens, relying on this method of keeping up with the doings of her friends, much as a stockbroker might turn to the *Financial Times* for the movements of the market. But Ferdel would have been interested to discover that Amy, far from being shocked, was actually in a curious way rather turned on by the Mirabella Prey saga.

That is to say, it was the actress's amorous connection with Ferdel which excited Amy (after all, she had been watching Mirabella Prey's films since she was *so* high, as she put it with a little bubble of malice to Ione, never dreaming that one day . . .) Amy found the actress's public posturings and declared warm love for the animal kingdom, on the contrary, slightly irritating. Where animals were concerned, Amy thought there should be lots of nice ones about, preferably dogs, just as she thought there should be a lot of nice servants about, preferably of dog-like devotion. Towards both dogs and servants, Amy was demonstratively and genuinely affectionate – in private. She just did not think this a proper subject for boasting about in the newspapers.

Here then was Mirabella Prey on the subject of her famous cheetah: 'I'd die for him,' she was quoted as saying, 'I'll never give him up.'

'How fatuous,' thought Amy. (For Amy, unlike most readers of the *Daily Exclusive*, assumed Mirabella Prey was actually talking about the cheetah.)

'I'd certainly never give you up, you silly old dogs. I just don't need to tell the whole world about it.' Princess Amy patted the grizzled snout of one of the two middle-aged cocker spaniels lying huddled beside her bed. 'You darling, darling old doggies.' Happy stirred and snuffled; Boobie did not move. Year ago they had been enthusiastically christened Hapsburg and Bourbon by Amy's historically minded governess, a woman much moved by the thought of Amy's grand European ancestry. In view of Amy's future grand European marriage, it was perhaps just as well that the dogs' original names, like the dynasties themselves, had receded effectively into history.

Sitting, still at breakfast, in the gloomy dining-room of the Eaton Square flat, Prince Ferdinand read to the end of the cheetah story and gave yet another sigh, the third of the morning; where Mirabella was concerned, he had a feeling there might be more sighs to come. Unlike Amy, he picked up the message of the piece – from 'cheet-her' to 'I'll never give him up' – perfectly well. It was bad news, not so much that Mirabella was talking to the Press, something she had never been averse to doing, her career in a manner of speaking demanding it, but that she was now condescending to gossip columnists. Unlike Amy again, Ferdel had never heard of Little Mary, she of the *Daily Exclusive* who was alleged to double as Miss Mouse of the Mousehole column in *Jolly Joke*; but he recognized trouble when he read it.

Trouble. Royal Trouble, to adapt the words of the gossip column's headline. There was more than one kind of royal trouble this morning. Ferdel took a letter from the pocket of his silk dressing-grown and then put it back. Where women were concerned, he decided that he was inclined to suffer from a sense of guilt first thing in the morning, a kind of emotional hangover; it might therefore be better to ponder this particular missive a little later on, say after the first Bloody Mary of the day at noon. Besides, threats were so tiresome, especially threats from women, when Ferdel was precluded from stifling them – the threats, that is – by a well-established method. This consisted of a quick immediate telephone call, a short passionate declaration, a more prolonged passionate embrace at a date to suit both parties, followed by a handsome gift bestowed by Ferdel. By the time this ritual was completed, the subject of the threat was quite forgotten; so that the threatener seldom noticed that Ferdel had not actually succumbed to it.

He could not carry out any of these steps now. Could he not? No, he really could not. Not even the first one? Not even the third one, followed discreetly by the fourth one? No, he really could not. Under the circumstances it might be better to throw the letter away, after the others, and forget about it. Probably Amy was too busy chatting on the telephone to her innumerable English girlfriends to read this diatribe from the so-called Little Mary. Ferdel took the letter out of his pocket and threw it, barely crumpled, into the wastepaper basket. He gave no thought as to what might become of the letter; that would have been as uncharacteristic as wondering who washed up his breakfast things, still standing on the heavily polished table before him.

'Trouble,' said Taplow, the English butler/chauffeur of Ferdel's absent aunt, when he later retrieved the letter from its resting place and flattened it again without difficulty. (It was Taplow who had cleared the Prince's breakfast table and re-polished the heavy table.) 'She's still writing to him. That's the third this week. Horrible, the things she says. I told you there'd be trouble.'

'She's foreign,' commented Mrs Taplow without looking at him. She was polishing the silver, a task which traditionally fell to the butler; but in the case of the Taplows, it had sometimes been commented upon by employers that Mrs Taplow was really the more masculine of the two. Although she referred on occasion briefly to 'Jossie', most people assumed unthinkingly that the Taplows were childless. Certainly Taplow, a big, soft, stately man, had something of the feminine about him; there was thus an impression, only a vague one, but vaguely disquieting, that there was some kind of sex reversal in their relationship.

'A foreign spitfire,' added Mrs Taplow after a pause.

'Spitfires aren't—'

'I was quoting the paper, Kenneth,' Mrs Taplow narrowed her eyes and inspected her handiwork. 'She loves him, that's all. She has a foreign way of putting it.'

'She loves him, does she? God knows why.'

'He's got what it takes. I'm quoting the papers again, Kenneth.' There was something disagreeably coy about her expression. 'Did you read the *Sunday Exclusive*? What *she* said, Mirabella. "All night passion"; that was the story.' Mrs Taplow picked up another fork and jabbed it gently but firmly into the green baize cloth. 'Again and again and again. That's what she said.' Mrs Taplow jabbed the fork in time with her words. Taplow looked away.

'I'm thinking of the security angle, Lizzie, you do appreciate that,' he said after a while, fingering the letter. 'Gossip has never interested me, I can say that with my hand on my heart. You should know that, Lizzie: gossip writers and sneak photographers, I've no time for them.' He paused. 'But security, yes. We have a responsibility here. I've been asked, *we've* been asked, to report anything odd. They're jittery about this wedding, it's obvious. So we have to report anything odd.'

'Is it odd for a woman scorned to write that kind of letter?'

'Well, what do you think, Lizzie?' Taplow abandoned the letter and looked directly at his wife.

'I've never been a woman scorned, Kenneth,' replied Mrs Taplow equably, 'so I wouldn't have the least idea.'

'Well then, look at this now – all this about blood for example. Isn't that odd? If it's not odd, I tell you I certainly find it quite disgusting.'

Mrs Taplow put down her cloth and took the letter. She adjusted the small spectacles on her nose, which had hung round her neck on a cord, low enough to give the impression of a chatelaine's keys.

'This blood to which you're referring is the blood of animals,' she said at last; she sounded very patient. 'Not his blood, Kenneth, but the blood of innocent animals. Innocent animals which have already been slaughtered. She, Mirabella, is not threatening to shed our Prince's blood. It's a matter of fact, Kenneth, that she is not.'

'It is a matter of fact, Lizzie, as you put it, that she is threatening to come and daub him, and anybody near him, including HRH, with buckets of animals' blood, innocent animals' blood or not, that is disgusting, Lizzie, which we have discussed before – in a certain connection—' He stopped.

'It hasn't happened yet.' Ignoring his last remark, Mrs Taplow spoke with an air of unshaken patience.

'I'm telling the police. Before it happens. Yes, I know what that will mean, Lizzie. Believe me, I do. Detectives all over the place. It's bad enough when HRH pays us one of her little visits. I am well aware of all that, Lizzie. And when I drive him, that detective always sitting in the front, making small talk as if it was *normal* him sitting there!' Taplow snorted. 'But then again, they might move him. Have you thought of that?'

'Move him?' For the first time Mrs Taplow sounded a little surprised.

'Move him to CP. There's masses of room at the Palace since the old Duke died. Self-contained flat, etc., etc. No suggestion of impropriety, naturally. The detective who spoke to me was in two minds about the whole thing anyway; thought our Prince might well be better off all along at CP.'

'And how will you explain the fact that you read his letters?'

'I'm going to tell the truth,' replied Taplow loftily. 'Find me that number, Lizzie. I don't trust these professional animal lovers, I don't trust them one inch. A violent lot. Are you going to disagree?'

'And what is that supposed to mean, Kenneth?' enquired Mrs Taplow, her composure restored.

'I was thinking of the Trooping the Colour. And the Opening of Parliament last year. Was that or was it not violent? Talk about blood – there was enough blood about then, the horses' blood, innocent horses, Lizzie.'

'If you're referring to Innoright, Kenneth, as I believe you are, Innoright had nothing whatsoever to do with the Opening of Parliament incident. You know perfectly well that Innoright is non-violent.' Mrs Taplow, with deliberation, drew out a small poster from the drawer beneath the table, on which the word INNORIGHT in red was clearly visible. A variety of animals' faces peered out of the letters, amongst which a tiger and a monkey could be distinguished.

'"Innoright abhors all violence." Do you hear that, Kenneth? And here it is again: "Innoright specifically does not seek to correct the violence which humanity shows towards innocent animals by violent means towards humanity itself, in so far as humanity itself is innocent."'

'Whatever that means, which to me, frankly, is somewhat obscure, give me the number. I'm ringing the police. We are here to serve, Lizzie.'

'We have paid the price for that,' murmured his wife.

But before Taplow could touch the receiver, the telephone began to ring. In spite of the perturbation of moments before, Taplow's voice was automatically grave and gentle as he answered it. 'Yes, Ma'am, I'll put you through to His Highness straight away.' Taplow turned to his wife with a raised eyebrow.

'Trouble?'

'HRH sounded quite hysterical. Unlike her. Maybe *she* got a letter.'

What Princess Amy was in the process of repeating frenziedly to Prince Ferdinand on the telephone was not however on the subject of letters.

'It's disgusting,' she was saying over and over again. 'Disgusting, Ferdel, I can't tell you how disgusting it is.'

'My poor little darling,' began Ferdel once or twice. 'Poor little Amy.'

'No, but it's disgusting. Blood everywhere. Animals' blood! Ugh! It stinks. It's like living in a slaughterhouse.'

'But your guards, my darling, the police, all those detectives—'

'They did it at night from the park side. It wasn't found till Mama set off in her helicopter this morning. They managed to stop her seeing it, thank heaven. They're whitewashing it now.'

'Amy, what does it say?'

'What does it matter what it says?' Amy almost shrieked down the telephone. 'It's just so disgusting. Oh, it's that thing for animals. No, not the usual one, this is another one, INNO-something or other.'

'Ah,' Ferdel breathed a long sigh, which might almost sound like relief.

'Anyway what's it to do with me? I love animals,' Amy went on. She added quite sharply: 'She's not the only one who loves animals you know.' It was the only reference made by either of them to the entry in the morning's gossip column.

It was left to a Chief Superintendent from the Royalty and Diplomatic Protection Department (generally known as the RDPD) to inform Prince Ferdinand later in the day that Innoright's bloody message on the Palace wall had actually read, in a grim parody of the AMY MEANS I LOVE YOU button: AMY MEANS TROUBLE — AND SO DO WE.

4

Underground Plan

The heavy-set man – perhaps something in the City? – who got on the Tube at Hampstead, waited for several stops before he took the evening paper from beneath his arm and glanced casually at the headline. The letters were black and enormous: PALACE OUTRAGE, and then PRINCESS IN DANGER?

'Dreadful!' exclaimed the pleasant-looking woman sitting next to him. She nudged her companion and pointed to the paper's headline, now virtually in her face since the heavy-set man had opened the paper somewhere at the start and was reading it. The respectable-looking woman sounded pleasurably indignant.

'Tch,' went her companion, also a woman, also middle-aged.

The train stopped at Old Street. Some people got out – one woman from the opposite end of the carriage – but the train as a whole was not full. It was that short lull in mid-afternoon before the office workers started scurrying home in their hordes, and after the comparative intensity of the lunchtime movements.

Once the train started again, Monkey turned to the City pages at the back of the evening paper. The meeting had begun, which meant that Chicken and Pussy no longer enjoyed their privilege of talking to each other as though they were friends (in reality Chicken and Pussy had never met until Innoright brought them together and never now met outside 'working hours' for reasons of security).

Tom, who was lounging by the doors, sat down in the empty seat next to Monkey. Beagle, already seated by the small door at the end of the carriage, moved up until he was next to Lamb, who was on the other side of Monkey. Fox came next. Before he moved, Fox had gazed anxiously out of the window at the departing platform, as though worried whether he had missed his proper stop; he also consulted a small paper map of the

Underground and then looked up at the map on the upper side of the carriage, as though comparing the two. Fox sat down with an air of relief.

It was all standard practice. The routine had been laid down several months earlier when this particular cell of the main Innoright Group had been founded – by Monkey, who had hand-picked the members from Innoright protest meetings, studying their record cards for suitable biographical details. In view of the nature of The Plan he wanted a special mixture of daring, practicality and imagination: plus true commitment to the cause that held them together. In theory, of course, any member of Innoright should possess such commitment. But in practice Monkey (a founder of Innoright to which he had privately devoted much of his City-made fortune) discovered that members differed radically in their particular angle of interest; this meant that they also differed radically in what they were prepared to do for Innoright.

Members who were particularly horrified by vivisection for example could not easily be induced to lobby food shops, regarding them as very much secondary objects of attack so long as laboratory conditions remained iniquitous. Other members believed with equal passion that the animals used for scientific research were at least living in conditions over which some control was exerted by law, whereas the lives of battery hens ... But the six people Monkey had picked to be part of his team were all of them more persuaded by the general nature of Innoright's philosophy than by any particular part of it. The innocent should never suffer at the hands of the guilty, guilty in the first place because of their torture of the innocent. In that cause, Monkey's team, he was convinced, would do anything, anything that might be asked of them by Innoright, as represented by Monkey. It was an awe-inspiring thought. It was a good thought. Monkey liked being in control of things.

Because Monkey was in control, it was Monkey who had laid down the necessity for a constantly changing meeting-place so that they could not afterwards be easily identified as knowing each other. To avoid suspicion.

'"Afterwards"?' asked Lamb, 'What do you mean by "afterwards"? I thought we were going to declare ourselves. That was the whole point.'

'Finally, yes. But you don't imagine, my dear Miss Lamb, that there will be no *hue and cry*.' Monkey had a way of putting words in italics with his resonant voice. He looked round and raised an eyebrow. 'We want no eager landlady coming forward with information about our constant meetings, no one afterwards to connect the seven of us. After all, we are sufficiently disparate, are we not, for such a connection not to be immediately suspected.'

They were certainly disparate, in Monkey's phrase. Although the second thing those members picked by Monkey had in common was a certain convenient flexibility of employment, if not actual lack of it, the reasons for this varying considerably with the members' different ages and classes.

The cell had held its first rendezvous at the National Portrait Gallery, gathering on Monkey's instructions by a huge royal portrait (that appealed to his sense of humour). He chose the study of King George VI, Queen Elizabeth and the two young Princesses over a family breakfast table, hung at the head of a staircase, garishly coloured, impossible to miss. On Monkey's instructions also, at this first encounter they divided into plausible groups; that is to say, Lamb, who might have been Monkey's docile daughter, stood close by him; while Chicken and Pussy chatted animatedly to each other.

'Look at Princess Margaret Rose! What a little poppet! To think that now her own children . . .' The words flowed happily.

Beagle, in baggy grey cotton trousers (in spite of the spring cold), loose whitish T-shirt, camouflage jacket, trainer shoes without socks, lounged alone. The trouble with Beagle was that he looked not so much implausible as subtly menacing in the context of the National Portrait Gallery. He even attracted the attention of one of the uniformed attendants who spoke to him.

'I'm unemployed, right? And it's free here, right? Any other questions?' was Beagle's response.

'You're asked not to touch the frames of the pictures,' said the attendant pleasantly. 'That's right,' said a young man with a rather high voice standing next to Beagle, self-importantly. 'There's a lot of history here, you know, and it belongs to everyone.' It was Fox. Beagle glared at him. Lamb, close to Monkey, felt the older man stir angrily.

'Just what we don't want to happen,' he muttered, 'calling attention to us. Beagle mustn't do that. And what Fox said was unnecessary.'

It was then that Lamb came up with the idea of rendezvousing on the Tube, 'where you sit next to absolutely anybody without thinking twice about it,' as she put it and then blushed (although Lamb rarely blushed). She blushed because Beagle looked at her, a hard slightly mocking look. Afterwards Beagle told Lamb that was when he first decided to have her.

'You were so sweet and innocent, Lambkin, so polite. One of these days, Beagle to have a taste of Lamb. That was the resolution.'

At the time Lamb corrected her statement to 'where everybody meets everybody'. And so – after an appreciative hum, hum, a raising of the upper lip and eyebrow from Monkey, the Underground Plan was born.

It proved strangely easy to carry out, given that Lamb's original unguarded remark – 'you sit next to absolutely anybody without thinking twice about it' – was undeniably true about the London Underground system; even if opinions might vary as to who 'absolutely anybody' was. The seven members of the cell were all of them physically common or unremarkable types – which was in fact the third principle on which Monkey had selected them originally.

Beagle for example was, to the outward eye, an apparent loafer of vaguely aggressive demeanour; a prejudiced observer might put him down as unemployed 'and happy with it; the sort who doesn't even want to work'. But there were after all many such travelling by Tube. In essence, Beagle's medium height, his neat features, lightish-brown hair, lightly tanned skin all combined to make him unremarkable: a common type. It was Lamb who knew that the body beneath the T-shirt and baggy trousers was hard, muscular – and scarred.

Pussy on the other hand had an air of silent self-righteousness, the air of one waiting for someone to light up a cigarette in order to ask them to extinguish it, which made her a common enough type too. She was also the mistress of the uninteresting-looking plastic shopping-bag, providing herself with an extraordinary variety of them as the weeks passed; what the logos of the bags had in common was that you could not possibly want to know more about the contents of any bag emblazoned with them. Pussy, although fat, was not so fat that you would remember her for exceptional obesity; just heavy, in the way that some women over a certain age are inclined to spread in the hips and bosom so that the waist is gradually eliminated.

In the same way, Fox, although on the short side, was certainly no dwarf; his lack of height was not even particularly noticeable unless he was standing side by side with a girl, say, Lamb. Slender as Lamb was, she topped Fox by an inch or two. The most noticeable thing about Fox originally had been his habit of bringing his mongrel dog, an aged bulldoggish sort of animal, to Innoright meetings. The hairless dog, with its crushed apologetic face, had made an odd contrast with the neatly dressed young man.

The dog, called Noel – 'for Coward, because as a result of my training, he doesn't get into fights' – had caused some dissension at early Innoright meetings; his continued presence being in the end responsible for the Innoright rule that meetings were, 'without prejudice', for human beings only. This was because some Innoright members had strong views on domestic pets – 'no better than Negro slaves on plantations' – and others equally strong views in the opposite direction. Monkey, while assuring Fox that Noel's presence at meetings had been perfectly acceptable to him personally, had delicately persuaded him to leave Noel behind for the cell meetings also, on grounds of Noel's noticeability.

Tom was vaguely foreign looking – but the foreignness was sufficiently unspecific for him to merge into the vast confluence of youngish foreign looking men on the Underground who might be students or at least carrying students' cards. His complexion was darkish – but it was olive-dark, not brown, and might even be the product of a recent holiday in the sun. Spanish or Portuguese blood? Possibly. Not Asian, at least probably not Asian: Tom was tall. Iranian or an Arab of some sort? Could be. Something Middle Eastern was certainly plausible. In general Tom might have been the kind of actor who plays foreign parts on television, minor characters in established series, never more than half seen or half remembered by the general public. It was the fact that Tom could vary the racial impression which he gave, which had persuaded Monkey to enrol him when he was produced by Beagle (Monkey had had to reject the idea of recruiting a handsome black from East Ham, of Nigerian descent, a founder member of Innoright, because his ethnic origin was too easily identifiable).

As for Monkey, Chicken, Lamb, their particular types, the City gent, the neatly if drably dressed woman of a certain age, the nice girl in her thoroughly Sloane-Ranger clothes, these types reproduced themselves endlessly around them.

'Nothing exceptional about us.' It was Monkey's theme song.

'Except what we're going to do, darling,' murmured Tom.

'No connections between us.' It was Monkey's other constantly reiterated cry.

'Except that we're all members of Innoright.' This time Tom spoke louder.

'Correction. We all *were* members of Innoright. Beagle resigned in protest against current policy, on my instructions. As a matter of fact, Lamb never joined, only went to a couple of meetings and met Beagle. I'm a member, so is Pussy.'

'I was a very early member, a founder member, I think you'll find, unlike Pussy,' put in Chicken in her comfortably firm voice, the voice of the teacher who will not be overlooked in the midst of the class. 'I have consistently voted *against* the amalgamation of Innoright with other groups on the grounds that—'

'Absolutely, my dear Miss, or should I say Mrs, Chicken?' Monkey interrupted her hurriedly; this was no time for that hoary old Innoright issue concerning its links with other groups.

'Absolutely. And Fox here was, like myself, a founder member. But he too has resigned. On my instructions.'

'The treatment of Noel—' began Fox in a mutinous voice; he had been becoming visibly restive during Chicken's speech.

'Provided the perfect excuse,' finished Monkey neatly. 'So you see, Tom, no secrets about it, all carefully worked out, except we don't hand about our membership list in the first place. And you? It's news to me that you are a member. *Are* you a member? Under what name?'

'I vouch for Tom.' Beagle, leaping to Tom's defence again.

At recent meetings these frictions had been stronger than ever, as the date on which the Plan had to be carried out drew closer and could not of its very nature be postponed. And yet, as Lamb said privately to Beagle afterwards, these arguments, these niggling disagreements were ludicrous, really. She wished she could tell Beagle her worry about Tom, the way he kept looking at her and other things. But she had to remember Tom was Beagle's friend.

Instead she said: 'We all want the same thing.'

'Innocent Rights,' said Beagle, and he took the lobe of Lamb's delicate ear in his fingers and gave it a little sharp nip.

This afternoon Monkey was angry. Lamb could tell by the way he sucked down his lower lip.

'What was all that about?' he asked Tom in a low voice, pointing to the headline in the *Standard*, PALACE OUTRAGE (although Tom had actually asked him if he could look up the time of a film – another agreed code).

'It was fun, darling.'

'*Fun*? Fun for who?'

'For us.'

'And the blood? Fun for the animals? You know how careful we are. We simply cannot afford to fall into *their* trap of violence—'

'It wasn't animals' blood. Cool down, Monko.'

'It wasn't *human* blood! Are you crazy?'

'It was paint, Monkey, paint. Oxblood, I think it's called. I'll get you the name if you want to repaint your posh dining-room.'

'Yes,' Beagle chipped in impudently. 'We thought we'd give the little Princess an early wedding present. Anything wrong with that? And advertise our presence, as it were. A trailer for the big show.'

Monkey was silent. Lamb supposed that he did not trust himself to speak. He turned over the page of his newspaper and then turned it back.

'Any luck with the shoes, dear?' Chicken spoke to Pussy in her adopted character, which she was not supposed to do during a meeting.

'Nothing in beige leather at all,' Pussy responded gallantly, scuffling in one of her plastic bags. 'Not a real beige anyway; plenty of cream and canary. I settled for taupe.'

Actually Pussy, like many of the members of Innoright, avoided leather in all its forms and thus her shoe shopping took rather a different form as she searched for synthetic footwear, made in large comfortable sizes for her heavy feet. The avoiding of leather was not however mandatory for members of Innoright (it was not considered in the same light as fur, for example). Monkey's polished shoes looked like leather as did Lamb's; one could not be quite sure about Chicken's classic shoes, possibly patent leather, possibly imitation.

Just as Pussy had not in fact been searching for beige leather, so Pussy was not actually the harmless if slightly fussy woman she appeared to be. Pussy, together with her only child, a daughter called Caro (otherwise known as Otter) had been responsible for some of the most daring night-raids on those boutiques, beauty shops and stores which stocked cosmetics notoriously tested out on animals. This was because Caro-Otter was, or rather had been, a model. But Otter (like her mother) was cunning; she had not advertised her strong views on the protection of animals to her agent, beyond declining gracefully to model fur coats (and that was by now a not uncommon stance among top models). Instead she had seized every opportunity to garner information as to which products were actually 'guilty'.

Then by night with Pussy she had poured super-glue into locks, and sprayed walls with the red Innoright logo with its huge pathetic animals' eyes gazing out of the letter O. Otter and Pussy had a particular taste for paint-stripping the cars of the smart young (male) managing directors of cosmetic firms who dated Otter following a photographic session on behalf of their products. However mother and daughter were also careful to paint-strip women's cars as well; the fact that it was not so emotionally satisfying was, they agreed, no reason to avoid such a necessary task.

But Otter was dead, dead in a car crash, the car driven by one of those smart young executives who was dating Otter and had dined rather too well in the process. (The man himself had survived.) She would have been twenty-two this month – the same age as Princess Amy, something which Pussy occasionally bore in mind when looking at newspaper photographs of nubile Amy, Amy smiling fetchingly into the camera, 5' 3", plump and privileged Amy who was alive while 5' 10" attenuated willowy Otter lay in her grave.

Pussy had become quite ruthless since Otter's death, and her single-handed attack on butchers' shops (including the savaging of an Alsatian which guarded one shop at night) had caused some disquiet among the Innoright Overground Group who had not been consulted.

'Even if Alsatians are incurable meat-eaters, as you know we regard that as human failure,' began the Chairman. 'Besides which, the whole subject of canine re-education towards vegetarianism is in its infancy, and Innoright Overground policy—'

'That Alsatian tore a cat to pieces last week,' said Pussy coldly.

'Yes, but surely using a *knitting-needle*—'

Monkey thought of that conversation now as he gazed at Pussy's broad slightly flushed face. He had been given a free hand to choose his own team by the Innoright Overground, and had thus not mentioned to them that he had chosen the woman who was known as Pussy. He had believed at the time that he could handle her, use her dedication, her madness springing from heartbreak, for the good of the cause. As with Beagle in the National Portrait Gallery, Monkey hoped he had not made a mistake.

Monkey put down the paper again. As though none of the preceding conversation had taken place, Monkey and the others had a series of quick, efficient, half-muttered exchanges on the subject of weaponry and the Lair. Whatever their dissensions, progress was being made. Fox was short and to the point. He announced that he had followed up those mysterious contacts to which he had referred at an earlier meeting, and expected to be able to provide the desired weapons – 'purely symbolic of course,' as he put it – at the appropriate moment.

Monkey, who knew about Fox's background, was not surprised; the others, if they were impressed, tried to hide it.

It was Tom who drew the meeting to a close with a sudden surprising announcement.

'Going to the Press Conference, aren't I, darling? Who's a clever boy, then? The Royal Press Conference, yes, not Number Ten and the Pri-jolly Minister. The Royal Press Conference.'

Beagle smiled sardonically and said nothing. Pussy, Chicken and Fox stared. Lamb shivered. The train was drawing into a station. The doors began to open.

Tom swung on the strap above Monkey's head and was half way out of the doors before anyone dared react.

Tom darted back to pick up a packet he had left – presumably deliberately – on his seat. Impudently he blew a kiss: was it in *my* direction, thought Lamb guiltily.

'Tell you more next week; look for me on telly in the meantime; creating a disturbance, Oxblood paint and all. No, Monko, that's a joke.'

'Circle Line between Paddington and Moorgate,' was all Monkey had time to say before Tom was gone. The stiffness of his tone reminded the others that according to the Underground Plan it was Monkey's right to leave the train first.

5

Sex and Security

'Surely we can't ask her *that*.' Jemima Shore leant over Rick Vancy's shoulder and gazed at the list of questions, neatly typed out under the heading of 'TUS: From the Desk of Richard Vancy.'

'Oh, I guess we can. Kind of late on, when she's relaxed.' Rick Vancy spoke most agreeably. It was his habitual tone, Jemima had noticed. Since his arrival in England, Rick had not lost his temper or raised his voice on a single occasion; indeed, his voice actually got yet more agreeable when times were trying. His appearance was agreeable too: he might even have been English with his fair hair, high narrow bony forehead; an English intellectual, or rather film star playing an English intellectual since, come to think of it, English intellectuals did not actually look like the late and much lamented Leslie Howard in real life.

But Rick Vancy was not English, in spite of vague rumours that his mother had been English and equally vague counter-rumours that it was actually Rick Vancy's first wife who had been English, or that Rick Vancy's first wife, herself American, was now married to an Englishman. There was even a suggestion that Rick Vancy had been to Cambridge – the University; but this rumour, coming as it did from an Oxford man in the shape of Jamie Grand, Jemima put down to his characteristic sense of mischief; the editor of *Literature* was wont to discover alumni of Cambridge University in the most extraordinary places. The real truth, thought Jemima, was that the English were simply unable to accept that anyone could look as 'English' as Rick Vancy undoubtedly did and not have some ancestral connection with the country. It was either a rather touching form of possessiveness or less touching snobbishness.

The fact that Rick Vancy did show a certain degree of Anglicization as time wore on, Jemima attributed to an admirable ability to study his surroundings rather than to youthful experiences or genetic inheritance.

His clothes for example: when Jemima first met Rick (at his suggestion, for a drink in the Palm Court of the Ritz) most of his garments seemed to have been bought in St James's including, improbably, a waistcoat. Rick eyed Jemima's Katherine Hamnett total look speculatively; the next time they met, all traces of St James's were gone and Rick Vancy was wearing something like the masculine equivalent of Jemima's radical chic. The result was that he no longer looked like an American aping an Englishman, but quite as English as anyone else at the Groucho Club (Jemima's suggestion); that is to say, aiming to look American.

'Surely we can't ask her that?' The question to which Jemima was pointing read: 'Your Royal Highness, if you will pardon me saying so, you are a very beautiful young woman. How do you feel about the other very beautiful women with whom your fiancé has been linked in the past?'

Rick furrowed his clear forehead and re-read the question. 'Yeah, I get you. You mean it's sexist,' he said after a pause. 'Have to phrase it round another way.'

'No, you dummy, this is England, not so much sexist as impossible. Bang goes our exclusive interview. We'll be lucky if we get to talk to her dogs if you ask something like that.' For a moment, Jemima looked puzzled. 'Besides, I thought all the questions had to be handed in to the Palace. Rick, for God's sake, you don't mean you put this down on the list. No, I see you didn't. It was going to be a little surprise—'

'I thought this was going to be a fun programme,' groaned Rick, taking out a gold pencil and scoring through the offending question. (Earlier when he had lent the pencil to Jemima, she had noted it had been presented to him for 'exceptional broadcasting services' during the most recent Hostage Crisis.) 'That's what they promised me back in the States. "Richard, have yourself some fun," they said to me, "after Iran, Beirut, the Libya problem, Syria and all the rest of it, you deserve to have yourself some fun." So out goes the sex angle, is that it? Can you be serious? I see you are. So what's left? Security, that's what's left. Out goes sex, in comes security. Not nearly so much fun. Now sex *and* security, that would have been great.'

'I am sure you can have a great deal of fun with the security angle,' suggested Jemima in what she intended to be a tone of gentle mockery.

But Rick responded quite seriously: 'Yeah, that's right. I think I can. If we play it up: the fairy story that turned into a nightmare; correction, for the time being, the fairy story that *may* turn into a nightmare, and then when it does – well, the possibilities are awesome, aren't they?' He leant back and gave an appreciative sigh.

'Mmm. Opium, isn't it? No, not for the people, though I suppose Royalty is the new religion with you guys. Your perfume I meant. Mmm. Listen, I don't anticipate any problems on this one. Happily, I was able to question the Ayatollah Khomeini on security, compared to which

Buckingham Palace, or whichever palace is involved, should present no problem at all.' Rick Vancy, eyes closed, was by now leaning so far back that he was almost touching Jemima.

Privately, Jemima thought that the Palace could probably hold its own with the Ayatollah in its silence over security matters, but that would be for Rick Vancy to find out for himself. She also thought that if Rick Vancy was into perfume-guessing, he might find more problems in that direction too than he anticipated.

Aloud she said: 'Miss Dior actually. The perfume. Opium comes on rather too strong for me.'

'Then I'm going to get you a huge bottle of Opium; to see if I can make you change your mind.' But Rick Vancy leant gracefully forward again as he spoke.

Rick and Jemima attended the Royal Wedding Press Conference attended by two historical researchers hired by TUS; one was English, one was American, both brandishing enormous folders full of genealogical details concerning the happy couple. Rick explained this was because 'we don't want to look cheapskates compared to CBS, NBC, ABC and co. Somebody had the bright idea of hiring a couple of royal biographers, titled ladies, I think, there's a whole crowd of them in your country, they do a family act on this kind of show, but anyhow the supply had run out by the time we got to think of it.'

The conference itself was being held in the large modern Republican Hotel in Plantagenet Square, Mayfair (Rick Vancy thought the combination of names awesome: it took Jemima some time to see why). Cumberland Palace was deemed too small to handle the ravening hordes of Press expected to attend; hence the exclusive nature of Jemima's projected interview with the happy couple at a later date. (Something, she had learned, whose genesis lay in the bridegroom's business interests in the States ... but no one was being too precise about that.) This would, she had been promised, take place in the Palace drawing-room, the Palace garden or whatever area the demands of the English summer dictated.

There was a security check at a large modern desk in the hotel foyer – rather a British check, Jemima felt. Passes were scrutinized and checked against a list, but no serious attempt was made to match passes to faces. After that, the arrangements irresistibly reminded her of some huge children's party, with journalists as clamouring already-spoilt children while sets of presents were handed out. The 'presents' were contained in zipped-up plastic holders stamped in gold with a variety of symbols including coats of arms, bells, flowers and horseshoes, the formality of the heraldry contrasting rather oddly with the rest. Their colour, Jemima noted, was not quite Amy Blue, although the unusual searing turquoise of the plastic indicated that a gallant attempt had been made to match it.

Were these folders actually being presented by Cumberland Palace?

Had Royalty really gone down into the marketplace this time? Jemima wondered. The answer, she discovered, was both yes and no: yes if you considered such *objets d'art* inherently vulgar and demeaning, even to a Press Conference; no if you accepted that a large sum had been paid to the Princess's favourite charity for the honour of manufacturing and distributing them. In short, the holders and their contents were the gift of a rival television station. Since the name of the television station was writ small, and that of the charity writ large, Jemima supposed that the answer to her original question must be no ... She started to leaf through her own folder.

Inside each folder were two thick dossiers on the ancestry of the bride and bridegroom, which looked imposing as well as substantial until a quick glance inside revealed that there was not much here that any quick-witted journalist could not have found out from *Debrett's Peerage* or *Burke's*. TUS's English researcher was a girl in her twenties called Susanna Blanding; her figure was quite plump although the features in the makeup-less face beneath the mass of untidy dark curly hair were in contrast delicate and rather pretty. She was smoking, however, as she entered the room and looked distraught at being asked to stop. Clearly historical research was a nerve-wracking profession.

Jemima watched Susanna as she opened the embossed blue cover; her expression was first apprehensive, then relieved, finally indignant.

'I've covered all of this,' she hissed at the American researcher who was reading the document quite happily. 'In here.' She tapped her own voluminous genealogical documentation.

'Is that so?' The American, a laid-back youth called simply Curt (what on earth were his credentials? Jemima wondered) went on reading.

'There are at least two mistakes on the first page,' went on Susanna Blanding in a louder voice. 'I wouldn't take it all that seriously as a work of reference, if I were you. You might feed in wrong information.'

'Is that so?' repeated Curt; he was almost as gentle in his tone as Rick Vancy. 'Listen to this: the Prince's grandmother was a Russian Grand-duchess who danced with Rasputin and bequeathed jewellery worth four million pounds. The so-called unlucky Rasputin sapphires alone were worth—'

'Great-grandmother,' put in Susanna sharply without any attempt to moderate her tone. 'And the Rasputin story is poppy-cock! What were they supposed to dance? Cossack war dances? As for the unlucky sapphires, in here I point out—'

'Anything you say,' said Curt pacifically, continuing to read. Once or twice he was heard to murmur, 'quite amazing,' which incurred sharp looks from Susanna Blanding.

The other 'presents' were less controversial if more childish: a huge unfolding family tree showing Princess Amy's place in the British Royal

Family. Susanna glowered at it although she could not immediately spot an error beyond an irritated aside: 'That's the *sovereign*'s coat of arms at the top; now you do realize, Curt, that Princess Amy herself has no right—' But by this time a plethora of objects, including a paper-knife with the royal cipher, pencils and biros with more gold symbols stamped on them and even AMY MEANS I LOVE YOU buttons were pouring out of the turquoise plastic. Susanna stuffed them in the pockets of her baggy velvet jacket, worn over a man's striped shirt belted at the waist and a short tight – too tight – dark-grey skirt. That left her free to vet the sheaf of large glossy photographs provided including one of the bridal coach.

'Would you say that was the Scottish State Coach?' she asked anxiously, enmity temporarily forgotten, 'because if not—' Curt was however busy pinning on his AMY MEANS I LOVE YOU button – special blue and gold version, with a photograph of the Princess, smiling rather shyly, taken several years back, crowning the message. He evidently had no views on this important question, and Susanna sank back again in renewed disgust.

At the Press Conference itself, it was the topic of sex which reared its ugly head first before that of security. A French reporter, interrupting details of arrangements for the Great Day itself with great politeness, enquired of the Palace spokesman whether Mademoiselle Mirabella Prey would be at the wedding breakfast. Major Pat Smylie-Porter, as opening royal bat, was however more than equal to this query. (Jemima suspected that the Major might prove a cool customer when she noticed that he sported an AMY MEANS I LOVE YOU button in the lapel of his dark-grey suit instead of the expected carnation.) He bent on the questioner – a small dark man in neat denims with a large handbag over his shoulder – a benevolent gaze. Jemima was reminded of a wartime story in which an English officer put in charge of a platoon of Jewish refugee intellectuals, anxious to fight for their adopted country, announced that he anticipated no problems 'since he was used to native troops'.

'A very private affair, the wedding breakfast,' beamed the Major. 'So private I haven't even seen the list m'self. No idea who's on it, no idea at all. But I can tell you what they're going to eat—' He shuffled through a sheaf of papers. 'Princess Chicken, is that right?' The Major chuckled, 'Sounds a bit odd, I must admit. Now where are we? Here we are. *Poulet à la Princesse*! Sounds better in French, doesn't it. Even my French. Now you're going to ask me for the recipe, and I'm afraid I can't tell you that either.' So the Major bumbled purposefully on, as though pinpointing possible trouble spots, darting little glances the while from beneath bushy eyebrows, which were very black compared to his silvered hair. In this way he was possibly more prepared than the rest of the restlessly heterogeneous assembly for the sudden irruption of a loud and strident voice talking very fast.

There was a general stir. Susanna Blanding turned and glared: she looked quite shocked at this apparent affront to majesty. Even Curt sat up a little straighter in his chair. A few moments later, Susanna, handing her clipboard to Jemima, left, as though such a distressing intervention had made a quick puff at a cigarette absolutely essential. On return, she certainly reeked of smoke.

'Talking of Princess Chicken,' shouted the questioner from somewhere on the far side of the large room. 'What about the Animal Rights demo outside Cumberland Palace the other day? Have there been any further threats from Innoright or any other Animal Rights group? Aren't you worried about security? What happens if—'

The heckler – for that was the impression these rapid questions gave – was cut short by something, or else the other journalists simply took the opportunity to join in. Jemima had a brief glimpse of him: darkish, possibly Arab she thought. Then a host of questions merged into a babble, in which the words 'security', 'incident', 'precautions' could be discerned. Jemima was just wondering wryly how the imperturbable Major would deal with this one – riot of native troops? – when his voice boomed out extremely loudly across the tumult. He had used the simple expedient of turning his microphone to its ultimate pitch.

'Gentlemen, I beg your pardon, ladies, ladies, gentlemen, one question at a time please. Now the gentleman there, would you wait for the microphone please, and repeat the question?'

A young woman, nicely but plainly dressed, crossed the platform and whispered in the Major's ear. She looked rather strained, but the Major merely beamed again; the expression of sheer good humour on his face made it difficult to believe the irruption had ever taken place.

'Good news,' he said. 'Their Royal Highnesses are on their way from the Palace. So we won't have time for very many more unprepared questions. I'm sure you'd all far rather talk to them than an old buffer like me,' he chuckled again and then pointed to where a movable microphone was now installed. This time Jemima had a better view of the questioner: no, not an Arab; in fact his face was vaguely familiar and she wondered if she had seen him recently on television, or had she interviewed him for her programme on child brides? He had the kind of face which was familiar without being memorable.

'Jean-Pierre Schwarz-Albert,' stated the questioner giving the name of a foreign news agency and now speaking quite slowly in a voice without a trace of an accent. 'In view of the animal rights slogan painted on the walls of Cumberland Palace by Innoright,' he emphasized the word, then repeated it, 'Innoright, I wondered what arrangements the Palace was making if there was some form of incident or demonstration on the route?'

'Now I'm sure you won't expect me to give you the full security arrangements made by our excellent police,' replied the Major; he glanced at a piece of paper handed to him by the neatly dressed girl. 'As to the painting, that was an isolated incident of which there will be no repetition. Security has been stepped up at the Palace. Next question—'

As the next questioner – 'Judith Spandau, Michigan TV' – began to speak, also on the subject of security, Jemima continued to gaze curiously at Jean-Pierre Schwarz-Albert. He in turn was gazing fixedly at the stage; there was something rather frightening about the intensity of his expression; Jemima shivered. Then she realized that Rick Vancy was nudging her.

'Hey listen, what we want to know is when do they tell us?' he whispered, 'will they bring it to us live? If not, exactly when do we get the news?'

'What news?' Jemima whispered back.

'An assassination attempt or whatever. Will we get full coverage?'

Jemima realized that it was her duty to her transatlantic employers to ask some form of question on this subject. She for one definitely did not expect there to be an assassination attempt, or any other kind of violence shown towards the bridal couple – this was Britain for God's sake, and Princess Amy was scarcely in the position of an American President – but she could see that her conviction was not shared by the rest of her colleagues. Question after question referred to 'live pictures' of something euphemistically described as 'an unexpected incident'. What was actually being asked of course was whether live pictures would be shown of dead people . . .

'Ask him whether Prince Ferdinand will wear a bullet-proof waistcoat in the open landau,' hissed Rick Vancy.

'What about poor little Amy?' countered Jemima. 'Is she going to be left out? Surely I should ask first whether she's going to wear a bullet-proof bra?'

Rick Vancy frowned. 'I guess that's rather tacky, isn't it?'

'I hear they're going to video any kind of rough stuff and show it later when the high-ups have okayed it,' commented Rick's neighbour, a fellow American.

'That could be the next month or *year*, where this bunch is concerned,' groaned Rick.

Jemima stood up. She caught the eye of the neatly dressed girl who had just returned to the platform and realized from her briefing that this was the Princess's lady-in-waiting, Ione Quentin, to whom she had spoken on the telephone about her interview. She had not recognized her. Susanna Blanding and Ione Quentin, both equally English looking, represented two opposing but eternal types of English womanhood: the one inconspicuous through elegance, the other conspicuous through lack of it. Yet in features they were not dissimilar. Ione Quentin for her part looked relieved at seeing a face she recognized, an *English* face, the face of a person guaranteed not to ask awkward questions; she directed the Major's attention in the direction of Jemima.

'Jemima Shore, Television United States—' she began. But it was too late. A further emissary, this time male, equally neatly dressed, had joined the couple on the platform and was in his turn whispering in the Major's ear.

'I am so sorry Miss Shore, I am so sorry ladies and gentlemen,' exclaimed the Major, giving Jemima a special beam as he picked up his sheaf of notes, 'but their Royal Highnesses are actually here two minutes early. That's what really efficient security does for you, it whizzes you through our dreadful London traffic. I am sure under the circumstances—'

Jemima, privately rather relieved (after all she had an exclusive interview coming), sat down.

There was a general stir as the royal couple were introduced on to the platform, preceded by a couple of security men solemnly carrying two velvet chairs upholstered in Princess Amy blue. All present stood up, or in the case of cameramen snapped furiously away, jockeying furiously for position at one and the same time. In the hubbub a disturbance on the far side of the room passed quite unnoticed.

No one, naturally, paid much attention to the one journalist who wanted to leave the room just as the royal couple were entering it. Such a bizarre course of behaviour – to attend the Major's briefing and then miss the conference proper – was hardly believable. The cliché, 'all eyes were fixed on the bride', was for once fully justified, as the world's Press goggled happily at Princess Amy in her – thank Heaven – turquoise-blue dress, and scribbled away with equal delight at the sight of the enormous glittering ring displayed on the small plump white hand which rested on her fiancé's discreetly dark-blue sleeve. So that afterwards it was remarkably difficult to piece together when it was that the man who called himself Jean-Pierre Schwarz-Albert had left the conference hall.

Had he taken the opportunity of the royal couple's entrance to elbow his way through the throng? Or had it been slightly later? When Princess Amy was answering questions? (In that attractively modest manner, head drooping slightly, which made her actual voice, clear, upper class, even slightly bossy in timbre, always come as a slight surprise.) His neighbour at the briefing spoke of a note being handed to him, a note which presumably caused him to leave; but in the excitement of the royal occasion, could not be precise as to when the note had been received. Afterwards, when the exact moment became of some import, those who had to trace Schwarz-Albert's movements wearily found that it was like questioning people about an incident which had occurred at the same time as the winning goal in the World Cup. Even if someone was prepared to come up with an answer, you could never be quite sure it was reliable.

'You'd think they were doing it on purpose,' moaned Detective Superintendent Portsmouth of Central Squad, otherwise known as Pompey of the Yard, petulantly, to his youthful-looking assistant Detective Sergeant Vaillant. But Vaillant, knowing better than to speak when his superior was in this kind of mood, merely nodded his head sympathetically and looked as sage as he judged permissible under the circumstances.

6

Frightening People

The death of Jean-Pierre Schwarz-Albert, journalist, although a subject of much interest to Detective Superintendent Portsmouth, received curiously little immediate attention in the Press and was not even mentioned on the television news. Perhaps there was something odd about this; or perhaps on the other hand the lack of interest, like the general indifference at the time, was simply due to the enormous attention lavished on the Press Conference given by Prince Ferdinand and Princess Amy.

Certainly the latter event was generally rated – by the media at least – a resounding success. The headline in the *Daily Exclusive* the next morning summed it up very fairly: AMY MEANS WE ALL LOVE YOU. Or as Rick Vancy confided happily to Jemima over a late lunch at Le Caprice: 'She's a real star, that girl. How do they get to train them?'

'The Royals? I don't think they do. It's the luck of the draw. Some of them are just much better at it than others. I agree with you that little Amy is quite brilliant. Ferdy's performance was a bit lacklustre, I thought. Do you notice the way he always looks as if he'd had a very late night?'

Rick considered the point. 'No, I went for that. Same as I liked the bags under his eyes; pointed up her performance. She the fresh young lamb; he the world-weary old wolf. Maybe they planned it that way.'

'Maybe they did,' agreed Jemima cautiously, sipping the champagne with which Rick had declared that they should launch their official collaboration.

About the same time, in Cumberland Palace, however, the fresh young lamb was enquiring the whereabouts of the world-weary old wolf with more than a little petulance; Rick Vancy might have been surprised at the abrasiveness with which Princess Amy was questioning Ione Quentin about the Prince's message.

Princess Amy was drinking Malvern water (unlike Jemima Shore and Rick Vancy, she had no taste for champagne or indeed any form of alcohol). Ione Quentin, looking exhausted in comparison to her employer whose cheeks continued to bloom pinkly despite – or perhaps because of – her recent ordeal, nursed the sherry for which she had been compelled, slightly embarrassedly, to ask: 'Ma'am, do you think I might—'

Amy stared at her with the huge almost circular blue eyes which made her photograph so well. 'Don't be ridiculous, Ione. Have whatever you like. Make yourself a Bloody Mary if you like, the way Ferdel does. And talking of Ferdel—' The famous pout was much in evidence.

Ione Quentin began all over again: 'An old friend from abroad, Ma'am, a last-minute arrangement. He wasn't able to speak to you personally because of the Press Conference. Mr Taplow came and picked him up, I believe, in the Prince's aunt's car. No, I don't know where they're having lunch, Ma'am. At the flat, possibly?'

Even to Ione Quentin the Prince's story sounded pretty thin and she frankly could not imagine – would in fact very much like to have known – why he had suddenly abandoned his fiancée at the last minute, leaving the faithful Ione, as usual, to placate. Out loud, however, Ione Quentin continued to deliver the message in her usual pleasantly neutral voice. 'You remember Mr Taplow, Ma'am,' she added, as though hoping to distract. 'He was the Duke's chauffeur in the country for absolutely ages. Rather creepy. You used to play with his little girl, funny little thing. No, it was a *boy* with long hair and sort of girl's clothes. Princess Sophie told me she used to tease him—'

'Oh really?' It was clear that Princess Amy was not the slightest bit interested in the Taplows.

'Boys as girls. It's all wrong,' pursued Ione, 'as your nephew Jamie would say. He's making such a fuss about his page's suit, isn't he? When it's so divinely pretty—'

Suddenly to Ione's surprise Princess Amy burst out laughing in a way that made her look much younger than her twenty-two years; she had a ringing schoolgirl's laugh (something which the Press seldom heard). 'I say Ione, you don't suppose this old friend from abroad is seven foot tall with long black hair like a witch and sports a puma in her luggage and talks like zeez? I read in the *Clueless* that *she'd* arrived.' Ione breathed a sigh of silent relief; Amy in this mood helped to make up for the other less enchanting mood which had preceded it.

'What cheek, eh you old doggie?' went on Amy, patting one of the ancient spaniels. It was snuffling at the high-heeled white sandal which Amy had discarded now that there was no need for her to try to level up against her tall fiancé. 'Standing me up like that, his dewy bride.'

'You *did* look dewy, Ma'am' responded Ione quite sincerely. 'It went terribly well, didn't it? Everybody thought you were wonderful. My cousin Susanna Blanding – she was there – rang up Lydia last night and told her you were wonderful.'

'Susanna Blanding? What was *she* doing there?'

'Oh, she's with one of those amazing American TV stations. She's awfully bright, especially about history, always has been. She wrote that book about young princesses down the ages, don't you remember? *Dear and Royal Sister*. She sent it to you. It sold awfully well. And she's always on those quizzes on telly, the brainy ones. Now she's making a fortune out of the wedding.'

'Making a fortune out of *one*?' But Princess Amy sounded very pleased. Susanna Blanding was evidently a far better note to strike than the Taplows and their son. Then she added in a different voice: 'Lydia – how is Lydia?'

'Going on very well, thank you, Ma'am,' said Ione quickly, a shade too quickly. 'But as I was saying, the way you dealt with that dreadful American who kept going on about your self-image—'

'What on earth was all that about?' Amy pointed her neat little stockinged foot – she had the shapely legs and pretty ankles of some plump women; in fact her whole appearance was an intriguing mixture of things which were notably large (her eyes, her bosom) and things which were notably small like her hands and feet and ankles. 'Was she going on about my lack of A levels? So drear. What does Ferdel care about my A levels? He's never even *heard* of A levels.'

'I think she was going on about your attitude to feminism, Ma'am.'

'*Feminism!*' cried Amy in a voice of outrage, 'Whatever will they ask one about next? And I wish they wouldn't keep going on about animals and hunting and all that. Those people are just crazy. I don't hunt, far too terrifying, took the opportunity to give it up when Daddy died. Quel relief! Giving up hunting I mean. Not poor old Daddy. So what's it all to do with me?'

'There's a lot of it about at the moment,' said Ione diplomatically. 'Animal Rights is flavour of the month where demos are concerned. Hence the questions. The Cumberland Palace incident didn't help, and I suppose there *might* just be further demonstrations before the wedding. Coming to which, Ma'am, there is just one thing I ought to tell you—'

As Princess Amy fished for her white sandal with one toe (the spaniel Happy – or was it Boobie? – thought it was a game), Ione Quentin broke the news of the death of Jean-Pierre Schwarz-Albert. Like the rest of the public, Princess Amy did not find the death – having never known of the life – of a French journalist profoundly interesting.

'How sad,' she remarked rather absently, at the end of her lady-in-waiting's recitation. 'Does one have to do anything about it? Write to anyone? I mean, was he fearfully brave or anything? Do we watch him on telly all the time?'

'Oh no, Ma'am, he was French,' replied Ione, in a tone that made it clear that the answer to all these questions was in the negative. Amy kicked her shoes aside again. She yawned. She was still yawning and contemplating the short unpainted nails on her small hand, weighed down by its huge aquamarine ring set in diamonds (true Amy blue) when Ione spoke again.

'Yes, Ione? Oh God, why won't my boring nails grow. Look at yours – positive talons. It's not fair – sorry, yes?'

'Just one more thing, Ma'am.'

Amy groaned. 'More unpleasantness. I know it. You always say "Just one more thing" when it's unpleasant. This is the second "one more thing" in five minutes.'

'The French journalist had a number of Animal Rights stickers in his pocket,' continued Ione rather coldly; then her eyes fell on her own nails, not particularly long, but neatly painted a delicate pink; her expression lightened. Princess Amy on the other hand gave a little pout.

'How drear! Actually at our Press Conference? *Very* drear. How on earth did he get in? I hope he doesn't do it again.'

'He's dead, Ma'am,' said Ione patiently.

'Well I jolly well hope there aren't any more like him, frightening Animal Rights people, I mean, among the journalists. They're bad enough as they are, them and their questions.' Princess Amy's pout deepened and for an instant she bore a strong resemblance to the late Duke of Cumberland when some household arrangement had gone awry. 'Now Ione, let's forget about the drear journalists. I'm not marrying *them*. What did Ferdel say exactly . . . ?'

A few miles away Princess Amy's royal disregard for the subject of dead French journalists was not shared by Detective Superintendent Portsmouth (although he might have been more sympathetic to her views on the Press generally).

'Dead!' cried Detective Superintendent Portsmouth, and then, after pausing as though searching for the *mot juste*, added impressively: 'As a doornail.'

'To coin a phrase,' remarked Detective Sergeant Vaillant smartly, and gave another of those sage nods which had caused Pompey of the Yard to mark him down as a bright lad.

Young Vaillant had however misjudged his moment. Pompey was in an irritable mood, suffering from what he mentally termed royal sciatica since his first bad attack had been at the time of the wedding of the Prince of Wales. On that occasion Mrs Portsmouth had caused him to plant out rows of loyal red and white begonias, interspersed with blue lobelias, in their garden before the season or, for that matter, Pompey was ready. Prince Andrew's wedding had called for backbreaking work with tri-coloured geraniums, more sciatica. Currently Mrs Portsmouth was massing petunias, crimson streaked with white, by the back door for the attack and wishing out loud that nature had created something properly red, white and blue.

Nothing, as Vaillant well knew, put his superior in a worse mood than being the brawn for Mrs Portsmouth's brains where gardening was concerned; indeed, had he noticed the tiny trace of earth under Pompey's normally immaculate fingernails, he would not have risked his smart remark or anything like it but would have confined himself to the nod.

'Given the state of the city, I'm inclined to think that it was done on purpose to annoy us,' went on Pompey, giving Vaillant a malevolent look. 'To coin a phrase as you would put it. Certainly someone did something on purpose. To put it another way, a good many people did a good many things on purpose, leaving us poor critters to figure out who did which to what.'

Vaillant knew better this time and merely nodded.

'For example the late Mr Schwarz-Albert did a good many things on purpose. Including painting Cumberland Palace red.'

'We're sure of that, are we, sir?' enquired Vaillant in his most sympathetic manner. Pompey ignored him.

'So what was he doing stone dead with a souvenir paper-knife in his back in the corner of the lounge of the Republican Hotel?'

Pompey spoke in a tone remarkably close to a groan, something that Vaillant ascribed to his physical condition rather than to any faintheartedness over the case. 'Answer me that one. Was he about to transfigure the lounge with violent red pleas for animal rights when he was struck down by someone with an even more violent dislike for Animal Rights activists? He was struck down—' as Vaillant leant even more sympathetically forward – 'and with one of these. Sharp little buggers.'

Pompey reached in a drawer and drew out a paper-knife similar to those presented to the avid Royalty-observers at the Press Conference. At the time the knife, surmounted by Princess Amy's cypher in blue, had seemed yet another example of royal journalistic kitsch; now, looking at it, Vaillant felt that the strong slender blade had assumed an altogether more sinister aspect.

'Here's one of them. Masses of them about, of course. A thousand manufactured. Quite a job tracing them. At the same time, shouldn't be allowed, should it, giving something as sharp as this to a lot of journalists.'

'They're not children—' murmured Vaillant. Pompey merely cocked an eyebrow.

'At least we know the murder weapon. Although we've kept quiet about the weapon for the time being to the Press. The hotel cooperated: *they* didn't want any bad publicity. We'll release that titbit when its suits us, not before. We also know the approximate time. But who and why:

that, my boy, is what we are here to find out. At the moment it's strictly person unknown.'

'What do we know about him, sir? Beyond the fact that he had a valid Press pass to the conference?'

'Give me that bit of paper.' Pompey stretched forward. The movement made him wince. He stopped. 'Go on then, read it out, boy.'

'Jean-Pierre Schwarz-Albert, journalist. A.k.a. Animal Rights activist. Known to have joined several Animal Rights movements, most recently Innoright – Innoright? Reason to believe he was part of the Innoright cell that made the red-paint raid on Cumberland Palace last—' Vaillant stopped.

'Reason to believe, sir?' he enquired delicately. 'Information received? You don't mean – we've got a source around that neck of the woods?'

Pompey grunted. 'Something of the sort. As you know, we've all been scared silly about these Animal Rights loonies ever since the Westminster Square incident. Yes, loonies. I said loonies and I meant loonies. They're insane in other words. Terrorists and insane. You can't begin to predict what they'll do. Far be it from me to call for the return of your wandering Irish terrorist, let alone your friendly neighbourhood Arab—' Pompey grunted again and then coughed to show it was one of his jokes.

Vaillant, alerted, gave a discreet smile.

'But these fellows,' went on Pompey, 'men and women, the women being among the worst by the way, you've no idea what they'll think of next. So many amateurs getting into the game, too, none of them on our books already. Not playing the game by the rules, because they don't know what the rules are.'

Perceiving this was not a joke, Vaillant asked: 'Has terrorism got rules, sir?'

'The only rule in terrorism is that things will always be different from the last time. You know that. But terrorists, like any other professionals, have patterns of behaviour, and, even more to the point, professional links. They're not in the main criminals, but they do become criminals. In short, somewhere along the way, generally quite soon along the way, your idealistic terrorist meets up with the criminal fraternity. And that's where we come in.'

'Because we meet up with the criminal fraternity quite soon along the way too. In the line of work,' added Vaillant hastily.

'Exactly so. Of course we've got our links with the criminal fraternity – how would we get on without them? How would they get on without them? And that leads us to the terrorists; or in certain cases leads them to us. But these amateurs' – Pompey exclaimed with disgust – 'many of them have never done anything wrong before in their life.' He stopped and then added in a sombre voice: 'But when they do plunge in – just think of Westminster Square again. The most frightful wilful destruction I can remember. And I've been a policeman all my life.'

'Frightening people, sir.'

'Frightening indeed. So that's when we decided to infiltrate them. Take them seriously, especially with this wedding coming up. We've been lucky twice – Charles and Andy. Got them home and dry, if you get my meaning. And the young ladies too of course,' Pompey added hastily in case Vaillant had what Pompey mentally termed 'Views' on the subject of the opposite sex. 'That still doesn't necessarily mean that we'll be lucky the third time. Unless we take all the proper precautions.'

'No such thing as luck in our business,' pronounced Vaillant sententiously. It was one of Pompey's own phrases. Vaillant was rewarded with an approving glance.

'And this time,' pursued Pompey, 'we have a royal young lady at the centre of it all. A born princess and a born prince. What's more, a prince who's a foreigner. He could attract all sorts—'

'He *has* attracted all sorts if you believe the *Sunday Clueless*,' began Vaillant recklessly and then stopped. Pompey appeared not to have heard.

'What's more, a prince with an international sporting reputation. And by the way, my boy, when I say sporting, I am not referring to the *Exclusive's* intimate revelations. Fancy reading that rubbish!'

Vaillant blushed: 'It was in the line of duty, sir, background material.'

'Ah, just so. I must tell that to Mrs Pompey. She read it too, I believe, while I was pulling up the bulbs in the garden, ready for her begonias. Could it have been background material for her too, do you suppose?'

But this time wild horses would not have dragged a reply from Detective Sergeant Vaillant.

'Photographs of our Prince killing this, that and the other plastered all over the Press. That could bring the nasties right out of the woodwork. So, as I was saying, we had a source inside it, a good chap too. Joined a lot of these organizations to get animal credibility as it were. Then concentrated on one of them: a small one. Innoright. Innocent Rights. Get it?

'He told us it was mainly full of nice innocent people who love Pussy and Rover and don't like the idea of any harm coming to them, let alone being cut up by nasty scientists. Hardly frightening people. Then there's the vegetarian brigade, nothing wrong with them either, I've got lots of sympathy for that, and as for these chicken factories, the calves – you should hear Mrs Portsmouth on that subject. I sometimes worry about my steak and chips.' Pompey laughed and after a moment Vaillant (who did as a matter of fact have vegetarian leanings, although no 'Views' on women's rights) laughed too.

'Then our source got on to something more serious,' continued Pompey. 'Thought that Innoright might be up to something. Or *Inner*

Innoright was up to something. By being all helpful about the place, and making friends, one particular friend, he stumbled on one or two clues.'

'Clues?'

'People who were supposed to have formally resigned from Innoright in protest against this, that and the other. Putting it on record. Then still dealing with it secretly. Odd that. The last message he gave definitely implied there was something rather frightening going on. Connected in some way to the wedding.'

'That was the last message. So what does he say now about all this?'

'He doesn't say anything. Because when last seen, he had a bright blue paper-knife stuck in him; which makes it difficult. Oh, didn't I make it clear?' Pompey gave Vaillant the full benefit of his most foxy smile.

'Jean-Pierre Schwarz-Albert was our man inside Innoright.'

7

Across Your Body

A few miles away from both Pompey at Scotland Yard (shoes eased off) and Princess Amy at Cumberland Palace (shoes kicked off) yet another pair of shoes was lying loose. Ladies' shoes. However these ladies' shoes, except that they were also high-heeled, bore little similarity to those of Princess Amy. The shoes on the hearthrug in Eaton Square were in another sense of the word hardly ladylike. They were shiny black patent with inlets of glinting mirror glass and slashes of silver leather; the heels were extraordinarily spindly.

'Mirabella,' said Prince Ferdinand, breathing heavily, 'you are insane.' For the woman who had stepped out of the shoes had also stepped out of her clothes, that is to say, a black crêpe dress ornamented with similar silver and glass motifs lay on the floor beside the shoes, the glass segments winking oddly as they caught the light; the impression was of fallen Christmas-tree ornaments.

Mirabella Prey raised her arms above her head in a graceful arc and pointed one toe in an equally graceful balletic position. The effect was not however of the ballet with its detachment and exquisite formality, but of something more primitive, a mating dance perhaps. Mirabella's naked body, sinuous (how many workouts, dance routines, exercises?) and brown (how many summers in Greece and Marbella?) could have been photographed as she stood, her face just slightly in the shade, her black hair flowing down between her small high breasts, for the cover of some Health and Beauty book.

As Ferdel, still breathing heavily, concentrated on this reflection to calm him, he realized that the thought was not a random one – Mirabella had appeared in just such a pose, with the sketchy addition of a highly cut-away black leotard, on the cover of her own best-selling book of exercises, every exercise based on the natural movements of the wild cat

373

family or something of the sort. What had it been called? *Wild Woman, Good Life?* No, the other way round, *Wild Life, Good Woman.* That sounded even less plausible. He gave up, feeling calmer; all proceeds went towards the protection of wild life, of that he was quite certain. Exotic animals, naturally.

'*Alors, mon Prince, je te plais encore?*' Mirabella let her arms sink into some form of suppliant position; she managed nonetheless to continue to look uncommonly predatory.

'Mirabella, you are crazy,' replied Ferdel carefully in English, taking a step back. Suppliant or not, he did not trust her. Mirabella stretched out one beautiful brown arm in his direction; the arm was not bare unlike the body from which it sprang, for on the arm glistened an enamel and diamond bracelet fastened with a puma's head. Ferdel recognized it because he had given it to Mirabella as – hopefully – a farewell present; he still remembered the fuss Mirabella had made about the anatomical details of the puma which the jeweller had stupidly confused with those of a leopard. Then he stepped forward again and picked up the glittering black crêpe heap on the floor.

'Cover yourself. At once.'

'Oh Ferdel,' purred Mirabella without moving. 'You are squairre,' – she extended the word. 'The leetle princess, she does that to you so soon? *Merde, alors.*' Mirabella put her hand down as if to cover the noticeably large square black shadow on her brown body; the gesture could conceivably in another woman have been one of Eve-like modesty; in Mirabella however it was quite clearly one of Eve-like invitation.

'Darling, why don't we fuck?' she purred again, in an accent which was surely heavier than her usual one. 'Just once, or maybe more than once. I like this room very much, *très homme*, it reminds me of you. It would be so amusing' – she perceived Ferdel's wince – 'Darling, if you're tired . . .'

'Dress and get out. I have nothing more to say.' Ferdel flung the clothes at her. He looked so intensely angry, his mouth a thin even line, that this time Mirabella herself took a pace back. The glittering clothes landed at her feet.

So she was still naked when the heavy polished doors opened abruptly and the butler Taplow, in shirt sleeves and an apron over his striped trousers, half fell, was half propelled into the room. Behind him, scarcely more appropriately dressed in jeans, anoraks, hoods and those creepy stocking masks which obliterate the features by substituting other less human ones, were two figures. One of them held an automatic pistol. Taplow was gabbling something like 'Your Highness, I'm sorry.'

Then the taller of the two men – they both seemed to be men although one could not be absolutely sure – pushed Taplow right down on to the floor and put his foot on the butler's white-shirted back. The pistol was now pointing unwaveringly in the direction of the Prince. All this time,

Mirabella, although not directly threatened by any weapon, had stood still, holding her position of a lascivious Eve. Her clothes remained in the black and glittering heap at her feet. Ferdel made a movement, perhaps towards her clothes, perhaps towards the stationary and naked woman. Instantly the taller of the intruders, his foot remaining on Taplow's back, turned his weapon in the direction of the woman.

'Prince,' he said in a muffled voice, more muffled than perhaps a mere stocking mask would explain, 'You will now do what we say.'

Ferdel made a gesture with his hands – long hands held high in the air, narrow lips curling slightly – which seemed to indicate both politely and disdainfully that in view of the threat to the woman he had little choice.

'Stand beside the lady.' Ferdel hesitated an instant, noted the unaltered position of the gun, and walked slowly and coolly, sauntered as it were, in the direction of Mirabella.

'Take her hand.'

This time there was a perceptible pause before the Prince did as he was commanded. After a moment the tall man in the stocking mask gave a small imperious wave of the pistol, still held on the woman.

'Take it. We mean what we say.'

The Prince picked up Mirabella's hand with its many glittering rings, in his. There was a tiny clink: possibly one of her rings had clashed with his heavy gold signet ring. Then there was a sudden radiant flash as the diamond bracelet with the puma's head slid like a falling star along her naked arm. Ferdel's face was expressionless.

The short man then stepped forward and, raised on his toes, pulled at the Prince's dark-blue knitted silk tie. He succeeded in loosening it. Then he undid the top button of his shirt.

'Take off his jacket.' The muffled voice of the man with the gun gave the order. At the same time the man with the gun edged his front foot forward, the other still planted on Taplow's back. Taplow however was apparently so inert – was he conscious? his back was heaving in an odd way – that the pressure of the foot hardly seemed necessary.

As the short man struggled to remove Ferdel's dark-blue jacket, the Prince neither obstructed nor helped him; that in itself made it a difficult operation in view of the Prince's superior height. Eventually the jacket lay on the floor, joining the heap of Mirabella's clothes. Ferdel shrugged his shoulders as though to settle himself in his new garb and for a moment seemed about to put his hand up to his neck as though to assure himself that the shirt was properly set without the tie. It was obviously a characteristic gesture and as such not intended to be threatening. A look at the man with the gun however stayed his hand. Ferdel, who had not glanced directly at Mirabella throughout the episode, now stared ahead, her hand held stiffly in his.

The pair of them, the Prince in his dark formal trousers and white shirt, his black polished shoes, the woman naked, had the air of some corrupt painting.

'Do it.' The tall man's muffled voice was now louder as if he had gained confidence. 'Do it quickly.' Then the short man produced from some inner pocket a copy of the day's paper – it happened to be the *Daily Exclusive*. Ferdel's expression changed for a moment when he saw it and he glanced involuntarily in Mirabella's direction. The short man stuck the *Daily Exclusive* into Mirabella's left hand. Her instinctive gesture to hide herself, with the paper, was it seemed what was wanted.

'Across your body.'

Mirabella began to tremble slightly; the paper quivered. While it was still quivering, the short man backed away from the pair of them, and producing what was only too clearly a camera, began to snap quickly, efficiently, fast, with a series of flashes. It was over almost before it began; beyond a series of blinks, Ferdel moved not at all. Mirabella continued to tremble.

'Right. We quit.' The tall man gestured to the little photographer to precede him out of the door. The last thing he did in the room itself was to scatter a series of white and red papers like benisons behind him. Taplow gave a kind of groan as the pressure on his neck was released. Finally the tall man backed out preparatory to shutting the heavy doors behind them both. There was the sound of a key turning in the lock.

The three of them, Taplow, Mirabella and the Prince, were left in the grand room which Mirabella had described only recently – but how long ago it seemed – as *'très homme.'* Taplow was now audibly groaning, almost sobbing.

Then Mirabella began to scream: the sound of her screams echoed rather horribly in the high-ceilinged room.

'It's all your fault, all your fault. You should 'ave loved me,' she cried. 'All you wanted was to . . .' A vivid scream of words, verbs, all meaning roughly the same thing, of which 'screw' and 'stuff' were the mildest, followed. Hysterically, without bothering to clothe herself, kicking aside a heap which included in fact the Prince's jacket, Mirabella began to pummel his chest with her fists.

Ferdel caught her hands in his. 'Stop that,' he said, 'Put your clothes on at once. And this time I mean what I say.'

'It was you,' began Mirabella again. But the Prince merely transferred both her wrists to one hand and slapped her face hard. Now the noise of Mirabella's sobs joined the sucking and groaning noise of Taplow on the floor.

'Get up,' said Ferdel curtly. The big man rose lumberingly to his knees, and then, panting, to his feet.

'Your Highness,' he began, as Mirabella, crying more quietly, arranged herself in her clothes, long black hair tangling with the black glinting dress, sobs gradually diminishing.

'Where's that bloody detective?' Ferdel, having reassumed his jacket, was fastening his tie, stretching his neck as he gazed at himself in the huge gilt-framed Chippendale mirror over the fireplace. 'What are these people for?' Ferdel's English was generally impeccable, the product of English schooldays; nevertheless his words suggested a European aristocrat speaking of peasants.

'Your Highness, we must ring the police—' began Taplow.

'First of all we must get out of here. Where is she? The woman. Your wife.'

'She went out shopping. She said.'

'And the detective?'

'He's coming back this evening. When you go to the Embassy dinner, sir.'

'I shall speak to him. How did this happen? It's – it's monstrous. This Press of yours. How can the government let them do it?'

'I'm so sorry, Your Highness,' wailed Taplow.

'It was not the Press,' said Mirabella in a sulky voice. 'Not how you mean it.' She was standing parallel with Ferdel, but at a distance, sharing the wide mirror to repair her make-up. Like Ferdel adjusting his tie, she made her own series of little *moues* into the mirror as she patted her high cheekbones with a series of dark and light powders.

Ferdel swung round and looked at her.

'Ah. So they are friends of yours. These charming people. Your idea. I thought you were not capable of that. I was wrong.'

'They lo-o-ve animals. That is nice.' Mirabella's lip trembled.

'They love animals! They *are* animals.' Ferdel started to stride up and down the room while Taplow, no longer shuddering, gaped at him. Suddenly the Prince stopped, whirled round and headed for Mirabella again. His expression was momentarily so fierce that the woman, wobbling slightly on her high heels, collapsed into one of the large leather chairs. From this lowly position, Mirabella's enormous eyes brimmed with tears. She looked a great deal more submissive than at any other point during her interview with the Prince.

'What happens now? What happens to the pictures? The filthy pictures? Do we see them in the filthy Press?'

'Oh Ferdel, you are so cross, it's ridiculous.' Mirabella attempted a light laugh.

'And you are not cross? Then I shall give you something to be cross about.' In response the Prince dived at her wrist and wrenched quite cruelly the jewelled bracelet fastened with the puma's head. He bent it violently; it snapped. He hurled it down into the fireplace where the pieces lay sadly glittering.

Mirabella gasped. After that she remained rigid. Taplow by now had resumed the impassive expression of the perfect butler, one whom nothing more could faze – not more naked female visitants, not more photographers, not more valuable jewellery broken and cast aside.

Ferdel turned back to Mirabella and eyed her speculatively. His gaze swept from her earrings, pendant and sparkling, to her many rings and the bracelets, less beautiful but possibly equally fragile, on her other arm.

'So. One more dead animal. Now you will tell me about this "feelthy" plot. At once.'

'It's to help the poor animals. It's not a plot. You will not see these photographs in the Press, not if you are sensible, they say. They are good people, not' – Mirabella cast around for the word – 'not horrid blackmailers.'

The Prince lifted an eyebrow; his face was hard in repose, and for a moment the skull of the older man he would become, lips too narrow, nose straight but long, deep incisions beside the narrow mouth, showed beneath the surface of the bonhomous man of pleasure, still in his prime.

'They wish you, they wish you and her – the leetle Princess – to speak to everybody. About animals. That is all. It is a nice thing to do, Ferdel, not a nasty thing.' Mirabella attempted a little winning smile. She fluttered her eyelashes. 'And then they will give you back the boring photographs. And they will trouble you no more. *Je te promis.*'

'Unfortunately our Press Conference was yesterday,' replied the Prince in a sombre voice.

'I know, but there is this woman, yes, you will speak to her? The woman with red hair, what is her name? You will speak to her, yes? You will speak to her on television. That is what they say. And with the leetle Princess, you will be very, very nice about the animals. Oh yes, my darling, you will.' There was something artificial, almost automatic about Mirabella's wheedling voice; she was evidently still upset in some way by the recent episode, but whether by the Prince's anger, her own outburst, or even (despite her complicity) the photographic session itself, was hard to say.

'I shall do nothing—' began the Prince. Before he could say anything more, there was a noise of the key in the lock. Then the heavy doors opened and Mrs Taplow, a strange expression which might have been anticipation or dread on her face, entered the room.

Whatever her expression betokened, she stopped abruptly at the scene before her, and stood in the doorway. It was noticeable that she did not look in the direction of her husband.

'Taplow,' said the Prince sharply, 'Leave the room. Take your wife. And no talk, nothing. I shall speak to you later. In the meantime no talk, no telephone calls, nothing. Both of you.'

'Sir' – Taplow gave a little bow. Mrs Taplow hesitated, then bobbed.

The Taplows retreated from the room, shutting the door behind them. Once the door was shut, the Prince moved swiftly across the room, opened it again and removed the key from the lock outside. He then locked the door from the inside. Ferdel stood looking at Mirabella. Something had changed about his expression; no longer quite so hard, it was more speculative, even anticipatory.

'So, Mirabella, friend of the animals, we shall talk. We are quite alone here. I do not expect further interruptions – I hope I am right about that, my dear? I would not want the return of those other animals, or rather friends of the animals, your friends? Good. And by the way, you had better keep quiet about the fact you know them – knew them. Understood?' Mirabella nodded.

He walked towards her.

'Understood. So we are in agreement once more. I am glad. You see – what was it you suggested an hour ago? Let's fuck. Ah, you don't feel like it now? After what has happened, you don't think it would be amusing. A pity. You see I disagree. After what has happened, for the first time, I think it *would* be amusing. Very amusing.'

He had reached her. The Prince stretched out his hand, the white shirt cuff protruding from the dark sleeve, in the direction of the tiny diamonded buttons which fastened her black crépe bodice. He started, with a faint smile, to unbutton them.

Mirabella did not attempt to stop him. She was trembling slightly.

It was only much later when she said something low, like *'mon Prince'*, and he responded, equally low, *'Ach Gott*, Mirabella', that an observer might have supposed that the coupling carried out so violently on the carpet in front of the fireplace – the man first devouring the woman with his lips, then forcing her to take him in hers, finally subduing her harshly with his body – that action begun with violent possession had in fact ended in some kind of tenderness on both sides.

8
Royal Gossip

Lamb was lingering unhappily on the platform at Sloane Square station waiting for the Circle Line train; trains of the other lines came and went with what she felt was unfair rapidity. Lamb was unhappy first of all because she wondered whether, due to some vagary of the erratic Circle Line, she had missed the appropriate train. Life on the regularly flowing Central Line was infinitely simpler: there was always trouble when Monkey indicated the rendezvous was to be on the Circle or the District ... Lamb always felt anxious. Lamb stopped herself. Lamb was not supposed to feel anxious.

The second cause for Lamb's unhappiness was, she decided, a legitimate one because it threatened the success of the Underground Plan. There were crowds of people, many of them foreign, standing on the platform, and not just because the Circle Line train was a long time in coming. London was filling up with tourists, some of them undoubtedly attracted by the coming spectacle of the Royal Wedding, others simply part of some slightly dazed routine which induced them to 'do London'. Then there were bodies, bodies of ordinary travellers. Goodness knows where they had been during the cold dull months of early spring; like bears they were out in the open now. Lamb allowed herself to worry about the question of security in these more crowded circumstances.

So far the Underground Plan, as devised by Monkey (and as suggested originally by Lamb, let her not forget, that was *Lamb's* idea), had surely been successful. No one could possibly have realized, could they, that the disparate group of travellers engaged in seeming casual conversation in their series of moving venues, had in fact been engaged in conspiracy. Of course there had been other meetings where necessary, mainly in one particular private place, but the Underground had generally served to establish contact. And now?

The Circle Line train was signalled on the indicator, and almost immediately arrived. As Lamb had feared, there was a rush towards it. When she achieved the last carriage, as was the practice, the first person she saw was Monkey strap-hanging. Beagle was next to him, lounging upright in his characteristic stance and being Beagle, disdaining to touch the strap; Lamb felt the familiar stab of fear, longing and, she had to face it, probably desire when she saw Beagle. Chicken was standing up, standing up and reading a paperback book called *Man and the Natural World*. Lamb recognized the book: Chicken had been reading it for some time. When Lamb had admired the cover, showing a variety of animals fleeing a forest fire, including a rather lovable if primitive lion, Chicken took the opportunity to explain that this famous painting, in a museum in Oxford, was not really so admirable since it depicted the classical myth whereby man discovered fire and in so doing succeeded in subordinating the animals to his sway.

Lamb nodded with apparent humility. She was good at appearing to look humble. Secretly she still thought the painting was rather lovely. Why not liberate it from the museum one day? As a symbol that animals were no longer subordinated. One day. The Underground Plan had to come first. All the same, it was an idea. Lamb pointed out to herself how she was absolutely full of ideas these days.

Unlike Chicken, Fox was sitting down – trust him. Lamb did not like Fox. Although he sometimes talked plaintively·to Lamb (naming no names) about his unhappy childhood, a father who had never understood his artistic leanings – only Noel the dog really seemed to understand *them* – Lamb thought rather crossly that the main effect on Fox had been to make him extraordinarily self-centred ... which was not the same thing at all as having artistic leanings.

Trust Pussy too to manage to get a seat when she arrived, which would be at the next stop, Sloane Square. With her mess of logoed plastic shopping bags about her, like sandbags surrounding her stout person, Pussy was not above demanding the right to sit down; she generally chose an inoffensive-looking young person, but on one occasion Pussy's black sense of humour (which oddly enough she did not lack) had led her to pick on Beagle. Lamb still remembered the look on Beagle's face when he refused.

'You must be joking,' was all he said; it was the expression which was frightening, a kind of naked glee at the opportunity to wound, insult.

'Right in character, Puss,' said Beagle later, 'Catch the sort of person I am getting up for any old cow with her plastic shopping battering rams.'

'I shall remember that, Beagle,' replied Pussy quite equably. 'You see if I don't. I have my own character too, you know.' And the incident apparently passed off. All the same Lamb wondered what Monkey thought of a complicated plan, involving watertight procedures in which at least two of the characters involved cordially disliked each other – not to use a stronger word. Better far when they loved each other, like Beagle and Lamb. *Did* Beagle love her? He hated what he described her as standing for, he had always made that quite clear; but then so in a sense did Lamb herself. If something in Beagle's background made him peculiarly violent at times, frighteningly so, towards the notion of Lamb's upbringing, did she not share his distaste? Hence Innoright, hence her participation in the cell. Hence, so her doctor, the nice one, had said certain other things in Lamb's past. But Lamb loved too, she loved animals, the innocent, sometimes with a quite unbearable love. And she loved Beagle, whatever his past. Did he, then, love her?

Lamb could just imagine Beagle's reply if asked such a question; because she had worked towards it in the past: 'This *is* love, my Lambkin,' he had said upon one occasion, putting her hand firmly on his groin, with its large moulded lump inside the skinny jeans. 'And this is for you.' But now Pussy was getting into the carriage. That left Tom, due to arrive at Victoria.

Then Lamb noticed that Monkey was carrying an umbrella. How had she not noticed it before? No, Monkey must have somehow masked it with his body until five out of the six members of the Underground Plan cell were present; that still left Tom unaccounted for. Wait, Monkey had a blue handkerchief in his breast pocket where normally a white one was customary. Now *that* he had definitely put in place within the last few minutes; she couldn't have missed the blue handkerchief, which, coupled with the umbrella meant . . . Yes, meeting abandoned for the time being, same route to be tried again in four hours' time, same procedure. Any cell member unable to do that for personal reasons to tell the person closest to them in the carriage.

Perhaps Monkey like Lamb found the crowds oppressive. This was certainly no occasion for any kind of planning meeting. Four hours brought them well past the rush hour to another theoretically dead period, office workers vanished. The Underground Plan involved three possible times of day, the third (which would be used following an evening cancellation) being at ten-thirty the next morning. But everyone found that time difficult, and it had so far only been used once.

'Good news,' Beagle was saying in her ear. 'We're really into something.' Then he patted her bottom, felt it really, followed the shape of it with his hand . . . Lamb gave Beagle a look of unforced indignation. 'My place afterwards,' he murmured. And was gone. Lamb left at the next station without further contact of any description with the rest of the cell.

Yes, she thought rather bitterly, seven o'clock was no problem to her. What did she have to do that was more important than Innoright? What did she have to *do*, come to think of it? But Lamb stopped that train of thought at once, that really was not the way to think, not in any way, not ever according to the instructions of the nice doctor. And although Lamb would never dream of telling the nice doctor what she was up to at Innoright, she still had a feeling that he, the doctor, would not totally disapprove. Lamb was after all thinking of others just as the doctor had told her to do, and at the same time valuing herself.

'Better to love others than hate yourself.' Lamb was definitely loving others – the others being the animals. And Beagle.

Lamb picked up a taxi outside the Tube station and went home.

Lamb's sister looked up when Lamb entered the house; the front door of the little Chelsea house which they shared opened directly into the sitting-room. The first sight which should have met Lamb's eyes at this point was a large oil portrait – over-large for the small room – which hung in a dominating fashion over the fireplace. It showed a man in military uniform; he had an incongruously fierce air amid the girlish chintzes with which the room was decorated. But Lamb took care not to look at the portrait and thus avoided the ferocious gaze which her father appeared to be bestowing upon the room's inhabitants. The nice young doctor had talked to her at length about 'finding your own way of dealing with your father's memory'. Lamb's own way was to refuse to look at the portrait altogether otherwise she found rage, what was worse, helpless rage, welling up inside her.

It helped Lamb to inspect automatically instead the various photographs of her mother which stood in silver frames on the occasional tables, chintz-draped, scattered about the room. An observer would have noted the strong resemblance between Lamb and her mother, even down to the tense expression they shared; but between the girl now standing (unseeing) beneath the portrait and the portrait's subject, it was difficult to see any resemblance at all.

'Good day, darling?' enquired Lamb's sister as Lamb entered. Her low-heeled court shoes had been kicked off and she was reading the evening paper. The tone was perhaps artificially bright, as though the conventional enquiry masked, for once, some real concern about the nature of Lamb's day.

'Mmm. Went to the Tate. Awfully crowded. And you?'

'Good day, bad day. You know how it goes. I've got the evening off. Am I going to make you some supper? Promise not a whisper of meat anywhere, or fish, no bouillon or naughty stock cubes, Chef gave me this wonderful recipe. I'm longing to try it.'

'I'm afraid I have to go out,' replied Lamb, 'and don't frown.'

'I'm not frowning,' said her sister mildly. 'I haven't said a word.'

'Well, your look was worried. I can't bear that. You're not supposed to worry about me, I'm supposed to worry about me if anyone does. It's called taking responsibility for myself. I have to go out. Do you find that odd? As a matter of fact I said I'd go to a film with Janey. It's a long one. I might be quite late.' Lamb was aware that she was speaking too rapidly.

'Sounds fun!'

'I don't know that it will be all that fun,' began Lamb in a slightly childish voice. She stopped. 'I may be late, that's all. Janey does go on a bit these days. Her parents' divorce. The whole thing.'

'But that was ages ago. I mean, you told me she'd finally got over it the last time you saw her. You were so relieved. Anyway, darling, I don't think Janey really should burden you of all people with things like that—'

It was the turn of Lamb's sister to stop. Then:

'Darling Lydia,' resumed Lamb's sister, Ione Quentin, in the same equable voice she was wont to use to Princess Amy in order to smooth over an awkward moment. 'Why *not* go to a cinema indeed? I'll try the recipe another night. I'm whacked as it happens. P.A. *not* in a good mood because Ferdel failed to show . . . Really that man, although I can't help fancying him when he's actually there. He looks a bit like Daddy, don't you think? Pictures of Daddy as a young man; not as you remember him. And of course P.A. fancies him like mad, so she gets all jealous.' Ione Quentin stopped. 'Am I boring you, darling? I'm sure you don't want to hear all this. Tell me what you saw at the Tate.'

'No, no, go on,' Lydia Quentin, known in some circles as Lamb, spoke with evident sincerity. 'I love hearing about your life at CP. I like the little details. Go on about Ferdel. So what did he do? Go on about everything. What about all those awful wedding arrangements? You're so clever, Nonie, I really love hearing it.'

The Quentin sisters settled down for a nice royal gossip until such time as Lydia Quentin had to leave again to keep her appointment at South Kensington station.

About this time, in other parts of the city, various other forms of what might also be termed royal gossip were taking place. For example, it would probably be legitimate to term the remarks made by a man leaning over some emerging photographic prints, as royal gossip; even if the remarks themselves were too scabrous to be printed in any actual gossip column.

As for Jemima Shore, sprawling on the white carpet of her Holland Park Mansions flat, with Midnight flumped down blackly beside her, she might be said at the very least to be studying royal gossip. All about her were notes, charts and newspaper cuttings, preparatory to her exclusive interview with the royal couple in the near future. When the telephone rang, she realized that it must be Rick Vancy making one of those checking calls from his car telephone which somehow seemed to her to do little more than establish Rick Vancy's ability to drive and digress (on topics of the day) at one and the same time.

Jemima stretched out her hand without looking to where her own neat little telephone had been deposited on the carpet. In the course of the stretch, her hand encountered Midnight who moved out of the way with a small indignant cry.

'Hi,' said Jemima. 'How's the traffic?' – hoping he would not tell her.

There was a short silence. Then a voice – not Rick's – began speaking, and continued to do so at some length, carefully as from a prepared statement.

At one point Jemima did interrupt: '*What?*' The voice continued to speak. Then: 'Who are you?'

A little later she said: 'That's out of the question. Absolutely out of the question,' she repeated firmly, 'whoever you are. And whatever it is you say you've got.'

9

A Dangerous Connection

'It may have been successful, Beagle,' Monkey was remarking in his (to Beagle) irritatingly lofty voice. 'But it was extremely dangerous.'

Monkey's suit was the habitual pin-stripe; with the handkerchief in the breast pocket once more white, the first impression was of the respectable city gentleman Monkey presented to the outside world. But Monkey was palpably disturbed by recent events: how could Beagle so blithely ignore *orders* when orders, correctly given, correctly carried out, were to be the secret of their success? Because of the emotion of this moment, Monkey's simian quality, conveyed by his long curved hairless upper lip, the unduly splayed nostrils, was more in evidence than usual. Twirling his umbrella, Monkey today had, thought Lamb, the air of some heavy and slightly desolate primate.

'Careful planning, my old Monk, careful planning,' replied Beagle easily. 'Careful planning eliminates danger. Chicken here took the photographs. No sweat, no problem. No difficulty. No laughs. No tears. Well, maybe just a few. But I assure you it was totally non-violent. The pistol was a fake or rather it was a true-blue pistol, but unloaded. As used in some lethal drawing-room tragedy. Supplied by Foxy. All by agreement as you might say. A gentleman's agreement.'

'Shouldn't we say a lady's agreement, Beagle?' Chicken as usual sounded earnest; but all the same there was a new ease about her, even an air of happiness. Pussy in contrast looked heavier than usual (like Monkey) and her expression as she gazed downwards at her single plastic shopping-bag was sombre.

'A lady's agreement, indeed, Chick. In more senses than one. So: no sweat, good photos, and now we use them.'

'In fact,' continued Beagle, 'as you know, I've already set it up. Now don't panic, Monko – you agreed' – and as Monkey appeared to be about

386

to speak – 'don't give me a lot of shit about orders, orders correctly carried out and all that shit. I really don't give a fuck for orders, never have, my orders being of course different—' Beagle smiled: but it was demonstrably not a smile intended to rob his words of offence. 'It just happened, right? Right and *Innoright*. There was I, photographing this lovely lady, clothes on, or most of them, and we get talking. Well, it was natural, wasn't it? We've got a lot in common, so we get friendly.' Beagle winked with meaning, a parody of a lewd wink perhaps, but a lewd wink none the less.

In spite of herself, in spite of everything she had learned about self-esteem from the nice doctor, Lamb felt a violent lurch of jealousy, followed by the kind of spasm which just might turn to depression . . . She would not, could not let it do so. Quickly, Lamb cast up counter-images on her mental screen to blot out the pictures already forming there of Beagle and Mirabella Prey, Mirabella's black hair, how very black, how very thick it must be everywhere, even where concealed by the *Daily Exclusive*, Mirabella and Beagle . . . Instead, Lamb concentrated on other images, in themselves far more horrific but which actually served as mantras to calm her down, restore her to her sense of purpose.

The image of a pet cat called Snowdrop came first; the young white cat with a pink nose and occasional tabby patches which Lamb had loved as a child and which had vanished one day from a London street. Lamb imagined the cat with wires through her nose, and other wires applied strategically to parts of her body; Snowdrop's eyes gazed in silent terror and despair into Lamb's own, but in spite of her terror, Snowdrop had to remain mute because she no longer had a tongue or at any rate a tongue that she could use . . . Lamb thought of the work of saving Snowdrop and all the other cats who vanished mysteriously in cities, from such a fate. She was already calmer and did not need to pass on to her next image, culled years ago from an Animal Rights handout, which involved a beagle, a cigarette, more wires, and the connection between smoking and human lung cancer. (A beagle! How odd! That Lamb had never been able to forget the expression in that dog's eyes had surely been an omen.)

Beagle was speaking again. 'So I find out for her where the Prince is staying, that's not difficult, Fleet Street being what it is, and get a message to him to come home quick which as a matter of fact is not all that difficult either.' Lamb closed her eyes and the wraith of poor Snowdrop floated away into the recesses of her mind for when it was next needed.

'It's easy, Monkey, so easy,' Beagle was saying. 'We're laughing. Just imagine them getting their knickers in a twist at Cumberland Palace. But there's nothing, bloody nothing, that they can do about it. 'Course no English paper will print them – you don't need to tell me that, I work for them, don't I? But abroad, that's quite another matter. I work for them too, don't I? And the date and all on the copy of the London *Clueless.* No way they can wriggle out of it.'

'The date and the paper was my idea,' put in Chicken. 'I got it from the hostages, those American ones, or was it the Prime Minister of Italy? Both, I believe. They always photograph them with a daily paper to establish veracity. I fancy it was a professional touch.'

'But the Underground Plan—' Monkey for once sounded irresolute.

'This is a development of the Underground Plan, a stage along the way. Can't you see that?' In contrast to Monkey's gloom Beagle was increasingly cheerful. 'Just as we're no longer meeting in the Underground at this very moment, are we? Too dangerous at this stage. We've adjourned to my pad, as on previous occasions, have we not? And very nice too, I think you'll agree, if a little sparsely furnished. No prying landladies *here.*'

Lamb looked around. Pussy was perched uncomfortably on a low curved white chair, her big knees held tightly together. That was because there were no other chairs visible, only the white cushions on the painted, shiny black floor. Monkey was standing, as was Beagle; some ridiculous prejudice had made Lamb avoid sitting on the bed – the familiar bed – when she first came in, leaving Chicken and Fox to sit on it together. The slightly built man and the precise woman, adjoining but not touching, had the air of puppet monarchs.

The kingdom over which they ruled was literally an animal kingdom. Enormous blown-up photographs of animals covered the walls: animals without bodies, faces only, staring with huge bewildered eyes at the puny humans below them, faces of seals in particular (plenty of seals – Beagle might perhaps have chosen the code name Seal, given his preference for them). There was one mother seal, her coat slightly speckled in the photograph, who crouched protectively over her snow-white baby: that was Lamb's favourite. When Lamb first got to know Beagle, she had imagined rather vaguely that he was the sort of person who would turn out to live in a squat. Just as she had imagined him to be unemployed.

'A squat!' he had repeated disdainfully. 'A squat brings you into contact with people – and I don't just mean the police. I have a perfectly good studio. And then I have this private place. As you can see, I'm for living privately with the animals.' He had gestured towards the nearest seal's face: with its neat muzzle and wide-apart eyes it looked pretty and rather plaintive, like an attractive girl; where the average photographer might have covered his wall with the faces of glamorous models, big eyed and long eyelashed, Beagle had his plaintive seals with long, appealing whiskers instead of eyelashes. Beagle's whole face changed and softened when he looked in their direction.

But then Beagle, thought Lamb, even if he was a photographer, was not an average one. And the room where he lived, although situated near newly fashionable Covent Garden, was not an average room. In many ways it was an ideal rendezvous for the cell – once the Underground had become too dangerous for detailed plotting – because it was situated over a deserted shop apparently awaiting conversion. There was a side door and a narrow staircase, and another door at the back of the staircase, leading out to a tiny mews yard. On the edge of the shining new Covent Garden development, yet not part of it, the dingy property was like something shipwrecked from another time.

'What about the owner of the shop?' Lamb had asked.

'The owner is sympathetic to our cause,' was all that Beagle replied, leaving Lamb to wonder whether Beagle was not the owner of the shop. At least there was no inquisitive shopkeeper to monitor their arrivals and departures, the sort that Monkey feared. Was Beagle's flat suitable perhaps for the Lair? Was that the intention? But now Fox was speaking.

'I wish one could have introduced an animal, say a *dog*, into the picture! Otherwise, it could seem a little, well, *sensational* . . .' Fox, who had the prints on his lap, sounded rather wistful; his voice trailed away as Beagle gave him a look of undisguised contempt.

'Do you introduce a dog into *your* work,' he began and then broke off. 'Oh, what's the use? Let's discuss the statement. Right, Monko? Right, Chick?' Lamb thought with a little stab of pain that Beagle seemed to be assuming some kind of inner command, now that he and Chicken had carried out this successful form of raid; then she laughed at herself. She could hardly be jealous of Chicken, now that would be ridiculous. Lamb, like the others, concentrated on the statement that Prince Ferdinand and Princess Amy would be asked to make on television on the subject of innocent rights . . .

'Where's Tom?' asked Fox suddenly. He had been silent during most of the discussion but Beagle's brutal dismissal of the notion of an animal – possibly a dog – lending the photographs some kind of symbolic dignity had evidently riled him; or maybe the exchange had raised painful memories of Noel's rejection at the main Innoright meetings.

There was silence. As a matter of fact Lamb had been wondering for some time why Tom's absence had not been explained; why Monkey for example had given the signal to abandon the earlier rendezvous before Victoria where Tom was due to join the train. There had been no explanation of that at the time, but then things had happened fast once she had glimpsed Monkey's blue handkerchief; Beagle, she remembered, had been in a state of exhilaration – but that was presumably explained by the successful photographic raid on Prince Ferdinand.

'Where's Tom?' repeated Fox stubbornly. 'Monkey, I think you should tell us. You're the leader.'

Monkey cleared his throat and raised one eyebrow. 'I regret to tell you all – Tom is dead.'

'Dead!' exclaimed Fox, petulance abandoned. Lamb at the same time was experiencing a feeling of overwhelming relief: now she would no longer worry over Tom, lie awake at night worrying; above all she would no longer have to keep her fear of Tom from Beagle – his friend.

'How dreadful! He was so young!' That was Chicken, as though talking of some former pupil.

'What does age have to do with it?' Pussy sounded as if she was preparing to be difficult on some minor point: she did not appear to be particularly surprised or even distressed.

'Well, wasn't it – a heart attack? Something like that?' Chicken again.

'Was it?' Pussy was increasingly captious.

'As a matter of fact it wasn't.' This was Beagle. 'As a matter of fact the police are treating Tom's death as murder. How about that, then?' He faced them, hands on his thin hips, smiling faintly. Like Pussy, he chose to express no regrets.

Lamb realized that she was the only one who hadn't said anything.

'How dreadful!' she exclaimed, echoing Chicken, whose sentiments, if banal, had been appropriate. She added piously: 'It's even more dreadful if he was murdered, of course.'

'How do you know all this, Beagle?' – Fox, high complaining voice.

'Can I tell them, Monkey?' Beagle was for once almost deferential. It occurred to Lamb that although Monkey knew that Tom was dead, he had not broken the news to them until pressed by Fox about Tom's whereabouts.

Monkey nodded.

'I was there,' announced Beagle. 'No, no, not literally there,' – a shade of the old impatience returned. 'I wasn't there when he was killed. No one was there when he was killed – except the killer that is. But I was at the Press Conference. Or rather I came late for the Press Conference, last job took longer than expected, but I did get there. Part of my work, isn't it? Photographing Royals – Royals of all sorts and in all sorts of positions.'

Beagle pointed his trainer shoe in the direction of Prince Ferdinand and Mirabella, still lying on the floor beneath the sad soulful gaze of the seals.

'Tom was there too: he was a journalist. You didn't know that? Some of you knew that. He was a mate of mine, at least you all knew that. That's how we met, working together. That's how I knew he was a good bloke where animals were concerned. We cooked up something – but that's another story.'

'He was killed *there*?' Fox was still incredulous. 'At the Royal Press Conference, the one we saw on TV? But I watched that—'

'Not there. In the hotel lounge outside. Somebody went and stabbed him, cool as you please. The lounge had been full of people, was currently empty because of the conference, empty save for Tom – Tom and his murderer.'

'Go on,' said Monkey slowly. 'They've a right to hear the rest of the story.'

'Afterwards the police questioned everyone – everyone at the conference, I suppose. Must have taken a bit of time. Not the Prince and Princess, I dare say. Everyone else. Anyway they questioned me, because we were mates, as I told you.'

'Who, who killed him?' began Lamb rather tremulously.

'*Why* was he killed?' exclaimed Chicken at the same time much more strongly, making Lamb realize that her question could be construed as being nothing more than inane, whereas Chicken as usual was able to make an intelligent case for her intervention. 'When you know why, you know who, as they say in all the best detective stories.'

'On that subject, Chick, you might feel like being in touch with the police,' remarked Beagle, staring at Chicken. 'If you're that interested. I'm sure they would be interested. To meet you.'

Chicken stared back, but Lamb had the impression that she was just slightly ruffled. Fox burst in, breaking the moment of tension: 'I hope you won't dream of any such thing, Chicken. We don't want him connected to us now in any way. Now that he's safely dead.'

'Safely dead,' observed Pussy. 'Now that's an odd way of putting it.' Nobody seemed to pay her any attention.

'It could be dangerous, well, dangerous for the Plan,' pursued Fox. 'A dangerous connection.'

'He is connected to us. He was connected to us when he was alive and he's connected to us now he's dead.' Beagle's smile had faded. He sounded quite savage.

'What are you trying to say?' demanded Fox.

Beagle looked at Monkey. Monkey nodded once more.

'I am trying to say that Tom was a spy, a nark, an informer.' Beagle spoke with increasing passion. 'I'm glad he's dead in a manner of speaking because he would probably have ended by betraying the whole fucking Plan. In another way, I'm furious he's dead because it's brought all of us, and the Plan, into danger. From this, chaps, you may gather definitively that I did not kill him. In case you're getting any funny ideas.'

Monkey lifted an eyebrow, preparatory to making one of his more sonorous statements. 'From what Beagle tells me, we may have to change the Underground Plan. Tom knew far too much – well, he knew a great deal, if not everything. We'll have to rethink.'

'At least let's be positive!' cried Chicken encouragingly. 'The photographic coup, now that's going to help our cause a great deal. It'll be quite exciting watching the interview, won't it, and seeing them making the first really strong statement on behalf of the innocent that this Royal

Family has ever made. I honestly don't count Prince Charles and the underprivileged, I mean a man who goes hunting . . .'

'Can they now refuse?' enquired Lamb. Her voice to her own ears was anxious; but then anxiety on this particular subject was comprehensible.

'We've made them an offer they can't refuse, in the words of the movie,' replied Monkey. 'This is the text.' He pointed to it. 'And the presenter, Jemima Whats-it, is ready to receive it.'

'So easy,' murmured Fox. 'If we can do this with mere photographs, what can't we do with our little Royal Madam herself.'

Pussy smiled ruminatively, as though at some image in her mind, not necessarily a pleasant one.

'You know the new Underground Plan,' began Lamb slowly. Tom was dead. She knew that she must now eliminate all the familiar feelings of anxiety, it was vital to proceed calmly, this was how she was justifying her whole existence, wasn't it?

'I have an idea,' went on Lamb. 'A new idea which might work . . .' She explained, her confidence growing as she spoke.

'I could help on that,' said Beagle. 'Fox, you could help me.'

'I could help you both,' contributed Chicken firmly. 'It's my special interest, you see.'

So they plotted, as the seals continued to gaze mutely down on the various and varied faces of the people who had constituted themselves their human saviours.

10
Speaking up for Animals

The terrible screaming which filled Cumberland Palace would, thought Ione Quentin, remain in her ears long after many sounds more generally associated with royal life (the noise of the bands, the noise of the crowds laughing and murmuring and clapping, the noise of the ceremonial horses clattering in the early morning) were forgotten.

'Ma'am, it'll be all right. They'll take care of it.'

Princess Amy gave another scream which sounded something like: 'They won't, they won't, they won't,' though the connection was not clear. One word, 'animals', could be discerned, and then the words became incomprehensible and finally turned into sobs. When the sobs were diminishing, Ione risked another gentle touch to the royal shoulder. Princess Amy raised herself on one elbow and gazed at her lady-in-waiting. Tears – aided by screams – had washed away most of her make-up: but the long eyelashes surrounding the enormous eyes which were her best feature were spiky-black with a mixture of tears and mascara. The full pouting mouth for once made Princess Amy look more like an injured child than a sulky young woman.

Unbidden and irreverent thoughts came to Ione Quentin's mind: one of these unbidden thoughts concerned Prince Ferdinand. Ione thought it was a pity the Prince could not glimpse his fiancée now. Ione, whose language, at least to herself, could be surprisingly robust, thought: for once P.A. looks positively fuckable. If P.F. saw her now, he might not waste quite so much energy in other directions . . .

Ione Quentin hurriedly pulled herself up and concentrated on the matter in hand. She put her arms round Amy's shoulders and Amy turned and buried her face in Ione's neat cream-coloured silk shirt, the shirt she wore so often (or something identical) that it was like a uniform. The feeling of Amy snuffling into the shirt, wet and still gasping or sobbing mildly, reminded Ione briefly of a pug puppy they had had as a child. Was that the pug Lydia had adored, the baby pug with a hernia who had to be put down? Another profitless line of thought. The sobs had turned to mere shudders of the frame held against hers. The worst was over.

Wait, thought Ione, what am I saying? The worst is only just beginning.

If the worst was just beginning, nevertheless Ione Quentin's arm round the weeping Princess Amy represented the last link in a long chain of shock, horror and disbelief since Innoright – or its representative – had rung Jemima Shore and requested certain public statements from the royal couple. Otherwise certain photographs would be released to the continental and American Press, and shown at least to the British Press.

'As if they'd dream of printing such filth!' one important person at another even more important palace had exclaimed, apprised of the emergency.

'Oh, I don't know,' murmured Major Pat Smylie-Porter, taking another long look at Mirabella's sinuous naked frame. 'Things ain't what they used to be where the Press is concerned, we all know that. Her without him perhaps. A Page Two picture.'

'Don't you mean Page Three?' rapped back the important person irritably. 'And anyway the wretched woman is hardly built for that kind of thing, our own horse would be—' He stopped to find Major Pat gazing blandly back at him.

On the other hand there was nothing bland about Rick Vancy, his usual calm tinged with manifest disgust at the idea of TUS's sacrosanct exclusive interview being tampered with by some 'unfocused friends of the animal kingdom', as he termed Innoright. To Jemima Shore, he remarked over lunch at Le Caprice: 'They have to find these gross people and they have to find them fast. Or find the photographs, and the negatives, *all* the negatives. We have to deaccessify them, correction, your police have to deaccessify them. What are your police doing?'

'Maybe we should send for the CIA,' suggested Jemima Shore sweetly.

'For Chrissake, those bunglers,' began Rick Vancy, before realizing that he had once again failed to identify a British joke; he really had to work on the whole subject of British jokes, thought Rick Vancy wearily, once this crazy business was over. A fun programme indeed! Even the animals were getting in on the act, it appeared, and that was not turning out to be much fun either.

From long experience, Rick Vancy knew himself to be a man of naturally liberal stance on every issue, without being so wildly liberal that TUS became greatly alarmed: it was good for them to be just a little alarmed, at least from time to time. For example, Rick Vancy was critical of the US government on Nicaragua ('a revolution with *no* right to survive?') and stern towards the British government on Northern Ireland ('a colony with *any* right to survive?'). In a seemingly relaxed fashion, Rick Vancy, with his moral eyes half shut, could sense the public mood at its most liberal and push his own position just a little bit further in order to adopt that hard-hitting stance upon which his admirers counted.

But animals! The ecology was one thing: that could be political to put it mildly and generally was, but animal rights pure and simple! Animal rights when there was nuclear energy for or against, chemical warfare for or against, on another level Afghanistan for or against the Russian presence, Cambodia for or against the Vietnamese presence, or just the Middle East for or against, if you could put it like that, and after many years of sage reporting, Rick Vancy thought that you almost could. Either you cared or you didn't care, but you went there and reported anyway, with luck returning. And as a matter of fact, Rick Vancy did care.

With all this to be considered, Rick Vancy felt he might pass a lifetime of activity without getting around to animal rights for or against ... Not that Rick himself wasn't an animal lover; two English sheepdogs had graced the first Vancy marriage to a Norwegian (the one that was sometimes supposed to have involved an Englishwoman, maybe on the strength of the dogs). Another live-in relationship sans marriage which *had* involved an Englishwoman had also encompassed a relationship with a rat. Yes, a rat, Goddammit, a tame or tame-ish domestic rat, the marks of whose bites were still with him long after the scars left by crazy English Tammy, herself a bit of a biter, had faded. And Goddammit once more, Rick had been fond of that rat! He shared memories with that rat.

Some of this Rick thought of expressing to Jemima, irked, he had to admit, that their relationship remained friendly and nothing more. Frankly, this was not what he had been led to expect in New York. Lunch at Le Caprice was all very well: in fact it was very agreeable. And Rick Vancy had noted with quiet satisfaction the moment when the corner table had become his table and stopped being inevitably Jemima's. So that Jemima, giving a last-minute lunch to her old friend Jamie Grand, the powerful presenter of the new arts programme *Literature Now!* had had to bow ruefully in Rick's direction, seeing him already installed there.

On the other hand, thought Rick, however socially gratifying, this had probably not helped his cause with Jemima. Rick had a sudden inspiration. Would an account of some of Tammy's odder practices, with or without the rat, turn Jemima on? Maybe all Englishwomen of roughly Tammy's age and background shared the same odd predilection for domestic rats in intimate situations. Maybe the rat was the key ...

'Hey, did you ever know a woman who owned a rat, called Tammy?' he began. 'The woman I mean, not the rat.' Since Jemima continued to look politely blank, he added: 'The woman was called Tammy. No, forget it. Listen, these people are sick. Isn't that right? All the causes in the world, all the dying babies in Ethiopia, all the dying babies in the Sudan—'

'All the dying *girl* babies,' put in Jemima who suddenly remembered she had completed a programme on female infanticide (tentative title: *Death is a Chauvinist*) shortly before leaving Megalith, and wondered what on earth had happened to it.

'Exactly. All the damn babies. And these guys go for animal rights. To me that's crazy. It's either crazy or it's sick. And given what they're asking us to do, it's sick. Come on, Jemima, give. These are your Brits for Chrissake. Do they just hate society? Is that it? Or just hate us humble humans without getting as far as a dangerously complicated concept like society?'

'I'm not sure about this lot,' said Jemima honestly, bringing her mind reluctantly back from the fate of *Death is a Chauvinist* (a private call to Cherry perhaps?). 'There are some very obviously violent ones around, animal liberationists, you read about them in the newspapers, horrifying manifestoes, threatening to burn, wreck, kill, whatever. Up till recently they tended to threaten but on the whole not perform. Or not perform particularly drastically. Then there was that incident in Westminster Square. You must have read about that. Ghastly! Carnage, that's the only word. The word everybody used and for once the right word. The fact that only, repeat only, horses were actually killed made it worse somehow.'

Rick looked at her quizzically. 'Better to have we horrid or humble humans knocked off than horses?'

'Does one have to choose?' countered Jemima. 'No, no, I mean that it's surely specially frightful that people would kill or rather in most cases hideously maim – so they had to be destroyed – the very species they were allegedly trying to help.'

'The old terrorist situation. The innocent tend to suffer along with the guilty. And I guess you have to locate these guys somewhere in the terrorist pantheon.'

'Innoright itself hasn't so far committed an act of terrorism as such,' Jemima pointed out. 'And I should add that according to my pal Pompey – the policeman – Innoright doesn't exactly have a *violent* reputation. More crazy than sick, to accept your distinction.'

'Oddballs?'

'What they're asking is not all that odd. If you believe what they believe. Not that we're going to give it to them,' added Jemima hastily, in case Rick Vancy's suspicions about the general British softness on the subject of the fate of animals as opposed to the fate of the human race in general should be confirmed. 'It's the principle of speaking up for animals. They feel no one does it, or no one of sufficient importance in the public mind. The Prince and Princess will do it, put it on the map for good. That's all.'

She was eating fish as usual, having politely described herself as 'almost a vegetarian' when she first met Rick (today: *salade tiède à lotte*). Rick on the other hand as he invariably did was eating chopped steak. And now that he knew Jemima better, he had slipped into drinking what she privately termed the Puritan champagne – Perrier water. I may be 'almost a vegetarian' thought Jemima, but he's 'almost a teetotaller' without liking to admit it. She herself was drinking white wine. To be frank, had it not been for Rick's sneaky abstemiousness, she would normally have diluted it with some of the Puritan champagne; as it was, she felt she must stand up for the rights of Sancerre to be drunk unadulterated.

'That's all!' echoed Rick. He pushed aside the steak (he always ate exactly two-thirds of it, as though he had measured it in advance, Jemima noticed) and began to tick off the Innoright demands: 'No more animal laboratory experiments of any sort, even in the cause of medicine, experiments on human beings if necessary instead.'

'Experiments on the human beings who benefit from the results,' corrected Jemima. 'That's what it said. Not the actual sick of course, just members of the human as opposed to the animal species.'

'Okay, okay.' He went on: 'In no particular order: no more fur coats or fur garments or trimmings. Leather not mentioned, I note. They're soft on leather. So-called Fur Law to be introduced. All existing fur coats to be sold abroad, proceeds to go to the rehabilitation of animals rescued from scientific laboratories, factory farms etc. Any woman seen wearing a fur coat in the street—' Rick broke off. 'Do you know something? This is fundamentalist rubbish. That clause about women wearing fur coats in the streets and the right of citizen's arrest, it reminds me of Iran, women without the veil, Pakistan, women with make-up—'

'Is it a fundamental liberty to wear a fur coat?' began Jemima. She stopped. 'Listen Rick, I'm not trying to argue the toss. If I were to be honest, I suppose like most people here, and doubtless a good many people in the States, I have to face the fact that I simply shudder away from the subject of animal experiments. Just imagine if anyone were to lay a finger on Midnight!'

'Cats not rats,' thought Rick irrelevantly. 'No wonder she didn't relate to Tammy and her rat.'

'On the other hand,' went on Jemima, 'leukaemia in children, for example, animals who suffer to save children from leukaemia, animals versus children – I just don't want to think about it. And I'm supposed to be an investigator!'

'You've never gotten around to making a programme about it.'

Jemima smiled. 'Now that's an idea. Instead of our exclusive interview with P.A. and P.F., I make a programme about Innoright. I show the famous photographs. I interview Mirabella Prey. The only problem being: where are the people behind all this? How do I lure them on to the silver screen? Any ideas?'

'This is the point, sweetheart. Where are they? And what are the police doing about finding them?'

'I may as well tell you one more thing, Rick. Now this is not crazy, this is serious. Far from killing, one of them was recently actually killed. A journalist who was a member of Innoright. One of them, one of the Innoright members died recently, was killed at a conference. Treated by the police as murder. Not much publicity, not exactly covered up, just not stressed when all attention was on the royal couple.'

'Jesus!' Rick took a quick restorative swig of the Puritan champagne. 'Murder! And what are the police doing about that?'

On the subject of what the police were doing about that – that being the unaccidental death of Jean-Pierre Schwarz-Albert – more voices than the plaintive voice of Rick Vancy were being raised. For example, Detective Superintendent John Portsmouth found his murder hunt suddenly interrupted by a series of interested enquiries concerning Animal Rights activists in general, Innoright in particular.

'Everybody keeps telling me in their panicky way that there has to be a connection,' observed Pompey stolidly to Detective Sergeant Vaillant as they sat alone, at the end of the day, in the incident room set up for the murder of Schwarz-Albert a.k.a. Tom, a member of the Innoright cell. 'And then they ask me will I please inform them what the connection is? The man dies. The photographs are taken. The threats are made: unless HRH speaks up—'

'Unless HRH and HH speak up—' corrected Vaillant.

'Unless they both speak up. But it's her they're after – cousin of the Monarch, member of the British Royal Family and all that. Could be seen by the ignorant – and a good many of *them* around – as some form of royal proclamation. A balance to all that hunting by You-know-who and all that shooting by You-know-who-else. Back to the connection. What I say is: if there is a connection, will those who know what it is, please inform me?'

Pompey gazed at Vaillant.

'So far as you know we've drawn a series of blanks. And not for want of trying. The photographer has an alibi, lots of witnesses that he came late, including the place of his other assignment which kept him. Still, we shan't forget him. Not us. We're having another look at him over the photographs of course. So are Special Branch. The film star – what's her name? Do you realize I know her figure better than I know her name?' Since Vaillant looked shocked, Pompey proceeded: 'She swears she can't identify him. Swears she has no idea who knew she was going there to confront the wretched bridegroom. Well, that's what she says.' He paused. 'But he allowed us to search his studio, positively offered it, so that must be clean. Then there are the two women,' Pompey added.

'The witnesses?'

Pompey pursued his train of thought. 'Odd that *two* women who made statements, apparently quite unconnected with each other – but we'll have to check that – should prove to be members of Innoright.'

'There's a lot of it about,' put in Vaillant helpfully.

'Ordinary rank and file members. All the same it's an odd coincidence. And—'

'In this office we don't believe in coincidences,' finished Vaillant.

'Charity Wadham, a teacher if I remember rightly. Meeting a friend for tea in the Republican lounge, unaware it had been blocked off for the Royal Press Conference. Friend went happily to the other lounge, Mrs Wadham strays into the wrong lounge and sees our man apparently sleeping. Friend confirms story. But Mrs Charity Wadham is a member of Innoright, a founder member, what's more. The other woman – what is her name? – something foreign, Muscovite . . .'

'Moscowitz.'

'Big woman,' went on Pompey. 'Rather gloomy. Appears to be Polish. Doesn't sound it, but looks it. Ordinary member of Innoright. She finally admitted that she popped into the Republican merely to go to the ladies for free – felt hot and tired after prolonged shopping in nearby Marks and Sparks. Subsequently rested in the empty Republican lounge. Except it wasn't empty. It contained the dead body of our friend. She didn't notice. And didn't notice Wadham's appearance either. Doesn't know Wadham anyway.'

'Plausible?'

'Why not? Innoright is a biggish organization, the outer layer of it, in some ways not unlike Greenpeace, with lots of different causes, all aspects of innocence abused is how they put it. Or some such phrase. Security all the while was concentrated on the actual conference inside the big double doors. The murderer certainly hit on a convenient moment to do it. No other clues.' Pompey sighed. 'With this interview business on top of it all, Special Branch not being very cooperative as usual, it beats me. Except I am not paid to be beaten. And nor, young fellow-me-lad, are you.'

'A message came from on high,' Vaillant spoke delicately, 'while you were talking to Mrs Pompey about – whatever it was you were talking about.'

'Sutton's seed catalogue!' exclaimed Pompey bitterly. 'She thinks I've hidden it on purpose. Go on.'

'The Palace has said no.'

'That's the message?'

'That's the drift of it,' murmured Vaillant.

'So the interview goes ahead? And no statement? No speaking up for the poor little animals from our young couple?'

'Not a dog's bark if you'll pardon the expression,' concluded Vaillant.

Pompey presumably did pardon the expression since he did not refer to it.

'Very interesting. Very interesting indeed,' was all he said. 'Have a look in the drawer will you and see if that damn catalogue is lurking. Do you suppose I ought to be grateful that Mrs Portsmouth is into flowers not animals?'

But Vaillant knew better than to answer that one.

11
Courtiers

'I guess I'm intrigued about *her*. I mean, how do you treat a guy when you find out he's been cheating on you? If you're a princess, that is?' added Rick Vancy.

'Just the same as any other girl?' suggested Jemima. 'Unless you choose to stab him with the sharp end of your tiara.'

'But how is that?' persisted Rick. 'We have to know this.' He sounded worried. 'Susanna, do you have anything on this?'

Susanna Blanding, researcher royal to TUS, her lap piled high with the memos, documents, notes and the various thick red books emblazoned with gold without which she seemed unable to move, was crouched in the back seat of Rick Vancy's car behind Jemima. Curt, her American colleague, whose whole role as TUS researcher had become no more precise over the last few days, was asleep beside her. They were all four on their way to Cumberland Palace. Rick was speaking in a lull between the many telephone calls both incoming and outgoing which were deemed necessary during the comparatively short journey from Jemima's flat to the Palace.

Susanna Blanding did not answer.

'Soo-zee, I'm talk-ing to you,' sang Rick in his melodious baritone voice, the voice which was as much part of his image as his English-film-star looks. 'Do you have anything on the kind of emotions which could be coming into play here? And Soo-zee, would you extinguish that cigarette?'

'Emotions, Rick?' panted Susanna, stubbing out the cigarette across Curt's recumbent body. Jemima wondered into what delightful reverie of eighteenth-century royal descent she had been plunged.

'Do you have anything relevant on Amy's emotional make-up? In confidence, maybe. Psychological reports? Doctors? Anything like that? Something to help us build up the correct picture of the way this young woman will respond to the unique pressures currently being imposed upon her. I guess I'm talking about strain here, Susanna. Strain and Amy's emotional stability.'

'I could research you some nice mad royal ancestors if you like.' Susanna Blanding spoke cautiously, feeling her way. 'For example the old Russian Princess, Amy's grandmother, was always said to be absolutely bonkers. Ended up thinking she was an Alpine goat: always wore a little bell round her neck and loved climbing stairs.'

Jemima took a quick look at Rick's face and decided to intervene speedily in the interests of Anglo-American accord.

'We don't exactly know he's been cheating on her,' she pointed out. 'After all, he did have his clothes on.'

'C'mon sweetheart – where clothes are concerned—' But perhaps fortunately Rick's rejoinder was cut off by the high loud bleeping of another incoming telephone call.

As they were slowing down for the small black police post at the entrance to the Palace drive, a slight young man in horn-rim glasses walking a dog could be seen parallel to them on the pavement. The dog, which had a vaguely bulldoggish aspect, lurched silently into the centre of the road, causing Rick to brake violently. Susanna Blanding bumped her nose and lost her papers. Curt woke up.

'Noel, Noel!' came the high well-modulated voice of the dog's owner. The young man patted his cowering animal and glared at the inhabitants of the car as if dogs not cars traditionally occupied the tarmac thoroughfare.

'Dogs should be banned from urban conurbations!' exclaimed Rick; Jemima thought his unusual irritability was probably due to the ordeal ahead, something outside his usual experience of war-stained statesmen. 'Do you know the figures on city-centre animal-related disease in children?'

'Daddy won't let Sabrina – that's my sister – bring Emma – that's her dog – to London,' contributed Susanna, anxious to restore herself to Rick Vancy's favour.

Cumberland Palace had a placid air of early Georgian elegance. Its low wall abutting Regent's Park (on which Tom and Beagle had once plastered the words AMY MEANS TROUBLE) was now free from any such excrescence. In its graceful sylvan setting, green lawns surrounding, the plash of oars on a lake heard nearby, this might have been a mansion in a country park; as it was its look of *rus in urbe* made the outer serenity especially delightful to behold.

The inner serenity of the Palace, in so far as it had ever existed, was however at this moment markedly disturbed.

Over the heads of the royal couple, Ione Quentin's eyes met those of Major Pat Smylie-Porter. The Major gazed steadily back at her without visible sign of either worry or exasperation, both of which would have been amply justified by the distressing circumstances in which the urbane Major Pat currently found himself. Nevertheless the steady look that passed between the two courtiers indicated that they understood each other perfectly; the situation, in a favourite cliché passed round Cumberland Palace in recent days, was desperate but not serious. As veterans of many similar situations – if never admittedly *quite* so serious – the two of them found themselves experiencing a certain not unpleasant quickening of the pulse at the challenge to their powers thus presented.

Although neither the Major nor Ione would have dreamt of phrasing it like that, certainly not to each other, they were aware of being needed. Never more than at the present time. And Ione Quentin, unmarried at thirty-one, highly competent and professional at her job, which despite its old-fashioned title of 'lady-in-waiting' often called for executive qualities, as though she was in fact the manager of a popular star – Amy being the star – the efficient self-controlled Ione Quentin liked to be needed. She knew that about herself.

Major Pat, looking at her one more moment before dropping his eyes and fixing his tie, thought involuntarily what a thoroughly good girl – woman really – Ione was. In Major Pat's opinion, Ione was very much Colonel Q's daughter beneath that ladylike exterior; although thank God she didn't look like the terrifying old boy (Major Pat's former commanding officer). Nor did she collect guns: Major Pat still remembered certain evenings in the Mess centring round Colonel Q's collection with an admiring shudder... All the same, Ione had something of Colonel Q's celebrated resourcefulness.

To put it another way, in the present crisis, thank God he had Ione aboard. Somewhere at the back of Major Pat's mind was another unspoken thought that he would probably end by marrying Ione one day, the Major being a widower with two increasingly recalcitrant teenage children. Ione would be good with them, God knew, given what she had been through with that pathetic drop-out sister of hers. Now *she* took after the late and disastrous Mrs Quentin. Lydia. Christ, would *she* have to live with them...?

Oddly enough in the same frozen moment, Ione's own thoughts had veered briefly, as they often did, to Lydia Quentin, a.k.a. Lamb. Lydia was staying out very late these days, nor had Ione, no fool, believed for one instant in the endless stories of cinemas with Janey, Melissa, Gaby and so on. Sadly, Ione knew too much about her sister. Something more would have to be done about Lydia...

The moment passed. Both the Major and Ione devoted themselves once more to the issue in hand.

Although the cameras had already been set up in the large Vienna Drawing-Room (so-called for its relics of the Congress, imported by some

Austrian ancestress) the couple were still seated in Amy's delicately furnished blue sitting-room.

'I want to see them,' Princess Amy was saying mutinously, 'I want to see the photographs. Otherwise I won't talk to the Press. Not to these Americans, not to anyone. I don't care.' She stuck out her lower lip. Recent events had thinned her somewhat. She looked very pretty indeed in an Amy-blue dress with an enormous white sailor collar, the picture marred only by the expression on her pouting face, somewhere between adult fury and girlish sulks.

Prince Ferdinand rolled his eyes.

'Please darling, be reasonable,' he began. Then he burst out: 'You're being utterly childish.'

'I'm being childish, am I?' Amy's voice rose. 'And you're grown up, I suppose. And that ghastly woman, is she grown up too? Is that the point? Go on, say it.'

A footman entered, dressed in the discreet dark-green semi-uniform of the Palace, adapted long ago by the Duke from his regimental dress. He bowed his neck in the same discreet traditional fashion. 'Your Royal Highness, Mr Richard Vancy and Miss Jemima Shore have arrived and are in the Vienna Drawing-Room.'

'Ma'am, do you not think it would be a good idea to join them?' suggested Ione in her agreeable, low voice.

Princess Amy looked at her; her expression was at its most Hanoverian, once again recalling her late father. Suddenly she stood up and gave a wide, ravishing smile. The sulky face was transformed, the pout totally vanished.

'Let's go then,' she said. 'On your heads be it.'

'And what is that supposed to mean, my love?' enquired the Prince in a voice of barely suppressed *ennui* as he rose to his feet. Major Pat thought that the Prince's sudden passionate wish to find himself a million miles away from this wayward girl, instead of being committed to marry her within weeks, was only too apparent.

'I was thinking of the threats made by those Animal Rights people,' replied Princess Amy, giving him a special smile, which was almost seraphic in its sweetness. 'That's all. Come along, darling.'

The Princess undoubtedly looked wonderful as she swayed out of the room on Ferdel's arm, although her high white heels hardly brought her up to her fiancé's shoulder. At the same time, Ione, seeing that particular expression, that glint in the royal blue eyes, feared something, without knowing quite what it might be.

The royal couple entered the Vienna Drawing-Room, dominated by the huge early nineteenth-century portrait of dancers at some grand ball held at the Congress, just as Jemima had finished explaining patiently to Rick Vancy: 'I curtsey modestly off camera because I'm British, and you don't bow on or off camera.' She wanted to add: 'Because you're a genuine American republican democrat quite uninterested in the doings of British Royalty – which only leaves unclear what your television station is doing here in the first place.' Instead she added: 'I'll begin with "Your Royal Highnesses" leaving you to continue the interview with "Prince Ferdinand" or "Princess Amy". None of this makes you – or me for that matter – a courtier.'

'The picture I have is that we're all courtiers here,' Rick responded with something less than his usual urbanity.

'Trust me,' murmured the (American) producer of the show yearningly, as she had indeed been murmuring yearningly at intervals since the project of the interview was first discussed.

Then Rick visibly cheered up at the sight of Princess Amy whose enchanting friendly smile, no less than her nubile figure, filled him with sudden hopes of achieving the first really *truly* informal interview with British Royalty ... Fergie was not a precedent. Remember after all that the Duchess of York, another lady with a nubile figure and an enchanting friendly smile, was not exactly Royalty to the palace born, having been actually born a commoner, a term which Susanna Blanding had recently dinned into his head. Unhesitatingly Rick Vancy dismissed from his mind all the many other really truly informal royal interviews: this and only this would be the one where the British Royals would be speaking as you have never heard them before, to coin the phrase that TUS would undoubtedly be using to promote it. After all no royal couple that he'd ever heard of (not Prince Charles and Princess Diana – another 'commoner' in Susanna's phrase; not Prince Andrew and Fergie, well, not exactly) had been threatened with recent scandalous pictures of him and her, her in this case being a naked film star ... Under the circumstances Princess Amy *had* to show herself yet more informal than anyone in the history of royal informality. As for Prince Ferdinand ...

As the Prince and Princess entered, Rick stood up. Jemima Shore gave her discreet curtsey and Susanna Blanding a curtsey which was both deeper and less graceful. To his discomfiture, Rick Vancy found himself instinctively starting to bend a knee with them: he compromised by giving a bow which was at least less ludicrous (and anyway the whole thing was off camera).

It was not until late on in the interview that the incident took place. By this time indeed the American producer was congratulating herself that the material would in fact need remarkably little editing before transmission, scheduled to be networked later that day in the States, making it an evening show in England.

Princess Amy gave vent to a series of unexceptional views on such matters as the family ('I love children, little children, I love my sisters' children, they're going to be our bridesmaids, I'm sure I'll love my children' – laughter – blush – 'our children'), and the man's position ('I love the idea of the man being the head of the family like they always have been, haven't they? It's traditional, isn't it? Although I'm also very very modern, aren't I, Ferdel?' Laughter, blush and even perhaps a slight pout). On being questioned about her new life in her fiancé's country, however, she declared more positively: 'I'm not just going to stick in the country and be a cabbage, that would be utterly drear.' (Sweet sidelong look at Ferdel, but a hint of steel here, too, thought Jemima: it was the first indication she had had that there might be more to Princess Amy than this pretty piglet in her pretty blue dress with its ruffled white collar.)

Prince Ferdinand for his part declared himself, equally impeccably, as looking forward to introducing Amy to her new country. 'And you will make a very pretty cabbage, darling – ouch—' So Amy followed what was presumably a royal pinch with a royal kiss on the cheek. At the same time Ferdel also stressed his English ancestry, his English schooldays, his English tastes – 'This shirt is English,' he told Rick Vancy, having observed that Rick was wearing a shirt from the same shirt-maker in St James's. 'Except for the coronet. That is not English.'

Ferdel even remembered, as an afterthought and tribute to the programme's origins, to point out his many links with the United States, including a year at an American university. Currently there were what he pleasantly described as 'sporting and business links'; but neither Rick on behalf of TUS nor the Prince himself, on his own behalf, saw any reason to give further prominence to what these links might be; even if in some publicly unacknowledged way, they had been responsible for the exclusive interview in the first place. Amy, he felt, would certainly enjoy the States with its friendly people . . .

It was left to Amy, extracting what was seen to be a sweet revenge for the cabbage episode, to exclaim: 'How fabulous! I'm *so* looking forward to seeing America! Now you've promised to take me, in front of all these cameras.' The cameras (in fact only two of them) recorded and the American producer passed Jemima a white card: I.D. WHEN AND WHERE VISIT. But this the Prince smilingly declined to do.

Because matters had really gone so swimmingly, if not exactly excitingly, neither Rick, Jemima, the producer, nor, least of all Prince Ferdinand was prepared for Amy's sudden departure from the not-exactly-scripted, but not-exactly-not-scripted either, shape of the inter-view. Only Ione Quentin might perhaps have warned them that something was afoot. But Ione, seated at the back of the drawing-room with Susanna Blanding, had retreated to that ladylike obscurity which her office guaranteed for her on these occasions.

'Oh, but I do have lots of views of my own,' exclaimed Amy airily as Jemima was questioning her concerning her wardrobe.

'Princess Amy, would you say that you are highly clothes-conscious? Or do you more or less leave it to the designers?'

'For example I feel very strongly about animals and things like that,' continued Princess Amy, leaning forward slightly; she sounded a little more breathless perhaps than previously, and her blue eyes were wide open, otherwise there was nothing to indicate the totally unexpected nature of her response. 'And where clothes are concerned, I hate fur coats, don't you? I hate things like that. I think there ought to be a Fur Law, now how about that? People jolly well shouldn't be allowed to wear fur coats. And then there's experimenting on animals and horrid things like that, it shouldn't be allowed, should it? Now what about a law about that too? I mean, it's us who take all the pills and medicines and things like that, not the poor animals, so why not experiment on us instead of—' Princess Amy's eyes roved round and in a moment of inspiration, fell upon Happy and Boobie, lying slumbering magnificently on the Savonnerie carpet in front of the fireplace. 'Instead of those poor old doggies?' Out of excitement or pity, Amy's voice broke. 'Too, too cruel,' she concluded.

About the same moment, another white card from the producer had reached Jemima's side of the table, with something similar in front of Rick. KEEP GOING read Jemima's card, continuing optimistically THIS MUST BE PLANNED. Rick's card read: ASK RE PALACE BLOOD DEMO.

'Your Royal Highness,' began Rick excitedly, democracy thrown to the winds in the new and invigorating atmosphere of a scoop: 'Now regarding your very warm and human feelings concerning animal rights, there was, was there not, a demonstration not so long ago—'

But by this time, Prince Ferdinand, leaning forward, had picked up his fiancée's small white hand with its gleaming aquamarine ring, and was giving it a distinctly continental kiss: 'I love you for your compassion for all wild things,' said the Prince seriously. 'You will love your new country where there is so much work to be done in this direction.' His eyes met hers, a shot which subsequently fascinated all those who pored over it at TUS later. Was it a look of princely command to which she responded? Was the whole thing set up to avoid the tiresome nuisance of those banned photographs marring the wedding? How had Prince Ferdel persuaded Princess Amy to do, in effect, his dirty work for him, since the photographs involved him not her? All these questions remained unanswered at TUS.

But that was later. At the time the TUS team allowed themselves to be dismissed courteously, more or less as arranged, with a few final platitudes about 'wishing you both every happiness', a few final curtseys from Jemima and Susanna Blanding, and a final bow from Rick (he reckoned they'd earned it). Only Curt and the American producer remaining sternly unbowed and uncurtseyed; but then since Curt had taken no active part whatsoever in the entire proceedings, his lack of gesture at least was not necessarily to be interpreted in any positive fashion.

Nevertheless the unvoiced tension, at least on the part of Rick and Jemima, as they drove away from the Palace, was considerable. As was the surprise and the excitement.

'There's that man with the funny-looking dog again, the one that nearly got itself killed,' remarked Jemima by way of light relief.

It was true: Fox and Noel, who had in fact been circling the Palace anxiously during the duration of the interview, had come to rest once more at their previous observation post by the Palace drive. Noel was manifestly exhausted: to tell the truth, the dog, unlike his master, was not a great walker and would in dog terms probably have agreed with Rick Vancy's irritable remarks that dogs should be banned from urban conurbations, since that meant master-led long city walks instead of more leisurely solitary country rambles. But Fox's excitement at the prospect of the revolutionary programme which was being enunciated within the white walls of the Palace, had meant he had been unable to keep himself – and Noel – away.

Somewhere in the distance the bark of sea-lions from the Zoo caused Jemima to think of Louis MacNeice and murmur poetically: 'Smell of French bread in Charlotte Square.' This in turn caused Susanna Blanding to say: 'I'm terribly hungry. That, or I must have a cigarette,' and Rick to suggest that they talked the whole thing through at Le Caprice. (Curt, with his enviable capacity for relaxation, had fallen asleep again.)

'Isn't that dynamite we have there with all that animals lib talk from *her*?' he remarked as he dialled the Caprice number on the car phone. 'Connections to the French lady only too easy to establish. Say, maybe *he* gets turned on by animals—'

'Maybe so, but it bothers me,' confessed Jemima. 'Why did the Palace – predictably – say no statement from them along the Innoright lines, we don't give in to blackmail etc., etc.? And then she made it. Whose plot was it, his, theirs – or hers?'

'Or those courtiers,' suggested Rick, 'those background figures, royal anchors, I guess.'

'Not Ione Quentin!' exclaimed Susanna in a shocked voice from the back seat. 'She's an absolute *pillar*. So's Major Pat. Still, you never know with the Palace. They can be awfully wily.'

'If it was her idea,' pursued Jemima. 'Why? That's what I want to know. Why do it?'

A few hours later when the programme 'Prince and Princess of Hearts' was being shown nationwide on British television, members of the Innoright cell who were watching it together, would echo the words of Jemima Shore more or less exactly.

'Why?' cried Lamb. 'When they said they wouldn't.'

'She said it – well, more or less,' Fox sounded bemused.

'She did not.' That was Pussy, four square.

The rest of the country turned their sets off with contented clicks.

'Listen to that, Kenneth,' said Mrs Taplow to her husband as they sat in their Eaton Square kitchen. 'HRH has turned out very nicely after all, I couldn't have put it better myself about loving animals.'

'Couldn't you, Lizzie? Are you sure?'

Mrs Taplow gave him a sharp look, then addressed herself once more to polishing the Prince's already exquisitely shiny leather shoes.

'You'd better get on with that, Kenneth,' she said after a moment; she spoke equably enough. 'Otherwise it will never be ready.' She pointed to some embroidery on the table: a royal crest was in the process of being created from silk and beads; it had the air of an intended wedding present. Taplow sighed but he obeyed her and picked up the embroidery; once he was immersed in its intricate design, however, his expression relaxed.

The Innoright members had no soothing tasks to which to turn.

'What do we do now?' Chicken turned to Monkey who was still gazing stolidly at the blank television screen.

'We go on with the Underground Plan,' replied Monkey sombrely. 'We don't release the photographs but we go on with the Plan. Mark Two. That wasn't the statement we asked for, the reasoned statement, that was just an outburst from an hysterical girl.'

'Grab her,' said Beagle with a laugh. 'Grab her all the same. She deserves it.' He laughed again. '*I* deserve it.'

Lamb, who tended to feel cold since her illness, experienced a special chill within her.

12

St Francis

'You're not really expecting anything to happen?' enquired Jemima of Pompey over their respective 'jars' (white wine and whisky) in Jemima's secluded top-floor flat overlooking Holland Park. Pompey had dropped in for an early drink on the way back from work to Mrs Pompey: his pretext being that Jemima needed a little off-the-record background briefing on security arrangements for the wedding.

'From our point of view something *has* happened,' pointed out Pompey: but his relaxed tone was not one that Detective Sergeant Vaillant, for example, would have recognized. 'A man was killed and we're not much nearer solving the case,' he added. 'One or two things have come up of course: there's a man with a dog. At the Republican, *with* the bloody dog that afternoon except they wouldn't let him in without a fuss. Said he was a humble fan of Princess Amy, always tried to follow her public appearances from *The Times*, nothing wrong with that, was there?'

'And was there? A good many people are like that.'

'True. But this man had once been a member of Innoright, resigned when there was some fuss about the very same unwelcome dog. We had some leads on him; small, of restricted growth I should say, works on and off for Leaviss – he mentioned the name of one of the leading theatrical costumiers – 'non-violent, or so we believe, but loves to distribute anti-vivisection posters in the most awkward places. Could well have been intending to do so at the Republican if the dog hadn't scuppered his plan.'

'The dagger – paper-knife – is odd, Pompey. It didn't *have* to be someone at the Press Conference, did it? Quite a few of them of course.'

'Quite a few paper-knives, too. And anyone could have helped themselves to the kit, including paper-knife, after the conference began.

Knives and kits not picked up remained at the checking-in desk. By then empty. Your Americans must all have had knives.'

'I'm currently using mine. Useful for dealing with royal memoranda from our industrious English researcher.' Jemima picked it up from the table in front of her and felt the point. 'Yes, bit of a mistake in manufacture, that. Very sharp indeed. Rick has presented his to the aforesaid industrious researcher, who claims to have buried hers somewhere in her historical files. Curt, the silent American, uses his to pick his teeth; when he's awake, that is.'

Jemima, discussing the new details of the case, thought how she had developed an excellent if unacknowledged working relationship with Pompey since their first association (over a television appeal for a missing child).

Jemima was tacitly allowed to give vent to her natural inquisitiveness by discussing those details of a case that Pompey found it discreet to reveal over a 'jar' (as a matter of fact not a few). Pompey on the other hand was a man on whom life with the hard-working albeit whimsical Vaillant sometimes palled. Besides, as he put it, the necessarily hothouse atmosphere of the incident room could also produce 'a wood for the trees' situation. In these moods he welcomed Jemima's proffered 'jars'; including contact with her aforesaid inquisitiveness.

It was true that Jemima's famous 'woman's instinct' was the subject of many traditional jokes between them in which Pompey gave way to heavy gallantry while defending the superior role of patient relentless investigation in the solution of a murder case. Jemima for her part generously allowed Pompey to term it a 'woman's instinct' from long usage (furthermore it did not do to argue overmuch with a contact). Nevertheless she contended strongly that the famous instinct was in fact no more than the thought process of a reasonable human being – not necessarily female.

'What about his own private life? Nothing there? Although I agree it's odd that whoever killed him should choose such a bizarre occasion as a Royal Press Conference if there was no connection. Odd or cunning.'

'Lamentably respectable,' replied Pompey. 'Unmarried. Not gay but no regular girlfriend. Several he took out confirm that.'

'That's *too* respectable,' said Jemima firmly.

'He took out that woman who's working for you once or twice, the writer who goes on history quizzes on the telly; Mrs Pompey likes her. Nothing in it, however.' In case Pompey should have seemed to imply that Mrs Pompey's taste had corrupted his official judgement, he added quickly: 'We checked it out. Talked to her.'

'She didn't tell *me*,' thought Jemima. 'But then, why should she? Besides, Susanna Blanding's attention at present is equally divided between the Cumberland family tree and Rick Vancy.'

'Then the woman Moscowitz – remember I told you about her? Going to sleep in the lounge with dead-as-a-doornail Schwarz-Albert lying there all along? We've checked her out, naturally. Seems her daughter was a well-known model who died in a rather hideous car crash. Caro Moss. Very beautiful, rather weird. Decapitated.'

'Ugh. I remember the case.' Jemima also remembered Caro Moss from the famous advertisements for health foods: an exquisite giraffe-like girl gazing up at a real-life giraffe munching leaves from a tree: 'Since I can't reach a tree,' ran the wistful faintly accented voice-over.

'Mother made a scene at the inquest, and again when the male driver was not sentenced to prison, only a fine.'

'One can hardly blame her,' Jemima reflected. 'No chance that Schwarz-Albert was the driver of the car and Mrs M the lurking figure of vengeance from the past, as in an Agatha Christie?'

'No chance at all,' replied Pompey coldly, who, unlike Jemima, did not retain a strong worship of Agatha Christie. 'Naturally we checked that out. Caro Moss's slaughterer – manslaughterer – is alive and well elsewhere.' He added with a return to joviality: 'So what does your woman's instinct say?'

'My perfectly good *reasoning* powers,' riposted Jemima, 'suggest that it isn't a coincidence your chap was killed at the Republican and at the conference. Someone took a risk – because it was a risk worth taking. Or because they didn't have another good opportunity. Yes, that must be it.'

Seeing that Pompey's brows were still drawn together at the mention of Agatha Christie, Jemima decided to return to the subject of the Royal Wedding. 'My question meant: are you – or they – expecting something to happen at the wedding itself?'

Since Pompey did not choose to answer, Jemima pressed on: 'Did you see the story in the *Exclusive*? A CITY PREPARES. Plus a lot of stuff about offices along the route being secretly commandeered. Either for some secret hidden marksmen. Or to prevent terrorists getting there first, it wasn't quite clear which. Some maps and photographs of likely angles. Explanations of how specially vulnerable this route is because it isn't the usual one from Clarence House or Buckingham Palace. The bride has to come from Regent's Park and they both go to the Palace for the wedding breakfast. Then Westminster Cathedral is bang in the middle of Victoria Street. A busy place. Lots of offices. Not cut off at the end like Westminster Abbey.'

'A CITY PREPARES indeed! It certainly loses nothing in the telling,' was Pompey's comment. 'That sort of thing only encourages the buggers of course: gives them some bright ideas about the weak links along the route, I always think. But what can you expect? In spite of their reputation Special Branch adore publicity. Always sneakily talking to the Press . . .'

Pompey seemed fortunately unaware just with whom he was sitting at the time of this less than generous comment concerning his colleagues.

'Am I naive in assuming the IRA are not interested since this is a Catholic wedding?' queried Jemima.

'It seems that Royal Weddings in general leave them cold,' grunted Pompey. Was he showing signs of sharing the feelings of the IRA on this issue if no other?

'I seem to remember that they made a statement to that effect at the time of Prince Andrew's bash. Unlike the rest of the world who get keener and keener. Has Mrs Pompey—'

'She has, God bless her. Red, white, and blue begonias. I planted them out at eleven o'clock last night. Ouch.' He winced.

'I went along the route today on a recce. And to the Cathedral with my American pals. Saw some very fine begonias on the way.' But Pompey only winced again as if in sympathy with fellow planters throughout London.

'A CITY PREPARES. More than one way of preparing,' was all he said.

Jemima had been well aware that it was necessary for her to follow the royal route if she was to be able to provide US audiences, sleepily awakening to this archaic British ceremony, with enough entrancing anecdotes to make it worth their while. TUS had provided a cheerful English driver named Harry but Jemima chose to sit in the back seat with Susanna Blanding. The latter sat with her head bowed over a clipboard, occasionally looking out of the window in order to reconcile passing buildings with her notes. Rick sat in the front seat (there was no sign of Curt, whose absence Rick explained rather vaguely along the lines of, 'I guess the guy slept late').

Unfortunately the comments of cheerful Harry – with which he had been enlightening tourists for years, so he told them – were somewhat at variance with those of Susanna. Nor did she accept the variance tamely. Rick had asked her not to smoke in the car, a prohibition which she had accepted but which undoubtedly increased her professional irritability.

'Queen Elizabeth II was *not* born at Number One London,' she explained indignantly at one point. 'Number One London is Apsley House, home of the Duke of Wellington as I would have thought absolutely anyone knew.' Susanna scowled at the driver's back.

'You win some, you lose some,' was all Harry said in reply, infuriatingly jovial. 'Any of you ladies like to know the origin of the Wellington Boot?'

Rick in the front seat moved restlessly: there was no telephone in the car, an administrative error he was determined should not be repeated.

'A lot of flat roofs round here,' he said suddenly. 'Susy sweetheart,' Rick turned round and gazed tenderly into her earnest face. 'Could you hold on that historical stuff for the time being? We have a security situation here that I'd like to talk through with Jemima.'

'Of course, Rick.' Susanna subsided. This confirmed Jemima's fear that Rick's handsome face and agreeable tones were making Susanna's heart beat significantly faster; it was noticeable that Susanna pardoned in Rick an almost total lack of interest in British history which she would have found unforgivable in anyone else.

'For instance, do you have some good assassination stuff there?' Since he was still looking at Susanna, it was she who answered, albeit hestitantly.

'Do you want historical assassinations? I can do you William the Silent. The Duke of Guise. That sort of thing. I'm afraid they do tend to be men, by the way. Unfortunately women weren't often assassinated in those underprivileged days.' As Jemima wryly noticed the principles of sexual equality being applied even in this unlikely area, Susanna continued more brightly: 'There was the Empress Elizabeth of Austria, of course – now she was assassinated. That was a good one. And it so happens that Prince Ferdinand himself is descended—'

'No, Susy, no.' The melodious tenderness was in danger of wearing thin.

'I take it you want the Roman Catholic Cathedral,' interrupted Harry, not necessarily out of any sense of diplomacy. 'See the spire if you duck and crane your head. Its exact height is—'

Rick Vancy found his fingers itching for a telephone to transport him to a wider world.

Just as Harry swung the large dark-blue car into the road leading to the Cathedral's piazza, Susanna gave a little squeak.

'Look! The Guards! Dressed up for rehearsal! Their history is absolutely fascinating—' She looked nervously at Rick's back. But even Rick was murmuring approvingly: 'Great pageantry.'

Suddenly to Jemima the scarlet-coated guards, their heavy cuirasses and plumed helmets gleaming in the sun, the jangling bridles and sweating flanks of the huge black horses, spoke not of pageantry – nor of history – but of violence and threat. Once upon a time men dressed like this or something like this, had ridden to battle to ride down other men dressed similarly. Now their role was apparently merely ceremonial: the visible guarding of the monarchy on occasions of official pageantry. Plus various clanking trots applauded by tourist London. Yet not so long ago men like this had died in London itself in an outbreak of terrorist bombing. Someone took the ceremonial sufficiently seriously to blow them to bits. Horses like this had suffered an even worse fate if you took the line that the horses had not voluntarily enlisted in the service of the State . . . And if the horses and guards were worth sacrificing, what price the equally ceremonial figures that they guarded?

As Rick observed in a most melodious voice: 'Where pageantry is concerned, the rest of the world is over the hill compared to you Brits.' Jemima shivered.

The lofty twilight interior of the great Byzantine-style cathedral, with its glinting mosaics and towering bands of green and rose marble, came as a relief. Jemima's morbid thoughts vanished as she observed with interest the considerable quantity of people – worshippers, tourists? – moving at some speed through the various aisles. It was four o'clock on a weekday afternoon. It was not just the advancing priests in their traditional long black vestments or the busy nuns (whose short skirts and briefly veiled, mainly uncovered hair would have been witnessed with horror by Jemima's old headmistress Mother Ancilla). There were quite as many lay people bustling about and the judicious development of the Catholic Church since Jemima's schooldays (a Protestant, she had attended a Catholic school) was attested by a large exhibition of photographs concerning relief in the third world.

'Good heavens, there's my cousin Lydia Quentin,' exclaimed Susanna. 'I didn't know she was a Catholic these days. Still I wouldn't put it past her. I wouldn't put anything past Lydia. Poor Ione, that's Princess Amy's lady-in-waiting, you know her, the ever calm one, she's had a ghastly time with Lydia. Ever since her father died, the famous Colonal Q, you've probably heard of him, *terrifying*! But rather marvellous. Then the house and everything had to be sold. What with that and her mother, Lydia picks up with the most terrible people – Moonies, Trots, people like that. Then Ione has to come and rescue her.' Susanna had on her important voice with which she generally imparted historical information. 'Now I suppose it's subversive nuns.'

Jemima gazed at a distinctly thin and rather pale girl. There was some resemblance to Ione Quentin, not only because both had dark hair; but where Ione radiated quiet strength, one would scarcely suppose that this frail creature possessed any strength at all. Cousin Susanna, with her sturdy frame, was a third version of the same model.

In one of the side chapels, behind a silver grille with its gates open, Lydia Quentin was kneeling as though in prayer in front of a large mosaic picture. Banks of little yellow candles twinkled on a stand outside. There was no nun, subversive or otherwise, to be seen. In fact Lydia Quentin was kneeling in a row with several other people and there were further people bent in prayer behind her. It struck Jemima that this was an especially popular shrine. The next door chapels were empty. Given the fact that their lips were moving in prayer, it occurred to her that this little group, if it was a group, might be taking part in some communal novena. Which said, the afternoon was an odd time for it to take place.

Jemima knew she should really be concentrating on the interior of the cathedral. This was her opportunity since TUS like all other foreign stations would not be allowed to have a camera inside the cathedral on the day itself. TUS would be obliged to take the BBC coverage with their own commentary superimposed as necessary. The TUS team would thus be installed in a specially built studio overlooking the piazza. All the same, curiosity – or perhaps even the famous instinct to which Pompey sometimes gallantly alluded – drove Jemima to investigate this popular or populated chapel further. The mosaic showed a man in monk's clothing, his hands outstretched, a group of birds perched upon them.

This must be the chapel of St Francis. White marble lettering surrounded by an acanthus border confirmed the fact. A rather less elegant wooden box nearby had a slit for donations and for candles (there was a large heap of candles in another box on the floor). Jemima wondered why she persisted in feeling the kneeling people were united in some common cause. The empty chapel next door was dedicated to St Paul; perhaps St Francis was more in keeping with the spirit of the times than St Paul. But then, further down, the chapel of St Patrick was empty too and it could certainly be argued that St Patrick had kept up with the times. For a moment she had even thought they were talking to each other instead of praying – which was absurd.

Lydia Quentin for example was kneeling next to a young man in a T-shirt with some conventionally protesting slogan on it. She was now gazing intensely in front of her. The young man turned his head and briefly his eyes met those of Jemima. There was no recognition in them although Jemima, with her distinctive colouring, apart from anything else, was used to the surprised flicker which the public sometimes accorded her, springing from the true late twentieth-century familiarity of television. Oddly enough, in this case it was Jemima who felt she might have seen the man somewhere before ... somewhere recently ... the wedding ... what was it ... the memory nagged at her and vanished.

It was fortunate that the man known to his fellow worshippers as Beagle was a sufficiently common type for there to be no certainty.

'Nosy bitch,' said Beagle in a low voice. 'If you'll pardon my language in this house of prayer. Jemima Shore Investigator as ever is. Not satisfied with that interview and all that royal rubbish.'

'Do you know her?' asked Chicken, kneeling on the other side of Beagle.

'I sat next to her at the Press Conference. I came in late. She won't remember. And even if she does – what's *she* doing here I want to know?'

'Same as us, I dare say,' murmured Chicken drily.

'Not *quite* the same as us, I hope, dear.' Pussy shifted the parcel at her feet and plunged her face once more into her hands.

Of the members of the Innoright cell, only Monkey was a practising Catholic. It was Monkey, with his usual sense of planning suffused with irony, who had suggested the cathedral for a meeting place, and the statue of St Francis, patron saint of animals, for the rendezvous.

'The Church. Another place where anyone sits next to anyone, as you put it, my dear Miss Lamb. Like the Underground.'

Fox, however, if not actually a Catholic (he had never been officially converted) was a man of romantic temperament who, in his single life with Noel, often dropped into Soho churches. He was not exactly seeking God, more enjoying the incense and music and above all admiring the vestments – a busman's holiday from his own work. When had he not loved costumes, dressing-up? It was a passion rooted deep in his unhappy childhood. Fox however had not turned his head at Jemima's approach. He took the opportunity of the respite to pray, a frequent prayer that he would somehow die with Noel; Noel who had been parked, panting, outside many churches and was in fact waiting panting outside the cathedral now.

Chicken, raised as an Anglican, had long ago abandoned that wishy-washy religion as she saw it, for a single-minded adherence to her campaign for the rights of the innocent. She felt marginally uncomfortable in her present Catholic situation but as a disciplined person, she was used to putting up with such things in the cause of Innoright. Pussy on the other hand, although she literally detested the Catholic Church for daring to state that animals, unlike slaughtering, meat-gorging humans, had no souls, had been raised by a Polish Catholic mother. She thus slumped down easily in her pew, crossed herself quite naturally and in general looked much like all the other middle-aged women with shopping bags scattered round the cathedral.

Jemima Shore wandered away to rejoin Susanna and Rick. Monkey was the last person to catch her eye: this was because this prosperous-looking person, conventionally dressed, appeared to be praying aloud.

'So, ladies and gentlemen of Innoright, fellow animals—' began Monkey again. Even at simulated prayer, Monkey's voice was sonorous.

It was some hours after this that Jemima, pouring another whisky for Pompey as she described her recce, remembered where she had seen Beagle. The recollection, including the group of disparate worshippers at the shrine of St Francis – St Francis, patron saint of animals, animal love, interesting that, there seemed to be a lot of it about, even within the cathedral's precincts – the recollection did not then seem important enough to relate. But it did seem important enough to file away in her memory, like one small piece of the mosaic on the cathedral walls. She thought of saying to Pompey: 'What was that photographer called? The one who was a friend of the murdered man? The one with the alibi?' That too would wait, if not for ever.

Thus it was part of her general thought process on the subject of the Princess, her security, and the past threat posed by Innoright, that she observed aloud to Pompey: 'They're at the opera tonight. I shall have to throw you out in order to get ready for Covent Garden. Royal Gala!'

'You to your garden and I to mine,' observed Pompey wistfully.

'Still, they'll be safe enough at the opera,' said Jemima.

13

Evening in a Good Cause

Against the red velvet frame of the box, Monkey looked both substantial and dignified in his white tie and tails. Moreover the crackling white waistcoat stretched smoothly over his broad chest unlike those of some of his contemporaries, sorted out from disuse for the occasion of the Royal Gala. But Monkey was used to white-tied City dinners; he was also used to benefits in aid of good causes of which the present Royal Gala might seem to be just one more example. Monkey even sported on his chest a minor medal incurred for philanthropic work and donations – in another life before Innoright.

For Monkey, however, it was not just one more evening in a good cause. Or not in the sense that the world generally would understand the phrase. The presence of Lamb beside him, thin shoulders peering out of a plain pale-pink satin dress with shoestring straps, signified that. Lamb herself was as appropriately dressed as Monkey. If her dress was slightly dowdy, an unusual lotus pattern diamond circlet sat upon her dark head. Ione Quentin, who had lent the dress (as a lady-in-waiting, she had numbers of such inconspicuous long dresses available, this one being cut sufficiently straight to accommodate Lamb's much slimmer figure) had also insisted on Lamb wearing the tiara.

'Mum's tiara,' said Lamb doubtfully, weighing it in her hand. The box in which the circlet had been housed was ancient battered red morocco, and the red velvet interior, unlike that of the Covent Garden box, distinctly shabby. But the diamonds shone in all their yellowish eighteenth-century lustre. 'I thought you usually wore it at this kind of bash.'

'P.A. won't mind. P.A. won't *notice*.' Ione, as so often with her sister, was determinedly cheerful. 'She's the veritable star of the show this evening. No other Royals going. Well, one or two royal-ish ones. The younger lot. But P.A. outranks them all. The Duchess, who frankly loathes the opera, has got one of her frequent convenient illnesses. P.A. loves that, of course; after all the Gala is for her – him too, naturally. Even if it was all rather last minute, slotted into the schedule. I told you.'

'Yes, you told me.' Lamb continued to weigh the tiara as though it represented a subject she was weighing up in her mind.

'Go on, Leelee, put it on.' Ione used the name from their childhood as she seldom did nowadays; it seemed to upset Lydia, reminding her of their mother who had never called her anything else. 'Besides it will help me to keep an eye on you. Also, I want to see what's his name. What *is* his name? The dirty old man who's taking you.'

'He's not a dirty old man.' Suddenly Lamb wore her intense look, the one that made Ione's heart sink, and Ione cursed herself. 'He's a very fine person who does a lot of good in the world, unlike all your lot with their show-off jewels. Princess Amy should meet *him* instead of that awful Gala committee. Do you know how much suffering—'

'But darling, it was a joke. I'm sure P.A. would *love* to meet him. You *said* he was a DOM, do you remember?' Ione hastily retrieved the tiara from Lamb's agitated hands and replaced it in the shabby box. 'And anyway I looked him up and saw that he married a sister of Mum's friend, Penelope, my godmother; wife deceased; no children; never remarried. So *I* said he must be looking for a young wife and you said, no, that's not what he's looking for, a wife, he's a Dirty Old Man. It was a joke,' concluded Ione patiently.

In the end Lamb wore the tiara. Ever since her illness she often did what people wanted in small things in order to save her energies for resistance when it really mattered. Lamb smiled to herself as she allowed Ione to fasten it on. She thought she might sell the tiara and give the money to Innoright. After everything was over. Then what would clever Nonie do? The tiara had after all been left to them jointly. Ione saw the smile on her sister's sad little face and was not reassured.

It would undoubtedly have surprised Lamb to learn that Ione's supposition concerning Mr Edward James Arthur Monck MBE's intentions were not really so wide of the mark. Or perhaps fantasies would be a better word than intentions. As Major Pat Smylie-Porter sometimes confidently dreamt of the day when he would marry Ione Quentin, Edward Monck also secretly dreamt from time to time of taking her sister as a second wife. He would review the years without his beloved Cynthia, she who had been so very different (not only physically) from Lamb and whose pointless death of an embolism during a minor operation had driven him on his first steps down the path of obsession. First making money – what else was there to do? – then giving it away – what else was there to do with it? Cynthia had left no children – finally Innoright, his own protest against a cruel world, and the Underground Plan, its supreme expression.

His mission accomplished, the Underground Plan accomplished, might he not allow himself at last the indulgence of a second bride, a child wife, one would combine in those two things, two attributes so long missing from his life?

Tonight was not the night for such dreams. Edward Monck a.k.a. Monkey, took one more quick look at Lamb's pale skin glimpsed above the smooth satin which virtually matched it and pointed his thoughts back sternly to the matter in hand.

At that moment there was a hush then a rustle in the audience. The starched white waistcoats crackled as their inhabitants struggled to their feet. Long skirts were retrieved uncomfortably from beneath the next-door seat. Like animals feeding together, who turn their heads in unison at a sudden noise, the whole audience now craned in one direction.

Princess Amy, a tiny shining figure, appeared in the Royal Box, in the centre of the right-hand tier of boxes facing the stage, followed by Prince Ferdinand, darkly handsome with the green sash of some appropriately Ruritanian order across his chest. While flunkeys in the flamboyant Opera House uniform were visibly hovering round them, the more discreet figures of Ione Quentin and Major Pat Smylie-Porter, the latter with several medals of a genuinely military nature on his chest as well as others gained in the royal service, could be discerned behind them.

Unlike Monkey and Lamb in their box on the opposite side, framed in red velvet alone, Princess Amy and Prince Ferdinand stood in a bower of blue flowers, swags cascading from the rim of the box itself, and great pilasters of blue surrounding them on either side. Was the blue a delicate tribute to Amy herself? But then speculation about such a comparatively minor matter as the flowers faded in favour of universally admiring exclamations concerning the Princess herself. Or rather almost universally admiring: an exception to the general chorus of admiration would have to be made in the case of Chicken and Pussy, sharing a second-tier box.

'Little Madam,' said Pussy to Chicken, putting down her impressive-looking binoculars. Lately she had taken to using Fox's phrase for Amy, rolling it succulently on her tongue, in preference to her own 'spoilt brat', 'I believe that was a fur stole that was being stowed away at the back. And after what she said on television! They're all the same. Hypocrites. I'd like to give her one.'

'You may soon have an opportunity,' murmured Chicken drily. But her words, as she intended, were drowned by the sound of the National Anthem. Chicken, believing herself to be potentially far more ruthless than Pussy – in a good cause and at the right moment – disapproved of the latter's habit of indulging in such blatantly vicious talk. Chicken rustled the score which as an opera lover (if mainly on Radio 3) she had brought in order to calm her nerves. With her usual forethought Chicken had taken care to remove all personal marks from the score; nevertheless she was aware that if anyone cared to look closely with their own binoculars into what was in effect a corner balcony box, next to the stage itself, they might be surprised to see an Indian woman sedulously following the musical score.

For some at least of Pussy's ill temper and Chicken's irritation was caused by the unaccustomed style of dress in which both women were attired: Indian and bejewelled would be the best way of describing it. As a matter of fact, Chicken and Pussy, with the connivance and advice of Fox, looked surprisingly convincing. It was true that neither of them would be taken for the kind of lissom Maharani of popular imagination (or the *Heat and Dust* style of film). But Pussy's dour build and basically dark complexion had needed very little adaptation to give her the characteristic phlegmatic look of an Eastern female; Chicken presented at first sight more of a problem. But: 'Nothing we can't overcome,' Fox insisted; his enthusiasm making him suddenly seem stronger, more forceful – or perhaps he merely displayed something more of his real character. So Pussy in voluminous turquoise, Chicken in neater red, inhabited their eyrie and gazed – across, to the right and downwards – at Princess Amy in the Royal Box. An observer might also have noticed that there were only two people in a box meant for four; although of course the restricted balcony view made this a practical measure. But who looked into a balcony box on the night of a gala?

These dissentient voices apart, it was generally agreed at the time – not only afterwards when such a retrospective judgement became perhaps inevitable – that 'little Amy' had never looked more beautiful. Expert analysis would indeed be needed to realize that what actually glittered at Amy's round white neck, at her little white ears, at the not inconsiderable cleft between her plump white breasts, and filleting her elaborately ringleted blonde hair, were the famous Russian sapphires belonging to Ferdel's great-grandmother (she who had or had not danced with Rasputin but had certainly known how to amass a wearable fortune in jewellery). Probably only Susanna Blanding, opera glasses trained, immediately recognized them for what they were. 'The so-called "Rasputin sapphires". Unlucky?' she murmured to Curt, without expecting an answer from this normally comatose source.

At the time it was Amy herself, eyes shining in palpable triumph at the applause her appearance evoked, rather than the provenance of her *parure*, which aroused the happily startled gasps of admiration.

She raised her plump little white hand – no ring but the engagement one – in a gracious royal wave and said something to Prince Ferdinand.

Once again it would need expert analysis – from lip-readers – to reveal what Princess Amy actually said. Fortunately there were none present, despite the increasing employment of them at such events as royal weddings so that the avid public might share the last-minute thoughts – or even, daring hope, last-minute second thoughts of the latest bride.

It was fortunate there was no lip-reader present because what Amy actually said to Ferdel as she smiled and waved was: 'You never told me that bitch was going to be here.'

There had indeed been a moment of more than usual awkwardness – or a moment of highly enjoyable drama, depending on your point of view – when Mirabella Prey's large limousine, of hearse-like length in the American style, had swung in to the pavement in front of the Royal Opera House just as the royal car was expected. There was no doubt in the minds of the numerous cameramen present, both for the newspapers and television, that enjoyable drama was the way to look at it; these representatives of television including Rick Vancy and Jemima Shore for TUS (looking for some footage for their Wedding Special).

As their driver, jovial Harry, he of the TUS London tour, would exclaim appreciatively later to his mates: 'Did you see her? Did you see her? Cor.' He shook his curly head under its blue cap, leaving no doubt that what he – along with millions watching the TV news – had seen was a ringside view of Mirabella's magnificent body.

Surely even that body had never been seen to greater advantage – certainly not in Beagle's infinitely cruder nude photographs. Tonight Mirabella's spangled white crêpe dress paid no more than a graceful tribute to the idea of concealing her small high breasts. In other places the dress was stretched so tight that the two slits on either side of the skirt revealed not only those celebrated long legs but also delicious brown thighs: the slits at least could be justified by the need to manoeuvre out of the car, which would otherwise have been quite impossible.

More was to come. As on-lookers – and cameras – found themselves transfixed by Mirabella's pièce de résistance, something which looked like a jewelled tiger's head in her exposed navel, the royal chauffeur for the night, Taplow, could be seen approaching at the wheel. Amy, unaware of what had happened, did however catch a glimpse of Mirabella's sinuous back just ahead of her as she stepped up the red carpet. She thought the presence of another individual so close vaguely odd: but by this time the Chairman of Covent Garden, having hissed: 'Get that woman out of here and into her seat and fast', was already bowing over the Princess's hand. What Ferdel's thoughts might be was not clear: he looked impassive. Did he perhaps recognize the famous back more swiftly? He had had after all ample opportunity to study it both in the distant and more recent past.

The Chairman of Covent Garden, one who like the centurion in the Bible was accustomed to say, 'Go, and he goeth', in his most recent command had reckoned without Mirabella Prey.

'I am c-c-crazy about this Gala,' she was saying to the eager pressmen in her thrilling husky voice. She paused naturally enough on the red carpet in order to do so: incidentally providing an opportunity for yet more revealing shots. 'You know I am doing so much work for this wonderful charity.'

No one had the gall to ask Mirabella if she knew what the charity in question, for which the Gala had been hastily assembled, actually was. But the exchange had been enough to enable Princess Amy, herself also in white, several inches shorter, weight about the same (very differently distributed) to catch up with her. This time the Chairman waited for no man to do his bidding and literally shoved the vagrant film star off the royal route. It was an action much misunderstood by those avidly watching the whole episode on television at home: for surely the Chairman was being not so much dreadfully unchivalrous towards Mirabella – the line generally taken – as wonderfully and vainly chivalrous towards Princess Amy, in a way of which Sir Walter Raleigh himself would have approved.

As it was, the Chairman's precipitate action merely enabled Mirabella, graceful to the last, to sweep a deep curtsey to the Prince and Princess as they passed. Ferdel looked straight ahead; Amy looked directly down, down Mirabella's cleavage as a matter of fact, or so the photographers made it appear.

IF LOOKS COULD KILL was one headline already planned for a morning newspaper. For once the headline was probably a pretty fair estimate of the Princess's feelings.

Now, safely installed in the Royal Box, Ferdel did not answer his fiancée's remark, hissed between her gritted teeth and smiling lips. Instead he lifted her white-gloved hand to his own lips and kissed it. It was a gesture which delighted one half of the audience (mainly female) and infuriated the other (predominantly male). 'So romantic' and 'Crafty foreign bugger' were the respective expressions most commonly used. No one in the audience was aware that as Ferdel lifted Amy's hand, he gave it a painful little nip, not in the least bit romantic, with his long brown fingers. If they had known, both halves of the audience would surely have been united in disapproval.

'What's the piece?' enquired Rick lazily of Jemima, 'They didn't give me anything on that.' Rick and Jemima were sitting in a box, with Curt and Susanna (the latter agreeably taking the fourth back seat on a high stool) which was directly opposite the royal one.

Because Princess Amy and Prince Ferdinand were the focus of everybody's attention – including Jemima's – it took some time for the latter to take in the existence of the box next door, although Jemima was actually sitting cheek-by-jowl with its inhabitants. She glanced to her left. She saw a thin young woman wearing whitish satin, cut rather too like a nightdress for Jemima's own taste; the diamond circlet on her head was however exquisite; it must be real. As Jemima recognized Susanna Blanding's cousin (and the lady-in-waiting's sister), Lydia Quentin, she realized that she had also seen her companion, a much older man, presumably her father, before. If he was her father he was a wealthy father, because he had installed two people only in a box meant for four. The same man had been with Lydia Quentin praying in Westminster Cathedral. But Susanna Blanding had said that the Quentins were horribly poor and their father, the celebrated Colonel Q, was dead . . . An escort then, an older escort, a much older escort. Why would a much older escort pray with a young girl in the middle of the afternoon? For rejuvenation? Filing the puzzle away at the back of her mind, Jemima returned her attention to Rick Vancy.

Like Prince Ferdinand, Rick looked remarkably handsome if slightly actorish in his white tie: his resemblance to Leslie Howard was more pronounced than ever. Rick's gift for verisimilitude was once more demonstrated by the fact that he had actually secured a tail-coat which fitted him, unlike his sidekick Curt who had only got as far as a dinner-jacket – which manifestly did not. 'The "piece" is *Otello*,' said Jemima.

'As in Shakespeare?'

'Exactly. Arias instead of soliloquies.'

'Isn't the particular story-line rather gross tonight?' Rick rolled one eye in the direction of the minor boxes opposite, where a couple of dignitaries in Arab dress could be seen (those in white ties might perhaps envy them their freedom of movement). Then he looked down at the elaborate Gala programme, magnificently inscribed, 'In the gracious presence of Her Royal Highness Princess Amy of Cumberland and His Highness Prince Ferdinand of . . .' A long string of foreign names followed, one of them actually sounding rather like Ruritania.

'Since it's for Eastern Relief, you could argue that *Otello* was in fact peculiarly appropriate,' suggested Jemima. 'Eastern Relief' was in fact a tactful umbrella name for Middle Eastern War Relief, its hasty organization due to the latest unpleasant twist in the situation in that area, where an increasing amount of homeless and sick of one country declined to receive the refugees of another. 'But I doubt whether anybody thought of the story of *Otello* at the time. More carried away by the unexpected presence of Ignazio Dorati in London due to a cancellation. He's behind Domingo and Pavarotti, but they, whoever "they" are, say he's going to be even better. At least in this part. And goodness, he's handsome. Look out for squeals at the curtain. He's a terrific favourite here.'

'So what do you know? Arabs at the opera.' Rick leant back and closed his eyes as the house lights dimmed and the first stormy bars of the overture were heard. Jemima hoped that he was not going to emulate his compatriot Curt in publicly going to sleep.

Whatever the Arabs thought of *Otello* – at charity prices, they must have paid a fortune for that box next door to the royal one, once again two people only occupying a box for four – the rest of the audience thrilled to it. Moreover, since Ignazio Dorati, not for nothing nicknamed El Dorado, made such a handsome bronzed fellow of the Moor, no insult to the Arab race could surely be intended. As for Mirabella Prey, sitting gorgeously in the front of the stalls circle, her lovely eyes glowed as the unfamiliar – to her – plot unfolded.

'I love this story – yes,' she exclaimed at one point to her escort. A Greek-looking person of heavy build, he wore gold jewellery which could be matched with that of many of the women in the audience. Mirabella's voice was however rather too loud for the regular opera-goers closer to her and there was some indignant shushing. Unabashed, Mirabella was later overheard comparing El Dorado to a puma, notoriously her favourite animal as her many admirers would testify. (The large puma bracelet flashing on her arm was either the broken one restored, or a re-creation.) Nor did the end of the opera dissatisfy her. Mirabella breathed an orgiastic sigh as the athletic Dorati straddled his plaintive but well-built Desdemona in order to strangle her.

'She's strong, that one.' Mirabella nodded approvingly. 'But he is stronger.'

By the time the great finale of the opera was over, the evil figure of Iago breaking loose to escape his just deserts, the whole of the audience from Princess Amy, the 'Rasputin' sapphires glittering at her throat, to a couple of obscure Indian women high up in a balcony box, with much humbler incrustations, seemed ready to erupt into applause. As the great red curtains fell, their clapping began to explode in rounds of wild energy like the sound of fireworks being released. First the whole company, then the company with the conductor, then the principals in ascending order of importance, appeared before the curtains, held back for them by the flunkeys. So that when the call came for which a high proportion of the audience had been holding back their ultimate ferocity: El Dorado himself, alone on the apron of the stage, not so much fireworks as thunder was the impression given.

There he stood, bowing, smiling, his face still mildly darkened, looking indeed much like the puma to which Mirabella had compared him, but a pleasant, cheerful panting puma, relaxing after the kill.

'El Dorado! El Dorado!' Monstrous bouquets in huge ugly cellophane wrappings were being carried on by the flunkeys and other single flowers began to rain down from the upper galleries. The whole audience, including Princess Amy and Prince Ferdinand, rose to its feet in tribute. Jemima, clapping away at Rick's side, was highly surprised to note that the inhabitants of the next box – Lydia Quentin and her elderly escort – had already left. Then she turned back to Ignazio Dorati. By now the sound was sufficiently all-consuming for it to take some moments for anybody, even the Covent Garden officials, to realize that the fireworks and the thunder had in fact been joined by another noise: that of an explosion. A minor explosion it was true, just enough to set off what appeared to be a smoke bomb in one of the balcony boxes. Smoke began to billow outwards.

But it was only when an enormous white banner was draped down from the farthest box on the right-hand balcony side, that heads actually began to turn away from El Dorado, still bowing and smiling on the stage, in the direction of the smoke. The logo of an animal's face, enormous sad eyes, dominated it. But to most people the words were even more striking:

INNORIGHT it read. PROTECT THE INNOCENT. And then: THE TRUE GOOD CAUSE.

As the audience, now staring and murmuring, began to take in something of what happened, and Covent Garden officials scurried in the direction of the banner – 'Get the police,' one of them was heard to say, 'there are enough of them outside' – two middle-aged women of inconspicuous appearance, one fat, one thin, emerged from the ladies' cloakroom on the upper level. Their dark dresses giving the impression of having done service in some office earlier in the day, the two women hastened down the side staircase. Someone else was talking about 'those damn Asians'.

'We must hurry, dear,' said the fat one, clutching her large plastic shopping bags to her. 'Do come on. We must make the last train home.'

'Wasn't he wonderful?' sighed the thinner of the two women. 'What a relief to have the full opera. The Zeffirelli film was definitely not for the purist.' She added: 'Don't worry, dear, we've got plenty of time.'

And Chicken was right. The timing worked out by Monkey, and gone over many times by the rest of the cell, had so far worked to perfection. The exactness of the royal schedule – characteristically exact – was of course a considerable help. As Ione Quentin often observed to her sister on this particular subject: 'When we say "Cars at 11.02", we at CP do not mean 11.03'.

So that Lamb entering the receiving room at the back of the Royal Box knew to the instant the moment at which the Prince and Princess were scheduled to desert the applauding audience and retire to the back room. Lamb smiled at Fitzgerald, the Princess's detective, whom she knew through Ione, and explained that she had arranged to make a presentation to Princess Amy; the detective nodded. The unscheduled confusion, caused by the Innoright banner, was as a matter of fact also working almost perfectly to the timetable they had planned. After that, several things happened at once, none of them expected within the royal receiving room, all of them planned by Monkey.

As Lamb said to Princess Amy, 'Ma'am, Ione said I could come—' the

Princess turned towards her with a faintly puzzled but still courteous air. After all, the evening had been full of the unexpected. It was Ione Quentin who cried: 'Leelee – no,' as two Arabs were revealed standing behind her.

Both men held automatic pistols. Both men were now masked beneath their Arab headdresses. To those outside, the loud plop of another smoke bomb, followed by more smoke billowing out, coming from a box adjacent to the royal one, created further pandemonium. But to those inside the box, there was the noise of a shot, a shot followed by a scream.

'Your Royal Highness,' said a muffled voice. 'You are to come with us.'

Elsewhere in Covent Garden, the noise and confusion following the Innoright demo still held sway, as sturdy men attempted to haul back the banner, with its defiant red legend: PROTECT THE INNOCENT.

14

'Palace Mystery'

In spite of the late hour, Major Smylie-Porter's voice was extraordinarily urbane on the telephone: 'Pat here ... Dear boy, this is probably the ultimate favour we shall ever ask you ...' And, added Major Smylie-Porter to himself, the ultimate test of my ability to handle anything, but anything, however big, big being not quite a big enough word. To his surprise, he found that at the same time he was uttering a rough prayer (surely he hadn't prayed since he was a young man in Malaya and those bandits attacked). He also found, going still further back to childhood, that he was keeping his fingers crossed.

But then Major Pat was well aware that for him personally this was the make or break of a so far modestly successful professional career. The retrieval of a twenty-two-year-old missing princess, not only that but the retrieval *without* such immediate attendant publicity, newspaper head-lines, clarion screams, blaring shrieks of anguish and excitement as to make the most impassive courtier blench, and as for the Monarch...

Here Major Pat checked his thoughts. Had he been a Catholic like Monkey (whom in some ways he resembled) Major Pat would have surely crossed himself at the thought of the Monarch to whom his devotion was both awed and total.

In short, the retrieval of Princess Amy *without pre-publicity* would place Major Pat in a strong position to be considered for yet higher office in a yet more august palace, when such a post should next become vacant.

First catch your hare, in the words of Mrs Beeton. The twenty-two-year-old Princess had yet to be retrieved, and retrieved in one piece, what's more. Surely the police could be trusted to do that, he thought, almost irritably, his finger reaching towards the next highly private number of a Press magnate or an editor or some other person within the mysterious purlieus of the BBC or the IBA ... or just one of those amazingly influential people who still, thank God – another sigh, the habit was catching – permeated English society. Many of them, thank God again, had been encountered at school or in the army or were even related to Major Pat, or possibly to his late wife, poor Louise.

Throughout the night he worked.

'Jumbo?' he began the next call, 'Paddles here.' The nicknames went back a long way; but there was nothing childish or frivolous about the total blanket which Major Pat, with the encouragement of the police and the agreement of certain august personages, was seeking to have imposed upon the news of Princess Amy's disappearance.

The price? The price would have to be paid. Like Rumpelstiltskin in the fairy story, the Press would be back for their due and promised payment. The full or at any rate fullish story of the hideous events which had led up to that disappearance, the mental anguish of the Princess (if nothing worse: only guessed at at the present time), the mental anguish of her *mother* (well, he did know all about that, the wretched Duchess having retreated into what in any other woman would have been described as an alcoholic stupor at the news, and for once the Major hardly blamed her). Newspapers and television from the BBC to the *Daily Exclusive*, would all have to receive the full or fullish story. When she was found.

That was the price of silence.

Ironically enough, it helped, it helped very much indeed, that most of the papers of the *Daily Clueless* calibre (long might that nickname remain apt) were happily obsessed with what they innocently took to be the main drama of the evening.

Pictures of Mirabella Prey, prettily outrageous in her white dress, wide questioning dark eyes fixed on Ferdel as he passed, were already being prepared for many a front page. As for Princess Amy's glance – a glance born in fact of sheer astonishment – that apparently icy expression, together with her jewels and upswept hair gave her quite a look of her ancestress Queen Victoria; at any rate the resemblance was sufficient for one newspaper, ignoring the rival claims of IF LOOKS COULD KILL, to try out the well-worn WE ARE NOT AMUSED.

Ione Quentin, lying in bed in a half-darkened room, gazed desperately at this particular paper, among those scattered on her white lace counterpane. Amused? To herself she said aloud: No, I should think not. Poor child, oh, poor child. Ione swung her legs over the edge of the bed and began slowly, methodically, as was her wont, to work out a plan of campaign.

Another helpful factor lay in the particular circumstances of Princess Amy's disappearance, or rather her *non*-appearance, at the front door of the Royal Opera House, immediately following the Gala. The bewildered Committee of the charity for whom the evening was being held, still in the ground-floor foyer to bid her farewell, assumed after a short while that the smoke bombs and the demo had caused the Princess to be smuggled out of a side entrance (which was, as a matter of fact, perfectly true). Outside, Bow Street, a narrow, crowded, two-way street at the best of times, was totally packed after the performance. A section of this crowd was stationary, and prepared to behave in quite an aggressive manner towards any force which might try to move it on.

These were the people, fervent monarchists or Amy-fanciers with I LOVE AMY buttons displayed, who waited by the royal car as, with Taplow at the wheel, it purred waiting for departure. But to be frank, at this hour of the night, the largest, most stationary – and most aggressive – portion of the crowd were milling round the Stage Door in adjacent Floral Street, or had somehow spilled over from the Stage Door crush on to the further pavements.

These were the expert fanciers of El Dorado, the would-be lovers, the aficionados, whom nothing, or nothing short of physical violence, seemed likely to budge from their stance. Not for a mild departure, deprived of their hero, had they raced down from the gallery and the amphitheatre; as they ran, they had either ignored such pathetic un-operatic distractions as the Innoright poster or assumed it to be yet another demonstration of adulation for Him. Even the first smoke bomb left such fanatics singularly unmoved, and by the time of the second one members of Innoright, impressed by the poster, might have been surprised at their disdain or sheer inattention. On the other hand a member of Innoright who was also an opera-goer such as Chicken was well able to anticipate such a Gadarene rush at the end of the evening – had indeed anticipated it, nay counted upon it, during the planning meetings of the Innoright cell.

In Floral Street, therefore, ordinary red programmes were there to be signed and there were also some of the elaborate Gala programmes to be seen. El Dorado was known to be generous towards his fans in this respect, and they would expect him to sign a fair amount before the time came to commence that late night roistering with his comrades by which he normally relaxed. There were photographs also to be seen: the black eyes, white teeth and merry smile of the famous face, framed by a romantic white frilly shirt open at the neck (Rodolfo in *Luisa Miller* was another favourite role) flashed before the gaze, as fans respectfully harboured their copies in the crush. These El Dorado would normally sign as well, particularly after what was generally agreed to have been a superb performance.

When an unexpected and quite violent irruption of police, followed by the speedy cordoning off of Floral Street, occurred, El Dorado's single-minded fans were still quite unmoved. Subsequent events – in any case getting late for the first editions of the morning newspapers – were literally chaotic.

Princess Amy's followers at the front Bow Street entrance were left with two contrary impressions: the first was that the Princess had left by another entrance (true enough) in order to elude them (not true); the second impression given by the police was that they were determined to push the crowd around in order to prevent them witnessing the Princess's departure from *this* entrance.

The continued presence of the royal car at the front, Taplow looking obviously bewildered at the wheel, did seem to militate against the first impression, but after a while even the royal car moved. Someone – a policeman – said something to Taplow: the cordon was lifted and the car departed, rapidly.

As for El Dorado's fans, in time they were more courteously instructed to disband: 'Mr Dorati has left by another entrance.' (This was indeed true, or about to be true, no one wanting to risk losing yet another star, in so far as anybody backstage had a glimmering of what had actually happened.) This instruction was however greeted by the Dorati fans not with apathy or resignation but with outright and vociferous protest.

In all this combined front-street and side-street drama, the noise of an ambulance which came to the side entrance, and to which a stretcher was rapidly and expertly carried, passed almost unnoticed. Stretchers and ambulances were not unknown at Covent Garden. Someone had fainted, a heart attack at worst – maybe the smoke was responsible – these things happened and were regrettable, none of this was particularly interesting to the populace at large since the person concerned was hardly likely to be Princess Amy or El Dorado. (Once again, true enough. The person concerned was the detective, Fitzgerald, shot in the chest in the line of duty, while trying vainly to protect his royal charges.)

Then Little Mary, she of the *Daily Exclusive* and *Jolly Joke*, decided to run her own special version of events. This involved Princess Amy deliberately leaving the Gala early without saying goodbye to the Chairman, the Gala Committee (again, all too true) owing to her disgust at the presence of Mirabella Prey. As a matter of fact, informed by a stringer of the Princess's unscheduled private exit, Little Mary had no reason to believe this was the actual reason for it: but she was currently carrying on a vendetta with a member of the Gala Committee and this seemed a good way of suggesting that a successful evening had in fact ended in failure.

As for the smoke bombs and the Innoright demo, the mention of smoke bombs could have been amusing if Little Mary had known exactly at whom they had been directed; the subject of animal rights on the other hand was inclined to be a slight drag where her readers were concerned in Little Mary's knowledgeable opinion. Their way of life might be threatened by such tiresome shenanigans: besides, bitchery concerning a good friend (she of the Gala Committee) was so much more amusing to read first thing in the morning.

It was all the more ironic that for once Little Mary by featuring the Mirabella Prey story earned the heartfelt gratitude of Major Pat Smylie-Porter and other loyal parties interested in the great cover-up. It was not that the news could, finally, be held for very long, for all Major Pat's heroic efforts, particularly in view of the enormous, if undercover, police operation now underway. It was just that by coincidence Little Mary did provide that titillating, if inaccurate, explanation for Amy's disappearance which the situation demanded for the more sophisticated. (For the rest, the Innoright demo and the smoke bombs were explanation enough.)

PALACE MYSTERY ran the headline of Little Mary's column. What was more, Little Mary, ever game to display a knowledge of the arts, managed to re-tell the plot of *Otello* in a way that linked Princess Amy, Prince Ferdinand and Mirabella Prey most satisfyingly if it might have outraged Boito and Verdi, let alone Shakespeare.

'PALACE MYSTERY,' repeated Major Pat, mopping his brow with his large white linen handkerchief. 'If only they knew.'

'PALACE MYSTERY,' echoed Jemima to Rick Vancy, with whom she was having (somewhat reluctantly) a working breakfast. At least she was allowed to stage it in her own flat and did not have to attend Rick's hotel. 'I do believe, Rick, that there was something odd about the way they went. Or does the demo explain it? I see the placard was awkward and not exactly conducive to the cause of Eastern Relief. Innoright strikes again! I must say that the smoke bomb or bombs were quite unpleasant: it says here there were at least two, and certainly we saw a second one in the Arabs' box, didn't we? After they'd left. But the *Guardian* only mentions one. It all happened so late: the Gala must have finished near to midnight.'

'Arabs at the opera! I never did buy that one,' was Rick's comment. 'So they were animal freaks like the rest of the world.' He shook his head as though the Middle East had let him down personally.

'PALACE MEES-TERY! So ridiculous. Why always this Palace, this Princess? The British are crazy about these things.' The voice today was husky as ever, but for once the effect was more cross than thrilling. The morning was never the best time for Mirabella Prey, who was woken at eight a.m. in her hotel suite by the *Evening Exclusive* (sometimes lovingly known as the *Even-more Clueless*), demanding her comment on the events of the previous night in general, and Little Mary's column in particular. Since Mirabella had recently taken much trouble to speak beguilingly to Little Mary, she was disconcerted to read a version of events in her column in which she featured most unflatteringly as Iago not Desdemona; worse still she was omitted altogether from the headline. Then other members of the Press began to ring too.

'Dulling,' purred Mirabella to one of her favourites. 'How silly this paper is: to you I am telling the true story. It is Theodoros who is loving the opera—' Then Mirabella talked at length about her new Greek-ish friend.

It was earlier that same morning that Pompey and Vaillant at Central Squad, still doggedly pursuing the solution to their own Palace Mystery (Death at the Palace Press Conference might have been a suitable title for that) had received a new and important piece of evidence. Thus the headline in the morning paper's gossip column passed more or less unnoticed, except for a brief appreciative chuckle from Pompey; which Vaillant thought it tactful to ignore.

'She was threatening him,' said a new witness who had come forward in answer to repeated police appeals. 'The foreign-looking chap, the one in your photograph. I was at this Underground station, I shall never forget it, I sat down on the bench with them, gave me quite a fright. Very intense she was; I would say she had burning eyes, to be exact.' The witness, who was in fact a man who had been at the time on his way to a creative writing school in Oxford Street, paused expectantly as though in search of commendation. 'Burning eyes and dark hair,' repeated the witness more lamely, before continuing:

'"I'll kill you," she said. "See if I don't. You think I won't but I will. I'm quite capable of it whatever you think." Or words to that effect.'

'We'd like to get the exact words, sir, if possible,' was Pompey's patient response. 'And a more detailed physical description. You see, burning eyes might mean a number of different things to different people.'

In the shocked Eaton Square household, or what was left of it, Prince Ferdinand having been removed to Cumberland Palace for safety, 'burning eyes' might also have been a suitable description to apply to Mrs Taplow's expression as she sat facing her husband. Taplow's head was bowed on his arms; the large man was weeping uncontrollably, without pretence. In part these were the tears of sheer exhaustion: Taplow's ordeal, begun so shockingly with the instructions given to him outside the Opera, had continued most of the night with the organization of the Prince's belongings, and other duties. It had started again very early in the morning when Taplow, red-eyed from lack of sleep, had decided to communicate certain facts to the police.

But there was a further hopelessness, beyond mere exhaustion, about Taplow, as he sat there weeping in front of his wife; her fiery gaze suggesting that she might pounce and devour him the moment he raised his head, like one of Mirabella Prey's favourite pumas. It was as though he wept not only for the frightful present but for decades of humiliating memories.

'I shall never forgive you for this, Kenneth, no matter what happens.' Mrs Taplow's voice was the more menacing for remaining low as though they might be overheard.

Taplow mumbled something.

'What's that, Kenneth?'

'Your *fault*, Lizzie,' and then more strongly: 'Your *fault*. All the dressing-up, encouraging him to be different. You dressed him up as a girl. That's where it started.'

'Seeing as he didn't have a man for a father,' his wife hissed back.

One way and another, neither Taplow had time to look at the morning paper. But a very senior policeman did, and exploded, as though in relief, to have something inanimate but actual to crush in his hand.

'PALACE MYSTERY indeed! Carefully planned from the beginning, the whole thing. So why was it a mystery to us? We knew about the threats to the wedding itself, so why didn't we know about all this?' He threw the paper aside and began ticking off on his fingers: 'Terrific timing throughout. The demo at the exact moment that singer was taking his bow. One smoke bomb set off up there to cause the maximum trouble and direct all the attention to that upper level, as distant as possible from the Royal Box. The next one set off in the box next door timed for the precise moment of the grab, so that the getaway is covered by the second wave of chaos.'

'Someone knew their opera form all right!' (Chicken would have been proud to hear him.) 'Seats, no, boxes paid for in cash. The Indian women who unrolled the banner and set off the first smoke bomb must have been in the plot. If they *were* Indians, which we doubt. Easy to escape down the stairs from the balcony level and saris only too easily disposed of. There's a pretty unused Ladies right there behind the balcony boxes.'

His expression darkened to one of ferocity as he continued to tick off: 'And while we're on the subject of foreign dress, HRH bound, gagged, possibly drugged, we're not sure, and bundled into some Arab robe, yashmak, chador, whatever, face hidden, *nose* hidden in one of these sinister black jobs, and supported, carried rather, down the stairs and out of the Royal Box private entrance, deserted on the night of a Gala, out to a waiting car by two solicitous Arabs, supporting her! Important sheikhs,' he almost shouted. 'A car with a chauffeur, a chauffeur in cap, ready there waiting. Planned to the minute.'

The very senior policeman looked round as though for something else to crush. 'How's Fitzgerald?' he concluded, the anger draining from his voice.

It was only a short while later that his most trusted assistant returned and said: 'The good news is: we think we know where they're holding her. The bad news is that we've received their demands. And this time, with Fitzgerald in mind, we know they're serious.'

15

Violence

'I've lost one of my new Russian earrings, Ferdel will be so cross.' For the first time since her abduction, Princess Amy's face crumpled and she began to cry. Dishevelled, the blonde ringlets now a wreck of the formal lacquered hair style, her face dirty, and still the Rasputin sapphires gleaming at her throat and weighing down her creased white dress at the breast, Princess Amy looked like Cinderella just after midnight struck. Already the finery was disintegrating; rags and ashes would soon follow.

'Don't worry, it will be found, people always find things like that. Besides, we are not interested in your jewels. Only in you.' Through her brown nylon-stocking mask, Pussy's voice sounded muffled and horrible. The effect on Princess Amy was to stop her new-found tears abruptly: at the same moment involuntarily she wrinkled her nose in disgust. It was actually the strong smell of Pussy's lavender water which disgusted her, reminding her of a tormenting governess in childhood.

'You're supposed to make friends with your captors,' thought Princess Amy. 'I've read about it, and there was that cousin of Ferdel's in Italy, that boy, he did it and it worked. But I'll never be able to make friends with *you*. You're really cruel under that awful mask. I know it.'

Amy, carried down the special stairs and out of the side entrance used for private visits to the Royal Box in Arab woman's clothing, had not been drugged, as the senior policeman suspected. She had been gagged, her disguise hiding the gag. Beagle, who did the gagging (as he also bound the other inhabitants of the box including the Royal Box Steward who had been serving the party) did it expertly. It was something he told the cell that he had learned from some kind of military anti-terrorist manual borrowed from a friend. Wherever he had learnt it, it seemed to work.

'She is sick,' was Beagle's reply to a reaction of surprise from the attendant at the bottom of the stairs. 'It is the smoke,' he muttered, rather than spoke, in some vaguely foreign accent, his face stained, shrouded under his own Arab headdress, robes flowing. 'We must go to the car.'

Both Fox and Beagle were carrying loaded pistols: but only Fox knew that they were loaded since at meetings Fox had carefully promised a couple of *unloaded* 9mm. Berettas, looking absolutely for real, via theatrical contacts for supplying such, made at Leaviss. He had already successfully supplied something similar to Beagle on the occasion of the photographic foray; but Beagle's pistol had had a solid barrel. For the climactic night of the abduction, however, Fox had obtained pistols used for firing blanks – and replaced the blanks.

Nevertheless Fox stoutly maintained that his decision to load them with real bullets was absolutely the right one. He also defended his shooting of the Princess's detective, who had flung himself forward as the 'Arabs' produced their weapons, even in the face of Monkey's appalled reaction.

'That was violence, Fox. We agreed that simulated weapons should be taken: that it would be enough to frighten them.'

Yet Fox was almost blithely impenitent. He merely pointed out that the detective's precipitate action would have in fact scuppered the whole plan if Fox's weapon had not been loaded. He seemed to think the detective had been quite unreasonable in his behaviour. Fox argued this on the grounds that it had been decided in advance that the sight of a Beretta pointed at the Princess's temple would immobilize him, as indeed it had immobilized the other occupants of the box – Prince Ferdinand, Major Smylie-Porter and the flunkey; Lamb had immobilized Ione Quentin by her own method of flinging herself into her arms and hugging her as if for protection.

Fox even regarded himself as a bit of a hero. Monkey on the other hand thought there was something positively frightening about the way that Fox, a young man apparently dedicated to a life of non-violence, shrugged off what Monkey himself considered to be a serious crime against a fellow human being: Innoright was after all specific in *not* condemning the whole of humanity in favour of the animal kingdom.

At this point – in the car – they had no idea whether the man had lived or died: probably the latter, judging from what Beagle had told Monkey briefly in the getaway car.

Monkey, dark uniform cap hiding his high forehead and receding hairline, scarf round his neck to conceal the white tie, had been satisfied that he looked the image of some rich Arab's chauffeur, at the wheel of a large, dark-blue Mercedes with elegant darkened glass windows; leaving the opera discreetly early, Monkey had brought the car up from where Chicken had parked it earlier in the evening. This chauffeur waited ready just at the side entrance for a quick, a very quick departure; it was something Monkey, with his awareness of such procedures, had arranged in advance, knowing that the police presence would be concentrated on the front entrance from which the royal party was scheduled to leave.

Fox had hired the car from a company who leased out such things for films (although it was currently showing false number plates). In the meantime the whole operation of the getaway had needed and received immaculate timing, where possible rehearsed, where not, estimated, discussed and re-estimated.

Monkey thought fleetingly that where violence was concerned, you could never really judge a character in advance until the pressure came. Out of Beagle and Fox, two young men who had little in common but their age, he would have backed Beagle any day over Fox to pull the trigger. Was it Beagle who had killed Tom? Monkey had always secretly dreaded that it might prove to be so. Or was perhaps Beagle's vaunted air of violence a mere carapace for a softer nature? They would soon find out. (In any case, there was a flaw in Monkey's reasoning about Beagle: it was Beagle who did not know that the guns were loaded whereas Fox, who had procured them, did.)

That had been Monkey's real mistake; underestimating not only Fox's streak of viciousness but also his independence. If only people would carry out orders! . . . Coolly – he prided himself on his driving – Monkey drew the Mercedes with its false number plates into the little yard at the back of Beagle's lair. The distance from the Opera House was so short that the whole journey had taken a matter of minutes even though Monkey had driven fast, but not too fast, to avoid giving the impression of escape.

Chicken and Pussy were waiting. As Fox and Beagle, Arab costumes discarded, carried the wrapped body of the Princess through the narrow back entrance (she was surprisingly heavy for such a small person, thought Fox, panting), Monkey moved over into the passenger seat of the car. Chicken got swiftly into the driver's seat. As well as long white gloves, she was now wearing a fake tiara and diamond earrings supplied, had they known it, by Leaviss; but the opulent fur jacket which she wore was real. It had belonged to Monkey's wife Cynthia and he had given it to her long before he appreciated the cruelty and violence involved in the fur trade. He liked to think that she too would have wanted to abandon it had she lived; as it was, this last ceremonial and sacrificial use of the jacket in the cause was to Monkey's way of thinking, absolutely appropriate.

Monkey removed his cap and scarf, to reveal his white tie and tail-coat once more. Pussy removed the false number plates. In a small street off the Law Courts, deserted at this hour, Monkey and Chicken abandoned the hired Mercedes (and the Arab robes in the boot) for Monkey's own car, an ancient but highly polished Rolls, which he had left there before the Gala. Monkey and Chicken together, he with his medals, she with her tiara, now conveyed (he felt) the perfect image of a prosperous opera-goer and his wife; the latter driving as being the more sober of the two following the necessary refreshments in the interval to make opera at least palatable to a tired businessman.

Only a short while after the Princess's body had been taken from the Opera House, Monkey arrived back at his flat in South Eaton Place. There Carmencita, his Spanish housekeeper, had laid out a cold supper for two: she, like Monkey, entertained secret sentimental hopes of the sweet little Miss Quentin even if she was a bit young for her stately employer (and needed fattening up – but then Carmencita would do that). Composedly, Monkey sat down to eat both portions of the cold supper. There was only a slight tremble in his hands and that he cured by draining a small glass of brandy more or less at a gulp before he began to eat.

Chicken, dressed once more in her inconspicuous clothes (Monkey would now dispose of the jacket and tiara as Pussy had disposed of the saris en route), walked to Victoria and hailed a taxi home. She left Monkey to work his way through gazpacho and cold Spanish pancakes: unlike Lamb, he needed no fattening up but Carmencita was such an excellent cook, particularly now she had been trained to vegetarianism, that it seemed a pity to waste the food. He was magisterially confident that he, the master planner, knew where all the members of the cell were. It had gone right and in the morning Innoright would deliver their demands. At least, it had gone *almost* right: but already under the influence of the brandy and some excellent burgundy, Monkey was beginning to forget about the injuries to the detective. Sooner or later, he would fit that into the scheme of things, as he had fitted in the death of Tom: part of the means which the noble end justified.

Momentarily however the trembling had returned: Monkey drank some more burgundy – from the other glass, forgetting in his temporary agitation that Lamb never touched alcohol. Now he was restored. He put down his glass and raised one eyebrow: for a moment he looked purely simian, a very clever ape indeed.

But Monkey did not know where all the members of the cell were. He did not for example know where Lamb herself was. He imagined that when the hue and cry at the Opera House itself was over, the immediate horror of the abduction understood if not accepted, she would be taken together with that unnervingly correct sister (now she would be an obstacle to his romantic dreams) back to their Chelsea flat.

That was not the case.

'What the hell are you doing here?' asked Beagle, coldly furious. 'You could have got yourself shot coming to the door like that. He's a bloody maniac, our Foxy.' Beagle hesitated; in spite of his anger his voice remained low. He pointed to the ceiling. Lamb imagined masked Fox and masked Pussy, the former still armed, holding the Princess captive under the sad gaze of the wide-eyed seals in the blown-up photographs.

'Look at you,' he went on, taking her thin bare arm in his fingers. 'Wearing a fucking crown through the streets of London' – with his other hand he touched the tiara – 'No coat. This is the English summer, okay? Not your favourite Port-oh-feeno.' (Lamb had once unwisely revealed her predilection for the Italian resort.) 'Dress which reveals your boobs, if you *had* any boobs.'

Lamb's eyes were enormous in her pale face. 'I wanted to be with you,' she began, and then altered it to: 'I wanted to be of help.'

'Obey orders, my dear Miss Lamb, obey orders. That's the way to be of help.' Beagle mimicked Monkey. Nevertheless the anger was fading and he relaxed his grip on her arm. 'You're shivering. Better put on something else. I'll get you some jeans and a jersey from upstairs. Even though you'll swim in them. It's bad enough having our little Madam looking like something out of a bodice-ripping movie without you too.'

'How is – she?' Lamb found her lips were too dry to pronounce Princess Amy's name and her heart was pittering very rapidly as she watched Beagle's reaction.

'The patient is as well as can be expected. Phew! Am I glad to leave my mask off?' He made towards Lamb as if to pull the stocking down over her head. 'Do you want to go up and have a look? I'll prepare you for the operating theatre.'

Lamb shrank back. 'No, no, I don't want to – besides it's far too dangerous.'

'Dangerous!' Beagle gave a short low laugh. 'That's rich. Do you realize what Foxy has gone and done? He's shot a fucking policeman. That little wimp, didn't know he had it in him, did I? In short, darling, that's torn it. We're for it. They'll never let us get away with that. Oh yes, darling, kidnapping a Princess to call attention to a good cause is one thing, particularly if we treat her nice; shooting a policeman is quite another. He hasn't even chucked his gun away: mine went down a fucking drain right away.'

He whistled. 'Oh, we're for it all right, the lot of us. Including that pompous bastard, Monkey – he's got his eye on you, by the way, hasn't he? The only question is, how we go – and who we take with us. And what we do before we go. I've a few plans meself.'

Pussy appeared silently at the door of the barred and shuttered ground-floor room, which had the outward appearance of a small grocer's shop in disrepair. In fact, it was not in disrepair but very well prepared. Behind the dusty tins lay fresh new ones, the deep freeze was working and stocked with supplies ... Lamb had a moment to think how specially gross Pussy looked in her mask (unconsciously echoing the earlier thoughts of Princess Amy) before Pussy took it off.

'Lamb!' she exclaimed, crossly.

'Leave her be, Puss.' Lamb was relieved to find that Beagle now sounded protective. 'She can't go upstairs but she can stand guard down here. When she's got some proper clothes on and got rid of all this tat.' He touched the tiara again. 'What happens to this, then?'

'I'm going to sell it and give the proceeds to Innoright,' said Lamb, with a defiant look at Pussy.

'There's a good girl. Now Pussy, that lets you and Fox get on with the delivery of the demands: two heads being better than one. You've got to ring Monkey at the agreed time and the telephone here has been disconnected as you know. Why don't you take Fox to your flat? You've never been connected as a pair.'

'He wants to be alone with her.' The thought flashed unbidden: Princess Amy with her bodice ripped . . .

Pussy frowned. Latterly her original dislike of Beagle had faded in favour of an irrational dislike of Lamb: it was irrational, for Lamb, unlike Beagle, had humbly sought to placate the sombre older woman. Lamb was not to know that Pussy's unstable loves and hates, all springing from her daughter's death, had now veered round and focused on young upper-class women who played with the cause, leaving Caro-Otter to die for it. (For that was how Pussy had now come to view Otter's death in the car crash.) Young upper-class women such as Lamb.

Another thing that Lamb did not know about Pussy was that, with the intuition of another obsessive character, she had easily caught a whiff of Lamb's jealous fears concerning Beagle.

'Just as you say, dear,' replied Pussy to Beagle with something like a smile. (Pussy's smile, thought Lamb, always had something unpleasant about it, even at the best of times.) 'You take over upstairs, throw down the clothes for our little Lamb here, or send them down with that naughty Mr Fox. After what happened, he probably shouldn't be here anyway, I'm sure I don't know what Monkey will say about *him*. That'll leave the lovebirds together,' she added.

What lovebirds? asked the now awakened monster in Lamb's breast. What lovebirds does she mean? Pussy's smile was by now positively malevolent. 'No more violence, mind. Protect the innocent. Don't forget.'

When Fox came down bearing a pair of Beagle's jeans and a khaki jersey, it came quite naturally to Lamb to say to him: 'Look, Fox, give me your gun. You shouldn't be found carrying that thing. I'll look after it.'

'Careful how you handle it, it's still loaded. I'm not sure how many I've fired.' Fox still sounded almost blithe on the subject.

'I'll get rid of it, I mean,' said Lamb. 'It's nice to think that for once I can do something really helpful.'

Once she was alone, Lamb sat with the pistol listening for the sounds which might come from the room upstairs, the room where Beagle and Princess Amy were now also alone – alone with each other.

'What are you going to do with me?' Then: 'This won't work, you know. You won't get away with it.' Finally: 'I think you had just better let me go.'

To her surprise, Princess Amy managed quite a creditably imperious tone: which was what she intended. The tears which the loss of the sapphire earring had temporarily evoked were gone. She had no intention of giving anyone the satisfaction of seeing her crying again – if she could help it. Was it acting pure and simple, or an imitation of her revered if notoriously tetchy father? Not acting: 'I was never any good at acting at school,' she thought, 'and as for imitating Daddy, well, I can't even begin to imagine Daddy in this situation. He'd have *exploded* long ago.' Even in her present dire situation, the idea of the late Duke of Cumberland captured by terrorists after an Opera Gala had a certain grim humour about it.

'I suppose I'm behaving *like* their idea of a Princess,' thought Princess Amy. 'I only hope I can keep it up. Goodness knows, I'm not being treated like one.'

'I'm going to let you sleep.' Beagle spoke in a voice which was both reasonable and distinct, so that unlike Pussy he did not sound, as well as look, menacing.

'Sleep! Where?'

Beagle pointed to the large low bed in the corner of the room.

'I assure you I have no intention of sleeping. Not with you in the room. As a matter of fact' – and as Princess Amy spoke she decided it was true – 'as a matter of fact, I'm hungry.'

'You can have food. We have food. You can even have a drink if you like. Wine, and I believe there's some whisky. The vintage may not be what you're used to—'

'I never drink,' interrupted Amy coldly. 'My mouth hurts. I would like a drink of water.'

Beagle went to the basin and poured out some water into a china mug with the Innoright logo on it. Princess Amy made a grimace.

'I assure you it's quite clean,' he said.

'How do you expect me to drink it like this? Please undo my hands. I shan't try to escape. I'll give you – my parole, I think it's called.'

Beagle considered. Amy's ankles were bound as were her hands: she was also bound to the white chair in which she sat, the single chair in the room. Shouting would get her nowhere above the deserted shop. It seemed safe enough to comply (despite Monkey's explicit instructions to the contrary); besides which, he had his own reasons for wishing to do so. He undid the ropes round Princess Amy's wrists and handed her the cup of water which she gulped down.

'Will you try to sleep if I get you some food? It's better for you. You've got to wait till morning anyway.'

'Wait for what? What do you want anyway? You're the same people who took those horrible photographs. You must be. Who are you?' Amy's glance wandered to the blown-up pictures of the seals on the walls. 'Did you take these?' Beagle nodded.

'So it was probably you who photographed *them*—' she thought. No, she mustn't let herself dwell on that, not think about Ferdel. Oddly enough it was the thought of Ferdel – where was he? what was happening to him? would he try to rescue her? or was that only in fairy stories? – which had produced her sudden rush of tears earlier. 'Who are you?' she repeated instead.

'Innoright.' He turned the logo on the mug towards her. 'And we are the same people who took the photographs. Innoright: protection of the innocent. That's what it's all about. Now how do you feel about that, Your Royal Highness?' The title sounded vaguely sarcastic on Beagle's lips.

'You know how I feel about it,' replied Amy with spirit; she found that talking – rather than thinking – was reviving her. She just wished that this unknown young man (she assumed he was quite young from the style of his clothes) would take his mask off. All the masks, including his, were so creepy. 'I said all those things on television. I *love* animals. Everyone knows I love animals. Besides, it's nothing to do with me. Talk about protecting the innocent! I *am* innocent,' concluded Princess Amy firmly.

'You're a Royal, aren't you? Where the innocent are concerned you're a royal symbol of oppression.'

'Are you sort of Communists?' ventured Princess Amy, her tone beginning to waver: this kind of language was both more familiar and more worrying. 'I mean, as well as being terribly keen on animal rights,' she added hurriedly.

'Personally, I'm a keen monarchist,' replied Beagle. 'And I'm specially keen on princesses. And out of princesses, I'm specially keen on you, Your Royal Highness. Or should I say My Royal Hostage?' Princess Amy guessed that he was smiling behind the mask; that thought did not reassure her either.

'Look, I'll show you something,' he said suddenly. Beagle took a small key and unlocked the cupboard beneath the basin. He drew out further rolls of photographs and started to strew them round the floor, on the boards, on the white cushions, finally on the bed. These were not photographs of seals, or indeed of animals, wild or domestic. With increasing apprehension, Princess Amy recognized herself in a series of enormous images, some clearly cropped from bygone royal functions (at which she had in fact cut an extremely minor figure) some snatched as she entered the Cumberland Palace gates. One actually showed her leaning out of the first-floor window at Cumberland Palace, laughing. Laughing! What on earth had she been laughing *at*? Don't brood, *talk*, Amy told herself fiercely.

'So you see, Your Royal Highness, you're my little private passion,' observed Beagle pleasantly. He stood over the photographs on the floor for a moment, gazed at Amy as though to compare them, and finally rolled them all up again. 'Now will you go to sleep? With or without food. I wouldn't let any harm come to you, would I? No violence. My little private passion.'

16

In a Secret Place

'They're holding her. In a secret place,' said Ione Quentin. 'Now will you help me?'

Jemima Shore's first reaction was that Princess Amy's normally equable lady-in-waiting had taken leave of her senses; presumably under the strain of the wedding preparations. But wasn't that exactly what she was hired for? A talent for calm administration. Oh well, people went mad at all sorts of awkward moments and for all sorts of awkward reasons.

Ione Quentin's arrival at Jemima's Holland Park Mansions flat had several bizarre aspects to it. For one thing, her name on the intercom had not been immediately recognizable (Jemima tended to think of her merely as 'the lady-in-waiting') so that Jemima took her at first to be some importunate fan; Megalith was not supposed to divulge her address, but there had been visits in the past and after all Megalith was no longer bound to protect her. Jemima did distinguish the word 'help' and decided she was not in the mood for offering kindness to strangers.

It was Rick Vancy, lingering after the so-called working breakfast (actually coffee and orange juice with bran muffins), who rolled his eyes and said: 'Hey, that sounds interesting. I haven't seen you in your sleuth's role before. I'm kind of curious to watch how you operate.' At which point Jemima decided that in order to get rid of Rick Vancy ('I'm afraid I never allow outsiders in on this kind of thing,' she observed sweetly), she would pay the price of attending to a distraught member of the public.

Rick Vancy, thus dismissed, passed Ione Quentin coming up the stairs; he too did not recognize her, or not immediately. He did place her a minute after she had been admitted to the top-floor flat but by then it was too late – too late to satisfy his curiosity about the nature of her mission. He made a mental note to enquire what that was all about when he next talked to Jemima. (It would probably be gross to call her from the car, and the woman, Quentin, might still be there.) Is Jemima holding out on me over something, he wondered. Much later Rick Vancy would curse the rare impulse towards reticence which had possessed him at this precise moment.

In the meantime Jemima was staring at Ione. Both women remained standing. 'Why are you telling me this? Surely the police – my God, what are *they* doing about it?' And the journalist in Jemima caused her to add in spite of herself: 'Why hasn't anything appeared in the Press?'

Ione explained in a surprisingly steady voice just why nothing, so far, had emerged. Agitated at the beginning, or merely nervous, she had regained her poise, it seemed. 'They want to get her back first. Naturally. A free hand to act. I suppose it always happens in kidnapping cases if one did but know: they try to keep it all quiet. But they won't get her back. Not without your help. And my help.'

Ione was looking straight at Jemima as though willing her to agree; there was something fierce, almost domineering about her gaze; suddenly she flinched. It was in fact the cat Midnight who had wandered insouciantly through the open balcony window and was now rubbing himself against Ione's leg. 'Oh, a cat. I thought—' she managed a smile. 'I'm not like Lydia, I'm not a terrific animal lover, I'm afraid. Humans very much first.'

'Lydia?'

'My little sister, Lydia. That's the point. That's why I'm here. I'm afraid she's terribly involved in all this. I know she is. She led them into the box, the men who grabbed the Princess. She asked if she could present her host to Princess Amy – he's some kind of philanthropist. So I arranged it. That's how they got in, not the philanthropist but some Arabs, or men dressed as Arabs. And now she's vanished. She ran off, didn't come home with me. That's exactly why you've got to help me.'

'Lydia Quentin!' exclaimed Jemima. The girl in the box next to her at the opera. The man in the box: that man who had also been at prayer in Westminster Cathedral. She had a vision of the intense face of her neighbour at Covent Garden, eyes staring ahead, staring indeed at the Royal Box. 'Burning eyes.' Where had she heard that phrase and heard it extremely recently? Pompey who had called her only minutes ago about the new witness in his murder case. Was that Lydia Quentin? She felt she was on the edge of understanding. For the time being she turned back to Ione.

'Miss Quentin, what can *I* do?' But to tell the truth Jemima was attending to Ione with only half her mind. The other half of her attention was focused on the fact that here she was, Jemima Shore Investigator, being presented with the scoop of her career, the scoop of anyone's career, and what on earth could she do about it, what on earth *should* she do about it?

Ione's voice cut across these thoughts.

'You see, Jemima, I know where they're holding her.' The fact that Ione addressed her unasked by her Christian name was now the single sign of disturbance that she displayed. What an incredible woman! thought Jemima. She witnesses her mistress kidnapped, abducted, or whatever you like to call it, she has reason to think her own sister is involved and she's still as cool and collected as if she's wearing a hat and white gloves at Ascot.

'Then you *must* go to the police—'

'If I go to the police, something ghastly will happen. I know it. She might even kill herself.'

'Oh surely not, Ione' – since they were friends – 'I would imagine that's the last thing she would do! Not that I know her as you do of course. One interview and that's all. All the same I thought she came across as surprisingly spirited, for Royalty, if I may say so without offence. Not at all the suicidal type.'

'Royalty?' Ione looked fleetingly puzzled. 'Oh Royalty. No, Jemima, I'm not talking about Princess Amy. I'm talking about Lydia. My sister.'

Jemima reflected that under the circumstances it was a fairly amazing thing to say but then the circumstances themselves were fairly amazing. And Ione Quentin was adding to them, minute by minute, in this tale she was unfolding.

'There's this man who got hold of her, I know he did, got hold of her and made her do all sorts of things. She's so impressionable, Lydia, and she's been badly ill. She's really not responsible for what she does, you must see that. You made that programme, I watched it when Lydia was – well, in pretty terrible shape. *Look To The Weak.* It helped me get through. I've done what I can since our mother killed herself, that's when it all started, really started. Lydia adored our mother. It was such a shock.' Ione paused. 'But she was always – fragile is the word I use. Or weak – your word. She had a little collapse once when a dog had to be put down when it bit someone, a grown-up who was teasing it. Our father as a matter of fact. Leelee said all sorts of wild things about putting down the grown-up instead – Daddy, that is. He was terribly strict – they didn't get on. She hated all his shooting and things like that. And he was so much older. She was easily upset, you see. Tender hearted. She loved animals, Jemima. She thought they were innocent! She's always felt so guilty herself. This photographer, the man who got hold of her, played on that.'

'Animals and innocence. So this is Innoright. And a photographer—' The shape of the conspiracy was beginning to appear to Jemima: an intense girl, a middle-aged businessman, and a rangy-looking young photographer who had come late to the Republican Hotel and sat next to her. All of these, and perhaps some others, had been gathered in that chapel at Westminster Cathedral. Was she at the same time stumbling towards a solution of Pompey's murder? In the meantime Ione continued to pour out her confidences concerning her sister.

'Of course it's Innoright! I've tried so hard to save her from it all. I used to go through all her things but she got cunning. Then I took to following her; there were certain stories she always told me about cinemas with girlfriends, late nights listening to their troubles. Whatever she told me about listening to other people's troubles, I knew she was, well, in trouble herself. I was always wary then. Poor darling, it wasn't so difficult to follow her, thinking she was so clever with her changing Tubes and her codes and all that. In many ways Lydia is still a baby.'

'This man, I gather, is not a baby.'

'He has this place in Covent Garden,' continued Ione as if Jemima had not spoken. 'I'm sure that's where they are. Horribly sordid. But that's not the point. If we went together we could talk to her. It could all be settled. Quietly. I'd take her away, take Leelee away. I do realize she'd have to go away—'

'Whether you're right or wrong, we *must* tell the police.' Jemima displayed a firmness at least equal to Ione's. 'These people are dangerous maniacs. No, not your sister. The others. As for your sister—' she stopped. She thought Ione Quentin had probably got enough to cope with at the present time. Besides it was important to keep her contentedly, or more or less contentedly, in line with what Jemima now proposed to do. For the time being, 'dangerous maniacs', politely excluding Lydia Quentin with her burning eyes, was appropriate enough.

'Dangerous maniacs' was however the mildest of the terms currently being used at Scotland Yard where the Innoright demands had just been received. Chicken had delivered them: she had been chosen as the least conspicuous of the cell (of those not currently involved in other tasks such as the guarding of the Princess). Moreover she assumed a traffic warden's uniform to do so, courtesy of Leaviss, which in a true sense made her even less conspicuous. Shortly after Chicken delivered the flat envelope to Scotland Yard, Fox telephoned to advise of the demands' arrival.

Fox was deputed by Monkey to do so: Monkey did not trust his own rather plummy voice to be sufficiently concealed, besides which he had been seen publicly with Lamb. Fox made the call from Pussy's flat, taking care, he hoped, to deepen his own naturally rather high voice. (Fox, a frustrated actor-turned-costumier, was proud to perform the task.) Pussy's flat was arranged, he found, like some kind of chapel; but as Beagle's secret studio was dedicated to animals, Pussy's flat centred round huge photographs of a blonde girl with long hair. Fox vaguely recognized her: wasn't that some well-known model? But Fox was not interested in Pussy's private life: having telephoned as arranged, his chief concern was to get back to Noel.

'Would you be interested in meeting Noel? That's my dog,' he could not resist asking in the temporary mood of exhilaration which seized him after he had made the call.

'A *pet*?' Pussy's voice, the voice of one referring to some truly barbaric practice, was icy; too late Fox remembered Pussy's views about pets and the story, the hideous story, about Pussy and the Alsatian. If she were to lay a finger on Noel! Pussy was dangerous. That sort of thing was the work of a maniac . . .

'Dangerous maniacs!' The phrase, with others considerably less agreeable, continued to be bandied about Scotland Yard.

'Princess Anne held up in The Mall, attempted kidnapping, that man in Her Majesty's bedroom wanting to talk to her or so he said, and now this – at the opera of all places – where will it end?' intoned a senior policeman in a doleful litany.

'It's simple, now, isn't it?' said an even more senior policeman patiently. 'Now we know where she is. We agree to them all, these demands, don't we? For the time being.'

One of his colleagues began to list the demands in a kind of rising frenzy. 'So where do you suggest we start?' he ended aggressively. 'The free-zone for animals in Windsor Great Park, for example? Incorporating the animals in the Windsor Wild Life Park – I think I'm quoting correctly. The whole of Windsor Great Park to be running wild with sweet little wolves and tigers and seals and dolphins right up to the castle itself. Correction: seals and dolphins don't run.

'Shall we start there?' he went on. 'Or the airlift to Africa and India perhaps, the airlift of all the animals in British zoos hailing from there? Shall we begin with the airlift perchance? Seeing as I note the Windsor Great Park scheme merely needs a public broadcast to inaugurate it. No problem, that.

'Or, let me see, Regent's Park, another free-zone, no, I beg its pardon, Innozones is what they will be called. Zones for innocents.' His voice rose and he was almost screaming. 'Isn't that lovely? Lions and tigers milling all about the American Ambassador's residence. That should take care of our security problems there nicely. No more guards necessary.'

As the senior policeman remained impassive, his colleague looked at the paper again and made a visible effort to control himself. 'As a matter of pure interest, if we do promise all this, what guarantee have they got, Innoright, these nutters, that the demands will be carried out? Once we've got her back.'

'The idea is: it's pledged, it will be done.'

'And you're talking about the *government*,' he snorted. 'Government pledges! Where have these people been living? Who on earth believes *government* pledges? Now I know they're seriously crazy.'

The patience in the voice of the very senior policeman was by now almost saint-like: 'No, not the government. The Monarch. Not likely to break the royal word, given in public. That's the idea. In the meantime, shouldn't you be seeing about those snipers, there's a good chap. I must get back to the Home Secretary. Now why didn't they think of grabbing him?' The very senior policeman sounded quite wistful.

As a matter of fact, when Jemima Shore succeeded in getting through to the right quarters – 'I have, or think I have, some information about a certain missing person' – the Home Secretary proved to be her chief problem too. That achievement of the right quarters was itself only performed with the help of Pompey – desperately sought and found at home on garden duty. It was illogical, Jemima realized, to be disappointed that the whereabouts of the 'missing person' were already known; even if those whereabouts had not been known for very long. In another way she found she was relieved that Ione Quentin's story was not a total fantasy produced by an overworked brain: and that too was illogical.

'Acting on information received,' was the only eludication she received. 'I am afraid we are not authorized to tell you any more at the present time.' Information received: who? Clearly not Ione Quentin. But who? A traitor in the ranks – the ranks of Innoright?

It was when Jemima pressed the claims of Ione Quentin, accompanied by herself, as an intermediary, that she found the image of the Home Secretary conjured up against her, an image which was defeated by the unexpected aid of a psychiatrist. This expert on sieges suggested that the calming presence of Ione, as the Princess' lady-in-waiting, was in itself desirable. Cumberland Palace, in a situation where everything seemed wrong, could see nothing particularly wrong with that. It even gave Major Smylie-Porter a vague feeling of relief that Ione should be involved. The family were beyond thinking of matters in those terms. As the Duchess of Cumberland kept to her darkened room, Amy's sisters, the vivacious Princess Sophie and the melancholy Princess Harriet, inhabited the Vienna Drawing-Room with their amiably undistinguished husbands – Scots and French respectively. Were any of them safe? In their distracted state, the sisters took refuge, as it were, in fears for their own children. The Vienna Drawing-Room was made into a kind of redoubt, at least in their imagination.

Thus the great ballroom picture, in its ornate golden frame, which had only recently formed the background to Amy and Ferdel's interview, now looked down upon the golden heads of Amy's little nephews and nieces: Jamie and Jack and Alexander, Isabelle and Chantal and Béatrice. All six of them owed their presence in London to their appointment as pages and bridesmaids at the Royal Wedding.

The Princesses had not the heart to interrupt the excited games of the children as they raced in and out of the famous silk and gilded 'Vienna' furniture. Ferdel, smoking heavily – a habit which came as a surprise to his future sisters-in-law – hardly appeared to notice them, even when baby Béatrice, the smallest and blondest, clasped him round his dark-blue trouser leg.

'I love you,' she cried, gazing up at him. Ferdel smiled rather vaguely in her direction as though she was some importunate dog – or rather puppy.

Little Jamie, sensing the abstraction of the grown-ups and seeking to turn it to his advantage, asked loudly: 'Mum, why can't I wear my kilt at the wedding instead of that silly page's suit? It makes me look like a girl. I want to wear my kilt,' he concluded in an even more stentorian voice.

'I think that is a skirt—' piped French Isabelle in her know-all way till she was shushed by Princess Harriet. But when Princess Sophie, normally a stern mother, responded by bursting into sobs, even Jamie was abashed. Putting his finger in his mouth, a gesture he was thought to have abandoned, he ran over to his father who was sitting in the window (wondering in point of fact whether it would be bad taste to ask for a dram of whisky so early).

'Come on, old chap,' said his father gently, disturbed from his reverie. He drew Jamie on to his lap. 'Let's be specially nice today, shall we? Mum's having –' He paused. '– a specially difficult time,' he ended rather lamely.

All in all, the attendance of Jemima Shore upon Ione Quentin, at the latter's suggestion, passed almost unnoticed in the devastated community of Cumberland Palace. It was in this way that Jemima found herself travelling in a police car, beside Ione, through the bedecked streets of London – bedecked in a way that seemed particularly bizarre to Jemima, since the decorations were all for a wedding that seemed at the moment peculiarly unlikely to take place.

There were displays in the shop windows: brides in numerous guestimates of Princess Amy's wedding dress, ranging from the super-frilly to the super-sleek. Prince Ferdinand for the most part had to make do with Ruritanian-type uniforms: since no one was quite clear just what he could wear at the ceremony. The *cognoscenti* knew that a European Catholic wedding involved a white tie and tails; but a sombre baffled statement from Cumberland Palace had not made it quite clear whether this would be the case at Westminster Cathedral. Maybe, as more than one shop-window dresser decided, one could let the imagination roam? As a result, Jemima was whirled past various wax dummies of Prince Ferdinand, bending over the hand of his fiancée, and wearing a variety of white, green and even pale-blue uniforms, which would not have disgraced the male lead of an operetta.

'We're still in a kidnap situation,' said the policeman who appeared to be in charge to Jemima; he spoke, in a seemingly offhand manner, from his position in the back seat between the two women. Ione Quentin's outward demeanour was impassive but Jemima noticed she had twisted a small white handkerchief so tightly round her wrist that it had the look of a tourniquet.

'A kidnap situation?' It was Jemima who asked the question; Ione did not – or could not – speak.

'A kidnap situation, not a siege. That is to say, we know where she is, but they don't know we know. We'd like to avoid a siege, if possible. Just get *her* out quietly' – a pause and then some emphasis – 'All the same, we have marksmen in place.' Another pause, 'Naturally.'

'Naturally,' echoed Jemima. Ione still said nothing. Then she murmured something desperate, and Jemima, turning, saw that there were tears in her eyes. Jemima realized that what Ione had actually said was: 'Marksmen.' She added more distinctly: 'She may be killed.'

The policeman gave her a slightly cold glance. 'Miss Quentin, it is our sincere aim that no one should be killed. Not even the killer.'

'The killer?' repeated Jemima.

'Detective-Sergeant Fitzgerald, who was shot in the Royal Box whilst attempting to prevent the abduction, died in hospital shortly before you telephoned. The person or persons we have reason to believe are holding HRH . . .' still that pause, then: '. . . are wanted on a charge of murder.'

After that there was silence in the car and even when they arrived at the edge of the Covent Garden backwater, where operations were being directed from a hidden police command post, Jemima said very little.

Ione Quentin, twisting the tight white tourniquet, said nothing at all.

17

End of a Fairy Tale

Princess Amy woke up first. It took only an instant for the horror to return: an instant in which she realized that the curious dark object next to her, lying on the pillow beside her, was a masked head. For a moment she thought – some battered but beloved toy of her childhood; then reality, terrible reality, flooded in.

'I must not cry.' Sayings of the past came back. That governess, the cruel one: 'Tears don't help.' Her father, overheard saying gruffly to her mother: 'Now Henriette, here's my handkerchief, you know I can't bear to see a woman cry.' (What long-forgotten peccadillo had he committed to make her mother cry?) She braced herself. One of her wrists was tied to Beagle's and the other to the bed, but her ankles were not tied. She gave a tentative wriggle.

Beagle was awake immediately at that; her movement must have disturbed him. He had not in fact intended to fall asleep at all, not only for reasons of security (although Lamb was guarding the house downstairs) but also to have time to reflect, to savour . . .

'I want to see your face,' said Princess Amy. She spoke softly but urgently as she struggled in vain to sit up until Beagle co-operated by sitting up with her. Then she had to lean awkwardly against the wall until he bent to release her other hand.

'No, not to identify you,' she went on. 'You know why. I want to *see* you.' She had the impression it had been removed at some point in the long night – but then darkness had surrounded her, had surrounded them both.

There was a long pause while the other figure on the bed, still disfigured, appeared to consider her proposition. Then Beagle took off his mask. In the eerie morning light filtering through the heavy shutters, Princess Amy stared at him. Then she put up her newly freed hand and touched his cheek. It was in no way a tender gesture, more an enquiry or a gesture of exploration.

'Recognize me?' he asked. There was something almost pleading about Beagle's question. 'Amy,' he added. The Princess dropped her hand.

'How should I recognize you?' she asked coldly.

'We've met before. We played together. You once gave me a toy dog for Christmas, black and white spotted. Somewhere I've still got it.'

Amy's expression showed quite clearly that she feared, apart from everything else, she now had to cope with madness.

'Oh don't worry, Your Royal Highness.' This time Beagle spoke with something of his old familiar and sardonic tone. 'I don't expect you to remember. You must have played with so many people. And given away cart-loads of spotted toy dogs. I'll end the dreadful suspense. I'm Josh Taplow these days, Jossie when you used to know me. Jossie Taplow the chauffeur's son. That's right, Taplow who used to work for you and now works for His Highness Prince Ferdinand, your oh-so-noble fiancé—'

'I *do* remember,' said Amy slightly incredulously. 'Jossie Taplow. Ione said something the other day. Didn't you have long hair? And you were dressed—' She stopped.

'Like a girl. But of course I'm not a girl. Explains a lot, no doubt. And I expect that toy dog explains a lot too, an early love of animals, even when stuffed.' Beagle laughed. It was not a pleasant sound.

'So your *father's* involved—'

'Oh, don't blame him, Your Royal Highness. He's been blamed enough already. Principally by my mother. She *is* involved in a way: not that she knew everything. But she's always backed me up – unlike my father who at one point chose to term me the rotten apple. Charming! As a result I haven't spoken to him for years.'

Princess Amy said nothing.

Beagle went on almost eagerly: 'This place is actually in my mother's name, you know, so as to keep it *really* quiet. No links to me. And it is *really* quiet, isn't it, Your Royal Highness? As I was saying, I'm sure the shrinks will blame my mother for everything, including setting up this flat, if they ever get hold of me.'

Since the Princess was still silent, Beagle turned her face towards him. 'So what do you think of all that?' he asked.

'I think – I'm sorry for you,' said Princess Amy slowly. It was not true. She was not in the slightest bit sorry for Beagle; all her energies in that direction were occupied in trying not to feel sorry for herself. But it occurred to her, if only she could keep calm and think *straight*, that there must be some kind of advantage to her in this weird conversation. Jossie Taplow! Princess Amy did not even remember him as clearly as she had pretended; that had been mere instinct, keep the man talking, don't give up, don't despair. But a recent casual remark by her lady-in-waiting about dressing little boys as girls had stuck in her mind because Ione had connected it to her nephew Jamie's repeated complaints about the girlish nature of his page's suit.

'Boys as girls! It's all wrong.' All wrong indeed.

'Yes, I'm sorry for you,' she repeated more strongly.

It was at that moment that Lamb, alone in her self-imposed vigil at the door, cramped, stiff, icy with a despair as acute in its own way as that which Princess Amy was trying to keep at bay, decided that death was the only answer.

She wondered how she would make out with the automatic pistol: was it easy to fire? With some confused idea of target practice, Lamb fired two shots rapidly into the door jamb.

When the sound of shots – and the instantaneous police reaction outside – reached Beagle upstairs, he recognized it to be disaster. He had been half expecting it of course. For one thing Beagle knew that he should not have taken off his mask and that some time in the remote past his mother (who liked such things) had read some silly fairy story to Jossie a.k.a. Beagle (who did not) in which a princess persuaded a prince fatally to unmask . . . everyone turned into an animal, no, a swan. Or was it only the prince? In this case the story was somewhat different: Beagle was already the animal and nothing could turn him back into a prince. Beagle, once Jossie, jerked himself into the present.

Ever since the wounding – or possibly death – of the detective, Beagle had been seized with a feeling of doom. He knew the disaster to be irreversible. There would be no kingdom of the innocent now, he was aware of that. He was doomed. As he had told Lamb the night before, it was more a case of who or how many he took with him. And yet – it had been worth it, hadn't it? What he had planned, worked and waited for, in one way he had achieved it. Beagle, aware, since Lamb's unwise shots, of the strong police presence outside, felt none of the sick tension and fear which had possessed him throughout the Royal Gala, leading up to the climactic abduction from the box.

When the noise of the loud-hailer reached him, the strong voice of authority reverberating in the tiny mews, he knew that control had already passed from Innoright, in so far as they had ever had it. It was over, all over. Wasn't it? And no fucking fairy-tale ending either. Not for this prince. He was still, in a strange way, happy.

But it wasn't all over. Not for Lamb at any rate, crouching outside the studio door. She gripped the pistol in her hand. Lamb, intent on what now seemed to her the only possible solution as dictated by a mind already beginning to spin away, away from all it had once held dear, had not heard or not taken in the police reaction outside. Despite a childhood spent despising and protesting against such country pursuits as shooting, she was confident that in an atavistic way she now knew quite enough about the gun to use it – just as she had managed easily to fire it downstairs. Colonel Q's daughter . . . Somewhere in her spiralling state, Lamb managed to be grimly grateful for that loathsome upbringing. That horrifying collection of guns, guns for killing *animals*; her father used to display to them in the library, making her feel utterly powerless and distraught. ('Just smile and say nothing, Leelee,' Ione used to urge her. 'Above all don't cry; Daddy hates tears.')

Lamb did hear the loud-hailer. She heard it without taking in the full import of the words, more taking the echoing sound as a kind of call to action – her predetermined action, the action which she had sometimes turned over in her mind in the past, during the long nights, caught as she was in the bondage of her jealousy, her lust – and her despair. The image of suffering Snowdrop, her calming mantra, had long ago vanished to be replaced by that of Colonel Q, the hunter.

To Beagle and Princess Amy, frozen the pair of them like the figures on a Grecian urn – what mad pursuit, what maiden loth – the words declaimed by the loud-hailer were not only totally audible but immediately and totally understandable.

'. . . We have you completely surrounded. Do not attempt to escape. You are surrounded. There are marksmen on the roof. Throw your weapons out of the window . . . Do not attempt to escape.' The loud-hailer continued to give its sonorous message. Then: 'Do you hear us? Send out your prisoner. You may indicate with a white cloth or some other other signal that you are sending out your prisoner . . . We can see where you are holding your prisoner. Repeat. We see you . . . We have you surrounded.'

How could they see us? wondered Beagle. Those new X-ray spy cameras no doubt. Their range was extraordinary even if their use in surveillance circles, British as well as Iron Curtain, was not advertised to the general public. Then he wondered how they had traced the lair. The possibility of confession by Mrs Taplow, betrayal by his father, had not occurred to him, when another quite different voice, the unmistakeably well-bred and surprisingly collected voice of Ione Quentin, was heard. Beagle immediately assumed Lamb to be in some way responsible for the betrayal.

Ione Quentin was addressing her sister: 'Lydia, no harm will come to you if you surrender, Lydia . . .'

'The bitch,' he thought, 'I should never have got tangled up with her. I have to admit that royal connection turned me on. And she was raving for it. But she's a loony. Never trust loonies. It should be a motto, Innoright's motto. Protect the innocent! Avoid the loonies. Just supposing there's a difference.'

Princess Amy remained silent. She could not trust herself to speak, since the prospect of rescue had the effect of diminishing rather than increasing her reserves of courage. At Beagle's side she began trembling violently. The voice of the police – and wasn't that Ione? – by bringing reality into what had been a kind of hideous dream sequence, fundamentally unreal however horrible, actually terrified her.

Was he now finally going to kill her? But he didn't seem to have a gun. Would he let her go? She must try and assert control again, she must, she had been getting somewhere with him, hadn't she? They had even been in an odd way friendly this morning, they had talked about the past, he had talked about his mother, that was a good sign, wasn't it? Above all, she must stop trembling. She suddenly remembered his name, his childhood name. She would use it.

'What are you going to do with me, *Jossie*?' enquired Princess Amy in a small hoarse voice, the best she could manage.

Hearing her say 'Jossie' – and aware perhaps of the effort it had cost her, otherwise how explain his ironic smile? – Beagle began to guide Princess Amy, still bonded to him at the wrist, in the direction of the shuttered window.

What had he intended to do? Was he going to open the window? And was he then going to show her, tattered but like the princess disguised as a goose-girl in another fairy story, still recognizably Her Royal Highness Amy Antoinette Marguerite Caroline, Princess of Cumberland... But the exact intentions of Jocelyn Taplow, photographer, a.k.a. Beagle, would never be known for certain and in so far as they subsequently became a matter for debate, it was an academic debate at best.

For it was at this point that Lamb, touched off finally herself to action by that whispered breathless 'Jossie,' pushed open the door of the room. The blown-up images of Princess Amy were still strewn about; Beagle had pinned some of them up to cover the huge photographs of the seals. Lamb thought confusedly that the seals who survived were gazing at her reproachfully as though at an act of betrayal; but that was wrong: it was Beagle who had been the betrayer. She tore down the photograph next to her with her left hand.

What happened then, unlike Beagle's intentions, did subsequently become the subject of quite hectic debate – none of it academic. Nevertheless, for all this debate, the exact course of these events, too, would never be known for sure, even if in this case some kind of official solution had to be proposed. Witnesses, as so often with a violent but unpremeditated crime, witnesses and their actual state of mind at the time of the crime were the problem.

Certainly Beagle shouted: 'Don't shoot!' as Lamb lunged forward with her pistol and having lunged forward apparently recklessly, stood quite steadily with the pistol levelled in the direction of – but that was when the questions began. Was Lamb's pistol levelled in fact at Princess Amy or was it all along levelled at *him*, Beagle, Josh Taplow, the man with whom she had had some crazed and mixed-up sexual relationship?

Princess Amy cowered instinctively backwards, tried to put up both hands to cover her face, made it with the free hand, but the use of the bound wrist pulled Beagle closer to her.

'No! Don't shoot!' shouted Beagle and at least one person – Princess Amy – believed afterwards that he had actually been trying to save her from the shots fired at point-blank range by Lamb in rapid succession. Certainly his body fell heavily down across hers as if he were already curled around her. He had protected her, taken the fire and fallen. That was Princess Amy's version of events; and she herself was quite convinced that she had been Lydia Quentin's original target: 'I saw her expression,' was her succinct shuddering comment.

All Lamb herself said afterwards was: 'Look what you've done. I've killed him. You've made me kill him,' as she stood with her now empty pistol gazing with her huge mad eyes across the blood-strewn body of Beagle, still half supported by Amy, half dangling. And that could be taken either way. Just as Beagle's cry of 'Don't shoot!' could have been an attempt to save himself rather than the Princess. But that way, of course, he would have pulled the Princess in front of him rather than vice versa. Wouldn't he? At all events, Beagle was not there to give his own version of it all since he had died very shortly after Lamb's attack, probably before the police actually reached him.

He did say or rather mutter something more as the heavily armed besiegers, at the sound of the shots, burst in from the roof, through the windows, burst in from everywhere, even out of the air, as it seemed to the two people left alive inside the house. Amy heard the word 'Innocent' but that could have meant anything, including a reference to Innoright itself. The last words she could distinguish as Beagle still looked up towards her from the floor to which he had now sunk, pulling her towards him, his eyes beginning to glaze over, a main artery close to the heart hit, as it was found afterwards, were 'Your Royal Hostage'. And that once again proved nothing either way; only that Beagle still knew who Amy was as he entered the straight towards death.

Did the word 'hostage' mean that Beagle still understood what he had done? 'My Royal Hostage' would have been a testimony to that. 'Your Royal Hostage' on the other hand was probably only Beagle's confused attempt to pay Princess Amy her due with what turned out to be quite literally his dying breath.

18

The Questions

'The wedding will go ahead. As planned,' said Jemima Shore to Rick Vancy, still holding the car telephone in her hand. Privately she thought it was amusing that the only truly important message that Rick Vancy had received while travelling in his car, had been taken by her, Jemima. This was because the profound shock – to Rick Vancy, let alone to the rest of the world – of recent events had had the unfortunate effect of making Rick take up smoking again. And he was currently lighting a cigarette – his fourth during the journey between Jemima's flat and the TUS office.

'I do not believe it!' Then: 'I simply do have to have a cigarette.' That was Rick Vancy's reaction not only when he heard of the traumatic course of the siege but also that Jemima herself had been in a certain sense involved. His reaction was in itself a mixture of outrage – what *about* her contract with TUS? – and admiration for the kind of upper-class British person whose contacts enabled her to be present somehow even at the dénouement of a British royal siege.

What she did not tell Rick about was the mixture of frustration, apprehension and excitement which had possessed her at the hidden police command post as she stood beside the rigid figure of Ione Quentin. In truth, the initial frustration of being a passive onlooker at the drama soon faded in face of her fears for the outcome. Admiring the extraordinary self-control of the police, given the exceptional nature of the hostage involved – up till the moment when the shots were heard inside the house – Jemima herself found it difficult to maintain an equivalent calm.

She knew that their calm was preserved in the interests of efficiency; perhaps if she had had something to do beyond supporting Ione, she too might have found it easier to stop her thoughts dwelling on the awful possibilities of the siege ending in some innocent death. '*Some* innocent death'? Since Princess Amy was, it seemed, the only person who could be described as innocent inside the shuttered shop, she had to face the fact that it was her death or injury that she dreaded.

Jemima knew that she should follow the example of Ione Quentin whose excited speeches in Jemima's flat had been succeeded by a marble self-control. Even her use of the loud-hailer as directed by the police – 'Lydia, no harm will come to you . . .' – might have been the work of a professional politician used to addressing crowds. Was such discipline the product of a highly disciplined upbringing? For Jemima remembered that Ione's father, that father whom Lydia had much disliked for his severity, had been a well-known soldier. Colonel Q. Yes, that was it. The discipline might not have done Lydia much good, but it had certainly produced impressive results in her sister.

Jemima only saw Colonel Q's elder daughter break down once as Lydia was led away by the police, her small figure muffled in some kind of blanket, jean-clad legs just visible beneath it.

'Leelee,' said Ione in a low voice. Then she straightened her shoulders.

None of this did Jemima choose to confide to Rick Vancy; for one thing she was still sorting out much of it in her own mind, as an orderly person goes through drawers tidying them one by one. That went for the dramatic end of the siege. And then her initial frustration at her own passivity was not something she wanted to share with Rick; let him believe she had herself played a prominent part in the end of the siege . . .

'I just do not credit it,' repeated Rick Vancy, and he shook his distinguished head, now subtly enhanced by an English hair-cut, even as Susanna Blanding wordlessly handed over her own packet of Marlboros. (Curt silently helped himself to one on the way, which must have been loyalty, since he had never hitherto been perceived to be a smoker.)

The reaction of the rest of the world was equally incredulous even if the manner of implementing that disbelief was not necessarily that of Rick Vancy. Now that the Press was released from its self-imposed silence and Major Pat was left to pay with those 'exclusive' releases, the debts of honour he had incurred throughout that long summer night of negotiation, the floodgates were well and truly unloosed. Yet it was remarkable that for once even the most lurid headline could scarcely be accused of exaggeration. That was the trouble. On the principle of crying 'Wolf!', the Press had presented the public with so many previous headlines all the way from PRINCESS: WEDDING SCARE (something vague to do with high buildings along the route), to PRINCESS: WEDDING FEARS (a lack of American tourists to buy souvenirs), that even the blazing thirty-point letters with which the *Daily Exclusive* led next morning: PRINCESS AMY SAFE – were somehow not quite as dramatic as the story itself, related in much smaller print beneath.

The staider papers, with more space at their command, a far calmer track record, had the advantage; it was generally felt, not only within the confines of the Times building, that *The Times* in its sonorous lengthy leader under the headline A BRIDE FOR ALL SEASONS had, for once, spoken for the nation more effectively than the *Daily Clueless*.

But that was all in public. Private reactions varied. Mirabella Prey, for example, put in a call to Prince Ferdinand (which he refused to take). So then she sent round a note to Cumberland Palace which contained some unwelcome phrases to linger in his mind, although the Prince only remembered them roughly afterwards. This was because he read the note through quickly, or rather read it half-through, then crumpled it and threw it away in that negligent way of his; except that now there would be no Taplow to unscrew the paper, only the impeccable and truly discreet servants of Cumberland Palace.

He did not therefore read as far as Mirabella's announcement of her future plans: life on a Greek or at least Greekish island with her Greekish admirer. The admirer was founding a wild animal sanctuary in her honour. This coincidental realization of the Innoright plans for Windsor Great Park, Regent's Park and other royal parks (if not generally perceived as such) was in fact broken to the world in general by Miss Mary of the *Daily Clueless* the next day.

'LOVE AMONG THE LEOPARDS! How too, too sweet,' exclaimed Princess Amy on this occasion when she read Miss Mary's column. 'I hope they *eat* her,' she added generously.

Mirabella's phrases, roughly remembered, which haunted Ferdel in spite of himself went as follows: 'So now she is a heroine, your little Princess. You will admire her and who knows, perhaps at last you will love her. I congratulate the little white mouse. How was she in the hands of the sexy photographer ... Often these so prim English girls ...' It was at that point that Ferdel had crumpled the paper. He should have known better than to read anything penned by Mirabella: that ever maddening ability of hers to get under his skin ... However, he was no longer thinking of Mirabella now, there being plenty to think about nearer home, to put it mildly. And Prince Ferdinand was still wondering quite how he *could* put it, put it mildly that is. There was a question which was torturing him, to be frank, beneath the smooth and tender caring surface which he had exhibited ever since Amy's return.

It was not a question which affected his admiration. Admire her! Ye Gods, he admired her. The pluck, the spirit, the *endurance*, even including the last dreadful incident and the removal of her own lady-in-waiting's sister, to say nothing of his own chauffeur's son lying there in pools of blood ... Somewhere at the very bottom of Prince Ferdinand's horrified reflections was surprise that *servants*, royal servants should somehow feature so strongly in all this. (For he did not in the very last analysis distinguish between Ione Quentin, the lady-in-waiting, and Taplow the chauffeur: both were to him and perhaps finally to Amy – servants.) And how bravely Amy had handled all the rest of it, including even, with courage beyond any reasonable expectation, allowing a very short Press Conference to be held at Cumberland Palace!

'Otherwise, Ma'am,' admitted Major Pat ruefully, 'they'll never believe you're all in one piece.'

'I jolly well am all in one piece, aren't I?' replied Princess Amy with a touch of new asperity in her voice, or perhaps it was sheer exhaustion. 'Which is more than you can say for my sapphires. Did no one ever find that earring? Ione, now did you ask—'

But there was of course no Ione to ask. Amanda, the young secretary at the Palace who had been helping with the wedding arrangements, seconded to a more senior position, was, in Amy's opinion, simply not a patch on Ione in competence, knowledge or tact. So grievously in fact did Amy, in her first flustered moments of return, miss Ione's calming presence and all it meant in terms of security and comfort that for a long time she simply could not understand why it was no longer possible for Ione to attend her.

'But why *can't* one be here, Mummy?' she cried angrily, used to having her own ways in all things with the Duchess, an arrangement which generally suited them both splendidly. The willowy Duchess, wafer thin to the point of emaciation (Amy had inherited her father's tendency to embonpoint), could do no more than sigh; tears – hers – were clearly not far away. Of the Princesses Sophie and Harriet, the one knew herself to be too plain-spoken (in the circumstances) and the other too nerve-wracked like her mother, to do anything; they rolled their eyes at each other, those huge slightly exophthalmic blue eyes which all three sisters had in common.

It was Prince Ferdinand who softly explained: 'My darling, you must understand: it is just not possible. Poor Ione. We are all of us so sorry for her. But the sister, you know, she is—' How to put it? Yes: 'In the hands of the police. Ione must rest at home. It is very difficult for her. She is, she *was*, devoted to her sister, and that this should happen to *you*! She is naturally quite shattered. Besides, it would not be – quite *suitable*, would it, darling?'

'In the hands of the police, is she? Well, I hope they keep her in their hands. I shall never forget her expression. Did I tell you, Amanda—' The thought of Lydia Quentin a.k.a. Lamb did at least distract Princess Amy from her lost sapphires – and her lost lady-in-waiting.

As for Princess Amy's decision – for it was finally her decision to go ahead with the wedding on the same date and with exactly the same arrangements (at least outwardly: what the police now did was their own business), that too was, as far as Prince Ferdinand was concerned, beyond praise.

It was not only the feeling of relief which such a decision gave to the nation as a whole: things could not be *that* bad, could not have been that bad, the poor little Princess couldn't be in that bad a state. Nor yet the commercially based relief of all those whose arrangements (and profits) depended on a given Royal Wedding on a given royal day: not least among these TUS and Rick Vancy of TUS, booked to leave for the Middle East immediately afterwards. But Ferdel himself had a deep-seated almost superstitious feeling that if the wedding did take place exactly as arranged, then his own relationship with Amy, that too would be restored to its original state. This relationship, which Ferdel believed would be the basis of a long and happy married life, was certainly not lacking in physical passion; all the same he knew it to be *au fond* more affectionate than passionate. If not precisely an arranged marriage, theirs was a marriage of convenience, great convenience. In such a relationship, affection was more important than passion.

But Ferdel could not forget one particular conversation with Amy following her release. In the immediate aftermath she had been almost totally distraught and in the course of her distraction had made, or at least begun to make, certain statements, highly frightening statements about her captivity, the import of which Ferdel had simply not dared think through at the time. The conversation came later. He would really like to obliterate the memory of it, as he wished to forget Mirabella's lethal phrase 'the sexy photographer'; alas, he was unable to do so.

How odd to feel what must be jealousy for virtually the first time in his life! (In principle Ferdel considered jealousy a terrible waste of energy.) To feel it in this situation and to feel it on behalf of *Amy*! Of all women in the world. When he thought of all the other delightful creatures he had known and their composite behaviour, exotic, sensual, provoking, none of whom had managed to arouse his jealousy although many had tried. Ah well. Did jealousy perhaps come with age? Another horrible suggestion.

Amy had been encircled by Ferdel's arms when the disturbing conversation in question took place. It was when he allowed himself to say (and in retrospect that had been his mistake): 'Amy, my darling, exactly what happened? You said such odd things when you first came back. He didn't – My God, my darling—' In his agitation, Ferdel found he was gripping both Amy's arms till she winced; he was also gazing at her most intensely.

A curious expression crossed Princess Amy's face. It was not that pop-eyed capacity for right royal indignation she had inherited from the late Duke, still less the air of sweet resignation characteristic of her mother, but seldom seen on her own very different features. No, Prince Ferdinand found it quite impossible to analyse the exact nature of Princess Amy's curious expression: in another older, more sophisticated, woman he might even have detected a very faint air of triumph there, but that was to be ruled out where Amy was concerned. Nor could Ferdel analyse quite why he found her look so disquieting, nor why some inclination of future trouble reached him, and from the direction he had least expected it. For an instant he was looking once more into the eyes of Eve, into whose beautiful and challenging eyes in one form or another he had been gazing all his adult years.

Of the two of them, Prince Ferdinand was the first to look away. After all, he had always known how to handle women, hadn't he? He gathered Amy more closely into his arms so that she nestled there.

'My little one,' he said over the top of her head, 'I'm going to protect you so carefully in the future. No harm will ever come to you,' he added very firmly. 'Thank God, no real harm *has* come to you.'

Still Princess Amy, her face buried in his shoulder, said nothing. But then, come to think of it, what was there to say?

Elsewhere there were other questions in the air, some – but not all – of which received more satisfactory answers than that posed *malgré lui* by the anxious Prince Ferdinand. For his part, he never returned to this particular interrogation just as Princess Amy herself never enquired again after her lost sapphire earring. Since she had decided that never never in a thousand years would she wear those hateful *evil* sapphires again, the whole subject might be allowed to lapse; thus the Rasputin sapphires were locked away once more (minus one earring) waiting like Camus' plague for their next malevolent appearance on the European scene. The comparison was that of Susanna Blanding who alone among observers had appreciated the historic and superstitious significance of the jewellery adorning Princess Amy at the moment of her abduction.

One of the important questions posed elsewhere concerned the extent of the Innoright conspiracy and the fate of the conspirators. Innoright Overground, the parent organization, expressed itself properly appalled by the events of the abduction and hastened to disavow, root and branch, the behaviour of its cell. Files were flung open with wild-eyed haste, protestations of non-violence, appeals to the Innoright charter and the Innoright motto – Protection of the Innocent and Princess Amy *was* innocent – filled the air. It was nevertheless only a matter of time before Innoright, as its honest members sadly realized, went into voluntary disbandment.

Non-violence as a policy was hard to sustain in view of the death of the detective; and there were other details to take into account, deaths which not only bit into the very structure of Innoright but also demonstrated clearly that the criminal cell had in fact been closely involved with the central organization. The death of Monkey a.k.a. Edward James Arthur

Monck MBE was one such example, which together with the revelations concerning his participation in the cell, caused the keenest anguish among the members. Generous and kindly, if some might say endowed with an over-managerial manner, Mr Monck had after all been one of the founders of Innoright.

On the other hand, from another point of view, Monkey's death did answer one question: the question of whether he had been involved in the abduction itself as well as in its organization. Princess Amy was understandably unable to state whether he had actually driven the getaway car, but Monkey, in a carefully explicit note to the police, laid down his own actions; at the same time regretting the death of the detective and 'the discourtesy to HRH Princess Amy'.

Monkey gave much thought to the manner of his death: it was after all to be his last plan. When the news of Princess Amy's rescue broke, he considered at first a last meal in South Eaton Place, a fine Burgundy (but no meat-eating: dying was no time to desert one's principles) and a host of fine pills which he prudently kept by him. Many dreams were over, dreams of Lamb (what had become of her? Under arrest, poor child), dreams of a world made safe for the innocent, were over.

He would go to join Cynthia. As a Catholic of his own particular variety, Monkey did not rate such an action as a sin: once again – as with the detective's death – joining Cynthia was the end to justify it. Monkey was in the process of writing a last note of command for Carmencita – DO NOT ENTER THE LIBRARY. E.J.A.M. – when the appropriate last plan was revealed to him. Cocking an eyebrow, at his most agreeably simian, Monkey destroyed the note. Carefully he attired himself in his City clothes, dark pin-stripe suit including a blue handkerchief in his breast pocket, an umbrella – and a bowler. The umbrella and blue handkerchief indicated postponement and the bowler signified after all the final abandonment of the Underground Plan; and with Monkey's death on the electric rails of the Underground just outside Sloane Square station, it could be said that the final abandonment of the Underground Plan had taken place.

Fox died too, adopting the same solution as Monkey (which would have pleased the latter: at the last, Fox was obediently following his lead in a way that he signally failed to do on the night of the abduction). Fox's choice of death-place was Tottenham Court Road Tube station – Fox being aware that the lead of the costumes from Leaviss made it only a matter of time before the police reached him. All his emotions were by this time bound up in his dread of parting from Noel, which was how he viewed the prospect of long imprisonment. It was ironic that the dog Noel, who had nothing of his master's death wish, used his notorious cowardice to pull back at the last moment from the drop, and thus survived the experience. So that Fox's last wish of a death together with

Noel, like his wish for a free kingdom of the animals, was not to be granted.

The police did reach Mrs Charity Wadham a.k.a. Chicken quite quickly, but Mrs Charity Wadham made no attempt to kill herself. She saw absolutely no need. Chicken was reached via a number of routes: not only her appreciation of Ignazio Dorati but her condemnation of Zeffirelli's film on the stairs leaving the Royal Opera House was recollected by one witness, who had turned to look at her: the witness in question had particularly enjoyed the Zeffirelli film of *Otello*. Most telling of all, the abandoned saris were found wrapped round Chicken's score of *Otello* – a substantial mistake on Pussy's part but perhaps she had been unconsciously jealous of Chicken's paraded knowledge of the opera during its performance. What with Chicken's condescending remark concerning Zeffirelli and her score-book, she had certainly paid dearly for this knowledge. There were plenty of finger-prints there to identify Chicken with the score-reading Indian woman, even if one of Chicken's teaching associates to whom it had once belonged, had not recognized the score.

Two questions in all this remained unanswered. The identity of the second 'Indian' woman, the masked 'cruel' woman who had guarded Princess Amy, assuming that they were one and the same person, remained officially unproved. Chicken resolutely refused to say anything on the subject; in fact she refused to make any statement at all, refused a lawyer (one was assigned), refused to consider her defence and merely announced her determination of pleading 'Guilty' and accepting her sentence whatever it might be. Chicken was confident in herself that she would never talk, never break, despising Monkey and Fox for their abject solutions. How like men! Women were so much stronger when it came to the point.

Chicken gave no trouble on remand in prison, however; was pleasant, respectful, nice to the young girls who were her fellow inmates: even if they were not particularly nice back to her since she was held to have laid hands on Princess Amy, by now a genuinely popular folk heroine. It was a consolation that the problems with her diet gave her opportunity to administer well-turned little lectures on the cruel treatment of battery hens. Vegetarianism proving a far more sympathetic subject, Chicken somewhat redeemed herself. Even in Holloway, thought Chicken, once a teacher, always a teacher.

The charges against Chicken were serious enough but she was not, so far as the police were concerned, on a charge of murder or even of conspiracy to murder since it was accepted that she had not been present at the incident in the Royal Box. So, one way and another, Chicken was confident of holding out, serving her sentence – for the cause. Setting herself up to be a model prisoner, one day she would emerge – and work for it again with equal determination, or perhaps even greater strength, forged by the iron years of martyrdom in prison. But she would not trust *men* – men like Fox with their ineradicable and fatal tendency to violence – next time.

So the question of Chicken's accomplice, of the sixth conspirator, for want of definite proof remained officially open.

That meant that Pussy – for the time being – went free. There was nothing specific to connect her with Chicken in the absence of the latter's hoped-for confession. The witness who remembered Chicken's disparaging comment on Zeffirelli's film had no recollection, and maddeningly was not even sure if Chicken had *had* a companion, although he admitted that the remark could hardly have been made to the blank wall of the staircase. Like Chicken, he had been in a hurry.

Princess Amy never saw fit to mention the characteristic smell of lavender water which had linked Pussy to her hated governess; along with many other details of that horrendous time, she had suppressed it. In any case, such olfactory evidence would surely never have stood up in a court of law. And Pussy had been careful to keep her gloves on during her period guarding the Princess.

No, the police wanted proper evidence to arrest Mrs Pussy Moscowitz and in their patient way they were convinced that with time they would get it. In the meantime they were watching Pussy.

That left Pussy free, like the rest of the world, to watch the Royal Wedding. She could either watch it on television in the flat dominated by huge pictures of Caro-Otter or maybe, as Pussy put it to herself, with one of her malevolent smiles, she would take her place among the crowds: 'To see how the little Madam is getting on.'

Another question which remained unanswered was the question of the killer of Jean-Pierre Schwarz-Albert a.k.a. Tom. It was the subject of yet another conversation between Jemima and Pompey, this time in the Groucho Club where Pompey sat nursing a whisky and showing a gallant appreciation of the various literary luminaries by whom he was surrounded.

'Anita Bainbridge!' he exclaimed at one point, 'I must tell my wife. One of her real favourites.' Jemima thought it best not to intervene. Then more sombre matters occupied them.

'It's all very well the shouting and the cheering, and the gutsy little Princess – and my word, she is gutsy – but I've still got my case,' complained Pompey. 'Work to do. I can't fit my murder to Taplow, the photographer; the little costumier is a possibility, just as he always was, except that the hotel is adamant he couldn't have got where necessary with the dog. The woman they're holding for abduction, the teacher, Wadham, will say nothing except she's guilty of the abduction but that she abhors violence.'

'Pompey—' said Jemima slowly. 'There's another woman of course. I've been thinking about it, working out a theory. Testing something I said to you a long time ago. That murder and now the Royal Wedding still to come. Tell me about the police watch. Who are they watching?'

19

Living Doll

The problem, Jemima speedily realized, was to find a language of lyrical freshness which had not been used before; or was not being currently used by all the other hundreds and thousands of commentators upon the Royal Wedding of Princess Amy and Prince Ferdinand. Since the problem rapidly proved insoluble (what could you say that wasn't almost audibly being said in other television studios close at hand?) Jemima decided not to try and solve it. Instead she gave herself up to the enjoyment of the occasion; or to be precise, wished to give herself up to it. It was still impossible to disregard completely, in one part of her mind, the implications of her last conversation with Pompey and she trusted that Pompey himself had not disregarded them. All this was, however, for another day – or she devoutly hoped it was.

In the meantime journalistic tasks, the very reverse of humdrum, awaited her in the more-or-less plastic studio erected by TUS on the roof of a building at an angle to Westminster Cathedral. TUS's studio-in-the-sky jostled with those of other famous American TV stations. On the narrow stairs which led up to the roof from the main building, a mock-Georgian office block, Jemima was amused to encounter other British notabilities ranging from the truly notable to the notable-for-being-notable who would give their own confident Best-of-Britain commentaries to be beamed around the US. She hoped she could still count herself amongst them despite her recent sacking from Megalith.

Among historical experts, Susanna Blanding was there, of course, notebooks, red books and all; her role was actually to crouch beneath the semi-circular simulated studio table at which Jemima sat, bemicrophoned and be-earplugged (to receive what was another form of royal command – from the producer) along with Rick Vancy. And along with Curt. The latter's perpetually sleepy stance had been abandoned overnight for a bright-eyed look which was almost disconcerting; his eyes positively glittered with innocent enthusiasm, and preppy, Jemima supposed, was probably the right word for the clothes in which he was now attired. This alien image – if not to the US, but then Curt would not be seen on camera – was in marked contrast to Rick Vancy's studiedly quiet British attire and Jemima's own sharply elegant emerald-green Jean Muir jacket (all that would be visible of her, she devoutly hoped, since she was wearing training shoes for long-term comfort, which could hardly be said to accord with her tight black skirt and sheer dark stockings.)

As usual, Susanna's own wardrobe did not bear thinking about. Taken all in all, her crouching position, with a noiseless electronic typewriter to tap out news flashes and hand them up from below to the team, reminded Jemima of that of a crusader's dog carved at the end of its master's tomb. It was by now quite clear that where Susanna was concerned Rick was the crusader.

For the time being, Jemima had better things to think about than Susanna's potential problems in this direction. Other wardrobes claimed her attention, notably that of the Royal Family about to come on view, described in a series of Press releases evidently composed by the various designers involved, and accompanied by illustrative sketches. Where the sketches were concerned, Jemima would come to see them as an endearing triumph of hope over experience; that is, when she got her first glimpse of the dignified but, dare one say it, ever-so-slightly dumpy incumbents of the dresses and compared them to the slim long-necked swans of the artist's imagination. At the same time the Keatsian language entranced her, words like azure and malachite abounded where, contemplating the reality, it was difficult not to conclude that humbler words such as blue and green would have done just as well.

Jemima found that her mind was still half distracted by those other nagging fears: but she *must* put them aside, this was not the time or place, if only because Jemima, not being a natural fashion journalist, knew that she needed all her concentration to interpret the Keatsian language to American viewers (waking up after all to an extremely early breakfast by US time). At this moment the final Press release was handed to her from below by Susanna. This was the one everyone had been waiting for: *the* Press release, *the* sketch, *the* dress itself . . .

The sketch now before her showed in effect an enchanting doll. On the evidence of this, Jemima had no difficulty in believing that Princess Amy bridal dolls would be bestsellers for many years to come. As for the fluttering Princess Amy blue bows (the traditional 'something blue') which were depicted nestling at the shoulder and somewhere in the endless bouffant train (eighteen feet long: six inches longer than that of the Duchess of York, the Press release proudly proclaimed), those belonged perhaps more to the world of the chocolate box. Jemima also had no difficulty in believing that chocolate boxes, mugs, plates, thimbles and so forth, depicting Princess Amy in all her bridal glory, would also be bestsellers for many years to come.

All the same, why shouldn't poor little Princess Amy look like a living doll if that was how she wanted to look? Given her ordeal, which had so nearly ended in her being not so much a living doll as a dead one. It was time to think again about her own personal language of lyrical freshness. What about some historical and artistic comparisons? Winterhalter, Greuze, Gainsborough: these were names to conjure with and she only hoped that Susanna Blanding, somewhere in her copious notes, had had the forethought to conjure with them.

Jemima gazed down at the little television monitor flush with the desk before her. The only public alteration to arrangements made at the instigation of the police, was to have the bride leave from one of the other royal palaces in The Mall, as other royal brides had done in recent years, instead of from Cumberland Palace itself, which being sited in Regent's Park, involved a far longer and less controllable route. The crowds in The Mall were quite as deep as Jemima remembered from shots of other weddings involving members of the Royal Family closer to succession. The abduction, however distressing for its subject, had undoubtedly been good for business: that is, if you had the temerity to regard the public attendance at a Royal Wedding as a form of business.

She could see numerous placards being held up echoing the theme of the celebrated buttons: AMY MEANS I LOVE YOU, now occasionally altered to AMY MEANS I ADORE YOU, and there were balloons, and here and there paper hats of Amy blue bearing the same message. Then there were some new-style placards bearing the allusive message: AMY NOT ANIMALS. Jemima learnt later that a few rash protesters had emerged bearing placards which read on the contrary: WE LOVE ANIMALS NOT AMY.

Regrettably if understandably, these small groups were manhandled by the crowd and forced to disband, their placards pulled apart; equally regrettably perhaps, there was little or no interference from the police during these scattered episodes. The police, standing with their backs to the route facing the crowds (an innovation at the wedding of the Prince of Wales), maintained an impassive stance. They were watching of course: watching not only these – the few – who proclaimed their animal rights sympathies but watching for those who might share these sympathies without proclaiming them.

There were no Innoright posters, placards or buttons, no Innoright balloons or paper hats. The sad-eyed logo was signally absent from the proceedings. Pussy, having reached a decision to attend personally instead of making do with television – 'to see the little Madam one last time for myself', as she put it – took care to wear nothing and carry nothing that might connect her with Innoright. Weddings of healthy young women generally made her feel physically sick with rage when she thought of Caro-Otter who would never have a wedding, but for the time being she knew she must subjugate her revulsion.

Pussy installed herself on a small portable seat near the front of the crowd in the piazza of the Cathedral. It was not, to be honest, that she had arrived all that early to achieve such an advantageous position: just that Pussy, heavily pressing, was a difficult force to resist when it came to having her own way. Her present desire was to watch the wedding from a convenient spot at the bottom of one of the stands in the piazza, amid the crowds but not swamped by them, and she achieved it.

Pussy took out a plastic box of sweet pastries and proceeded to lick round the chocolate coating of one. She needed sweetness, and sustenance. Pussy, unlike some of those near her, did not offer to share her pastries with the policeman in front of them. Pussy, watched by the impassive policeman, and watching him, licked resolutely on.

Jemima, from her perch roughly above Pussy's head, studied the order of events and the official programme with its seemingly endless list of coaches and carriages and cars and mounted escorts and so forth and so on. (No official mention of armed escorts and so forth and so on, although one would imagine that in view of recent events the practice at recent royal weddings of substituting policemen for various bewigged coachmen on the boxes of the coaches would scarcely be abandoned at this one.)

'She's killed herself!' exclaimed Susanna Blanding suddenly from her crouching position, holding headphones with which she was listening to the news flash. 'Killed herself in prison. Lydia! How on earth did they let her? My God, poor old Ione, this will kill her, sorry, unfortunate use of language. Well, perhaps it's for the best. Think of the trial and all that. Which reminds me—'

Still sounding rather shocked, but ever dutiful, Susanna began scurrying through her notes and the order of the procession.

'What have we here? Ah yes, do you have this, Jemima? Rick – it needn't bother you. "The Hon. Amanda Macpherson-Wynne, Acting Lady-in-waiting to HRH, etc., etc., will travel in the second carriage in place of Miss Ione Quentin."'

'I have that,' said Jemima, thinking with pity, certainly no vindictive satisfaction, of the intense girl she had seen praying – as she had then thought – at the statue of St Francis. Even if Susanna, in her practical way, was right, and death, self-sought death (and how *had* she managed to achieve it? Some dereliction of care there?) was the best solution to that particular tragic life, she could not mark the event, like any youthful suicide, without some pang of emotion for what once might have been prevented.

Poor Ione. As Susanna, her cousin, had charitably and percipiently said.

It was while the first cascade of roaring cheers came through on the monitor, greeting Princess Amy as she was drawn slowly in her coach out of the gates of the royal palace into the Mall, that Jemima, looking in her monitor as the television cameras raked the crowds now here now there, saw a face she recognized.

'My God!' she thought. 'I don't believe it. How could they have let her? They were going to watch her. She's right there. I *saw* her.'

Subsequently, Jemima's chief memory of the events which followed centred on the fearful and frustrating experience, comparable only to a nightmare which sometimes plagued her of swimming through mud, of trying to move rapidly through a crowd which was profoundly and determinedly stationary. Only the trainer shoes were helpful and seemed like an extraordinary piece of prescience.

'It must have been like Jean Louis Barrault in *Les Enfants du Paradis*,' observed a film buff friend wisely afterwards. 'You remember, looking for Arletty as the crowd all swirled, revelling in the opposite direction.'

'This revelling crowd was not swirling in *any* direction,' countered Jemima rather sharply, for she too had seen the movie many times. 'That was the whole point. It was standing stock still and revelling if you want to put it like that, on its stationary feet and in its position which it had risen at dawn or even slept out all night to protect.'

At the time it was the thought of that face in the crowd which impelled her forward, a killer's face, above all a desperate face, and she must get there, no time now for phone calls, no good to appeal to the many policemen on the route, certainly no time to appeal to a higher authority.

So that it was in fact at the exact moment, in the antiphonal rise and fall of the cheering, of Princess Amy's own arrival in the piazza, that Jemima managed to get within striking distance of her prey. And it was at the moment of arrival too, that Jemima, whose determined path beaten through the crowd had not passed unregarded, was herself seized by the authoritative hand of the law.

Jemima, pulled back temporarily from engagement with the person she had sought, was able to witness for herself the moment when Princess Amy, pointing the toe of her plain but immensely high-heeled white satin shoe, stepped gingerly out of her coach.

The flowing white train with its occasional blue bows was bundled out after her and then fanned out on the pavement before the Cathedral by the designer, energetically aided by the cooing little French bridesmaids, Amy's nieces. Beneath the soft white tulle veil gleamed diamonds – some respectable British tiara one supposed, in view of the dismal track record of the Russian sapphires. Amy's distinguished and ancient French grandfather, who was to give her away, eased himself stiffly out of the coach and stood for all his age erectly beside her, a tall figure compared to her tiny one.

Beneath the drifting veil, lifting slightly in the breeze, Princess Amy's expression was impossible to discern. More strongly than ever, Jemima had the impression of a doll, a doll at the centre of these hieratic ceremonies, but still mercifully a living doll.

'Let me go,' cried Jemima, and then more forcibly: '*Stop* her.' For one moment Jemima did succeed in getting free and ran a short way, elbowing amid the crowd, only to be grasped yet more firmly by someone in plain clothes who was evidently a policeman.

'She must go into the Cathedral,' thought Jemima desperately, 'Once she's inside, she's safe. Don't just *stand* there . . .'

Still the Princess stood, poised, inscrutable, in her ivory tower of lace and tulle and diamonds, on the verge of taking the arm of her towering grandfather, but still half facing the cheering crowds on the piazza.

'I'll just have to shout, I'll just have to bellow,' thought Jemima. 'There's no other way. We're quite close. I hope to hell she can hear me.'

'Ione!' she yelled.

Although Jemima's frantic appeal, half scream, half cry, had to reach the ears of Ione Quentin, now in the front row of the crowd, over all the other noise, the cheers, the chomping of the horses, the jangling of their bridles, the music now swelling from inside the Cathedral, reach her it did. It must have reached her, because Ione Quentin hesitated just one instant, still with the concealed weapon in her hand, and turned her head, as it were involuntarily, sideways.

One instant was enough. In that instant Princess Amy put her hand at last on her grandfather's arm and began to move gracefully and, thank God, inexorably into the interior of the Cathedral.

Behind her, and still quite unknown to the bridal cortège, Ione Quentin, former lady-in-waiting to HRH Princess Amy of Cumberland, collapsed in the savage grip of three policemen.

20

But Who's to Answer?

Afterwards Jemima Shore's decision to abandon her post was much criticized – by TUS that is, and by Rick Vancy in particular. TUS behaved with what was considered by Jemima's agent to be a strange lack of moral fibre in trying to withhold her fee on the grounds that she had never actually commented on the wedding itself – not at the crucial moment anyway. Fortunately it was not for nothing that Jemima's agent, a girl in her twenties, was already known as the Dragon of Drury Lane (where her office was) and the matter, months later, was finally sorted out to the Dragon's, if not TUS's satisfaction.

Some of Rick's bitterness could probably be ascribed to the fact that TUS did not in the event find itself with only one presenter in the shape of Rick himself for the arrival of the bride. When Jemima precipitately and clumsily unhooked herself from her position, and fled the plastic studio-in-the-sky there was a short anxious cry from the producer: 'Is she sick or something?' followed by the imperious command, 'Cut the anchor.' This sounded strangely nautical to English ears, along the lines of 'abandon ship'. But it merely meant that the freelance British cameraman hired for the occasion, who happened to be Jemima's friend Spike Thompson, formerly of Megalith, should swing away from the 'anchor' in the shape of Jemima and concentrate on the wedding scenes below.

Spike, like the Dragon of Drury Lane, was in his own way more than equal to the occasion. He swung his camera neatly away from Jemima's seat, pausing only to file away the notion of further financial claims against TUS for services beyond the call of contract (Spike Thompson's claims in this respect being a legend in his lifetime, held by many of the mean-hearted to be at least partly responsible for the recent coup at Megalith). A minute later he had his camera unerringly focused on the resplendent figure of Curt, already installed, bemicrophoned and be-earplugged in Jemima's place. So now there were two 'anchors' on the TUS desk again, if you preferred the more exciting American phrase to the calmer British notion of presenters.

The rest, as many at TUS (but not Rick Vancy and not Susanna Blanding) would murmur with awe afterwards, was history: British history. Where, oh where, had the somnolent Curt acquired that intimate knowledge of every detail of the wedding ceremony, that intimate command of anecdote about every royal personage, that intimacy – one had to use the word since a sense of intimacy combined with pageantry subsequently became his trademark as a broadcaster – with every facet of British history from the Conquest onwards? By the time Curt's dazzling reputation had been established, outclassing coast to coast and rating for rating the laid-back style so sedulously cultivated by Rick Vancy during his weeks in Britain, it was far too late for Susanna Blanding's indignant cry from the depths: 'None of this is in my notes. I do believe he's making it all up.' A star had been born. For this at least Rick Vancy would always blame Jemima Shore.

Jemima Shore on the other hand would always blame herself for not being more emphatically direct to Pompey in their last conversation about Ione Quentin's responsibility for the murder of Schwarz-Albert at the Republican Hotel. Notions of opportunity came to her: she remembered seeing Ione Quentin leave the stage where Major Pat was holding forth at rather an odd moment in the proceedings, given her role in it all. She must have had the note delivered then, the note which drew Schwarz-Albert out of the Press Conference. Then she boldly took advantage of the royal arrival and the royal question-and-answer session for the killing itself, knowing full well how absorbed the general attention would be in the inner room. She had only to remember to remove the note from the body, and of course Ione had easy access to the 'Royal' paper-knives, besides knowing in advance how sharp they were.

Notions of motive also passed through Jemima's mind. Who but Ione Quentin, who would, in her own phrase, 'do anything' for her sister, had such a strong motive to eliminate the inquisitive Schwarz-Albert? The other members of Innoright could merely have ejected him, but Lydia's terrifying personal vulnerability, to say nothing of her royal connection, made her a soft target for Schwarz-Albert's machinations. Did he plan to use her for further information against her comrades? If so, Ione, who regularly went through her sister's things and even followed her, as she told Jemima, would have known. As Jemima had pointed out intuitively to Pompey, the Republican Hotel represented an opportunity for Ione – who had the list of attendances at her command – an opportunity which might not come again.

With Ione, whatever her normal feelings outside the influence of madness towards Princess Amy, Lydia always came first. (Not that Lydia herself reciprocated those feelings: she had shown the total self-absorption of the mad – or the fanatic – throughout, using her sister's royal position shamelessly without regard to the consequences for Ione. She would never even have known of Ione's daring deed on her behalf . . . for Ione, as ever solicitous of Lydia's welfare, would have kept her own counsel on that.) It was Lydia towards whom Ione's thoughts turned, not her royal mistress, at the moment of the abduction. That amazing conversation had given Jemima the vital clue; just as Ione's conduct at the siege, pondered over later, had brought Jemima to a full realization of the cold-blooded indifference Ione showed to Princess Amy's fate within the shuttered shop – compared to that of her sister. So Jemima's enforced passivity on that occasion had not been wasted after all. It had enabled her to see that someone capable of such indifference was in the final analysis ruthless: in Ione Quentin's case, a ruthless killer.

Perhaps Pompey was right and like the tortoise he was, he would have reached Ione sooner or later: after all he had his creative-writing witness from the Underground who described the woman with 'burning eyes' threatening Schwarz-Albert. (Only the burning eyes in question belonged of course to Ione, not Lydia Quentin, as Jemima had surmised.) But by that time Princess Amy might have been dead; like Taplow, the photographer, and Lydia Quentin herself. As for the latter, Pompey had a few old-fashioned remarks concerning those who permitted, or at least had not prevented, her from committing suicide. The macabre detail that it was a long sharp pin, originally part of the Quentin tiara worn at the fatal Gala, which Lydia had secreted about her and with which she performed the opening of her veins at the wrist, did not make things any better in Pompey's opinion.

At least Ione, driven finally to craziness by her beloved sister's death, had failed in her last mad rash attempt.

'It would never have worked,' Pompey comfortingly assured Jemima. 'Though I grant you she shouldn't have been there in the first place – our failure entirely, so much police presence needed elsewhere, that was the trouble.'

He patted her knee. They were seated in the Groucho Club again, Pompey confessing himself to have taken quite a fancy to the place, especially since Mrs Pompey had recently approved all late home-comings from this particular quarter; the literary gleanings were to be her reward. Detective Sergeant Vaillant had dropped his superior there with some reluctance, or rather he had left him there with some reluctance; he meditated some off-the-record conferences with Jemima Shore himself one day – starting at the Groucho Club.

'There was a good deal of focus on the other one, of course,' continued Pompey. 'The big woman with the model daughter. But do you know all she did? Munched her way through a box of chocolate biscuits, then cried with happiness along with all the rest of them at the sight of the bride coming out of the Cathedral. Finally queued up to see the wedding flowers inside the Cathedral after the ceremony. Even then they kept a pretty close eye, naturally. But what should she do then? Never looked at the flowers but went and lit a candle to some statue or other. Harmless as you please – if you call the saints and all that sort of thing harmless which, I have to admit,' concluded Pompey generously, 'many do.'

It was true. Pussy had not lit a candle since her own violent rejection of the Catholic religion years ago; but some kind of cathartic experience had happened to her as she watched Princess Amy, married at last, on the arm of her handsome husband, standing on the steps of the Cathedral, laughing and waving as the bells began to peal out overhead, joined, so it seemed, by all the bells of London. Not rage and bitterness but overwhelming sorrow swept over her; she wept not for happiness as her covert watchers had supposed but for loss, a loss which no anger could hope to assuage.

So Pussy lit a candle for her daughter Caro in front of the statue of St Francis in Westminster Cathedral. Unaware of Lamb's suicide and thinking of her held in prison, she lit a candle for her too, another gesture of reconciliation towards those young women who could not really be held responsible for the death of her own daughter.

'You did very well, my dear, very well,' Pompey conceded.

'And my instinct? What you call my woman's instinct and I call my rational good sense. Did that do well?' demanded Jemima; but she knew she would never win this particular argument with Pompey. A team . . . long might they remain so.

As for Ione Quentin: 'A cool customer,' was Pompey's final verdict. 'But she'll probably end up in Broadmoor. Given the circumstances.'

'You mean – she shouldn't.'

'No, no, that's the solution all right. She's totally deranged according to the prison doctor. By the way, it seems the mother, the Quentin mother, committed suicide. Started Lydia off on her particular course. Something very unstable in that family.'

'And the famous father – Colonel Q, you remember him – was obviously a monster, at least where Lydia Quentin was concerned. What a recipe for disaster! Martinet for a father, depressive for a mother. Ione told me that Lydia wanted to have her father put down in revenge for the death of a pet dog that *he* put down, when she was quite small!'

'Now we know it was a recipe for disaster for both of them,' pointed out Pompey. 'Even if it took this particular crisis to bring out the craziness in the elder girl. But when she did go off her rocker, she still had all that lethal courage she must have got from the war-hero father. Talk about the female of the species—' But that did not seem a particularly profitable line of conversation to pursue with Jemima, so Pompey sighed and returned to the subject of Ione Quentin's future.

'"Given the circumstances" just meant being a lady-in-waiting – serving, servitude, perpetual attendance. Might begin to give you some funny ideas, I suppose.'

'I have to say that the rest of them seem all right,' murmured Jemima. But perhaps Pompey was merely ruminating on his own servitude, in horticultural terms at least, to Mrs Pompey.

Others would have sweeter memories of the Royal Wedding than Jemima Shore. Major Pat Smylie-Porter, for example, had some sweet memories, while shuddering away from what-might-have-been in every sense of the word, not only the demise of his royal mistress, but those secret hopes concerning Ione . . . but these were now repressed deep into his unconscious, as only Major Pat knew how to repress inconvenient and strong emotions. His sweet memories included not only arrangements perfectly carried out – and God knew what a triumph that was under the circumstances – but the particular way young Amanda Macpherson-Wynne, acting lady-in-waiting to Princess Amy, had carried out her new role, staunchly and discreetly. Major Pat intended to keep a fatherly, well a not entirely fatherly, eye upon young Amanda in the future.

The sweetest moment for Jemima herself came on her return to her flat from the Groucho Club following her drink with Pompey. She saw from the red light on her answering machine that there had been at least one call, and from the number registered on the machine itself, she discovered that there had in fact been a positive host of callers – or calls. The telephone rang again as she patted the purring Midnight, draping himself round her legs and arching his tail as one who had been unfed for weeks (a gross libel on Jemima's cleaning lady Mrs B). Jemima decided to ignore the noise.

'A telephone that rings but who's to answer—' she hummed. But Cole Porter did not know about the 1980s' solution of the answerphone. The noise stopped as the machine began to click.

Around Jemima literature concerning Royal Weddings, past and present, still proliferated while Princess Amy's radiant face, veil flung back, gazed up at her – in full colour – from the heap of morning papers. Most of the papers had chosen for their front page the balcony shot in which Prince Ferdinand – crafty foreign bugger or romantic hero according to taste – held Amy's hand to his lips and implanted upon it a deep deep kiss while gazing romantically – or craftily – into her eyes. It was a specially popular picture since the lip-readers, not present at the Royal Gala, had been out in force on this occasion.

What Prince Ferdinand said, looking so soulfully at Amy, was: 'A dream come true.'

A minute later Princess Amy, who could do no wrong, won even more hearts by exclaiming in rather a different mode: 'Hey, Prince Charming, you're treading on my train!' And then she added, surely roguishly: 'This is your wife speaking.'

A good deal of pictorial attention was also paid to little Jamie Beauregard, who had revenged his defeat over the kilt, by concealing his dirk in the beribboned tie of his page's knee breeches. He brandished it aloft in triumph on the balcony where his furious mother could not reach him; but for once this was a weapon which caused no one (other than the aforesaid mother, who would make him pay later), any anxiety.

Prince Ferdel's own comment: 'I'd like to wring that boy's neck,' although dutifully translated by the lip-readers was ignored on grounds of taste by all papers except the *Daily Clueless*.

'Marriage!' thought Jemima. 'I wish them the joy of it.' She picked up the papers and the notes and the family trees – all Susanna Blanding's patient work – and began to stuff them into the wastepaper basket. (She had an awful feeling that some of the numerous calls on her machine must have come from a sobbing Susanna, Rick having departed that morning for the Middle East.)

Feeling herself in a reckless mood, Jemima added: 'And I wish Cass and Flora Hereford the joy of it too.' The moment she had framed the thought, she realized to her surprise that it was true. She was free of all that. Weddings, marriage, royal or otherwise, was simply not for her.

Pity under the circumstances about the career, the TUS fiasco and the Megalith one which had preceded it. Oh well, there was always Midnight . . . She would end her days as an unemployed spinster alone with her cat. That thought seemed to call either for tears or for celebration. Finding the latter preferable, especially since Midnight, an independent cat who liked to choose his own moment of embrace, had jumped out of her arms with an indignant mew, she routed out a bottle of champagne from the fridge. She realized wryly that it was the bottle given to her in tribute by a member of the Press on the day she had been sacked by Megalith and appointed by TUS.

Jemima had just opened the bottle when the telephone rang yet again. This time she decided to answer it. Susanna or no Susanna, what could she lose?

'Where are you?' cried the instantly recognizable voice of Cy Fredericks without any preliminaries. It was not only the instantly recognizable voice of Cy Fredericks, it was also the instantly recognizable voice of Cy Fredericks in a state of great agitation. 'Didn't you get my messages? Where are you? Why aren't you *here*?' Then, virtually without pause, 'Jem, my Jem, we have plans, wonderful new plans, most exciting plans, I can't wait to see you and tell you everything—'

'Cy darling, where are *you*?' But Jemima should have known better than to ask. Such a question, even at the calmest of times, had been known to cast Cy into a fearful state of uncertainty and these were definitely not the calmest of times.

'Miss Lewis,' she heard him shout in the familiar manner. 'Where am I? Miss Lewis, where are *you*?'

'I'm here, Mr Fredericks,' Miss Lewis's voice cutting in on the line had a soothing timbre which was equally familiar. 'Mr Fredericks is back at Megalith, Miss Shore,' she continued. 'There have been a few, er . . .' – discreet pause – 'changes recently and in short Mr Fredericks has been . . .' – another discreet pause – 'reinstated.'

'Only I'm now President,' boomed Cy's voice, interrupting. 'Tell her I'm President, not Chairman, President-for-life. We've all the time in the world. And tell her to get here as soon as possible.' Evidently seeing no irony in his last statement, Cy Fredericks flung down the telephone, leaving Jemima alone on the line with the ever-helpful Miss Lewis.

'Can you possibly get him to wait till I finish this glass of champagne?' asked Jemima Shore Investigator.